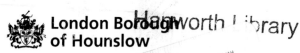

First Published in Great Britain 2017
By Mills & Boon, an imprint of HarperCollins*Publishers*
1 London Bridge Street, London, SE1 9GF

COME FLY WITH ME... © 2017 Harlequin Books S. A.

English Girl In New York, *Moonlight In Paris* and *Just One More Night* were first published in Great Britain by Harlequin (UK) Limited.

English Girl In New York © 2014 Scarlet Wilson
Moonlight In Paris © 2014 Pamela Hearon Hodges
Just One More Night © 2014 Fiona Gillibrand

ISBN: 978-0-263-92955-3

05-0317

Our policy is to use papers that are natural, renewable and recyclable products and made from wood grown in sustainable forests.The logging and manufacturing processes conform to the legal environmental regulations of the country of origin.

Printed and bound in Spain
by CPI, Barcelona

ENGLISH GIRL IN NEW YORK

BY
SCARLET WILSON

Scarlet Wilson wrote her first story aged eight and has never stopped. Her family have fond memories of *Shirley and the Magic Purse*, with its army of mice, all with names beginning with the letter 'M'. An avid reader, Scarlet started with every Enid Blyton book, moved on to the Chalet School series and many years later found Mills & Boon.

She trained and worked as a nurse and health visitor, and currently works in public health. For her, finding Mills & Boon Medical Romance was a match made in heaven. She is delighted to find herself among the authors she has read for many years.

Scarlet lives on the West Coast of Scotland with her fiancé and their two sons.

My first Mills & Boon® Romance story has to be dedicated to my own three personal heroes, Kevin, Elliott and Rhys Bain.

This story is set in New York, and they helped me celebrate my 40th in New York in style!

Also to my editor Carly Byrne, who is soon to have her own adventure! Thank you for your support, and I hope to collaborate with you on lots more stories. x

CHAPTER ONE

THE SUBWAY RATTLED into the station, the doors opened and Carrie felt herself swept along with the huddled masses on the platform, barely even looking up from her hunched position in her woefully thin coat. It had looked better on the internet. Really. It had.

She resisted the temptation to snuggle into the body in front of her as the carriage packed even tighter than normal. Just about every train in the city had ground to a halt after the quick deluge of snow.

The streets had gone from tired, grey and bustling to a complete white-out with only vaguely recognisable shapes in a matter of hours.

An unprecedented freak snowstorm, they were calling it.

In October.

In the middle of New York.

The news reporters were having a field day—well, only the ones lucky enough to be in the studio. The ones out in the field? Not so much.

And Carrie appreciated why. Her winter coat wasn't due to be delivered for another two weeks. She could die before then. Her fingers had lost all colour and sensation ten minutes ago. Thank goodness she didn't have a dripping nose because at these temperatures it would freeze midway.

'They've stopped some of the buses,' muttered the woman next to her. 'I'm going to have to make about three changes to get home tonight.'

An involuntary shiver stole down her spine. *Please let the train get to the end of the line.* This part of the subway didn't stay underground the whole way; parts of it emerged into the elements and she could already see the thick white flakes of snow landing around them.

A year in New York had sounded great at the time. Magical even.

A chance to get away from her own *annus horribilis.*

A chance to escape everyone she knew, her history and her demons.

The only thing she'd taken with her was her exemplary work record.

In the black fog that had been last year it had been her one consistently bright shining star.

She should have known as soon as her boss had invited her into his office and asked her to sit down, giving her that half sympathetic, half cut-throat look. He'd cleared his throat. 'Carrie, we need someone to go to New York and represent the London office, leading on the project team for the next year. I understand this year has been difficult for you. But you were my first thought for the job. Of course, if it feels like too much—or the timing is wrong…' His voice had tailed off. The implication was clear. There were already two interns snapping at her heels, anxious to trample her on the way past.

She'd bit her lip. 'No. The timing is perfect. A new place will be just what I need. A new challenge. A chance for some time away.'

He'd nodded and extended his hand towards her.

'Congratulations. Don't worry about a thing. The firm has an apartment in Greenwich Village in the borough of Manhattan. It's a nice, safe area—easily commutable. You'll like it there.'

She'd nodded numbly, trying not to run her tongue along her suddenly dry lips. 'How long until I have to go?'

He'd cleared his throat, as if a little tickle had appeared. 'Three weeks.' The words were followed by a hasty smile. 'One of the partners will be leaving for business in Japan. He needs to brief you before he leaves.'

She'd tried hard not to let the horror of the time frame appear on her face as she'd stood up and straightened her skirt. 'Three weeks will be fine. Perfectly manageable.' Her voice had wavered and she'd hoped he didn't notice.

He'd stood up quickly. 'Perfect, Carrie. I'm sure you'll do a wonderful job for us.'

The train pulled into another station and Carrie felt the shuffle of bodies around her as the passengers edged even closer together to let the hordes of people on the platform board. It seemed as if the whole of New York City had been sent home early.

A cold hand brushed against hers and a woman gave her a tired smile. 'They've closed Central Park—one of the trees collapsed under the weight of the snow. I've never heard of that before.' She rolled her eyes. 'I'm just praying the school buses get home. Some of the roads are closed because they don't have enough snow ploughs and the grit wasn't due to be delivered for another two weeks.' Her face was flushed as she continued to talk. 'I've never seen it so bad, have you? I bet we're all snowed in for the next few days.'

Carrie gave a rueful shrug of her shoulders. 'I'm not

from around here. I'm from London. This is my first time in New York.'

The woman gave a little sigh. 'Poor you. Well, welcome to the madhouse.'

Carrie watched as the train pulled out of the station. It didn't seem to pick up speed at all, just crawled along slowly. Was there snow on the tracks, or was it the weight of too many passengers, desperate to get home before the transport system shut down completely? *Please, just two more stops.* Then she would be home.

Home. Was it home?

The apartment in West Village was gorgeous. Not quite a penthouse, but part of a brownstone and well out of her budget. West Village was perfect. It was like some tucked away part of London, full of gorgeous shops, coffee houses and restaurants. But it still wasn't home.

Today, in the midst of this snowstorm, she wanted to go home to the smell of soup bubbling on the stove. She wanted to go home to the sound of a bubble bath being run, with candles lit around the edges. She wanted to go home somewhere with the curtains pulled, a fire flickering and a warm glow.

Anything other than her own footsteps echoing across the wooden floor in the empty apartment, and knowing that the next time she'd talk to another human being it would be with the man who ran the coffee stall across the street on the way to work the next morning.

She wrinkled her nose. It might not even come to that. The sky was darkening quickly. Maybe the woman next to her was right. Maybe they would end up snowed in. She might not speak to another human being for days.

She shifted the bag containing the laptop in her hands. She had enough work to last for days. The boss had been clear. Take enough to keep busy—don't worry about getting into the office. If the snow continued she couldn't count on seeing any of her workmates.

The people in her apartment block nodded on the way past, but there had never been a conversation. Never a friendly greeting. Maybe they were just used to the apartment being used by business people, staying for a few weeks and then leaving again. It would hardly seem worthwhile to reach out and make friends.

A shiver crept down her spine and her mind started to race.

Did she have emergency supplies? Were there any already in the apartment? How would she feel being snowed in in New York, where it felt as if she didn't know a single person?

Sure, she had met people at work over the past two months. She'd even been out for a few after-work drinks. But the office she worked in wasn't a friendly, sociable place. It was a fast-paced, frenetic, meet-the-deadline-before-you-die kind of place. She had colleagues, but she wasn't too sure she had friends.

The train shuddered to a halt at Fourteenth Street and the door opened. 'Everybody out!'

Her head jerked up and the carriage collectively groaned.

'What?'

'No way!'

'What's happening?'

A guard was next to the door. 'This is the last stop, folks. Snow on the tracks. All trains are stopping. Everybody out.'

Carrie glanced at the sign. Fourteenth Street. One subway stop away from the apartment. She glanced down at her red suede ankle boots. She could kiss these babies goodbye. The ground outside was covered in thick,

mucky slush. She didn't even want to think about what
they'd look like by the time she reached the apartment.

The crowd spilled out onto the platform and up towards the mezzanine level of the station on Fourteenth
Street. Carrie could hear panicked voices all around
her trying to plan alternative routes home. At least she
knew she could walk from here, no matter how bad it
was outside.

The sky had darkened rapidly, with thick grey clouds
hanging overhead, continuing their deluge of snow.

Snow. It was such a pretty thing. The kind of thing you
spent hours cutting out of paper as a kid, trying to make
a snowflake. Then sticking on a blue piece of card and
putting on the classroom wall or attaching to a piece of
string and hanging from the Christmas tree.

It didn't look like this in the storybooks. Thick wads
of snow piled at the edges of the street, blanketing the
road and stopping all traffic. The whiteness gone, leaving mounds of grey, icy sludge.

There was a creaking noise behind her and across the
street, followed by a flood of shouts. 'Move! Quickly!'

In slow motion she watched as a large pile of snow
slowly slid from a roof four storeys above the street. The
people beneath were hurrying past, blissfully unaware
of what was happening above their heads.

It was like a slow-moving action scene from a movie.
All the inevitability of knowing what was about to happen without being able to intervene. Her breath caught
in her throat. A woman in a red coat. A little boy. An
elderly couple walking hand in hand. A few businessmen with their coat collars turned up, talking intently
on their phones.

There was a flash of navy blue. The woman in the red
coat and little boy were flung rapidly from the sidewalk

into the middle of the empty street. The elderly couple pressed up against a glass shop window as some frantic shouts alerted the businessmen.

The snow fell with a thick, deafening thump. A cloud of powdered snow lifting into the air and a deluge of muddy splatters landing on her face.

Then, for a few seconds, there was silence. Complete silence.

It was broken first by the whimpers of a crying child— the little boy who had landed in the road. Seconds later chaos erupted. Onlookers dashed to the aid of the woman and small child, helping them to their feet and ushering them over to a nearby coffee shop. A few moments later someone guided the elderly couple from under the shelter of the shop's awning where they had been protected from the worst of the deluge.

'Where's the cop?'

'What happened to the cop?'

A policeman. Was that who had dived to the rescue? Her eyes caught the flicker of the blue lights of the NYPD car parked on the street. It was such a common sight in New York that she'd stopped registering them.

Some frantic digging and a few choice expletives later and one of New York's finest, along with one of the businessmen, emerged from the snow.

Someone jolted her from behind and her feet started to automatically move along the sludgy sidewalk. There was nothing she could do here.

Her own heart was pounding in her chest. Fat use she would be anyway. She didn't have a single medical skill to offer, and the street was awash with people rushing to help. She could see the cop brushing snow angrily from his uniform. He looked vaguely familiar but she couldn't place him. He was holding his wrist at a funny angle and looking frantically around, trying to account for all the people he had tried to save.

A tissue appeared under her nose. 'Better give your face a wipe,' said another woman, gesturing towards her mud-splattered coat, shoes and face.

Carrie turned towards the nearest shop window and did a double take. She looked like something the cat had dragged in. 'Thanks,' she muttered as she lifted the tissue to her face, smudging the mud further across her cheek. Her bright green coat was a write-off. The dry-clean-only label floated inside her mind. No dry-cleaning in the world could solve this mess.

She stared up at the darkening sky. It was time to go home. Whether it felt like home or not.

Daniel Cooper coughed and spluttered. His New York skyline had just turned into a heavy mix of grey-white snow. Wasn't snow supposed to be light and fluffy? Why did it feel as if someone were bench-pressing on top of him? A pain shot up his arm. He tried his best to ignore it. *Mind over matter. Mind over matter.*

There was noise above him, and shuffling. He spluttered. Snow was getting up his nose. It was strange being under here. Almost surreal.

He didn't feel as if he was suffocating. The snow wasn't tightly packed around his face. He just couldn't move. And Dan didn't like feeling as if things were out of his control.

The scuffling above him continued and then a few pairs of strong arms pulled him upwards from the snow. His head whipped around, instantly looking to see if the mother and child were safe.

There. On the other side of the sidewalk. He could see the flash of her red coat. Throwing them towards the street probably hadn't been the wisest move in the world, but the street was deep in snow, with not a car in sight. People were crowded around them but they were both safe, if a little shocked. The woman lifted her head and caught his eye. One of her hands was wrapped around her son, holding him close to her side, the other hand she placed on her chest. She looked stunned, her gaze registering the huge mound of snow that they would have been caught under, the horror on her face apparent. *Thank you,* she mouthed at him.

He smiled. The air left his lungs in a whoosh of relief. Snow was sticking to the back of his neck, turning into water that was trickling down his spine. As if he weren't wet enough already.

The elderly couple. Where were they? And why was his wrist still aching so badly? He spun back around. The elderly couple were being escorted across the street towards a sidewalk café. Thank goodness. He gave a shiver. He didn't even want to think about the broken bones they could have suffered—or the head injuries.

'Buddy, your wrist, are you hurt?' A man in a thick wool coat was standing in front of him, concern written all over his face.

Dan looked down. The thing he was trying to ignore. The thing he was trying to block from his mind. He glanced at the pile of snow he'd been buried under. There, in amongst the debris, were some slate shingles. Who knew how many had fallen from the roof above. He was just lucky that one had hit his wrist instead of his head.

Darn it. His eyes met those of the concerned citizen in front of him. 'I'll see about it later,' he muttered. 'I'm sure it will be fine. Let me make sure everyone's okay.'

The man wrinkled his brow. 'They've called an ambulance for the other guy.' He nodded towards the sidewalk, where one of the businessmen was sitting, looking pale-faced and decidedly queasy. Truth be told, he felt a little like that himself. Not that he'd ever let anyone know.

He tried to brush some of the snow from his uniform. 'Who knows how long the ambulance will take to get here. We might be better taking them to be checked over at the clinic on Sixteenth Street.' He signalled across the street to another cop who'd appeared and was crossing quickly towards him. 'Can you talk to dispatch and see how long it will take the ambulance to get here?'

The other cop shook his head and threw up his hands. 'The whole city is practically shut down. I wouldn't count on anyone getting here any time soon.' He looked around him. 'I'll check how many people need attention—' he nodded towards Dan '—you included, then we'll get everyone round to the clinic.' He rolled his eyes. 'It's gonna be a long shift.'

Dan grimaced. The city was in crisis right now. People would be stranded with no way of getting home. Flights were cancelled. Most of the public transport was shutting down. How much use would he be with an injured wrist?

A prickle of unease swept over him as he looked at the streets crowded with people. He should be doing his job, helping people, not sloping off to a clinic nearby.

He hated that. He hated the elements that were out of his control. He looked at the crowds spilling out onto the sidewalk from Fourteenth Street station and took a deep breath.

Things could only get worse.

Carrie stared out of the window. The sun had well and truly disappeared and the streets were glistening with snow. Not the horrible sludge she'd trudged through earlier—but freshly fallen, white snow. The kind that looked almost inviting from the confines of a warmly lit apartment.

Her stomach rumbled and she pressed her hand against it. Thank goodness Mr Meltzer lived above his store. Every other store in the area had pulled their shutters and closed. She glanced at the supplies on the counter. Emergency milk, water, bread, bagels, cheese, macaroni and chocolate. Comfort food. If she was going to be snowed in in New York she had every intention of eating whatever she liked. It would probably do her some good. After the stress of last year she still hadn't regained the weight she'd lost. Gaining a few pounds would help fill out her clothes. It was so strange that some women wanted to diet away to almost nothing—whereas all she wanted was to get her curves back again.

Her ears pricked up. There it was again. That strange sound that had brought her to the window in the first place. This apartment was full of odd noises—most of which she'd gotten used to. Rattling pipes with trapped air, squeaking doors and floorboards, sneaky unexplained drafts. But this one was different. Was it coming from outside?

She pressed her nose up against the glass, her breath steaming the space around her. The street appeared deathly quiet. Who would venture out on a night like this? The twenty-four-hour news channels were full of *Stay indoors. Don't make any journeys that aren't absolutely necessary.* Anyone, with any sense, would be safely indoors.

She pushed open the window a little, letting in a blast of cold air. Thank goodness for thermal jammies, bed socks and an embossed dressing gown.

She held her breath and listened. There it was again. It was like a mew. Was it a cat? Downstairs, in the apartment underneath, she could hear the faint thump of music. It must be the cop. He obviously wouldn't be able to hear a thing. She didn't even know his name. Only that he must be a cop because of the uniform he wore. Tall, dark and handsome. But he hadn't looked in her direction once since she'd arrived.

Who had left their cat out on a night like this? Her conscience was pricked. What should she do? Maybe it was just a little cat confused by the snow and couldn't find its way home. Should she go downstairs and investigate? She glanced down at her nightwear. It would only take a few seconds. No one would see her.

She could grab the cat from the doorway and bring it in for the night. Maybe give it a little water and let it curl in front of the fire. A cat. The thought warmed her from the inside out. She'd never had a cat before. It might be nice to borrow someone else's for the night and keep it safe. At least she would have someone to talk to.

She opened her door and glanced out onto the landing. Everyone else was safely ensconced in their apartments. Her feet padded down the flights of stairs, reaching the doorway in less than a minute. She unlocked the heavy door of the brownstone and pulled it open.

No.

It couldn't be.

She blinked and shut the door again. Fast.

Her heart thudded against her chest. One. Two. Three. Four. Five. Her brain was playing horrible tricks on her. Letting her think she was safe and things were safely locked away before springing something out of the blue on her.

Maybe she wasn't even awake. Maybe she'd fallen asleep on the sofa upstairs, in front of the flickering fire, and would wake up in a pool of sweat.

One. Two. Three. Four. Five.

She turned the handle again, oh-so-slowly, and prayed her imagination would get under control. Things like this didn't happen to people like her.

This time her reaction was different. This time the cold night air was sucked into her lungs with a force she didn't think she possessed. Every hair on her body stood instantly on end—and it wasn't from the cold.

It was a baby. Someone had left a baby on her doorstep.

CHAPTER TWO

FOR A SECOND, Carrie couldn't move. Her brain wouldn't compute. Her body wouldn't function.

Her ears were amplifying the sound. The little mew, mew, mew she'd thought she'd heard was actually a whimper. A whimper that was sounding more frightening by the second.

Her immediate instinct was to run—fast. Get away from this whole situation to keep the fortress around her heart firmly in place and to keep herself sheltered from harm. No good could come of this.

But she couldn't fight the natural instinct inside her—no matter how hard she tried. So she did what any mother would do: she picked up the little bundle and held it close to her chest.

Even the blanket was cold. And the shock of picking up the bundle chilled her.

Oh, no. The baby.

She didn't think. She didn't contemplate. She walked straight over to the nearest door—the one with the thudding music—and banged loudly with her fist. 'Help! I need help!'

Nothing happened for a few seconds. Then the music switched off and she heard the sound of bare feet on the wooden floor. The door opened and she held her breath.

There he was. In all his glory. Scruffy dark hair, too-tired eyes and bare-chested, with only a pair of jeans clinging to his hips—and a bright pink plaster cast on his wrist. She blinked. Trying to take in the unexpected sight. His brow wrinkled. 'What the—?'

She pushed past him into the heat of his apartment.

'I need help. I found this baby on our doorstep.'

'A baby?' He looked stunned, then reached over and put a hand around her shoulders, pulling her further inside the apartment and guiding her into a chair next to the fire.

'What do I do? What do I do with a baby? Why would someone do this?' She was babbling and she couldn't help it. She was in a strange half-naked man's apartment in New York, with an abandoned baby and her pyjamas on.

This really couldn't be happening.

Her brain was shouting messages at her. But she wasn't listening. She couldn't listen. *Get out of here.*

She stared down at the little face bundled in the blanket. The baby's eyes were screwed shut and its brow wrinkled. Was it a girl? Or a boy? Something shifted inside her. This was hard. This was so hard.

She shouldn't be here. She absolutely shouldn't be here. She was the last person in the world qualified to look after a baby.

But even though her brain was screaming those thoughts at her, her body wasn't listening. Because she'd lifted her hand, extended one finger and was stroking it down the perfect little cold cheek.

Dan Cooper's day had just gone from unlucky to ridiculous. He recognised her. Of course he recognised her. She was the girl with the sad eyes from upstairs.

But now she didn't look sad. She looked panicked.

He was conscious that her gaze had drifted across his bare abdomen. If she hadn't been banging on the door so insistently he would have pulled on a shirt first. Instead, he tried to keep his back from her line of vision as he grabbed the T-shirt lying across the back of his sofa.

He looked back at her. Now she didn't look panicked. She'd stopped babbling. In fact, she'd stopped talking completely. Now she just sat in front of the fire staring at the baby. She looked mesmerised.

His cop instinct kicked into gear. *Please don't let her be a crazy.* The last thing he needed today was a crazy.

He walked over and touched her hand, kneeling down to look into her eyes. He'd heard some bizarre tales in his time but this one took the biscuit. 'What's your name?'

She gave him only a cursory glance—as if she couldn't bear to tear her eyes away from the baby. 'Carrie. Carrie McKenzie. I live upstairs.'

He nodded. The accent drew his attention. The apartment upstairs was used by a business in the city. They often had staff from their multinational partners staying there. His brain was racing. He'd seen this girl, but had never spoken to her. She always looked so sad—as if she had the weight of the world on her shoulders.

He racked his brain. Had she been pregnant? Would he have noticed? Could she have given birth unaided upstairs?

His eyes swept over her. Pyjamas and a dressing gown. Could camouflage anything.

He took a deep breath. Time was of the essence here. He had to ask. He had to cover all the bases. 'Carrie—is this your baby?'

Her head jerked up. 'What?' She looked horrified. And then there was something—something else. 'Of course not!'

A feeling of relief swept over him. He'd been a cop long enough to know a genuine response when he saw one. Thank goodness. Last thing he needed right now was a crazy neighbour with a baby.

He reached over and pulled the fleecy blanket down from around the baby's face. The baby was breathing, but its cheeks were pale.

The nearest children's hospital was Angel's, all the way up next to Central Park. They wouldn't possibly be able to reach there in this weather. And it was likely that the ambulance service had ground to a halt. He had to prioritise. Even though he wasn't an expert, the baby seemed okay.

He stood up. 'How did you find the baby?'

Her brow wrinkled. 'I heard a noise. I thought it was a cat. I came downstairs to see.'

He couldn't hide the disbelief in his voice. 'You thought a baby was a cat?'

Her blue eyes narrowed as they met his. His tone had obviously annoyed her. 'Well, you know, it was kinda hard to hear with your music blaring.'

He ignored the sarcasm, even though it humoured him. Maybe Miss Sad-Eyes had some spunk after all. 'How long since you first heard it?' This was important. This was really important.

She shook her head. 'I don't know. Five minutes? Maybe a little more?'

His feet moved quickly. He grabbed for the jacket that hung behind the door and shoved his bare feet into his baseball boots.

She stood up. 'Where are you going? Don't leave me alone. I don't know the first thing about babies.'

He turned to her. 'Carrie, someone left this baby on our doorstep.' His eyes went to the window, to the heavy snow falling on the window ledge as he slid his arms into his jacket. 'Outside, there could be someone in trouble. Someone could be hurt. I need to go and check.'

She bit her lip and glanced at the baby before giving a small cursory nod of her head. He stepped outside into the bitter cold, glancing both ways, trying to decide which way to go. There was nothing in the snow. Any tracks that had been left had been covered within minutes; the snow was falling thick and fast.

He walked to the other side of the street and looked over at their building. Why here? Why had someone left their baby here?

There were some lights on in the other apartment buildings on the street. But most of the lights were in the second or third storeys. Theirs was the only building with lights on in the first floor. It made sense. Someone had wanted this baby found quickly.

He walked briskly down the street. Looking for anything—any sign, any clue. He ducked down a few alleyways, checking behind Dumpsters, looking in receded doorways.

Nothing. Nobody.

He turned and started back the other way. Checking the alleys on the other side of the street and in the opposite direction. His feet moving quickly through the sludgy snow.

He should have stopped and pulled some socks on. The thin canvas of his baseball boots was soaked through already. The temperature must have dropped by several degrees since the sun had gone down. He'd only been out here a few minutes and already he was freezing.

He looked up and his heart skipped a beat. Carrie was standing at his window, holding the baby in her arms.

There was a look of pure desperation on her face—as if she were willing him to find the mother of this child.

It was a sight he'd never expected to see. A woman, holding a child, in his apartment. She'd pulled up his blinds fully and the expanse of the apartment he called home was visible behind her. His large, lumpy but comfortable sofa. His grandmother's old high-back chair. His kitchen table. His dresser unit. His kitchen worktop. The picture hanging above the fireplace.

Something niggled at him. His apartment was his space. He'd rarely ever had a relationship that resulted in him 'bringing someone over'. He could count on one hand the number of girlfriends who'd ever made it over his doorway. And even then it seemed to put them on an automatic countdown to disaster.

He didn't really do long-term relationships. Oh, he dated—but after a few months, once they started to get that hopeful look in their eyes, he always found a way to let them down gently. They eventually got the message. It was better that way.

So seeing Carrie standing in his apartment with a baby in her arms took the wind clean out of his sails. The sooner all this was over with, the better.

Still, she was cute. And even better—from London. She'd have no plans to stay around here. Maybe a little flirting to pass the time?

He gave himself a little shake and had another look around. There was no one out here. The streets were completely empty.

It was so funny being on the outside looking in. He loved his home. He cherished it. But he'd never really taken a moment to stand outside and stare in—to see what the world must see on their way past if he hadn't pulled the blinds. His grandmother had left it to him in her will and he knew how lucky he was. There was no way a single guy on a cop's salary could have afforded a place like this.

But it was his. And he didn't even owe anything on it. All he had to do was cover the bills.

A little thought crept into his mind. He hadn't quite pulled the blinds fully tonight. He just hadn't gotten round to it. Was that why someone had left their baby here?

Did they see into his home and think it would be a safe place to leave a baby?

It sent a shudder down his spine. The thought that a few minutes ago someone could have been out here having those kind of thoughts.

The snowfall was getting even heavier—he could barely see ten feet in front of him. This was pointless. He was never going to find any clues in this weather. He had to concentrate on the immediate. He had to concentrate on the baby.

He hurried back into the apartment. Carrie turned to face him. 'Nothing?' The anxiety in her voice was obvious. Was she just a concerned citizen? Or was it something else?

He shook his head and pulled off his jacket, hanging it back up behind the door.

He walked over to where she was standing at the window and had another quick look out into the deserted street, searching for something, anything—a shadow, a movement. But there was nothing. Just the silence of the street outside.

He stood next to her, watching the way she cradled the baby in her arms. She was holding the baby, but he could sense she was uneasy. She'd said she didn't know the first thing about babies—well, neither did he. And in a snow-storm like this, it was unlikely they could get any help.

Most of the people who stayed around here were pro-fessionals. He couldn't think of a single family that stayed on this street. There were a couple of older people who had lived here for years. Mrs Van Dyke upstairs, but her family had long since moved away. There really wasn't anyone they could call on for help.

He watched her. The way her blue eyes were fixed on the face of the baby, still swaddled in its blanket. It was then he noticed the way her arms were trembling. It was slight—ever so slight. Making her chestnut curls waver and the pink flush of her cheeks seem heated.

She was beautiful. Now that he was close enough to take a good look at her, Carrie McKenzie was beautiful. Even if she didn't know it herself. Even with the realm of sadness in her blue eyes. He wondered what they looked like when they were happy. Did they sparkle, like the sun glinting off a turquoise-blue sea?

They were standing too close. He was sure his warm breath must be dancing across her skin. He could smell the orange scent of her bath oils, still present on her skin. He liked it. It was nicer than the cloying scent of some perfumes that women wore. The ones that prick-led your nose from the other side of the room. This was like a warm summer's day. Here, in his living room, in the middle of a snowstorm in New York.

She looked up at him with those sad blue eyes. She didn't pull away from him. She didn't seem to think he had invaded her personal space. It was quite unnerving. He couldn't remember the last time he'd been this close to a beautiful woman in his apartment—and certainly not one in her nightwear.

A smile danced across his face. If he'd ever pictured

a woman in his apartment in her nightwear it certainly hadn't been in fluffy pyjamas and bed socks. She blinked and it snapped him out of his wayward thoughts and back to the current situation.

'I don't even know your name,' she whispered.

Wow. He hadn't even introduced himself. What kind of a New Yorker was he that his neighbour didn't even know his name? His grandma would kill him for his lack of manners and hospitality.

Why hadn't he ever introduced himself? Was it because he was so used to the constant flow of traffic up above him that he hadn't thought it worth his while? The thought shamed him. Because this woman definitely looked as if she could do with a friend. 'Dan. Daniel Cooper.'

'Daniel,' she repeated, as if she were trying to associate his face with the name. Her lips curled upwards. 'It's nice to meet you, Daniel,' she whispered, her gaze steady on his. 'Even if I am barely dressed.' He liked that about her. Even though her arms were trembling and she was clearly out of her depth, she could still look him clear in the eye and make a joke at her own expense.

The baby let out a whimper, reminding them of its presence, and he jerked back to reality. 'Maybe it's time to find out whether we've had a boy or a girl.' He raised his eyebrows at her and held out his hands to take the bundle from her.

It only took a few seconds to relieve her of the weight. There was a noticeable sigh of relief in her shoulders as she handed the baby over.

He walked closer to the fire and unwound the little blanket. His cast made it awkward. There were no baby clothes underneath—no diaper. Just a little wrinkled towel. Carrie let out a gasp, lifting her hand to her mouth at the sight of a piece of string and a barely shrivelled umbilical cord.

Dan sucked in a deep breath. 'Well, like I said, I'm no expert but I guess this means we have a newborn.' A million thoughts started to flood into his head but he tried to push them aside. 'And I guess I should say congratulations, we've got a boy.' He rewrapped the blanket and lifted the little one onto his shoulder, trying to take in the enormity of the situation.

'I have a friend who works at Angel's, the children's hospital. Let me give her a call.'

'Her?'

He lifted his head. It was just the way she said the word *her*. As if it implied something else entirely.

'Yes. She's a paediatrician. Since neither of us know what we're doing and we can't get any immediate help, I guess she's the best bet we've got.'

He walked over to the phone and dialled quickly, putting the phone onto speaker as he adjusted the baby on his shoulder, away from his cast. 'Can you page Dr Adams for me? Tell her it's Sergeant Cooper and it's an emergency. Thanks.'

It only took a few seconds to connect. 'Dan? What's up?'

The relief he felt was instant. Shana was the best kids' doctor that he knew. She would tell him exactly what to do.

'Hi, Shana. I've got a bit of a problem. I've had a baby dumped on my doorstep and from the looks of it, it's a newborn.'

'What?' He could hear the incredulous tone in her voice. 'In this weather?'

'Exactly.'

Shana didn't mess around. She was straight down to business. 'Is the baby breathing?'

'Yes.'

'How cold? Do you have a thermometer? What's the baby's colour? And how is it responding?'

Carrie burst in. 'We think he was outside for just over five minutes. His skin was cold when I brought him in— and he was pale. But he's started to warm up. He looks pinker now.' Her brow was furrowed. 'Do you have a thermometer, Dan?' She was shaking her head. 'I don't.'

'Who's that?'

Daniel cleared his throat. 'That's Carrie, my neighbour from upstairs. It was she who heard the baby crying. And no, Shana, we don't have a thermometer.'

'No matter. Crying? Now that's a good sign. That's a positive.'

Carrie shook her head. 'Not crying exactly, more like a whimper.'

'Any noise is good noise. You said he's a newborn. Is the cord still attached? Is it tied off?'

'Yes, it's tied with a piece of string. Doesn't look the cleanest. But the baby was only wrapped up in a blanket. No clothes. No diaper.'

'Sounds like no preparation. I wonder if the mother had any prenatal care. Does the baby look full term?'

Daniel shrugged and looked at Carrie, who shook her head and mouthed, *I don't know.*

'To be honest, Shana, neither of us are sure. I guess he looks okay. What does a full-term baby look like?'

'Does he have a sucking reflex? Is he trying to root?'

'What? I have no idea what you're talking about.' He was trying hard not to panic. This was all second nature to Shana. These types of questions were the ones she asked day in, day out. To him it all sounded like double Dutch.

They could hear the sound of muffled laughter at the other end of the phone. 'One of you, scrub your hands thoroughly under the tap then brush your finger around the side of the baby's mouth. I want to know if he turns towards it, as if he's trying to breastfeed or bottlefeed.'

Daniel nodded at Carrie, who walked over to the sink and started scrubbing her hands. 'Give us a second, Shana.'

Carrie dried her hands and then walked back over and lifted her finger hesitantly to the side of the baby's mouth. It took a few gentle brushes to establish that the little guy was reacting to her touch, turning towards it and opening his mouth.

'Yes, Shana. We think he is responding.'

'Good. That's a sign that he's around full term.' She gave an audible sigh. 'Okay, Daniel, you're not going to like this.'

'What?' Did she think something was wrong with the baby?

'There's no way I can send anyone from Angel's to get that baby. Our emergency room is packed and the roads around us are completely impassable. And from the weather report it's going to be like that for a few days.'

'Is that the good news or the bad news?' The mild feeling of panic was starting to rise.

Shana let out a laugh. 'Probably both. It sounds as if your baby is doing okay. Thank goodness. He will need a proper assessment as soon as possible. I'll put the necessary call in to social services, but they are on the other side of the city from you and everyone is in crisis right now. It will be a few days before they get to you. In the meantime the first thing you need to do is feed the little guy. Do you have somewhere local you can get some supplies?'

Blank. His brain had instantly gone blank. He'd never had any reason to look for baby supplies before. Where on earth would he get them?

Carrie touched his arm. 'Mr Meltzer stays above his store. I'm sure he'll have some powdered baby milk and diapers we can buy.'

Instant relief, followed by a sickening feeling in the pit of his stomach. 'Shana, you can't seriously expect us to look after a baby. Me, Shana? Seriously?'

'Daniel Cooper, you're one of the most responsible guys I know. I can't think of a single other person I would trust with a newborn baby right now. You're like any brand-new parent. None of them have experience. They just learn as they go. You'll need to do the same.'

'But they have nine months to get used to the idea. They read dozens of books about what to do—'

'And you have your own personal paediatrician at the other end of a phone. Not that I think you'll need me.'

Daniel could feel his heartbeat quicken in his chest. He wasn't afraid—not really. As a New York cop he'd dealt with most things in life. He'd had a gun pulled on him, a knife—on more than one occasion. He'd stopped a young girl from being abducted once, and managed to resist the temptation of doing what he really wanted to the potential kidnapper. He'd even talked a guy down from the edge of a rooftop before. But this? Looking after a baby? Why did it seem more intimidating than anything else?

'Shana, I don't think I'm the best person for the job.'

'Why not? You're practical. You're resourceful. And right now you're the best that baby's got.' She was beginning to sound exasperated. Angel's must be under an enormous amount of pressure right now, and he really didn't want to add to it. 'You've even got some help from your neighbour.'

He glanced over at Carrie, who was shaking her head frantically. *No,* she was mouthing.

'Suck it up, Daniel—and call me if you have any problems.' There was a click at the other end of the phone.

Carrie's chin was practically bouncing off the floor. 'Suck it up, Daniel? Suck it up? That's what she says to you?' Her voice was getting higher pitched by the second and the baby was starting to squirm in his arms, reacting to the noise.

Reactions? Was that a good sign, too? He really didn't have a clue.

He shrugged. 'She's my best friend's older sister. It isn't the first time Shana's told me to suck it up—and it won't be the last.' He walked over to the sofa and sank down onto the cushions. This little guy weighed more than he thought. Or maybe it was just because he couldn't swap him between his arms.

'I'm going to have to put a call in to the station, to let my captain know about the abandoned baby.'

Carrie sagged down next to him on the sofa. She shook her head and squeezed her eyes shut. 'I know we've just met, Daniel, but I'm sorry. I just can't help you with this. I can't do it. Babies—' she hesitated '—they're just not my thing. I won't be any help anyway. I don't know a thing about babies.'

He stared at her. Hard. 'You've got to be joking, right?'

Her eyes opened and widened. It was clear she was instantly on the defence. 'No. Why?'

He shook his head in disbelief. 'You turn up at my door with a baby, and now you're expecting to dump it on me in the middle of a snowstorm.'

When he said the words out loud they were even worse than the thoughts in his head.

Her face paled. 'But I...'

'I nothing.' A grin appeared on his face. 'Suck it up, Carrie.'

She drew back from him and he could sense her taking some deep breaths. 'It's not quite like that.'

He shook his head. There was no way she was leaving him high and dry. He waved his cast at her. 'What am I supposed to do? How am I supposed to bath a baby with one of these? Sure, I can probably manage to feed a baby and make up some bottles. But be practical, Carrie. I'm hardly the ideal babysitter right now.' He could see her staring at his pink cast and trying to work things out in her head. 'Least you can do is give me some help.'

Her cheeks flushed with colour, as if she'd just realised how mean it looked to walk away.

She pointed at his cast. 'How did you end up with that anyway? And what made you pick a pink cast?'

He snorted. '*Pick* isn't the word I would choose. There was an accident earlier today, a tonne of snow fell off a roof and I got trapped underneath it pushing people out of the way.'

Her eyes widened. 'On Fourteenth Street? That was you?'

He sat up a little straighter. 'How do you know about that?'

'I was there. I saw it happen.' She tilted her head to the side and stared at him again. 'I didn't realise it was you—I mean, I didn't know you.' She reached over and touched his cast. 'I remember. I remember seeing you hold your wrist at a funny angle. I guess it's broken, then?'

He nodded.

'And the pink?'

He smiled. 'It seems that today was the biggest day in the world for fractures at the clinic on Sixteenth Street.' He waved his wrist. 'Pink was the only colour they had left.'

She started to laugh. 'I can just imagine the look on your face when they told you that.'

He started to laugh, too. 'I was less than impressed. The air might have been a little blue.'

'Not pink?'

'Definitely not pink.'

She shook her head. 'That was really scary. I just remember the noise and the shouts. What about that woman in the red coat and her little boy? And that elderly couple?'

She really had been there. And she could remember the details. The lady could be a cop. 'All checked out and okay. One of the businessmen twisted his ankle and the other was being assessed for a head injury. He kept being sick.'

'Wow. Thank goodness you were there.'

Her words struck a chord with him. He hadn't really thought about that. He'd been too angry at breaking his wrist and being out of action for the NYPD. He hadn't really had time to stop to think about what could have happened to that elderly couple, or the woman and her young son.

A vision flashed in his eyes. The woman in the red coat cradling her son with one arm as if he was the most precious thing on earth. Then looking at him, with her hand on her heart, and mouthing, *Thank you.* He hadn't really had time to talk to her properly, but that one action had been more than enough for him. He didn't do this job for the thanks.

The little bundle shifted in his arms and started to

whimper again. There was colour coming into the baby's cheeks and his tongue was starting to play around the edge of his mouth. He sighed. 'I guess our boy is getting hungry. I'll give Mr Meltzer a call and see if he can open the store so we can get some supplies. Know anything about making baby bottles?'

Carrie shook her head quite forcefully. 'I've told you—I can't help. This isn't my thing.'

But Dan was already on his feet, shifting his weight and moving the baby into her arms, whether she was ready or not. 'My computer's right next to you. Do an internet search while I'm gone.' He flicked through the nearby phone directory and punched a number into his phone. 'I'll only be five minutes.'

He grabbed his jacket and headed for the door again. What was her problem? He wasn't so chauvinistic that he expected all women to want to be mothers, but he did expect any responsible adult to help out in an emergency situation.

Maybe it was just the cop in him. Maybe his expectations of the average person were too high. But he'd seen the way she'd looked at the baby. She might not have experience, but she couldn't hide the tenderness in her eyes.

Maybe she was just uncomfortable with the pyjama situation. Maybe he should offer to let her go back upstairs and get changed.

He pressed the send button on his phone as he headed along the white street. Whatever it was, she'd better get over it quick. There was no way he was doing this on his own.

Carrie sat frozen on the sofa.

This wasn't happening. This couldn't be happening.

There was a weight pressed firmly against her chest.

Like a huge dumb-bell just sitting there, taunting her to try and pull some air into her lungs.

He was scowling at her again. The baby. Nearly as much as Daniel Cooper had scowled at her when she'd tried to pull out all the lame excuses under the sun to get out of here.

It must make her seem like a bitch. But right now she didn't care.

She could feel tears starting to flood into her eyes. This was someone's precious baby. Someone's living, breathing, precious bundle. What on earth could happen in this life that would make you leave a baby on someone's doorstep in the middle of a snowstorm?

It wasn't fair. Life wasn't fair.

Last time she'd held a baby it hadn't been moving. Its little chest didn't have the rise and fall that this little boy's had. It didn't have the pink flush to its cheeks.

She blinked back the tears. The tightening in her chest was getting worse.

It.

A terrible term.

But she couldn't use any other right now. She couldn't think about her daughter. She couldn't think about Ruby McKenzie. She couldn't let that name invade her thoughts.

Because then she would spiral downwards. Then she would remember the nursery and pram. Then she would remember the routine check at the midwife's, followed by the urgent scan. Then she would remember the forty-eight-hour labour, with no cry of joy at the end of it.

Then she would remember the disintegration of her five-year relationship, as both of them struggled to cope with their bereavement.

The whimpering was getting worse, turning into full-blown screams.

She'd have given anything to hear the screams of her daughter. She'd have given anything to see her daughter screw up her face and let out a yell like that.

She shifted the baby onto her shoulder. Five minutes. Dan would be back in five minutes.

She put her hand on the keyboard of the computer and did a quick search. If she could keep her mind on something else, she could fight back the feelings. She could stop them from enveloping her. *How to sterilise and prepare bottles.*

She read the screen in front of her, scanning quickly. Her hand automatically moving and patting the baby on the back. She could do this. She could help him make a bottle and then leave.

He couldn't expect any more. She couldn't *give* any more.

She could feel herself pulling in—withdrawing inside herself. Turning into someone else. Stepping outside herself to a place where there was no hurt, no memories. Switching off.

It was the only way she'd coped before. And it was the only way she could cope now.

She glanced at the clock. Ten minutes maximum.

She could keep this face painted in place for ten minutes when he got back. That was how long it would take to sterilise the bottle, make up the powdered milk and leave him positioned on the sofa.

Her eyes registered something on the screen. Darn it! Cooled boiled water. How long did the water have to cool for before it was suitable to give a baby?

Maybe he'd only just boiled the kettle. She juggled the baby in her arms and walked over to the kitchen countertop, putting her hand on the side of the kettle. Stone cold. She picked it up and gave it a shake—and practically empty.

Nightmare.

She ran the tap and filled the kettle, putting it back into position and flicking the switch for it to boil.

Then she felt it—and heard it.

That first little squelchy noise. Followed by a warm feeling where her hand was resting on the baby's bottom.

No nappy. This little boy had no nappy on.

Her heart sank like a stone as she felt the warm feeling spread across her stomach. Could this night really get any worse?

CHAPTER THREE

DAN ENDED THE CALL on his phone. His captain had let out the loudest, heartiest laugh he'd ever heard when he'd told him about the baby. It hadn't helped.

He could hear pandemonium in the background at the station. He should be there helping. Instead of doing a late-night recce for baby supplies.

Mr Meltzer, on the other hand, had been full of concern. Loading up supplies on the counter and waving his hand at Dan's offer of payment.

'If I help the little guy get a better start in life that's all I need.'

The words tormented him. Ground into him in a way they shouldn't. If only everyone felt like Mr Meltzer.

He pushed open the door to the apartment building and kicked the snow off his favourite baseball boots. They were really beyond repair.

Carrie was waiting and she pulled open the inside door. 'Did you get some milk?'

He nodded and dumped the bags on the counter.

'Wow, how much stuff did you get?'

He pulled his arms out of his jacket. 'Who knew a baby needed so much? Mr Meltzer just kept pulling things off his shelves and saying, "You better take some of that".'

Carrie tipped one of the bags upside down. 'Please tell me you got some nappies and dummies. We need both—now.'

'What? What are you talking about?'

She waved her hand in the air. 'Oh, you Americans. Nappies—diapers. And dummies—what do you call them? Pacifiers? He's starting to get restless and it will take a little time to sterilise the bottles.' She rummaged through the bags. 'You did get bottles, didn't you?'

'What's that smell?' He wrinkled his nose and caught sight of the expression on her face. 'Oh, no. You're joking. He can't have. He hasn't eaten yet.' He pulled out a pack of baby wipes. 'I take it we'll need these?'

She nodded. 'Do you have a towel we can lay him on? I'd say getting a nappy on the little guy is a priority.'

Dan walked over to the laundry cupboard and started throwing things about. 'I know I've got a brand-new set of towels in here somewhere. My friend Dave just got married. He was drowning in the things. Ah, here we are!' He pulled out some navy blue towels and laid one down on the rug, a little away from the fireplace. He glanced at his cast. It was more inconvenient than he first thought—to say nothing about the constant ache that was coming from his wrist. 'Can you do this?'

He could see her taking a deep breath. 'Fine,' she muttered through gritted teeth. She grabbed the bag of diapers from the counter, along with the wipes and some diaper sacks. 'Did you get some cream?'

'Cream? What for?'

'For putting on the baby's bum, of course. Everyone knows you put cream on a baby to stop them from getting nappy rash.'

He shrugged his shoulders. 'Mr Meltzer didn't seem to know—and he knew everything else.' He pulled something from a second plastic bag. 'Look—ready-made formula in a carton. We've got the powdered stuff, too, but he said this was ready to use.'

She scowled at him as she laid the baby down on the fresh towel and peeled back the blanket.

'Eww!'

'Yuck!'

The smell was awful and filled the apartment instantly. The baby, on the other hand, seemed to quite like the freedom the open blanket gave and started to kick his legs.

'How can all that stuff come from one tiny little thing?' He really wanted to pinch his nose shut.

Carrie was shaking her head, too, as she made a dive for the baby wipes. 'I have no idea, but the next one is yours.'

He looked at her in horror. 'No way.' He waved his pink cast again. 'Can you imagine getting a bit of that caught on here? It would stink forever. I would smell like this for the next six weeks.' He shook his head. 'At least you can wash your hands.'

Carrie was deep in concentration, wiping and thrusting the dirty wipes into the supposedly scented diaper sack. She pulled out one of the diapers and held it up. 'Well, at least you seemed to have got the right size.'

Dan bit his lip. 'Actually, there was a whole shelf of the things. Mr Meltzer picked them out.'

She raised her eyebrow. 'Can you ask him to come babysit, too, please? He seems to be the only person around here who knows anything about babies.'

'I tried. He wasn't buying it.'

Carrie positioned the diaper under the clean little bottom and snapped the tapes into place. 'There, that's better. Pity the smell hasn't disappeared.' She picked up the blanket by the corner. 'This will need washing. Where's your machine?'

'In the basement.'

She let out a sigh. 'I don't get that about New York. Why does everyone have their washing machine in the basement?' She waved her hands around. 'You've plenty of room in here. Why isn't your washing machine in the kitchen? Everyone in London has their washing machine in their flat. You don't have to walk down miles of stairs to do the laundry.'

'Worried about leaving your underwear unguarded?'

There it was again. That cheeky element coming out. He couldn't help it. She seemed so uptight at times.

Just as he suspected, a pink colour flooded her cheeks. He could almost hear the ticking of her brain trying to find a way to change the subject quickly.

She nodded over to the counter. 'We need to sterilise the bottles.'

'I think he gave me some tablets for that.' Dan started to root around in one of the bags.

'He probably did, but according to the internet the bottles would need to be in the sterilising solution for thirty minutes. It only takes ten minutes if we boil them. That way you can use the ready-made formula and get it into him quicker.'

'What about one of these? Can we give him a pacifier in the meantime?'

Carrie shook her head. 'I think we need to sterilise them, too. And we need to use only cooled boiled water with the powdered milk. But I've no idea how long water takes to cool once you've boiled it. And I don't know whether we should put the milk in the fridge or keep it at room temperature—everyone seems to have a different opinion on the internet.' She was getting more harassed by the second, the words rattling out of her mouth and her face becoming more flushed. 'I told you—I'm not an expert in all this. I have no idea what I'm doing!'

Something clenched in his stomach. He could sense the feelings overwhelming her, and he had a whole host of some himself.

Deep down, having a woman in his apartment—without an expiry date—was freaking him out. But these weren't normal circumstances. He *needed* Carrie Mc-Kenzie's help. He couldn't do this on his own and right now he could sense she wanted to cut and run.

He was feeling a bit flustered himself. Flustered that some gorgeous Brit was in his space. But this wasn't about him. This wasn't about Daniel Cooper and the fact he liked his own space. This wasn't about the fact his relationships only lasted a few months because he didn't want anyone getting comfortable in his home—comfortable enough to start asking questions. This was about a baby. A baby who needed help from two people.

So, he did what his grandma had always taught him. Her voice echoed in his head. *You get the best out of people when you compliment them—when you thank them for what they do.*

He reached over and touched Carrie's hand. She was getting flustered again, starting to get upset. 'Carrie McKenzie?' He kept his voice low.

'What?' she snapped at him.

Yep, he was right. Her eyes had a waterlogged sheen. She was just about to start crying.

He gave her hand a little squeeze. 'I think you're doing a great job.'

The world had just stopped because she wasn't really in it.

This was one of those crazy dreams. The kind that

had your worst type of nightmare and a knight in shining armour thrown in, too. The kind that made no sense whatsoever.

She wasn't here. She wasn't awake.

Her earlier thought had been true. She was actually fast asleep on the sofa upstairs. She would wake up in a few minutes and this would all be over. This would all be something she could shrug off and forget about.

Except those dark brown eyes were still looking at her.

Still looking as if he understood a whole lot more than he was letting on. As if he'd noticed the fact she was seconds away from cracking and bursting into floods of tears.

But he couldn't, could he? Because he didn't really know her at all.

Daniel Cooper was an all-action New York cop. The kind of guy from a romance movie who stole the heroine's heart and rode off into the sunset with her. A good guy.

The kind of guy who looked after an abandoned baby.

She was trying to swallow. Her mouth was drier than a desert, and it felt as if a giant turtle had started nesting at the back of her throat.

She looked down to where his hand covered hers. It was nice. It *felt* nice.

And that was the thing that scared her most.

When was the last time someone had touched her like that? At the funeral? There had been a lot of hand squeezing then. Comfort. Reassurance. Pity.

Not the same as this.

He smiled at her. A crooked kind of smile, revealing straight white teeth.

A sexy kind of smile. The kind that could take her mind off the nightmare she was currently in.

There was a yelp from the towel. Dan moved his hand

and looked down. 'I guess baby's getting hungry. I'll stick the bottles in the pot.'

Carrie left the baby on the towel and started to look through the bags on the counter. Five prepacked cartons of formula, two different kinds of powder, more dummies and a whole mountain's worth of baby wipes.

She folded her arms across her chest as she watched Dan dangle the bottles and teats from his fingertips into the boiling water. 'Clothes, Dan. What are we going to put on him?'

His brow wrinkled and he shook his head. 'Darn it, I knew I'd forgotten something. There weren't any baby clothes in the general store, and there's no place else around here that sells any. Can't we just leave him in the diaper?'

Carrie shook her head. 'Want me to do a search on that?' She started to pace. 'Don't you know anyone around here with kids who might still have some baby clothes? How long have you stayed here?'

He blinked and his lips thinned. As if he was trying to decide how to answer the question. He averted his eyes and started busying himself with the coffee maker. 'I've lived here on and off my whole life. This was my grandma's place.'

'Was it?' She was surprised but it made perfect sense. After all, how did a young guy on a cop's salary afford a gorgeous brownstone West Village apartment? She looked around, starting to take in the decor of the place. There were a few older items that didn't look quite 'him'. A rocker pushed in the corner near the window, a small antique-style table just at the front door, currently collecting mail and keys, a dresser in the more modern-style kitchen. It was kind of nice, to see the old mixed in with the new. 'It's a lovely place. Big, too. You're a lucky guy.'

He made a noise. More like a snort. 'Yeah, I guess. Just born lucky, me.'

Carrie froze, not really knowing how to respond. What did that mean?

But he must have realised his faux pas because he changed the subject quickly. 'The ten minutes will be up soon. Once we've fed the little guy I'll go on up to Mrs Van Dyke's place. Her family used to stay here. She might have some things in storage we could use.'

'Mrs Van Dyke? Which one is she? Is she the one on the second floor who looks as if she came over on the Mayflower and is about six hundred years old?'

He raised his eyebrows. 'Watch it. According to her, her family were amongst the original Dutch settlers. And I don't think she's quite six hundred years old. She's as sharp as a stick, and she hasn't aged in the past twenty-five years.' He gave her a wink as he switched off the burner. 'Maybe you should ask her what cream she uses.'

Carrie picked up an unopened packet of pacifiers and tossed them at his head. They bounced off the wall behind him.

'Careful, careful, we've got a baby in the apartment. We don't want anything to hit him.' He glanced at his watch. 'On second thought, it's getting kind of late. Maybe it's too late to go knocking on Mrs Van Dyke's door.' His gaze was still fixed on the baby, lying on the floor, grizzling impatiently for his milk.

Carrie folded her arms as she stood next to him. 'You've got to be kidding. Mrs Van Dyke is up watching TV until four a.m. most nights. And I take it she's getting a little deaf, because I can't get to sleep in my apartment because of the *Diagnosis Murder* or *Murder, She Wrote* reruns that I hear booming across the hall. Seriously, the woman needs a hearing aid.'

'And seriously? She'll be far too proud to get one.'

There was something nice about that. The fact that he knew his elderly neighbour so well that he could tell exactly why she didn't have a hearing aid. 'So what was wrong with me, then?' She couldn't help it. The words just spilled out.

'What do you mean?'

'You obviously know your other neighbours well, but it was too much trouble to even say hello to me in the foyer.'

The colour flooded into his cheeks. Unflappable Dan was finally flapping. He could deal with a tonne of snow falling from a roof, he could deal with a baby dumped on his doorstep, but this? This was making him avert his eyes and struggle to find some words.

'Yeah, I'm sorry about that. I just assumed you were staying for only a few days. Most of the others seemed like ships that pass in the night.'

'I've been here two months, Dan. Eight long weeks—' she let out a little sigh '—and to be honest, this isn't the friendliest place I've ever stayed.'

He cringed. 'I can hear my grandmother shouting in my ear right now. Shaming me on my bad manners. I did see you—but you always looked like you had a hundred and one things on your mind. You never really looked in the mood to talk.'

This time Carrie felt like cringing. There was a reason Dan was a cop. He was good at reading people. Good at getting to the heart of the matter. And she had only herself to blame for this, because it was she who'd called him on his behaviour.

She gave a little shrug, trying to brush it off. 'Maybe a cheery good morning would have been enough.'

She walked over and lifted the pot, tipping the boiling water into the sink.

He appeared at her back, his chin practically resting on her shoulder, as he lifted the plastic bottles and teats out onto the worktop with a clean dish towel. 'You're right, Carrie. You're absolutely right. I should have said hello. I should have said good morning.'

She turned her head slightly. He wasn't quite touching her, but she could feel the heat emanating from his body. She wanted to step away, to jerk backwards, but her body wasn't letting her.

Her lips were curving into a smile—even though she was telling them not to—as she stared into those brown eyes again. It was nice. Being up close to someone again. His lips were only inches from hers. She wondered if he was having the same kind of thoughts she was. The kind of thoughts that made her forget there was a baby in the room...until he let out an angry wail from the floor.

They jumped back, both at the same time. She reached for one of the cartons. 'Do you have a pair of scissors?'

He opened a drawer, pulled out the scissors, snipped the edge of the carton and upended the contents into one of the cooled bottles. Carrie picked up one of the teats by the edge of its rim and placed it on the bottle, screwing it in place with the retaining ring.

The bottle sat on the middle of the counter and they stared at each other for a few seconds.

'Don't we need to heat the milk up now?'

She shook her head. 'According to the internet, room temperature is fine.'

'Oh, okay.'

Silence. And some deep breathing, followed by a whole host of screams from the floor. It was like a Mexican stand-off.

'So, who is going to do this?'

'You. Definitely you.'

'But what if I do it wrong?'

'What if I do it wrong? Don't you dare suggest that I can do it better because I'm a girl.'

He raised his eyebrows. 'Oh, I'd never refer to you as a girl.'

'Stop it. He's mad. Just feed him.' She opened one of the kitchen drawers and handed him a dish towel. 'Here, put this over you.'

'What do I need that for?'

'In case he pukes on you.'

'Ewww…'

Dan picked up the bottle, holding it between his hands as if it were a medical specimen. He squinted at the markings on the side of the bottle. 'How much do I give him?'

'I don't know.'

'Well, look it up on the internet while I start.'

Relief. Instant relief. She wasn't going to be left to feed the baby. She could sit on the other side of the room and do a search on the computer.

Dan picked up the baby from the floor and settled him on his lap, resting him in the crook of his arm that had his cast in place. He held the bottle with his other hand and brushed the teat against the baby's cheek.

There were some angry noises, and some whimpering, before finally the baby managed to latch on to the teat and suck—furiously.

Carrie was holding her breath on the other side of the room, watching with a fist clenched around her heart. A baby's first feed.

One of those little moments. The little moments that a parent should share with a child.

Daniel seemed equally transfixed. He glanced over at her. 'Wow. Just wow. Look at him go. He's starving.'

And he was. His little cheeks showed he was sucking furiously. But it was Dan who had her attention. The rapt look on his face, and the way the little body seemed to fit so easily, so snugly against his frame.

Her mouth was dry and the hairs were standing up on the back of her neck. Worse than that, she could feel the tears pooling around her eyes again.

What was wrong with her? This had nothing to do with her. Nothing to do with her situation. She shouldn't be feeling like this. She shouldn't be feeling as if she couldn't breathe and the walls were closing in around her.

But Dan looked so natural, even though he kept shifting in the chair. He looked as if he was born to do this. Born to be a father. Born to be a parent.

The thing that she'd been denied.

She glanced at the screen and stood up quickly.

She had to leave now, while he was trapped in his chair and before the tears started to fall. She needed some breathing space.

'You should stop after every ounce of milk, Dan. Take the bottle out and wind the baby. I'm sorry. I have to go.'

'What? Carrie? Wait a minute, what does *wind* mean? How do I know how much an ounce is?'

But she couldn't stop. She couldn't listen.

'Carrie? Come back.'

But her feet were already on the stairs, pounding their way back up to the sanctuary of her solitude.

CHAPTER FOUR

DAN STARED AT the wall. What had just happened?

One minute she seemed fine, next minute a bundle of nerves, ready to jump out of her skin at the slightest noise.

She'd caught him unawares. She'd caught him while he was in no position to run after her. Probably planned it all along.

Still, it wasn't as if she could go anywhere. The city was at a standstill and if this little guy started screaming she was right upstairs. Whether she liked it or not.

He shifted on the sofa. The little guy was feeding fast and furious. Was this normal?

He heard some rumbling, the noises of the milk hitting the baby's stomach. How much was an ounce anyway? And how on earth could he tell if the baby had drunk that much when the bottle was tipped up sideways? At this rate he was going to need Shana on speed dial. He glanced at the clock and let out a sigh.

This was going to be a long, long night.

Carrie slammed the apartment door behind her and slid down behind it. Her mind was on a spin cycle. She couldn't think a single rational thought right now.

What Dan must think of her.

She tried to take some slow, deep breaths. Anything

to stop her heart clamouring in her chest. Anything to stop the cold prickle across her shoulder blades.

She sagged her head into her hands. *Calm down. Calm down.*

This was ridiculous. Avoiding babies for the past year was one thing. Body-swerving pregnant friends and brand-new mothers was almost understandable.

But this wasn't. She had to stop with the self-pity. She had to get some perspective here.

What would she have done if Dan hadn't been in the building?

There was no way she would have left that baby on the doorstep. No matter how hard the task of looking after him.

And if she'd phoned the police department and they couldn't send anyone out? What would she have done then?

She lifted her head from her hands. She would have had a five-minute panic. A five-minute feeling of *this can't be happening to me*.

Then what?

There was a creeping realisation in her brain. She pushed herself back up the door. Her breathing easing, her heartbeat steadying.

Then she would have sucked it up. She would have sucked it up and got on with it.

Because that was what any responsible adult would do.

She strode over to the bedroom, shedding her dressing gown and bed socks and pulling her pyjama top over her head. She found the bra she'd discarded earlier and fastened it back in place, pulling on some skinny jeans and a pink T-shirt.

Her pink baseball boots were in the bottom of her cupboard and she pushed her feet into them.

There. She was ready.

But her stomach started to flutter again.

The light in the bathroom flickered. Was the light bulb going to blow again? Which it seemed to do with an annoying regularity. She walked inside and ran the tap, splashing some cold water over her face.

She stared into the mirror, watching the drops of water drip off her face. Dan would have labelled her a nutjob by now. He probably wouldn't want her help any more.

But the expression on his face was imprinted on her brain. He'd looked stunned. As if he couldn't under-stand—but he wanted to.

She picked up the white towel next to the sink and dried off her face. Her make-up was right next to her. Should she put some on? Like some camouflage? Would it help her face him again?

Her fingers hesitated over the make-up bag. It was late at night. She'd been barefaced and in her pyjamas. He wouldn't expect anything else.

But it might give her the courage she needed. It might make her feel as if she had some armour to face the world.

She pulled out some mascara and a little cream blusher, rubbing some on to her cheeks and then a touch on her lips. There. She was ready.

She crossed the room in long strides before any doubts could creep into place. There was no point in locking her apartment door. She would only be down two flights of stairs.

She placed her hand on the balustrade, ready to go down, and then halted. The television was booming from the apartment across the hall. Mrs Van Dyke.

The neighbour she'd only glimpsed in passing and never spoken to. The neighbour who might have some baby supplies they could use.

She hesitated and then knocked loudly on the door. 'Mrs Van Dyke? It's Carrie from across the hall. Daniel Cooper sent me up.'

She waited a few minutes, imagining it might take the little old lady some time to get out of her chair and over to the door—praying she'd actually heard her above the theme tune from *Murder, She Wrote*.

She could hear the creaking of the floorboards and then the door opened and the old wizened face stared out at her. Oh, boy. She really could be six hundred years old.

'And what do you want, young lady?'

Carrie jerked back a little. She had such a strong, authoritative voice, it almost reminded her of her old headmistress back in London.

She took a deep breath. 'I'm sorry to disturb you, Mrs Van Dyke, but we found a baby on the doorstep and Dan said you might be able to help.'

As the words tumbled out of her mouth she knew she could have phrased it better. If this old dear keeled over in shock it would be all her fault.

But Mrs Van Dyke was obviously made of sterner stuff.

'Oh, dear. What a terrible thing to happen. What does Dan need?'

Just like that. No beating about the bush. No preamble. Just straight to the point. Wonderful.

'We got some things from Mr Meltzer's store. He opened it specially to help out. We've got nappies—I mean, diapers—and pacifiers and bottles and milk.'

There was a gleam of amusement in the old lady's eyes. 'Just as well. I doubt I would have had any of those.'

Carrie shook her head. 'Of course. I mean—what we don't have is any baby clothes. Or any clean blankets. Do you have anything like that? Dan wondered if you might have some things packed away.'

Mrs Van Dyke nodded slowly and opened the door a little wider. 'I might have a few things that you can use, but most of them will be at the back of my cupboards. Come in, and I'll see what I can do.'

Carrie stepped into the apartment and stifled her surprise. 'Wow. What a nice place you have here.'

Clutter. Everywhere.

The floor was clear, but that was pretty much it.

There was no getting away from it—Mrs Van Dyke was clearly a hoarder.

She gave a smile and stepped further, keeping her elbows tight in against her sides for fear of tipping something off one of the tables or shelves next to her.

On second thoughts, Mrs Van Dyke wasn't your typical hoarder. Not the kind you saw on TV with twelve skips outside their house so it could be emptied by environmental health.

There were no piles of papers, magazines or mail. In fact, the only newspaper she could see was clearly deposited in the trash. And all the surfaces in the apartment sparkled. There was no dust anywhere. Just…clutter. Things. Ornaments. Pictures. Photo frames. Wooden carvings. Tiny dolls. Ceramics. The place was full of them.

No wonder Dan had thought she might have something they could use.

'They're mementos. They're not junk. Everything holds a memory that's special to me, or my family.'

Carrie jumped. Mrs Van Dyke seemed to move up silently behind her. Had she been so obvious with her staring?

'Of course not,' she said quickly.

Mrs Van Dyke picked up the nearest ornament. 'My husband used to carve things. This one he gave me on our first anniversary. A perfect rose.'

Carrie bent down and looked closely. It really was a thing of beauty. She couldn't even see the marks where the wood had been whittled away—it was perfectly smooth.

'It's beautiful.'

Mrs Van Dyke nodded. 'Yes, it is.' She walked slowly through the apartment, pointing as she went. 'This was the globe he bought me at Coney Island. This was a china plate of my grandmother's—all the way from Holland. This—' she held up another carving, this time of a pair of hands interlinked, one an adult's and one a child's '—is what he carved for me after our son Peter died when he was seven.'

Carrie's hand flew to her mouth. 'Oh, I'm so sorry.'

Mrs Van Dyke ran her finger gently over the carving as she sat it back down. 'It shows that we'd always be linked together, forever.'

She reached a door and gestured to Carrie. 'This is my box room. This is where I keep most of my things.'

Carrie was still taken aback by her comment about her son, so she pushed the door open without really thinking. She let out a gasp of laughter. 'You're not joking—it *is* a box room.' And it was. Filled with boxes from floor to ceiling. But there was no randomness about the room. Every box was clearly labelled and facing the door, and there was a thin path between the boxes. Room enough for someone of slim build to slip through.

'The boxes you're looking for are near the back.' She touched Carrie's shoulder. 'Your baby—is it a boy or a girl?'

Just the way she said it—*your baby*—temporarily

threw her for a second. It took her a moment to collect her thoughts. 'It's a boy. It's definitely a boy.'

Mrs Van Dyke nodded. 'Straight to the back, on the left-hand side somewhere, near the bottom, you'll find a box with David's name on it. And behind it, you might find something else that's useful.'

Carrie breathed in and squeezed through the gap. The labelling was meticulous, every item neatly catalogued. Did this really make Mrs Van Dyke a hoarder? Weren't those people usually quite disorganised and chaotic? Because Mrs Van Dyke was none of those things.

The box with David's baby things was almost at the bottom of a pile. Carrie knelt down and started to gingerly edge it out, keeping her eyes on the teetering boxes near the top. The whole room had the potential to collapse like dominoes—probably at the expense of Mrs Van Dyke, who was standing in the doorway.

She pushed her shoulder against the pile, trying to support some of the weight wobbling above her as she gave a final tug to get the box out.

In that tiny millisecond between the boxes above landing safely in place, still in their tower, she saw what was behind the stack and it made her catch her breath.

A beautifully carved wooden cradle.

She should have guessed. With all the other carefully carved items of wood in the apartment, it made sense that Mr Van Dyke would have made a cradle for his children. She weaved her way back through the piles, careful not to knock any with her box, before sitting it at the door next to Mrs Van Dyke. 'Do you want to have a look through this to see what you think might be appropriate?'

She chose her words carefully. Mrs Van Dyke had already revealed she'd lost one child; there might be items in this box that would hold special memories for her.

Items she might not want to give away. 'I'll go and try and get the cradle.'

It took ten minutes of carefully inching past boxes, tilting the cradle one way then another, before she finally managed to get out of the room.

She sat the cradle on the floor. Mrs Van Dyke was sitting in a chair with the open box on her lap, setting things in neat piles next to her.

Now that she had the cradle in the light of the room she was able to appreciate how fine the carving was. The cradle actually rocked. Something Carrie hadn't seen in years. The wooden spindles were beautifully turned, with a variety of ducks and bunnies carved at either end on the outside of the crib. Something like this would cost a small fortune these days.

She ran her fingers over the dark woodwork. 'This is absolutely beautiful. It looks like the kind of thing you would see in a stately home. Did your husband really make this himself?'

Mrs Van Dyke's eyes lit up at the mention of her husband. She smiled proudly. 'Yes, he did. It took him nearly four months.' She leaned forward and touched the cradle, letting it rock gently. 'This held all five of my children. Just for the first few months—they quickly outgrew it.'

'Are you sure we can borrow it? It looks like a precious family heirloom.'

Mrs Van Dyke nodded. 'A cradle is only really a cradle when it holds a baby. That's its job. You'll bring it back, mind?'

Carrie nodded. 'Social services have been called—' she held out her hands '—but with the snowstorm it might be a few days before they can collect the baby.'

Mrs Van Dyke handed her a small pile of clothes. 'I'm

sorry. I didn't keep too much. There's some vests, socks and some hand-knitted cardigans. Oh, and a blanket.'

'These will be great. Thank you so much. I'll launder them and bring them back to you in a few days.' She fingered the edge of the intricately crocheted blanket. 'This is beautiful and it looks brand new. Are you sure we can use this?'

Mrs Van Dyke smiled and shook her head. 'It's not new. I made a new blanket for every child. This was the final one. You're welcome to use it.'

Carrie smiled gratefully. 'Thank you, it's gorgeous and I'm sure it will be perfect.' She sat the clothes inside the cradle and picked it up. 'I'm sure Dan will be really grateful to you, too. If there's anything you need in the next few days be sure to let us know. We can ask Mr Meltzer to open his store again.'

Mrs Van Dyke shook her head. 'I'll be fine. My pantry is well stocked.'

Carrie walked over to the door. 'Thanks, Mrs Van Dyke.' She opened the door and gave a little smile. 'You have a beautiful home here.'

Mrs Van Dyke smiled. 'And you're welcome in it any time.'

Carrie juggled the cradle in her hands and closed the door behind her quietly.

Wow. Not what she'd expected at all.

Mrs Van Dyke was lovely, a real pleasure to be around. And she could imagine that Mrs Van Dyke could regale Carrie with hundreds of stories about her life and her family.

She thought of the little carving of a mother's and child's hands interlinked. It was heartbreaking—and it was beautiful. It hadn't felt right to ask any questions about her son Peter. She'd only just met Mrs Van Dyke and that would be intrusive.

But she'd felt the *connection*. The connection that only another mother who had lost a child could feel.

Obviously she hadn't said anything to Mrs Van Dyke. The woman hardly knew her. But that little feeling in the pit of her stomach had told her that this woman would be able to understand exactly how she felt.

Their circumstances were obviously different. Mrs Van Dyke had spent seven years loving and cherishing her son, getting to know his thoughts and quirks, growing together as mother, child and part of a family. Carrie had missed out on all that.

She'd spent seven months with her hands on her growing stomach, with a whole host of hopes and expectations for her child. In her head she'd been making plans for the future. Plans that involved a child.

None of those plans had been for a future without her daughter.

Her hands were starting to shake a little. Was it from the weight in her hands—or was it from the thoughts in her head?

A cradle is only really a cradle when it holds a baby.

How true.

She'd loved the white cot she'd bought for her daughter. But it hadn't been nearly as beautiful as this one. It had been dismantled and packed off to the nearest charity shop, along with the pram, because she couldn't bear to look at them.

Hopefully some other baby had benefitted from them.

Carrie walked down the stairs carefully, making sure she didn't bang the cradle on the way. Who knew what Dan would say to her? She wouldn't be surprised if he let rip with some choice words.

Her ears pricked up. Crying—no, wailing. The baby was screaming at the top of his lungs. Her steps quickened and she pushed open Dan's door with her shoulder.

'Dan, what on earth is going on?'

Dan's ears were throbbing. Weren't there environmental laws about noise? No one seemed to have told this little guy.

He changed him over to the other shoulder. This had been going on for the past fifteen minutes. What on earth had gone wrong?

He screwed up his face. Why was he even thinking that? He knew exactly what had gone wrong. The little guy had nearly finished the entire bottle without burping once. And according to what he'd read on the internet—that wasn't good.

He tried to switch off from the screaming. Tried to focus his mind elsewhere. Who would leave a baby outside in the cold?

The thought had been preying on his mind since the second Carrie had found the baby. Sure, he'd done the cop thing and made a half-hearted attempt to look for the mother—to see if someone was in trouble out there.

But truth be told—he wasn't that sure he wanted to find her.

Some people just weren't fit to be parents. Fact.

He was living proof and had the scars to back up his theory.

Even twenty-five years ago social services had tried to support his mother to keep him, when the truth of the matter was they should have got him the hell out of there.

Thank goodness his grandmother had realised what the scars on his back were. The guys in the station thought they were chicken-pox scars, and he wasn't about to tell them any different. But cigarettes left a nasty permanent burn.

The expression on Carrie's face had said it all. She'd felt compassion; she'd felt pity for the person who'd left this baby behind. He felt differently. Maybe this little guy was going to get the start in life he deserved.

There was a light tap at the door, then it was shouldered open. Carrie—with a wooden crib in her hands.

She wrinkled her nose at the noise. 'What did you do?' She crossed the room and sat the crib at his feet. Had she been with Mrs Van Dyke all this time? It was the only place she could have got the crib.

He shrugged his shoulders. 'Fed him.'

She shook her head. 'He shouldn't be squealing like that. Give him here.' She held out her arms and he hesitated. What was going on? This woman had hightailed it out of here as if there were a fire licking at her heels. Now she was back as if nothing had happened?

He placed his hand protectively on the little guy's back. 'What happened, Carrie?' He didn't care how blunt it sounded. He didn't care how much help he really wanted right now. He needed her to be straight with him.

She looked him straight in the eye. But he could see it—the waver. The hesitation in her blue eyes. 'I needed a little space for five minutes. And now—I've had it. I spent a little time with Mrs Van Dyke. She's great. I wish I'd had the opportunity to speak to her before today.' She walked over to the sink and lifted one of the pacifiers out of the sterilising solution. 'Has this been in there thirty minutes?'

He glanced at the clock and nodded, watching as she put the pacifier in the baby's mouth and lifted him from his shoulder. 'Let's try something else, then.' She sat down on the sofa and laid the baby across her lap, face down, gently rubbing his back.

Dan looked at the crib and shook his head. 'I hadn't even thought about where he was going to sleep.'

Carrie smiled. The kind of smile that changed the whole expression on her face. There it was. That little glimpse again of who she could be if she let herself.

'Neither did I. I asked Mrs Van Dyke if she had any clothes and it was she who suggested the crib.' She peered over at him as she continued to rub the baby's back. 'We don't have a mattress, though. Do you have something we could put inside?'

Dan tried to rack his brain. 'What about those new towels? We used one earlier, but I have plenty left. I could fold some of them to make a mattress for the crib.'

'That sounds perfect. I don't have a lot of clothes. A few cardigans, some embroidered vests and some socks. She also gave me a beautiful crocheted blanket. It looks brand new.'

The baby had stopped crying. Dan turned his head just in time to see a little pull up of the legs and to hear the loudest burp known to man.

'There we go. Is that better, little guy?' Carrie had turned him over and lifted him up again, staring him in the face. She put him back on her shoulder and kept gently rubbing his back. Her tongue ran along her lips. 'I remember somebody mentioning that trapped wind makes a baby cranky.'

Dan let out a snort. 'Cranky? You call that cranky? You only had to listen to five minutes of it.'

She bit her lip. 'Yes, I know. Sorry.' He could see her take a deep breath. 'I find this difficult, Dan. And I'm not sure I'll be much help.' She stood up and walked over to the window with the baby on her shoulder. 'I can't help feeling really sorry for whoever is out there. Why didn't they think they could take care of their baby? I wish I could help them.'

There it was again. The sympathy vote. The thing he just couldn't understand.

'Maybe they don't want our help. Maybe they just weren't designed to be a parent. There's a good chance they didn't have any prenatal care for the baby. Why on earth would they leave a baby on a doorstep? They didn't even ring the doorbell! This little guy could have frozen out there—he wasn't properly dressed or even fed. No diaper. He could have died during delivery. This isn't a person who wants a baby, Carrie. This is a person who has no sense of duty or responsibility.'

She spun around. 'You don't know that, Dan. You don't know anything. This could be an underage girl's baby. She might have been terrified to tell anyone she was pregnant—afraid of the repercussions. What if she was abused? What if she lives with her abuser? Have you thought of that?'

He was trying not to get mad. He was trying not to shout. He took a long, slow breath, his eyes lifting to meet hers. 'It could also be the baby of someone who wasn't interested in prenatal care. Someone who wasn't interested in making sure their baby was delivered safely. Someone who doesn't really care what happens to their baby.'

There was a tremble in her voice. 'You don't know that, Dan.' She looked down at the baby. 'You don't know anything. I just can't imagine what would make someone dump their baby on a doorstep. But I've got to believe they were desperate and wanted their baby to get help.' Her hand stroked the baby's head. 'A baby is a precious gift. I don't know any mother who would give their baby up willingly.'

'Then I guess our experiences of life are different.' The words were out before he knew it. No hesitation. No regrets.

Her eyes met his. It was as if she was trying to take stock of what he'd just said. As if she was trying to see inside his head.

He gave himself a shake and walked over next to her. 'I agree with you, Carrie. I think babies are precious and they should be treated with respect. So I think we should do something.' He lifted his finger and touched the baby's cheek.

'What?'

'I think we should give our baby a name.'

CHAPTER FIVE

SHE LOOKED STUNNED.

As if he'd just suggested packing up the car and heading off into the sunset with a baby in tow.

'What? We can't keep calling him "the little guy". You know what happens with abandoned babies. At some point somebody, somewhere gives them a name.'

'But we don't have any right. This isn't our baby.' She gave a little shake as if the thought was too alarming.

'Actually, right now, he is our baby. And might continue to be so for the next few days. We have to call him something in the meantime. Calling him "baby", "him" or "it", it's just not right. You know it isn't.'

She'd started pacing now. Walking about the apartment. Her eyes refusing to meet with his. 'Well, what's your suggestion, genius? Do you want to call him Dan?'

She was mocking him. For some reason, she was uncomfortable with this.

'I don't want to call him Dan. That will just get confusing. I'm trying to make this *less* confusing, not more.' He looked at her again; her pacing was slowing. 'What kind of names do you like?'

'I'm not naming him.' The words snapped out of her mouth.

'Why not?'

'Because he's not my baby.'

He shook his head. 'We know this. That's not the point. Let's find something we can agree on. Do you like crazy names like Moonwind or Shooting Star? Do you like modern names, celebrity names or something more traditional?'

Her chin was on the floor. 'Moonwind? Shooting Star? You've got to be kidding?'

He shook his head and rolled his eyes. 'You forget. I'm a cop in New York. I've heard everything.'

'Wow.' She sat back down on the sofa and picked up the bottle of milk. 'I'm going to try and give him a little more of this.' She watched as his mouth closed around the teat and he started to suck. 'I guess I like more traditional names,' she finally said.

'Plain? Like John or Joe or Bob?'

'No. They are too plain. Something proud. Something that makes you sit up and take notice.'

'I thought you'd ruled out Moonwind?'

There was a sparkle in her eyes as she turned to him. 'How about really traditional? How about something biblical?'

'Now you're really testing me. I'll need to think back to my Sunday school days.'

'Then you do that. How about Joseph? Or Isaac, or Jeremiah?'

He grabbed the first names that sprang into his mind. 'Noah, or David, or Goliath?' he countered. He wanted to make her smile again. And it worked. She was sitting up a little straighter. Trying to beat him at this game.

He could see her start to rack her brains. 'Peter, Paul or Matthew?'

'Adam, Moses or Joshua?'

There was silence for a few seconds as they both concentrated hard.

'Abraham.'

'Abraham.'

Their voices intermingled. And a smile appeared across both their faces.

Carrie stared down at the baby. 'Abraham,' she whispered. 'Now there's a proud name. What do you think of that one?'

He sat down next to her. 'Abraham, I like it. Also the name of one of our finest presidents. It's perfect.'

'It does seem perfect.' She was staring down at the little face as he sucked at the bottle. She nodded. 'You're right. We do need to give him a name—even if it's temporary. What a pity his mum didn't leave a note with what she'd called him.' There was a wistfulness in her voice. The sympathy vote that grated on him.

'Might have been better if she'd actually left some clothes. Or some diapers. Or anything at all to show us she cared about her son.'

Carrie gave the tiniest shake of her head as she eased the bottle out of Abraham's mouth, then sat him upright, putting her hand under his chin to support his head while she rubbed his back. 'Let's see if we can get a burp out of you this time.'

She turned to face him. 'You're really hard on people, Dan. And I find it really strange. You didn't hesitate to try and help this baby. You weren't even too upset when Shana told you that you'd need to keep him a while. We have no idea what's happened here. Can you at least try to give his mother the benefit of the doubt?'

'No.'

Just like that. Blunt and to the point.

Abraham arched his back and let out a big burp.

'Good boy.' His head started to sag. 'He's tired. Maybe we should put him down to sleep.'

Dan nodded and started folding up the towels he'd pulled from his cupboard, forming a makeshift kind of mattress in the crib. 'What do you think?'

'Perfect.' She had to put him down. She had to put him down now. She was starting to feel a little overwhelmed again. A baby cuddling into the nape of her neck and giving little sighs of comfort was making a whole host of emotions wash over her. None that she wanted to share.

She adjusted Abraham and laid him down in the crib, covering him with the hand-knitted shawl, and held her breath, waiting to see if he would stir.

It took her a few seconds to realise Dan was holding his breath right next to her.

But Abraham was out cold. His first feed had been a success.

'Darn it. Do you think we should have changed his nappy again?'

Dan raised his eyebrows. 'I think if you touch Abraham right now and wake him up I will kill you.'

She gave a little laugh. 'It's kind of strange, isn't it? Standing here waiting to see if he'll wake up again?'

Dan straightened his back. 'What time is it?' He looked over at the kitchen clock. 'Ten-thirty? Wow. No wonder I'm starved. I haven't eaten dinner. What about you? Are you hungry, Carrie?'

She shook her head. 'Maybe I should go.'

'You are joking, right?'

She shook her head firmly. All of a sudden there wasn't a baby as a barrier between the two of them.

All of sudden there wasn't a whole lot of space between them. And it was as if a little switch had been flicked.

Everything about Dan was making her feel self-conscious. How was her hair? Was her make-up still in place?

She'd spent the past few months going around in a fog. It had never once crossed her mind how she looked to the opposite sex.

But there was something about Dan. Something about being in close proximity to him that was making her feel uncomfortable. She didn't want to have to think about all those kinds of feelings resurrecting themselves. Not when she knew where they could eventually lead.

Now, she was fixating on his straight white teeth, the little lines of fatigue around his eyes and the sincerity in his face.

Then he snapped her out of it by giving her a cheeky wink and folding his arms across his chest. 'If I have to arrest you, I will.'

She jolted out of her daze. 'Arrest me?'

He smiled. 'To keep you here. To force you to help me look after Abraham overnight. What do I know about a newborn baby?'

'And what do I know?' She felt the rage surge inside her along with something else she couldn't quite work out. 'Because I'm a woman you think I should know about babies?'

'No.' His words were firm and strangely calming. They must have taught him that in cop school. How to calm a raging bull. 'I think you're another human being and two heads are better than one.'

It sounded logical. It sounded sensible. And it made all the chauvinistic arguments that had leaped into her head feel pathetic.

She didn't want to spend the night with a new baby. How on earth would she cope? It could end up bringing back a whole host of memories she didn't know how to deal with.

Then there was Dan. With his short dark hair and big brown eyes that made her skin itch. No, that made her skin *tingle*.

Every now and then he flirted with her, as if it was his natural demeanour. Flirting with women was obviously second nature to a guy like him. But it wasn't second nature for her. And she just didn't have the defences for it yet. She didn't want to be drawn in by his twinkling eyes and cheeky grins. She would look like some hapless teenager around him. This was feeling more awkward by the minute.

Carrie walked back over to the window, sneaking a look at Abraham on the way past.

'How long do you think he'll sleep?'

She shook her head. 'Yet another thing I'll need to look up. Isn't it usually around four hours for new babies?'

Dan glanced at the clock. 'So we've got until two-thirty.' He smiled. 'Do you want the night shift or shall I?'

Carrie hesitated. 'I'm not sure about this, Dan. I told you I've got no experience with babies. How am I supposed to know if something is wrong or not? I can't read everything you're supposed to know about babies in a few hours. What if we do something we shouldn't?'

He lifted his hands. 'We can only do our best. And anyway, look at you earlier—you were a natural.'

The words sent a chill down her spine. She knew he didn't mean for that to happen—he probably meant the words as a compliment. But her mind and body just couldn't react that way.

She was trying to partition this whole experience in her head. Put it inside a little box that could be safely stowed away somewhere.

Somewhere safe.

This was hard. And the reality was, it was only going to get harder. She'd felt herself waver a few moments before when Abraham had snuggled into her neck and she'd caught that distinctive baby scent in her nostrils.

She knew it was time to back off. To give herself a little space. And if she could keep doing that she might actually survive this experience.

And let's face it. Dan was hardly a strain on the eyes.

Why hadn't they ever spoken before? Had she really seemed so unapproachable? So caught up in her own world?

She watched as he looked in his cupboards, trying to find something to eat. Eventually he pulled some glasses and a bottle of soda from the cupboard. She could see the taut muscles across his back through his thin T-shirt. She tried not to stare at the outline of his behind in the well-worn jeans.

Her eyes automatically went downwards. Would he look at her the same way? Maybe she should have given some more thought to what she was wearing.

'I see you've finally got some clothes on.'

She gave a little smile as she walked over and sat down at the table. 'I didn't really have time to think earlier. I don't often roam around strange men's apartments in my nightclothes.'

'You don't?' He had a gleam in his eyes. He was trying to lighten the mood. Ease the stress they were both under. 'Is your apartment cold upstairs? You were bundled up like you live in an igloo.'

She took a sip of the soda he'd just poured for her. 'No. It was comfort clothes. I was freezing when I got in—I ruined my suede boots walking in that mucky slush. My raincoat was covered in muddy splatters and all I could think about was getting inside, heating up and eating myself silly.'

He tilted his head as he sat down. In this dim light in the kitchen he had really dark brown eyes. Comforting kind of eyes. The kind you could lose yourself in.

'And what does eating yourself silly involve?'

She shrugged. 'Chocolate. In all varieties. Macaroni cheese. Grilled bagels with melted cheese. Porridge. Pancakes.' She pointed towards the ceiling. 'I bought some stuff at Mr Meltzer's before I came home. I was worried I'd be stuck inside for a few days with no comfort foods.' She gave him a grin and shook her head. 'Believe me, that would *not* be pretty.'

He eyed her closely, the smell of pizza starting to fill the apartment. 'And would you be willing to share some of your stash?'

Her smile widened. The atmosphere was changing between them. They were going from frantic neighbours to something else entirely. Were they flirting here? Was that what was happening? It had been so long for Carrie she wasn't sure she remembered how.

She rested her elbows on the table, sitting her head in her hands. 'Oh, I don't know about sharing. I might be willing to trade.'

'Aha, a wolf in sheep's clothing.'

'What does that mean?'

The gleam wasn't disappearing; in fact, if it was possible, it was getting naughtier. 'You come down here with your innocent smiles, woolly socks and grandma pyjamas—not forgetting an abandoned baby—with your tales of a huge pirate haul of comfort foods upstairs, and now you're trying to hold me to ransom.' He leaned back in his chair and tapped the surface of the table. 'You're not really a grandma-pyjamas girl, are you? That was all just a ruse—you're really a sexy negligee kind of girl.' He lifted his hand and tapped his chin. 'The question is, what colour?'

She could feel her cheeks start to pink up. She hadn't been imagining it. He was flirting with her. And the thing that amazed her—or terrified her—was she wanted to flirt right back. Could she trade her bagels for a kiss?

Wow. That thought made the blood rush into her cheeks. 'What's wrong with grandma pyjamas? They hide a multitude of sins.'

He didn't hesitate. 'You don't have any sins to hide.'

She felt her breath stall. She couldn't breathe in. She definitely couldn't breathe out. She was stuck in that no man's land. He'd said it so quickly. He didn't even have to think about it twice.

What did that mean?

She made a vague attempt to laugh it off—feeling like a nervous teenager instead of a capable twenty-seven-year-old woman. 'You're a man. You really have no knowledge of water-filled bras or hold-your-gut-in underwear.'

He leaned across the table towards her. A cheeky smile across his face. 'And you have no need for either.'

He stayed there. Inches away from her face. Letting her see the tiny, fine laughter lines around his eyes and the smattering of freckles across his cheeks.

Up close and personal Daniel Cooper looked good enough to eat.

And then there was the smell. His cologne. It was affecting her senses. Everything seemed heightened.

Her skin prickled, her hairs standing upright. Her mouth felt dry, her tongue running across her lips.

She couldn't take her eyes off his mouth. Or maybe it was his brown eyes. The kind you could melt into. Both were distracting her. Both were making entirely inappropriate thoughts about a man she hardly knew invade her brain and send a warm feeling to her stomach.

A feeling she hadn't felt since…

It was like a bucket of cold water being tipped over her head. That, and the awareness of the little contented noises from the crib off to the side.

That was why she was here.

Not for any other reason. Dan wasn't interested in her. Not really. He just didn't want to be stuck with some strange baby on his own. He'd made that perfectly clear.

The rest?

She hardly knew the guy, and with handsome looks and a job like his? He probably had women eating out of the palm of his hand.

The thought made her pull back in her chair, her sudden movement causing him to blink and a wrinkle to appear on his brow.

She fixed her eyes on the table. They were safe there.

'Don't you have a friend you can call to help you with Abraham overnight? I'm sure you must have plenty of female friends who'd be willing to give you a hand.'

'What does that mean?'

She shrugged, trying to look complacent. Trying to pretend she hadn't just almost asked him out loud if he had a girlfriend. 'It means there must be someone other than me who can give you a hand.'

He shook his head. 'All the female cops I know are currently run off their feet on duty. My friends who are married all stay too far away to get here and help.' He rolled his eyes. 'And the past few female companions I've had—I wouldn't let within fifty feet of this little guy.'

She almost choked on her soda. 'Then maybe you should be more selective with your female friends.' It was

meant to sound playful, but it came out like a chastise-
ment. All because her insides were wound up so tightly.

He shrugged his shoulders. 'Maybe I should.'

It was left hanging in the air between them.

She had no idea what to make of that. She shifted uncomfortably in the chair. 'You mean there's absolutely
no one you can ask to help you out?'

'Just you.'

'Dan…' She looked out at the falling snow. If it were
even possible, it seemed to be falling even heavier.

She looked around the apartment and threw her hands
in the air. 'I don't like this, Dan. I don't know you and
you don't know me. It doesn't matter that you're a cop and
one of the "good guys".' She put her fingers in the air and
made the sign. 'Baby or no baby, I can't stay in an apartment with some strange guy. I'm just not comfortable.'

He leaned back in his chair, watching her with those
intense brown eyes.

'What if I promise not to come near you at night? You
can sleep in my room and I'll sleep on the sofa. We can
move the crib during the night. That way—you'll still
have some privacy but we'll both know the other is there
if we need a hand.'

Her. In a room by herself with Abraham in a crib. She
was going to throw up right there and then.

And then Dan did something. He reached across the
table and took her hand. 'I need help, Carrie. I need you.
Don't say you can't do it.'

A lump a mile wide appeared in her throat.

He was leaning towards her in the dim light. Her eyes
fixated on his lips. What was wrong with her? And what
was wrong with her emotions?

Everything about her wanted to run right now.

But her ethics and her goodwill were making her

stay. She couldn't abandon Abraham right now. His own mother had already done that.

She had been the one to find him. She should be the one responsible for him.

'I feel really awkward about all this, Dan.' She sighed.

'Then let's see if we can make you feel unawkward.'

'Is that even a word?'

'It is now.' He put his head in his hands. 'So, Carrie McKenzie, what's your favourite movie?'

'What?' It was so not what she was expecting. She was expecting him to pry. To ask why she'd reacted like that. To ask what had been wrong with her this whole evening.

The question was totally random and took her by surprise. It took a few seconds for her brain to think of an appropriate response. 'If it's adults' it's *Dirty Dancing.* If it's kids' then definitely *Toy Story.* What kind of a question is that anyway?'

'A getting-to-know-you question,' he said as he took a sip of his soda. Just like that. So matter-of-fact. Boy, this guy didn't mess around. He raised his eyebrows at her. 'What? You've never been on a date and done the getting-to-know-you questions before?'

She opened her mouth to react, to ask what he meant, then stopped herself dead. He was being casual. He was being cool. And anything she would say right now would be distinctly *uncool.*

One moment she'd been staring into his eyes wondering what it would be like to kiss him—next they were having a first-date kind of conversation.

She took a deep breath. 'It's been a while,' she said quietly. 'I guess I'm out of practice.'

'How long?'

His question was fired back straight away. She could tell a lie here and try and pretend to be blasé. But it just didn't suit her. 'About seven years.' She lifted her head and looked him straight in the eye. She'd had to think about that. Had it really been that long? She'd dated Mark for five years before she was pregnant with Ruby, and it had been more than a year since then. To Dan's credit he didn't even blink, no smart remarks, no more questions. It was as if he just filed the information away for use at a later date.

She shouldn't have said anything. It was time to move things back to the original question. Get off this subject completely. 'You do realise I had to leave out the musicals—for obvious reasons.'

The eyebrows lifted even further. 'What obvious reasons?'

She shrugged. 'I couldn't possibly count them. I'll have you know I know the words to every song of every musical ever made.' She gave him a cheeky wink. 'And some of the dance moves.'

He leaned across the table towards her. 'The thing that scares me about that is—I believe you.' He kept his eyes fixed on hers. 'I might ask to see some of those dance moves.'

She gulped. Colour was rushing to her cheeks. She'd been premature with that wink. Trying to appear sassier and way cooler than she actually was. Maybe not her best idea. Especially when she could almost feel the heat radiating from him. It was time to get this back to safer territory. 'What about you?' That was easy. That kept everything on an even keel.

'Definitely *The Great Escape,* with Steve McQueen on the motorbike. Nothing can beat that.'

She nodded. She'd watched the movie a hundred times—knew some of the lines by heart. 'And a kids' movie?'

He had the good grace to look a little bashful. 'You

might be surprised. But I love *Finding Nemo*. I love Marlin and Dory. It's one of those movies that you turn the TV on, walk past and find yourself sucked in for two hours. Just like that.' He snapped his fingers.

She couldn't help the smile that was plastered on her face. 'I wouldn't have taken you for a *Finding Nemo* kind of guy.'

He took another sip of soda. 'See? There's lots you don't know about me. And vice versa. Are you feeling a little less awkward now.'

She let out a little laugh. 'Just because I know what films you like doesn't mean I feel comfortable about staying in your apartment overnight.'

He nodded slowly. 'So, what brought you to New York, then, Carrie? I know your business owns the apartment upstairs, but why you? Why now?'

There it was. The killer question—sneaked on in there when her defences were down. She should have seen this coming.

How could she answer that? How could she answer any of that without giving herself away?

She picked up her glass and walked over to the sink. 'I'll do the dishes.' She started running the hot water and putting some washing-up liquid into the basin. 'Seems only fair.'

'But what if we're not finished yet?'

He knew. He knew exactly what she was doing. Distraction. Avoidance.

She jumped. His voice was just at her shoulder. His warm breath next to her ear. 'What do you mean?' Darn it. Her voice was wavering. He would have heard it. He would know the effect he was having on her.

So much for acting cool.

He slid his glass in next to hers, his arms on either side of her body, capturing her between them.

She could feel him up against her. One part of her wanted to relax. To let herself relax against him as if this was the most natural thing in the world.

But her frantically beating heart wouldn't let her. And her oxygen-deprived brain wasn't playing ball, either.

She watched the bubbles form in the warm water. Letting them come halfway up her arms.

And what did he mean anyhow?

His hands slid into the basin next to hers. His head coming forward and almost resting on her shoulder. 'I mean, what if we're not finished with this conversation? What if I think you just avoided my question and I want to know why?' His hands were over hers now and her breath hitched in her chest. 'What if I want to get to know you a little better, Carrie McKenzie? Despite our unusual meeting—and despite our chaperone.'

He lifted up a finger and held it in the air. It was covered in bubbles, with the light reflecting off them revealing a rainbow of colours. She couldn't speak. She didn't know what to say—how to respond. Plus she was mesmerised by the bubbles popping one by one. He gave a little laugh, moved his finger and smudged the bubbles on her nose.

She breathed in quickly in surprise, inhaling half the bubbles, leading to a coughing fit. All she could hear was Dan's hearty laughter as she half choked to death, doubled over, then she felt his hand on her back, sharply at first, giving a few knocks to ease her choking, then soothing, rubbing her back while she caught her breath again.

She finally stood upright, his hand still positioned on her back, damp from being in the sink. His other hand fell naturally to her hip.

She turned her head to look at him. 'What was that for?'

'Fun.' He was grinning at her. Showing off his perfect teeth and American good-boy looks.

It was like temptation all in one package.

She bit her lip. 'You've got me all wet.' She squirmed as she pulled her T-shirt from her back. Then cringed at her words. No! She hadn't really said that out loud, had she? She could feel the blood rush to her cheeks. *Please don't let him take anything from that.*

But he just gave her that sexy smile again. 'We can't have that. Do you want something else to wear?' He walked towards one of the doors in the apartment—most likely his bedroom. 'I'm sure I've something in here for you.'

It was blatant. It was obvious. He was full of it.

She folded her arms across her chest. She should be insulted, but the truth was she wasn't really. She was a tiny bit flattered.

She shook her head. 'You were the college playboy, weren't you?'

He leaned against the doorjamb. 'What if I was?'

'Then you should be used to women thinking you're too big for your boots.'

The tension in the air was killing her. If this were a movie she would just walk over, wink and lead him into the bedroom.

He sighed and looked skyward. 'I love it when you talk dirty to me. It's the accent. It's killing me. Every time you talk I just—'

There was a little grunt from the corner of the room and they both leaped about a foot in the air.

Every other thought was pushed out of the window.

In the blink of an eye they were both at the side of the crib, leaning overtop the still-sleeping baby.

'Did that mean something?' asked Dan.

'How am I supposed to know?' she whispered back.

She watched Abraham's little chest rise and fall, rise and fall. It was soothing. It was calming.

'Did we decide on who was doing the night shift?'

She wanted to say no. She wanted to say she couldn't do it and retreat back upstairs to the safety of her silent apartment.

She wanted to put the random flirtations out of her head.

But there was so much churning around in her mind. This baby. Abraham.

He didn't have a mother to comfort him right now. Being around him was hard. Being around him was torture.

But what if this was something she had to do? What if this was something she had to get past?

Sure, she'd grieved for her daughter. She'd wept a bucketload of tears and spent weeks thinking 'what if?' She'd watched her relationship slowly but surely disintegrate around her and Mark. They'd both known it was inevitable, but that hadn't made the parting any easier.

So she'd been bereft. She'd been empty.

But had she allowed herself to heal?

And Dan wasn't anything like Mark. Mark hadn't walked from their relationship—he'd practically run.

And here was Dan stepping in, and taking responsibility—albeit temporarily—for an unknown baby on their doorstep. Maybe for five minutes she should stop judging all men by Mark's standard. Maybe she should take a little time to get to know someone like Dan. Someone who might restore her faith in humanity again.

And did she even know how to do that?

She straightened up, pushing her hands into her back and cricking her spine. Dan was at her back again. 'Carrie, are you okay? Is there something you want to tell me?'

This was it. This was her opportunity to tell him why she was acting so strangely around him and this baby. This was a chance for her to be honest.

This was a chance to clear the air between them.

But she was torn. There was a buzz between them.

They were both feeling it. She liked the flirtation. It made her feel good. It made her feel normal again. Even though there was nothing about this situation that was normal.

She barely knew Dan, but just being in his company made her feel safe. The way he'd reacted to the abandoned baby. The way he'd immediately gone out into the snowstorm to look for the mother, even if he really didn't want to. The way he wasn't afraid to roll up his sleeves and help take care of a baby, even with no experience.

But what would happen right now if she told him?

She could almost get out a huge crystal ball and predict it. The moment she said the words, *'I had a stillbirth last year. My daughter died,'* it would kill anything between them stone dead. It would destroy this buzz in the air.

It would destroy the first feel-good feelings she'd felt in over a year.

So, no matter how hard this was, and for what were totally selfish reasons, she wanted to stay. She might feel a sense of duty, a sense of responsibility towards Abraham, but that wasn't all she was feeling.

And right now she wanted to do something for herself. For Carrie.

Was that really so selfish?

She took a deep breath and turned around to face him.

It would be so easy. It would be so easy to lean forward just a little and see what might happen.

To see if this buzz in the air could amount to anything.

To hold her breath and see if he was sensing what she was feeling—or to see that it had been *so* long that her reactions were completely off. Completely wrong.

He reached up and touched her cheek. 'Carrie?'

She swallowed, biting back the words she really wanted to say and containing the actions she really wanted to take.

She didn't want anything to destroy that tiny little buzz that was currently in her stomach. It felt precious to her. As if it was finally the start of something new.

'How about I take the first shift? I'll sleep on the sofa next to the crib and do the first feed and change at night. You can take over after that.'

She kept her voice steady and her words firm.

She could see something flicker behind his eyes. The questions that he really wanted to ask. He nodded and gave her a little smile.

'Welcome to your first night shift, Carrie McKenzie.'

She watched his retreating back as she sat down on the sofa.

Was she wrong about all this?

Only time, and a whole heap of snow, would tell.

CHAPTER SIX

CARRIE STRETCHED ON the sofa and groaned. The early morning sun was trying to creep through the blinds. It was brighter than normal, which probably meant it was reflecting off the newly laid white snow. All thoughts of everything returning to normal today vanished in the drop of a snowflake.

There was no getting away from it—Baby Abraham was hard work.

She hadn't had time last night to feel sorry for herself and neither had Dan—because Abraham had screamed for three hours solid. She certainly hadn't had time for any romantic dreams. It seemed neither of them had the knack for feeding and burping a new baby.

'Carrie?' Dan came stumbling through the doorway, bleary-eyed, his hair all rumpled and his low-slung jeans skimming his hips.

She screwed up her eyes. Bare-chested. He was bare-chested again. Did the guy always walk about like this? Her brain couldn't cope with a cute naked guy this early in the morning, especially when she was sleep-deprived.

She pointed her finger at him. 'If you wake him, I swear, Dan Cooper, I'll come over there and—'

'Cook me pancakes?'

She sighed and sagged back down onto the sofa, landing on another uncomfortable lump. 'You have the worst sofa known to man.' She twisted on her side and thumped at the lump. 'Oh, it's deceptive. It looks comfortable. When you sit down, you sink into it and think, *Wow!* But sleeping on it?' She blew her hair off her forehead. 'Not a chance!'

'Wanna take the bed tomorrow night?'

With or without you?

She pushed the wayward thought out of her head. How did parents ever go on to have more than one child? Hanky-panky must be the last thing on their minds.

She stood up and stretched. Abraham had finally quietened down around an hour ago. He was now looking all angelic, breathing steadily as if sleeping came easily to him.

'The offer of pancakes sounds good. Do you think you can cook them without waking His Lordship? Because at this rate, ancient or not, Mrs Van Dyke's going to have to take her turn babysitting.'

Dan nodded. 'Right there with you, Carrie. For some reason I thought this would be a breeze. You've no idea how many times I nearly picked up the phone to call Shana last night and beg her to come and pick him up.'

Carrie leaned against the door, giving him her sternest stare. 'Well, maybe you need to think about that a little more.'

'What do you mean?'

'You've been pretty down on Abraham's mum. We're presuming he was just born. But what if he's actually a few days old? Maybe she was struggling to cope. Maybe she's young—or old—and didn't have any help. Maybe she's sick.'

The dark cloud quickly descended over Dan's face again. 'Stop it, Carrie. Stop trying to make excuses for her. And if Abraham's not newly born, then where were his diapers? Where were his clothes? And no matter how hard she was finding it to cope—is that really a good enough reason to dump a baby on a freezing doorstep?'

She shrugged her shoulders. 'I'm just throwing it out there, Dan. I'm not trying to make excuses for anyone. What I am going to do is take a shower and change my clothes.' She headed over to the door. 'I'll be back in ten minutes and I expect my breakfast to be waiting.' She gave him a wink.

He lifted his eyebrows. 'Hmm, getting all feisty now, are we? I think I preferred you when you were all *please help me with this baby.*'

She picked up the nearest cushion and tossed it at his head. 'No, you didn't,' she said as she headed out the door.

'No. I didn't,' he breathed as he watched her head upstairs.

Carrie took a few moments to pull open her blinds and look outside.

A complete white-out with no signs of life. Not a single footprint on the sidewalk. Every car was covered in snow, with not a single chance of moving anywhere soon. It seemed that New York City would remain at a standstill for another day.

For a moment she wished she were in the middle of Central Park. Maybe standing at Belvedere Castle and looking out over the Great Lawn, or standing on Bow Bridge watching the frozen lake. It would be gorgeous there right now.

She didn't care that it was closed because of the snowfall. She didn't care about the potential for falling trees.

All she could think about was how peaceful it would be right now—and how beautiful.

But with daydreams like this, was she just looking for another opportunity to hide away?

She tried to push the thoughts from her head. There was too much going on in there. What with virtually bare baby and bare-chested Dan, her head was spinning.

She switched on the shower and walked through to her bedroom, stripping off her clothes and pulling her dressing gown on while she waited for the water to heat.

The contents of her wardrobe seemed to mock her. A sparkly sequin T-shirt. Trying too hard. A red cardigan. Impersonating Mrs Van Dyke. A plain jumper. Frumpy.

She pulled out another set of jeans and a bright blue cap-sleeved sweater. It would have to do.

Her eyes caught sight of the silver box beneath her bed and her heart flipped over.

It was calling her. It was willing her to open it.

She couldn't help it. It was automatic. She knelt down and touched it, pulling it out from under the bed and sitting it on top of the bed in front of her.

Her precious memories, all stored in a little box. But how could she look at them now after she'd just been holding another baby?

It almost seemed like a betrayal.

She ran the palm of her hand over the lid of the box. Just doing it made her heartbeat quicken. She could feel the threat of tears at the backs of her eyes.

She couldn't think about this now. She just couldn't.

Steam was starting to emerge from the bathroom. The shower was beckoning. She couldn't open the box. Not now. Not while she was in the middle of all this.

For the contents of that box she needed space. She needed time.

She needed the ability to cry where no one could hear. No one could interrupt.

She sucked air into her lungs. Not now. She had to be strong. She had to be focused. Her hand moved again—one last final touch of the silver box of memories—before she tore herself away and headed inside, closing the door firmly behind her.

There was a whimper in the corner. Dan's pancakes were sizzling; was the noise going to wake the baby? He sure hoped not. He didn't know if he could take another cry-fest.

The television newscaster looked tired. He'd probably been stuck inside the New York studio all night. The yellow information strip ran along the bottom of the news constantly. Telling them how much snow had fallen, how the city was stranded, all businesses were closed, food supplies couldn't get in. Nothing about how to look after a newborn baby.

It was time to do an internet search again. They must have done something wrong last night. There was no way a baby would cry like that for nothing. At least he hoped not.

He tossed the pancakes and his stomach growled loudly. He was starving and they smelled great.

A jar of raspberry jam landed on the counter next to him. She was back. And she smelled like wild flowers—even better than pancakes.

'What's that for?'

'The pancakes.'

'Jelly?' He shook his head. 'Pancakes need bacon and maple syrup. That's what a real pancake wants.'

She opened his fridge. 'Pancakes need butter and raspberry jam. It's the only way to eat them.'

He wrinkled his nose, watching as she flicked on the kettle.

'And tea. Pancakes need tea.'

He grimaced. 'You might be out of luck, then. I've only got extra-strong coffee.'

She waved a bag at him. 'Just as well I brought my own, then.'

Dan served the pancakes onto two plates and carried them over to the table, pulling some syrup from his empty cupboards and lifting the brewing coffee pot. 'I can't tempt you, then?'

Something flickered in her eyes. Something else. Something different. She gave him a hesitant smile. 'I'm an English girl. It's tea and butter and jam all the way.'

They both knew that the flirtation was continuing.

And right now he wanted to tempt her. The cop in him wanted to forget about the mountain of paperwork he'd need to complete about this baby. The cop in him wanted to forget about the investigation that would have to be carried out.

The guy in him wanted to concentrate on the woman in the lovely blue sweater sitting at his table with her jar of raspberry jam. He wanted to reach over to touch the curls that were coiling around her face, springing free from the clip that was trying to hold them back. He wanted to see if he could say something to make her cheeks flush even pinker than they currently were. He wanted a chance to stare into those cornflower-blue eyes and ask her what she was hiding from him. What she was guarding herself from.

He lifted the maple syrup and squirted it onto his pancakes. She was concentrating on spreading butter on her pancakes smoothly and evenly with one hand while stirring her tea with the other hand.

He'd opened the blinds partly to let a little natural light into the apartment. And seeing Carrie McKenzie in the cold light of day was more than just a little shock to his system.

The girl was beautiful. From the little sprinkle of freckles over her nose to the way she wrinkled her brow when she was concentrating.

He'd felt a pull towards her last night, when he'd seen her in the dim lights of his apartment. But now he had a chance to look at her—to really look at her—and all he could think about was why on earth he hadn't noticed her before.

How on earth could he have stayed in an apartment building with someone so incredibly pretty and not have noticed? He could just imagine the cops at the station if they ever got wind of that.

Carrie put a teaspoon into the jam jar and spread some jam onto her pancakes. 'Are you going to watch me eat them, too?' she asked, a smile spreading across her face.

He jerked backwards in his seat. 'Sorry. I was just thinking.'

'About Abraham?'

Wow. No, Abraham was the last thing he'd been thinking about, and as if in indignation there was a squawk from the crib. Dan set down his cutlery, gave a sigh and waved his hand at her as she went to stand up. 'Stay where you are—you're still eating. I'm finished. Maybe he's hungry again. I sterilised the bottles so we should be fine.'

It was amazing how quickly you could learn to make a baby bottle. A few minutes later he lifted Abraham from the crib and settled him onto his shoulder for a bit.

'Carrie? Does he look okay to you? What do you think about his colour?'

She set down her mug of tea and walked over. 'It's kind of hard to tell.' She shrugged her shoulders. 'We don't really know anything about the ethnicity of his parents, so I'm not entirely sure what normal will look like for him.'

She walked over to the window and pulled the blinds up completely. 'Bring him over here so I can get a better look at him.'

Dan carried him over and they stood for a few seconds looking at him in the daylight. 'He looks a tiny bit yellow, don't you think?'

She nodded. 'Jaundice. Isn't it supposed to be quite common in newborns?'

He gave her that smile again. The why-are-you-asking-me-something-I-couldn't-possibly-know smile.

They both glanced at the computer. Carrie took a few seconds to punch in the words and then—nothing.

She turned towards him. 'Looks like your internet has just died.'

'Really? It's usually really reliable. Must be the weather.'

She stared out the window. 'It must be something to do with the snow. I hope the power supply doesn't get hokey. That sometimes happens in storms back home.'

He looked at her with an amused expression on his face. 'Hokey?'

She raised her eyebrows. 'What? It's a word.'

'Really? Where?'

She gave him a sarcastic smile. 'I'd look it up for you online but your internet is down.'

'Ha-ha. Seriously—what are we going to do about Abraham? Do you think it's dangerous? I mean, he's drinking okay and—' he wrinkled his nose '—he certainly knows how to poo.'

She raised her eyebrows at him. 'Really? Again? Then maybe you should phone a friend. It's a bit like the blind leading the blind here. I guess you'll need to phone Shana. There really isn't anyone else we can ask.'

He gave her a smile as he walked over to put Abraham on the dark towel to change him. He could only imagine the chaos going on at Angel's Children's Hospital right now. Last thing he wanted to do was add to Shana's headache. But he wanted to make sure that Abraham was safe in his care. Screamer or not, he wanted to do the best he could for this baby.

'Do you think this is how all new parents feel? As if they don't know anything at all?'

Carrie turned her back and walked over to the countertop, picking up her mug of tea. Trying to find the words that would counteract the tight feeling in her chest. She was trying so hard. So hard not to let these things creep up on her. Then—out of the blue—some random comment would just cut her in two.

She set her mouth in a straight line. 'Most new parents would have a whole host of textbooks or family to ask—we don't.'

He pulled his mobile from his pocket. 'I guess I'll phone Shana, then.' He dialled the number and waited for Shana to be paged, pressing the button to put her on speakerphone as he wrestled with Abraham's nappy.

'What?'

Not good. She sounded snarky. 'Shana, it's Dan.'

'Is the baby okay?' Straight to the point as usual. Did she ever stop—just for a second?

He took a deep breath. 'We're not sure. Abraham looks kinda yellow. Carrie thinks he might be jaundiced.'

'Who is Abraham?'

'The baby. Who did you think I was asking about?'

'Oh, so you've given him a name. Abraham—I like it.'

'I'm glad I've got your approval. What about his colour?'

'More common in breastfed babies—but not unusual. It could be jaundice.' It was clear she was thinking out loud. 'Could be serious if it's appeared within twenty-four hours of birth—but then we don't know that, do we?'

'So what do we do now?'

'Ideally, I'd like to check him over and draw some blood.'

'Well, that's not gonna happen any time soon. What should we do in the meantime?'

'Monitor him—I mean, watch him. Make sure he feeds regularly and he's not too sleepy. Don't be afraid to wake him up to feed him. Let him get some natural light onto his skin. Put his crib next to the window and keep a close eye on his colour. If you think it's getting worse—or he has any other symptoms—phone me, straight away. Check the whites of his eyes. If they start to turn yellow you need to call me.'

Dan couldn't help it. He lifted a sleepy eyelid immediately, much to the disgust of Abraham, who squealed loudly at being disturbed.

Shana let out a laugh at the other end of the phone. 'If he's that annoyed, he's doing okay. But let me know if you're concerned.' She ended the call abruptly—probably a thousand other things to do.

Dan stared at the receiver in his hand. 'She never even told me if she contacted social services,' he murmured.

'Probably too busy.' He jumped at the quiet voice in his ear. He should have realised she'd stepped closer to him. The wave of wild flowers seemed like her trademark scent.

He held his breath. Did she realise she was standing so

close? Was there something, somewhere that kept pulling them closer together? Because it sure felt like it.

Her gaze dropped to the floor and he was sorry, because he liked when she was so close he could see the other little flecks of colour in her cornflower-blue eyes. Tiny little fragments of green that you could only see up close. She tugged at the bottom of her sweater, obviously feeling a little self-conscious.

'I heard a little of that,' she said. 'Shall I move his crib over to the window?'

He nodded and she moved swiftly, pulling all the blinds up completely and drowning the room in the reflected brilliant white light from outside. He flinched, his hand on Abraham's back. 'Wow. Well, if that can't beat a bit of jaundice I don't know what will.'

She turned around and shot him a killer smile.

His reactions were automatic. Abraham was put down in the brightly lit crib and Dan found himself standing right at her side.

He was obviously going stir-crazy. Being trapped in his apartment with a beautiful lady was playing havoc with his senses. He was going to have to try and find some other way to distract himself.

All his usual self-control was flying out the window around Carrie McKenzie and he had no idea why.

She was hiding something from him. And who could blame her? They hardly knew each other. He couldn't expect her to tell him her every dark secret.

But Dan's instincts were good. Probably due to his experiences as a child. Experiences that had affected his ability to form real, trusting relationships with women.

So why was it that the first time he ever really wanted to get to know someone, he picked the one woman who was clearly hiding something? Was he crazy?

He had to do something—anything—to distract himself from all this. 'Any plans today, Carrie?'

She folded her arms across her chest. 'Apart from strapping on my jet pack to fly across New York, get to work, put in a ten-hour day, find some groceries and clothes for a stranded baby, no, nothing at all.' She was shaking her head, staring out at the five-foot-deep snow. She was obviously as stir-crazy as he was.

He waved his pink cast at her. 'Well, I'm going to go swimming. Then I'm going to strap on my skis—can't waste good snow like this—and finally I'm going to ship Shana over here to check out Abraham and make sure he's okay.' He gave her a little smile. 'And if she could bring some beers, sodas and a fresh pizza, that would be great.'

Carrie leaned against the window and sighed. 'What are we going to do all day?'

'If we can't play our imaginary games?'

Carrie counted off on her fingers. 'We could have a soapathon. You know, watch all the soaps that you haven't for years. Watch them all day.' Her brow wrinkled. 'I don't really know the names of any of the soaps in America. Are they any good?'

He shook his head. 'Next idea.'

She looked around. 'We could reorganise. Everyone needs a spring clean. It could be the perfect time.'

'Get your hands off my stuff, McKenzie,' he growled at her. 'Anyway, haven't you already realised there's nothing in my cupboards to reorganise?'

She laughed. 'Okay. I didn't think you'd go for that one.

'Do you have games? Board games? I could challenge you.' She could obviously see him racking his brain. 'Chess?' She was getting desperate.

'I might have some board games. But they will be years old. Some are probably originals.'

He walked over to a cupboard and went down on his hands and knees, crawling right inside. She heard some groans as some sports-kit bags, rackets and balls shot past her ankles. 'Need some help in there?'

There was a little cloud of dust followed by a coughing fit and Dan crawled out with a pile of games in his hands. He held them out towards her. 'How about these?'

She carried them over to the table. 'Wow. You were right—some of these are originals.' And even better than being originals, they all showed visible signs of wear and tear. It was obvious that these games had been used and loved at some point in their history. 'I think these would be perfect.'

He appeared at her side, a big smudge across his cheek. 'What does the winner get?'

She couldn't help it. Her fingers reached up to wipe the smudge from his cheek. He froze, then caught her hand in his before she could pull it away. 'What does the winner of this games tournament get?'

His words were quiet this time, the jokey aspect removed, and she could sense the feeling hanging in the air between them.

A whole variety of answers sprang to mind; some of them would make her hair curl and save her hours at the hairdressers.

Then a safe option shot into her mind. 'Can you bake?'

'What?' He looked stunned. He'd obviously had something else in mind.

'I said can you bake?'

'I suppose so. My grandmother baked all the time. But it's been years since I've tried anything like that.

Anyhow, you've seen my cupboards. Old Mother Hubbard had nothing on me. I don't have any ingredients.'

'But I do. There—it's settled. The loser has to make the winner a cake. Just what we need on a day like this.'

'You'd trust me to make you a cake?'

'I love cake. I'd trust anyone to make me a cake.' She held out her hand. 'Do we have a deal?'

He hesitated for just a second, before his competitive edge took over. 'I'm a chocolate cake kind of guy. You better get your apron out.'

The waft of baking filled the whole apartment. It had been years since the place had smelled like this. It only made him miss his grandmother more.

Apple pie. That had been the thing she'd baked most frequently. And it was the smell he most associated with his grandmother. Freshly baked juicy apples bubbling under the surface of the golden pie, topped with a sprinkling of sugar. Bliss.

Now the smell was a little different. The timer on the oven buzzed. He hadn't even known that his oven had a timer, let alone how to use it. But Carrie had insisted it was essential to bake the perfect cake.

Or cakes as it had turned out.

The game marathon had resulted in a dead heat.

And now his kitchen was filled with the smells of chocolate cake and carrot cake. He pulled the door open as a waft of heat flooded out from the oven. The chocolate cake that Carrie had baked for him looked spectacular. His carrot cake? Not so much. A little charred on top. But nothing that the mound of frosting she'd made him prepare couldn't hide.

He lifted both out and watched as she tipped them onto a wire rack to cool—yet another thing she'd brought down from her apartment upstairs. Along with the mixing bowls, spatulas, ingredients and cake tins. She probably had more of her possessions currently in his apartment than her own.

Baking was definitely her thing. She seemed relaxed, she seemed happy and she liked it. Even Abraham seemed to be more chilled out. Two feeds, lots of wind and no crying fits. Finally things were starting to settle.

'We need to let the cakes cool before we ice them. So let's give them a minute.' She pulled out some plates from the cupboard, then shook her head and went back to look for more.

'What's wrong with my plates'?

'Nothing.' Her voice was muffled as she crouched in one of his kitchen cupboards. 'But cake-eating is an art form. You have to have better plates than those. Aha.' She pulled herself back out of the cupboard with something in her hand. 'These are much better.'

She stood up and put the fine bone china plates on the countertop. White with tiny red flowers painted on them. Another remnant of his grandmother. She'd used them for eating cake, too—probably why they were now hidden in the depths of his cupboards.

The lights flickered around them.

'Uh-oh,' murmured Carrie. 'That's the third time that's happened now.'

Dan walked over next to her. 'This could be a problem.'

She turned to face him. 'Why?'

'Because I don't have any candles.'

She looked at him in mock horror and held up her hands. 'You don't? What kind of emergency guy are you? Aren't you cops supposed to be prepared for anything?'

He didn't move, just kept his eyes fixed on her face.

'Not everything.' His voice was quiet, barely a whisper. There was no mistaking the alternative meaning.

She looked up at him. He was only inches from her face, inches from her lips. The lights flickered again, so he moved a little closer, his hand resting on her hip.

She didn't move. Not an inch. Her tongue came out slowly and ran along her lips, as if, without even realising it, she was preparing them for kissing.

She could feel the pull. She could feel the same draw that he felt. He wasn't wrong about this—he could tell.

It had been there all day and they had been dancing around the edges of it. But now it wasn't hiding any more. It was right there in front of them.

His fingers pressed into her hip, pulling her pelvis a little closer to his, giving her every opportunity to object—to resist.

But she didn't.

He leaned forward. 'Carrie McKenzie, I'm going to kiss you now.' His voice was low, trying to entice her to edge forward to hear it.

But she didn't do that.

She did something totally unexpected. She lifted her hands and wrapped them around his neck. 'It's about time,' she whispered as she rose up on her toes to meet his lips.

Honey. She tasted of honey. Was there honey in the chocolate cake she'd just baked? At least that was what it felt like. The kiss started out shy—tentative. He didn't want her to feel forced. He didn't want her to feel as if she couldn't say no. He just prayed she wouldn't.

Her fingers wound up across his shorn hairline as the kiss deepened. As her tongue teased with his. Then she let out a little sigh that almost undid him completely.

He should pull back. He should let her out of his arms

to give her time to think about this. There was still so much about Carrie McKenzie he didn't know.

But right now he didn't want to. Letting her go was the last thing he wanted to do right now. Not when she seemed to be matching him move for move.

And in an instant everything was black.

They jumped apart, then instantly moved back together again, bashing noses.

'Oops.' Carrie started to giggle as she rubbed her nose. 'I guess that will be the power cut, then.'

'I guess it is. Do you have any candles?'

'Yeah, I have some upstairs in my apartment. Not the emergency kind. More the bathroom kind.'

'What's a bathroom kind of candle?'

'The scented kind. The kind you light around your bath.'

He shook his head. 'I guess I'll take your word for it. We'll need something.'

'I'll go up and get them.'

He slipped his hand into hers. 'Let me come with you.'

'What about the baby?' She glanced over in the direction of the silent crib.

'Leave the door open. We'll only be a few minutes. He's sleeping. Nothing's going to happen.'

He liked holding her hand. It felt right inside his. It fitted.

They stumbled towards the door, leaving it wide open, and stepped out into the hallway. There was no light in the hall at all. No street lights shining in. No gentle glow underneath the opposite door. It was weird. He couldn't remember the last time there had been a power cut— probably why he didn't have any candles. He reached out for the banister and started up the stairs, giving her a gentle tug behind him.

They reached her door and she glanced in the direction of Mrs Van Dyke's apartment. 'Do you think we should check on her?'

'Maybe. Do you have any extra candles she could have?'

She let out a little laugh. 'Oh, I have a whole year's supply in here.' She pushed open the door to her apartment and walked over to the bathroom, bending down and pulling things from one of the cupboards.

Dan looked around as best he could. It took a few seconds for his eyes to adjust to the dark. The only available light was the moonlight outside, streaming in through one of the windows.

Neat. Tidy. Everything in its place.

There was nothing strange about that. Lots of women he knew were tidy. But there was something else. Something he couldn't quite put his finger on.

He moved across the room, putting his hand on the back of the leather sofa.

This wasn't Carrie's place, so she wouldn't have chosen any of the furnishings. But she'd been here for a few months now.

The darkness wasn't helping. Nor was the sight of Carrie's behind in her jeans as she bent over the cupboards and pulled out an array of candles.

She walked back over, fumbled through a drawer for a box of matches and lit the candle she was holding in a glass jar. The warm light spread up around her face, illuminating her like some TV movie star.

Candlelight suited her. Her pale skin glowed, her brown curly hair shiny and her eyes bright. She smiled as she held it out towards him and the aroma from the melting wax started to emerge.

He wrinkled his nose. 'What is that? Washing powder?'

She waved her hand in the air to waft the smell a little further. 'Close. Cotton fresh. I've also got lavender, orange, cinnamon, raspberry, spring dew and rain shower.'

'Sheesh. Who names these candles?'

She lit another one and moved over next to him again. 'I think it would be a great job. Right up there with naming paint shades.'

'You'd have a field day doing that.'

'You can bet on it. Imagine the fun. Shades of yellow—sunshine rays or daffodil petals. Shades of purple—sugared violet, lavender dreams or amethyst infusion.' Even in this dim light he could see the twinkle in her eyes and the enthusiasm in her voice were completely natural.

'Wow. You weren't joking, were you?' He took a little step closer.

She shook her head slowly. 'I don't know how the careers advisor missed it from my career matches.'

He could see her automatic reaction. She was drawn towards him.

A thought jumped into his head, tearing him away from the impure thoughts starting to filter through his brain. He groaned. 'What about the power? How can we sterilise the bottles and make the milk for Abraham?'

She touched his arm and an electric current shot straight up towards his shoulder, sending his brain straight back to his original thoughts. There was hesitation. She'd noticed it, too. 'We should be fine,' she said quietly, lifting her eyes slowly to meet his. 'I had just boiled the kettle and resterilised the bottles. We can make up one when we go back downstairs.' She was staring at him. Even in the dark light he could see the way her pupils had widened, taking over most of her eyes. Natural in the dark, but it didn't feel like that kind of response. It felt like another entirely.

He set his candle down on a nearby side table, letting the glow shine upwards, emphasising the curve of her breasts and hips. He couldn't pretend any more. He couldn't hide his reactions. He didn't want to.

He put his hand on her hip, pulling her closer, leaving her with a candle jar clutched to her chest. 'So, not only am I marooned here—' he waved his other hand around '—in a snowstorm, with the power out, with a lady who found a baby on the doorstep and knows all the words to every musical known to man—' his hand came back to rest on her other hip, pulling her even closer with only the burning candle between them '—I find out she's also slightly crazy. With career ambitions even the career-matching machine couldn't have predicted.'

There was hesitancy there. A little apprehension—even though they had been lip-locked a few minutes ago. But Carrie was gradually relaxing. He could feel the tension leaving her arms and her body easing into his. She moved the flickering candle from between them, pressing her warm breasts against his chest. If she moved any more, things could start to get out of hand.

But she was smiling. A happy, relaxed smile. A warm smile. The kind he'd only glimpsed on a few rare occasions over the past two days. The kind that showed she'd let her guard down. The metal portcullis that was kept firmly in place was starting to ease up—ever so gently.

It revealed the real Carrie McKenzie. The kind of person she could be—if she was brave enough. The kind of person he'd like to know more about—be it vertical or horizontal.

Stop it! He tried to push those thoughts from his crowded head. Carrie just wasn't that kind of girl. And instead of lessening the attraction it only heightened it.

He reached up and pulled one of her long chestnut curls from behind her ear. 'I like your hair down. It's beautiful. Really flattering.' He hesitated a second as his finger brushed the side of her face. He didn't want to push this. He didn't want to scare her off.

Even though his male urges were giving him a whole other vibe his brain kept jumping in to keep him in check. 'Sexy,' he murmured, holding his breath to see the effect of his words.

He could almost predict she would tense and pull away. It was the biggest part of Carrie that he'd seen over the past couple of days.

But something had changed. The dim lights, the candles or just her new relaxed state meant that instead of pulling away she brushed closer against him and rested her hands on his shoulders. 'Sexy—I like that.' Her breath was dancing against his skin. He had to let her be the one to make the move. He had to be sure about this.

Those few seconds seemed like forever.

But she did move. Her body pressed against his a little more firmly and he felt her rise up on her tiptoes. Her lips brushed gently against his, then with a little more confidence her kisses became surer. His hands moved to her ribs; he could feel her deep breaths against the palms of his hands. He couldn't stop them. He wanted to do more.

She had one hand on his back, the other at the side of his face as she deepened their kiss, teasing him with her tongue.

It was driving him crazy. *She* was driving him crazy.

He wanted to release the emotions and passions that were currently stifled in his chest doing their best impression of a smouldering volcano. But Carrie had to feel in control. He could sense how important that was.

He had to concentrate. He couldn't lose himself in this. It was far too tempting. Far too tempting by half.

All he had to do was edge his hands a little higher and then he would feel her warm skin, be able to cup the warm mounds of her breasts and...

He stepped back. Slowly, pulling his lips apart from hers. Careful to let her know he hadn't suddenly changed his mind about this.

His voice was hoarse. Too much pent-up expectation. 'I hate to remind you, Carrie McKenzie, but we have a sleeping baby downstairs. We've only been gone a few minutes but if you distract me for another second...' He let his voice drift off, leaving her in no doubt as to his meaning.

He wasn't pulling away from her because he didn't want to kiss her.

He was pulling away because right now he *should*.

She bit her lip.

A tiny movement. And one that could be the complete undoing of him. He wanted to slam her apartment door shut and drag her through to the bedroom. And forget about everything else and everyone.

But on the floor underneath them lay a little boy. He'd already been abandoned by one adult. He certainly didn't need to be abandoned by two others.

Daniel's sense of duty ground down on his chest.

He tugged at his jeans, trying to adjust them. Some human reactions were as natural as breathing.

Others he would have to control.

She nodded. 'Let me grab a few things that I might need.' She picked up one of the candles and walked over to her bedroom, opening a cupboard and pulling a few items of clothing out.

In the flickering candlelight he could make out the outline of her bed and possessions scattered around the room. A smile danced across his lips. Carrie McKenzie's bedroom. Would he ever get an invite into there?

It wasn't entirely what he'd expected. No flowers. No pink.

A bright green duvet, a mountain of pillows and a matching fleece comforter across the bottom of the bed. An electronic tablet and a few books were scattered on the bedside table, along with a few other obligatory candles. He wondered what scent they were. What scent she liked to fall asleep to.

A silver box lay on top of the bedclothes.

Her eyes flickered over to it and there was something—was it panic?—before she moved quickly, picked up the box and tucked it under the bed. She tucked the assorted clothes under her arm and appeared under his nose. 'Ready.'

It was just a little too bright. A little too forced. As if she was trying to distract him.

He'd just been kissing this woman but there were still parts of her she wanted to keep hidden. A tiny flare of anger lit in his stomach, only for him to extinguish it almost as quickly. He should know better than most. Everyone had secrets they wanted to hide. Parts of their life they wanted to remain hidden. Why should Carrie be any different?

'Let's go. We need to check on Abraham, and Mrs Van Dyke.'

He turned to follow her out of the door. And then it hit him.

That was what was wrong with this place.

There was nothing really of *Carrie*.

Oh, she might have her candles and a few books.

But there were no photos. Not a single one.

It sent a strange sensation down his spine. Every woman he'd ever known had pictures of their friends and family dotted around. Even he had some family pictures in various places around his apartment.

Carrie didn't have one. Not a single one.

What did that mean? She'd been here two months, surely enough time to get some family snaps out. Wasn't there anyone to miss back home?

'Dan, what's wrong? Let's go.' Carrie stuck her head back around the door, her impatience clear. Or was it her hurry to get him out of her apartment?

With one last look around he followed her out and pulled the door shut behind him.

There was more to Carrie McKenzie than met the eye.

And he was determined to get to the bottom of it.

CHAPTER SEVEN

WHEN CARRIE OPENED her eyes that morning it was to a totally different sight.

Blue walls and white bed linen.

The disorientation was over in an instant. She drew in a deep breath. It was strange waking up in someone else's bed.

She'd felt like that the first few nights in the apartment upstairs. Then, after a week, she hadn't even noticed. It just proved to her how much *home* in London hadn't really felt like *home* any more.

Dan's place was much more lived-in than hers. But then, he'd spent most of his life here. In amongst the state-of-the-art television and digital sound system, there were tiny ornaments, old picture frames and the odd piece of antique furniture. The little dark wood side table next to the door was her favourite. He hadn't really said much about how he'd ended up living with his grandmother and she didn't want to pry.

Just as she didn't want him to pry too much, either.

An unconscious smile crept across her face. He'd kissed her.

And she'd kissed him back.

Her first kiss since…

And it felt nice. It felt good.

Actually it felt a lot more than all that. Nice and good made it sound like a safe kiss. A kiss that was taking her on the road to recovery.

But Dan's kiss had ignited a whole lot more than that in her. She almost couldn't sleep last night when they'd parted. It was amazing how long you could lie staring up at the ceiling while your brain was on a spin cycle.

She looked around the room. A pair of his boots were on the floor, along with a pair of jeans slung across a chair. She could almost still see the shape of his body in those jeans. And it sent another lot of little pulses skittering across her skin.

Dan had decided to do the night shift last night. She was almost sure another two slices of her chocolate cake had been the appropriate bribe for him to spend the night on his lumpy sofa.

Abraham. He appeared in her thoughts like a flash and she sat upright in bed.

She hadn't heard him. She hadn't heard him at all.

A chill spread across her body instantly, reaching straight down into the pit of her stomach. Sending its icy tendrils around her heart.

No. Surely not.

She was up and out of the bedroom before her feet even felt as if they'd touched the wooden floor. Her steps across the floor the quickest she'd ever moved. Her breath caught in her throat and she leaned over the crib.

Empty. It was empty.

She spun around. 'Dan—' And stopped dead.

Dan was upright on the sofa, fast asleep with Abraham tucked against his shoulder. She'd obviously missed quite a bit last night. Why hadn't he woken her up? More importantly, why hadn't she heard?

In her haste across the room she hadn't even looked

over at his slumped frame. She'd been so focused on Abraham. So focused on the baby.

Dan's eyes flickered open and he lifted his hand covered in the cast to rub his sleep-ridden eyes. 'Wake my baby and I'll kill you,' he growled, echoing her words from the day before.

'I'm sorry,' she gasped. 'I just woke up and realised I hadn't heard him all night. I thought something was wrong. Then he wasn't in the crib and I—' She stopped to draw breath, conscious of the look on Dan's face. 'What? What is it?'

The coldness of the wooden floor was starting to seep through her toes and up her legs, making goosebumps erupt on her skin—her woefully exposed skin.

'Oh!' She lifted her arms across her breasts. Some body reactions weren't for public view.

Dan had been right about her other nightwear. Her tiny satin nightie covered her bum and not much more. Last night she'd been wearing her dressing gown—her eternal protection—and hadn't removed it until she'd climbed into bed. The power had come back on and the temperature in the apartment was warmer than usual, both having agreed that due to the lack of appropriate clothing for Abraham they needed to raise the temperature slightly. So she couldn't have bundled up in her usual fleece pyjamas—not without melting completely—and Dan would never see her in her nightie anyway, would he? Until now.

The cold floor had the ultimate effect on her body. Her nipples were firmly pressed into the sides of her arms across her chest. They had obviously been the feature that had caught his attention.

'Give me a second,' she blurted as she made a run for the bedroom and the sanctity of her dressing gown.

Too late she realised how much her slight nightie must have flapped around her behind, leaving little to the imagination.

She emerged a few minutes later, trying not to look completely flustered.

'I'll make breakfast this morning,' she said brightly. 'It was American yesterday—you made pancakes. So I think it will be tea, toast and marmalade this morning.'

Dan couldn't wipe the smile off his face, even though she was trying desperately to change the earlier subject. He shook his head. 'I sense distraction techniques, Carrie McKenzie. But since I'm a gentleman with an empty stomach I'll let it go. As for toast and marmalade? No, you don't. You sabotaged the pancakes with your butter and jam. And don't even think about making me tea after the night I've had. I need coffee. With at least three shots.'

Guilt surged through her and she sat down next to him. She was safe now; she was completely covered. 'Was Abraham really bad last night? I'm so sorry. I never heard a thing.'

'I noticed.' He shook his head and gave her a weary smile. 'If I'd needed you, Carrie, I would have woken you up. But it was fine.' He paused. 'Well, actually, it wasn't fine, but I closed the door so you wouldn't hear. I figured this was hard enough for you and a night with no sleep wouldn't help.'

She was stunned.

It was no secret she hadn't managed to hide things from Dan. He'd already asked her on more than one occasion what was wrong and she hadn't responded. Because she didn't feel ready to.

It had only been a few days. And she didn't know him that well—not really. But Dan had taken actions last night to make sure she had some respite. He was reading her better than she could have ever thought. Was it the cop instincts? Did he just know when to push and when to back off?

Did they even teach things like that in cop school? Or was he just good at reading her? At sensing when things were tough and she needed to step back. She wasn't ready to share. Or was she?

Her friends back home all knew about the stillbirth. And they either tiptoed around her or tried to make her talk. Neither way worked for her.

She needed to talk when *she* was ready. Not when they were ready.

Maybe it would be easier to share with someone from outside her circle of friends. Someone who could be impartial and not try to hit her with a whole host of advice about what to do and how she should feel.

Dan was the first guy to cause her stomach to flutter in a whole year. She'd thought that part of her had died. And nothing would cause it to wake up again. But the close proximity was definitely a factor. How much of a risk would it be to tell him, to trust him?

Looking at the snow outside, they could be here for at least another whole day. The flickering TV in the corner of the room still had the yellow strip running across the news report, telling about more snowfall and more people cut off from their family and friends. 'I see there's going to be more snow.' She nodded at the TV.

He sighed. 'Yeah.' He shrugged his shoulders as his eyes met hers. 'Seems like we're not going anywhere fast.'

'At least the electric shower will be working. And the kettle and hob. I'll be able to sterilise things and make some more bottles for Abraham.' The practical things. The things that always came into her brain first.

But there was something else there. Something else drumming away inside her head.

They were stuck here. For at least another day.

Another day with delectable Dan.

Another day with a baby. Could she cope? Could she do this again?

It was as if something happened inside. A little flare sparked inside her brain. This was it. This was her chance.

If only she had the courage.

She held out her hands towards Abraham. Would Dan notice they were trembling? 'May I?'

He nodded and handed over the half-sleeping babe to her. Abraham didn't seem to mind who was holding him. He snuggled instantly into her shoulder, obviously preferring the upright position.

There was a loud splurging noise, closely followed by a smell creeping around the apartment. Carrie wrinkled her nose. 'Oh, Abraham. How could you?'

Her hand felt along his back and came into contact with a little splurge at the side of the nappy and half-way up his back. She let out a sigh and set him down in the crib.

'I guess it's going to be a bath for you, little sir.'

'How are we going to manage that? We don't have a baby bath.'

Carrie walked over to the deep kitchen sink. 'We'll improvise. This is the best we've got. Don't you remember ever getting bathed in the kitchen sink as a child?'

He shook his head. 'Can't say that I do. Is it an English tradition?'

Carrie had started to scrub the sink within an inch of her life. 'I guess it must be, then. My gran's got some pictures of me sitting bare naked in her kitchen sink. I thought everyone did that.'

She filled the sink with some tepid water and baby bubble bath before testing the temperature. She stripped Abraham's clothes and put them in a bucket of cold water to soak. Dan wrinkled his nose. 'I'm going to wash these? Really? Wouldn't it be better just putting them in the garbage?'

Carrie shook her head. 'We don't have that luxury, Dan. We only have a few things that fit him. They'll just need to be soaked and then boil washed.'

Dan lifted the bucket and headed down to the laundry. 'Be back in five,' he said.

Carrie lifted Abraham from the towel he was squirming on. 'Let's see if we can get this all off you,' she said as she gently lowered him into the warm water.

The expression on his face was priceless. First he squirmed. Then he let out a little yelp of dismay. It only lasted for a few seconds before the shock of being cold disappeared and his little body picked up the surrounding warm water. He gave a little shudder. Then started to kick his legs.

She smiled. His first baby bath.

Her first baby bath. And it was just the two of them.

There was something about it that was so nice. She knew this should be a moment that he shared with his mother. But it was almost as if this were meant to be. She watched as his little legs stretched out and kicked in the water in the sink. She lapped the water over his stomach and chest. He let out a range of little noises. If she didn't know better she could imagine he was almost smiling.

Some babies screamed when they hit the bathwater, hating being stripped of their warm cocoonlike clothes. But not Abraham. He seemed to relish it, enjoying kicking his legs in the water.

She lifted some cotton wool balls, being careful to

make sure he was entirely clean. Turning his position slightly, so she could make sure there was nothing left on his back.

That was when it happened.

That was when he gave a little judder.

She knew instinctively something was wrong. She turned him over, her hands struggling to hold his slippery body as she panicked. He was pale. Deathly pale. Almost as if he was holding his breath.

No. No!

She let out a scream. She couldn't help it. The whole world had just started to close in all around her. She grabbed him beneath the arms and thrust the dripping baby into Dan's arms as he strode back through the door.

'Carrie, what's wrong?'

She couldn't stop. She couldn't breathe. Her feet carried her outside the apartment door and out onto the steps. The cold snow-covered steps where she'd found him. As soon as she reached the cold air it was as if her legs gave way and she collapsed down onto the steps, struggling to catch her breath.

There were tiny little black spots around her vision. She put her head between her legs and told herself to breathe slowly. But nothing could stop the clamouring in her chest.

That sight. That pale little body. That still little chest. It had been too much for her. That momentary second of panic had made her head spin. No one should have to go through that twice in their life.

No one was meant to experience that again.

Breathe. In through her nose, out through her mouth. And again. Breathe. In through her nose and out through her mouth.

She tried to get control. Her senses were picking up

something else. A noise. A background noise. A baby crying.

Then she started to sob. Uncontrollably sob. Abraham was fine. She knew that. She'd panicked. If she'd stopped to think—even for a moment—she would have realised he'd only been holding his breath for a second. But she couldn't. She didn't possess those rational kinds of thoughts any more. And she doubted she ever would.

Then she felt it, a hand creeping around her shoulders and a body sitting on the step next to her. The heat of another body touching hers. The comfort of an arm around her shoulders and the feeling of somewhere she could lay her head.

But he didn't speak. Dan just held her. She didn't know how long passed. She didn't know how long she sobbed. All she knew was his arms were around her and he was holding her—as if he would never let go.

His hand was stroking her hair. It was bitter cold out here, but neither of them seemed to notice. 'Tell me, Carrie,' he whispered. 'Tell me how to help you.'

'You can't, Dan.' It was a relief to say the words out loud. 'I panicked. I thought Abraham had stopped breathing.'

'He's fine, Carrie. Abraham is absolutely fine.' His voice washed over her, like a calm, soothing tonic. He lifted her chin towards his face. 'But you're not.' His finger traced the track of tears down her cheek. 'You're not fine, Carrie. Tell me why not.'

It was time. It was time to tell the truth. 'Why do you struggle with babies?'

The million-dollar question.

'Because I had one.'

She heard his intake of breath, but to his credit he never reacted the way she expected. There was a few moments' silence while he obviously contemplated her news. 'When did you have one?' His voice was low, comforting. The question wasn't intrusive. He made it feel like an everyday conversation.

'Last year.'

'Oh.'

'Yes, oh.' A shiver danced along her spine. Was it a reaction to the cold? Or was it a reaction to saying those words out loud?

Dan stood up and pulled her along with him. 'Let's do this inside. Let's do this inside with Abraham.'

Even now he didn't want to leave the baby on his own. Dan was being a good parent. It made this seem so much easier.

Abraham was wrapped in a towel, his bare toes kicking at the air above. As Dan closed the door behind them, shutting out the cold winter air, she knew what she had to do. She knew what would help her through this.

She picked up the kicking bundle and held him close to her chest, taking some deep breaths in and out.

She couldn't think of a single reason why this made her feel better. The thought of holding another baby in her arms had terrified her for so long. But the past few days had been cathartic.

Never, in a million years, would she have thought that holding another baby in her arms while she talked about the one she had lost would feel okay. Would actually feel quite right. If she'd ever planned to share, it would never have been like this.

'It wasn't too long ago.' Her words were firmer than she expected. She'd always thought that she'd never be able to get them out.

Maybe it was because she was with Dan. Maybe it was because he was literally a captive audience with no place to go. Maybe it was because she knew he couldn't run out on her if he didn't like what he heard. Maybe it was because she was beginning to feel as if she could tell this guy anything.

'Fifteenth of May last year, I had a little girl. Ruby. She was stillborn.'

There was silence.

It seemed important. Even though she hated the word *stillborn* it seemed important to her to tell him what had happened to her baby. She didn't want him to think she'd given her baby up for adoption, or done the same as Abraham's mother and abandoned her.

What was he thinking? And then a warm hand crept up and covered hers, squeezing gently. 'I'm sorry you lost your daughter, Carrie. That must have been a terrible time for you.'

The quiet acknowledgement made tears spring to her eyes. 'Thank you, Dan,' she whispered.

For Ruby. He was expressing his sorrow for the loss of her daughter. For Ruby. Some people didn't like to acknowledge a baby who had been lost. Some people didn't even want to say their names. It was easier to pretend they'd never existed. After all, babies who had never drawn breath in this world, they practically hadn't been here.

Except Ruby had been here.

She'd kicked under her mother's expanding stomach for seven months. She'd twisted and turned in the middle of the night, constantly having dancing competitions that kept her mother awake into the small hours. Sometimes a little foot or hand had been clearly visible as Carrie had lain watching her belly.

Ruby McKenzie had definitely existed. And it was so

nice to finally talk about her. Talk about her in a normal way instead of in hushed, quiet tones.

'Is that what's in the silver box upstairs?'

Now he had surprised her. 'How do you know about the box?'

'I saw it sitting on your bed when we were in your apartment. I saw the way you looked at it.' He gave her a little smile. 'It's pretty. And it seemed important.' His finger traced along the knuckles of her hand, small circular motions. 'Your place. You didn't have pictures up. For a woman, that struck me as strange. I figured you had a good reason and didn't want to ask.'

A tear slid down her cheek. 'I'm trying to get away from memories. That's why I'm in New York. It seemed like a good time to get away. Everything and everyone back home just reminded me of last year. It made sense. Coming here, getting away from it all.'

Dan traced his finger from her hand to her breastbone. His voice was intense. 'You can't get away from what's in here, Carrie. It stays with you all the time—no matter where you go.'

Wow. Her breath caught in her throat.

It was the way he said the words. The understanding. How could Dan be so in tune with things? There was an intensity she hadn't seen before. A darkening of his brown eyes from caramel tones to deep chocolate colours.

He knew. He understood her straight away, and she didn't know why.

'I know that. But sometimes what's in here feels easier if you've got room to deal with it yourself.' Easier than everyone clamouring around you, suffocating you with *their* grief.

'And has it been? Has it been easier, Carrie?'

'I thought it was. I thought I was coming to terms

with things.' Her eyes went down to Abraham. 'Until now. Until him.' She could hear the waver in her voice, feel the tremble in her throat. She desperately wanted to keep it together. She wanted to put her thoughts, feelings and frustrations into words—in a way she'd never managed before.

But Dan's reaction was flooring her. She couldn't have asked for more.

Dan shook his head. 'No wonder you didn't want to help out. No wonder you tried to make excuses.' His eyes were still heavy with weariness and she could see the lines on his face. He was fighting fatigue with every bone in his body.

He turned around on the sofa so he was facing her entirely. 'I'm sorry, Carrie. I had no idea how hard this was for you. But I really needed your help. I couldn't do this on my own. I don't know the first thing about babies.'

The gentle tears were still flowing. 'And neither do I, Dan. I never got the chance to find out. And I'm so worried I'll do something wrong. What if I caused Ruby to be stillborn? What if it was something I did? Something I ate? I'm not sure I should be around babies. I'm terrified that I'll do something wrong. What if he's sick and I don't know it? What if the jaundice gets worse instead of better?' She shook her head. 'I've already held one dead baby in my arms. I couldn't live with myself if anything happened to Abraham.'

Panic was welling up inside her and threatening to take over.

Some things were still too much for her. Still too raw.

Dan put his hands on her shoulders. 'Don't, Carrie. Don't do this to yourself. We've spoken to Shana. You heard what she said. As soon as possible, she'll arrange to examine Abraham and make sure everything is fine.

Nothing happened today when you bathed him. Abraham must have just held his breath. As soon as you handed him to me, it was almost as if he let out a little squawk. It was nothing you did, Carrie. Nothing at all. As for doing something wrong—I'm more likely to do that than you. You're a natural. Everything you do is right. No matter how hard you're finding this, you still make a much better parent than I do. I couldn't even get a diaper on straight!' He pressed his fingers into the tops of her arms. 'I don't know what happened to Ruby, but I don't believe for a second it was your fault. Did they ever tell you? What did the medical examiner say?'

Carrie took a deep breath. 'Nothing. They found nothing. Although she was early Ruby was the right size and weight. There was nothing wrong with my placenta. There was nothing wrong with the umbilical cord. I hadn't been in an accident. I didn't have any infections. My blood pressure was fine. They couldn't give me a single reason why Ruby stopped moving that day. She was perfect. She was perfect in every way.'

Her voice was cracking now. Her head was filling with pictures of that room. The expression on the radiographer's face as she swept Carrie's abdomen, trying to find a heartbeat with no success. The quiet way she had spoken, mentioning she needed to look for a colleague before disappearing out of the door.

And Carrie, sitting in the semi-dark room, knowing, just *knowing,* that life was about to change in an unimaginable way. Placing her hands on her stomach, ignoring the gel, and just talking to her baby. Telling her that Mummy loved her. Forever and ever.

Ruby's name had been picked weeks before. The hand-painted letters already adorned the door of the room in their flat that had been dedicated as the nursery. The nursery that Ruby would never see—never live in.

She could see the empathy on Dan's face. He understood. He understood the pure frustration of having no reason, no answer to the worst thing that could happen to her.

He lifted his heavy eyelids with caution. 'What about Ruby's dad?'

'What about Ruby's dad?' She shook her head. A small bit of guilt still weighed on her soul. 'Mark was a good guy. But neither of us could cope with what happened. Things just fell apart. He got another job and moved away. He's met someone now. And I'm happy for him. We just couldn't stay together—it was far too hard. Like having a permanent reminder etched on your brain.'

'Seems to me that Ruby will be permanently etched on your brain anyhow. Whether you're with Mark or not.'

She stared at him. That was blunt and to the point. And for the first time Dan had a deep crease across his forehead. A crease she wanted to reach up and smooth away with her fingers.

She was feeling it. This connection to Dan. Just as he was feeling it, too.

Mark was a chapter of her life that was over. And although she thought about Ruby frequently, she barely ever thought about Mark.

Dan's last remark seemed almost protective, and a tiny bit territorial. And the strangest thing was she didn't mind. Why had she been so scared to talk about this?

It wasn't comfortable. It wasn't comfortable at all. But Dan seemed to understand more than she would have expected him to.

And Dan was everything Mark wasn't. Mark couldn't bear to be around her once she'd lost Ruby. It was too hard. Too hard for them both. But Dan was nothing like that. She couldn't imagine Mark in this situation. Looking after an abandoned baby. Mark would have wanted nothing to do with that at all. But Dan had taken it all in his stride. A totally different kind of man.

And timing was everything. If New York hadn't been hit by this freak snowstorm she and Dan might never have talked. Might never have got to know each other and started to show these little glimmers of trust.

She sagged back on the sofa as Abraham let out a little sigh, his warm breath against her neck. 'I don't ever want to forget my daughter, Daniel. I couldn't, and I wouldn't ever want to. I have things in the box, her first scan, her scan at twenty weeks. A few little things that I'd bought for her that she never got to wear.' She stared off into the distance. 'I had to buy something new. Something for very premature babies to put on her. And some photos. I have some photos. But—'

She broke off, unable to finish. The photographs were just too painful.

His hand was wrapped back around hers again. 'So, how do you feel about helping me with Abraham? I know it's hard for you, Carrie. But I really need your help.' His words were said with caution, as if he didn't want to cause her any more pain.

She took a few moments before she answered, trying to sort it all out in her brain. 'It's strange. It's not quite what I'd expected. I've avoided babies for months. Any of my friends who were pregnant and delivered, I just made excuses not to see them and sent a present. I think they all understood. Most of them felt awkward around me anyway. I thought Abraham would be my worst nightmare.'

'And?'

'And—' she looked down at the little face, snuggled

against her shoulder '—I won't pretend it's not hard. I won't pretend that I don't sometimes just need a minute. Just need a little space. But it's not as bad as I expected.'

The heat from Abraham's little body was penetrating through her dressing gown, like an additional hot-water bottle. But it felt good. It felt natural. It didn't make her want to run screaming from the room. Not in the way she would have expected.

'Then can you do this, Carrie? Can you keep helping me for the next day or so?' He pointed to the TV. 'It doesn't look like New York is opening back up for business any time soon.' He touched her arm, and she could sense the frustration he was trying to hide from her. 'I'll understand, Carrie. I'll understand if you say no and want to go back up to your apartment and stay there.'

She thought about it. There was no hiding the fact that for a few moments she actually considered it. But just at that point Abraham moved and snuggled even closer to her neck.

What was up there for her? An empty apartment with no one to talk to. There was only so much news she could watch on TV saying the same things over and over again.

There were only so many times she could rearrange her wardrobe and shoes. There were only so many times she could reread her favourite books.

She sucked in a deep breath. He was watching her. *He* was holding *his* breath, waiting for her response. 'You understand now, but you didn't understand a couple of nights ago.' She could remember the stunned expression on his face when she'd bolted for the door.

He nodded in defeat. 'You're right. I thought you were distinctly weird. But I was crazy and desperate enough not to care.' He pointed to his chest. 'But I know, Carrie, I know in here if someone is a good person. And don't think it's anything about being a cop. I've been like this since I was a kid. I always knew who had a good heart— no matter what their appearance or surroundings. And I always knew who to steer clear of, no matter what they told me.'

There were shadows in his eyes. He was revealing a tiny part of himself here. Maybe without even knowing it. And that was the second time this had happened. First with the comment about things always staying inside you, and now about knowing people—who to stay away from. How had he learned that lesson? It was painful to even think about it.

She reached up and touched the side of his face with her free hand. Bristles. Dan hadn't managed to shave yet and they felt good beneath her smooth skin. She even liked the sound.

'And do you want to steer clear of me, Dan?' He was staring at her with those dark brown eyes. Pulling her in. Thank goodness she was sitting or her legs would currently be like jelly.

There was comfort here. Because she knew what he was about to say. Didn't doubt it for a second. This connection was the truest thing she'd felt in a long time.

He gave her that sexy smile. The one that made her stomach flip over. 'Not for a second,' he whispered, and leaned forward and brushed his lips against hers.

It was beautiful. The gentlest of kisses.

Just as well. She still had Abraham in her arms. Under any other circumstances she might feel the urge to throw her dressing gown to the wind and jump up onto his lap.

He was concentrating solely on her mouth. His hand still only brushing the side of her face as their kiss deepened and his tongue edged its way into her mouth.

She could feel the heat rush through her, warming

her chilled legs and feet and spreading to a whole host of other places.

She could concentrate solely on this. She could concentrate solely on Dan. Once he started kissing her nothing else mattered. Her brain didn't have room for a single thought.

But as if sensing where this could go, Dan pulled back.

And for a second she felt lost. Until she opened her eyes again and realised he was smiling at her.

'What do you think, Carrie McKenzie? Will you be my partner in crime? Can Abraham and I count on you?'

She narrowed her eyes at him. Boy, he was good. With his fancy words and his kisses. His help-the-baby plea. This man could charm the birds out of the trees.

Just as well she was the only bird around.

She lifted her eyebrows. 'Are you doing this for the chocolate cake?'

He smiled. 'I'm definitely doing it for the chocolate cake.'

'Well, that makes us even, 'cause I'm doing this for the carrot cake—and the pancakes.' She liked this. She liked that they could fall back into flirting so easily, even after her monumental revelation.

'Just what I like—a woman with her priorities in order.' He pushed himself up from the sofa and held out his hands for Abraham.

'Don't you want me to take a turn for a while?'

'Oh, no.' He shook his head firmly as he gathered Abraham into his arms and took a long look at her bare legs and painted toenails. 'What I want is for you to put some clothes on. You're *way* too distracting without them.'

She stood up, deliberately letting her dressing gown open, just to annoy him. 'Well, we wouldn't want any distractions, would we?' she teased as she headed to the door.

There was some colour in his cheeks. A guy like Dan couldn't be embarrassed. Not when he looked like that. He must have women throwing themselves at him all the time—particularly when he was in uniform.

She saw him shifting uncomfortably, adjusting himself. No! She'd caused an age-old reaction with a few cheeky words and a flash of skin. Her cheeks started to blush, too.

And then she started to smile.

It was starting to feel as if she had some control back. As if everything in life wouldn't just slip through her fingers like grains of sand on the beach.

She turned the handle on the door.

'Carrie?'

She spun around.

Dan was standing with Abraham in his arms. Looking every inch the gorgeous family man. Looking every inch like the man she pictured in her dreams about the life she wanted to have.

'Hurry back.'

She tried to think of something witty or clever to say. But she had nothing.

'Absolutely,' she muttered as she sped up the stairs as fast as her legs would carry her.

Her brain had just flipped into a spin cycle again.

It was certifiable. Daniel Cooper was driving her crazy.

CHAPTER EIGHT

By now Dan should have been a crumpled heap on the floor. He'd spent most of last night walking the floor with a sometimes whimpering, sometimes screaming baby. At one point he'd put Abraham back in the crib and gone to stand in the kitchen for a few minutes to catch his breath.

But from the moment Carrie had appeared, all bright-eyed and bushy-tailed after a good night's sleep, he'd felt instantly invigorated.

There was something about her brown curls, blue eyes and flash of skin that was slowly but surely driving him crazy.

And now he knew.

Now he understood.

Well, not entirely. God willing he'd never really understand what it felt like to lose a child. But at least now he had an explanation for the shadows beneath her eyes. The moments of panic that he'd seen and recognised. Her abruptness. Her lack of confidence in herself.

What he couldn't understand was why Carrie couldn't see what he could see. A remarkably caring and competent woman who seemed to have a real empathy with this little baby.

For some reason Carrie's news reassured him a little. He'd known there was something wrong but hadn't quite been able to put his finger on it. His instincts told him she was a good person and not a crazed baby-snatcher or madly unstable.

Carrie McKenzie was probably the bravest woman he'd ever met. And that included his grandmother.

She'd put the needs of this little baby—a child she didn't know—before her own needs, even though it was apparent at times her heart was clearly breaking. How many other people did he know who could have done this?

A smile danced across his lips as he remembered her reaction to Shana's 'suck it up' comment. No wonder she'd been so horrified.

This was truly her worst nightmare and she'd just lived through thirty-odd hours of it, with only a few minor hiccups along the way.

He'd been right to let her sleep. It seemed to have given her new strength and the confidence to share. And he was glad she'd shared.

He'd just resisted the temptation to gather her into his arms and try to take her pain away. Because something told him this was all new for her. Sharing about this was all new for her, and he had to let her go at her own pace.

And while it seemed the most unlikely solution, holding Abraham had seemed to give her comfort at that moment. Which was why he'd resorted to the smallest movement—the hand squeeze—to show his support.

What did this mean now for them?

Now that she'd shared he'd given her the opportunity to walk away. To stop making things so hard on herself. But she was determined to stay and help. And his sense of relief was overwhelming. If left to himself, he was sure he could muddle through. But having someone else there—even a little reluctantly—was more help than she could imagine.

As for the kiss?

How much was Carrie ready to move on?

Because being in a confined space with her was going to drive him crazy—in a good way. Now that he'd tasted her sweet lips and felt the warmth of her body next to his it just made him crave her all the more.

Carrie wasn't like any other woman that he'd met.

Girls in New York weren't shy. *Reserved* was an extinct term around here.

He was used to women throwing themselves at him, in pursuit of either a relationship or something far hotter.

It was just the way of the world these days.

But truth be told, it wasn't really Dan's world. It wasn't really the family values his grandmother had brought him up with. They, in themselves, were almost laughable. His mother certainly hadn't had any family values—no matter what her family had taught her. And that had reflected badly on Dan.

His grandmother had patched him up, fought fiercely for him and his mother's name was never mentioned in the house again.

And that was fine with him. For years she haunted his dreams most nights anyway.

But Carrie McKenzie, with her too-blue eyes and quiet nature, was slowly but surely getting under his skin in a way no other woman had.

It was clear there were some aspects of life they disagreed on. But did that mean it would be pointless to pursue anything else? Dan wasn't sure. He still had his own demons to deal with. And the situation with Abraham was only heightening a whole host of emotions he'd buried for so long.

His stomach grumbled loudly just as Carrie burst back through the door, wearing a pink shirt and jeans, her hair tied up in a loose knot. She laughed at the sound of his stomach. 'You called?'

He nodded at her hands that were clutched to her chest holding a jar of lemon marmalade. 'It's getting to the stage I won't even fight you about the toast and marmalade. You've starved me so long I'm ready to concede.' He walked over to the crib and laid Abraham back down.

She strode over to the toaster and slid the last of the bread into place. 'I'll concede on one thing. I'll make you coffee instead of tea—but only since you had such a bad night. I might make some scones this afternoon and make you drink tea, then.'

He felt his ears literally prick up. The cupboards' supplies were getting low—even though it had only been a few days. The cakes yesterday had been a real boost. Scones today? Even better.

'I've never really had the scone things. What do you have them with?'

She shrugged. 'It should be jam and cream, but jam and butter will do. Do you want fruit scones or plain?'

He rolled his eyes upwards. 'I take it bacon's not an option?' He smiled at the horrified expression on her face. 'You've got a secret stash of dried fruit up there, too?'

She put her hand on her hip and gave him a sassy look. 'I've got a whole host of things you know nothing about up there.'

He let out a stream of air through his lips. 'Woman, you're going to drive me crazy.'

The toast popped behind her and she started spreading butter and marmalade, pulled out two plates and mugs and finished making breakfast in record time.

It was almost as if Abraham had an inbuilt antenna.

As soon as Carrie's backside hovered above the chair he started to grizzle in his crib. She glanced at the clock. 'When did he have his last feed?'

Dan looked at his watch. 'I think it was around four. This little guy is like clockwork. He couldn't possibly let it go any more than four hours.'

'It must be my turn to feed him. Let me make up a bottle.' She picked out the bottle and teat from the sterilising solution and measured out the formula. 'I wish we could get some more of the ready-made formula. It's so much easier.' She peered into the contents of the formula tub. 'How many bottles does this make? I know it's only a small can but it seems to be going down mighty quickly.' She turned back to face him.

Dan wasn't listening. He was staring at the toast and lemon marmalade as if it had sprouted legs and run across the floor.

'Dan? Dan? What's wrong.'

He took another bite of the toast. 'This is much nicer than I remember. Or maybe it's just that I'm so hungry that I would eat anything.' He stared at the toast. 'I always thought marmalade was—you know—yeuch.' He let a shiver go down his spine. 'I don't remember it tasting like this.'

She gave him a smile. 'It's one of my secrets. You probably had orange marmalade as a child. I don't like it, either. This is much nicer, made with lemons. I brought it with me from London.'

He narrowed his eyes. 'Where do you keep the jar?'

She tapped the side of her nose. 'Aha, that's a secret. You'll never make me tell.'

'Never?' He stood up, his chair skidding across the floor and his hands on her hips in an instant. She could hardly even remember him crossing the space.

Oh, no. Those come-to-bed eyes again. The kind that gave her ideas she really shouldn't be having at this time of day.

He didn't wait. He didn't ask. He just claimed her lips as his own. His hand coming up and cupping her cheek. There was an element of ownership in his actions.

But the strange thing was, instead of being annoying, it sent little sparks of heat all the way down to the tips of her toes.

The past year had been lonely. The past year had been more than lonely. The past year had been dark and bleak and, at times, scary.

Sometimes she felt as if the black cloud around her would never lift, no matter how hard she tried.

For the first time she was feeling something other than despair. Other than hopelessness.

Maybe her senses were overreacting. Maybe it had just been too long since she'd been in a position like this, where her hormones couldn't keep themselves in check.

All she knew was she wanted Daniel Cooper's lips on hers. She wanted Daniel Cooper pressed up against her. She wanted to feel his arms around her body, touching her skin, stroking her cheek…

She wound her arms around his neck as his hands found their way to the bare skin at the small of her back. Would his fingers creep any lower? Or any higher? She wasn't quite sure which way she wanted them to go.

There was a howl from the corner of the room and they jerked apart instantly.

Baby. There was a baby in the room. She made to move towards the crib. 'Don't. I'll do it,' he said, his hands still pressed firmly against her hips.

'But you did all of last night.' She touched his shoulder. 'You're exhausted, Dan. You really should get some sleep.'

He nodded. 'And I will, as soon as you've eaten. You haven't had a chance yet. Finish breakfast, then come and take over from me.'

She eyed her toast with oodles of butter and marmalade and her steaming-hot cup of tea. How long would it take her? Five minutes? Then she could take over from Dan for a good part of the day.

From the shadows under his eyes it was clear that he needed a few hours' sleep. Could she cope with Abraham on her own for a few hours?

No matter how hard she was trying here, the thought still struck fear in her heart. What if something happened? What if she did something wrong?

The truth was she felt safer when Dan was around. Even though he told her she was doing a great job she wasn't sure she wanted to do it alone.

One of the little cardigans was hanging on the side of the crib and the solution was with her in an instant. Of course! That was what she would do. She would take Abraham upstairs to visit Mrs Van Dyke—at least then she wouldn't be on her own. And even though Mrs Van Dyke was elderly she had lots of experience with babies. She might even be able to give Carrie some tips.

She looked over to the sofa. Dan was already taking the bottle out of Abraham's mouth. He was feeding really quickly. A thought crossed her mind. 'Is your internet working yet?'

Dan shrugged his shoulders. He was deep in concentration. 'Haven't checked yet. Why?'

'Do you think there's any way we could weigh Abraham? Maybe we aren't giving him enough milk. He always seems to gulp really quickly then gets lots of wind.'

The news anchor was telling the same story over and over again. Wasn't she wearing that same suit jacket a few days ago? Pictures filled the screen of stranded cars, a collapsed tree in Central Park, aerial shots of all the roads completely covered in snow. More pictures of people being rescued by police and, in some cases, helicopters. It looked as if there had been barely any improvements in the past two days. Her voice was starting to annoy Carrie.

'Snow ploughs cleared most of New York State Thruway the I-87 this morning, only for the hard work to be destroyed less than three hours later after another record deluge of snow. Some people had been waiting two days to get their cars out of the snowdrifts, only to get snowed back in a few miles down the thruway. Emergency services can't give an estimate on how much longer it will take to clear the thruway again. They are stressing that people in the area should only travel in emergency cases. Every resource possible is currently being used to try and restore the fluctuating power supplies to the city. Some areas of the city have been without power for more than twenty-four hours. Authorities assure us that all power supplies should be connected in the next twelve hours.'

Dan pointed at the screen. 'That's the bad news. Now wait for it—here comes the good news story.'

Carrie turned back to the screen. She definitely had seen that jacket before. Wardrobe at the news station must be as closed down as the rest of New York.

'And finally, community kitchens are springing up all over New York City. The latest is in Manhattan's Lower East Side at Sara D. Roosevelt Park and the locals have been enjoying the opportunity to gather somewhere with some hot food and heating.' The camera shot to children building a giant snowman in the park and several residents holding cups with something steaming hot inside.

'Wow, that snowman is enormous. There's no way a kid made that. They couldn't reach that high.'

'Do I sense a little snowman envy?' Dan had an amused expression on his face.

Carrie shrugged. 'Maybe. Can't even tell you the last time I made a snowman. I must have been around ten. Back home in London I don't even have a garden.'

Dan headed over to the back window, juggling Abraham in his arms. It was time for winding again. 'Most of the apartments around here don't have gardens. But there are gardens. Have you managed to get to Washington Square Park yet?'

She joined him at the window, looking out over the snow-covered back alley. 'If I even thought we'd have a chance of making it there I'd ask you to take me.' She reached over and touched Abraham's little hand. 'But we pretty much can't take this little guy anywhere with no proper clothes, jacket or snowsuit. I guess that means we're stranded.'

It was the wrong thing to say. Almost as soon as she said the words she wanted to pull them back. She could instantly see Dan's back and shoulders stiffen, the atmosphere changing around them in a second.

'I guess the actions of others impact on us all.'

She was still touching Abraham's hand, letting his little fingers connect with hers. 'We don't know, Dan. We don't know anything.'

He spun around to face her. 'Of course we do. Look at him. Look at this defenceless little baby. Left out in the cold with hardly any clothes. He could have died out there, Carrie. He could have died.'

'Don't. Don't say that. I don't even want to think about that. I can't think about that.'

She stared him down. He had to know how much his

words impacted on her. How she couldn't even bear to think the thoughts he was putting in her head.

'Why are you so critical, Dan? You must see a whole host of things in your line of work. I thought that would make you more sympathetic to people out there. Not sit as judge and master.'

'I don't judge.' His words were snapped and Abraham flinched at the rise in his voice.

'Well, I think you do. I think that's what you've done since the second I found Abraham and brought him to you.'

He opened his mouth, obviously ready to hit her with a torrent of abuse. But good sense waylaid him. She could almost see him biting his tongue and it annoyed her. She didn't want Dan to hide things from her. He should tell her how he really felt. It didn't matter that they would disagree.

'Spit it out, Dan.'

'I don't think that's wise.' His words were growled through clenched teeth.

She walked right up to him, her face directly under his chin. He was angry. She could tell he was angry. But she wasn't intimidated at all. Dan would never direct his anger at her.

'So, you can kiss me to death, but you can't tell me how you feel?'

Dan walked over to the crib, placed Abraham down and raked his hand through his short hair, his hand coming around and scraping at the bristles on his chin. 'Just leave it, Carrie.'

'Why? Isn't it normal to disagree about things? I just can't understand why the guy who was prepared to risk his life for a bunch of strangers can't take a minute to show a little compassion to a woman who is clearly desperate.' She pointed over at the crib. 'No woman in her right mind would abandon her baby. Not without good reason. I bet she's lying crying and terrified right now. I bet the past two nights she hasn't slept a wink with worry over how her son is doing.'

He shook his head. 'You're wrong, Carrie. You're more than wrong. Good people don't do things like this. Good people don't abandon their babies or make them suffer. Everyone who has the responsibility for children should put their needs first—before their own.'

She wrinkled her brow. 'What are you getting at, Dan? What need do you think Abraham's mother was putting first?'

He couldn't meet her eyes. He couldn't look at her. His eyes were fixed either on the floor or the ceiling. He walked towards the window, staring out at the snow-covered street, his hands on his hips. 'Drugs, Carrie. I think his mother was looking for her next fix.'

Carrie's hand flew up to her mouth. It hadn't even occurred to her. It hadn't even crossed her mind.

Maybe she was too innocent. Maybe she'd lived a sheltered life.

'No.' She crossed quickly to the crib and looked down at Abraham. His eyelids were fluttering, as if he was trying to focus on the changing shapes around him. He looked so innocent. So peaceful. The thought of his mother being a drug user horrified Carrie.

She hadn't lived her life in a plastic bubble. There had been women who clearly had drug problems in the maternity unit next to her's. But they were in the unit, being monitored for the sake of their babies. Although they had other issues in their lives, their babies' health was still important to them.

She reached out and stroked Abraham's skin. It still

had the slightest touch of yellow, but these things wouldn't disappear overnight. Could his mother really have been taking drugs? It was just unimaginable to Carrie.

She felt a little surge of adrenalin rise inside her. 'No, Dan. No way. It can't be that. It just can't be. We would know. Abraham would be showing signs. Drug addicts' babies show signs of withdrawal, don't they? If Abraham's mother was an addict he would be screaming by now.'

'Hasn't he screamed the past two nights?'

She shook her head firmly. It didn't matter that she was no expert. She'd heard enough to know a little of the background. 'He would be sick, Dan. He would be *really* sick. And Abraham's not. Look at him.' She walked around to the other side of the crib to give Dan a clear view. 'He's not sick like that. Sure, he gets hungry and has wind. He pulls his little knees up to his chest. That's colic. Nothing else. And there are pages and pages on the internet about that.' She folded her arms across her chest. 'If we had a baby in withdrawal right now, we'd need Shana to airlift him to the hospital. There's no two ways about it.'

It was clear from the tight expression on Dan's face that he wasn't ready to concede. He wasn't ready to consider he was wrong.

She could feel her hackles rising. She could feel they were on the precipice of a major argument and she just didn't want to go there. All her protective vibes were coming out, standing over Abraham like some lioness guarding her cub. But why would she have to guard him against Dan? The man who'd opened his door and welcomed them both in?

She took a deep breath. 'Dan, you're tired and you're cranky. I know what that feels like. Let's leave this. Go and sleep for a few hours. I'm going to take Abraham upstairs to see Mrs Van Dyke. She'll be happy to see him and, who knows, she might even give me some tips.'

She could see he still wanted to argue with her but fatigue was eating away at every movement he made. His shoulders were slumped, his muscular frame sagging.

'Fine. I'll go to sleep.' He stalked off towards the bedroom—the bed she'd recently vacated—before he halted and turned around. 'Mrs Van Dyke, ask her if she needs anything. Anything at all. I can phone Mr Meltzer and go back along to the shop in a few hours and get us some more supplies. We'll need things for Abraham anyhow.'

There it was. Even in his inner turmoil, the real Dan Cooper could still shine through. He was still thinking about others, still concerned about his elderly neighbour.

She picked up Abraham from the crib, tapping her finger on his button nose and smiling at him.

Just when she thought Dan had gone he appeared at her elbow, bending over and dropping a gentle kiss on Abraham's forehead.

'I'm not going to let anything happen to this little guy, Carrie. Nothing at all.' His words were whispered, but firm, and he turned and walked off to the bedroom, closing the door behind him.

CHAPTER NINE

CARRIE WALKED UP the stairs slowly, Abraham cradled in her arms.

The way that Dan had come over and kissed him had almost undone her. She was ready to fight with him, to argue with him over his unforgiving point of view.

But Daniel Cooper was a good guy—his most recent action only proved that. There was so much more to this than she could see. Maybe she'd been so wrapped up in her own grief and struggling with her own ability to cope with the situation that she'd totally missed something with Dan.

It just didn't figure for a warm-hearted Everyman hero to have such black-and-white views. To be so blinkered. Maybe it was time for her to crawl out of the sandbox and get back in the playground—to start to consider those around her.

She reached Mrs Van Dyke's door and gave a little knock. 'Mrs Van Dyke? It's Carrie from across the hall. May I come in?'

She heard the faint shout from the other side of the door, once again almost drowned out by the theme tune of *Diagnosis Murder*. She turned the handle and walked in, crossing the room and kneeling next to Mrs Van Dyke's brown leather armchair.

She adjusted Abraham from her shoulder, laying him between her hands so Mrs Van Dyke could have a clear look at him. 'Guess who I brought to visit,' she said quietly.

Mrs Van Dyke reached out for the remote control and silenced the television. 'Well, who do we have here?' she asked, one frail finger reaching out and tracing down the side of Abraham's cheek.

'We call him Abraham. It's been three days now and there's still no sign of his mother.'

'May I?' Mrs Van Dyke held out her thin arms. For a second Carrie hesitated, instant protective waves flooding through her, wondering about the steadiness of Mrs Van Dyke's hands. But she pushed the thoughts from her mind. This woman had held more babies, more little lives in her hands than Carrie probably would in this lifetime. She had a wealth of experience to which Carrie really needed even the tiniest exposure.

She placed Abraham in her shaky hands and watched as Mrs Van Dyke repositioned him on her lap, with her hand gently supporting his head as she leaned over and spoke to him quietly, all the while stroking one cheek with her bent finger.

It was magical. Even though Mrs Van Dyke was obviously feeling the effects of age, from her misshapen joints to her thin frame, a new life and sparkle seemed to come into her eyes when talking to Abraham. It was as if he released a little spark of life into her.

Carrie couldn't hear what she was saying. It was as if she were having an entirely private conversation with him. His little blue eyes had opened and were watching her intensely. Could he even focus yet? Carrie wasn't sure. But the conversation brought a smile to her face.

Abraham was wearing one of the beautiful hand-knitted blue cardigans that Mrs Van Dyke had given her, along with the white crocheted shawl. The recognition made Mrs Van Dyke smile all the more as she fingered the delicate wool. They still had hardly any clothes for him and without Mrs Van Dyke's contribution Abraham would have spent most of the time wrapped in a towel.

Carrie settled onto the antique-style leather sofa. 'Dan asked me to check if you needed anything. He's hoping to give Mr Meltzer a ring and go along to the shop later. Can you give me a list of what you're running short of?'

A smile danced across Mrs Van Dyke's lips. 'He's such a good boy, my Daniel.'

She almost made it sound as if he were one of her own. 'I'm surprised he didn't come up himself.'

Carrie felt her cheeks flush. She wasn't quite sure what to say. 'He's really tired. Abraham kept him awake most of the night. I told him to get some sleep and I would come up and see you.' It almost made them sound like some old married couple. She was hoping that would pass Mrs Van Dyke by.

But the old lady was far too wily for that. The smile remained on her lips and as she regarded Carrie carefully with her pale grey eyes it was almost as if she were sizing up her suitability. 'I could do with some things,' she said slowly.

'No problem. What do you need?'

'Some powdered milk—there won't be any fresh milk left. And some chocolate biscuits and some tins of soup.'

'What kind of soup do you like?'

Mrs Van Dyke smiled as she played with Abraham on her lap. 'Oh, don't worry about that. Daniel knows exactly what to get me.' She eyed Carrie again. 'Sometimes I wonder what I'd do without him.'

The words seemed to drip with loyalty and devotion to Daniel. These two had known each other for most of Daniel's life. How much had they shared?

Carrie pushed the queries out of her head. She was fascinated by how content Abraham looked, how placid he was on Mrs Van Dyke's lap, with her wholehearted attention. 'You're much better at this than me. Maybe you can give me some tips.'

Mrs Van Dyke raised her head. 'Tips? Why would you need tips?'

'Because I'm not very good at this. I think he's feeding too quickly. He gets lots of wind and screams half the night.' She pointed over at his little frame. 'I've no idea what he weighs. So I don't know if we're giving him enough milk or not. This baby stuff is all so confusing.'

Mrs Van Dyke gave her a gentle smile as Abraham wrapped his tiny fingers around her gnarled one. 'I'm sure you're much better at this than you think you are. He's around six pounds,' she said.

'How do you know that?' Carrie asked in wonder.

Mrs Van Dyke smiled. 'I just do. Years of experience. I think he might have been a few weeks early.' She touched his face again. 'But his jaundice will settle in a few days. Have you been putting him next to the window, letting the daylight get to him?'

Carrie nodded. 'Dan has a friend who is a paediatrician at Angel's Hospital. She told us what to do. I just wish we could actually get him there so he could be checked over.'

'He doesn't need to be checked. He's fine. As for the wind—he's a new baby. It will settle.' She slid her hands under his arms and sat him upright. 'It's a big adjustment being out in the big bad world. A few days ago he was in a dark cocoon, being fed and looked after. Now he's got to learn to do it for himself.'

Carrie felt a prickle of unease. 'I wish Dan felt like that.'

Mrs Van Dyke's eyes were on her in a flash. 'Felt like what?' There was the tiniest sharp edge to her voice. A protective element. Just like the way Carrie felt towards Abraham. It heightened Carrie's awareness. Mrs Van Dyke had known Daniel since he was a child. What else did she know?

Carrie gave a sigh. 'Dan doesn't think that Abraham's mother cared about him at all. He doesn't think she looked after him. He thinks she might have been a drug user.'

She could see Mrs Van Dyke's shoulders stiffen and straighten slightly. Maybe she was wrong to use the drug word around someone so elderly.

But Mrs Van Dyke just shook her head. 'No.' Her eyes were focused entirely on Abraham. 'His mother wasn't a drug user.'

Carrie leaned back against the leather sofa. Even though it looked ancient, it was firm and comfortable. Much more comfortable than Dan's modern one. How many people had rested on this sofa over the years, laid their hands on the slightly worn armrests and heard the pearls of wisdom from Mrs Van Dyke?

'Then what happened?' She gave a sigh. 'I just can't get my head around it. I keep thinking of all the reasons in the world that would make you give up your baby, and none of them are good enough. None of them come even close. I keep thinking of alternatives—all reasons a mum could keep her baby. None of them lead to this.'

'Not every woman will have the life that you've had, Carrie.' The words were quiet, almost whispered and spoken with years of experience. The intensity of them brought an unexpected flood of tears to Carrie's eyes.

Her voice wavered. 'You say that as if I've lived a charmed life.'

'Haven't you?'

She shook her head firmly. 'I don't think so. Last year I lost my daughter. I had a stillbirth.' She looked over at Abraham, her voice still wavering. 'I came to New York to get away from babies—to get away from the memories.'

Mrs Van Dyke was silent for a few moments. Maybe Carrie had stunned her with her news, but, in truth, Mrs Van Dyke didn't look as if anyone would have the capability of stunning her.

Her answer was measured. 'It seems as if we've shared the heartache of the loss of a child. At least with Peter, I had a chance to get to know him a little. To get to share a little part of his life. I'm sorry you didn't get that opportunity, Carrie.'

The sincerity in her words was clear. She meant every single one of them. And even though Carrie didn't know her well, it gave her more comfort than she'd had in a long time. Maybe this was all on her. She'd kept so much bottled up inside for so long. She didn't want to share. And now, in New York, the only two people she'd shared with had shown her sincerity and compassion—even though they were virtual strangers.

'You had five children, didn't you?'

Mrs Van Dyke nodded. 'Peter was my youngest. David, Ronald, Anne and Lisbeth all have families of their own now.'

'Are any of them still in New York?'

There was a sadness in Mrs Van Dyke's eyes. 'Sadly, no. David's in Boston. Ronald's in Washington. Lisbeth married a lovely Dutch man and is back in Holland. Anne found herself a cowboy and lives on a ranch in Texas. She spends most of her time trying to persuade me to go and live with her and her family.' Mrs Van Dyke showed some pride in her eyes. 'She has a beautiful home—a beautiful family. But I find Texas far too hot. I visit. Daniel takes me to the airport and I go and stay with Anne for part of the winter. But New York is home to me now. It always will be.' She hesitated for a moment, before looking at Carrie with her pale grey eyes. 'And Peter's here, of course. I would never leave my son.'

It was as if a million tiny caterpillars decided to run over her skin. Tiny light pinpricks all over.

Ruby. Her tiny white remembrance plaque in a cemetery in London. She'd visited it the day she left and wondered if anyone would put flowers there while she was gone. The chances were unlikely. Most people had moved on.

Part of her felt sympathy for Mrs Van Dyke not wanting to leave her beloved son. Should she feel guilty for coming to New York? All she felt was sad. Ruby wasn't there any more. Her talismans were in the box upstairs and in her heart—not on the little white plaque next to hundreds of others.

She was trying to put things into perspective. Her past situation and the current one. Trying to find a reason for Abraham's mother's behaviour.

Mrs Van Dyke's voice cut through her thoughts. 'You have to remember, Carrie. Our children belong to God. We're only given them on loan from heaven. Sometimes God calls them home sooner than we expected.'

The words of the wise. A woman who'd had years to get over the death of her young son, but it was clearly still as raw today as it had been at the time. But here she was, with the help of her faith, rationalising the world around her. Getting some comfort from it.

Carrie moved from the sofa and knelt on the ground next to Mrs Van Dyke's armchair. 'Then why would we waste any of that precious time? Why would we want to miss out on the first feed, the first smile? It's all far too precious, far too fleeting to give it up so easily. I can't believe that Abraham's mother doesn't care. I can't believe she abandoned him without a second thought.'

'It's a sad world, Carrie. But sometimes we have to realise that not everyone has the same moral standing and beliefs that you and I have. Not everyone values babies and children the way that they should.'

It was a complete turnaround. The absolute opposite of what she'd expected Mrs Van Dyke to say. But as she watched the elderly face, she realised Mrs Van Dyke was lost—stuck in a memory someplace. She wasn't talking about the here and now; she was remembering something from long ago.

It sent a horrible, uncomfortable feeling down her spine. She'd seen the awful newscasts about abused and battered children. She'd seen the adverts for foster carers for children whose parents didn't want them any more. The last thing she wanted was for Abraham to end up in any of those categories. It was just unthinkable.

She was staring at him again. Transfixed by his beautiful skin and blinking blue eyes. 'I just can't think of him like that. I just have the oddest feeling—' she put her hand on her heart '—right here, that I'm right about him. I can't explain it, but I just think that Abraham's mother didn't abandon him because she didn't love him. I think it's just the opposite. She abandoned him because she *did* love him.'

Mrs Van Dyke sat back in her chair, cradling Abraham

in her arms. Carrie was almost envious of her years of experience. The strength she had to draw on. It radiated from her. Being around Mrs Van Dyke was like being enveloped in some warm, knowledgeable blanket. She could only hope that one day she would be like that, too.

After a few moments she eventually spoke. 'It seems to me like it's time to ask some hard questions, Carrie.'

The words made her a little uncomfortable. Could Mrs Van Dyke read her thoughts? See all the things that were floating around her brain about Daniel? That would really make her cheeks flush, because some of those thoughts were X-rated.

But surely Mrs Van Dyke had no inkling that anything had happened between them. She hadn't even seen them together. She couldn't possibly know.

'What kind of questions?' she finally asked.

'The kind of questions you're skirting around about. Why exactly would a mother leave a baby on our doorstep? What reasons could she possibly have? And why this doorstep? Why not another?'

Carrie sat back in her chair. All the things that had been circling in her brain for the past few days. Even though they were in the background, she hadn't really focused on them, or given them the attention they deserved. Looking after Abraham, and trying to decipher her emotions towards Daniel, had taken up all her time and energy.

It was time to sit back and take a deep breath. To look at things from a new angle, a new perspective.

'I guess I need to take some time to think about this,' she said quietly.

'I guess you do.'

It was like being in the presence of an all-knowing

seer. A person who knew what was happening but left you to find it out for yourself.

She stood up and walked over to pick up Abraham again. Just holding him close seemed to give her comfort. It was amazing how quickly she was becoming attached to this tiny person.

'I'll get Dan to bring your shopping up later.'

'That's perfect, Carrie.' She gave a little nod of her head. 'You've taken on a big job, and I commend you for it. But Abraham is someone else's baby. It's so easy to love them, and it's so hard to let them go. You need to protect yourself. You need to look after your own heart.'

Carrie placed her hand across Abraham's back. 'I know that. I know that this won't last. As soon as the snow clears, Abraham will go to Angel's to be assessed. Social services already know about him. I'm sure they will already have somewhere for him to go.'

She nodded towards the television. The title for a new episode of *Diagnosis Murder* was just beginning to roll. 'I'll let you get back to your television.' Had she really been up here for an hour? 'Thank you for letting us visit, Mrs Van Dyke.'

'No, thank *you,* Carrie. I hope I'll be seeing you again soon.'

'I hope so, too.'

She headed towards the door. Even before she opened it Abraham twitched in her arms as Mrs Van Dyke reached for the remote control and the sound boomed around the apartment again.

Carrie smiled as she closed the door behind her.

She lifted her head. It was as if her own doorway was beckoning from across the hall. She'd barely been in there for the past few days. Just twice for a shower, a change of clothes or to pick up some baking ingredients.

Last time she'd been in there Dan had kissed her.

After this morning that almost seemed like a lifetime ago.

She propped Abraham up on her shoulder. She knew exactly what she was going to do now. She wanted to leave Dan to sleep a little longer. Hopefully then he would be in the mood to talk.

In the meantime she and Abraham would have some quiet time together. It didn't feel like a betrayal to have him in her arms any more. It just felt right. As if he belonged there.

But most importantly she had someone she wanted him to meet. Someone she wanted to talk to him about.

To let him know that there was room in her heart for everyone.

CHAPTER TEN

THREE HOURS LATER she was back downstairs. Abraham had slept for a few hours while she sat quietly and looked through the things in Ruby's box.

It was the first time she'd ever managed to do it without breaking her heart. She was still sad, a few tears had still slid down her cheeks. But this time it hadn't been so hard to put the things back in the box. It hadn't felt as if her life was over. It hadn't felt as if there was nothing to fight for any more.

And that wasn't just because Abraham was in her arms. It was because she was beginning to feel different.

Daniel appeared in the doorway, his hair rumpled and sticking up in every direction but the right one. 'Hey, how long did I sleep?'

She glanced at her watch. 'We've been gone for four hours. We had to come back down because Abraham needed another bottle.' She hesitated for a second. 'We need some more supplies, and Mrs Van Dyke needs some things. How would you feel about leaving Abraham with her for a little while?'

He nodded and rubbed the sleep out of his eyes. 'I think that sounds like a plan.'

'Are we almost out of nappies already?'

Dan looked over and nodded, staring into the bottom

of the powdered-milk can. 'We're almost out of everything. I definitely need to buy some more coffee. It's the only thing that keeps me awake. I'm usually never this tired.'

Carrie walked over to him, leaving Abraham to kick his legs freely on the towel for a few minutes. 'You're usually never looking after a baby. How do you do on night shifts?'

He gave her a rueful look. 'The busy nights are fine. The quiet nights? I drink about six cups.'

'Will Mr Meltzer have anything left?'

Dan shook his head. 'No. We'll need to go further afield. Do you have rain boots?'

'Wellies? Sure I do.'

'Then get them. Go and get changed and I'll make a few calls to see where we can get some supplies. Are you okay walking a few blocks?'

'Of course. Do you want me to take Abraham up to Mrs Van Dyke?'

He shook his head. 'No, I'll do it. You go and get changed.'

She should have known. Dan wanted to check on Mrs Van Dyke himself. He really was a good guy. So why was he so down on Abraham's mother? It just didn't fit with the rest of his demeanour.

Ten minutes later she was ready. Her pink wool coat, purple scarf and purple woolly hat pulled down over her ears. Her wellies firmly in place with her jeans tucked inside.

The nip of frost was still in the air as they stepped outside. Dan pushed a piece of paper into his pocket and held out his gloved hand towards her.

Carrie hesitated for just a second. There was nothing in this. He was being mannerly and making sure she didn't fall over in the snow. This wasn't about the kiss that they'd shared—not at all.

She put her hand in his. 'How far do we need to go?'

The snow was deeper than she'd expected. Not quite deep enough to reach the tops of her wellies, but not too far off it. 'A few blocks,' he murmured.

It only took a few minutes for her to realise that trudging through the snow was harder work than she first thought. She could feel her cheeks flush and her breathing get harder. This was the most exercise she'd had in days. But there was something almost magical about being the first set of footprints in the clean, bright snow.

They walked for ten minutes before they came across their first snowman. He was built in the middle of the sidewalk at a peculiar angle. The hat had slipped and one of the stones that had been an eye had fallen out.

Dan smiled as she stopped to admire him. 'Oh, no. Here she goes. Snowman envy again.'

'What do you mean?'

'I saw your face when you watched the news report. The shops we're visiting are right next to Washington Square Park. If you really want we could stop and build one.'

She shook her head. 'But I didn't bring a carrot. Every good snowman needs a carrot for a nose.' She smiled. 'Actually, I'd much prefer to do a snow angel. Less work, more fun.'

They walked around the edge of the park towards the shops. There were a number of independent stores with lights on inside. Dan pushed open one of the doors quickly and shouted through to the back. 'Aidan, are you there?'

'Hi, Dan.' The guy appeared quickly from the back of the shop. 'Sorry, the phone keeps going ever since I got here. Seems the whole world needs supplies right now.' He nodded to the bags on the counter. 'I think I've got everything you requested—including the baby supplies. Anything you want to tell me, buddy?'

He looked from Dan to Carrie, and back again. 'It's not what you think. We found a baby on our doorstep a few days ago. Social services can't get through to pick him up and we need some supplies to take care of him.'

Dan's face was a bit flushed. As if he knew exactly what Aidan had been thinking. Was he embarrassed? Was he embarrassed that people might think they were actually a couple?

'This is my neighbour Carrie. She's giving me a hand with the baby.'

It seemed so.

Aidan nodded at Carrie and rang up the purchases on the register. 'Hopefully this will last only another day or so. Then you'll both be able to stop playing babysitter.'

The phone started ringing again and he headed back through to the back of the store. Dan had picked up the bags from the counter but seemed frozen. A bit like Carrie.

Another day or so. Abraham would be gone in a matter of days—maybe hours. What would happen to him then? Would he just get lost in the New York care system and be handed out to a foster family? The thought made Carrie feel sick. Before she'd been worried about Dan being embarrassed by her. Now, she realised she had much more to worry about.

She was going to have to say goodbye to another baby.

They walked out into the clear day. The snow was still thick everywhere, but the sky was clear and bright. Maybe this was the beginning of the end of the bad weather. Maybe it was time to move forward.

Dan seemed as lost in his thoughts as Carrie. Was he thinking about Abraham, too, or was he thinking about her?

They reached the edge of the park, near the Washington Arch. There were a few figures dotted around the park and a whole host of snowmen. 'Look.' Carrie pointed. 'It's like a whole little family.' She stood next to the father snowman and looked down at the carefully erected snow family. 'Dad, mum, a son and a daughter. How cute.' Her voice had a wistful tone that she couldn't help. Even the snow people had happy families.

Dan lifted his eyebrows at her. 'Snow angels?' he asked.

She wanted him to say so much more. She wanted to know how he was feeling. But Dan just wouldn't reveal that side of himself to her. In a way he was even more closed off to her than Mark had been.

She gave a little nod. 'Snow angels.' This could be the last thing they would do together. She might as well have a little fun.

They found a bit of untouched ground. 'It's perfect,' said Carrie. 'Are you ready?'

She walked as gingerly as she could in her wellies and turned around holding her hands open wide. Dan left the bags on the ground and stood next to her, hands wide, their fingers almost touching. 'You do realise you're about to get soaked, right, Brit girl?'

'It's a question of whether I care or not,' she responded as she leaned backwards, arms wide, letting herself disappear in a puff of powdery snow. She waved her hands through the snow as fast as she could, laughing, as Dan tried to keep up with her. Snow was soaking through her coat quickly, edging in around her neck and up her coat sleeves.

Then she felt it, her fingers brushing his, and she stopped.

She turned her head to face his. All of a sudden it seemed as if they were the only two people in New York. The only two people in this park, in this universe.

Dan moved. His breathing just as quick as hers. The warm air spilling into the cold around him, and then he was on her. His legs on either side of her, his warm breath colliding with her own.

'What are you doing to me, Carrie McKenzie?' His brown eyes were full of confusion and it made her heart squeeze. There it was. For the first time. Daniel Cooper stripped bare.

'What are you doing to me, Daniel Cooper? I thought I was doing fine till I met you.'

She pushed her neck up, catching his cold lips with hers. Wrapping her hands around his neck and pulling him even closer. She didn't mind the cold snow seeping through her coat around her shoulders and hips. She pushed aside the fact that a few minutes ago she'd felt a little hurt when he'd introduced her as his neighbour. She was as confused about all this as he was.

She'd told him everything. She'd told him about Ruby. She'd told him about Mark. But how much did she know about Daniel Cooper? And why did she feel as if she'd only scraped the surface?

In a few days the snow would be cleared, Abraham would be gone and their lives would return to normal. But what was normal any more? What would happen to her and Dan? An occasional hello on the stairs? She couldn't bear that.

He pulled away and stood up, holding out his hands to pull her up from the snow. 'Let's go, Carrie. You'll catch your death out here.'

The moment was past. It was over. Just as they would soon be.

She swallowed the lump in her throat. Now the wet patches were starting to feel uncomfortable. Starting to make her notice the cold air around them.

'I guess it's time to get back,' she said quietly.

'I guess it is.' He picked up the bags and started towards the exit, leaving her feeling as if she'd just imagined their kiss.

Two hours later, dried off and with clean clothes, Carrie finished making coffee for Dan and tea for herself, before adding the fruit scones that she'd made upstairs to a plate. Baby Abraham was in a good mood and feeding happily after being picked up from Mrs Van Dyke's.

Dan grinned at her. 'I wondered what the smell was. Do you know it drifted down the stairs and woke me up earlier? Not that I'm complaining.'

'Butter and raspberry jam. I hope you like them.'

'I'm sure I will.' He held her gaze for a minute and it made her wonder what he was thinking about. Was he regretting having her help with Abraham? Because she wasn't regretting it for a second.

'What did you do when I was sleeping—apart from baking?'

'I went upstairs and visited with Mrs Van Dyke. She's lovely—really lovely. Abraham seemed to like her, too.'

'Everybody likes her. She's just one of those people.'

'Was she good friends with your grandmother?'

Dan nodded. 'They lived in the same apartment block for sixty years and spoke to each other every day. Things were a bit different in those days—they used to borrow from each other all the time. There was hardly a day that went by where my grandmother didn't send me up the stairs to borrow or return something.'

'Did you meet her family?'

Dan adjusted himself in the seat as he fed Abraham. He looked slightly uncomfortable. 'They were all a good bit older than me.'

'The same age as your mother?' She couldn't help it. Both of them were tiptoeing around the issue. She didn't want to ask him about his mother, and he hadn't volunteered any information.

'Yeah, around about the same age.'

Nothing else. It was his prime opportunity to tell her a little more and he hadn't taken it. Should she give up? Maybe some things were best left secret. But it just felt so strange.

She took a deep breath.

'How come you ended up staying with your grandmother? Was your mum sick?'

Dan let out a laugh, causing Abraham to startle in his arms. But it wasn't a happy laugh. It was one filled with anger and resentment. 'Oh, yeah, she was sick all right.'

'What does that mean?'

'It means that some people shouldn't be mothers, Carrie.'

He didn't hesitate with his words and it made the breath catch in her throat.

What did that mean? Was that just aimed at his mother? Or was it aimed at her, too?

Was this why he was so screwed up about Abraham? He thought Abraham's mother wasn't fit to have a child?

'Is your mother still alive, Dan?' It seemed the natural question.

'No.' His words were curt and sharp. 'She died ten years ago. Drug overdose.'

The words were a shock and not what she was expecting to hear. Lots of people she knew had lost their mum or dad to various illnesses, cancer or some tragic accident. But no one had ever had a parent die from a drug overdose. One boy that Carrie had gone to school with had died a few years ago from drugs, but that was the only person she knew.

Chills were flooding over her body. Dan's reactions were acidic, obviously affected by years of bitter experience. What kind of a relationship had he had with his mother? It couldn't have been good.

'I'm sorry, Dan. I'm sorry that your mother died of a drug overdose. That must have been awful for you.'

He stood up as Abraham finished his bottle and propped him up onto his shoulder. 'It wasn't awful at all. I hadn't seen her in years. Nor did I want to.'

Carrie was at a loss. Should she ask more questions or just stay quiet? There was that horrible choice between seeming nosey or seeming uninterested. The last thing she wanted to do was upset Dan—he'd been so good to her. But she also wanted to support him as much as he'd supported her. Surely there was something she could do.

And then she remembered. His touch, and how much it had meant to her.

She walked over and laid her hand on his arm. His eyes went to her hand, just for a second, then lifted to meet her eyes.

She could see the hesitation, the wariness in them. He'd revealed a little part of himself, but there was so much more. She'd shared the most important part of her. It had hurt. It had felt as if she were exposing herself to the world. Taking her heart right out of her body and leaving it for the world to spear.

And what hurt most here was that Dan didn't feel

ready or able to share with her. Had she totally mis-read the situation? She'd thought they had connected. She thought that there might even have been a chance of something more. But if Dan couldn't share with her now, how on earth could they go any further?

The television flashed in the background. Pictures of snow being cleared in some areas, with aerial shots of previously deserted streets now with a few people on them, or a single car slowly edging its way along. The snow was finally going to stop. New York was going to return to a sense of normality.

Maybe it was for the best. Abraham would be able to go to Angel's Hospital and be checked over by Shana. That was good, except it made her want to run over and snatch him out of Dan's arms.

How much longer would she be able to cuddle him? Would this be their last night together? And what hurt more, the thought of being separated from Abraham, or the thought of not having a reason to spend time with Dan any more?

It was almost as if Abraham sensed her discomfort. He chose that precise moment to pull his little legs up, let out a squeal and projectile vomit all over Dan's shoulder.

Her reactions were instant. She held out her arms to take Abraham from him.

'Yeuch!' Dan pulled his T-shirt over his head, trying to stop the icky baby sick from soaking through. It was an almost unconscious act and she tried not to be dis-tracted by his flat abdomen and obvious pecs. If only her stomach looked like that.

But it didn't—ever. No matter what the TV ads said, women's abdomens just weren't designed to look like that, even *before* they'd had a baby.

Stifling a sigh, she pretended to fuss over Abraham

as Daniel walked past on his way to the laundry basket. What about his shoulders? And his back? Was the view from behind just as good?

She tried to take a surreptitious glance and her breath caught in her throat. While Daniel's torso was something a model would be envious of—his back was entirely different.

Scars. Chicken-pox scars all across his back. She winced inwardly, remembering how itchy she'd been as a child when she was covered with the spots. She'd only had a few on her back and they'd driven her insane because she couldn't—probably thankfully—get to them to scratch them.

'This is my favourite T-shirt,' he moaned as he flung it into the laundry basket. 'I bet no matter what I use, I'll never get rid of that smell.'

He looked up and caught sight of her face. She felt her cheeks flush and looked down at Abraham again.

But it was too late. He'd seen the expression that she'd tried to hide. He'd seen the shock. And maybe a little bit of horror.

She wanted to take back the past few seconds. She wanted to stand here with a smile fixed on her face. But it was too late.

Dan made to walk past, heading to his bedroom to get another T-shirt and cover up, the shadows apparent in his eyes. But something made her act. She put Abraham down in the crib and grabbed Dan's arm on the way past.

'What?' he snapped.

'Stop, Dan. Just stop for a second.'

She had no medical background. She had no training whatsoever. But something had registered in her brain. Something inside was screaming at her.

She nervously reached her fingers up and touched his

back. He flinched, obviously annoyed at her touch. His voice was lower. 'What are you doing, Carrie?'

Her fingers were trembling. She was almost scared to touch his flesh. But something was wrong. Something was very wrong.

The scars weren't what she'd expected. She had chicken-pox scars herself. And she and her fellow friends had spent many teenage years debating over how to hide their various scars.

Chicken-pox scars were pitted and uneven. No two looked the same.

But that wasn't the case on Dan's back. All his scars looked the same. Uniformly pitted circles across his back with not a single one on his chest, arms or face. Nothing about this was right.

Her pinkie fitted inside the little uniform scars. They were all the same diameter, all perfect scars, but of differing depth. Almost as if…

'Oh, Dan.' Her hand flew to her mouth and tears sprang to her eyes. She'd seen scars like these before. But only single ones, caused by accident by foolish friends.

These hadn't been caused by accident. These had been inflicted on a little boy. One at a time. Cigarette burns. She couldn't even begin to imagine what kind of a person could do this to a child. What kind of a person could willingly and knowingly inflict this kind of pain on another human being. It was beyond unthinkable.

Everything fell into place. Dan's reactions. His feelings towards his mother. The fact he'd ended up staying with his grandmother.

She reached her hands up around his neck and pulled him towards her. 'Oh, Dan, I'm so sorry. Your mother did this to you, didn't she?'

He was frozen. Frozen to the spot at his secret being exposed.

Even as her hands had wrapped around his neck her fingers had brushed against some of the scars. It was so unfair. So cruel. It made her feel sick to her stomach.

Finally, he answered. 'Yes. Yes, she did.' She could feel the rigid tension disperse from his muscles.

He walked back over and sagged down on the sofa, Carrie at his side. She didn't want to leave him—not for a second. Carrie couldn't stop the tears that were flowing now. Tears for a damaged child. Tears for a ruined childhood.

She shook her head. 'Why? Why would she do something like that? Why would *anyone* behave like that towards a child?'

The words he spoke were detached. 'Not everyone is like you, Carrie. Not everyone is like Mrs Van Dyke or my grandmother.' The words were catching in his throat, raw with emotion. 'My mother should never have had children. I was a mistake. She never wanted me. I ruined her drug habit. As soon as her doctor knew she was pregnant my mother was put on a reducing programme—even all those years ago. She couldn't wait to get her next fix. When she didn't use, she was indifferent to me, when she did use, she was just downright nasty. My grandmother tried time and time again to get her to give me up. Most of the time my mother kept moving around the city, trying to stay out of the way of my grandmother, social services and the drug dealers she owed money to.' He ran his fingers through his hair. 'Drugs aren't a new problem in New York. They're an old one. One that affected me since before I was even born.'

His other hand was sitting on his lap and she intertwined her fingers with his.

Touch. The one thing she knew to do that felt right.

So many things were making sense to her now. So many of the words that he'd spoken, or, more importantly, not spoken. So many of his underlying beliefs and tensions became crystal clear, including his prejudices towards Abraham's mother.

She would probably feel the same herself if she'd been in his shoes. But something still didn't sit right in her stomach about this whole situation.

She squeezed his hand. 'So how did you end up with your grandmother, then?'

'The cops phoned her. Our latest set of neighbours heard the screams once too often.' Carrie flinched. She didn't like any of the pictures her mind was currently conjuring up. 'They were concerned—but didn't want to get involved. Fortunately for me, one of their friends was a cop.'

'And he just picked you up and took you out of there?'

Dan shook his head. It was apparent he didn't like the details. 'It was more complicated than that. Social services were involved, as well as the police—it took a little time to sort out. But from the second I set eyes on the cop in my mother's house I knew I would be safe. There was just something about the guy. He wasn't leaving without me—no matter what happened.'

She gave him a smile. 'I guess he paved your way to the police academy.'

'I guess he did. He even gave me a reference eighteen years later when I needed it.'

'And what did your grandmother say?'

He shook his head. 'Nothing. Nothing at all. My mother's

name was never mentioned again. As far as I know she never had any more contact with my mother. Neither of us did. I can only ever remember a woman from social services coming to the door once. That was it. Nothing else.'

There was silence for a few seconds, as if both of them were lost in their thoughts. 'Thank you,' Carrie whispered.

'For what?' He looked confused.

'For sharing with me.'

'But I didn't. Not exactly.'

'It doesn't matter. Now I understand why you're so concerned about Abraham.'

They both turned towards the crib. 'I can't allow him to have a life like that, Carrie. If his mother didn't want him, then maybe this is the best thing for him. To go to loving parents who do want him. There are thousands of people out there who can't have kids of their own, just waiting for a baby like Abraham.'

Carrie hesitated. She didn't want to upset him. What he said made sense, but it still just didn't ring true with her.

'I get that, Daniel. I do. But I still think there's something else—something that we're both missing here.'

'Like what?'

She stood up and walked over to the window. The newscaster had been right. She could see the difference in the snow outside. It wasn't quite so deep. It wasn't quite so white. No freshly lain snow was replacing its supplies and what was there was beginning to disintegrate, to turn to the grey slush that had been on the streets before.

This time tomorrow Abraham would be gone. Gone forever. And the thought made her heart break.

She turned to face him again, her arms folded across

her chest. 'Why here, Dan? Why this house? There are plenty of nice houses on this street. What made Abraham's mother leave him *here?*' She pointed downwards, emphasising her words.

Daniel lifted his hands. 'What do you mean, Carrie? We've been through this. The lights were on. This place was a safe bet. Even if the mother didn't ring the bell.'

'That's it.' She was across the room in a flash, a little light going on in her brain. 'A safe bet. Don't you get it?' She grabbed hold of his arms.

'Get what?'

Her frustration was mounting. 'Dan, I knew you were a cop—even though you'd never spoken to me. I saw you every day in your uniform. Walking along this street and into our apartment building.'

'So?' A wrinkle appeared on his brow.

'So!' Her face was inches from his. The compassion in her eyes more prominent than anything he'd ever seen. 'What's a safer bet than a cop? If you had to leave a baby at anyone's door, who would you choose, Dan? Who would you choose?'

A horrible feeling of realisation started to wash over his skin. A horrible feeling that he'd missed something really important.

'You think the baby was left here because someone knew I was a cop?'

'I *know* he was. Think about it, Dan. It makes perfect sense. If I wanted to keep my baby safe—and couldn't tell anyone about it—where safer than at a cop's door.'

'But who? Who would do something like that?'

Their eyes met. It was as if a mutual thought had just appeared in their heads. One that left a sinking feeling in his stomach. But Carrie wasn't about to stand back and leave things unsaid. Leave possibilities unchallenged.

She looked at Abraham again and tried to keep the tremble from her voice. 'Dan, is there any chance—any possibility at all—that Abraham could be your baby?'

'What? No! Of course not.' There was pain in her eyes. Hurt there for him to see. It didn't matter to her how painful the suggestion was, Abraham came first. She was thinking only of him.

It was there, in that split second, that he knew. Carrie McKenzie was the girl for him. He loved her, with his whole heart. The past few days had let deep emotions build, heartbreaking secrets revealed by both of them.

But as he looked at her flushed face, her blue eyes trying to mask the pain she didn't want him to see, her teeth biting her plump bottom lip as she tried to digest his answer, he absolutely knew. This was a woman who was prepared to push her feelings aside for a child she had no responsibility for, no connection with. If he pulled her to the side right now and told her there was a strong likelihood that Abraham was his—even though that wasn't a possibility—he knew she would just nod quietly and say nothing. All for the sake of the child.

The one thing he'd never been able to do—connect with a woman—he'd found here, in his own home and right on his doorstep. His fractured relationship with his mother had made him erect barriers even he couldn't see. But here, and now, with Carrie McKenzie, they were gone. She wasn't shying away from him because he'd been an abused child. She was only trying to understand him better.

'Are you sure?' She was struggling with the words,

trying to be steady and rational even though he knew inside she wasn't.

It only took a step to reach her and touch her cheek— no, cradle her cheek in his hand. 'I promise you, Carrie. There's no chance that Abraham is mine. That's not why he's been left here.'

There were tears brimming in her eyes. Tears of relief? She let the air out of her lungs with a little whoosh. Her bottom lip was trembling and he ached to kiss her. But it wasn't the time. They were on the precipice of something here. The precipice of something for them and something for Abraham. And they both had too much duty and responsibility to know what came first.

He didn't ever want to do that to her again. He didn't ever want to do anything to cause Carrie McKenzie even a second of hurt, a second of pain. Once was enough. She was far too precious to him for that.

She looked at him with her big blue eyes, words hovering on her lips, before she broke eye contact and looked down at the floor. Anything they had to say to each other would have to wait, if just for a few hours. She lifted her head again. 'Then it must be someone else, Dan. Someone that knows you're a cop and trusts you.'

He tried to rack his brain. 'I just can't think, Carrie. Most of my friends don't stay around here. And none of them are pregnant.' He glanced towards the window again. 'And the snow might be beginning to clear now, but it was thick on Monday night. It could only have been someone around here, someone local….' His voice tailed off and he pressed his hand against the window.

'What if it isn't a friend, Dan? What if it's a neighbour? Or someone you've come into contact with because of your job? Is there anyone around here you've been called out to see?'

'I usually work in the middle of the city. I've only ever covered a few shifts down here. It doesn't do any good covering your own patch.'

'Who did you get called out to see when you visited? Anyone that sticks in your mind?'

He felt the blood rush from his head right down to his toes. He could be sick, right now, all over the floor.

He made a mad dash for the phone, pressing the numbers furiously. 'It's Daniel Cooper. I need to speak to the captain. Now!'

'Dan, what is it? What have you remembered?'

He shook his head. He didn't have time for small talk. All he could do was pray that some of the roads had cleared and help would be available if needed.'

'Captain, it's Dan. This baby? Yes, he's fine. But I think I know who put him here. Look up Mary and Frank Shankland…. Yes, that's them. A list of domestics as long as your arm. Last time I was there, she was pregnant, he was mad and he'd beat her so badly she lost the baby. Told her if she ever got pregnant again, he'd do the same.'

Carrie's hand flew to her mouth. 'Oh, no! That's awful.'

Dan lifted his hand to silence her as he listened to the other end of the phone. 'That's why she was unprepared. She couldn't buy anything for this baby or else he might notice. She must have hidden her pregnancy from him. How are the roads? Can you send a unit? I'm going there. Now.'

He slammed down the phone and headed straight for the door. 'Wait, Dan, you can't go there alone. Look at your hand—you're already injured. How will you be able to protect her with a broken wrist?'

He spun around, his eyes furious. 'I can't, no, I *won't* wait another second, Carrie. Why didn't I think of this? After what he did to Mary the last time, we'll be lucky if she's still alive.' He pointed over to the crib. 'Take care of Abraham. Take care of Abraham for his mother. And just pray I get there in time.'

And in an instant he was gone.

CHAPTER ELEVEN

IT WAS THE longest two hours of Carrie's life. Every time she heard a siren her heart was in her mouth. Every time she heard the start-up of a car engine she would run to the window to peer outside.

Abraham was perfect. He fed and winded like a little dream. It was as if he knew how stressed and on edge she was. The noise of the snow plough coming down the street nearly tipped her over the edge. Most of the snow was starting to melt and it merely ploughed the dirty slush ahead of it.

Finally, there was a flashing blue light and the sound of a door slamming. She ran and opened Dan's apartment door.

There was a scuff mark on his cheek, as if he'd hit a wall. And his clothes, although still intact, were definitely rumpled. As if someone had clutched them in a tight grip.

Behind him, a uniformed officer was lurking, obviously waiting to hear their interaction. She couldn't stop herself. With Abraham in one arm, her other was wrapped around Dan's neck in an instant. 'Are you okay? Are you hurt? What about Abraham's mother? Please tell me that she's okay?'

Dan turned and nodded to the other cop. 'Give me five minutes, Ben. I'll be right out.' It was then Carrie noticed the baby car seat in Ben's hands. He nodded at Dan, and left it sitting next to the door.

Dan closed the door and leaned against it for a few seconds, catching his breath, before finally leaning over and dropping a kiss first on Abraham's head and then on Carrie's.

He walked over to the sofa and put his head in his hands.

Her heart was breaking for him. It was obvious he was blaming himself for this. Even though it had been entirely out of his control.

She sat next to him, the length of her thigh in contact with his. Even the slightest touch gave her a little comfort. But she couldn't find the patience to wait. Two hours had been long enough. She had to know. She had to know Abraham still had a mother.

'What happened, Dan? Does Abraham belong to Mary Shankland?'

He nodded and lifted his head from his hands. His eyes were heavy with fatigue and strain. 'It was just as I suspected. She hid the pregnancy and gave birth in secret. She knew she would have to hide him from Frank, and thought she would have made it to a women's shelter or a hospital. But everything conspired against her.' He held up his hands. 'The weather. The snow. Then Abraham came four weeks early. She was desperate. She didn't know what to do. Frank was at the pub and was due home any minute. She didn't have time to pack up the kids and leave, and they didn't have anywhere to go.' He shook his head in frustration. 'She couldn't even get through to emergency services.'

'So she left the baby here, with you?' Carrie wrinkled her nose. 'Why didn't she ring the bell? Why didn't she ask for your help?'

He thumped his hand on the table. 'She did, Carrie! She did ring the bell. My darn music was on too loud. I never heard it. Frank was due back any minute and she'd left the children by themselves. She had to get back home before he knew anything was wrong.' He turned to face her, his eyes full of sorrow. 'If you hadn't been upstairs and heard Abraham...' He was shaking his head, obviously imagining the worst.

She clutched at his hand. 'But I did, Dan. And Abraham's safe.' She took a little moment to look at the sleeping baby on her lap. Perfect. Perfect in every way. And more importantly, safe. Something squeezed at her heart. Every baby like Abraham and every child like Dan had the right to be safe. Had the right to be cared for and loved. Had the right to be treated with respect. If only everyone in this world felt the same.

'How are Mary and the other kids?'

Dan nodded slowly, letting a long stream of air out through his pursed lips. 'She's safe now. We arrived just as Frank was kicking off. It looks as if his temper has got worse and worse over the past few days with the family being snowed in together. Mary was crouched in a corner sheltering her youngest son.' The words sent a horrible shiver down her spine.

'Oh, those poor children.'

He nodded. 'Frank's been arrested. Mary is being checked over at Grace Jordan Hospital.' He reached over and touched Abraham's tiny fingers. 'I almost couldn't persuade her to go. She wanted to come straight here and check on Abraham. It was awful, Carrie. The tears of pure relief when she saw me and knew that I was there to help. It was a look I recognised.' He shook his head again. 'I should have got there sooner. I should have known.'

'But you didn't know, Dan. *We* didn't know.'

'But you didn't let your past history cloud your judgement—stop you from looking at other possibilities.'

'Of course I did, Dan! How many times did I tell you I couldn't do this? I couldn't look after Abraham? I couldn't help you?'

But Dan was still fixated on his own failings. 'I shouldn't even be doing this job. How can I be a good cop when I can't even think straight?'

'Stop it. Stop it right now. You're the finest cop I've ever met, Dan Cooper. You have the biggest, kindest heart in the world. You can't help what happened to you in the past. And even though you had a crummy mother with a terrible addiction, even though you experienced things a child should never experience, it's shaped you, Dan. It's made you become the fine man that you are.' She reached over and touched his cheek. 'You feel passionately about things. You have a clear sense of right and wrong. You have the courage of your convictions. You looked at the example of the cop who looked out for you and used him as your role model. Him, Dan—not your mother. He would be proud of you. I know he would. Just like your grandmother would be.' She could feel her eyes pooling with tears. 'I couldn't have got through the past few days without you.' She looked at Abraham in her lap. 'No, *we* couldn't have got through the past few days without you.'

The tension seemed to dispel from his muscles, the frustration to abate from his eyes. He reached over and cupped her cheek, brushing her curls behind her ears. 'Carrie, you know what I need to do now, don't you? I need to take Abraham to Angel's. Shana is waiting to see him. And I need to reunite him with his mother.'

Carrie could feel the pooled tears start to spill down her cheeks. Of course. This was what she'd always wanted to happen. For Abraham to be safe, to be returned to his mother. So why did it feel as if her heart were breaking?

These past few days had been hard. But they'd also been wonderful. She finally felt healed. She finally felt as if she could start to live again.

And she'd found someone she wanted to do that with.

But their cosy little bubble was about to burst. The snow was melting. Things would get back to normal. New York would get back to normal.

Dan would get back to normal. There would be no reason for them to be stuck in his apartment together. There would no reason for her to be in his life at all.

She tried to concentrate. She tried to focus. Last thing she wanted to do was appear like a blubbing wreck.

Abraham's eyes flickered open and she leaned over him. 'Well, Abraham, it's time to say goodbye. Or maybe I should call you Baby Shankland now?' She raised her eyebrows at Dan and he shook his head and gave her a sad little smile.

'Mary loved the name. He's definitely going to stay an Abraham.'

A tiny bit of the pressure in her chest felt relieved. He wouldn't have another name. He'd have the name that they'd given him—together. At least that little part of their time together would live on, even if nothing else did.

She ran her finger lightly over his face, touching his forehead, his eyelids, his nose, his cheeks and his mouth. Trying to savour every second, trying to imprint on her brain everything about him. Something caught her eye. His little soft fontanelle, it was pulsing. She could see the proof of his heartbeat right before her eyes. She hadn't noticed it before and it gave her even more comfort than she could have imagined.

She tried not to let her voice shake. 'I'm going to wish

you a long, happy and healthy life, Abraham. I'm going to tell you that you're blessed. You're blessed to have a mother who did her best to protect you. And every time I see snow I'm going to think of you and remember you here—' she pressed her hand to her chest '—in my heart. Now and always.'

She wrapped him a little tighter in Mrs Van Dyke's crocheted shawl. She was sure Mrs Van Dyke wouldn't mind it going to a good home. She couldn't even lift her head to look at Dan right now. She already knew he was holding out his hands, waiting for Abraham, to take him away.

She must have paused. She must have waited just a little too long. Because his hand touched her arm. 'Carrie.' It wasn't a question. It was a prompt, in the quietest, subtlest way.

She put one final kiss on Abraham's forehead and held him out with shaky hands. It took all her self-control not to snatch him back from Dan's grasp.

She felt his hand on her shoulder. A tight squeeze. Followed by his voice murmuring in her ear. 'I don't know how long I'll be, Carrie. I could be all night. I need to stay with Abraham at the hospital, then fill out a mountain of paperwork downtown.'

She was nodding automatically at his words. Not really taking any of them in.

Her heart was thudding in her chest. Was this it? Was this it for them, too?

Dan hadn't said anything. She had no idea what would happen next.

All she knew was she wanted him to stay. She wanted him to stay with her. She wanted him to wrap his arms around her and tell her that everything would be okay. She wanted him to reach out and tuck her hair behind her ears. She wanted him to look at her the way he had the night before, right before he'd kissed her. She wanted to feel her heartbeat quicken and flutter in her chest as it did when they were together.

Anything other than this horrible leaden feeling that was there right now.

He released his fingers on her shoulder and she heard his footsteps heading for the door.

No words. He hadn't said anything to her. He hadn't told her to stay. He hadn't told her to go.

She heard the final hesitant steps and then the click of the door behind her.

It sounded so final. It sounded like the end of everything.

And it probably was.

And then the sobs that had been stifled in her chest finally erupted.

CHAPTER TWELVE

DAN'S WHOLE BODY wanted to go into shutdown mode. But his brain was buzzing. It had been twenty-four hours since he'd slept.

The check-over at the hospital for Mary Shankland had taken much longer than expected. She had three broken ribs and a minor head injury. It had taken hours before she was cleared for transfer and Dan didn't want anyone else to have the job of reuniting her with her son.

He wouldn't have missed it for the world.

Abraham was fine and healthy. He'd even managed to squirt a little pee all over Shana, much to Dan's amusement, as she'd examined him.

But the real heart-stopping moment had been when Mary finally got to hold her baby in her arms. She sobbed and sobbed, telling him how much she loved him and how she just wanted to protect him. The hospital social worker had been standing by to help find the family alternative accommodation and to assess them. And even though Frank had been taken to jail, a temporary restraining order had been put into place to protect the family in the meantime. All of which added to the mountain of paperwork toppling over on his desk.

His captain had been as understanding as could be. But there were still professional requirements that Dan had to fulfil. Pages and pages of paperwork that had to be completed before he could leave the station and get back home to Carrie.

Back home to where he wanted to be.

Back home to the one he wanted to be with.

Things had been too hard. Taking Abraham away from Carrie had been hard, and he'd tried his best not to make it any more difficult than it already was.

There was so much to say. So much to do. He didn't have a single doubt in his head about Carrie McKenzie. But would she have any doubts about him? There was only one way to find out.

He'd made three pit stops on his way home, his stomach churning the whole way. Thankfully the New York florist he'd visited hadn't even flinched when he'd asked her for 'rose-coloured' roses. There might have been a slight glimmer of a smile while she'd walked to her back storeroom and reappeared with beautiful, rich pink-coloured roses with the tiniest hint of red, and tied them with a matching satin ribbon.

Perfect. Just like the roses his grandmother used to fill the apartment with. It was time to do that all over again.

He walked up the stairs to his apartment building with trepidation in his heart. As he pushed open the door to his apartment he already knew she wasn't there. He could feel it. Just her presence in a room made it light up.

His feet were on the stairs in an instant, thudding upstairs and knocking on the door of her apartment. The snow had started to clear, but most people hadn't returned to work yet; the subway still wasn't completely open.

Please don't be at work. Please don't be at work.

'Carrie? Are you there? It's Dan. I need to speak to you.' He waited a few seconds, then dropped to his knees and tried to peer through the keyhole.

The door behind him creaked open. Mrs Van Dyke's thin frame and loose cardigans filled the doorway. 'I think the person you're looking for is in here,' she whispered.

'She is? What's she doing?'

Mrs Van Dyke shrugged. 'It appears I need some help with tidying up. She's in my spare room.'

He hurried inside, knowing exactly where to go. That was just like Carrie. Now that she knew about Mrs Van Dyke's hoarding she would be doing her best to try and help. He walked over to the room, hearing the muffled noises of falling cardboard boxes inside.

'Yikes!'

His heartbeat accelerated as he elbowed his way into the room, past the teetering piles and fallen boxes, finally reaching Carrie in a heap on the floor. He grasped her hand and pulled her upwards, straight into his arms.

'Dan!' She looked dazed, and it took him a few moments to steady her. Then the arms that had rested on his shoulders fell back to her sides.

'What do you want, Dan?' She sounded sad, tired even.

'I wanted to see you.'

'Why? Why did you want to see me, Dan?'

He reached up and touched her cheek. 'I wanted to speak to you. I wanted to make sure you were okay.'

Her hand reached up and covered his. 'I'm fine, Daniel. I'm just glad that Abraham is back with his mother.'

His gut was twisting. She was still hurting, still in pain because of the whole situation he'd allowed her to become involved in.

'Abraham is fine. Mary Shankland is fine—well, not really, but she will be. But what I'm most interested in is you, Carrie. Are you fine?'

Her eyelids widened, as if she was surprised at his words.

He pulled her a little closer. 'I've been thinking about you all night and all day. I couldn't get away—I had a mountain of paperwork to fill out. I'm so sorry I had to leave you, Carrie. I know how hard it was. But I had to take Abraham back to his mother. I had to make sure they were both okay. Even though the person I wanted to be with was you.'

'It was?' Her lips were trembling. Her whole body was trembling.

'Of course it was, Carrie.'

'But you didn't say anything. You didn't ask me to stay.' She was shaking her head as if she was trying to make sense of things.

'I couldn't, Carrie. I didn't want to start a conversation with you that I couldn't finish. Not when I had things to sort out. I wanted us to have time. Time to talk. Time to see what you wanted.' He brushed her hair behind her ear and whispered, 'What do you want, Carrie? What do you want to happen now?'

She was hesitating. As if she was scared to say the words out loud. He was praying inside it was because she was nervous and not because she wanted to let him down gently.

He lifted up the hand-tied bouquet and handed it to her. 'My grandmother's favourite roses. I bought you some, to say thank you for helping me these past few days.'

'Oh.' The little spark that had lit up her eyes disappeared. He wasn't doing this right. He wasn't saying the right things. None of this was working out how he'd planned.

'They're beautiful. Thank you.' She was disappointed. She'd been hoping for something more. And so had he.

He moved forward, pulling her close, and whispered in her ear, 'Look closely, Carrie.'

She held up the bouquet to her nose and took a deep breath, savouring the smell of the roses. 'Where did you get them in the middle of this snow, Dan? They must have cost a fortune.' She still hadn't noticed. She still hadn't seen what he'd done.

He held up the bag he had in his other hand and pulled out a bundle—also tied with pink ribbon. She looked surprised and took the bundle from his hands. It was DVDs. *The Great Escape, Dirty Dancing, Finding Nemo, Toy Story* and a whole host of musicals. A little smile appeared on her face. 'What did you get these for, Dan?'

He gulped. He was going to have to spell it out. 'I figured if we were staying in a lot, we might need to expand our DVD collection. I thought we'd start with some favourites for us both.'

Her eyes finally caught sight of it. The key hanging from the pink ribbon on the bouquet. 'What's this for?'

'It's for you.'

'For me?' Her smile was starting to broaden and the sparkle to appear in her eyes again.

He caught a whiff of her scent. Freesias. More subtle than the roses. Sweeter. Something he could happily smell for the rest of his life. Who needed candles?

He pressed his hands firmly on her hips, pulling her closer to him. 'What's the point of having two apartments when we could easily have one?'

She wound her hands around his neck. 'One?'

He nodded and smiled. 'One.'

'What about the getting-to-know-you dates?'

'What about them?'

'Aren't we missing some stuff out here?'

'Honey, if you want to do some getting-to-know-you, then I'm your man.'

He bent to kiss her.

'You know, Dan, I think you could be right.'

'Carrie McKenzie, you're killing me. Will you look inside the roses, please?'

She wrinkled her nose and caught the glint of a diamond nestled inside one of the roses.

He sighed. 'Finally!'

He got down on one knee. 'Carrie McKenzie, I've never connected with anyone the way I've connected with you. I don't care where we stay, whether it's here or in London. All I know is I want us to be together. Carrie McKenzie, will you be my wife?'

He slid the ring onto her finger. She smiled. 'Aren't you supposed to wait for an answer?' She held up the ring, watching the perfect diamond glint in the sun.

He whispered in her ear, 'I'm not going to risk it. I'm hoping it's a yes.'

'Oh, it's definitely a yes,' she whispered as she wrapped her hands around his neck and started kissing him.

* * * * *

MOONLIGHT IN PARIS

BY
PAMELA HEARON

Pamela Hearon grew up in Paducah, a small city in western Kentucky that infuses its inhabitants with Southern values, Southern hospitality and a very distinct Southern accent. There she found the inspiration for her quirky characters, the perfect backdrop for the stories she wanted to tell and the beginnings of her narrative voice. She is a 2013 RITA® Award finalist for her first Mills & Boon Cherish novel, *Out of the Depths*. Visit Pamela at her website (www.pamelahearon.com) or on Facebook and Twitter.

To my precious daughter, Heather...
the one true masterpiece of my life.

ACKNOWLEDGMENTS

Writing a book requires gleaning information from many sources and sometimes becoming annoying in the process, I'm sure. I'm always amazed by the willingness of people to share their knowledge and experiences that add authenticity to my story. . .and I'm filled with gratitude.

As a small show of my appreciation, I'd like to thank the following people: Coroner Phil Hileman for his expertise on accidental death and suicide; susan barack for her contact in Paris; steve and Jackie beatty for sharing the opportunity for a Paris vacation; sandra Jones, Angela Campbell, Maggie Van Well and Cynthia D'Alba for their suggestions, ideas, plotting help and patience; Kimberly lang for always having the time to talk me through the loopholes and gaps; Agent Jennifer Weltz for her wisdom, insight and approachability; and editor Karen reid for her gentle guidance, fabulous editing and her innate ability to just "get me."

Above all, I want to thank my loving husband, Dick, who stays beside me through it all and encourages me to continue following this dream.

CHAPTER ONE

"I'VE ALWAYS HEARD life can change in an instant. Guess I'm living proof, huh?"

Tara O'Malley threw a glance out the window to the tangled mass of metal that had been her motorcycle. It sat on prominent display today in her parents' front yard—a grim reminder to passing motorists that motorcycles travel at the same speed as cars. Tomorrow, it would be junked.

Her mom sat the butter dish in the middle of the table and dropped a quick kiss on the top of Tara's head. "*Living* is the important word in that sentence."

"Yeah, I know." Tara focused her attention back to the app on her phone where she was entering all the family's medical history. Her accident had made her aware of the need to have such information at her fingertips, but it was Taylor Grove's blood drive in her honor today that made her finally sit down and fill in the blanks. "What was Thea's blood type?"

"A...same as mine," her mom answered absently. "Do you think Emma would stop and get a bag of ice on her way into town? I'm afraid we might run low."

"I'll call her." Tara pulled up her favorites list and thumbed her best friend's number.

"Hey," Emma answered on the first ring.

"Hey, would you stop and get a bag of ice? Mama's afraid we'll run out. And while I'm thinking about it, would you resend that class schedule for this week? I couldn't get the one from the office to open, and I keep forgetting

when the junior high students are coming for their tours."
The last full week of school was always crammed with so
many activities that it was hard to fit in a lesson.

"Sure. I'm just leaving Paducah. Does your mom need
anything else? Paper plates? Paper cups?"

"Do you need anything else, Mama? Are we using paper
plates?"

Faith shook her head. "No, I'm doing Memorial Day like
Thanksgiving in May this year. I just need enough people
to eat all the food."

"She says to bring people." Tara relayed the message.

"I haven't eaten all day, so I'm bringing a three-meal
appetite," Emma promised. "Be there in forty-five minutes or so."

"Okay. See you then." Tara pressed the button to end
the call, and, before she could think, reached to rub the
burning itch on her right hand. As had happened so many
times over the past two months since her accident, her
breath caught at the empty space her pinkie and ring fingers had occupied, and she sent up a quick prayer of thanks
that two fingers and a spleen were all she'd lost. She traced
the bright red scar that stopped halfway up her arm. "I'm
thinking I might get another tattoo. Maybe some leaves
that will make this look like a vine."

That got her mom's attention. Faith shot her daughter
a pointed look. "Your dad will disown you. He took your
first one pretty well only because it's hidden, and the second with a grain of salt, but he threatened to write you out
of the will over the last one."

Tara didn't mention the two they knew nothing about.
She grinned, remembering the aggravated look on her dad's
face when she'd shown off the Celtic symbol for life just
beneath her left earlobe. When she'd explained it was in
memory of Grandma O'Malley and their Irish roots, he'd
held his tongue, but the hard set of his jaw had indicated
his displeasure.

Tara often referred to her dad as the closest thing to a saint she'd ever known. As the preacher at the lone church in Taylor's Grove, Kentucky, Sawyer O'Malley sought to lead a life above reproach, and for the most part, he'd been successful. A loving and faithful wife...three relatively good kids.

Thea and Trenton had both gone through some rebellious stages during their teenage years, but it was just regular teenage stuff—a little drinking, some partying. But Tara, the "good girl," had been the surprise to everyone, including herself.

Five years ago, her fiancé, Louis, returned from a mission trip in Honduras with a brand-new wife—an event that threw Tara's world into a tailspin. Louis, her boyfriend of eight years, had been the only guy she'd ever dated. They'd even signed pledge cards that vowed chastity until marriage. Then he'd shown up with a wife, leaving Tara as an oddity—that rare twenty-three-year-old with her virginity still intact.

She'd made quick work of making up for all the lost time.

"Are Louis and Marta bringing their brood?"

Her mom answered with an affirmative nod as she slid the giant pan of macaroni and cheese into the oven.

Tara's ex and his wife hadn't lost any time, either. Three children in five years. And though it had taken a couple of years, Tara was glad she and Louis were friends again. She liked his family—especially Marta and her quiet, kind ways.

Tara set her phone down, feeling guilty that her mom was so busy, and she was doing nothing of great importance. "I'm not an invalid, Mama. Can I at least set the table?"

Her mom chewed her lip for a moment. "All right, you can set the table. But I'll get Lacy's china myself." She disappeared into the other room.

Tara took the hint. Grandma O'Malley's Belleek table-ware was too precious to risk being carried by someone with newly missing fingers.

Trenton came in through the back door, arms laden with cartons of soft drinks and bottled water. With the blood drive in Tara's honor going on, the annual O'Malley Memorial Day Dinner had swelled to triple the usual number of people. The entire day had been very humbling.

"Hey, pinky."

Tara snorted and rolled her eyes at her brother's twisted sense of humor. He'd labeled her with the new nickname before she'd even gotten out of the hospital.

"Would you help me with the chicken?" He found an open spot on the drink-and-dessert table, and unloaded his arms. "I've got to get all those pieces turned and basted, and the ribs need a close eye kept on them."

"Sure." She eased out of her chair, still aware of the tightness from the scar where her ruptured spleen had been removed. "But I need to know your blood type first. I'm filling in an emergency app for our family."

"AB," he answered.

Tara keyed in the information, and then frowned as she glanced down the chart. "What's with this?"

Her dad came in from the garage just in time to hear her question. "What's with what, lovebug?" Slipping an arm around her shoulder, he gave her a quick hug and a peck on her temple.

She pointed to the chart. "It doesn't make sense. Trent's AB like you. Thea's A like Mama. I'm the only O negative in the bunch."

Her mom came in from the dining room with Grandma O'Malley's china stacked to just below her chin. Sawyer moved quickly in her direction, ready to alleviate her of the load as Tara continued voicing her thoughts to no one particular. "Is that even possible? Can an A and an AB produce an O?" She laughed. "Maybe we need a paternity test, Dad, to see if I'm really yours."

Faith's loud intake of breath drew everyone's attention. Her eyes went wide with a horrific look of mingled shock, pain and undeniable guilt an instant before twelve of Grandma O'Malley's treasured china plates crashed to the floor.

FAITH ISABEL FRANKLIN O'Malley had never wanted to die before, but the past seven hours had convinced her that death would be preferable to the excruciating pain she was presently feeling. It was as if she was dangling from a cord attached through her heart and the organ was being ripped slowly from her body. She'd been aware of every second of every minute of every hour that had brought her closer to this time when it would be just the immediate family.

Time for her confession.

People had started arriving before the broken china could be disposed of, so the mess and loss of family heirlooms made a convenient cover for the tears she couldn't bring under control. Sawyer, Tara and Trenton watched her with guarded expressions throughout the afternoon, and even Thea, soon after her arrival, began questioning the family quietly about what was going on.

Their looks of pain had been almost more than Faith could bear, but Sawyer's blessing for the food had been her major undoing. She'd lost it completely when he gave his thanks for the spared life of Tara, his beloved daughter. His voice had cracked at the words, and Faith and the rest of her family knew the reason behind the falter.

She knew that he knew. They all knew.

She also knew the next few minutes could bring her family crashing down around her. The china had served as a warning.

Her hands lay on the table in front of her. She clenched and unclenched them, twisted her fingers, then her rings.

She swallowed hard, trying to clear the way for the words, knowing in her heart there were no "right" ones—none that could ever make this anything but what it was.

"His name was Jacques Martin," she said at last, finding no preamble that could ease her into the subject. "He was from France. Paris."

Tara's eyes widened at the news. She sat up straighter in her chair and rubbed the side of her hand vigorously— a common gesture for her since the accident.

Faith shifted her eyes to her husband. "We spent one night together. Graduation. He left to go back to Paris the next day."

Sawyer rubbed his temples as his eyes squeezed closed, and she felt the squeeze in her heart. Was he praying? No. More likely he was running through the timeline, letting all the pieces fall into place.

Their college graduations had been on the same day, hundreds of miles apart. He'd been in Texas while she'd remained in Kentucky. By the time he moved back home ten days later, the pregnancy test had already read *positive*. Another test ten days after that had been all it took to convince him they were going to have a baby—together. They'd eloped, to no one's surprise after four long years apart.

Deception had been easy. But twenty-eight years had woven the lie tightly into the center of the fabric of their lives. Now, it was starting to unravel.

No one said anything. Everyone was avoiding eye contact with her except Tara, who sat staring with tear-filled eyes, pulling at her bottom lip. That gesture was unadulterated Sawyer, but Tara's wide, curvy mouth was the spitting image of her biological father's. Faith had always found it ironic that Tara's mouth served as the constant reminder of the lie that remained a secret.

Until seven hours ago.

Trenton stood up quickly, the force sending his chair

backward across the wood floor. "I don't think I want to hear this," he announced. "Whatever happened back then is between you two." He folded both arms around Tara's neck and rested his chin on her head. "Pinky's my sister. Wholly and completely with none of that half stuff. Nothing's ever going to change that." He clapped his dad on the back and planted a quick kiss to the top of Faith's head before strolling casually from the room.

Thea scooted over into the seat Trenton had vacated, weaving her hand under Tara's thick mane of red hair until she located her sister's shoulder. She pulled her close—cheeks touching, tears mingling—as she shot Faith a "how could you?" look. "I feel the same way," she said. "We've never been just sisters. We've always been closer than that. There's no way anything can make us any different than what we are."

Tara's chin quivered as she nodded.

Faith's spirit lightened momentarily at the show of solidarity. Maybe things were going to be okay after all. But one glance at Sawyer told her that wasn't so. Her husband was a preacher. A man who made his living talking. He'd counseled hundreds of couples with marital problems through the years, always knowing exactly what to say to clear the air of the fallout from unfaithfulness.

His silence grated her heart into tiny slivers like lemon zest.

"So whatever became of this…Jacques Martin?" Tara's voice held the same strained edge it had when she realized her two fingers were gone.

"I never saw, never heard from him again," Faith answered, then added, "I never wanted to. I had all I needed and wanted with you all." Blood pounded in her temples. How could she make them understand? "Jacques was…" Someone she'd had too much alcohol with that night. Someone she'd gotten carried away celebrating with. Someone who'd helped her bear the loneliness of not being with the person she loved on one of the most important days of her life. "He was someone I barely knew."

Sawyer swerved around to face Tara and gathered her partial hand into both of his. "You're my daughter, love-bug. The daughter of my heart. Like Trenton said, nothing's ever going to change that." He pressed their knotted hands against his chest. "I hold you right here, and nothing will ever break that grip."

Faith watched the tears overflow from her daughter's eyes, unaware of her own until she felt a drop on her arm.

Tara nodded. "I love you, Dad." She paused and Faith held her breath and prayed that those words would be repeated to her.

They weren't. Instead, Tara stood, pulling her hand from Sawyer's grip. "I really, really need to go home. I need time alone to process this."

Thea followed her to her feet.

A different fear gripped Faith's insides, a familiar one since Tara's accident. It recurred every time one of her children left her house to drive back to their own homes. "Will you be okay making the drive back to Paducah? You want me to call Emma?"

"I'm leaving, too. I'll take you home," Thea offered.

Tara shook her head. "I don't want to be with anyone. I'll be okay."

Faith stood and reached for her, and her daughter hugged her then, but her arms felt limp and lifeless with no emotion behind them. Her parting hug with her dad had a bit more vitality, but not much.

Faith's breathing grew shallow when Thea didn't hug her or Sawyer, but she did take Tara's hand to lead the way out.

As Tara slid the patio door closed behind her, Faith turned her attention back to her husband. They stood beside the table where their family had shared thousands of happy mealtimes. Would those be enough to blot out the anguish of today?

She took Sawyer's hand and tilted her head in silent question.

"It's not the action, Faith. It's the deception. The betrayal."

He pulled his hand away and headed for his study, locking the door behind him.

CHAPTER TWO

"BUT HOW ARE YOU HANDLING it, really? And none of that 'I'm okay' stuff. I held your hair when you threw up your first beer, so I've seen you at your worst." Emma blew on her spoonful of tomato soup, waiting for an answer.

Tara reached behind her chair to shut the door to Emma's office, pondering how to put her feelings into words. "You remember that weird, uneasy feeling inside you the first Christmas you no longer believed in Santa Claus? It's kind of like that. I remember knowing the presents were still downstairs, waiting to be opened. But the magical quality was gone forever. That's the way I feel. Like some kind of wonderful something has slipped away, and I'll never be able to get it back."

Emma's eyebrows knitted. "But you haven't really lost anything. Your dad is still your dad...."

"But I've lost who I thought I was. Everything I accounted to my Irish heritage—my red hair, my fair complexion, my love of Guinness. I've only talked myself into believing they had significance." Tara popped a grape into her mouth. "And that makes me wonder what other things I've believed in that were actually of no significance."

"Well, maybe you need to talk to somebody." Emma tore open a package of oyster crackers and sprinkled them over the top of her soup. "You know—" she shrugged as she stirred them in "—a professional."

"You're a professional guidance counselor with a master's in counseling. I'm talking to you."

Tara watched her friend's eyebrows disappear beneath her wispy bangs. "Doctors don't operate on family members, and counselors don't counsel family."

"But we're not—"

"We're just as close."

"Who I really want to talk to is Jacques Martin." Tara blurted out the idea that had kept her awake most of the night. "I just want to take off for Paris and find my birth father."

"And what good would that do?"

Tara thought about that question while she nibbled on a carrot. What good *would* it do? "Mostly it would satisfy my curiosity," she admitted. "I can't stop wondering what he looks like, what his personality is like. Do I have his nose? His laugh?"

"Your mom can tell you that."

Tara's throat tightened around a bite of carrot. She dropped the rest of it back into the plastic container, her appetite suddenly gone. "I can't talk to her any more about him. At least, not yet."

"I understand." The sympathy in her friend's voice made Tara's throat tighten again. "So what difference would it make if you found out those things about him?" Emma gave a quick nod in Tara's direction. "You rub your lip when you're thinking about something just like Sawyer does. No matter where those little things come from, they make up *you*."

Self-consciously, Tara dropped her hand from her mouth. "I just want to look Jacques Martin in the eye and say 'I'm your daughter' and see his reaction."

Emma eyed her warily. "Can't you just let your imagination play out that scene for you? Paris is way too big a city to find somebody with only a name to go on. And it's very expensive from what I hear."

Tara shrugged and glanced out the window to avoid

eye contact. "I have my inheritance from Grandma." She cringed at Emma's outraged gasp.

"You're serious! You've actually given this some thought…and have a plan. It's a crazy idea, Tara—one you need to get out of your head right now."

Emma's gray eyes bored into her, causing Tara's cheeks to burn. "Thought you weren't going to counsel."

"I'm not counseling. I'm giving my best friend a verbal shake to wake her up." Emma ran her fingertips through her short bob, fluffing the soft, chestnut ends. "Finding him would take a feat of magic. He might've moved. Might not want to be found. Some people don't. Or…or he might be dead. Have you thought about that?"

"That's another thing. Family medical history is important." Tara held up her half hand. "Emergencies happen. Diseases strike. It would be great to at least have a hint of what else I might come up against in the future. Mama's family doesn't have any heart disease, but what if it's in his genes?"

"Then you do all the right things to keep your heart healthy no matter what."

Tara looked at her friend in earnest. "Even if I didn't find him, I could learn about my French heritage. The Irish thing I've always been so proud of has been jerked away from me, and now I want to replace it with *something*. I want to find out who I *am*."

Emma looked at her long and hard, the steel in her gaze softening to a down-gray. "Know what?" She reached across the desk to place her hand on top of Tara's. "I'm wrong. If it means that much to you, I think you should do it."

"Really?" Tara jolted at Emma's change of heart. "Because I'm thinking I want to do it soon. Like as soon as school is out."

"That's short notice. Can you make all the arrangements that quickly?"

Tara shrugged. "I don't know. Maybe through a travel agent."

"That will run the cost up even more. Do you know anyone who might know somebody over there?" Emma drummed the desk with her spoon. "What about Josh Essex?"

Tara hadn't gotten far enough in her planning to consider that the French teacher might have connections in Paris, but it was a good idea—he did usually take students to Paris during the summer.

"He was eating lunch in the teachers' lounge when I got my soda." Emma got up quickly, abandoning her soup and crackers. "Let's go talk to him now."

"CAN WE PLAY SOME CATCH, Dad?"

Dylan had disappeared a couple of minutes earlier, and now stood in the doorway of the flat holding a ball and wearing the St. Louis Cardinals ball cap, jersey and glove that had arrived from his grandmother that day.

Like I could refuse. Garrett gave a wry smile. "Sure. Just let me get the dishwasher loaded."

Dylan set the ball and glove in the chair he'd vacated earlier and picked up his plate to help clear the table, something he rarely did. No doubt he was anxious to try out his new equipment.

"Watch your step," Garrett warned as the six-year-old caught his toe on the frame of the sliding patio door.

When the Paris weather permitted, they ate every meal possible out here on the terrace. The wide expanse of concrete wasn't anywhere near as large as their backyard had been in St. Louis, but life had its trade-offs. For a second-story flat, the extra living space the terrace afforded was well worth the small amount of extra rent. Although several other flats had windows that looked out on it, only one other had a door leading to it. And that one had been empty for over a year, so Garrett and his son had gotten used to having the entire space to themselves.

They made quick work of loading the dishwasher, and then Garrett grabbed his own glove as they headed back out to their makeshift practice field.

Dylan punched the new leather with his fist. "I'm ready for a fastball."

That drew a laugh. "One fastball comin' up." Garrett made a wild show of winding up, watching his son's eyes grow huge in anticipation. At the last second, he slowed down enough to toss the ball toward the boy's padded palm.

Dylan kept his eye on the ball, stretching his arm out to full length and spreading his glove open as far as his short fingers would allow.

The ball landed with a *thump,* and a pleased grin split Dylan's face as he hoisted the glove and ball over his head in a triumphant gesture. "Freese makes the play!" he yelled.

"How 'bout we send a picture of you and your new stuff to Nana and Papa?"

"And Gram and Grandpa, too."

Garrett snapped the picture and messaged it to both his parents and Angela's. Then he laid the phone down within easy reach to listen for the calls that were sure to come.

His mom and his deceased wife's mother called every time he sent a picture of Dylan, which was often. The distance was hard for them.

They'd all done their damnedest to talk Garrett out of the voluntary move to Paris three years ago when the brewery he worked for was bought out by a Belgian company. Only his dad had fully understood his need to escape from the constant reminder of his wife's suicide. And his guilt.

No matter how they felt about it, the move hadn't been a mistake.

Dylan mimicked Garrett's windup, minus the slow down at the end. The ball he released sailed wide past his father, who broke into a run to catch it on the bounce. His timing was off. He missed and wasn't able to catch up to it until it hit the back wall.

"Dad! Your phone's ringing," Dylan called.

By the time Garrett got back to answer it, he was winded. *"Allô."* He breathed heavily into the phone. *"C'est Garrett."*

"Well, your French has definitely gotten better, but the creepy heavy breathing makes me wonder if I've caught you at a bad time. My math says it should be around dinner time there."

Garrett laughed, recognizing the voice of his teammate from college Josh Essex. "Actually, it's pitch-and-catch after dinner, Josh."

"Is that the new French phrase for hooking up? 'Cause, if it is, my seniors will want to know."

"By the time I get around to…" Dylan was within hearing distance, so Garrett veered away from what he'd been about to say. "To needing *that* information, the *deed* will probably be obsolete."

"I can't even bear that thought." Josh chuckled. "How's Dylan doing?"

"Growing too fast for me to keep him in jeans. We've resorted to rolled cuffs and belts."

"Well, let's hope cuffs, belts and, of course, the *deed* never go out of style."

"I hear you," Garrett agreed. "And to what do I owe the pleasure of this call, Monsieur Essex? Especially in the middle of your work day."

"I have a friend—a colleague—who's wanting to come to Paris in a couple of weeks and plans to stay a month. Does your building have any short-term rentals?"

Garrett's eyes cut to the flat across the way, and then wandered on around the terrace to the window boxes devoid of flowers—a dead giveaway in spring and summer that spaces were empty. "Yeah, probably. Hold on." He fished his wallet out of his back pocket and thumbed through the cards until he found the one he wanted. "You have a pen handy?"

"I'm just waiting on you."

"Here's the number to call." Garrett read it off slowly. "That's the main office of the company that owns my building. They'll have listings of what's available."

"Got it. Thanks."

"Will we be seeing you this summer?" For the past three years, Josh had brought groups of his students for ten-day tours of the City of Lights. The visits had certainly been the highlight of the summer for Garrett, who tried to deny to himself how much he missed the U.S.

Josh's sigh was fraught with frustration. "I don't have too many interested, and a couple who were had to drop out. June 20 is the cutoff, and I'm still not sure."

Garrett didn't know who was more disappointed, he or Josh. "That's too bad."

"Yeah, well, it's the damn economy. How about you? You and Dylan planning a trip stateside any time soon?"

Garrett had been thinking this might be the year to go home for Christmas, but he was keeping mum on it in case he backed out. "Economy here's just as bad. I might have to hock Dylan to buy tickets."

Dylan perked up at the mention of his name, but not enough to tear his concentration away from his task. The ball he was bouncing off the wall shot back at him. He missed it, but not for lack of trying. Garrett took that as a sure sign his boy was meant for the big leagues, and the thought made him smile.

The familiar jangle of a school bell reverberated in the background. "Gotta go, man." Garrett could tell his friend was on the move. "It's the last week of school, and I'm showing *The Diving Bell and the Butterfly* to my third-year students."

"Great movie." Garrett motioned a thumbs-up to Dylan, who'd made a successful catch. "I hope you get enough students to make your group, so we'll get to see you."

"Me, too." The background sounds heightened as lockers slamming joined the mix. "And thanks for the number. Maybe I'll see you in a couple of months."

"We'll look forward to it. See you, man."

"Later, dude."

The call ended before Garrett realized he hadn't asked who needed a flat for a month—hadn't even asked if the interested party was male or female. Man, he was slipping.

While he liked the idea of having someone from close to home in the building, he hoped whoever it was wasn't interested in the flat across from them. He and Dylan would hate to give up their private recreation area. Would hate to give up their privacy, in general.

After the years of chaos with Angela, this terrace had become his and Dylan's oasis of tranquility. Beyond the walls was one of the most exciting cities in the world, but here was quiet space.

He didn't want anything to interfere with that.

Not even for a month.

CHAPTER THREE

TARA BREATHED A RELIEVED sigh as the key turned in the lock. Getting lost twice in the maze of dark, windowless corridors had her convinced she'd entered some kind of Parisian warp zone and might never find the flat she'd rented. The lights in the hallways were on a timer, and didn't stay on very long. Just finding the switches was like being on a treasure hunt…blindfolded…with no map.

Elbowing the door open, she rolled the duffel into the small foyer, dropping it and her shoulder bag as she took in her new surroundings.

"Well…thank you, Josh…and whomever you got that number from." Tara tried to recall the name—some college friend of Josh's. It didn't matter. What did matter was that this place, with its warm wood floors and modern furniture, was cheery and chic and perfect for a month's stay. She would have to pick out a nice thank-you gift for the French teacher.

A quick tour found the rest of the apartment much to her liking, too. The bathroom seemed antiquated with its pull-chain to flush the toilet, but the living room and the bedroom both looked out on a terrace rimmed with ivy-covered lattice work and flower pots brimming with color.

A notebook lay prominently on the dining table. Lettering across its front spelled out the word *tenant* in several languages. She flipped the book open to the section labeled English. Coming to Paris had been such a quick decision that there'd been no time to study the French language in any depth. She'd hoped her two years of high school and college Spanish would help, but it hadn't yet.

Everyone she'd been in contact with so far had spoken at least a little English, except for Madame LeClerc at the front desk. Hand gestures had been the language that had landed Tara the key to the flat. There were a few other gestures she'd wanted to use with the awful woman, but she would have hated to get kicked out before she got moved in.

Inside the notebook, Tara found a note of welcome, which she scanned for important information. "Oven temperature displayed in Celsius…shutters on a timer, which can be reset to your schedule…take key when you leave as the door locks automatically…terrace shared by one other flat…call if you are in need of any assistance."

The words blurred on the page. The excitement of being in Paris for the first time and facing the opportunity to find her birth father was fast losing ground to jet lag. What she needed was a breath of fresh air, and with rain imminent, she'd better make it quick.

She unlatched the sliding door and stepped outside into the heat of the sultry morning, careful to close the door behind her so as to not allow any of the precious air conditioning to escape.

Latticework placed strategically around the large concrete patio gave some definition to what area belonged with each of the flats. Her section was a bit smaller than the other, but still quite large.

The sliding door to the other flat directly across from hers was open as were many of the windows of other flats. Vague sounds of morning with families and children drifted through.

Around the corner from her door and several yards away, a railing hung with flowerboxes added an explosion of color to the gray day. Below lay a courtyard with a lovely formal garden and a huge wooden door that looked as if it was left over from the Middle Ages.

She heard a shout, and a boy who looked to be eight or nine ran through the courtyard below, trying to make it to the wooden door ahead of something—or someone. At that point, the first drop of rain hit the top of her head.

Maybe the boy was trying to beat the impending downpour?

But then a second shout filtered up toward her, and two more boys appeared, larger and older than the first, who was frantically working to open the massive door.

One of the older boys pounced on the child from behind, pinning his arms behind his back while the third boy approached menacingly.

Tara's schoolteacher persona pushed to the forefront. She had to do something, but if she vaulted over the railing, she'd break her neck. And there was no way she could find her way back downstairs to that area in time to save the boy from whatever the ruffians had in mind for him. In desperation, she used her teacher voice and yelled over the railing, "Hey! Stop that! Leave him alone."

The older boy paused midstride and turned toward the voice. He looked up with a sneer and made a gesture toward her that needed no translation. When he started back toward the younger boy, the child started to shriek and thrash about.

A whirring sound nearby jerked Tara's attention from the tableau below to the sight of metal shutters closing over the windows of her flat. *Mechanical storm shutters. Thank heavens!* They would buy her more time here.

A shout obviously from an adult male came from below, and then a short, burly guy appeared, and the big boys immediately stopped their attack. With the rain coming harder, Tara could feel her curly hair growing bushier by the second, but she had to stay long enough to make sure everything was okay.

Even without understanding the language, she caught the word *papa* from all three boys often enough to figure out they were siblings and *Papa* was taking care of things. And just in time, as the sky opened up then, and rain pelted her full force.

Relieved that she was no longer needed, she sprinted in the direction of her door and rounded the corner, letting out a shriek of her own. "Eek! No!"

Storm shutters had been installed over the door, as well. She got there just in time to see them clamp down tightly, a metal fortress barring anything—or anyone—from entrance.

Frantically, she looked for a button. Surely there was an override. Lifting a metal flap exposed a numerical keypad, but, try as she might, she couldn't recall anything about a code in the note she'd read. She tried a few random numbers…0000…1234…but soon gave up, realizing the futility. She wasn't even sure it would be a four-number code.

"Damn it!" She gave the metal a swift kick. The barrier didn't budge, but the action bruised her toe and her ego.

She was already soaked. The lemony, cotton sundress, which had made her feel so chic, now clung to her legs, directing the water flow into sodden ballet flats. She squished back around the corner, checking the windows, hoping for a breakdown somewhere in the system, but finding everything in dismally perfect working order.

She would have to wait it out. Crossing her arms, she leaned against the wall, and she was surveying her surroundings when the open door gaped at her from across the terrace. How many times had her dad preached about the open doors in life and choosing the right way?

Shielding her eyes from the pelting rain, she studied the door. No movement came from that apartment. The owners might be gone…might be trusting souls who left their back door open because they usually had no neighbors.

If she cut through their flat, she could find her way back down to Madame LeClerc—not a pleasant thought, but standing in a downpour wasn't exactly the way she'd pictured her first hour in Paris, either. She could get…*beg*… the spare key, come back up and let herself in through her own front door.

While she pondered the plan, the sky grew blacker, and despite the heat, she began to get chilled.

A crack of lightning nearby made the decision for her. She loped across the terrace toward the safety of the open door, praying the occupants had left for work…or at least had a good sense of humor.

She paused for a few seconds just inside the door and knocked on the wall. *"Bonjour?"* she called. She was met by silence, but the luscious aroma of fresh coffee told her that the owners were out of bed…or awake, anyway. The scent had a magnetic pull that drew her a couple of steps deeper into the room.

"Bonjour?" she repeated, at a total loss to say anything else in her limited French. She cocked her head and listened, becoming aware of a sound only when it stopped. Running water, which she'd initially attributed to the rain outside. But this was inside. Someone who was in the shower had now gotten out.

Good Lord! Her predicament thudded into her stomach full force. What if the owner wasn't sympathetic *or* amused? What if he or she called the police? She was in a foreign country where she knew no one.

Wouldn't that be a lovely way to meet the father who didn't know she existed? *Hi there. I'm the daughter you didn't realize you had. Would you mind coming to the police station to bail me out?*

She shivered—not from a chill this time.

Thunder was coming right on top of the lightning, so going back outside was unthinkable. She'd choose arrest over electrocution any day.

Most people paused in the bathroom to put on lotion or shave after a shower. Maybe she could still make it out the front door without getting caught.

She started to tiptoe across the floor when the squish between her toes reminded her how wet her shoes were. Toeing out of them, she clasped the soggy slippers in her hand.

She crossed the room and turned down a hallway only to find light creeping from beneath the door along with a shower-fresh scent.

An about-face focused her on the door at the other end, where the hallway widened into a small foyer with a desk and, obviously, the front door.

She tiptoed as fast as she could in its direction, not even hesitating as the floor creaked and groaned beneath her.

A little boy appeared through a doorway to her right, rubbing the sleep from his eyes.

He took one look at her and let out a terrified shriek.

HIS SON'S SCREAM propelled Garrett out of the bathroom with the towel he'd been drying himself off with still in his grip and his brain moving at warp speed to assess the situation before him.

Dylan's eyes lost some of their terror as he scampered to safety behind his dad, but the same look remained fixed in the eyes of the stranger standing in their foyer—a young woman...obviously deranged.

Garrett scanned her quickly for a weapon but didn't spot anything. The way the yellow dress plastered against her body would make it difficult to hide anything. She looked as though she'd just stepped out of the shower herself... fully clothed. The bright red bush of hair that sprouted from her head was tipped in blue and had an undeniable Medusa quality about it. The hand she used to push it out of her eyes was only half there.

Nine years with Angela made him a freakin' expert on handling crazy women. No sudden moves. No shouting. But he gripped the towel tighter, thinking he could throw it over her head, then tackle her and keep her pinned while Dylan called the police.

"Pardon." Her voice shook on the word as she raised her hands to shoulder height, one palm out in a show of surrender, the other clutching a pair of shoes. "Um...*bonjour?*"

Garrett tilted an ear in her direction to pick up more of the weird accent.

"*Je...Je* got locked out of my flat in the rain." She kept her hands up, but flicked her fingers in the direction of the door that opened onto the terrace.

The accent dropped a pin on the map in Garrett's brain—America...and most definitely the South. His guard dropped a smidgen by sheer reflex. "You're American," he said, at last.

"Oh, you speak English. Thank God." The woman's shoulders sagged and her eyes closed momentarily as if she were actually in prayer as she said those words. Her hands dropped limply to her sides. "I just got here." Her eyes flicked from him to the terrace door. "I'm renting that apartment over yonder." As she made jerky movements with her head in the direction of the terrace, the words came streaming as fast as her drawl would allow. "The automatic storm shutters closed, and I don't know how to get them open." Her eyes came back to him, flitted downward and upward just as quickly before a crimson flush started to steal its way from the neckline of her dress into her cheeks. "And I left my key inside on the table, so even if I get back to my apartment, I can't get in." She gave a frustrated sigh, running her fingers through her hair and squeezing the roots. "I'll have to beg another one from Madame LeClerc, which won't be easy because I'm pretty sure she already hates me."

The Southern accent had started to lull Garrett into complacency. He relaxed completely when she called Madame LeClerc by name. Nobody got by Ironpants LeClerc without a confirmed reason to be in the building. He dropped the idea of using the towel to subdue the young woman, and used it instead in a more appropriate manner by wrapping it around his middle. "So you're our new neighbor? Which flat are you in?" he asked as a final test of her veracity.

"Four C," she answered, somehow making the phrase three syllables long. "We share the terrace."

"She talks funny, Dad." Dylan had moved around to stand beside Garrett—not clinging, but Garrett was aware of the shoulder pressing into his thigh.

The woman squatted down to be on eye level with his son. "Bless your heart. I'm so sorry, scaring you like that." She offered her half hand for Dylan to shake. "I'm Tara O'Malley, by the way."

Garrett felt his son tense as he gazed at the three fingers extended in his direction. Tara O'Malley didn't move forward, just waited patiently as if she expected him to sniff it first. Finally Dylan stepped forward and took the hand, shaking it vigorously. "I'm Dylan Hughes."

Pride swelled in Garrett's chest. He offered his hand and helped Tara up as they shook. "I'm Dylan's dad. Garrett Hughes."

"Oh!" Tara's face broke into a wide smile. "You're Josh Essex's friend. The one who gave him the number I used to find my flat."

Garrett cringed inwardly as the pieces fell into place. "That's right." He was at least partially responsible for the crazy woman being here. "You and Josh work together?" Disbelief was evident in his voice, but the woman standing before him—who sported a tattoo beneath her ear, a pierced eyebrow and blue-tipped hair—didn't look like any of the high school teachers he'd had. Of course, his teachers had all been Catholic nuns.

"I teach freshman English at Paducah Tilghman." A subtle rise of one of her eyebrows seemed to add, "So there."

Apparently the mention of Josh's name loosened Dylan's tongue. "What happened to your hand?" He pointed blatantly at her disfigurement.

"Dylan—" Garrett started to correct him.

"No, it's okay." Tara gave him a small smile, but then sobered when she looked back at Dylan. "Motorcycle accident."

"Cool!" Dylan's voice was filled with awe.

Bona fide crazy, Garrett thought.

Tara continued to address Dylan. "Yeah, motorcycles can be very cool, but they can also be very dangerous. Sometimes people driving cars don't notice them, or they think of them as a bicycle. So don't ever get on one without a helmet, and don't ride too fast."

"I won't," Dylan assured her.

"Well." She sighed, and Garrett followed her eyes to the rain that was coming down so hard that her flat across the way was barely visible. "I've been enough trouble to y'all this morning. I'll just mosey on back to my place."

"Stay and have breakfast with us!" Dylan blurted, and Garrett's jaw tightened at the suggestion.

"Oh, no, I can't. I'm soaked to the skin. My hair's a mess."

Garrett's logical side urged him to let her go on her way, but his emotional side, which was being suckered by the sultry, Southern accent, chided him for even entertaining the possibility.

"You can't go out in this," he said, ignoring the warning sirens blaring in his brain. "Although we're just across the terrace, we're actually on opposite sides of the building. You'd have to go literally halfway around the block to get back to the main entrance."

"Well…"

She chewed her bottom lip as a visible shiver ran through her, making her suddenly appear delicate and fragile. Garrett felt a stirring below and realized he was still standing there wearing nothing but a towel.

"I'll go get dressed and find you some dry clothes to put on. I think this rain has set in for a while." He motioned to the pot of French-pressed coffee on the counter in the kitchen. "Help yourself to some coffee. We'll be right back."

"I'll bring you some clothes!" Dylan was obviously excited to have an unexpected guest for breakfast. He ran ahead into Garrett's bedroom.

Garrett lost no time rifling through a bottom drawer for the long shorts he shot hoops in. No doubt they would swallow Tara, but they had a drawstring that might, at least, help her keep them up. He grabbed a T-shirt from another drawer and thrust the pair toward Dylan, who was still in his pajamas. "Take these to our guest, sport, then go get dressed."

A smile spread across his son's face. "I like her, Dad. She's cool." He ran from the room, clutching the bundle.

"Of course you like her." Garrett muttered under his breath as he closed the door. "She's crazy. Just like your mom."

He wasted no time getting dressed. Time alone between his son and the crazy woman wasn't going to happen.

CHAPTER FOUR

PEOPLE STAYING AT bed-and-breakfasts do this all the time, Tara told herself as she passed the plate of croissants to the little boy who'd insisted on sitting beside her. Of course, it would probably have been easier to convince herself there was nothing weird about eating breakfast in a new country with total strangers if she hadn't seen one of them naked a few minutes earlier.

She tried to focus on the inch-long scar that cut diagonally through the left side of Garrett's upper lip—the one that disappeared almost completely when he smiled—rather than let her mind wander to the foot-long one on his thigh that pointed like an arrow to his masculine assets.

"I finally decided it was time to see Paris." She answered Dylan's last question just shy of the complete truth. "How long have you lived here?"

Dylan piped up before his dad could answer. "Three years. We moved here when I was three, but I'll be seven soon, so I guess then I'll have to start saying we've been here four years."

Garrett used his spoon to point at his son. "Quit talking so much, sport, and eat your breakfast."

With a grin that could charm the sweet spot from a Louisville Slugger, Dylan opened his mouth wide and shoveled in a spoonful of Greek yogurt and fresh berries.

The boy's grin was a replica of his dad's, as was the sandy color of his hair. But the jade-green hue of his eyes was a far cry from the walnut-brown of his elder's.

No mention had been made of a wife or mother. And something about Garrett Hughes's manner seemed stand-offish, despite the fact he'd invited her to stay for breakfast. If he'd kidnapped his son and moved to a foreign country, Josh Essex would've let her in on that, wouldn't he?

"So you're originally from St. Louis?" Tara probed, trying to get Garrett to continue where he'd left off before Dylan had started in with questions again.

Garrett held up the carafe as a question, and Tara offered her cup in response. "I grew up in St. Louis," he said, "and moved back there after college. Not too long after my wife died—"

Ah, a widower. "I'm so sorry." She took another sip of the incredibly strong brew and settled a hand on her chest to check for any hair it might cause to sprout through the T-shirt.

"Thanks." Garrett acknowledged her condolences with a curt nod. "The brewery I worked for was bought out by a Belgian company that was expanding. Dylan and I moved here with that expansion."

"How exciting that must've been."

Garrett shrugged one of his broad shoulders, and even though a sport coat now covered it, Tara's mind flashed back to how it had looked unclothed and damp from the shower. "It came at the right time," he answered.

The concoction Garrett called coffee had chased away any effects of jet lag and set her mouth to chatty mode. "And what do you do at the brewery?"

"I'm head of the marketing department."

The formality of the country she was visiting struck her as she wiped away the last remains of the buttery croissant from her lips with the linen napkin that had been part of her place setting. "Were you already fluent in French before you moved here?"

Her question brought a low chuckle from Garrett that tickled at the bottom of her spine. "Whether I'm fluent *now* is still debatable." He jutted his chin in his son's direction. "Dylan's the language wizard. He speaks it like a native."

Dylan paused, the spoon halfway to his mouth. *"C'est vrai, Tara. Je parle le français très bien. La langue n'est pas difficile."* He cocked his head and grinned, looking like the cat that ate the berry-and-yogurt-covered canary.

Garrett shook his head as his mouth rose at one end. "And he's obviously quite modest about it."

Tara smiled, her heart touched by the endearing relationship between these two. Would she and Jacques Martin ever have anything that approached this? The thought caused her hand to tremble as she set her cup back on its saucer. "How did you get so good, Dylan?"

"Only French at school. Only English at home."

"And speaking of school, we need to be on our way." Garrett stood and started clearing the table. "Go brush your teeth and get your stuff, bud. We'll walk Tara down to the front entrance."

Hearing her name from Garrett's lips sent an unexpected, pleasant zing through Tara. She gathered her and Dylan's dishes as the child hurried to the bathroom.

"With our key, we can get in the courtyard below and take the shortcut through the building." Garrett loaded the dishwasher while he talked, and Tara stored the items that needed to be refrigerated. "Madame LeClerc is quite taken by Dylan. If she balks about giving up the extra key, he'll be able to talk it out of her."

Tara glanced around, noting that everything was done. "I'll change back into my dress as soon as Dylan gets out of the bathroom."

"Don't bother." Garrett's eyes met hers, and then darted away as he waved at the outfit she had on. "You can return those…whenever."

Tara's stomach did a quick flip. She'd just been given an invitation to come back. A little offhanded, maybe. But, nonetheless, an invitation.

"EARTH TO FAITH. Can you hear me?"

Sue Marsden's annoyed tone broke through the deep fog of Faith O'Malley's thoughts. She glanced around the small circle of women who made up the Ladies' Prayer Group, noting all twelve eyes were on her.

Being the preacher's wife, she was used to that, but she still hated it…had always hated it. Living in the glass house had taught her to never throw rocks, but that wouldn't stop the community from verbally stoning her if word got out of what she'd done.

Sue Marsden would be the first to start flinging.

"I'm…I'm sorry. What did you say?" Even that comment was an admission that she hadn't been listening and would give Sue something to gossip about later.

Sue gave that laugh of hers, which wasn't really a laugh at all but more of a *tsk-tsk.* "I asked if you had any prayer requests. We are a prayer group. Remember?"

We don't have enough time for my list, lady.

Prayer requests from the group too often gave Sue her weekly start on new items of gossip.

Time and again, Faith had seen it happen, had warned the group that what was shared within the group should stay within the group.

But Sue's pious contention was that the more prayers rallied on a person's behalf, the better the chance of God's listening. She'd back her ideas with much Bible-thumping and scripture quoting. And, yes, the prayer chain she'd formed after Tara's accident had been much appreciated.

But to have the matters of Faith's heart bandied about Taylor's Grove like an item in a tabloid was unthinkable, and even the slightest hint of turmoil in the O'Malley household would start the rumor mill turning.

On the other hand, if she didn't share *something,* the ladies would think she was being either secretive or uppity. She'd walked this tightrope for years and knew well how to perform on it without losing her balance.

"Tara called this morning," she said, at last. "She got to Paris last night around midnight our time. I'd like y'all to remember her in your prayers…her safety."

Nell Bradley spoke up. "I've worried so about her ever since I heard she was gallivanting off to a foreign country. And in such a hurry about it. I'll never understand why kids these days have to have everything right now."

"Well, I'm not at all surprised." Sue waved her hand dismissively. "Ever since she and Louis broke up, Tara's been a different person. She has a capricious nature that none of us had ever seen. She needed someone like Louis to keep her reined in."

The comment jarred Faith's composure, causing it to slip. "Tara's twenty-eight. She doesn't need anyone to rein her in. Certainly not a man."

"You can't be okay with all her shenanigans, Faith. Motor-cycles and tattoos." Sue rolled her eyes. "Last Sunday, she came to church with her hair tipped in blue, for heaven's sake."

That brought out the lioness in Faith. No one was al-lowed to attack her cubs…her pride. "Sue, I am very proud of my daughter," Faith said quietly before she gave a swipe, claws extended. "And, yes, her hair might be tipped in blue, but, at least, she was *in church* last Sunday."

The astonished looks of amusement told her that every-one picked up on the thinly veiled reference to Sue's daugh-ter Quinn, who made it a habit of sleeping in on Sunday.

Faith's cheeks burned with shame that she'd stooped to Sue's level and had given everyone a story to repeat this week.

Well, at least the talk would focus on her and not Tara.

A muscle twitched in Sue's jaw, proof that she'd felt the stinging blow. "Let's pray," she snapped.

Faith bowed her head and took deep breaths to slow her racing heart.

Another week had passed and her secrets were still se-cure by all indications.

No one had mentioned the increase in Trenton's visits home as opposed to the decrease in Thea's.

No one had brought up the haunted look in Sawyer's eyes, or the despair that Faith felt was surely reflected in her own.

No one knew that they hadn't touched each other for going on four weeks now. That the happy faces they put on in public dissolved once they stepped through their door at home. That Sawyer pulled away every time she tried to reach out to him. That their conversations were cordial, but lacked any kind of intimacy, as if they were acquaintances meeting on the street.

That he'd moved into Trenton's room.

That her family was fractured just like she was on the inside.

That she was searching desperately for something to hold them together. To hold *her* together before she fell apart completely.

No one knew what she was going through.

No one could ever know

Amen.

CHAPTER FIVE

HENRI LEANED FORWARD in his seat across the table and lowered his voice to a conspiratorial whisper. "Now that we are alone, perhaps you should share with me some details about your *unsettling* morning, eh? Is Dylan well?"

"Damn, I'm sorry." Guilt took a swipe at Garrett's insides. He should've realized that his friend would jump to the conclusion that the unsettling morning he referred to in their meeting might mean something had happened to Dylan. "Yeah, he's fine. But we both got quite a scare."

"Pourquoi? What happened?"

The approaching media blitz for Soulard Beer had the head of production wringing his hands, but Garrett's marketing staff and Henri's IT staff had been treated to a well-earned lunch with the company's owners. They'd be working late again tonight, so they'd been told to take their time getting back to the office. Garrett and Henri intended to do just that.

"I'd just gotten out of the shower, and I'm standing there buck naked, when all of a sudden, Dylan lets out a scream that would've made even your well-lacquered hair stand on end."

Henri smirked at the mention of his perfect coif. "Jealousy does not sit well on you, *mon ami.* Now, quickly, tell me what happened to Dylan."

"Dylan was fine. But I go running out with a towel in my hand—" Garrett held up his napkin in his fist "—and there stands a woman in my foyer, who's also dripping wet, but she's fully clothed."

"Did Dylan allow this woman into your flat?"

The threat of a lecture to Dylan lay in Henri's tone, so Garrett hurried on to reassure him. "No. She came in through the terrace door, which I'd left open. Turns out she's an American who's renting the empty flat that shares our terrace. In fact, she's a friend of Josh Essex. You remember Josh?"

Henri nodded, and Garrett continued his tale. "She just arrived this morning, and was on the terrace when the rain started, and her storm shutters closed. She was locked out in a downpour, so she came over to our place."

"But what made Dylan scream?"

"Well, for one thing, she startled him. He'd just woken up. But, damn, Henri, you should've seen her. She looked like something out of a slasher movie."

The side of Henri's mouth twitched. "*Oui?* A woman in a wet T-shirt? I am thinking that is not so terrible."

Garrett shook his head. "No, you're not getting the picture. She had on this yellow dress that's soaked and clinging to her, and she's got bright red hair—" he held his hands out beside his head to indicate how far Tara's had stuck out "—with the curls tipped in blue. Her eyebrow's pierced, and she's got a couple of tattoos. One on the side of her neck, and one right above her ass."

Henri's head cocked in interest. "And how do you know this?"

Garrett gave a sheepish grin. "The wet dress was practically transparent, so I noticed that one when she walked past me."

"Ah, *oui.* It is always a man's duty to check out a woman's ass if it is presented."

"Exactly," Garrett agreed. "But the really freaky part was, on top of all this other stuff, half of her right hand is missing. She lost it in a motorcycle accident."

"Mon dieu!"

"Yeah, exactly. And, of course, Dylan goes from being terrified to being fascinated in about fifteen seconds and invites her to stay for breakfast."

Henri laughed. "So, did she behave herself at breakfast?"

"Oh, yeah…sure. She was very nice, in fact. She's from Kentucky, and she's got this strong Southern accent."

"Mmm." Henri smacked his lips appreciatively. "Two very sexy things, *oui?* An American woman speaking French with the American accent, and a woman from the southern United States saying anything at all."

Garrett didn't respond. He shifted in his seat, uncomfortable with the ideas of Tara and sexy being linked.

Henri dabbed the sides of his mouth with a napkin-swathed finger. "I see you brood all morning and now I have to wonder why an unexpected breakfast with a-little-wild-yet-nice woman would make you do that?"

Garrett twirled the demitasse spoon between his thumb and index finger. "She made me uncomfortable."

"But you said she was very nice." Henri's bottom lip protruded in the quintessential French pout. Garrett had noticed Dylan doing the same thing lately.

"Oh, I don't think she's dangerous or anything…"

Henri pressed him more. "Then what is it about this woman that bothers you?"

"I don't know." Garrett was beginning to wish he hadn't brought up this morning's escapade. He'd only meant to entertain his friend with the story, and now Henri was trying to turn it into some deep analysis that Garrett was in no mood for. No doubt, the woman had dug up some buried emotions, but it was better to leave them in that dark hole within his psyche.

"Then you are in luck, my friend. I am the world's greatest expert on…" Henri gave a vague nod in the direction of a middle-aged brunette wearing a power suit with a one-button jacket and, by all appearances, nothing underneath. "A-little-wild-yet-nice women—this new neighbor reminds you of Angela, *oui?*"

"No, not really." Garrett shifted his gaze away from Henri's knowing smirk. "Maybe a little…"

"*Mais…?*"

"When Angela went off her meds, there was no telling what she might do. She might disappear for hours with no hint of where she was and come home with a new piercing or another tattoo." Garrett tossed the spoon on the table. "And once, after Dylan was born, when she wouldn't take her meds and was swinging from one extreme to the other, she dyed her hair a hideous shade of pink."

Every time he thought he was over his pity and his anger toward his wife, something would happen and those emotions would wash over him, drenching him and making him feel just as exposed as Tara had been in that damn transparent dress. He picked up the spoon again so he could have something to squeeze and transfer the emotion to.

"Many women have colored hair and piercings and tattoos, Garrett." Henri checked his reflection in his own spoon and adjusted his tie. "This woman. This…"

"Tara. Tara O'Malley."

Henri leaned forward again, peering closely at Garrett. "This Tara O'Malley is not Angela."

"But she's obviously got some of the same idiosyncrasies."

Henri's face broke into a wide grin. "You like her."

Garrett saw where this was going. "Don't. Don't even start with all your matchmaking nonsense. Even if I liked her, which I don't, at least not like you're thinking…she's only here for a month. I don't want Dylan getting attached to anyone who's just going to leave."

"Pfft!" Henri waved away his argument. "You have already picked up on something within her that attracts you."

He wagged his finger "And *you* don't want to get attached to her, either."

Garrett opened his mouth to stretch away the tightness in his jaw. "You're such a damn know-it-all, Henri. But you're wrong this time. I'm not worried about getting attached to that freakin' woman. She's not my type." He ran his hand through his hair. "The thing is, despite all my efforts to be everything he needs, Dylan misses having a mom. He's vulnerable with women. I sure as hell don't want anybody who's just passing through—be it Tara O'Malley or someone else—to get close to my son. He doesn't need another major loss in his life."

Snap!

Garrett opened his hand and sheepishly dropped on the table two pieces of metal that *had* been a demitasse spoon.

"We will charge that to the company, *oui?*" Henri calmly adjusted his starched cuffs until the perfect amount showed from below the sleeve of his suit coat. "A spoon that is broken can be quickly replaced. The heart that is broken requires a longer time."

MOTHER NATURE PROVIDED Tara with the perfect excuse to give in to the jet lag and slightly delay both her exploration of Paris and her search for Jacques Martin. She napped the rainy day away until late afternoon gave way to clear skies at last.

Calls were made to her family and Emma to let them know she'd arrived safely. They'd all been entertained by her tale of the morning's adventure. And they'd all mentioned how typical it was for her to have such a strange thing happen, as weirdness seemed to keep her in its sights—but she'd only shared with Emma the splendid details of Garrett's atypical nude appearance.

Need for sustenance finally prodded her out to rue du Parc Royal in search of a market, but not before she double-checked to make sure the key to her flat was in her possession. With no Garrett or Dylan in tow, it was doubtful that Madame LeClerc would give up the extra key a second time without requiring a pound of flesh as a deposit.

The third *arrondissement*, part of the area commonly known as le Marais, was every bit as charming and quaint as Josh had described. Narrow, cobblestone streets were lined with small, yet elegant boutiques and art galleries. Cafés occupied nearly every corner, and entire blocks were taken up by sprawling apartment buildings, whose ancient courtyards were protected by electronically locked wrought-iron gates that allowed spectacular views but no access.

Cars parked willy-nilly along the curb—and some up on the uneven stone walkways—gave the area a delightfully chaotic touch. Pedestrian traffic was heavy, and since the sidewalks were too narrow to accommodate two people passing, most people walked in the streets, stepping aside to let the occasional automobile by while dodging the plethora of bicycles.

A market turned up just two blocks from her building, but she passed it by for the chance to explore a bit longer with empty arms. A few more blocks brought her to a wide avenue—boulevard Beaumarchais—with one specialty food shop after another lining its sidewalks.

A variety of savory sausages hanging in the window of the *charcuterie* made her mouth water, enticing her to give it a go.

"Bonjour, mademoiselle," the elderly butcher called as soon as the bell heralded her entrance.

"Bonjour," she answered, to which he immediately replied something she didn't understand. *"Je voudrais..."* She didn't know the word for sausage, so she simply pointed to the kind she wanted in the case.

He smiled. "English?"

"Oui. Yes." She gave a grateful nod.

He pulled the sausage from the case and cut off a small

piece for her to try. The bite filled her mouth with a salty, savory burst that begged for a chardonnay to wash it down. Her accompanying "Mmm" brought a proud smile to the butcher's lips.

"Is very good, *oui?*"

"It's delicious. I can't wait to have a glass of wine with it."

"But of course." Obviously, the wine was a given. "How much would you like?"

"A quarter pound?"

His eyebrows drew in. "No pounds in France. Kilos."

Tara cringed. *Kilos?* She had no idea. "Um…" She hesitated.

The butcher picked up on her distress. "How many people?"

"One. Just me."

He tilted his head and gave her a glance as if sizing her up. "No, *mademoiselle*. You are too beautiful to eat alone. This is Paris!" He gave a dramatic sweep of his arm toward the street. "Find someone to share."

Tara's cheeks warmed. She'd already laundered the borrowed clothes and had thought about inviting Garrett and Dylan over for a light meal to repay their hospitality when she returned his things—having bought too much food for just her would be the perfect excuse.

The butcher's mouth turned up in a knowing grin. "Ah, I see you have someone in your thoughts. *Bien.*" Using his knife as an appendage, he pointed to where he thought the cut should be made. "Enough for two, *oui?*"

"Actually, three." Tara held up three fingers. "But one is a little boy with a big appetite."

He laughed pleasantly and moved the knife over a couple more inches before making the cut and wrapping the portion in the quintessential white paper. He insisted she try some of the fresh pâté, which was exquisite, and she bought some of that also.

Before she left, he gave specific instructions on what to

pair the purchases with. "Serve with *le fromage,* the honey, *une baguette, les cornichons* and, of course, *le vin.* If you do this, you will never eat alone."

She thanked him and left the shop feeling as if she'd made a new friend. He'd given her advice on where to find the best of everything on his list, even pointing out the specific shops that were his personal favorites, so those were her next few stops.

Everyone who waited on her immediately switched to English as soon as she started trying to speak French. Josh had told her that just the effort on her part would be appreciated, and that seemed to hold true. The Parisians, it appeared, would rather speak English than hear their beautiful language butchered by her American tongue.

The two cloth totes provided with the apartment filled up quickly with the butcher's suggestions and the fresh produce from the open-air market. After tasting the samples, she couldn't pass up the tender asparagus spears or even the turnips, which she would never have considered serving raw at home.

She had to rein in her sweet tooth at the *pâtisserie* with its shelves crammed with decadent, scrumptious-looking pastries. She escaped with only three items by promising herself she could have one treat each day.

Who was she kidding? Everything she ate for the next month was sure to be a treat. Like the butcher said, this was Paris!

She purchased a small bouquet of daisies from a wizened old woman who stood on the street corner with two pails of flowers—they would be perfect for what she had planned. And two bottles of wine—one white and one red—from the wine shop filled her second tote to the top, giving her arms as much weight as they could bear for the walk home.

Once she moved away from the wide avenue, the side streets all looked the same. Twice she lost her bearings and had to backtrack to the park with the rose garden surrounding the statue of the man on the horse, but eventually she found her way back to the apartment building and surly Madame LeClerc.

This time, Tara would follow her dad's lifelong advice to win over the enemy with love. She held out the bouquet of daisies and said the little speech she'd looked up in the phrase book and memorized before she left to go shopping. *"Bonjour, madame. Merci beaucoup pour votre aide ce matin."*

The woman looked stunned, her eyes moving from Tara's face to the daisies and back. For an uncomfortable moment, Tara thought she was going to refuse them. But then, the woman's demeanor changed. She smiled a smile so sweet, Tara would've thought it impossible a few minutes before.

"Merci, mademoiselle." Madame LeClerc's voice shook a little as she spoke. *"Merci beaucoup."* She lifted the flowers to her nose for a quick sniff as she buzzed Tara through.

Thanks, Dad.

The thought closed her throat as she headed up the stairs. She hoped her mom and dad had worked out their problems. Oh, they'd tried to act as if everything was okay when she and Thea and Trenton were around. But there was a heaviness that pervaded the atmosphere around them, as if the elephant in the room was sitting on everyone's chest. How long would it take until someone from the church took notice? If Sue Marsden got the slightest whiff of the juicy tale that lay within her grasp, she would burn up the telephone lines.

Tara unlocked her door and entered her flat, her shoulders now heavy with guilt. She tried to distract herself by putting her purchases away. It was too late for regrets. She was here to find her birth father, and she was prepared to face any ramifications that may come.

Her good friend Summer Delaney had once talked to her about the ripple effect—how every action is like a rock thrown into the pond of our lives. The first ripple causes a second, then a third. They multiply and spread, yet they're all connected at the source. And there's no stopping any of them.

Her mom and Jacques Martin had thrown a rock into the water one night, and twenty-eight years later, the ripples just kept coming.

She poured herself a glass of wine. Grabbing her laptop, her handheld GPS and the phone book from the apartment, she headed out to the terrace to kick off the official search for the stranger who gave her life.

CHAPTER SIX

"HI, TARA!"

Dylan sprinted across the terrace, a baseball glove clutched to his chest and a delighted grin on his face. When he came to an abrupt stop beside the table she was working on, Tara saw the ball nestled in the glove.

"Hi, Dylan. Have you been playing ball?"

"Not yet. My dad's not home."

An uneasiness gripped Tara's insides. "Do you stay home alone?"

Dylan shook his head. "Monique stays with me."

Ah, there's a Monique. Why she was surprised—maybe even a tad disappointed—by the news that her sexy neighbor had a woman in his life? He hadn't mentioned anyone that morning, but she should've figured a guy like him would be attached…on some level.

Right then, a petite young woman—maybe even a teenager—stepped onto the terrace. Her glossy black hair was pulled into a high ponytail and she had a cell phone to her ear.

"That's her." Dylan waved.

The woman spotted him and gave an answering wave, then went back inside.

"She talks on the phone a lot to Philippe. They're going to get married soon."

Tara scolded herself for the little flutter that news caused. "So Monique is your babysitter?"

"Yeah." His attention made an abrupt swerve to the small GPS device she held. "Whatcha doing?"

"Well." Getting into personal details wouldn't be prudent, but the child's curiosity was natural. "I may have some family in Paris. So, I'm looking up names in the phone book, then I'm using the laptop to map where that address is, and then I'm putting the address in my GPS to get directions in case I decide to visit…um, that location."

"Cool! Can I see?"

She handed over the small device and watched the child's unabashed wonder as he examined it thoroughly. The kids at the summer camp where she'd been a counselor had the same reaction, and that memory gave her an idea. "Have you ever been geocaching?"

Dylan shook his head. "What's that?"

"Here. I'll show you." She logged into the geocaching website she was a member of and typed *Paris* into the search box. A list, several pages long, appeared instantly. She pointed to a few of the items. "Each of these gives a description and the location of something that's been cached—that means hidden—here in Paris. But the location is given in latitude and longitude." When Dylan's bottom lip protruded in thought, she reminded herself he was only six. Precocious, but still only six. "Those are just numbers like addresses. Anyway, you put those numbers into the GPS, and it leads you to the thing that's hidden."

"Like a real treasure?" The child's jade eyes glowed with excitement.

"It's sort of a treasure—a small one, though. Usually, it's a little box with various items inside, and a notepad and pen. You get to choose an item to keep, and you leave behind one of your own. Once you sign and date the notepad to prove you were there, you hide it back where you found it."

"I want to do that! I want to go geochashtering!"

"Geocaching," she corrected. "And maybe we'll go sometime if it's okay with your dad."

"Can we go tonight? Right now?"

Tara chuckled at the child's enthusiasm. "No. We have to wait for your dad to say it's okay. Plus, he'd probably need to go with us, too, since I don't know my way around very well."

"He has to work late tonight, but he said he'd be home in time to play some pitch-and-catch, so maybe we can go when he gets home." The boy's exuberance had taken over his mouth, which was moving a mile a minute.

Tara held up her hand to slow him down. "Tonight's probably not a good night, Dylan. Your dad will be tired after working late, and y'all will have to eat."

"What's y'all mean?"

"You all. All of you, or in your case, both of you. But what I'm saying is, we can't go tonight, but we'll definitely try to go sometime while I'm here…if it's okay with your dad. Deal?"

"Deal." The glum look only stalled his face for a few seconds. "You want to play some catch?" He held up his ball and glove.

It was plain that she wasn't going to get much more done tonight. Besides, she'd been at her research for over two hours and was ready to stand up and move. "Sure. Do you have a glove I can use?"

"You can use Dad's." Dylan laid his gear on the chair and headed back to his flat in a run while Tara gathered her material and deposited it on the coffee table in her living room.

By the time she got back outside, the child had returned. He handed her a ball and a worn glove. "Will it hurt your hand to throw?"

What a sweetie—showing concern for her hand. Tara picked up the ball with her two fingers and thumb and wiggled it in front of his nose. "It will give me a mean curveball, I think."

His face relaxed in a grin, and he backed away a few feet and took his stance.

The man's glove swallowed her left hand. "Ready? Here it comes," she warned Dylan, and tossed the ball lightly.

He caught it easily and tossed it back. "You need to wind up." It was clear by his tone that he'd meant what he said to be an admonishment—he was not to be thought of as some wimpy, little kid.

Tara blew the dust off her high school softball career and wound up like a pro for the second pitch. She didn't let loose a fastball, but still threw one hard enough to bring a gleeful laugh from her opponent when he found the ball once again lodged in his glove. Dylan wound up and threw it back with surprising force for a kid his age.

"You've got a good arm, buddy."

His eyes gleamed with pleasure. "My dad says I've got his arm. He used to play in the minors."

Tara tucked away that interesting tidbit for conversation with Garrett later. "Well, no wonder you're good. It's in your genes."

Dylan's mouth drooped at the corners, and he pointed to his cotton shorts. "I'm not wearing jeans."

Tara laughed as she threw the ball back to him. The child's mastery of the language made her forget he was only six. "Not the kind of jeans you wear. The things you inherit…um, you get from your parents. That kind of genes."

"Oh, like my eyes. Dad says I got my mommy's eyes."

His words caught in Tara's chest, making her next breath heavier than the last. "Well, she must've had beautiful eyes. They're very handsome on you." She coughed to clear away the sudden congestion in her throat. Which of her own physical characteristics came from Jacques Martin? Eyes? Height? Build? She would have an answer soon perhaps.

Dylan's next pitch went a little wild, and she had to chase it down. When she got back into place, she moved the conversation to a less emotional common ground. "So, tell me about your school. Where do you go?"

"I attend *L'école primaire publique ave Maria.*" He was obviously enthused about the subject because for the next hour of pitch-and-catch, with frequent breaks, Dylan educated Tara on the French education system.

She learned that students only attended school four days a week, with Wednesdays as well as weekends off. But school days were long, lasting from eight-thirty to four-thirty.

This was the last week of school, and then Dylan would be on summer break for the months of July and August. Monique would be staying with him most days. And some days, he would go to Pierre's house. Pierre was his best friend and a baseball enthusiast, also.

During their game of catch, Monique came out to check on him occasionally. "She doesn't like to play catch," Dylan explained. "I usually just throw the ball against the wall until Dad comes home."

"What time is that?" It was already past seven-thirty, so Garrett was putting in a really long day.

"He's working late this week, but he'll be home by eight." The words were hardly out of his mouth before a deep voice brought their game to a halt.

"Dylan!" As if their conversation had transported him to the spot, Garrett stood in the doorway of their flat. The sport coat and tie he'd worn at breakfast were gone, and his white dress shirt and khaki pants accentuated the broad shoulders and narrow waist of his athletic form.

An image of his naked torso flashed across Tara's brain, and she felt her face heat in reaction.

"Hey, Dad." Dylan ran to meet him with a hug, which Garrett greeted with a smile.

But, as she headed his way, Tara watched the facial expression transform into a scowl when Garrett's eyes shifted up to meet hers.

DAMN IT! Garrett cursed his own shortsightedness. He should've told Monique not to allow Dylan to bother Tara. But he'd been so absorbed with work when she called to tell him they were home, he hadn't given it a thought.

A quick glance at the happiness on his son's face told him an attachment was already forming…and it was easy to see why.

The woman headed toward him held little resemblance to the freaky one he'd had breakfast with this morning. The wet yellow dress was gone, replaced by a pair of cream-colored shorts that showed off a set of long and toned legs. A peach T-shirt was the perfect complement to her fair complexion. No makeup disguised the adorable smattering of freckles that dotted her cheeks and nose. Had those even been there this morning? And what about the pierced eyebrow? Oh, yeah, there it was…. Her red curls—and a few of the blue ones—curved softly around her face and neck.

The entire effect was light and feminine, and Garrett fought down a wild urge to search among the curls for the tattoo nestled under her ear…with his mouth.

"Tara's a good catch, Dad."

The words stunned Garrett speechless for a couple of seconds, by which point she was already upon him.

Caution dimmed her bright eyes as she gave him a tentative smile. "We were just playing around some. I hope that's okay."

Garrett gathered his composure and shoved his sexual awareness to a deeper, safer place in his psyche. He took the glove she held out, searching for the appropriate words that wouldn't sound overly harsh in front of the boy. "Dylan shouldn't be interrupting your private time."

Her wariness gave way to a relieved smile. "He didn't interrupt anything. I had a good time." She held up what remained of her right hand, stretching the fingers apart. "It was good therapy—mentally and physically."

Garrett's spine stiffened at her words. If she needed

mental therapy, she needed to get it from someone other than Dylan.

Her thumb caught her middle finger, leaving her index finger pointed to the sky. "Oh, be right back." She turned and jogged across the terrace to her flat.

Garrett had no idea what she was up to, but he used the time to get Dylan out of hearing distance. "You need to go get washed up for dinner."

"Can we invite Tara to eat with us?"

Oh, hell. The entreaty in Dylan's eyes solidified that Garrett's fears were justified. He squatted down to eye level with his son—time for some damage control. "No, bud. Tara didn't come to Paris to visit with us. She's only going to be here for a month, which isn't really too long, so we need to leave her alone, and let her do what she wants with her time."

Dylan's bottom lip protruded in advance of his protest. "But—"

"No buts. You're not to bother Tara. Understand?"

Dylan sighed. "Yeah." He dropped his glove and ball inside the door and slunk off toward the bathroom, looking like a whipped puppy.

Garrett watched him until the bathroom door closed. When he turned back, Tara was headed toward him from across the terrace. He stepped out to meet her, sliding the door closed behind him.

The clothes he'd loaned her this morning were arranged in a neatly folded bundle, which she held out to him. "I figured out the washer and dryer, so these are clean."

Garrett took them from her. "Thanks. You didn't have to do that."

She slid her hands into her back pockets, which stretched her shirt tighter across her breasts. "Well, y'all didn't have to help me out this morning, but I sure did appreciate it. I...um..." She cleared her throat and tossed her head in the direction of her place, flashing the tattoo under her ear in

Garrett's direction. "I picked up some sausage and cheese and wine and a few nice pastries. I plan to have a light supper on the terrace, and I was wondering if you and Dylan would like to join me? Give me a chance to pay you back for breakfast?"

Her accent coupled with the expressive, vivid green eyes battered at Garrett's resolve, but the cautious voice inside him whispered its repeated warning about getting too friendly. "It's nice of you to offer, but I don't think we'd better. I work long hours, so dinnertime is special for Dylan and me. *Alone* time, you know?"

"Oh, sure." A deep blush crept up her neck into her face. "I should've thought of that."

The disappointment in her voice was palpable, but the first snip was made, and Garrett was determined to stop any more buds of friendship before they blossomed. "Well, there isn't a lot of privacy around here, so we'll try to respect yours as much as possible while you're here." A movement from the corner of his eye told him Dylan was headed back toward them. Garrett laid his hand on the door handle. "I'm sure you'll do the same for us," he added before sliding the door open and stepping back through it.

His escape wasn't quick enough to keep him from catching the hurt look in Tara's eyes—the same look that was reflected in his son's eyes when he met them.

"Now, how about some dinner?" Garrett clapped his hands together in a fake show of enthusiasm.

Dylan shrugged, looking like lead weights were attached to his shoulder. "I'm not very hungry."

Garrett's gut twisted at the words.

But they also told him without a doubt he'd done the right thing.

CHAPTER SEVEN

FAITH PUSHED THE BEIGE DRESS to one side, and studied the next one carefully—a sleeveless shift in a pretty shade of mint green that Sawyer had always liked on her. But, like everything else in her closet, it was modestly cut and gave no hint that the creature clothed in it had a clue that such a thing as sex existed.

Just once, she'd love to wear a dress that was a little provocative...that showed a little cleavage or more of her back than was strictly proper. Nothing vulgar. Just something feminine and sexy. Something that would remind her...and Sawyer...who she was at her center. The way God made her before the congregation of Taylor's Grove Church had molded her into who it wanted her to be.

The green dress was her best option for tonight, though.

Changing out of her white slacks and navy blue knit top into the new pink lace and satin bra and panties gave her a rush as if she was doing something scandalous...and fun. She paused to look in the mirror and evaluate the effect. A subtle attack was what she was going for. Just a touch of sexiness that would spur Sawyer on if she got him to the stage where he wanted to undress her.

The idea came to her after prayer group this morning. She'd never had to seduce her husband before, so shopping for sexy underwear this afternoon with that motive had been venturing into foreign territory.

Until four weeks ago, Sawyer had pursued her with a vigor that sometimes made her question all the jokes about middle age. She'd counted herself blessed to have someone who'd always made her feel attractive and desired despite the frumpy clothes and the weight gain that had crept up on her in her forties. They both understood that the preacher's wife had to be appropriately dressed at all times. They'd accepted that fact and had made ultimate use of their private time. And when all the kids finally moved out, she and Sawyer had had plenty of…how did the younger generation put it? *Bow-chicka-wow-wow?*

Well, this *chicka* was going to try her darnedest to coax the *wow-wow* out of the *bow* tonight.

She swiped on just a touch of foundation, and a light application of mascara defined her lashes. The salesperson had assured her that the pink lip gloss would make her lips irresistible. It looked like any other pink lip gloss, but maybe the extra price indicated it had some esoteric qualities perceived only by men. If the manufacturer truly wanted to make it irresistible, it would've been bacon-flavored.

A quick brush-through to fluff her hair, a squirt of cologne and a pair of beaded flip-flops finished the look that she hoped was casual yet sassy.

Back in the kitchen, the timer indicated it was time to put the cornbread in to bake alongside the meatloaf. The green beans were done, tomatoes sliced, and ears of fresh corn were buttered, wrapped in waxed paper and ready to be popped into the microwave.

New sexy underwear. Sawyer's favorite dress. His favorite meal. Fresh strawberries waited in a bowl on the counter, but she hoped she would be his dessert of choice.

Her heart skipped a beat when she heard the door open.

"Hey," he said as he entered the room.

She watched his eyes skim over her. "Hey," she answered, trying to keep it casual. "Supper's almost ready. You hungry?"

"Famished." He paused, and she saw his Adam's apple bob in his throat. "You, uh...you look pretty."

That's a start. Don't scare him away. "Thanks." She started the corn cooking in the microwave and pointed to the plate of tomatoes. "I was out in the garden—you can put those on the table—and I got sweaty and itchy. I had to take a shower to cool off. By tomorrow, we should have a nice mess of okra."

The light came on in his eyes—the one she hadn't seen in far too long—as it dawned on him that tonight she wasn't going to try to talk about their problems. She watched the transformation as his shoulders relaxed and the lines disappeared from between his eyebrows. With an easy, compatible fluidity, they fell into their routine of her dishing up the food and him setting the table, and for the first time since Memorial Day, her hopes ran high that perhaps the dry spell was over.

After supper, she set the second part of her plan into action. "Let's walk down to the park. Are you up for that?"

His hand hovered motionless for a moment before he placed the dish into the dishwasher. "Yeah. Sure. If you want."

Faith's pulse quickened. That he was willing to face the park together was a positive sign. She adjusted the strap of her new bra and smiled to herself.

Sawyer wiped off the countertops while she swept, and when the kitchen was clean, they started their stroll to the park at the center of town.

They'd managed to stay under the radar because, since Tara's accident, their park visits had become more sporadic rather than a daily occurrence. One or the other of them would show up a few times each week, armed with plausible excuses about the other's absence. Tonight's two-minute walk was a journey of a thousand miles as it was the first time they'd made it together since the Memorial Day Faith would never forget.

The park, which had no other official name because it was the only one in town, was the official gathering spot for the whole community. On any given night, you could catch up on the happenings of the day within a ten-minute period.

It was the park where everyone came after weddings to celebrate, after funerals to mourn and after births to pass out cigars and roses.

It was the park where Sawyer had proposed to her in the gazebo under the stars after everyone had gone home for the night.

It was the park where Tara had taken her first step in an endeavor to join the children playing on the swings.

The park at the center of town was the center of the town's life. The heart of Taylor's Grove.

As they approached, the sweet strains of "Gentle Annie" being played by Ollie Perkins on his violin met Faith's ears, and the poignant tune encouraged her to slip her hand into Sawyer's and pull him in the old man's direction. He didn't protest. While macular degeneration was doing its best to steal away the last vestiges of Ollie's sight, his ability to make the violin sing seemed to increase in an indirect proportion to what he lost. His renditions of Stephen Foster tunes could squeeze a tear from the devil himself.

Bobo Hudson vacated his seat beside Ollie and motioned for Faith to sit down. She could hardly refuse, but felt the sting of disappointment when she had to let go of Sawyer's hand.

Ollie finished his song. "Ev'nin', Faith." He turned his head slightly and nodded in her direction.

"How'd you know it was me?"

The disease had wiped out Ollie's central vision almost completely, but left a bit of the peripheral. He wiped his forehead with his trademark red bandanna. "I recognized your cologne."

She patted his knee affectionately. "You gonna play my favorite?"

She always requested "Shenandoah," and he always obliged, but, this time, he shook his head and tucked the bandanna between his chin and the chinrest on his instrument. "Nope, not yet, anyway. Got something different tonight. I was thinking today about Tara, and how she'd always ask for something Irish she could dance a jig to. Well, since she's in *Paree,* I thought we might just join her there, instead."

Faith cringed inwardly and cut her eyes to Sawyer, who blanched at Ollie's words as "Pigalle" rolled off the strings. The subject of Tara's being in Paris still cut Sawyer to the quick. He barely lasted until the song was over, then hurried away to join a small knot of men who always discussed the county's politics while they refereed the checker game between Johnny Bob Luther and Kimble Sparr. Faith, however, was stuck in Ollie's audience for a while longer.

She tried not to despair…hoped the mood of the evening hadn't been spoiled completely by Ollie's innocent comment.

When Al and Mary Jenkins walked up, Faith gave up her seat to them and found her way back to her husband's side. He and Tank Wallis were discussing how badly the crumbling steps on the front of the church needed repair. The project had been at the top of Sawyer's list for months now, but he couldn't get the maintenance committee, which Tank was the chairman of, to get off dead center with it.

"Some of those cracks are getting so big, it's just a matter of time before somebody catches a toe in one and breaks a hip," Sawyer declared.

"I hear you, Preacher, but it's not time to fix them until Sue says it's time."

The mention of Sue's name reminded Faith of their little verbal skirmish that morning, and with it came a flicker of irritation. The woman's power over the church, over the town and, yes, over Sawyer, was sickening.

Sue hadn't earned that power. Her daddy, Burl Yager,

was the one who sold a huge tract of land on Kentucky Lake to a developer. And it was Burl who built the Taylor's Grove Church out of that money and set up the trust fund that paid for the upkeep of the building, as well as the preacher's salary. Burl had been a fine man who loved the church and wanted it to thrive.

When Sawyer, as a teen, had surprised everyone in town by accepting God's call to become a minister, it was Burl who'd paid for his college and seminary study. But, when Burl died, Sue had inherited everything, except his benevolence. The church had tried to circumvent her ways by forming committees. But that had done little good. Sue held the purse strings.

"I'll talk to Sue again," Sawyer said, but his tone indicated he doubted that would do any good.

A chuckle rolled out of Tank's big belly. "Maybe you ought to send Faith this time." The big guy gave her a knowing wink. "Word from the prayer group says it's one to nothing in Faith's favor."

Sawyer sent her a questioning glance. He hadn't heard yet. Good. At least she could give him her side first.

She smiled and rolled her eyes. "No scorekeeping in Taylor's Grove. We're all playing for the same team." Turning her attention to Sawyer, she added, "Strawberries are going to get mushy if we don't get back and eat them pretty soon."

He nodded. "Can't let that happen. See you tomorrow, Tank." He patted his friend's shoulder in parting. They crossed Yager Circle and headed down Main Street before he finally asked, "So are you going to tell me what happened at prayer group?"

She dreaded bringing up the subject of Tara's trip, and related the incident to him as innocuously as possible, stressing Sue's general displeasure of Tara's nature.

Just as she'd hoped, his eyes flashed anger at Sue's snide comments, but his guarded chuckle about her own retort came with a warning. "You know she's not going to let you have the last word."

"I don't care." Which wasn't exactly the truth. She *did* care…too much. About Sue's opinion, and everybody else's in this antiquated fishbowl of a town. She and Sawyer turned up their driveway, bypassing the front door and going around to the patio doors in the back. "I just get so tired of her holier-than-thou attitude."

"You know better than to let Sue get to you." Sawyer opened the door, letting her pass through first, then followed her in. "She means well."

The irritation that started with the mention of Sue's name flickered higher. "You always take up for her."

"I just try to understand where she's coming from." He got two bowls from the cabinet and set them on the kitchen counter.

Faith clutched his arm, and pulled him around to look at her. "How about me? Have you tried to understand where I'm coming from?"

His look lasted a long moment, his lips pressed together in a thin line. "We're not talking about prayer group anymore, are we?"

"We're talking about the fact that you haven't touched me for nearly a month. Are you even trying to understand?"

The cloak of sadness that had been absent in his eyes during supper dropped back into place. "Faith, I can't—"

"Can't or won't?" Emotion sent a tremor through her body. "Why *can't* you understand? Why won't you *let* yourself understand?" She reached behind her and jerked the zipper of the shift down. "I love you." She pushed the dress off her shoulders and arms, exposing her breasts clad in pink. The dress caught on her hips. She hooked it with her thumbs and shoved it free to pool around her ankles. "You always forgive Sue. I want you to forgive me. I want you to want me." She stepped into him, sliding her arms around his waist, plastering her body against his.

His hands found her shoulders, and he pushed her gently away to hold her at arm's length. "I want that, too, Faith. I pray for that every night." He let go of her, his arms dropping like heavy weights to his side. "But, it's not happening. My prayers get clogged by other thoughts like, what if I lose Tara completely? What if she finds Jacques Martin and chooses him over me?"

"That's not going to happen, Sawyer."

"It could happen. The man was able to lure *you* away from me." He turned his gaze away from her toward the back window. "Oh, I know it was only one night and alcohol was involved. I get that. But your night with him caused a major change in us. It changed the way you relate to me. I tell myself that he gave us Tara…and she's so precious to me…but what if finding him changes the way she relates to me?"

Faith stayed quiet. She would let him talk and get it all out. Surely, that could only help.

He wiped a hand down his face, leaving a glistening dampness below his eyes, and turned back to her. "And every night I try to talk myself into going to you in our room." He looked her up and down, his face contorted with anguish. "You're a beautiful, vibrant woman, Faith."

She stepped into him again, pleading with her eyes. "Then do it. Make love to me. Please."

The anguish settled into a look of despair. "I can't." He took her hand and moved it slowly to his groin.

It was a familiar gesture, but it took on a surreal quality as her hand groped for something that wasn't there. Nothing. No detection of even the first stirring of an erection. The bulge she'd expected was instead a small mass as soft and pliable as putty.

His whisper was coarse and strangled. "I. Can't."

He released her hand, and she stepped away from him quickly. Her eyes blurred as she leaned over to gather her dress, snatching it up and making a dash for the bedroom.

She slammed the door and locked it behind her, then collapsed against it onto the floor as the wave of understanding washed over her.

Sawyer—the only man she'd ever loved—couldn't get an erection for her.

He didn't want her.

And maybe never would again.

TARA SAT AT the café in the shadow of the Eiffel Tower, still ogling the beauty of Paris's quintessential landmark while practicing her lines. The addresses of forty-three Jacques Martins were programmed into her GPS, and, though she was aware of the challenge she faced linguistically, she was armed emotionally for whatever happened. Or so she hoped.

Garrett Hughes's stuffy behavior last night had been good practice, reminding her that first impressions weren't always reliable. What a surprise he'd turned out to be— and not the pleasant kind. She'd been looking forward to some occasional American conversation while she was here, and yeah, maybe a little casual flirting, as well. But the guy had turned out to be a contrary curmudgeon who obviously resented her staking a claim to part of the terrace that he used like it was his sole dominion.

Well, he could go piss up a rope. She'd paid the rent for a month, and that gave her terrace privileges. Much as she liked the apartment, she wasn't going to spend all her time inside when she could be taking her meals and her books outdoors.

Besides, Dylan was a delight. He made her feel at home. And from where she was sitting at the moment, looking out over a park that could very likely hold a huge chunk of Taylor's Grove, it was obvious she wasn't at home anymore.

She signed the receipt the waiter brought and picked up her things. The GPS dangled from her wrist, where she could check it often. She punched up the set of coordinates for the maybe-father closest to the Eiffel Tower and began her first search, following the map toward the blinking dot. It was just like the geocaching she'd explained to Dylan yesterday, but with what could be a priceless treasure as the find rather than a box of trinkets.

The exquisite beauty of the city with its wide, tree-lined avenues and perfectly proportioned balances of lines and curves, man-made and natural, tempted Tara to forget the hunt and give in to the desire to explore. But her mind kept running ahead to her destination, and her heart pumped fast to keep up.

The map guided her around the final turn to a street filled with small boutiques rather than homes. The internet search had yielded all addresses—business and residential—that had a Jacques Martin linked to it, but she was surprised nonetheless...and maybe a little relieved...to see that the first address was that of a shop. Walking into a store was easier than ringing a private doorbell.

She stopped outside the address and took several deep breaths before pushing the door open and stepping inside. The strong, pervasive scent of formaldehyde greeted her from the bolts of materials hanging from chains, which covered the walls in brocades, damasks and linens. Her eyes and nose started to water simultaneously. The reaction was familiar, and her memory scampered back to hours she'd spent in fabric stores with Grandma O'Malley. She'd had the forethought to bring tissues in case the reunion with her father involved tears...of any kind.

She snatched one from her pocket and dabbed, trying not to smear her carefully applied mascara.

Several customers milled about, eyeing the rich colors in the woven tapestries, running their palms over the nap to change the shading of the velvet. Tara ran her fingertips across a bolt of deep brown fabric—its hue reminded her of Garrett's eyes.

Jerk, she reminded herself.

Soon, an elderly woman with silver hair pulled back into a severe bun turned her attention to Tara. A head-to-foot scan pinched her expression into a condescending sneer. *"Bonjour, mademoiselle."*

"Bonjour, madame." Tara's eyes jerked involuntarily to the door—yes, it was still there—before settling back on the woman. *"Je m'appelle Tara O'Malley. Je cherche Jacques Martin. Est-il ici?"*

A short pause allowed the woman time to exchange her sneer for a knowing smirk. *"Oui. Un instant."*

She disappeared into a back room, giving Tara time to become all-too-aware of the sound of her pulse *swishing* through her ears.

The woman appeared again, followed by a striking, middle-aged man in an impeccably cut gray suit that set off his salt-and-pepper hair, which was combed back and heavily gelled.

His age looked promising, and Tara's breath stopped as she scanned his face for a trace of anything familial and stalled on his mouth. It was wide like hers, and it curved upward into a smile as he approached.

"Bonjour, mademoiselle." His deep voice was pleasant and welcoming, and she felt her courage bolstered at the sound.

"Bonjour, Monsieur Martin?" He nodded and Tara extended her hand, pumping it a tad too enthusiastically when he took it. *"Je m'appelle* Tara O'Malley. I…uh…" She caught her breath before plunging into the script she had memorized. *"Je viens des États-Unis, et je cherche un ami de ma famille. Il s'appelle Jacques Martin. Il habitait à* Murray, Kentucky." A family friend who had lived in Murray, Kentucky had seemed like the most nonthreatening approach. She watched him closely for a reaction.

The man's gray eyes held a hint of disappointment as his smile thinned. *"Ah, ce n'est pas moi. Je suis désolé."*

Tara swallowed her own disappointment, becoming

aware of the way his thumb caressed her hand, which he still held, not even seeming to notice the missing digits. Obviously, they were coming at this conversation from very different angles.

She pulled her hand, but he gripped it tighter and leaned in to whisper something. She didn't understand the words, but his tone took on a smooth and oily quality like his hair. His mouth curved again into a leer that drove the scene past extreme *ick* and into dimensions all its own.

Tara jerked her hand from his, mortified at the turn things had taken. *"Au revoir, monsieur."* She didn't say thank you or try to ask her other memorized questions about whether he knew any other Jacques Martins she could contact. All she could think about was getting to the door and into fresh air. Once outside, the shudder that passed through her could've rocked a seismic score on the Richter scale as she allowed herself to express it verbally with a loud "eww!"

She took off at a fast walk, not even stopping to get her bearings for a couple of blocks. When she did, she was in front of Rodin's studio and museum—the perfect place to get her mind off of her creepy encounter with Jacques Martin number one.

The garden was especially inviting, quiet and relatively uncrowded compared to the area around the Eiffel Tower. She spent the entire afternoon in the shadow of *Balzac* and *The Thinker,* taking pictures of the statues and attaching them to text messages to family and friends.

Emma called as Tara boarded the metro late in the afternoon to head back home. She reacted with the proper "eww" as Tara related her tale of the first Jacques, and when she heard about Garrett Hughes's request for privacy, she replied with "What a jerk!"

As she had so often in their years together, Tara reminded herself how fortunate she was to have a best friend who viewed the world with a similar enough perspective to her own to make them compatible, yet still different enough to keep their conversations interesting.

Back at her flat, Tara poured a glass of wine and took it and her journal out to the terrace to write about the experiences of her day—another of Emma's suggestions to help her work through the emotion of her search for her birth father.

She'd thought the idea a little silly at first, but as she started to chronicle not only her emotions but her impressions as a first-time visitor to Paris, her hand flew across the pages, filling up one after another. She was especially surprised at the depth of disappointment today's encounter churned up. But plenty more addresses remained to be searched.

"Hi, Tara."

She looked up to see Dylan standing a few feet away, ball and glove in hand.

"Hi, Dylan. How are you today?"

"I'm fine." He stayed awkwardly planted to his spot. "What are you doing?"

She held up the book she'd been writing in. "I went to the Eiffel Tower and the Musée Rodin today, so I've been writing in my journal about those places. Have you ever been to the Musée Rodin?"

"Yeah, lots of times."

She patted the empty seat beside her. "Come tell me what you like best about it."

He hesitated for only a second, then hurried to plop down in the proffered seat. "Dad says I'm not supposed to bother you, but I don't guess I'm bothering you if you invite me. Isn't that right?"

Tara smiled at the child's honesty. "That's right. If I invite you, it means I want some company."

The warmth in Dylan's smile thawed the icy coating that had surrounded Tara's heart as she wrote her review of today's father search.

"What I like best about the Musée Rodin is the ice cream," he answered her original question. "But the statue I like best is *The Burghers of Calais*."

"That was my favorite, too!" Tara was intrigued that she and the six-year-old were both taken by the same piece out of all the choices. "Why do you like that one best?"

"Because my dad told me the story about those guys being heroes. They're not superheroes like Iron Man and Thor, but they saved a lot of people, so I like them."

"Yeah, me, too…for the same reason." Tara made a mental note to include this delightful conversation in her journal. "Is your dad home yet?"

Dylan shook his head. "He has to work late again tonight."

"Well, I wouldn't mind playing a little catch if you'd like."

Dylan shot out of his chair. "Cool! I'll get Dad's glove for you."

They played for almost an hour, but as it neared the time when Garrett had gotten home the night before, Tara thought about what the man had asked of her.

"Whew! I'm getting tired, Dylan." She faked it a little, but not too much. "I think I'd better call it a night and go grab a bite of supper."

"Okay."

She handed the glove back to him and ruffled her hand through his hair. "Thanks for playing with me. It was fun."

"Maybe we can play again tomorrow," he said and then hurried to add, "if I don't bother you."

"Maybe."

She gathered up her things and went inside as Dylan continued his game by throwing the ball against the wall by his terrace door.

Tara heated some soup and fixed a salad for a light meal. When she sat down at the table, she saw that Garrett had gotten home and was on the terrace playing catch with his indefatigable son.

The guy may be a jerk, but he was obviously doing something right. Dylan seemed well-adjusted and was a delight to be around.

Maybe giving them their private terrace time wasn't such a big deal. She could sacrifice a little.

The Burghers of Calais had been willing to sacrifice everything for the people they loved.

Watching Garrett play with his son—a single dad in a foreign country, a young man who lost his wife—it struck her that Rodin could have immortalized him, as well.

And she'd seen him naked.

Definitely statueworthy.

CHAPTER EIGHT

HENRI'S NOSTRILS FLARED as the coffee cup neared his nose. "Ahh!" He closed his eyes and breathed deeply, a look of something akin to ecstasy relaxing his features. "Is there a more delicious scent in the morning than freshly ground coffee?" He paused, and a wicked gleam lit his eyes. "*Peut-être* a freshly ground woman, *oui?*"

Garrett shrugged. "It's been so long since I've had a woman in the morning, I'm not sure my grinder would even work."

A uniquely French sound came from the back of Henri's throat. It combined humor, dismay and a touch of disdain, and Garrett had never been able to come close to mimicking it, though Dylan already had it perfected. "How are you and your American neighbor getting along?" The Frenchman took his first sip and smiled appreciatively. "You have not mentioned the wild woman in several days."

Garrett tried to take a sip, but the coffee in his cup was still too hot. "I haven't spoken to her since…" Since the day he'd been abrupt with her about giving him and Dylan their privacy…the day she'd looked so stung by his words. Occasionally, he'd see her wander out onto the terrace, but it was always a glimpse through the window. She never came out if he was outside. "For several days," he finished his answer.

"You share a terrace and, for several days, you do not speak with her?"

Coupled with the guilt he was feeling about the whole

Tara matter, the question irritated Garrett more than it should. "I told you before, I don't want her around Dylan."

"But Dylan goes to bed, does he not? There is much time to share a bottle of wine after he is asleep."

His friend knew him all too well. Last night, Garrett had started to do just that. After Dylan was asleep, he'd put on a Miles Davis CD and opened a bottle of an exquisite 2007 cabernet that begged to be shared.

Tara was out on the terrace with her own bottle, and she wasn't reading or writing in that book the way she usually did. She was simply sitting alone with her wine, illumined by the soft lights of the night around her, looking lovely and serene. Garrett had actually taken several steps toward the door before his own words had stopped him. *"There isn't a lot of privacy around here, so we'll try to respect yours as much as possible while you're here."*

Approaching her during her private time would be opening a can of worms, and would, of course, require an apology for his previous rudeness to her. Probably best to leave well enough alone.

But she'd been tempting.

Garrett raised his chin as a warning that he was tired of talking about this. "My wine and I did just fine all by ourselves. So, what do you have for me this morning?" He glided into another subject before Henri could make him feel worse. "Have the numbers stabilized enough for me to order my Ferrari?"

Henri handed him the morning's report. "No Ferraris yet, but someday soon, *peut-être.*"

While Garrett was certainly interested in the entire report, he couldn't keep his eyes from searching out the bottom of the right-hand column first. When he did, his heart skipped a beat, and he felt like skipping along with it. An 8 percent jump in sales in twenty-four hours.

Convincing the higher powers that the marginal analysis leaned toward a successful flighting strategy had been a bitch, but worth every penny they'd spent.

Of course, it was too soon to tell how deeply Soulard had penetrated the beer market, but the GPRs were promising. "Do you have the disaggregations yet?"

Henri's sigh implied that answering that question was beneath him. "They are printing now. Go drink your coffee—which is now too cold to be palatable, but your American tongue will probably not notice—and I will bring them to you."

Garrett went back to his office to wait for his friend, but he was too anxious to sit. He paced back and forth, allowing the numbers on the paper to absorb into his brain. Such detail so quickly was beyond his comprehension. He'd worked with plenty of IT specialists, but Henri Poulin was by far the best of the best. The man was a virtual magician with a computer, and he had a sixth sense for anticipating what information would be needed. More often than not, he and his staff had reports generated before they were even called for.

The man would be an asset to any company. Soulard Beer had simply managed to land him first.

As promised, Henri appeared within a few minutes, report in one hand, fresh coffee in the other. "*Voilà*. The market profile is much as you anticipated…with a pleasant surprise in the over-fifty range, *oui?*"

Garrett shook his head in astonishment at the number his right thumb hovered beside. A fluke mention of Soulard—thanks to a friend of a friend of one of the owners—during a television show watched mainly by an older crowd had sent sales soaring, though whether it was truly a penetrated market or a one-time thing only time would tell. But Garrett was hopeful.

"We're out there, Henri. We're really out there."

His friend nodded in agreement. "So tonight, instead

of the wine, which you did not share, you share the champagne with your American neighbor, *oui?*"

The mention of Tara brought another surge of guilt and frustration, heightened by Garrett's already overstimulated emotional state this morning. "Damn it, would you let that subject go?"

Tsk. Tsk. Henri clicked his tongue. "I hear you whine often that you miss your home. And yet, when the opportunity arises for you to enjoy the company of a young woman who is not only from your home but is also your nearest neighbor, you do not extend friendship to her."

The arch of his eyebrow made Garrett doubt that *friendship* was Henri's first choice of what he should extend in Tara's direction. But his friend's words hit their intended mark. "Just one more reason I don't need to be around her," he grumbled. "She'll only make me more homesick."

Henri found his reflection in the window glass and adjusted his tie. "The Americans always refer to the French as 'stuffy,' and yet you snub someone for no good reason and act like it is nothing." He shifted his gaze to bore directly into Garrett's. "You are the stuffy one."

Garrett held his tongue and grabbed his coffee cup instead. He took a giant swig, and a thought hit his chest simultaneously with the brew.

He and the coffee had a lot in common.

Both were cold and bitter.

TARA POISED HER PEN ABOVE the name. Instead of the dark red line that crossed off six Jacques Martins from her list, beside number seven she drew a red star.

He hadn't been her birth father, but he was one she wanted to remember, nonetheless.

Four days, seven prospects and no results that had moved her any closer to her goal. She knew it wasn't going to be easy, but she didn't know it was going to be this hard. Ringing doorbells, walking into shops, trying to converse with strangers in a language she had no grasp of. She was exhausted, and if her search took her all the way to the final name and she would have to go through this thirty-six more times, she wasn't sure her heart could take the battering.

The crowds at Paris's popular sites sometimes made her feel as though the air was being pressed from her lungs, so today she'd opted to get out of the city. Number seven lived in Giverny. She'd always wanted to see Monet's house and garden, so, although she'd much rather have been on a motorcycle with the wind whipping her hair, she'd caught the train to Vernon instead. A three-mile walk from there to the village of Giverny had brought her to the small, quaint cottage of number seven, and her breath had stuttered with hope at the sight.

A neighbor out in the yard next door had called to her— an old woman with kind eyes who spoke no English. But she knew the name Jacques Martin, and her eyes had filled with tears. She took Tara's half hand, caressing it gently while cooing words with sympathetic, grandmotherly sounds, and led her to the small cemetery at the end of the lane.

She pointed out a new grave—not fresh, but newer than those surrounding it—and left Tara with a parting pat on her back.

According to his tombstone, the birthdate of Giverny's Jacques Martin was May 27, 1942, which made him too old to be the man her mother had slept with. But Tara's heart squeezed just the same for the loss of this man she never knew. A plethora of bouquets said he was much loved, and fresher ones—even recent ones—said he was still missed.

She'd felt compelled to leave some of her own, so after touring Monet's gardens and house, she'd sought out a flower shop, and bought two small bouquets of daisies. One she'd left on the grave of Jacques Martin number seven, and one she'd left with his kind old neighbor who'd cried a tearful thanks.

Now, sitting on her terrace, chronicling the day's events in her journal, she felt mired up in melancholy. She needed some fun.

Dylan was throwing a ball against the wall beside their door. True to his word, he'd waved when he came out, but he hadn't come over, hadn't bothered her in the least.

"Hey, Dylan." She closed her journal and put away her pens. "Want a glass of Orangina?"

The boy's grin lifted her spirits faster than the shopping spree she'd been considering—and was definitely cheaper.

"Sure!" He sprinted over to her, dropping his ball and glove into a chair. "It's hot today." He wiped his sweaty face on his sleeve.

"Yeah," she agreed. "Almost too hot to play ball."

The boy answered with a vigorous shake of his head. "It's never too hot to play ball."

"Well, you sit here and catch your breath, and I'll go fix us a cool drink."

She left him at the table, but when she returned a couple of minutes later with the drinks, he was standing in the middle of the terrace with his babysitter, who was on the phone, crying and obviously frantic.

Tara's first thought was of Garrett. Had something happened to him? She rushed to Dylan's side. "What is it? What's wrong?"

Dylan's look was one of concern but he wasn't distraught, and Tara's heart slowed a tad as he took one of the lidded cups from her. "Thanks." He took a deep draw on the straw.

Keeping an ear to the conversation, he translated the blur of words for Tara. "Something's wrong with Monique's father. They've taken him to the hospital. That's her mom on the phone. She wants her to come to the hospital right now, but Monique doesn't want to take me."

"Tell her to go. You can stay with me until your dad gets home."

Dylan grabbed Monique's arm to get her attention and pointed to Tara. His words were too fast for Tara to pick up anything, but Monique's look of surprise and relief told her the message had been received. The babysitter nodded and spoke into the phone again briefly before hanging up and turning her attention to Tara. "Monsieur Hughes—"

"Garrett won't mind, I'm sure," Tara said. "Dylan will be fine with me, won't you, Dylan?"

Dylan spoke in French to Monique first. "I told her we're good friends," he said to Tara.

Tara wasn't sure if Monique understood English, so she shifted her gaze from the young woman to Dylan as she spoke. "I'll tell Garrett what happened. You just go on and be with your father."

"Thank you. Thank you very much." Monique's English was perfect. "I will call Monsieur Hughes later when I know more of my father's condition. My mother does not handle the crisis very well."

She ran to the door, stopping for a last look. "Oh, and Monsieur Hughes has an important meeting and will not be home until around nine-thirty. The dinner for Dylan is in the refrigerator. His bedtime is nine o'clock." She gave a quick wave before disappearing.

Tara checked her watch. It was only six-twenty, so she and her new charge had a few hours to fill. "Want to play some catch after all?"

"Can we go to the park instead? Monique and I go there a lot. It's close. Just down the street."

Tara wasn't sure which park he was referring to. There were several nearby. "Are you sure that would be okay with your dad?"

His eyes grew big, opening a window to his soul as he nodded. The look was too cute to be anything but honest. "It's okay as long as I have an adult with me."

Tara caved quickly. "Well, okay, then. But you'll have

to lead the way because I still don't know my way around the neighborhood very well."

"I know how to get there. We go there all the time. It's easy." The child slipped his hand into hers, catching her two fingers in his grip. His brow buckled with concern. "Does that hurt?"

"Nope. Just don't squeeze hard," she warned him.

His grasp was firm, but easy, as he led the way through their apartment. "Your hand feels weird. It's little. My dad's hands are great big."

Tara remembered Garrett's big hands. More than once during her nap after their first encounter, she'd fantasized about how big and warm those hands might feel on her naked back. But that was before he'd been a jerk. Since then, she'd banished such thoughts...or, at least, most of them.

Dylan guided her easily through the labyrinth of corridors to the ancient wooden door at the back of their building.

Le Parc Royal was just at the end of the block. As soon as they arrived, some children called Dylan by name, and he dropped Tara's hand to go join them in their game of what appeared to be freeze tag.

Tara found a spot on a bench close by and watched, fascinated. Dylan seemed to be popular and well accepted by the group. He had an obvious kind streak—staying close to the younger or slower children so they didn't have to stay frozen out of the game long.

His poor mother...missing out on all this. What a privilege it was to be able to sit here and watch him. An emotion stirred deep in Tara's chest that hit several vulnerable areas at once. Being a mother someday was her highest hope. Kids were one of the greatest treasures of life. But to have that treasure and then lose it? Her hand trembled as she pushed a curl out of her eye. Did Jacques Martin feel the same way? Would he be sorry he'd missed out on her childhood?

She shook away the melancholy that threatened for the second time that day and glanced at her hand, her constant reminder of the blessing of life.

"Boo!"

She jumped and let out a little squeal, which brought a hoot from Dylan, who'd sneaked up beside her.

"Are you hungry?"

She took his hint. "I *am* hungry. Shall we go eat supper?"

He cocked his head. "Is that another word for dinner?"

"Sort of. Supper's a light meal at night, like lunch is a light meal during the day," she explained. "Dinner's a big meal either time."

He thought about that for a moment. "I think I want dinner."

"Dinner it is."

He took the hand she extended without question, and they strolled home at a leisurely pace. Dylan must have decided it was time for her to learn the French language properly because, for the rest of the evening—through eating the shish kebabs Garrett had left to be grilled until she tucked him into bed—he pointed to things and drilled her on the correct word, insisting on proper pronunciation. By the time he fell asleep, she figured her French vocabulary had doubled.

Barely a week past the summer solstice, a hint of sun still lit the evening sky even though the clock read 9:33 p.m. Tara had just stepped out onto the terrace to enjoy the last remnants of sunset when she heard the *snick* of Garrett's key in the lock. She hurried back in to greet him.

He had a broad smile when he stepped through the door, which vanished the instant he saw her. "Tara? What are you doing here?"

The panic in his voice spurred her to the important matter first. "Dylan's fine. He's already asleep. Have you spoken with Monique?"

"No. I just got out of a long meeting." Panic had been replaced by disapproval. He dropped his keys and briefcase on the desk. "What's going on?"

Tara's hackles rose at his tone. She clipped out her response as if she were answering a police interrogation. "She got a call from her mom that her dad had been rushed to the hospital, and she needed to get there right away. She was upset and crying, so I told her to go on, and I stayed with Dylan."

"He's okay?" He stepped lightly over to his son's door and peeped in.

"He's fine." Her voice dropped to a normal level as her neck muscles loosened. "We went to the park, and he played really hard. Then we came back and grilled the shish kebabs you had fixed, and I threw a salad together. It was a lovely meal, which we topped off by sharing one of your bold cabernets. Dylan chose it," she taunted, keeping a straight face.

Garrett's eyes widened just like she'd seen Dylan's do so many times. "You let Dylan—" He stopped when her grin broke, and he gave her the first real smile she'd ever received from him. Her toes curled in reaction. "You're kidding, right?"

"Yeah. I had my own cabernet, and he had Orangina."

"You could've opened one of mine. I wouldn't have—" He was interrupted by his cell phone. *"Allô? C'est Garrett."* He paused. *"Oui, Monique..."*

Tara watched the easy manner they'd briefly reached a few moments before dissolve as Garrett spoke to the babysitter. His voice held sympathy, but Tara could also see a milder form of the panic settle into the crease between his brows. It may have been her imagination, but the scar that cut into his lip seemed to have deepened by the time the call ended.

"How's Monique's father?" she asked.

Garrett rubbed his brow. "Not well. It's his heart. They're talking about open-heart surgery, but they're trying to decide if he's strong enough to take it."

"Oh, the poor girl. She said her mom didn't handle crisis well, so she's got her hands full." Thinking about her dad, Sawyer, in the same situation caused her chest to tighten. "I assume Monique's going to need some time off? I sure would."

Garrett nodded absently. "At least a week, probably."

"What will you do with Dylan?"

"There's an after-school program until six. He hates staying for it, but we have to use it occasionally."

"But you haven't been getting home until later than that," she reminded him, immediately regretting doing so when he squeezed the bridge of his nose in frustration.

"Yes, well, normally, I could be off by then, but we've got this media blitz for another three days, so we're having to keep late hours."

"I'll keep him for you." The words came out before her brain fully processed the ramifications of what she was suggesting.

Garrett's head jerked toward her, and she got the feeling he'd forgotten she was there. "No. I couldn't ask you to do that."

"You didn't ask. I volunteered."

His hands went to his hips, and she saw his fingers tighten their hold. "I really appreciate what you did tonight, stepping in and taking care of him. I'm grateful. Really. But I don't think it's a good idea for you to be around Dylan too much."

That comment pushed her too far. Just what in the hell was he implying? "Look, Garrett, I don't know what your problem is with me." She realized her voice had risen. She lowered it to a whisper as she moved away from the child's door, and continued to spit out the words. "I'm a schoolteacher. Kids are my life. I love them, and I'm very good with them. Now, you can stick Dylan in that after-school program, which he hates, if you think that would be better than spending the time with me. But Dylan and I get along well. We genuinely *like* each other. So if you come to your senses and change your mind, you know where to find me."

She charged onto the terrace and crossed to her flat without looking back. Once at her place, she headed straight for the shower, where she could stand in the steam and let the hot spray beat away the day's frustration.

When she got out and dried off, she felt better—more relaxed—but still too wired to go to bed. She left her hair up in the clip and slipped into some loose cargo pants and a camisole, intending to plot out her Jacques Martin search for tomorrow.

She'd just gotten settled on the couch when she was startled by a soft knock on the sliding door that led to the terrace.

It could only be one of two people, and Dylan had been asleep for over an hour.

She looked out. Sure enough, it was Garrett. She slid the door open, but before she could speak, he held up a bottle of champagne and two glasses.

"I'm sorry. I've been rude to you and have been a terrible neighbor. I'd like to start over." He tilted his head toward the table on his side of the terrace. "Will you forgive me and join me for a drink? I just realized I have a lot to celebrate tonight."

CHAPTER NINE

"DOES THIS MEAN YOU'VE changed your mind about my keeping Dylan?" With her arms crossed firmly across her chest, Tara's green-eyed stare bored into Garrett, steady and unflinching—the quintessential teacher look.

Hell, he might as well confess everything. Her look had him convinced she'd find out anyway. "Yeah. I…um…I called Josh Essex after you left. He says you're a great teacher. Honest. Trustworthy. Always concerned about what's best for the kids."

His confession didn't relax her stance even the slightest. Her eyes tightened at the corners, and she tilted her head in question. "What else did he say?"

He gave a sheepish grin. "He said you have a lot of energy, and everybody wants you on their committees because you're willing to do most of the work."

She dropped her arms and her protective wall at last, answering his grin with one of her own and stepping out on the terrace to join him. "Okay, then. I get to babysit Dylan, so I have something to celebrate, as well."

Garrett pointed across the way, where he already had some candles lit on his table to drive away mosquitoes. "Is it okay with you if we sit over there…in case he wakes up?" He hoped the candles didn't look too presumptuous… or romantic.

"Sure." She nodded and turned to slide her door closed. A gentle night breeze caught some of the curls that had worked loose from the clip in the back of her hair. They stirred around her face, and his fingers twitched with an unsettling urge to brush them back and linger for a moment in their softness.

He shifted his gaze from the enticing curls, only to have it land on the tattoo below her ear. It looked different in the moonlight, like an exotic jewel embedded into her long, elegant neck at one of the tenderest areas. He imagined following the intricate design with the tip of his tongue… her warm breath quickening in response against his naked shoulder.

"Are we…waiting for something?"

Her question slapped him out of his inappropriate reverie. "No. I, uh, was just noticing the…" He wiggled his finger toward the area that had held him spellbound. "The, uh, tattoo on your neck. It must've hurt like hell."

"Not really." She held up her hand. "Compared to losing two fingers, it was a picnic."

"I'm sure. Well…" He gestured toward his table. *"Après vous."*

"So, what are you celebrating?" She gave him a sidelong glance as they crossed the imaginary line to his section of the common space. "Other than the fact that you came to your senses, I mean."

Josh had warned him the woman was known for not mincing words. He set the bottle and the glasses on the table and pulled the chair out for her to sit down, then began removing the foil from around the cork. "I think I told you before that I'm the head of marketing for Soulard Beer?" She nodded. "Well, we're in the middle of a media campaign. I don't want to jinx anything by talking too much about it, but suffice it to say that it appears the campaign has passed all our expectations." A small *pop* punctuated his words.

Tara rose to her feet again in overstated ceremony. He filled the two glasses she held out, then he took one and, continuing the drama, held it aloft. "Here's to Soulard Beer and the venture of your choice. May our successes continue to grow in direct correlation to our friendship."

"To Soulard, new friendships and successful ventures," she answered.

They clicked their glasses together and sipped. The candlelight heightened the color of the liquid to amber and cast a golden glow across Tara's face that was quite bewitching. Pleasant warmth from the shared toast and the fine drink bloomed in his chest making him happy he'd invited her to join him.

They sat, and Tara held her glass out again. "Here's to Dylan, one of the cutest, sweetest, most lovable kids I've had the pleasure of knowing."

Her words caused the muscles in Garrett's throat to constrict, making it difficult for the second sip of champagne to pass. "Tara…" Getting too personal would be a mistake, but she deserved to know where he was coming from in regards his son. "I need to explain my concerns about Dylan, so you don't think I'm a total asswipe."

"*Jerk* was my epithet of choice."

He let that mull in his mind as he swirled his glass, causing a tempest of bubbles to rise to the top. "Okay." He took another sip. "We'll go with jerk."

Tara settled back in her chair, stretching her long legs out in front of her as if preparing to hear a lengthy story.

He took a deep breath. Where to start? "It wasn't so much you personally, as much as…well, how certain things about you remind me of my wife."

"Oh…really?" Tara straightened, brows knitting in concern. "Is there a resemblance? Is that why Dylan took so quickly to me?"

"No, no, it's not like that. Angela was short, black haired, dark complexioned." Garrett wiped his hand down his face. Hell, he needed to just say it. He took another sip, hoping the bubbles would lighten the weight in his chest. "She was bipolar."

Tara's brows shot up. "Oh."

"When she took her medication, she was fine." He continued. "The problem was that she didn't like to take the medication. She said it repressed who she really was. During her pregnancy and then after Dylan was born, she went without it more and more often, and her mood swings flitted from one extreme to another. She could go from the most manic high to the most depressed low in a matter of hours. When I came home from work, I never knew if the woman who met me would be the same one who was there when I left or someone totally different."

Tara sat her glass down gently and leaned forward to clasp her hands on the table. "And what exactly is it about me that reminds you of her? I mean, you really don't even know me."

"I know. But when Angie would get on one of her highs, she would do things on the spur of the moment. She'd come home with a piercing or a tattoo." He waved his hand in her direction. "She had lots of them…said the pain made her feel real and alive."

While he talked, Tara had been listening intently, brushing a finger lightly up and down on her lips. She now used that finger to make figures in the air as if she were adding up some kind of imaginary math problem. "So, since that first day, it's been in your head that I might be mentally unstable because I have a few tattoos and a couple of piercings?"

"Well…" When she put it that way, his logic did sound a little weak. "You also admitted to the motorcycle wreck that cost you part of your hand…and your gorgeous red hair has blue streaks in it. Angie would do wild things like that to her hair, too."

Tara started like he'd pinched her, and Garrett grunted in frustration. He wasn't explaining himself very well and was probably pissing her off, beating around the bush with his dance of avoidance. "Oh, hell." He downed the remainder of his glass. Grabbing the bottle, he topped off Tara's glass and refilled his own. "I know I'm silly. I know that not everyone who has piercings and tattoos and blue hair is crazy like Angie. I know you're not crazy. And if I thought you were, Josh pretty well squelched that."

The side of Tara's mouth lifted in a half smile. "I grew up in a small town as the preacher's kid, and I was always held to a higher standard. I followed the rules and never got into trouble. But as an adult, I realized I'd never learned to express myself. I have a reason for all of these." She gestured to the ring in her eyebrow and the tattoo under her ear. "Play nice and maybe someday I'll tell you what they are."

It had to be the champagne because something about her words shot straight to Garrett's groin, causing a stiffness that made him shift uncomfortably in his seat. He shoved the idea of playing nicely with Tara from his mind. "I guess we all have our reasons for doing the things we do. And my objections to your being around Dylan go back to Angie. He lost his mom when he was three, and he has a definite soft spot for women." He was in too deep to turn around now, so he laid it all out. "I got involved with my French tutor when we first moved here. Big mistake. Dylan latched on to her, and it was really tough on the little guy when we broke up. Ever since, I've been trying like hell to protect him from getting too attached to someone who's only going to vanish from his life."

"Oh, Garrett." Tara dropped against the back of her chair, throwing her arms into the air. "I understand now. You're afraid Dylan will see me every day for a month, and then I'll be gone." Her finger settled on her lip again, brushing back and forth.

Garrett shifted in his seat again, wishing she'd stop calling attention to her luscious lips. "Exactly." His voice was hoarse, and he cleared his throat.

"But there have to be other women in Dylan's life that

he's attached to. Teachers? Grandmothers? How do you handle other situations?"

"Teachers he'll see occasionally even after he's left their classes. We call my mom and Angie's mom a lot, usually a couple of times a week."

She tipped her glass his direction. "If that works, then we have our answer. Even after I go home, I'll be as close as a phone call. Dylan can call me whenever he wants to, and I'll take his calls as long as he needs to make them. But I have a feeling he won't need them too long. People have a way of forgetting. Out of sight, out of mind, you know?" A shadow crossed her face, and Garrett got the feeling she wasn't just referring to Dylan, but he didn't press her about it. Whatever it was, it was none of his business.

That she understood and was taking his concern for his son so seriously filled him with gratitude. "You seem to know Dylan pretty well. Have you been spending time together I haven't been aware of?"

Tara's smile was gentle…and disarming. "We play catch almost every night before you get home."

"THAT'S TROUBLESOME." A GROWL of displeasure underscored his voice. "I gave him strict orders not to bother you. It's not like him to disobey. At least, I didn't *think* it was like him to disobey."

Tara hadn't meant to get her little friend in trouble. "Relax, Dad." She leaned across the table, laying a hand of reassurance on Garrett's. "He told me from the beginning that he wasn't supposed to bother me. He only comes over to my section if he's invited. And playing catch is usually my idea."

Garrett chuckled and turned his hand over to grasp hers. "So you're telling me you and my son have been having clandestine meetings for…?"

"About a week now." She filled in the blank.

He laughed and shook his head. "And here I thought I was keeping him safely out of your clutches."

He gave her fingers a light squeeze. It felt nice, and she squeezed back before letting go. "I'm the one caught in the clutches, I'm afraid. Dylan's a heart stealer."

Pride bloomed on his face. "Yeah, he's pretty special."

The second glass of champagne was making them bold, adding warmth to the conversation, convincing her she could get away with more than what would normally be proper. "Garrett, if you don't mind my asking—and you don't have to talk about it if you don't want to…"

"Suicide," he answered.

Tara recoiled at the word spoken so matter-of-factly, though the tense set of Garrett's jaw and the shadow that veiled his eyes belied a deep pain within.

His response hadn't been what she expected. *Cancer. A horrible accident.* Those she'd been prepared for. But suicide? How did one respond to that? "I'm—I'm sorry," she faltered. "I shouldn't have brought it up."

"It's okay." Garrett downed the remainder of his champagne in one gulp. He reached for the bottle. His hand hovered near it momentarily before he drew it back. "The coroner declared it an accident. She was texting and smashed her car into a tree. But there were no skid marks. No sign of any braking at all." His eyes found a faraway point to focus on—one from three years ago, if she were guessing. "The text was for me. It said, 'I hate you.'"

The icy words sent a shiver down Tara's spine despite the lingering heat of the evening. "That's horrible." Garrett's Adam's apple bobbed in agreement. "No," she corrected herself. "It's cruel. No one should have to live with something like that hanging over his head."

His gaze jerked back, crashing headlong into hers, and this time the pain wasn't hidden. It oozed from him like a sore that had lost its protective scab. "We don't get a choice in the matter, do we?"

"No. No, we don't." Emma had used those same words when they'd talked about the bizarre twist of Sawyer not being Tara's birth father. Her brain spun in circles, searching for a topic she could switch to. Anything that would shift them from this sad conversation. But how could she do that tactfully and without seeming callous?

"She got it in her head I was having an affair."

He didn't wait for any prompting, so obviously he wanted—maybe needed—to talk about this. Tara took a large gulp of champagne to dull her senses.

"I worried about leaving Dylan at home alone with her, but I had to work, so I hired a woman—a housekeeper to clean and cook, but mostly just to be there to keep an eye on things. I never even gave her a second look, but Angie was convinced we had a thing for each other." His hand mopped his face again, and he blew out a long breath. "The night she died, she flew into a rage because I'd given Sally a Christmas bonus that Angie thought was too much. The truth was, Sally was threatening to quit at the first of the year because Angie was getting so hard to deal with, so I'd hoped the extra money would be an incentive to stay on."

He paused and Tara stayed quiet, willing to let him have the floor as long as he wanted it.

"Sally left," he continued, "and I went to Dylan's room to check on him. Angie grabbed the keys and took off before I could stop her. I called the police. They said she hadn't committed a crime, but they'd keep an eye out. Thirty minutes later, I got the text and then a few minutes after that, I got the call from the police. She died on impact." He shrugged slowly as if a heavy barbell lay across his shoulders, or maybe the weight of the world. "End of story."

Tara rolled her shoulders forward and back to loosen the muscles, which had tightened considerably during his tale. She waited to see if he had anything else he wanted to add. When he didn't, she eased the subject in a different direction. "You and Dylan have been through a lot… and you've done a wonderful job of raising him alone."

The compliment brought a tender smile to Garrett's lips. "Thanks, but I can't take all the credit. Dylan probably learned early on to adapt to any situation. He's one of those kids who's easy to be with."

"I couldn't agree more. He's a very kind little boy." She filled him in on the details of Dylan's actions, which she'd observed at the park. As she'd seen so many times during parent-teacher conferences, Garrett's whole demeanor changed when she told him complimentary things about his child. Even parents who came in loaded for bear about a bad grade would calm down and leave with a smile when she told them what a great kid they had. The best part was that she didn't have to fake it. All of them were great kids to her. She didn't always like how they acted, but she always liked *them*.

She shared how touched she was by Dylan's actions toward her. "He doesn't mind holding my hand, but he's cautious and doesn't want to hurt it."

"I didn't mind holding your hand a few minutes ago, either." Garrett's mouth twisted up at the corner. "Fact is, it felt pretty nice."

So the man *was* capable of flirting after all! The heat started in her back and worked its way into her neck and face. She held up her half hand. "It used to feel twice as nice."

Garrett laughed at that. Reaching for the bottle once again, he filled her glass, then emptied the bottle into his own. "This evening took much too serious a turn. Weren't we supposed to be celebrating?"

"Yes, we were. And you also need to fill me in on Dylan's schedule so I'll know what time to be where."

He stood up. "Be right back."

He was gone for a couple of minutes. When he returned,

he handed her a sheet of paper. "Dylan's schedule. My friend Henri designed a spreadsheet for me."

She glanced down the entries, which included not only Dylan's school schedule but also his Wednesday schedule, Garrett's numbers and an array of other numbers. The man was nothing if not efficient—and so was his friend. "We haven't discussed it, but I'd like to keep Dylan until Monique is able to come back. Not just tomorrow. If that's all right with you."

Garrett gave his head an emphatic shake. "That's too long, Tara. You're only here for a month. I can't take an entire week of your time. And this is the last week of school. Next week, he'll be around all day."

At that moment, being with Dylan seemed more important than finding Jacques Martin, and she wasn't sure exactly why. It had to do with the privilege of being with him that she'd felt that afternoon while watching him play. Now that she knew the story of his mother's death, she had a fierce instinct to let him know he was worth every second of her time. And Jacques Martin wouldn't be going anywhere other than where he'd been for twenty-eight years. She could pick up the search for him when Monique got back, even if it wasn't for a couple weeks.

She tilted her glass in Garrett's direction. "Even all day will be fine. I've got lots of sightseeing to do. If it's okay with you, he can be my tour guide. I'm going to spend a day at the Louvre, and one at the Musée d'Orsay. And I also want to go to Notre-Dame and Sainte-Chapelle."

"He loves all those places." Garrett grew quiet for a moment, and when he spoke, his voice was steeped in gratitude—and sexy as all get-out. "You're sure you don't mind?"

"I'm sure. I told him I'd take him geocaching if you were okay with it. We can do that while we're exploring the city."

Garrett's heavy brows gathered in question, so she delved into more detail about the pastime. He leaned toward her, hanging on her every word just like Dylan had done when she explained it to him. "Hell!" He slapped the table lightly. "That even sounds like fun to me!"

Was he asking for an invitation? She ventured out to test the waters. "Then, maybe some evening we can all search for a cache together."

"I'd like that. I'd like that very much." A look came into his dark eyes that was part fun but part something else entirely, and a tingle that couldn't be attributed to the champagne zinged through her. Their gazes locked for a few seconds, charging the air between them with electricity.

They teetered at the edge of something momentarily before Garrett backed off. "So…tell me about the town you grew up in."

"You want to hear stories about Taylor's Grove?"

He grinned. "Actually, I just like to hear you talk."

"Well, if talking's what you want, I'm the girl for the job. When I go to talking, my mouth runs like the clatter bone of a goose's ass."

Garrett's laugh was deep and mellow, bringing a certain heat to the air around her that made her want to hear it again.

For the next half hour, Tara enthralled him with stories about life in her corner of small-town America. She told only the comedies, the things that would keep them laughing, staying away from the dramas that infused life in Taylor's Grove as surely as they did everywhere else— of which her own family was solid proof.

The champagne and camaraderie had finally worked its magic. Her muscles, which had been so tight before, were loose and relaxed, and she tried ineffectually to stifle a yawn that popped out unbidden. "Oh, wow, I'm getting sleepy."

Garrett looked at his watch. "Yeah, it's way past my bedtime, too. And I've got another long day tomorrow."

They stood up slowly…and reluctantly on Tara's part.

"I hate for nights like this to end." Garrett echoed her thoughts.

"Me, too. But we can pick up where we left off tomorrow night."

"I'd like that." Garrett's tone was husky again. He paused as if he was on the verge of saying something else, but then he picked up the glasses and the bottle. "Thanks for sharing my celebration and volunteering to keep Dylan."

"It's my pleasure." She started toward her flat, feeling Garrett's eyes on her, following her progress across the space they shared. When she got to her door, she turned to look back.

Sure enough, he hadn't moved. "Good night," he called.

She blew an impetuous, giddy kiss in response.

CHAPTER TEN

GARRETT FELT HIMSELF crashing. If the Soulard bigwigs didn't finish their speeches and toasts soon, he was going to fall face-first into the remains of his chocolate soufflé. The rich meal and the magnums of champagne made it impossible to comprehend all that was being said, and he was exhausted enough not to give a damn.

He wanted to be home with Dylan, and…okay, yes, with Tara. The two of them had barely scratched the surface the other night getting to know each other, and there was so much more he wanted to know. But for the third night in a row, he wasn't going to make it home before midnight— too late for any real interaction, which was probably just as well. The more he was around Tara, the more he liked her, and liking her too much would be dangerous territory for him and Dylan.

He took a sip of water to clear the fog from his brain. Thank God tonight was the end of the campaign and the outrageous hours.

Things weren't supposed to have been this hectic, but he could hardly complain. The day after his and Tara's celebration, one of the television programs—sort of a French version of *Entertainment Tonight*—had requested an interview with the company's owners, so the marketing department had been thrown into extra-double duty to write fresh, snazzy new lines that would make the owners look cool and hip for the young audience.

The interview had been taped this evening and then the

entire company had gone to Le Pamplemousse for an exquisite celebratory seven-course meal that had gone on for five hours and twenty-two minutes, but was almost over.

Tara had been so understanding about all of this, though how he would ever repay her was still up in the air. She acted miffed every time he brought up the subject of money.

The speaker's words faded as his imagination took over with some totally inappropriate things he could offer to make her stay in Paris more enjoyable for them both.

That his mind shouldn't drive on that side of the road was a no-brainer. His life was complicated enough without adding a fling with a neighbor into the mix. But the woman had wormed her way into his consciousness and parked her fine ass there—*not* thinking about her was impossible. An instant, full-blown erection made him shift in his seat, which woke him up just in time to stand and join in the cheer of what he could only hope was the final damn toast.

It was. Everyone around him hugged and said their adieus and made their French-equivalent promises to show up for work Monday *bright eyed and bushy tailed*. It was a good thing the weekend lay before them because they were going to have one hell of a collective hangover.

"Garrett!" Henri hurried from his table, and they clasped in a hug of camaraderie. *"C'est fini."*

"Oui, c'est fini, Henri." Garrett wasn't sure if they were discussing the campaign or the dinner, but he was thrilled both were done.

They hadn't chatted in days. Not since he and Tara had made their peace. A power outage Wednesday had sent Henri and his staff into panic mode and put them behind with the all-important reports everyone was expecting. And then Garrett and the marketing crew had gotten slammed. His friend was still unaware that Tara was watching Dylan, but tonight wasn't the time to bring it up. Henri would demand all the details.

"Veronique and Jean Luc will come to my house tomorrow." Henri's tired eyes brightened when he spoke of his youngest sister and her son. "Would you enjoy to come to dinner, also? The boys can play, and Dylan can stay the night, *peut-être?*"

Dylan would want to go. He and Jean Luc always had a great time together. But Garrett had really been looking forward to a dinner with Tara, and tomorrow night was the night he'd earmarked.

"Um, actually…you remember my American neighbor, Tara?"

Henri's chuckle was a low growl. *"Mais oui."*

"Well, Monique's father is in the hospital, and Tara has been keeping Dylan for me. I'd sort of promised her we'd make dinner for her tomorrow night. I owe it to her after all she's done this week."

Henri's face split into a wide grin. *"C'est parfait, Garrett. Prépare le dîner pour Tara.* Dylan will come to my house and stay for the night, and you will have the time alone."

Alone time with Tara, and Dylan nowhere around? Garrett's mouth went dry. Even the mention of it filled his head with all kinds of possibilities—dangerous thoughts involving the two of them naked and a treasure hunt where he would search her body for hidden tattoos. His head spun as all the blood in his torso headed southward.

Guilt took a swipe at him. "I've been away from Dylan a lot the past two weeks."

"Oui." Henri was always Dylan's champion. "But you will have the complete day together tomorrow. And Dylan will not want to miss the chance to have a sleepover with Jean Luc."

"That's true," Garrett admitted. But the chance for a sleepover with Tara was what he needed to get out of his mind. Maybe it would be better to go out to dinner? Give her a real night on the town to repay her for her help…

and avoid the risks that an intimate dinner on the terrace might lead to.

He clapped his friend on the back. "You're right, Henri. It's perfect. Dylan will be so excited. What time would you like him at your house?"

"I do not care, *mon ami*. But, if I were you, I would bring him as early as possible, *oui?* And allow him to stay late the next day, so you can *sleep*—" Henri half smiled and half leered at the young woman bussing the table "—for as long as you desire."

Garrett sucked a breath deep into his lungs. What he *desired* and what he *allowed* were two altogether different things.

He wouldn't even think of this as a date. This would be a nighttime sightseeing excursion with a friend.

And that was all.

FAITH COULDN'T STAND the pressure anymore.

What she was about to do would be a life-changing event for her and Sawyer, the kids, the church…maybe the whole town. But she couldn't bear one more second in this tortured hell of a life she'd been living for the past month.

This change was necessary. She'd tried suffering in silence. Remaining stoic. Facing the world with a calm demeanor and pretending everything was fine.

But everything wasn't fine, and her serene facade was crumbling. People were noticing her weight loss. Friends were whispering, speculating on illness. Cancer had been mentioned…and leukemia. Her mom had died of heart disease, so some people were betting on heredity.

If people were talking anyway, why not give them the truth to talk about?

She'd let a lie exist between her and Sawyer for twenty-eight years, and that lie had ended and come to light at long last. She refused to let another one take its place—at least, not for any longer.

All the lying ended today.

She grabbed a luggage handle with each hand and hauled the two pieces from the bedroom.

The door to Sawyer's study was closed. He always used Saturday morning to fine-tune his sermons.

The pot of coffee she'd heard him making a half hour before had barely a cup gone, and the paper sack of Ivadawn's cinnamon-glazed yeast doughnuts still bulged with its contents, a big grease mark soaking through the side.

The sights. The smells. Everything was as it had always been—and yet nothing was the same.

No doubt, Sawyer waited on the other side of the door for her knock—her bidding him to stop his studies a little while and share a cup of coffee and a doughnut.

Faith blinked, expecting tears, but she had none. She'd cried them all. Maybe that's where the weight had gone.

She pulled the luggage across the kitchen floor, the wheels making a racket on the tile. They beat out a *thunk-thunk* rhythm, squealing like piglets who'd been pushed off the hog's teat. She ignored their protest. She'd thought this through for days and had come to the conclusion that only a separation would give her any peace.

Being within touching distance of the man she loved yet not being allowed to touch him was a torture she could bear no longer.

She jockeyed the luggage through the door to the garage and popped the trunk with the button on the key fob. There were already a few items in there boxed up—just a few sentimental things from the kids that she wanted with her… homemade birthday cards and valentines…a few pictures.

She wasn't taking much.

She shuddered at the finality in the sound of the trunk slamming, closing her eyes and allowing the vibration to move through her and out.

"Faith?"

Her eyes flew open to find Sawyer standing in the doorway, his coffee cup poised chest high, a look of bewilderment on his face as if he'd forgotten where his mouth was.

"What are you doing?"

She stepped around the car to face him with nothing between them. "I'm leaving, Sawyer. I can't stand this. I was going to come back in—I wouldn't have left without saying goodbye."

"You're leaving?" His tone was the same one she'd heard when they got the call from the police about Tara's accident. "Where are you going?"

"To your mom's."

It was just across town—a few blocks away. The house was still fully furnished. They hadn't gotten rid of anything since Lacy died. It wasn't an ideal location. She'd still be smack-dab in the middle of the talk and the meddling. But it would give her a quiet space that wasn't a forced quiet, and it wouldn't cost their tight budget anything extra.

Sawyer's other hand came up to grip the coffee cup like he didn't trust the finger through the handle to hold the weight. "Faith, don't do this. Please don't do this." His normally calm voice shook with emotion. "I've counseled enough couples to know that people don't separate to work things out. People separate to start the process of living away from each other permanently."

She placed a trembling hand to her throat, feeling the steady pulse. Somehow she was living through this. "I don't know what I'm starting. I only know what I'm ending. The lie. I've had all I can take of the pussyfooting around town like everything's fine…pussyfooting around each other, trying to act like we're one thing when we both know we're something else entirely now. I don't know what that something else is, but I'm not getting any answers here. I need some alone time to sort things out for myself."

"I love you, Faith." His words sucked the air from her lungs. "I'm just having a hard time right now." He stepped into the garage, watching her closely like he did the deer in the backyard, afraid the wrong movement might send her scurrying.

She squared her shoulders to show him her leaving wasn't a fear-induced reaction. She'd thought it over for days and hadn't come to the decision lightly. "I know you are, Sawyer. And I'm so, so sorry for putting you through this. But what's done is done, and I can't take it back. But I also can't continue living in what feels like a perpetual state of punishment."

He leaned against his workbench, pushing some tools out of the way to clear a place for his cup. "I'm sorry. I don't mean to make you feel that way. I'm not trying to punish you." His hands thrust deeply into his pockets. "This isn't even about you. It's about me, and the lie I perpetuate week after week. Every Sunday I preach about love. How love is the answer to everything." He shrugged. "*I* love. And yet, my love isn't enough. I'm trying to figure out why." His hand came out of his pocket, balled into a fist that he rapped against his chest, punctuating his words. "I could understand if it had just been you. But it isn't enough for Tara, either. What am I missing? What do I need to change my message to? How do I lead people to the answer when *I* don't have the answer?"

Seeing him like this made her sick to her stomach. Sawyer—the rock…battered and broken into pebbles. "I don't have the answer, either. But this—" she wagged her finger between them "—isn't the way to find it. So I'm ready to try something else." She jerked the car door open.

Sawyer was there in two steps, holding the door to keep it open. "The whole town will know ten minutes after you get to Mom's. Maybe not even *that* long with Sue as your next-door neighbor."

The woman's name sent a surge through her. "You don't get it, Sawyer. I. Don't. Care. I *want* people to know. I'm tired of living a lie. I am who I am, and you and the town can try to pretend I'm someone else, but that doesn't make it so." She pressed the button on the key fob, and the garage door started grinding open.

"Then, let *me* go." Sawyer's eyes glistened with unshed tears. "You shouldn't have to be the one to leave when I'm the one with the problem."

Dear Lord! She was finally beginning to understand the depth of Sawyer's misery…and the mindset behind the impotence. She had to get out of there before the man broke completely. "I've thought this over, Sawyer. Stay. Leave. Do whatever you want. Just find your answers so we can start getting our lives back together."

"What about Tara? This will ruin her trip if she finds out."

"I thought about that, too." The past few nights, all she'd done was think, her mind wandering aimlessly, shifting directions like a rabbit being chased by a fox. But her focus always came back to Tara. "She's got enough on her plate over there. She doesn't need to be worrying about us, too. When I call Thea and Trent, I'll ask them not to say anything when they talk to her. I'll call Emma, too."

Faith climbed into the driver's seat and started the ignition. A small tug pulled the door from Sawyer's grasp, and he stepped out of the way.

She backed out of the driveway, leaving him standing there, a lost look on his face. With a push of the button, she lowered the garage door.

CHAPTER ELEVEN

THE EIFFEL TOWER was even more beautiful at night—an image in lacy, gold filigree, more stunning than any photo could possibly capture.

Tara just wanted to stand and drink it in.

"It's even better from over there. The Trocadéro." Garrett pointed to a crowded pavilion across the way. His hand found the small of her back, sending a delicious shiver up her spine. "But we'll have to hurry."

"Why? It doesn't appear to be going anywhere."

Garrett laughed and gave her a wink. "You'll see."

The wine served during the cruise had apparently worked some magic because Garrett had loosened up, at last. When he'd first picked her up, he'd been stiff and distant, treating this more like a guided tour than a date. Up until this moment, it was as if they'd reverted back to square one with the flirtation of the other night forgotten—at least, on his part. She, on the other hand, had been giving it all she had. That he'd finally touched her was encouraging.

The cruise had been beyond delightful. The views of Paris from the Seine with each movement of the boat bringing more opulence into view…the running commentary of fascinating tidbits told in the tour guide's sexy French-infused English…the undivided attention of the ruggedly handsome man sitting at her side. *Ooh-la-la!*

Now, walking toward the Trocadéro, she kept turning around, eyes constantly drawn back to the Eiffel Tower, half afraid it actually *might* disappear, the other half unwilling to miss a second of the view.

Garrett took her hand, causing the endorphins in her brain to break into a happy dance. Keeping her in tow, he threaded through the crowd, his urgency evident. She paused the questions and comments, keeping pace with his jog up the steps to the crowded top level of the pavilion, where they found an open space and fell against each other laughing and gasping.

"Whew!" Garrett checked his watch, then flung his arm around her shoulder and whirled around to face the landmark. A few seconds later, the Eiffel Tower erupted into a twinkling mass of brilliant white lights, diamonds encrusting the gold filigree—a royal brooch worn by the Queen of Cities.

"Oh, my gosh!" Tara squealed as the crowd shouted and broke into applause. Caught up in the excitement, she intertwined her fingers with the ones on her shoulder and tilted her head against the side of Garrett's face. "You're right. This *is* better." A blissful sigh accompanied her next breath.

"Told you."

She swiveled her head and watched the side of Garrett's mouth rise slowly in a lazy smile that oozed sexy. Her insides coiled with heat. "Don't give me that Mona Lisa smile, Garrett Hughes. I can't stand here gawking at you when I've got tourist business to take care of."

The twinkle in his eyes when he laughed made her even more reluctant to let go of his hand, but a video of the glistening tower to post on her Facebook page couldn't wait. Her heart skipped a beat, though, when she put her phone away, and his hand found hers again.

"C'mon." He bobbed his head in the direction of the landmark. "More good stuff awaits."

They wove their way through the crowd and back across the Seine via the Pont d'Iena, but the slower pace did nothing to calm her breathing. Garrett's sudden decision to stay in constant physical contact by holding her hand or resting an arm around her shoulders kept causing her breath to hitch. By the time they stood on the top level of the Eiffel Tower, she was dizzy with excitement and the effects of looking down from the thousand-foot height at the exquisite city below.

She closed her eyes for a moment and tried to recapture some calm. "I still can't believe I'm here, standing at the pinnacle of worldly sophistication. If Taylor's Grove could see me now…" She massaged her face, which ached from the smile she'd been wearing all night. When she opened her eyes, a lustrous golden dome caught her attention. "Ooh. What's that over yonder?"

"Yonder?" Garrett's deep laugh brought a flush of embarrassment to her face.

"Guess I haven't stood at the pinnacle long enough to absorb much of that sophistication, huh?"

"I wasn't making fun. That laugh was pure enjoyment. Hearing you say things like that brings home a lot closer." He pulled her around to face him, brushing a finger down her heated cheek. "I'd like to find a quiet place where I could close my eyes and just listen to you talk."

Oh, Lord! Heat moved through her again, having nothing to do with embarrassment. Were all guys in Paris hot? Or was it just something about being in this city? "Thanks," she murmured. "That was a nice thing to say." Over his shoulder, she could see the couple behind them locked in a kiss of romance novel quality.

So maybe it *was* the city.

Garrett leaned in so close she could feel his breath against her cheek. Was he about to kiss her? Her own breathing came to an abrupt halt.

Instead, he pointed. "The gold dome 'over yonder' is Hôtel des Invalides, Napoleon's tomb." His boyish grin, so much like Dylan's, said he was obviously pleased with the reference to their personal joke.

"*Hôtel des Invalides.*" She repeated the words, using her best French accent. Being short of breath made it sound even better. "Only the French language could make a tomb and a military museum sound so divine."

"It's pretty interesting, really." His eyes lit up. "We could go there tomorrow, if you'd like. Dylan loves it, and there's a tradition about touching the foot of the Mansart statue in the garden."

"I went one day last week although I think I missed the Mansart statue." Tara drooped her lip in a pretend pout and watched as Garrett's gaze moved to her mouth then back up slowly to tangle with her eyes. There was enough electricity in that look to keep the City of Lights in business for a while, but if he didn't kiss her soon, she was going to blow a breaker.

His eyes darkened. "Well, if you missed Mansart, we can't take any chances. There's another tradition we need to take advantage of right now." With a tilt of his head, he directed her gaze to the couple next to her, who were also enjoying a sensuous moment, oblivious to everyone around them. "Tradition says if you kiss on top of the Eiffel Tower, romance will forever spread out around you like the city below." He leaned toward her again, hesitating as if asking permission.

Tara answered him by meeting him halfway. Their lips touched, and she expected something short and chaste, but once her mouth settled on his, it felt so nice, she was in no hurry for it to end. Her hands found his waist and his hands found her back, and they relaxed against each other, warm and comfortable, yet pleasantly enticing. The kiss lasted much longer than she thought possible with no tongues involved.

She leaned back a little, meeting his gaze, but kept her hands where they were. Likewise, his stayed put. "I like this tradition," she said.

"Well, there's another one, too, you know."

She quirked an eyebrow. "You're making these up, aren't you?"

"Yeah." The side of his mouth rose in that yummy lop-sided grin.

"Well, tell me anyway."

Garrett cleared his throat. "If you kiss a second time, it means you'll come back."

"That's the Trevi Fountain in Rome. Surely you can be more imaginative than that."

"Okay, how about if you kiss a second time, your love will shine more brilliantly than the tower itself."

She pursed her lips, pretending to ponder it, and finally nodded. "Works for me."

His mouth covered hers again, but remained gentle even when she opened and met his tongue. There was no hurry... no urgency...just a long, languid kiss that left her knees weak and her lungs devoid of breath.

"You don't kiss like a girl from Taylor's Grove," Garrett whispered.

"Actually, I kiss *exactly* like a girl from Taylor's Grove," she whispered back. "We didn't have any movies, or teenage hangouts. The only thing to do was park by Kentucky Lake and make out until we got it down pat."

Garrett chuckled. "You did more than get it down pat. You perfected it."

Tara batted her eyes playfully at him. "I had more practice than everybody else. I was a virgin until I was twenty-three, so kissing was my forte."

A serious look settled on Garrett's face as he stepped back and took her hands. "That's a tidbit I never would've guessed. What other things am I going to learn about you that will surprise me?"

Her own recent surprise—the one that gave her a reason for being there—pricked her heart. "I'm still in the discovery stage myself." His brows buckled in question at her cryptic response, but she didn't give him a chance to ask whatever it was he was thinking. She was having too glorious a time at the moment to get into the subject of Jacques Martin. Instead, she pointed at the famous avenue in the distance with the arch at the end. "Champs-Élysées and Arc de Triomphe."

"Oui. L'avenue des Champs-Élysées et l'Arc de Triomphe," Garrett repeated in what sounded like perfect French to her no matter what Dylan said about his father's pronunciation.

She sighed. "You can take the girl out of Taylor's Grove, but you can't take Taylor's Grove out of the girl."

Garrett caught her chin with a finger and gently turned it toward him. "Don't *ever* lose the Taylor's Grove. It's pure gold." He touched his lips to hers again in the tenderest of kisses, and she gripped the railing tighter as her knees went weak.

Garrett pointed to the other side of the viewing deck. "Now, let's take a look over 'yonder.'"

They headed in the direction he'd indicated, not quite making it to the other side before Tara's cell phone rang. Her mom's name came up on the caller ID. "I need to take this. Do you mind?"

"You ask this of a single father?" He ran a finger down her arm. "Of course not."

Saturday night was an odd time for her mom to be calling. But then, it *was* two in the afternoon at home. She swiped the button to answer. "Hi, Mama."

"Hey, sweetpea. Just wanted to see what you're doing." Her mom's voice sounded tired. She'd probably been picking tomatoes from the garden. Or maybe canning, which was a job she hated.

"Actually, I'm having dinner with my neighbor Garrett."

"That's Dylan's father, isn't it?" The voice on the other end perked up a bit.

Tara winked at Garrett, who'd moved far enough away so as not to hear the conversation. "That's right. Dylan's spending the night with a friend, so Garrett's treating me to a night on the town. We've been on a Seine river cruise, and we watched the Eiffel Tower light up, which is the most gorgeous sight ever. I'm actually talking to you from the top of the tower right now."

"Oh! I'm sorry, sweetie. I—I didn't mean to interrupt your date. I'll, um, I'll let you go."

Tara's senses went on alert. Something wasn't right. She could hear it in the way her mom's voice strained and tightened all of a sudden—like she was trying to sound okay when she really wasn't. "What's wrong?"

There was a pause on the other end. "Nothing. I just haven't talked to you in a few days, and I wanted to see how you were doing."

Okay, so her mom was probably just worried about the Jacques Martin search. Tara didn't want to get into that. It might put a damper on what was turning out to be a fabulous night. "Well, I'm doing great." She threw an extra load of exuberance into her voice. "I've got lots to tell you, but it'll have to hold until sometime when I don't have somebody waiting for me. We're just about to head to dinner."

"Yes, I understand. I should let you go then."

Her mom's tone slipped into sad, and Tara's gut twisted. "Are you sure you're okay?"

"I'm fine. I'll talk to you tomorrow…or sometime soon."

Something unspoken niggled at Tara. "Wait, um, how's Dad?"

"He's…okay."

"Which means not great."

"He's still upset."

"But he sounded better when I talked to him yesterday." The last call from her dad had made her hopeful that everything at home was finally getting back to normal. At least, he talked about everyday things—the first tomatoes, the doe with triplets still in spots that had come into the backyard.

"It's me he's upset with. Not you." The voice on the other end of the line cracked. "I'm sorry. I'm calling from Grandma O'Malley's house, and it's just making me overly sentimental."

Ah! There it was. Mama was calling from Grandma's. She was finally going through things, deciding what to get rid of and what to keep. "Well, don't stay too long. No sense in working up a case of melancholy. All that stuff will still be there tomorrow and the next day and the day after that."

"Yeah, I don't know how long I'll be here…" Her mom's voice faded. "But, I'll let you go now. Enjoy your dinner."

Tara walked to where Garrett stood. "I will. Talk to you later."

"Bye, sweetpea. Love you."

"Love you, too. Bye." Tara blew out a long breath as she touched the button to end the call.

Garrett was watching her, concern hooding his deep-set eyes. "Is everything okay?"

She cocked her head and gave her brows and her shoulders a simultaneous shrug. "I wish I could say yes to that, but I'm not certain it'd be the truth."

"Why? What's going on?"

Tara chewed her lip, wondering how much to tell him. He'd been very forthcoming about his wife. And with Emma thousands of miles away, it would be nice to have someone to talk to. "I'll tell you all about it," she promised. "But not until after dinner."

"NOTRE-DAME IS GORGEOUS in the moonlight. So majestic." Tara's voice was full of wonder and awe—a pleasant, almost childlike quality that Garrett had noticed throughout their night out, beginning with the cruise. It had shifted his focus completely away from the platonic sightseeing tour he'd originally planned.

Attentive, appreciative and enthusiastic about everything he suggested, Tara had been the perfect date. It had been a long time since he'd spent time with a woman who had such a zeal for life, and it felt good. Damn good.

He'd gotten caught up in her enthusiasm, and somewhere between her dreamy sigh as the boat passed under Pont Neuf and her squeal as the Eiffel Tower shimmered to life, he'd thrown caution to the wind and allowed himself to think of this night as a date.

Now, with her back to him and his arms around her waist, she was snuggled against him with the breeze whipping her hair to the side, the moonlight glinting on that tattoo below her ear. This *all* felt pretty damn good.

"I was thinking the same thing about you," he answered, and she reached up and caressed his cheek in a gesture that, at that moment, seemed more intimate than a kiss.

He wasn't sure where the night was going to end, but it wouldn't be here on Pont Notre-Dame. Suddenly, he was anxious to get home. "You ready?" he murmured into her ear.

She nodded, breathing another of those dreamy sighs that made his breath catch, and slipped out of his arms, but only long enough to catch his hand. "Ready."

She was in such a good mood now, he hated to bring it up, but they still had the rest of the stroll home, and he was curious to know what had bothered her so much during the phone conversation at the Eiffel Tower. "When your mom called earlier, you seemed worried. Want to talk about it while we walk?"

"I suppose." She gave him a small smile. "Nothing could seem too bad when it's filtered by Paris in the early morning moonlight, right?"

Tara told her story with the same enthusiasm that infused everything she did, captivating him with her tale of a family torn apart by a secret over twenty-five-years old. Garrett could almost hear Grandma O'Malley's dishes breaking right along with the hearts of her family members. His own parents were still devoted to each other after thirty-seven years together, so putting himself in Tara's shoes made his gut twist. "This whole experience must be a nightmare for you." He pulled her against his side as they approached their building. "So how many of these Jacques Martins have you checked out so far?"

"Fourteen," she said dully, and the lack of inflection told Garrett just how much that answer bothered her.

"And you're just making cold house calls?"

She nodded. "My telephone French is even worse than my in-person French."

That made Garrett smile, but then an image of Tara walking naively into a seedy neighborhood popped into his mind and his grip on her shoulder tightened. "I don't want you doing that anymore. Paris is relatively safe to walk around in, but it's a city, and there are places you shouldn't be going—especially alone."

She shrugged. "I don't know how else to do it. I mean, if I do find him, and he doesn't want anything to do with me, at least I'll know what he looks like. I'll have that to—" her voice broke "—to keep with me."

Garrett glanced down and saw the hope glistening in her eyes. Tara was easy to read. She might be talking in terms of Jacques Martin not wanting anything to do with her, but her dreams lay in a different direction entirely.

She looked up at him, and her smile trembled. Beneath all that zest for life lay a fragile soul. Garrett was filled with several kinds of desire, but the most prominent at the moment was to protect her. He pulled her into his arms, kissing the top of her head. She melted against him, and he felt the warmth deep in his heart.

When he spoke his voice was huskier than he meant it to sound. "When we get to your flat, I want to see this list."

"ONE LAST GLASS OF WINE on the terrace?"

Tara kicked off her shoes as soon as they walked through her door.

Garrett's arms came around her from behind, and he kissed her neck. All of the touching tonight had put her senses on high alert, and this caress sent a shiver into all the right places.

"I was thinking champagne might be more appropriate," he answered.

She frowned. That did sound like the perfect ending to this date—or perhaps the second most perfect ending. "Sadly I don't have any champagne."

"I do, and my place is just a few yards away. I'll get it and some glasses. You get your list of addresses."

They met on the terrace a few minutes later, Garrett with an already-opened bottle of bubbly and two glasses, and Tara bearing her list of possible fathers.

Garrett held her chair for her and then pulled the other one close enough that their thighs touched when he sat. He lifted his glass. "To tonight." He gave her that half smile that made her toes curl.

"To tonight," she agreed, and took a sip. The bubbles tickled her nose, and left an effervescent trail from the tip of her tongue down the back of her throat and into her chest.

Garrett scooted her list over in front of him, and began talking to her about the addresses and making notes on where she would be safe to go alone and where she wouldn't.

"I won't be working so late this week, and I might even be able to take off a little early and go with you to these places." He'd put Xs by the four that were located in neighborhoods he didn't trust. "These two—" he pointed to one on rue Racine and one on rue de Condé "—are near the Luxembourg Gardens. Have you been there?"

She shook her head. "Not yet."

"The Sorbonne is in that area, and the Pantheon. That's where Foucault's pendulum is, which is really cool—Dylan loves it." He looked up from his list and peered closely at her. "You haven't been taking Dylan." It wasn't a question.

"No. I didn't think I should. What if there was a scene with one of the men?"

"But you've lost a lot of time this week, staying with him. Time you could've been using looking for your father."

"I've been able to get in about one place a day. And, if Monique gets back by Wednesday, I'll still have almost two weeks. I hope I don't have to go through all forty-three," she added.

Garrett pushed back in his chair with a disgusted sigh. "You should've said something earlier, Tara. You've made a huge sacrifice of your time."

"Being with Dylan isn't a sacrifice. Dylan's real and precious. Jacques Martin may not even still exist." The honesty in her words hit her hard, and she felt a tear slide down her cheek. "I may be looking for someone who has already passed away or somebody who won't want me even if I find him." A sob swelled in her throat, and she took a sip of champagne to wash it down. She would *not* allow this beautiful night to be marred by an emotional melt-down of any sort.

Garrett's hand cupped her chin, and he turned her face toward him. "I can't imagine anyone who has met you not wanting you."

He pressed his lips to hers gently, but it was like he'd touched her with a branding iron. She'd never experienced sizzle from a kiss like she did in that moment.

Her hand crept to the back of his neck and she pressed him closer, opening her mouth to the exploration of his tongue. She heard the subtle groan in the back of his throat as he breathed more fire into the embrace.

His arm slid around her waist, and he stood, pulling her with him and against him until the only separation of their bodies lay in the thin fabric of their clothing. She could feel his desire, and she rubbed her palms against his back to fan the flame higher. All the while he kept possession of her mouth in a kiss that made all the others of her life seem like child's play.

She knew without a doubt what she wanted, and she pulled her mouth away long enough to make her feelings known.

"Make love to me, Garrett."

She didn't have to ask twice.

In an instant, he'd bent down to brace an arm under her knees, and he lifted her as easily as he might lift a child. "Grab the list. Just leave the bottle and the glasses," he instructed, leaning her near enough to the table for her to grab her papers.

"Do you have condoms?" he asked, and she shook her head in response.

He inclined his head toward his flat. "Then my place it is."

He strode across the terrace with her in his arms, and she could almost understand what made ladies of yesteryear swoon. If she'd ever played out a scene that was swoon-worthy, this was it. Her heart was beating a strong cadence against her chest, making her wonder if he could feel it.

Between the two of them, they managed to maneuver the doorways without too much distraction, and soon he was laying her on his bed and placing the list on the bed-side table.

He sat, his weight pressing the mattress down and rolling her to her side. "Now, it's *my* turn." The back of his fingers brushed lightly across the fabric covering her breast, bringing immediate heat to the area…and others, as well.

She made an effort to give her voice full volume, but it came out as a whisper, heavy with desire. "To do what?"

His eyes held that mischievous twinkle, and he grinned. "To finally see *you* naked."

CHAPTER TWELVE

IT HAD BEEN A WHILE SINCE he'd undressed a woman—even longer since the woman had been as tall and lean as Tara—and Garrett wanted to prolong the experience as much as desire would allow.

He stretched out beside her on the bed, and immediately her hands began to unbutton his shirt. He grasped them gently and shook his head. "I'm glad you're eager, but I've fantasized about exploring your body and its tattoos for days. Can I have a little fun before we get to the serious stuff?"

"Ooh." Tara's eyes lit up. "You want to do some body geocaching?"

"Exactly. How many, um, caches, can I expect to find?"

She held up her left hand, fingers spread. "Five."

He took her hand and brushed his tongue across the tips of her fingers. "This will be my cache finder. Now, you have to lie still, and you can't give me any hints. Understood?"

She nodded and lay back against his pillow, arms at her side and eyes closed. Her hair spread out like a flower in bloom around her. Even the blue tips, which he'd found so strange in the beginning, now enhanced the effect, adding depth to the overall appeal of the woman.

He brushed back a lock that curled around her neck and bent his head to the mark below her ear that had kept him mesmerized for long periods of time in his daydreams.

With the tip of his tongue, he traced the pattern, feeling her responsive shiver at his touch.

The tattoo was an intricate triple spiral that he'd seen before but had never thought much about. "What does this one mean?" His tongue flicked lightly around one of the loops.

"It's the Celtic symbol for life, death and rebirth. Oh! That feels really nice." She wriggled beneath him. "I got it after my grandmother died. Ironically, she turned out not to be my biological grandmother, and I'm not even Irish—"

He cut off her speech with a kiss. "Shh."

She grinned, and he went back to tracing the tattoo slowly with his finger and then his tongue.

He allowed his tongue to wander to her earlobe, nibbling there for a while before moving on to the rim of her ear and the delicate skin behind it. She threaded her fingers through his hair and pressed him closer, her breath coming in pants with an occasional moan of pleasure. The erotic sounds urged him to hurry, but he reined his body in.

Her breath caught as he fingered the first button on the front of her pale blue dress and slid it through the hole. A small V appeared in the square neckline of the dress and deepened as each button gave way, each punctuated by a small gasp.

The third button confirmed what he'd already suspected—she wore no bra—and deep within the area between her breasts, a delicate green stem appeared. Two more buttons and he was able to lay the bodice open. He stopped for a moment to take in the sight.

Her breasts were small, but beautifully shaped with perky nipples, drawn tight with excitement. Below the right breast was a small daisy with a bright yellow center and white petals. Its stem wound across her torso from one side of her rib cage to the other.

"Number two." Garrett bent his head to trace the flower with his tongue, but the nipple was too enticing. He sucked it quickly into his mouth, and was rewarded with an appreciative squeal that lowered into a moan as Tara's back arched off the bed. He flicked his tongue on the very tip, then made a wet path to the daisy and around its many petals. "What's this one mean?" he asked, as he started across the stem.

"My deflowering. Giving up…my virginity at…at…oh!" Her words came in spurts, and Garrett watched her fist the sheet into her half hand. "Twenty-three…petals. Ah!"

As his tongue continued its journey, Garrett opened three more buttons to reveal a lace thong that matched the color of the dress. The vision shot directly to his groin and he hurried to undo the final buttons and lay the dress completely open.

Tara's pale body speckled with freckles against the blue material…with the delicate daisy and the wisp of blue lace…was worthy of the Louvre. A few small scars that he guessed were from her spleen removal were still visible, but they added an element of danger that spoke of her genuineness. When he sat back to look at her, she propped herself up on her elbows, arched her back in a languid pose and let her head drop back. The straps of the dress slid down her arms in slow motion, and Garrett's heartbeat accelerated.

To hell with the tattoo hunt. He wanted her. Now.

He hooked a thumb into the lace and tugged as she lifted her hips. The lace slid down her legs, exposing a small pink heart on her flat stomach, two inches above the top of her left thigh.

She gave him a coquettish grin. "That one's just for fun. Sort of a reward for getting this far, you know?"

"I think I'm ready to capture the prize." He stood up and pulled his shirt over his head.

"You're giving up mighty quickly." She punctuated the challenge in her voice with a raised eyebrow.

Garrett unfastened his belt and trousers, shucking them, his briefs and his socks in one fluid movement. "I'm not giving up. I just think it may be time to probe deeper into this mystery." He climbed into the bed, sheathing himself as quickly as his eager fingers would allow.

Tara reached out and brushed the back of her finger across his lips. "Will you use the same instrument you've been using?"

"I'll start with that one." He tried to sound official, but he couldn't hold back the grin that twitched his mouth. "But then I'll probably have to switch to something larger and more sensitive."

She gave a delighted laugh and opened her arms wide to greet him.

He met her embrace, rolling on top of her, covering her neck and shoulders with kisses, then sliding down to torture her time after time until she was wild with need.

She responded in kind, placing kisses, nips and licks on any part of his body that ventured near her mouth. Her touch burned through him like a set fuse. At last, she wrapped her legs around him, locking him into position, and if he'd had any thoughts of lingering, they were lost in a haze of lust.

He slid into her exquisite tightness, catching her erotic gasp on his tongue. Her fingernails scraped along his back as she met his thrusts, curving into him as her back arched higher.

He reached the edge but backed off, refusing to make the plunge without her.

"No!" She ground out the words through clenched teeth. "Don't…slow…oh! Oh, Garrett!" Her legs, her arms, her hands—it was as though every muscle in her body tightened its hold on him, taking control, throwing him over the precipice to join her in the free fall.

Time stopped, and they floated in midair, riding the currents up and down until they once again touched solid ground.

He collapsed on top of her but worried that his weight might be too much, so he rolled off, gathering her to him.

They each took a deep breath, and the single syllable exploded from both of their mouths simultaneously.

"Wow!"

TARA WOKE TO THE BRIGHT morning sun warming her front and Garrett's warm body spooning her from behind. His arm snuggled around her waist, holding her close and secure. She closed her eyes and listened to his slow, deep breathing, reliving the night before.

Garrett Hughes was the stuff of dreams. That he'd planned the perfect date for her spoke volumes, but nothing could compare to his lovemaking. It was as if he could read her mind, recognize all the subtleties and nuances of her movements and breaths. Time after time he'd brought her to climax, and even when he'd finally driven home, he'd held back until he was sure she would make it one last time with him.

She'd never had anyone like him, and—a lump formed in her throat—after she returned home, she might never again.

But she had last night…and hopefully there would be several more repeat performances before she returned to the States.

She sighed and an involuntary tremble of emotion shook her. Garrett's arm tightened around her, pulling her closer. "You cold?" His breath caught the back of her ear, making her shiver again.

"No. It's just my body's reaction to the nearness of you." She turned a little, so that her head rested against his cheek.

"Mmm. That's nice." She sensed his smile although she couldn't see his mouth. "Last night was pretty special."

A contented sigh escaped from her lungs as she nodded. "Yeah. It was."

Garrett raised himself up on an elbow, and the loss of his embrace rolled her onto her back. He caught her gaze and held it, brought her hand to his lips and placed a tender kiss to the palm. "I don't think I've ever enjoyed myself so much with anyone else. It was…fun…and hot…and—"

"Ooh-la-la?"

He chuckled. "Your French has certainly improved."

She cupped his cheek with her hand, brushing the thick growth of stubble with her thumb, then moved it over to brush the scar that cut through the top of his lip. "Did you get spiked here, too?" She hoped not. His tale of his thigh getting ripped open by a kid sliding into third base with metal spikes made her cringe, but she didn't even want to think about that happening to something as sweet as his lips.

He shook his head. "A memento from Angie. We were walking in our neighborhood late one night, and she ran over and climbed on our neighbor's trampoline and started jumping really high. I was sure she was going to break her neck, so I climbed on to get her off, and when I got hold of her, she head-butted me." He pointed to his front tooth and ran his finger along the next one beside it. "Lost two teeth, as well."

Little by little, Tara was piecing together the nightmare his life with Angie must've been, and it made her admire his strength and resilience all the more. "I'll kiss the boo-boo." She softly pressed her lips to the spot.

Garrett's hand traveled to the small of her back and caressed the site of her largest tattoo. "Tolkien's initials, eh? I knew something was there. I just couldn't make it out through that wet dress you had on when we first met."

She squeezed her eyes closed, feeling the heat creep into her face. "What a way to meet! I was soaked and frustrated, and you're standing there naked—"

"Trying to figure out if I could subdue you by throwing my towel over your head."

They laughed together, and then they laughed harder as the memory of the ludicrous situation loomed larger in their minds. She collapsed on top of him, and he rolled her onto her back and started kissing—and laughing—his way down to the tattoo of the small chain that circled her ankle—"a reminder to not be chained down by other people's ideas of who I should be," she had explained.

His finger and thumb encircled her ankle, adding a third dimension to the tattoo, and he gave a tug, parting her legs slightly. His lips began a steamy line of kisses that traveled up her calf.

"Oh, yeah." She wiggled her butt deeper into the bedclothes.

"I think I know the real meaning behind this tattoo." He tightened his grip on her ankle, and gave her that lopsided grin that made her insides melt.

"And what would that be?"

"I think…" He continued the line of kisses up the inside of her thigh. "I think you are…a slave…to your desires."

The next set of kisses continued upward, convincing her he was probably right.

CHAPTER THIRTEEN

GARRETT GAVE TARA A small tour as they hurried toward Henri's, pointing out some of the more interesting sites in this part of the city.

After surprising her with breakfast in bed—complete with chocolate croissants, an omelet extraordinaire, sausages and pureed strawberries mixed with champagne—Garrett had surprised her, and himself, even more by suggesting she go with him to pick up Dylan. One of her Jacques Martin addresses wasn't too far from Henri's house, and on the way home, they could go by another Jacques Martin address on île Saint-Louis.

He didn't want his time with her to end yet—and she didn't seem in a hurry to leave.

Though she'd confessed that meeting his best friend coupled with the prospect of meeting her birth father made her slightly queasy, not even that double whammy caused her to back down.

She'd returned to his apartment in the now-infamous yellow sundress, which was smart on her, and Garrett was proud to have her on his arm. So proud, in fact, that they'd gotten a later start than he'd hoped because he'd had an overwhelming desire to remove it.

Once they reached their destination, he guided her up the sidewalk to Henri's door, which flew open while he was still in the process of knocking.

"Hi, Dad." Dylan's eyes widened along with his grin. "Tara!" He rushed out to greet the surprise visitor with a hug, and Garrett's heart was divided. His son was thrilled to see Tara, and she him, but the affection they already shared wasn't going to make her goodbye easy for any of them.

Garrett shoved the thought from his mind. One bridge at a time. The one he'd crossed last night had landed him in Wonderland, and he would stay there as long as possible.

"Garrett? Entre, entre!" Henri's voice came from somewhere deeper inside the house.

Jean Luc and Veronique showed up close on Dylan's heels, both of them excited to see Garrett again, so he wasn't quite through the introductions when Henri entered the room.

His friend took one look at Tara—not a quick look, but a bold, head-to-toe-and-back ogle that made Garrett want to punch him in his handsome face—and immediately transformed into the sexy, suave Frenchman women flung themselves at. He stepped toward her, hand extended. *"Bonjour, Tara. Bienvenue chez moi."*

Garrett's hand instinctively went to the small of her back to stake his claim, but he reminded himself that he didn't have a claim on this woman—she was a free spirit who would be going away soon, disappearing out of their lives as suddenly as she'd popped in. He dropped his arm back to his side.

Tara gave Henri's hand a brisk shake. "Thank you, Henri. It's nice to meet you." As soon as she pulled her hand free, she caught Garrett's arm and latched on to the crook of his elbow.

Henri's eyes followed the movement, and his smile softened into a look of genuine affection. Then he shifted his gaze to Garrett and gave him a brotherly pat on the shoulder. "Can you stay? The boys help Veronique plant the lettuce."

"Please, Dad?" Dylan was always reluctant to leave any place where he was having fun.

Garrett was aware how anxious Tara was to check out

the two addresses they had, but he wanted Henri to spend a little time with her, too. "Okay." He nodded. "But only for a few minutes."

"It will only take a few minutes, and I will try to keep him clean," Veronique assured them with a smile as she followed the two boys outside.

Henri led Garrett and Tara into his living room with its low-slung, ultramodern furniture, which Garrett detested. The Italian leather in white and gray tones reminded him of a lounge that might be frequented by the storm troopers from *Star Wars*.

Their host indicated they were assigned to the love seat, throwing a wink Garrett's way while Tara was getting settled. It was a small piece with abrupt ends and no arm rests, and two people sitting on it made for cozy conditions.

Garrett started to protest, but they weren't staying long...and Tara's thigh pressed tightly against his was nice.

"Do you enjoy Paris, Tara?" Henri asked.

"Yes. Very much." She shot Garrett a grin that would've seemed innocent if she could've controlled the blush that crept into her cheeks. "It's a beautiful city. Photos can't do it justice."

"What sights have you seen?" Henri settled into his favorite chair that looked to Garrett like a giant check mark.

Tara started naming off the places she'd visited, and Garrett watched Henri's face tighten with concentration.

"You have the beautiful accent, but I am sorry that I do not understand all you say."

Tara laughed. "I've been encountering the same thing for two weeks now."

Garrett could tell that Henri hadn't picked up all of that, either, but it didn't seem to matter. His friend liked Tara, and he was glad for that. And if Tara felt uncomfortable, she didn't show it. She had a manner about her that put people at ease. Now it seemed silly that he'd gone out of his way to avoid being around her.

"Do you happen to know anyone around here named Jacques Martin?"

Tara's question startled Garrett, and he shifted in his seat. She turned to him and shrugged. "I figured I could just ask Henri about the address that's close by. It might save us some time."

"Tara is in Paris looking for someone," Garrett explained to the unspoken question in Henri's eyes.

"My birth father," she added. "I just found out about him, and I came to Paris to try to meet him. His name is Jacques Martin."

Garrett translated what Tara said into French, along with an abbreviated version of Tara's story, and how she'd been going to addresses she'd generated from the phone book and the internet.

When he finished, Henri shifted his attention back to Tara. "The world, she is small. *Oui,* I know of the Jacques Martin who lives near. But he is not of the age to be your father." His words were slow and distinct and edged with a tenderness Garrett had heard often when they spoke of Angie…or Dylan. "He is *peut-être* thirty or thirty-five."

Tara's shoulders had visibly stiffened with Henri's declaration that he knew such a man. Now they sank…and slumped…and Garrett's heart sank with them. He saw her lip tremble slightly before she caught it between her teeth, but she gathered her composure quickly. "Well, thank you anyway, Henri." She looked at Garrett and let out a deep breath. "Another one bites the dust, huh?"

Reflexively, his arm looped around her shoulder and gave it a squeeze. "That will just give us more time to spend looking for the right one."

She nodded and gave a tight smile that he sensed covered a flood of disappointment. She was strong, this one. And though she didn't need his arm anymore for physical or moral support, he left it around her anyway.

TARA AND GARRETT ROUNDED a corner and emerged from the cool shadow of a building into the bright sunlight. Dylan had been walking between them, holding both of their hands, but now he ran ahead to look into the window of a shop with a kite hanging outside. Despite the heat, Garrett tucked Tara's hand under his arm as they walked, bringing her right side into a contact that felt much more intimate than he probably meant it to. She realized with a smile that her body was still stuck on some kind of thrill mode from last night.

She'd had an adequate six hours of sleep, dozing off around four, a full hour after Garrett's soft snores started. But his kisses had flavored her dreams, and she'd woken to find his desire still raging. Then there had been break-fast and the visit with Henri. Hours had passed, yet she re-mained suffused with an excitement that made the events of last night seem only moments ago.

Now Garrett's hand casually caressed hers as if it had always been there, and they were heading to rue Dante, an address that housed a map shop owned by a Jacques Martin.

"Have you thought about what you'll say to your father when we find him?" Garrett shot her a sidelong glance as he maneuvered the two of them down the narrow sidewalk, all the while, keeping an eye on his son.

"I've gone over the scene in my head almost nonstop, but it plays out differently each time, depending on his re-action. I'll just play it by ear." Her cell phone rang before he had a chance to respond. "Hello?" she answered.

"Hey, lovebug."

The nickname brought a smile to her lips. "Hi, Dad. This is a surprise."

"Yeah, I haven't talked to you in a few days. Is, uh, ev-erything going okay over there?"

Worry tinged his tone. Was it related to this quest for her birth father, or was something else bothering him?

"Everything's wonderful. I'm having a great time."

"That's good. Thea said your neighbor is showing you the sights?"

So her mom had told Thea, but hadn't said anything to her dad. That meant Mama had figured out it was a bona fide date.

She didn't want her dad to get the wrong idea about Garrett—or maybe the right one—and she felt weird talking about him in front of him. She chose her words carefully. "Yeah, that's right. I'm taking in all the tourist attractions. In fact, my neighbor Garrett and his son and I are on Île Saint-Louis right now. We're going to visit Notre-Dame and Sainte-Chapelle this afternoon." She didn't mention their first destination on the island.

"Sounds like you have good neighbors."

She could almost hear her dad's inner voice convincing him this guy was just being neighborly. Taking her under his wings, which, of course, in her dad's point-of-view, would have to belong to angels.

"The best," she agreed.

"Well, I just wanted to hear your voice."

"And?" She laughed.

"And you sound like you're having the time of your life."

"I am, Dad."

"I'll let you go then. Love you, lovebug."

"Love you, Dad." She slid the phone into her pocket as Garrett and Dylan stopped in the middle of the block.

Garrett pointed to a small shop across the street. "That's the address."

This could be it. She swallowed and nodded. The sweet phone conversation that had brought home and Dad so close was suddenly replaced by what felt like an unknown, scary universe only a few yards away.

Garrett dropped her arm but held her hand as she stepped into the street, anchoring her to this side of the abyss.

"Are you sure you want to do this, Tara?" He spoke

low, like he might give away a secret if he raised his voice. Dylan held his other hand, but the child's attention was farther down the street.

She looked hard into his eyes. "I'm sure."

"Why?"

"Why?"

"You love your dad. I hear it in your voice. And he loves you. What will it do to *him* if you find the man who conceived you?" He leaned in and lowered his voice to a whisper. "And that's all he did, Tara. He merely deposited some sperm."

His last sentence jolted her, considering he'd done the same thing with her a few hours ago. Though, hopefully, the condoms caught all the frisky creatures. But was this his way of reminding her that one-night stands were no big deal?

She jerked her hand from his. "This isn't about my dad." His question was the same one her parents had asked her over and over when she started planning this trip. How many times would she have to explain her actions? "It's about me—about who I am. I need to know my true roots. Is that so difficult to understand?" Maybe it was to someone who'd always known who he was. "I always thought I knew who I was, but there's a half of me I know nothing about. I'm not trying to hurt anybody. I'm simply trying to know myself better."

Garrett gave a resolute nod, grabbed her hand again and tucked her arm under his, close to his side once more. "Then come on. Let's do this."

"Are we going to Berthillon, Dad?" Dylan tugged his father's hand and pointed.

Garrett stooped, not letting go of either hand. "We'll go a little later. But first, we're going to go in that shop over there. Tara is looking for someone."

"Like a geocache? But with people?" The child held

up the plastic ring from the canister they'd located a half
hour before.

"Just like that," Garrett agreed, and the thought that she
might be on the verge of finding a treasure made Tara's
heart race.

The three of them marched across the street to the door
beneath the engraved copper sign, which was worn to a
weathered green patina.

Garrett opened it and stood back for Tara to enter first.

An elderly gentleman rose to greet them from behind a
desk covered with neat stacks of paper weighted down by
miscellaneous items that included a jewel-encrusted sword
hilt and a marble ashtray in the shape of Italy.

*"Bonjour, monsieur. Je cherche Monsieur Jacques Mar-
tin."* The words she had practiced so often fell from Tara's
tongue.

"C'est moi. Je suis Jacques Martin."

Tara understood his answer—she'd heard it several
times before—and her heart sank with disappointment.
This gentleman had to be in his seventies, or eighties even.

"Parlez-vous anglais?" she asked.

The old man shook his head. *"Non."*

An uncomfortable silence hung in the air between them
as he waited for her to speak, curiosity plain in his eyes…
and maybe a hint of fear.

She wasn't sure what to do next. She couldn't just leave.
He deserved an explanation that she couldn't give him in
French. She turned to Garrett for help.

At just a glance from her, he picked up the conversation,
explaining their reason for being there. Tara watched the
transformation in the man's face as he gained understanding of their mission.

When Garrett asked if he knew any other Jacques Martins who might fit their criteria, the old man shook his
head, turning sympathetic eyes to Tara. *"Je suis désolé,
mademoiselle."*

Tara forced a half smile. *"Merci beaucoup."*

The gentleman said something else and Tara looked to Garrett for a translation, but it was Dylan who spoke up. "He said he wishes you were his daughter. It would be very nice to have a beautiful daughter like you." The child's arm went around her leg for a quick hug.

She blinked back the tears that stung her eyes. "Thank you." She ruffled Dylan's hair and nodded to the old gentleman. "That's very kind."

When she found her birth father—and that was the only possibility she was going to consider—she hoped his sentiments would be the same.

As they said their adieus, the old man squeezed her hand and said something.

"He said good luck," Dylan told her.

Back outside the shop, Garrett let go of Dylan's hand and nodded, and the child took off at a run. Garrett's arm slid around her shoulder with a comforting hug as they followed in his son's wake. "Don't be sad, okay? You still have a lot of Jacques Martins on your list."

"I know." Her breath left her in a huff. "I told myself this wasn't going to be easy, but it's hard to not get my hopes up. Every time I find one, I'm positive it's him."

Garrett leaned into her as they walked. "And I'll be here if it's not," he whispered. "Every time."

His breath caught on the rim of her ear and feathered down her neck, causing an unexpected shiver that slithered down her spine and coiled deep within her belly. A low chuckle confirmed he felt her response and had known what it would be. "I know what you need."

Fueled by the frustration of another false lead, irritation flickered inside Tara at Garrett's words—and the smugness behind them. Men's minds were like boomerangs that always came back to the same thing. "Not everything can be fixed by great sex," she pouted.

His eyes opened wide in surprise and then softened

with a playful glint as he nodded toward the storefront they were approaching and where Dylan was already waiting. "I thought maybe something from here would lift your spirits. Berthillon. World's best."

Her eyes followed his nod, her face heating at the conclusion she'd jumped to. "Ice cream!" She gave an embarrassed laugh. "Sorry."

"Never apologize when you've used *great* to describe it." The corner of his mouth twitched before it broke into one of his dazzling smiles. "But maybe this will cool you off." When he opened the door to the shop, the chilly air from inside did exactly that.

Sweetness hung in that same air as they entered, and Tara could taste the sugar on her tongue just from sniffing. Her mouth watered in anticipation as she looked over the list of flavors *du jour*.

"What would you like?" Garrett asked.

"A cup of strawberry," Dylan announced.

Despite the many choices, Tara's mind stalled on the sixth one down. "One scoop of cappuccino chocolate chip on a cone, please."

"My favorite." Garrett shifted his smile toward the young woman behind the counter, words flowing so smoothly from his lips that Tara could almost imagine them having their own flavor named after them.

The woman's eyes drifted lazily down Garrett as she leaned forward in open flirtation. The woman saw something she liked, and she put her message out there without hesitation.

Thea was like that.

Since birth, Tara's sister had dared the world to try to stick the *preacher's kid* label on her while Tara had tried to live up to the expectation—until she was twenty-three. The irony that Thea was the preacher's kid by blood while *she* was the bastard child squeezed at her again.

If she found her birth father, it would be news she'd

want to share. But how would that news go over in Taylor's Grove?

Garrett's low chuckle drew Tara out of her reverie. The woman behind the counter had evidently said something that tickled his fancy.

"She said she likes your tattoo." He handed Tara the cone. "And I said I do, too."

Tara didn't recognize the emotion that had flared briefly as jealousy until his words transformed it into butterflies in her stomach. "Thanks." She tipped the cone in his direction.

He grinned. *"Je t'en prie."*

He paused, and she realized he was waiting for her to take her first bite. When she did, the silky texture spread a burst of coffee flavor across her tongue, and she let out a groan of pure pleasure.

A lazy smile touched his lips. "I like that sound." He took a bite and tilted his head toward the door, calling to his son. "Come on, Dylan. Let's go back down by the river."

Dylan dropped another spoonful of sprinkles into his cup and ran to join them.

As they walked along the Seine, eating their ice cream and enjoying the shade from the hazelnut trees, Notre-Dame came into view—majestic and serene. They approached Pont Saint-Louis, which connected Île de la Cité with the small island they were on, and Tara pulled out her camera.

"Here. Let me get one of you." Garrett took the camera from her and handed her his cone. Using mostly hand gestures, he positioned her with her elbow on the wall of the bridge and Notre-Dame in the background, and took quite a few shots, moving farther away each time. In between, she gave quick licks to the ice cream, which threatened to melt all over her hands. Satisfied at last, Garrett returned to her, laughing as she took a huge swipe with her tongue on both cones. He slipped the camera back into her purse and zipped it closed.

"Dad, can I go over there and watch the puppet show?" Dylan pointed to a knot of children sitting on the lawn of the cathedral in front of a portable puppet stage. Their giggles and claps infused the air with happy sounds.

"Sure, sport. We'll be right here."

Tara and Garrett stepped off the bridge and moved to the side behind the group of kids.

Tara held Garrett's cone out to him, but he dropped his gaze to her mouth and paused. "You have chocolate on your lip."

As her tongue made a quick jaunt around her lips, he leaned down and caught it with his mouth, capturing and muting her startled gasp. Her grip tightened around the cones she still clutched in each hand. She became aware of his erection forming against her front and the stone wall against her back. Whoever made being between a rock and a hard place synonymous with trouble had never been kissed by Garrett in Paris.

The tender kiss made her brain go all fuzzy.

"Did you get it?" she asked.

"Did I get what?"

"The chocolate."

He laughed. "Yep. All gone." He took his cone from her. "Now I have a much sweeter taste in my mouth."

The kiss and the fire she'd felt in Garrett's touch brought heat to her lips. She cooled them by burying them deep in the ice cream and threw a worried glance in Dylan's direction, finding his attention glued to the puppet show. "What if Dylan had seen?"

Garrett took a lick from his cone, seeming to weigh his words. "He's seen me kiss people in the past, and he's never been traumatized by it."

"Well, yeah, of course. But we don't want him to get

the wrong idea that this is anything serious...like with you and your tutor."

"Yeah. You're right." He turned away to lean his back against the wall, and she felt the distancing in the move—both mental and physical.

Well, they'd had their night together...and their morning...and their afternoon. Twenty-four hours of romance was more than she'd ever expected on this trip. She should be grateful and satisfied that she had that to remember.

But Garrett's nearness made her feel hot and needy... and anything but satisfied.

When she took her next bite, the ice cream hung on the back of her tongue, making her shiver and causing a moment of excruciating brain freeze.

She remembered the admonishment her dad would give her when she did the same thing as a little girl.

"Don't bite off more than you can handle," he would say.

Now that she'd made love to Garrett, she knew exactly what her dad meant...though this time it had nothing to do with ice cream.

CHAPTER FOURTEEN

IT WAS 9:25 A.M. ON SUNDAY, and Faith was still in her pajamas. She couldn't remember the last time that had happened.

If ever.

Oh, she'd stayed home with the kids when they were sick, but she always gotten dressed, even if that just meant slipping on jeans and a T-shirt. When *she* was sick, getting dressed was a must because *her* being under the weather always brought the women with their casserole dishes. It wouldn't do for them to stop by unexpectedly and catch her in a robe. That would be snickered at in the community for three to five days, depending on what other gossip popped up in the meantime.

Sawyer was at church by now. What was he telling people? No one had paid any attention yesterday that she was at her mother-in-law's. It was commonplace for her or Sawyer or the kids to be running in and out. And she'd gone to their cabin on Kentucky Lake for the better part of the day. That's where she'd called the kids from. The situation didn't seem so dire when she sat on the dock, watching the sunset on the water.

It occurred to her that she should move in there rather than Lacy's, but that would leave Sawyer to face the community alone, and that hardly seemed fair since he was the innocent in all of this.

The Marsdens' house next door was dark when she'd returned. With any luck, they were out of town. But she hadn't heard anything about their being gone, so that was unlikely.

Still she could hope.

She took her coffee cup and wandered aimlessly around the house until she found herself on the screened-in back porch. The forsythia and spirea bushes, tall and gangly and in bad need of pruning, had formed a privacy hedge around the backyard. Lacy had said it amounted to laziness, but Faith always suspected it gave much-needed privacy from her neighbor's eagle eye…and serpent tongue.

Lacy's roses and hydrangeas were in full bloom, a living canvas of color, and the swing was usually the perfect place to enjoy the sight and scents, but she was too restless. She could, however, cut some of the blooms and bring the divine scent indoors. Maybe it would be good aromatherapy.

She pushed the door open and descended the steps, letting the spring slam it back.

Sawyer's beloved bass boat, a treasured inheritance from his dad, sat under the carport, covered and untouched since this ordeal started, despite her husband's passion for the sport. His best sermons usually contained some fishing stories. The day would come—soon, she hoped—when he'd hook the boat up and head for the lake. That would be her sign that healing had begun.

The dewy grass squished between her toes as she padded barefoot to the potting shed. Packets of unopened seeds lay in a pile on the potting bench next to the gloves and a hand trowel, placed there by hands that had expected to come back for them.

Well, hands were back—just not the same ones these items were waiting for.

Faith picked up the seeds and the tools and stalked out of the potting shed with a purpose. She was an action person. And until a better action came to her, this would do.

She dropped to her knees in the dirt, ramming her hand into one of the gloves with determination. Something squished in the tip of one of the fingers, wringing a startled cry from her tight throat.

She jerked the glove off and shook it. A black spider with long, crumpled legs fell out. It was dead, but she was terrified of the creatures and looking at it still raised goose bumps on her arms. Then her eyes caught the red hourglass shape on its back, bringing her to her feet with a squeal of horror. A black widow! "Eww!"

"Who's there?" a sharp voice demanded from the other side of the hedge.

Sue! Another black widow would've been preferable. Faith's flight-or-fight instinct kicked in, and she looked around wildly for a means of escape.

"Who's there, I said? Answer me, whoever you are, or I'm calling the sheriff."

A flush of heat spread through Faith, but with it came an awareness of the cool dirt beneath her feet, which were firmly planted in a yard that belonged to her and her family.

Fight it would be.

"Don't be alarmed, Sue. It's me. A spider scared me."

"Faith?"

She shouldn't have been surprised, considering who she was speaking with. Nevertheless, Faith was startled to see a pair of arms snaking through the middle of the thick bushes, pushing them aside, and leaving her completely exposed to her neighbor's gawk.

"What in the world are you doing here at nine forty-five on Sunday morning…in your pajamas? Why aren't you at Sunday School?"

"Why aren't *you* at Sunday School?" Oh, *that* was sure the perfect, snappy comeback.

"I'm not feeling well." Sue sniffed as if she needed to add evidence. A sneeze followed, which couldn't have been faked.

It ran through Faith's thoughts that she could beg off the same way. She could say she wasn't feeling well, which was actually the truth, and had come to Lacy's house so Sawyer wouldn't catch it. But, any way she tried to spin it would be a lie. And when the news broke, which it might've already done, she'd be caught in her lie—even if the truth was nobody's business.

She'd told Sawyer she didn't care who knew. She was tired of living a lie. No use starting a new one now.

"I'm going to live here for a while, Sue." She didn't have to try to keep emotion out of her voice. It was dull and lifeless with no effort needed.

"Why? Is something wrong with your house?"

"No. Nothing's wrong with the house."

"Well, I don't understand why y'all would move out of your house that's only—what? Twenty years old?—into this place that obviously needs so much work. It'll drive Sawyer crazy. He doesn't have time now to take care of everything at the church that needs doing, much less fix this place up."

"Sawyer isn't moving, Sue. Just me."

"What? Do you mean to tell me…?" Aghast was too light a term to describe the woman's face. "Wait just a minute."

The arms jerked from the shrubs, allowing the stems to shoot back upright into their intended positions. Before Faith could get her wits about her, Sue had made her way to the end of the hedge and was coming through the gate attached to the side of the house.

Faith met her by the Mr. Lincoln tea rose—Lacy's favorite.

"Do you mean to tell me you and Sawyer are separated?" Sue's voice was a hodgepodge of emotion with shades of disbelief, incredulity, curiosity and a tinge of unchecked amusement all balled together.

"That's correct."

"Why?" Sue's eyes narrowed and anger took top billing. "Has he been messing around on you?"

"No." Faith shook her head emphatically, wanting to squelch that rumor before it got wings. "Never. Sawyer's the most loyal, trustworthy husband who ever lived. He would never even *think* about cheating."

Sue crossed her arms, tapping her fingers against her bicep. "What is it then? I mean, why else do couples separate?"

"Couples separate for a lot of reasons, Sue. Sawyer and I have some things we need to straighten out, and I needed space to think. And time alone," she added.

If she picked up on the hint, Sue chose to ignore it. "Well, who all knows? I mean, is he going to make a public announcement this morning at church? The congregation has the right to know if their preacher and his wife are going to get a divorce."

"I didn't say anything about divorce." Faith interlocked her fingers to keep from lashing out at the silly ninny.

"No, of course you didn't. But if y'all are separated, certainly divorce is a possibility. Anybody with any sense knows that."

Faith took a deep breath, her head filling with the scent of Lacy's Mr. Lincolns. Her mother-in-law had lived by Sue for thirty-plus years and was one of the few people who truly cared about the woman. The thought cooled her temper and guided her words. "I pray it won't come to that. And I don't think it will, but whatever the outcome, Sawyer and I need the prayers of the community. And we need privacy."

Irritation flared in Sue's eyes as her mouth clamped shut. At least it had stopped her from saying whatever her next comment was going to be. "Privacy isn't something Taylor's Grove's very good at. We're all family here. We care about each other." She sneezed again, and pulled a tissue from the pocket of her khakis to wipe her nose, which was beginning to look raw.

"As long as people let that care guide their actions, I can't ask for anything more," Faith said.

"Yes, well…" Sue looked at her watch. "I'll leave you alone. Give you some of that privacy you need."

She turned and practically sprinted from the yard, leaving Faith to wonder why Sue had bolted the way she did.

Following a hunch, Faith went back into the house, changed out of her pajamas and took a seat in the living room next to the window.

Just as she suspected, Sue and her husband, Ed, left their house at 10:17 a.m. Their hurried pace gave away that they were trying hard to make the ten-thirty service at Taylor's Grove Church despite Sue's cold and the old people she'd be putting at risk with it.

As to what message they would hear, Faith couldn't be sure, but somehow Sawyer would manage to bring love into it.

She headed to the kitchen to pour herself another cup of coffee. She would need the caffeine. When church let out, her day was going to get very busy.

"I'M TELLING YOU, EMMA, if I'd made a list of things to include in my most perfect day, I could check most of them off. Finding the right Jacques Martin would be the only thing without a mark in front of it."

Emma's dreamy sigh came across clearly. "Mmm. I'm thrilled for you, and jealous down to my star-spangled toenails."

"Oh, that's right! Tuesday's the Fourth of July. It's weird being in a place that doesn't celebrate it." That Garrett had provided her with the best fireworks she'd ever experienced ran through her mind, but she didn't voice it. She'd gushed enough about him already. Any more and Emma would get the wrong idea.

"But you'll be there for Bastille Day, right? That's sort of the same thing, isn't it?"

"Yeah, that'll be my last day here. I fly out the morning of the fifteenth." Her gaze strayed across the terrace to Garrett's flat, where she watched the lights wink out in Dylan's bedroom, and followed Garrett's progression as he appeared in the foyer, headed toward his kitchen. Her stomach knotted and she changed the subject away from her leaving. "Are you going to the cabin for the Fourth?"

"I, uh." Emma coughed loudly into the phone. "Sorry! Something went down the wrong way. Your parents cancelled the picnic this year."

"Cancelled? Why?" The July Fourth picnic at the cabin on the lake had never been cancelled. It was a tradition.

"They're calling for the weather to be bad." Emma's explanation didn't make sense.

"If it rains, we've always just moved the picnic into the cabin."

"But this year, there's a chance of some really nasty weather. You know, tornadoes and stuff."

"Oh." Tara wasn't sure what "and stuff" referred to. Garrett appeared in his living room, sipping a glass of wine. He leaned over and picked something up from his coffee table, and a second later, strains of Miles Davis drifted through Tara's open window. "Garrett is so hot, Emma. I wish you could meet him."

"Well, maybe some time when he's in St. Louis, we'll run up there and do some shopping."

"Yeah, maybe we'll do that." He disappeared into his bedroom, and Tara's mind shifted back to the cancelled picnic. "Tornadoes and stuff, huh?"

"Yeah. Hey, uh, I hate to cut this off, but my cycling group is riding the Tunnel Hill Trail today."

"No problem. Talk to you soon."

"Hope tomorrow's even better than today for you! Bye!"

"Bye."

Tara stared at the phone for a minute. Something was up about the picnic. There was an edge to Emma's voice.

Mama had said Dad was down. Was he so depressed they would cancel the picnic?

She hit Trenton's number.

"Hey, pinky."

She laughed. Garrett and Dylan had been so accepting of her deformity, she'd almost forgotten about it while she'd been there. "Hey, bro. I was just talking to Emma, and she said the picnic was cancelled."

Trenton paused. "Yeah. Yeah, that's right."

"But it's never been cancelled before. If it stormed, we always just moved inside."

"Yeah, well, uh…tell me what you've seen since the last time we talked."

Was he changing the subject? "What is going on?"

"What do you mean?"

"I mean, the last time I told you about my sightseeing, you told me your eyes were glazing over, but tonight, you want to know all about it. What gives, Trent? I feel like I'm getting the run—"

"You're fading out, sis. Hello?"

Tara checked her connection. Five bars. "Quit messing with me, Trenton. Is everyth—"

"Hello? Hello? Sorry, sis. I think I've lost you."

"But you're coming in loud and clear."

Beep. Her phone read Call Ended. She called him back immediately, but it went straight to voice mail.

More angry now than worried, she punched Thea's number. It rang several times before going to voice mail. Was Thea avoiding her, too?

The air seemed hot suddenly, so she stepped out onto the terrace.

"You're pulling your lip. What's wrong?" Garrett was walking toward her with a glass of wine in each hand.

She held her phone out. "My family."

His chin buckled in concern. "Is somebody sick?"

"No." She ran her thumb and middle finger into the hair

at the top of her head, and flipped the sides out of her face. "They've cancelled the July Fourth picnic, which has never happened before, supposedly because of weather."

Garrett's shrug suggested she was overreacting. "That sounds plausible."

"Yeah, I guess." She stuffed her phone into the pocket of her shorts. "I'm probably just being paranoid. You were right about my dad being bothered by my looking for Jacques Martin, though. I think the whole situation's got him depressed."

Garrett held out a glass of wine to her. "Well, you're here, and the die is cast, so just roll with it."

"I hope I don't read 'em and weep."

He grinned. "That's poker, not craps."

"Oh." She took the glass he offered and tipped it in his direction. "Then let the good times roll." She took a sip of the tongue-pleasing, full-bodied wine. Garrett's wines were always superb. Or maybe it was the presence of the man who flavored the drink. "Speaking of which, I thought we decided it wouldn't be smart to spend the evening together."

After the afternoon's excursion, they'd returned to their respective flats, not wanting Dylan to get ideas about their time together. She'd stayed tucked away out of sight while they played their nightly game of catch and grilled their hot dogs.

"He's asleep. He won't see us together." Garrett's lips on hers made acquiescence much easier. With a hand at the small of her back, he guided her to the bench beside his door.

She helped him clear away the balls and gloves that littered the seat. "What if he wakes up?"

"He won't. He never does. The kid's always been a sound sleeper."

As soon as they sat, Garrett's arm went around her shoulder and pulled her close. She relaxed against him, his solidness and the wine making whatever was going on at home seem very far away. "I like Henri."

She felt the vibration of Garrett's chuckle against her shoulder blade. "He likes you, too, but he had a hard time understanding what you were saying."

She laughed. "Nobody's ever had to translate my English into regular English before. My kids at school are going to love this story."

"Henri's been a good friend. He took a liking to me as soon as we met, and he adores Dylan. I'm anxious to hear what he has to say about you tomorrow." He let loose with a growl, and his best Henri imitation. "*Mon Dieu*, Garrett, theese Tara, she has the voice of the angel but the look that ees hot as hell."

Tara giggled and pressed her palm to her hot face. "He's quite the lady's man, huh?"

"If you made that plural, you got it right. Henri can charm the clothes off a woman with the raise of an eyebrow."

She gave him a sidelong glance. "You don't do so bad yourself with that lazy, one-sided grin."

"Is that right?" Garrett sounded genuinely surprised. He leaned forward and looked her in the face. "Like this?" He did an exaggerated lift to the right side of his mouth that left a goofy expression on his face.

Tara tried to stifle her laugh, but it burst out, along with some wine-colored spit that landed on Garrett's nose. "Ack! I'm sorry!" The apology would've been more effective if she'd been able to control her laughter, which she couldn't.

Garrett closed his eyes and wiped his sleeve down his face, and his lips relaxed into a yummy, genuine smile. "It's okay. We've exchanged spit, as I recall. Along with other bodily fluids."

There it was. One side of his mouth dropped, leaving the other raised in that look that made her insides squirm. His eyes locked with hers and darkened. "It didn't work."

She cocked her head, holding his stare. "What didn't work?"

"Your clothes are still on." He leaned forward, touching his lips to hers. She opened her mouth to him, tasting the wine that seemed to have grown sweeter on his tongue. He followed as she leaned back into the bench. They both found the side table and managed to set their glasses on it without ever breaking contact with their mouths.

The kiss intensified when she ran her hands through his hair, pressing him close, inviting his tongue deeper. His arms encircled her with heat, on her neck, shoulder, breast. Reflexively, the small of her back came off the bench as she arched against him. He wasted no time accepting the offer, running his hand under her T-shirt and her bra, brushing her nipple with his thumb.

She came up for air, reluctantly pulling her mouth away. He continued to kiss the side of her lips, her cheek, her jaw line, and down to her neck, still brushing her nipple, driving her insane with the light touch. She needed more. So much more.

"We have to stop now," she warned, "if we're going to stop at all."

Garrett leaned his head back to look at her. His hand dropped from her breast, but the back of his fingers kept contact along her rib cage and stomach. "Why would we stop?"

"Dylan." The word came out on a gasp as he caught her other nipple between his fingers. "We don't want him to get…oh! To get…the wrong idea."

"He's sound asleep." He kissed her eyelids tenderly. "And we could be, too, in a couple of hours."

Tara raised her lips to his. "Are you asking me to spend the night?"

Garrett kissed her gently, and then backed his face away until they could actually focus on each other. His hand brushed her cheek. "I want you so badly. We can make love in my bed, and go to sleep in each other's arms. I'll set the alarm to wake us up and you can go back to your place before Dylan gets up. He won't even know you stayed the night."

The child would be in her charge all day tomorrow. If she was going to be on her best game, she needed a good rest tonight—and that wasn't going to happen if she and Garrett stopped now. She would spend the rest of the night in turmoil, aching to have him inside her.

"Okay, let's go."

He stopped to check on his son on their way to his bedroom.

She went on ahead and was waiting, naked and more than ready, when he met up with her two minutes later.

"I can't keep avoiding her calls, Mama. She's going to figure out something's up."

Faith had known that Thea would have the hardest time with the lie they were perpetrating on Tara. The two girls had always been close, had always shared everything. But she'd thought she could count on Trenton—Mr. I-can-keep-my-cool-in-all-situations. Apparently, he'd blown it, too—a fact that Thea had started their phone conversation with.

"She might suspect, Thea, but she can't know unless somebody tells her. I told her Sawyer was still having a hard time with things. Can't you just reiterate that?" Faith rubbed her throbbing temple, certain that any more pressure in her life would cause it to rupture. She'd talked to far too many people today, trying to explain the separation Sawyer had announced from the pulpit without giving away intimate details. She didn't need things with Tara to go awry now, too.

Her younger daughter sounded close to tears. "I can try. But you know how she always finagles secrets out of me."

Faith knew all too well. Christmas presents. Surprise parties. No secret was safe if Thea got hold of it. If her oldest child had any inkling something was up, she could easily get the youngest to sing like a canary, without even having to bribe her with seed.

"Can't you just be too busy to talk to her?" Faith suggested.

"And miss all the good stuff about the new guy?" Incredulity oozed over the line. "Not a chance."

"What new guy?" It was Faith's turn to be incredulous. "Has Tara met somebody in Paris?"

"Um…no. Of course not. I mean, they're just neighbors."

Faith knew that once Thea started crawdadding, you were mere seconds away from getting the lowdown. She pressed in quickly, overwhelming her younger daughter with questions. "Tara's involved with her neighbor? Dylan's father? What's his name? How do you know?"

"His name's Garrett, and, for one thing, *you* told me they went out."

Okay, she had her on that one. But Faith wasn't about to let this go. Tara was her firstborn, and it sounded as if she was going to need some direction from Mama. "But, I thought it was just an innocent date. That he was showing her the sights. Is there more to it than that?"

"No, no, of course not. All they did was visit some historic sites." Thea would be twirling her hair around her finger about now. She claimed it helped her concentrate, but it mostly let her family know she was withholding information.

"I thought they went to dinner, too."

"Well, yeah. That's what I meant. All they did was see sights and go to dinner. Emma just said that she really liked him."

Faith's head spun with that news. If Understatement Emma said "really liked," that meant Tara might be shopping for an engagement ring as they spoke. "Really likes him as in doing things she shouldn't even be thinking about doing because she doesn't know him well enough to be doing those things? Or thinking about them?"

"Uhh, geez, Mama, I've got to go. I totally forgot that I told my friend, uh, Melody that I'd help her, uh, move some furniture around today. I'd better get over there. Love you. Bye!"

Faith closed her eyes and groaned. Tara was sleeping with some Garrett guy in Paris. Her baby. Involved with somebody she hadn't known long enough to barely be friends with, much less lovers. Getting serious with someone she had no chance at a relationship with because everybody knew that long-distance relationships didn't work. Surely, she knew by now that "absence makes the heart grow fonder" was a fallacy. "Out of sight, out of mind" was the truth.

Or maybe Tara wasn't getting serious. Maybe this was just a fun fling. A month of sex and then head home without a backward glance. That was even worse.

Faith twirled her wedding band, which had grown loose on her finger. She and Sawyer had tried to instill a belief in their children that physical intimacy was the highest means of showing love, and sex was not something to be taken lightly.

Like I did.

Her past hadn't just come back to haunt her, it was claiming squatters rights smack-dab in the center of her life.

Well, she may not have been the perfect role model, but that wouldn't keep her from being the best mother she knew how to be. "But I did it" was an excuse parents used way too often. She'd done a lot of things she didn't want her kids to do, and she hoped they learned from her mistakes.

She picked up her phone and touched Tara's number.

Her daughter answered immediately. "Mama?"

Faith saw no use easing into this. Tara's frankness came straight from her own gene pool. "Thea tells me you're sleeping with your neighbor."

"She *what?*"

Anger and horror, but no denial. "Okay, she didn't come

right out and tell me, but you know how she loses her composure and can't think of what to say? Well, she just did that, and we were talking about you and your neighbor, so I'm pretty sure I've jumped to the right conclusion."

"I don't think this is something I want to talk about."

"Of course you don't. I knew you wouldn't. So don't talk. Just listen. You need to think about the consequences of what you're doing. You're setting yourself up for heartbreak because you're going to lose either way."

A noisy sigh came from the other end of the line, but Faith wouldn't relinquish the floor. At least Tara hadn't hung up on her. "If you fall in love with him, you're going to be leaving in two weeks, and everybody knows long-distance relationships don't work. And, if you're not in love and just doing this for fun, then you're following in my footsteps. And look where they led me."

"Mama…"

"I just don't want you to make the same mistakes I made, and I'll go to any lengths to keep that from happening."

"Like calling me in the middle of the night?"

Faith looked at her watch. Six-twenty. Which meant it was after one in the morning in Paris. The tide turned, and guilt swept over her. She'd disturbed her daughter's sleep and probably scared the wadding out of her, too. "Oh, sweetpea, I'm so sorry. I didn't even consider the time difference! Go back to sleep. I hope you're alone. I love you."

"Love you, too. Bye."

Faith dropped the phone on the table and picked up the photo that sat on one of Lacy's hand-crocheted doilies. Her family smiled back at her—her family as it used to be a couple of years ago. The family she wanted back. Smiling. Hugging. United.

With the first utterance of Jacques Martin's name, that family had vanished, and Tara had started looking for something to hold on to to keep her world upright.

Maybe that's what she was doing with this Garrett person. Perhaps he was giving her something in Paris to hold on to while the world shifted beneath her feet.

But, if Tara found her father, she might not need the other man to hold on to.

A flash of inspiration lifted Faith's spirit.

All this time, she'd been hoping Tara wouldn't find Jacques Martin. She'd been afraid of what it would do to Sawyer and the family.

But fear of the unknown was a crippling kind of fear. The kind that held you back when destiny was calling your name. It took *faith* to step out into the darkness, as her mama always told her. That's why she named Faith what she did.

Tomorrow, she would start with calls to Murray State University. Somewhere, someone would know something about Jacques Martin.

If Tara was determined to find her birth father, and if finding him would fill the void and keep her from making a huge mistake, then her mother would help her find him.

Faith would lead the way.

"SORRY ABOUT THAT." Tara shot Garrett an apologetic look and set the phone back on the bedside table.

He gave her a sleepy grin and reached up to brush her hair from her face. "It's okay. My mom does weird things like that, too."

Tara covered her eyes, hoping by some feat of magic the gesture would make her invisible. "No chance you didn't hear what she was saying, is there?"

It didn't work because Garrett found her hand with no trouble and pulled it away from her face. He faked a sorrowful expression, but the twinkle in his eye gave him away. "Nope."

She groaned her exasperation, sinking back down into the pillow.

He sat up enough to lean on an elbow. "But maybe she's right."

His voice was quiet, and it made Tara's heart thud in her chest. "You mean, you think we're making a mistake by having sex?"

His expression became somber, and the mirth left his eyes. But heat replaced it, along with a look the depth of which thrilled her and terrified her at the same time. "I mean, I think we're making a mistake if we believe we can walk away from this in thirteen days and treat it as if it meant nothing."

Thirteen days. He'd used the exact number rather than the more arbitrary two weeks. He was counting them, just like she was. A knot formed in her stomach, hearing him verbalize the same agitation she'd dealt with all afternoon. "What do we do about it, though?"

"I think the first thing to do is to be honest about what's really going on, so we know where we actually stand without any pretense. I'll go first." He rubbed his hand up and down her arm a few times, and she sensed he was trying to work up his courage. "I'm falling for you, Tara." She watched his Adam's apple bob as he swallowed hard. "My connection with you has been so swift and hard, it scares me. I've wanted to ignore it. Act like it wasn't there. But you've been on my mind for two weeks now, and, after that first touch Saturday night, I don't want to think about *not* touching you. I already *know* you. I think I've *always* known you. I've just been waiting for you to show up in my life. Does that make sense?"

She placed her hand against his chest, could feel his heart pounding at the sincerity of his words. "You said it prettier than I could, but I feel the same way. It depresses me to think about going home and leaving you and Dylan. I know that's crazy—I *have* to go home. But..." Emotion clogged her voice, and she cleared her throat. "What if the reason I'm here isn't to find my birth father? What if I'm here to find you and Dylan?"

He brushed a tear from her face that she hadn't realized was there. "I love that idea, and I love that it's in your mind. It tells me this isn't one-sided on my part."

She shook her head. "It's not one-sided on your part."

He touched his lips to hers. "But don't give up on finding your father yet. He may still be out there."

She felt her chin quiver, and she pressed her lips together to hold it still. "I'm not giving up, but I get my hopes up a little higher each time, and that makes me fall harder when it doesn't pan out."

"I wish I could snap my fingers and deliver the right Jacques Martin to you."

Garrett lay back and pulled her close against him in a hold that made her feel protected from any hurt the outside world might throw at her.

"So what do we do now?" she whispered.

"About Jacques Martin?"

"About us."

He kissed her forehead and her eyelids. "We handle it the same as the search for your father. We keep our hearts open to any possibility, and we believe that, if we're meant to be together, love will find a way."

Tara raised herself up this time, needing to see his eyes. "Love?"

He shrugged. "We can break out all the moves to dance around it, or we can call it what it is."

She cocked her head and smiled at his straightforwardness. "Love." She laughed. "Mama would be so horrified if she knew."

He gave her a tender smile. "You have good parents. Weird, but good."

"I know." She lay down, her head on his chest listening to his heart. It was a sweet sound, a gentle sound that would lull her to sleep very quickly. "If I were smart, I'd get up and go home right now so the alarm wouldn't have to wake us up so early."

"Mmm," he answered and she couldn't tell if the sound was affirmative or negative.

"But I've never been accused of being a brainiac."

"You couldn't be too smart, or you wouldn't have stayed a virgin until you were twenty-something. What a waste of talent."

She smiled and continued smiling until his breath slowed to the deep sounds of slumber.

CHAPTER FIFTEEN

"TARA, SHE IS LOVELY, Garrett."

Waiting in Garrett's office for him when he arrived, Henri was obviously anxious to talk. He had his cup of espresso in hand and one for Garrett, covered to keep it hot.

"*Bon matin, Henri.* It's good to see you, too." He gave his friend a smile. "I knew you'd like her."

"Her hair is very wild and crazy." Henri's hands flew above his head, gesticulating to make his point. "*Mais, ils sont fabuleux!*"

Henri never had a hair out of place, so it was interesting that he'd find Tara's wild curls fabulous.

"And her poor hand! *Mon Dieu!* Does it cause her pain?"

"She never complains about it, but she warns Dylan and me not to squeeze it too hard. She sustained some major injuries in that motorcycle wreck. It's amazing she's even here." A lump swelled in Garrett's throat at that thought. He tried to get rid of it by swallowing his espresso in one gulp, which garnered him a disapproving eye roll from his friend. "But, I'm thrilled she is." Even that felt like an understatement.

"*Oui, c'est évident.*" Henri paused, weighing what was coming next. "Can you share with me the circumstances of her father, this Jacques Martin? Did she recently learn of him, or has she known of him throughout her life and has only now the means or desire to search for him?"

Garrett didn't think Tara would mind, so he brought

his friend up to speed on the circumstances surrounding Tara's conception.

"Très interéssant." Henri thrust his bottom lip out and made a French sound that meant he was mulling something over. "And you say she found names and addresses in the telephone book and on the internet?"

"That's correct."

Henri shook his head. "Such lists would not be complete. He might be not listed. He has the cell phone, *probablement. Oui?*"

"Yeah. She knows that." He and Tara had already talked about her archaic means of searching. "But she's doing it the only way she knows how."

"Did she consider to hire a private detective?" His shrug suggested it was so obvious he shouldn't even have to mention it.

Garrett leaned back in his seat to get comfortable. He appreciated Henri's interest in Tara's predicament. Had his friend already figured out how very special she was to him?

"I suggested that, but she said she didn't know anyone in Paris who could recommend one, and she was afraid, if she hired someone blind, he'd turn out to be a shyster."

Henri's nose wrinkled like he smelled something unpleasant. *"Qu'est-ce que ça veut dire*—'shyster'?"

"A crook." Garrett explained. "Someone who cheats people out of their money."

"Ah!" Henri nodded. *"Je comprends.* But what if she finds this Jacques Martin, and *he* is the shyster?" His eyebrow lifted to make his point.

"We've discussed that, and she's aware that she'll have to be careful and trust her instincts," Garrett agreed. "She's a pretty good judge of character. She told me that if you'd looked her up and down one more time, she was going to ask you to leave a *few* clothes on her because she didn't want to catch a cold."

Henri had a good laugh at that. "It was the test for you,

mon ami. Not Tara. And it worked. Your hand made the fist very quickly."

Garrett recalled the flare of jealousy that had shot through him, and he had no doubt Henri was speaking the truth.

"But do not worry." Henri gave a dismissive wave of his hand. "I will allow you to keep Tara for yourself."

That pulled a laugh from Garrett. He'd never encountered a woman who would choose him over Henri—until Tara. But she left him no doubt as to who her choice would be, and it felt damn good to be the winner for once. Good enough that he had to rub it in a bit. "This is one you have no chance with. Did you see the way she latched on to my arm after you ogled her? She wasn't the least bit affected by your debonair French ways."

Henri's warm smile lit up his face. "The woman was blind. I have heard that the climaxes may cause that condition."

Garrett's face warmed at the truth in Henri's folklore, but he wouldn't cheapen what he had with Tara with locker-room talk. "Back to Jacques Martin." He made his point by switching to their former subject. "It doesn't look promising that she'll find him. It's like looking for a needle in a haystack."

Henri's nostrils flared. "What is this needle in the haystack I always hear of? American idioms do not make sense. Why would someone put a needle in a haystack? Would he be sewing in a hay field? Why would it not be like finding a needle in the pin cushion?" He crossed his arms imperiously, making Garrett certain Napoleon Bonaparte's blood ran in his friend's veins.

"I don't know, Henri. Make it a needle in a pin cushion if you want, but, either way, finding him is difficult and not likely to get any easier."

Henri drummed his fingers on the desk, staring at them for a minute. Then he slid his eyes up slowly to meet Garrett's. "You are falling in love with her. I see this in your eyes when you speak her name."

"Yeah, I, um…" The serious turn in the conversation was far removed from their usual banter. "I believe I am."

"Dylan is very fond of her. He brought her into most conversations during his visit." A hint of worry edged Henri's voice. "You had a fear this would happen."

The strong coffee…or something…made the muscles around Garrett's heart tighten. "But love's a process that takes time, Henri, and if the right woman comes along, I have to open myself up to the process. Unfortunately, that means opening Dylan up to it, too."

"And you think Tara could be the right one?"

Garrett took a deep breath, and the tightening loosened a smidgen. "Let's just say it feels right at this time."

Henri broke eye contact, brushing at something on the desk. "And when will she leave?"

"The fifteenth." The reality of the time they had left closed off Garrett's throat and made breathing impossible for a few seconds.

"If she found her birth father, would that change her plans? Would she stay longer, *peut-être?*"

Garrett hadn't considered that, but it was certainly a possibility. Extending her stay to get to know her father would make perfect sense. "I don't know. I guess that could change things. She has the summer off, so she wouldn't *have* to be back until the middle of August." His heart beat faster at the thought.

Henri pushed out of his chair. "Well, I must begin the work, *oui?*"

"What's your hurry?" His friend's swift change in manner was out of character. With the campaign over, Garrett had expected him to take it easy today.

"I have important things to do." Henri pointed his finger dramatically upward as he hurried from the room.

Garrett rolled his eyes at his friend's theatrics. "French-men." He chuckled. "Probably headed to the restroom."

"DO YOU SEE IT YET, Dylan?"

Tara glanced up anxiously into the sprawling tree where Dylan was searching.

"Not yet." The child caught the branch above his head and used it to make his way to the other side of the trunk.

Tara checked the cache finder again. The treasure had to be up in the tree. "I'll give you a couple more minutes, then we'll have to give up on this one." Her eyes darted around the park. No security guard in sight.

"I don't want to give—wait! I see something!" Dylan swung his arm over a branch and ducked under it. "There's a hole! And it's got something in it!"

The giddy excitement in his voice was infectious. Tara held her breath as he slid his hand in to retrieve what he'd found.

"Got it!" He held up a small plastic container in triumph.

"Drop it to me, so you have both hands to climb down." Tara held her arms out, and her partner did as he was in-structed.

Following the tradition to keep geocaches secret, they strolled leisurely with the treasure to the closest bench and pretended they were merely opening a mundane plastic box.

Dylan's bottom lip drooped in disappointment when he ripped the lid off and peered inside. "There aren't many items. Not like the one we found yesterday."

Tara gave him a pat. "Yeah, but that makes this one even better."

"Why?" He gave her one of those skeptical looks kids save for when they know adults aren't being completely truthful.

She flipped open the log. "This cache was hidden on March 3, 2011, and it's only been found…" She counted the entries. "Nine times. That means it's a really difficult cache to locate, and *you* found it!"

The grin that broke across his face was a duplicate of his dad's, making Tara's breath hitch. "Wow! That means we're good at this, aren't we?"

"We're better than good. We're freakin' awesome!" She held up her hand, but then thought better of allowing him to hit the one that had been injured. She switched to the other. "I want an official high-five for that. A high-three just won't do."

Dylan giggled and slapped his palm against hers. Then he dug in their Crown Royal pouch, which had been donated to the cause by Garrett, pulling out one of the special tokens he and Tara had made that morning, and traded it for a gold medallion with a fleur-de-lis embossed on it.

Then he shimmied up the tree and placed the cache back in the hole where he'd found it.

Tara was absorbed in watching Dylan and didn't hear the police officer approach. When the man spoke, she wheeled around to find him giving her a look that was none too friendly.

He shook a finger at Dylan, then at her, his voice stern and unyielding. She couldn't understand a word he said.

"I'm sorry." She had no idea how much a tree-climbing fine might run, but she didn't want to find out. "I don't understand what you're saying."

Dylan was making his way back down. "I un—"

"Be quiet, Dylan." She shot a silencing look his way.

The policeman's facial features lost their hard edge. *"Madame."* He spoke slowly and precisely. "To climb trees is not allowed. We warn of the danger." He pointed at the sign in front of their tree.

Tara willed her face to flush, and she touched her hand to the base of her throat for added drama. "Oh, I'm so sorry. My French isn't very good, so I didn't realize that's what it said. I should've checked my phrase book."

Dylan dropped from the bottom branch to land beside her. "But you said you wouldn't need that book as long as I—"

She pulled him to her, clamping her hand lightly over his mouth. "Shh, Dylan. Don't interrupt the adults." Then she turned her attention back to the police officer, smiling sweetly while thickening her Southern accent. "The visitor's guide said that the Luxembourg Gardens were a wonderful place to bring children." She played the sympathy move by wiping her face with her injured hand.

Just as she'd hoped, the policeman grimaced at the sight, caught himself and then gave her an overly cheery grin. "It is of no great importance, *madame*. Your son is safe."

Dylan nudged her leg at the policeman's error.

She ruffled his hair with her good hand and placed her other index finger to her lips. "Shh. Let the nice man finish what he's saying."

The policeman leaned toward Dylan and wagged his finger. "You may not climb these trees. And when you climb the trees at your home, you must always be very careful. Do you understand?"

Dylan nodded. "Yes, but I don't have any trees at my house."

"That is unfortunate." The man's chin buckled in a look of sympathy. "Perhaps someday you will." He turned his attention back to Tara. "*Au revoir, madame*. I hope you will enjoy your stay in Paris."

"You're very kind. Thank you." Tara gave a small wave as she guided Dylan toward the walkway.

"You sort of told that policeman some fibs." Dylan threw an accusing frown her way.

"Yes, I did," she admitted.

One corner of Dylan's mouth curved into a half smile that was identical to, and just as charming as, his father's. "You let him think we didn't know what that sign said."

"Yeah. I probably shouldn't have done that, but I didn't

want him to fine me—fine means paying money as a punishment for breaking a law."

"I know what it means. It makes Dad mad when people park on the sidewalk. He says he's glad they got a fine."

She chuckled at the child's honesty.

"You let him think I was your son, too."

His half smile burst into a full-blown grin that Tara answered with her own. "I didn't think that one would hurt anyone. It wasn't something he could fine me for. I mean, you'd look pretty weird with one of those yellow tickets stuck to your head."

His childish giggle filled her ears and warmed her heart at the same time.

"I wish you *were* my mom." He took her hand. "You're fun."

The air whooshed out of her lungs, but she managed a choked "Thanks, Dylan. You're fun, too."

Backed by the swiftness of a six-year-old's attention span, his face lost its smile. "Yesterday, Dad said you were trying to find your father. How'd you lose him?"

Oh, wow! This one was going to require the most finely honed of her teacher talents. "Well, your dad has told me that you lost your mother when you were three. That kind of lost means—"

"That she died, and now she's up in heaven."

"That's right. But I didn't lose my father that way. I think he lives here in Paris." Dylan's knitting brows said the explanation wasn't enough. "He moved away before I was born." She tried again. "So we've never gotten to meet. But I came to Paris to look for him."

"Do you have a mom?"

"Yes, I have a mom *and* a dad." She anticipated his next question. "A man named Sawyer married my mom. He loves me very much, and he's my dad just like *your* dad."

"Did they have sleepovers?"

Tara swallowed her startled gasp. If she'd learned anything from teaching, it was that sometimes a kid's wording could be wonky. "What do you mean?"

"My friend Michelle has a new dad. He used to eat with them a lot. And then he and her mom started having sleepovers, and they got married. Now she's going to get a new baby sister."

"Sometimes it happens that way," Tara agreed.

Dylan pinned her with that wide-eyed look that was so easy to read, and she braced for what was coming.

"You want to have a sleepover at our house tonight?"

"Thank you for asking, but that's probably not a good idea." She could read the disappointment in the child's dangling lower lip.

"Well, if you wanted to have sleepovers, that would be okay. Maybe you and my dad could get married and you could be my mom."

His suggestion was so innocent…and so earnest…it filled her heart to the point of breaking. "Let's sit a minute, okay?" She sat down on a nearby bench and pulled him into her lap. "You planted seeds with Veronique yesterday, didn't you?"

He nodded. "Veronique said they would grow into a salad."

"Well, see all these trees and flowers?" She motioned to the artfully landscaped area around them, and his eyes followed her gesture. "Each of these plants started from a seed, and each of them grew into something special. Now, I like you and your dad very much, and that's like planting a seed of friendship. Sometimes friendship grows like a flower. It's very beautiful, but it stays small. And sometimes friendship grows into something much bigger and stronger like a tree. That's the kind of friendship that becomes love. The thing is, both kinds of friendships, whether they're the *like* kind or the *love* kind, both need time to grow."

She paused, but for once the little boy didn't have any

questions. "So, like I said, you and your dad and I have planted the seed—" She drew his attention to a green sprout just popping from the ground. "But we don't know yet what it's going to grow into. We'll just have to wait and see." She pressed on, determined to keep her message up-beat. "I'll have to go back to my real home soon, but even after I leave Paris, our seed is going to continue to grow into something."

"You could stay with us."

"If I did, my mom and dad would *really* miss me, just like I'm going to miss you and your dad when I leave. But he and I have already decided that we'll talk on the phone a lot—talking is sort of like sunshine to a seed—and you're going to call me whenever you feel like it—like you do with your grandmas and grandpas. And after a few months, let's say like after Christmas, if it looks like we're going to grow into a tree, we'll make plans for me to come back for another visit…or for you to come visit me. Deal?"

He smiled and nodded. "Deal."

With no forewarning, he threw his arms around her neck. He was soft and warm, and the summer sweetness of the tree he'd climbed earlier still clung to him.

Just as suddenly, the tears that had been hovering close to the surface since the start of this conversation burst from Tara's eyes like a spring shower.

Dylan loosened his hold and sat back, gaping at her. "Are you crying?"

Tara sniffed. "We can't expect our seed to grow with just sunshine, can we?"

He shook his head.

She swiped at the tears, and flung the excess water from her fingers. "Then I'll water it, too."

He grinned and she pulled him into another quick hug. Her words had been playful and light—the exact opposite of the weight she carried in her heart.

Garrett's worst fear had come true. Dylan had imprinted

onto her like a newly hatched duckling. Problem was, she felt the same way about him and his dad.

Oh, she talked a good game. Give the seeds time to grow and all that. But when the time came for her to leave and these hugs were the goodbye kind, how would she ever be able to let go?

CHAPTER SIXTEEN

FAITH PUSHED THE BOX OUT of the way with her calf and pulled out the last one from the depths of the hall closet. She'd set a goal to work through a closet each day, throwing away what was of no use or sentimental value, boxing up the items the family might want to keep, and filling trash bags with things that could be donated to charity.

The job occupied a good part of her brain but didn't require too much concentration, and left plenty of room for wandering thoughts. The call to Murray State had proven futile this morning. The offices were closed until Wednesday due to the July Fourth holiday weekend. And the call to Sawyer had been just as futile.

He'd expressed no interest in helping sort through things when she'd let him know what she was up to. His voice sounded dull and listless, and she suspected he'd had another sleepless night. He'd told her to do whatever she saw fit with his mom's stuff. He trusted her to make the right decision. There had been no emotion in his tone.

What else could she expect? He'd been through the wringer yesterday, by all accounts—all seventeen accounts if she included both visitors and phone calls. She'd suggested that he take the boat out for a day of fishing and relaxation today, but he hadn't taken the bait.

Her heart fell at the sound of a knock on the front door. She stood motionless. Maybe if she didn't move, whoever it was would think she was out and would go away. She was tired of visitors and tired of talking.

Another knock, more persistent this time.

Snatching a washcloth from a box of linens, she wiped her sweaty face and headed to greet the unwelcome guest.

Ollie Perkins stood on the front porch, clutching his violin case in one hand and his red bandanna in the other.

"Hi, Ollie." Faith edged the screen door open slowly, giving him time to move out of its arching path.

"Morning, Faith." He raised the case in explanation of his visit. "Thought maybe your soul might be hankering for a little music to soothe it."

Faith choked at his words. When Lacy had lain too sick to get out of the bed, she would ask for Ollie to come soothe her soul with his music. He always obliged.

"Come in. My soul needs soothing for sure." She held the door wide. Once inside, Ollie stopped and glanced around the living room slowly, as if he were taking inventory of the furnishings.

"Wanted to make sure you hadn't moved anything." He grinned. "I'd hate to bang into one of Lacy's beloved lamps."

Faith reached to take his arm, but he moved toward a chair with a meaningful shuffle, so she let him do it on his own.

"How's your mom this morning, Ollie?"

"Fair to middlin'." He made short work of settling his case on the floor at his feet, and getting it open. "Tara doing okay over yonder in Paris?"

Faith nodded and then realized he couldn't see her. "She's enjoying herself. I talked to her last night." Heat crept into her face as she remembered the impulsive call she'd made and the conversation that had precipitated it. At least Ollie couldn't see her embarrassment.

"What d'ya need this morning? Hymns? Jigs? Reels? Any particular requests?"

Faith sat on the arm of the recliner. "I'm not sure what I need, Ollie. Just something pretty."

"How 'bout this?" The haunting melody of "Theme from *A Summer Place*" glided from his strings, and Faith slid from the arm of the chair onto the seat. The tune had been one of her mom's favorites.

She closed her eyes, letting the beautiful strains carry away some of the tension. As the last note died, she took a deep breath, and felt it plunge to a space long neglected at the bottom of her lungs.

"That was beautiful." She sighed. "I didn't realize you played that kind of music."

"I don't play it nearly often enough. Here's another."

Faith smiled as "Moon River" filled her ears. She could almost feel herself being pulled along by the current, peaceful and calm, not caring what lay "waiting 'round the bend."

On and on, Ollie played. One song after another with barely a pause in-between. Mostly romantic songs from movies, his choices revealed a side of him she'd never known.

An amiable silence fell between them, as if words were unnecessary and inadequate. Once, her phone rang and he'd stopped to let her answer. But the caller ID identified that it was Nell Bradley from the Ladies' Prayer Group. She let it go to voice mail.

"This one's my favorite. It's called 'Today.' A folk group called The New Christy Minstrels made it popular back in the '60s. The words are really pretty."

"Can you sing it?" Faith had never heard the old man sing, even at church, but there was such openness about him at the moment, he might be persuaded.

Her question drug a laugh from his belly. "My screeching would not be soothing to your soul. Look the words up sometime, though. You'll appreciate them."

The song, like all the others, was beautiful, and Faith was sorry when it ended…and intrigued. "What makes that one your favorite?"

Her visitor leaned over and put his violin back to rest in

its case before he answered her. He also mopped his face, and wiped his eyes, which had grown misty.

"I was in love once. That was our song."

Faith had never thought about Ollie in that way…as someone who would fall in love. He'd been devoted to his mom, had lived with her his entire life in the house he grew up in until she went to the nursing home. That another woman had ever been in his life seemed impossible. Who could it have been?

"I never knew that, Ollie."

"No one did." He leaned forward to rest his elbows on his knees, and somehow pinned her with his dead-on gaze. "He was married."

His words sent a shockwave through Faith's system. Her fingers reflexively tightened on the chair arms.

"Yes, sweet Faith, you heard me right. Have I shocked you?" His voice was quiet and smooth, holding no hint that he was asking for sympathy…or anything from her, for that matter.

"Yes," she answered. "I had no idea…"

"No one ever has, that I know of." He paused, but his rheumy gaze didn't waver. "You see, Faith, everybody's got something. There's not a person in Taylor's Grove hadn't been through an ordeal. That's what life is. How you come through it's the key." He leaned back, seeming more comfortable now with the conversation he'd dropped her into. "Loving is never wrong."

"But I didn't love him, Ollie. He was a one-night stand, and I haven't seen him since." Her mouth was moving, telling this old man her story, and she wasn't sure why. But it felt cathartic, and she didn't want to stop. "Tara was the result. That's why she's gone to Paris. To find him."

"You never told…anyone."

"Not until Memorial Day. The whole family found out at the same time. Sawyer included. Now he's questioning our relationship." She leaned forward, pressing the matter. "But that one incident doesn't define us, does it?"

"Only if you let it."

It was hard to believe that, with all the women in town Faith could've turned to, it was a seventy-seven-year-old man she was confiding in. But it felt right somehow. Ollie understood. And now she understood the passion always present in his music.

"What do I do now? I've apologized so many times, I can't say those words anymore with any feeling. But Sawyer can't get past my betrayal. I knew I was pregnant when we got married. I made him believe Tara was his."

"You accept the situation for what it is. And what it is is over and done with. We can't go back and change the past. Do you want me to talk to Sawyer?"

"No." She shook her head. "He has to decide on his own who to turn to."

Ollie closed the lid of the violin case and latched it. "Your secret's safe with me, Faith."

"And yours with me."

"I knew that before you told me. But as for Tara's lineage, I think that's Tara's choice to tell or not. People are making all kinds of speculations as to what this separation stems from. Nobody's focusing on the past. Everybody thinks y'all have been through a recent trauma. An affair or maybe a near-affair. I'll tell you though, some in our midst are out for blood and they don't care what the cause is or who's to blame."

"I...we anticipated that."

"I'm sure you've thought through everything. In the middle of the night when you shoulda been sleeping would be my guess." He picked up his case to leave.

Faith stood up to show him out. "Ollie? Whatever happened to the man you loved?"

"Died too young."

She hugged him like she would have one of her children. "I'm sorry things couldn't have been different for you two."

The old man sniffed and wiped his eyes on his bandanna. "'The universe is unfolding as it should.'"

How desperately she wanted to believe that...wanted to believe that somehow all of this was going to turn out okay. "Thank you for coming by." She gave his back a pat in parting. "You gave me an hour of sheer joy."

"No better compliment than that. Keep your chin up. This'll pass."

She watched him stroll down the steps and all the way to the sidewalk that ran along Main Street.

"Bless your heart, Ollie," she whispered as she closed the door. "If you can endure this town, so can I."

"I'M GLAD MONIQUE'S FATHER is doing well enough for her to come back, but I'm going to miss my time with Dylan. I talked to him about my leaving, by the way."

The subject dampened Tara's spirits even more than the rain that was keeping them from the terrace this evening. She'd fought tears all afternoon—weepiness wasn't usually in her nature.

"How did he take that news?" Garrett closed the terrace door against what was now a downpour as a streak of lightning lit the sky.

Tara secured her hair into a ponytail. The humidity was making it feel like a bush had sprouted on her head. "He didn't like it much." She reached for the bottle and divided the remainder of the wine between their two glasses.

Garrett flipped the air conditioner on. "I don't like it much, either."

An accompanying rumble of thunder added drama to his words, and jarred a renegade tear from Tara's eye. She brushed it away while Garrett's back was to her, determined not to spoil one of the precious few nights they had left.

"I guess it's back to the search for dear old Dad tomorrow." She cringed at the subject she'd changed to. Her futile search for Jacques Martin was the second most depressing thing on her mind.

Garrett sat down on the couch and patted the cushion next to him. "Maybe tomorrow will be the day."

"Maybe." She forced a smile she didn't feel as she handed him his glass and sat down.

Garrett stretched his legs out and put his arm across her shoulders, its weight a comfort, an anchor in this stormy emotional sea she was currently tossed about on. His fingertips brushed her temple, and she leaned against him. "What's the matter, love? You seem down tonight." His concern was edged with caution. He'd practiced those same words on Angie time after time, no doubt. Tara wanted no resemblance between her actions and those of his deceased wife.

"I'm just more emotional about this Jacques Martin stuff than I want to admit." She settled on the half truth, leaving out the part about him and Dylan, gnawing her bottom lip when it quivered.

"Don't give up hope." His fingertips brushed her forehead and her hair. "There's still time."

She nodded, but her mind was shaking its head. Time with him and Dylan was growing much too short. Another tear eased from her eye, catching on Garrett's finger as it brushed her cheek.

He leaned forward and looked directly into her face. "Oh, baby, don't cry," he said, and, of course, the gentleness in his manner opened her water works to full force. He took her glass from her, and set both of them on the coffee table.

"I'm s—sorry." She swiped at her eyes and tried to control the sobs, but the words came out on snubbed breaths. "I'm...usually...not the...crying...kind."

"I know." He kissed each of her eyelids. "I can tell."

"You...can?" Her breathing stuttered in her chest.

Garrett nodded. "You're the bravest woman I know. Facing the things you've gone through." He kissed her injured hand. "Coming here alone in search of a man you've never met." His labored sigh filled the space between them. "I've acted like such a coward at times. You put me to shame."

He leaned in and pressed his lips to hers. His touch was calm and warm. It stilled her...and excited her. "You should never feel that way because you have nothing to be ashamed of," she said. "You lived through hell and carried Dylan safely through it all."

A fleeting grimace touched his mouth and then it was gone, replaced by a small pucker that deepened the scar on his upper lip. "You know, maybe we haven't been making the most of the manpower available." He shifted to face her. "Why don't we split up the remainder of the names on your list? Between the two of us, we could get all of the Jacques Martins covered. You'd have to take the ones farther away, but I could cover the ones closer to the office and on my way home."

"You'd do that for me?"

He cupped her face in his hands, tilting it so she was looking directly into his. "I would do anything for you, Tara." His eyes took on a darker hue, and he kissed her with more fervor than before.

Her body stirred with longing, and she pressed closer. "Well, I'd like to do something for you...to repay your kindness." She gave him a soft smile. "Think Dylan's asleep?"

"Long ago."

She stood and held out her hand. "We can talk when he's awake. Let's make better use of our time alone."

She led the way to his bedroom.

Barely inside the door, he kissed her, long and hard, and the stirring intensified. The way this man affected her with just a kiss! Heat surged through her, every fiber sizzling.

They broke contact only briefly while she pulled his

T-shirt over his head and threw it on the bed. Then her eager palms sought the taut planes of his stomach muscles. His hands lost no time reciprocating, ridding her of her clothes. He grasped her rear and pressed her front against him.

With a little hop, her legs were around his waist, and he backed over to his bed, pausing only long enough to grab a condom from the drawer. He lay down, keeping her on top.

Astride him and in the driver's seat, she shifted into high gear and stomped on the gas.

Their lovemaking was fast and furious and wild like the storm that battered the window, leaving them sweaty and gasping for air.

But soon, and with what turned out to be fortuitous timing, a burst of lightning struck, followed immediately by a rolling concussion of thunder. It sent a chill through Tara and had her grabbing for Garrett's cast-off tee. She slipped into it just as the bedroom door flew open, and a terrified Dylan streaked into the room.

"Dad, the thunder's too loud!"

He drew up short at the side of the bed, the terror in his eyes giving way to confusion. "Tara?" His face broke into the wide grin she adored. "You decided to sleep over!" he crowed. "Why didn't you tell me?"

"Well." She looked to Garrett for help, but he answered her with an I've-got-nothing shrug. She glanced at the clock that read 12:43 a.m. "We just remembered that it's July Fourth, which is a holiday in the States. Why don't we make a tent and pretend we're camping out?"

"Cool! I'll go get my pillow!" The child ran from the room on a mission, and Tara and Garrett lost no time jumping from under the covers to don their shorts.

"Seriously? Sleeping on the floor?" Garrett speared her with a disgruntled look. "I've got to work tomorrow."

"Oh, shut up." She laughed and pulled the blanket from the bed. "And go find me some rope."

Garrett's frown dissolved into the same enthusiastic smile Dylan displayed. "Now you're talking."

He sprinted from the room, as well.

"For the tent!" she called after him.

CHAPTER SEVENTEEN

THE FIRST RAYS OF SUN caught the prism Lacy had always kept hanging in the side window of her bedroom, coloring the opposite wall with a rainbow that required no rain.

Faith was awake and had been for some time. As she watched the hues deepen, she was reminded of the story of Noah and his ark. If only her rainbow could be a sign like his had been—a promise that the storm was over…or maybe would be soon.

It was going to be a beautiful Fourth of July. Maybe she would call the kids and Emma and have a picnic at the cabin after all. Then they could stop lying to Tara.

An unexpected noise drew her from the bed to the front window. She cracked the blinds to find Sawyer hooking the bass boat onto his truck. Another good sign! If he felt like going fishing, it surely meant he was getting back to normal.

She held her breath, hoping he would knock on the door and invite her to go along. But when he got back in the truck and slammed the door, she let the breath out slowly, waving goodbye to him with an unseen hand.

They'd only spoken briefly since the conversation in the garage Saturday. Three days ago—though it seemed like three years.

She picked up the novel she'd been reading and wandered to the kitchen. Bacon and eggs sounded good for breakfast. Or an omelet perhaps. Her stomach had been so upset, food seemed like the enemy. But since Ollie's visit yesterday, she'd managed to eat lunch and supper, and breakfast was on her agenda for this morning.

She arranged some slices of bacon on the tray, and put them in the microwave to cook.

If the dear old man could go through what he had and never complain to anyone about the unfairness of things, she could certainly bear this. He had nothing except memories, but she'd actually been blessed.

She had Tara.

She picked up her phone and touched her precious daughter's number.

Tara answered on the first ring. "Hi, Mama."

Uh-oh. She sounded breathless. Oh, surely not. It was midafternoon over there.

"Hey, sweetpea. Have I caught you at a bad time?"

"No, a good time, actually. I could use some cheering up."

Faith assessed the situation quickly. Tara wasn't distraught. Just down. Man trouble? Had she seen the folly of her ways? "Why?" She used her sympathetic mom voice. "What's wrong?"

A long sigh whispered over the line. "I just located another wrong Jacques Martin."

"Oh, that's got to be hard. I know you had your hopes up."

"I've been thinking about this whole thing…my snap decision to try to come find him."

"Yeah," Faith agreed. "It was a bit hurried."

"Well, you know how you and Dad always taught us that everything happens for a reason? I'm thinking that the reason I'm here may not be to find Jacques Martin. Maybe I came here to meet Garrett and Dylan."

Emotion gripped Faith's heart and squeezed. "Oh my, Tara. That sounds way too serious."

"I am serious, Mama. I'm falling in love with him. Them."

"Honey." Faith switched to her let's-be-reasonable tone. "It's too soon to be thinking about that."

"And yet, here I am thinking about it. That's what makes me think it's real."

Arguing would do no good. Tara had Sawyer's stubborn streak, blood-relation or no. When either of their minds got set a certain way, they held on to the belief like a snapping turtle holds a stick...and they wouldn't let go till it thundered. "I don't know what to say."

"You don't have to say anything, Mama. Just be happy for me."

"I'm always happy for you, sweetpea. Happy for you in my life."

Tara's laugh sounded relieved. "Love you."

"Love you, too."

"By the way." Tara's tone changed. "Emma said the picnic was cancelled because of weather." It was a statement, but the question was evident.

"Well, it's turned out pretty after all, so I'm thinking we might throw one together." The microwave dinged, reminding Faith of the breakfast she'd started. "Your dad's already headed to the lake, in fact," she added for authenticity.

"Good. It sounds like things are back to normal."

Faith wouldn't answer that with a lie. "My bacon's ready, so I need to go, sweetpea. You be careful, now. You hear?"

"I hear. See ya."

"See ya."

Faith opened the microwave and set the bacon on the counter. Despite its mouth-watering aroma, her appetite had fled once again.

So Tara believed her reason for being in Paris was to meet Garrett.

"The universe is unfolding as it should." Ollie's words from yesterday scampered across Faith's brain, causing the hair to rise on the back of her neck.

Only one thing would change Tara's mind back to her

original intent…and shake her loose from the stick she was clamped on to.

Faith sent up a prayer for thunder in Paris…in the form of an address for the elusive Jacques Martin.

GARRETT ENDED THE CALL and gestured Henri to come in.

The Frenchman held a paper fisted in one hand and a mysterious expression on his face. He stepped in and closed the door behind him.

"What's up? You been watching those old Pink Panther movies again?" Garrett chuckled at the joke that his friend obviously didn't understand. "I was just talking to Marc Fornier. He's agreed to add Soulard to the beer flight dinners at le Verrou."

"C'est formidable!" As was his custom, Henri chose the armless chair at the north end of Garrett's desk. He perched on the edge, resembling a bird on a wire.

"Yeah, wonderful news for us."

Henri nodded. Garrett hadn't seen so much excitement in his eyes since they'd test-driven that Ferrari last year. "And I may have wonderful news for Tara." Henri pushed the paper he held across the desk.

Garrett scanned the document, a spreadsheet, much like the one Henri made for Dylan's activities, but this one held a list of names—well, actually the names were all Jacques Martin. Most had two columns of addresses, work and home, and a slew of other columns, some filled out and others empty.

Three names had been circled in red.

Garrett pulled his copy of Tara's list from his pocket and compared the two. They were totally different. He dropped the new one on the desk and spread his hands in question. "What is this?"

"Ce sont les Jacques Martins who are not in the telephone book or found easily over the internet." Henri's rigid posture hardly matched the nonchalant tone he affected.

His friend's manner, so different from his normally perfect composure, sent a chill up Garrett's spine. "Where did you get this information?"

"If I tell you, *mon ami,* I will have to kill you." His grin dissolved as quickly as it appeared. "*Vraiment,* Garrett, no one must know that I have done this."

"What did you do?" Garrett fought to control the panic in his voice. "Hack into a government website or something?"

"*Oui.*" Henri shrugged one shoulder. "Or something."

"Damn it! You could get arrested."

"*Oui,* and go to the prison for a very long time. *Mais seulement* if it becomes known. This is why you must tell no one." He wagged his finger. "Not Tara. Not anyone." The wagging finger dropped to point at the circled names. "But I am certain one of these is the correct man. The three are of the correct age to be the father, and all were in the U.S. during the right time."

Garrett's hands were sweating. He clenched and unclenched them, not sure if he should kiss Henri or kick his ass for pulling such a stunt. "How did you get your hands on all this?"

"Much information is available, *mon ami.* One only needs to know where to look." He gave a sly grin. "And how."

Garrett became aware of how fast his heart was racing when a drop of sweat ran into his eye. He wiped it off, then reached for his phone. "Tara could be meet—"

Henri snatched the phone from his hand. "Tread carefully, Garrett. These are men of means. They are not found easily *pour une raison.*"

Garrett jerked his hand back. "You mean they're crooks? They might be dangerous?"

"*Non.*" Henri's bottom lip drooped as he pondered the question, then he pinned Garrett with a meaningful stare.

"But there is some reason they—how do you put it?—'fly below the radar.'"

"Shit!" Garrett wiped his hand down his face.

Henri answered with a low chuckle. "*Oui,* and very deep. And, *s'il te plaît,* you must burn the document when you finish with it."

Garrett studied the names and addresses circled in red. If he made first contact with Tara's father, he could assess the situation and arrange for their meeting—and prepare them for each other.

He grabbed a pen and made the notes he needed, then returned the paper to his friend. "Do whatever you want with it, Henri. I have what I need."

Henri's perfect posture slumped in relief, but only slightly. "*Peut-être* Tara will stay in Paris a little longer *maintenant.* To know her father, *oui?*"

That Henri had gone to such measures to gain him and Dylan more time with Tara was staggering, and Garrett was overwhelmed with emotion. Loosening his tie did nothing to ease the tension in his neck and jaws. He leaned forward to capture Henri's gaze. "I'm speechless…that you would go to this extreme. You're a devoted friend, Henri, and Dylan and I are so blessed to have you in our lives."

Henri's Adam's apple bobbed, and for a split second, Garrett thought he saw mistiness in the Frenchman's eyes. "We are more than friends, Garrett. *Nous sommes frères.*"

Garrett stood and walked around the desk, pulling Henri to his feet and into a hug. "Brothers. I like that."

They slapped each other's backs extra hard to keep things on a mature male level, and then Garrett checked his watch. "If I leave now, I can go by the Kléber address on the way home."

He gathered the papers he'd been working on and stuffed them into his briefcase in the improbable event that he'd feel like looking at them once he got home. His gut told him tonight was going to be an exciting one with Tara.

Hell, every night was exciting with Tara.

Henri held the office door open for him to pass. *"Bonne chance,* Garrett." He added another hardy clap on Garrett's back.

"Thanks." Garrett headed toward the elevator, walking backward for one last acknowledgment to his friend. "I owe you," he called as the doors opened.

Henri's hands were in his pockets and he gave a shrug. *"Oui."*

Less than a half hour later, Garrett stood in the massive corridor of an ancient but elegant building that looked as if it had once housed a large corporation, but had now been divided into small, though impressive, suites.

The door his hand rested on had a thick, leaded glass window trimmed in rich mahogany. The etching on it read simply: *Jacques Martin, le concessionnaire.*

So this Jacques Martin was a distributor of goods although no hint was given as to the kind of goods distributed. But the location of his business spoke of his success.

Garrett pushed the door open to a small waiting room. Stepping inside was like hopping from one century to another. While just as elegant as its exterior, the office interior was very contemporary decked out in blue-gray walls with low, Italian leather sofas in the hue that he called purple but Henri insisted was *l'aubergine*—eggplant.

A young woman who looked as though she had been supplied by the Chanel School for Receptionists sat at a desk of sorts. Made either of glass or clear acrylic, it had no drawers and no real legs—except for the model-worthy ones that belonged to the receptionist. The workspace was nearly bare, holding only a small appointment book, an equally small pad, a pen, a cell phone and the elbows of the receptionist, though not her weight, as she sat very straight.

"Bonjour, monsieur." She greeted him with a tight smile. *"Comment puis-je vous aider?"*

"Bonjour, madame. Je m'appelle Garrett Hughes." He

concentrated to keep the question out of his voice. *"Je voudrais parler avec Monsieur Martin, s'il vous plaît."*

A question lit her eyes, gone as quickly as it appeared. She glanced at the appointment book. *"Avez-vous pris rendezvous?"*

Was he expected? Hell, no. Nor was the news he was bearing, if this turned out to be the right guy.

"Non. Je suis ici pour—" he chose his wording carefully *"—une affaire personnelle."* It didn't get much more personal than this.

A flare of color bloomed in the young woman's cheeks, but her manner remained cool and poised as she stood. *"Un moment."*

The tight, black dress clung to every curve of her body as she swayed to a door at the end of a long, narrow hallway. He watched her movements, imagining what the dress might look like on Tara, and found himself grinning at the image despite the nervousness that was causing his heart to beat a staccato rhythm.

The young woman rapped twice and stepped inside the office, though Garrett couldn't hear an invitation.

He stood waiting for two of the longest minutes of his life, and then the door opened again, and the young woman swayed out, followed by a middle-aged man with deep-set eyes and jet-black hair, combed back much like Henri's coif.

"Monsieur Hughes?" The man questioned, and Garrett's mouth went dry.

The lips. The mouth. It was the same one he had kissed a thousand times over the past week.

And it belonged to a man who, without a doubt, had to be Tara's father.

CHAPTER EIGHTEEN

GARRETT HAD BEEN LED into a false sense of security by Jacques Martin's easy, though cautious, manner.

The preliminaries had gone smoothly with the two men sitting across the desk from each other in Martin's office. Yes, he was Jacques Martin. Yes, he attended a year of college at Murray State University. His English was flawless, and he had shifted to it almost immediately.

The trouble started when Garrett asked if he remembered Faith Franklin.

A flash of recognition lit Martin's eyes at the mention of her name, or perhaps it was the sudden understanding of where this conversation was leading. His face drew in, as if he was concentrating hard. "No, I remember no person of that name."

Garrett had thought that might be the answer. He plunged ahead with the details of the story, assuring Jacques Martin that his memory was of no concern. "You and Ms. Franklin—Faith—celebrated together on graduation night. She admits that you both had too much to drink and ended up in bed together. A few weeks later, she found out she was pregnant from that encounter."

The Frenchman's face blanched. "That is impossible."

"But true." Garrett used the understating technique Henri was so fond of.

"Faith and I..." Jacques paused. "Had no relationship."

His use of the woman's given name convinced Garrett she was indeed remembered and hope flickered in his chest.

"Perhaps not, but you slept together, and a daughter was conceived. She's twenty-eight years old now."

Martin's white pallor seeped away, replaced by a red that had a purplish quality—though not quite *l'aubergine.* "And I suppose this person hired you to find me?" Resting on the desktop, his hand clenched and unclenched repeatedly.

"No." Garrett thought it best not to shift the focus to him and Tara. "She's a friend of mine, and she's come to Paris to find you."

"Surely with her hand out expecting part of my fortune."

The acid in his tone burned Garrett's insides as an image of Tara's injured hand flashed through his mind. "Tara's not like that. That's her name, by the way. Tara O'Malley. And she's not a…a gold digger. She's a wonderful person." Reminding himself to remain calm, he loosened his fingers from their tight grip and spread them wide to show he had nothing to hide—and neither did Tara. "She only wants to meet you. Nothing else."

Jacques snorted derisively, and then shrugged as if he were turning down a piece of chocolate. "I have no desire to meet her."

Garrett noticed his fingertips were leaving perspiration marks on Jacques Martin's antique cherrywood desk. He shifted farther back in his chair. "She's come a long way just hoping for a chance to meet you. She's a daughter you should be proud of."

Jacques's head tilted. "Is she?" He arched an eyebrow. "So are my other two children who were born to me by women other than my wife. My very jealous wife."

"But Tara is from a relationship twenty-eight years ag—"

Jacques Martin's fist slammed on the desk, but his voice was almost a whisper. "There was no relationship!"

Nothing good would come of engaging this man in a heated confrontation. Garrett backed off and tried for an offhand, man-to-man approach. "Surely, your wife wouldn't be threatened by anything that long ago, Monsieur Martin." He forced his lips up at the corners. "We all bear the sins of our youth."

The Frenchman leaned on his forearms, his tone conspiratorial and quiet. "My wife is young and beautiful—you met her when you arrived—and she is jealous of everything, even things that happened two years before she was born."

The new information slid into place, and the puzzle began to form a clearer picture in Garrett's mind. The young woman in the waiting room was a jealous trophy wife with a philandering husband who had two known children from outside his marriage. Now there was a third. Jacques Martin's character solidified, and if Garrett didn't care for him before, he disliked the man intensely now. He motioned with his head toward the door. "Your wife?"

"Yes, and my receptionist. Yvette is quite spoiled, and she detests sharing my fortune with the two other bastard children who surfaced. She threatens divorce *if*—" he placed meaningful weight on the word "—she learns of any further indiscretions. I have no desire to pay more alimony or look for a fourth wife yet, though I suspect I shall someday. Perhaps *then* I will arrange to meet your friend."

The statement was wrong on so many levels. Garrett had a strong desire to punch the Frenchman right in his arrogant pout. Believing Tara could have come from the loins of this asshole took a stretch of the imagination.

The two men eyed each other for a long moment, then Jacques Martin stood. "Now, Monsieur Hughes, I have work to do. If you will excuse me." He gestured toward the door.

Garrett stood and straightened to his full height, playing the intimidation card just for the hell of it. "I'll tell Tara you don't wish to see her, but I don't think that will keep her from coming anyway."

"If you do not want your friend hurt by rejection, I suggest you keep her away. If she comes here, I will refuse to see her." The man spoke as if he were referring to a cocktail mixed incorrectly.

Garrett's words pressed through gritted teeth. "Tara is a person. A beautiful, precious daughter." He paused, shifting his stance to throw one last curveball. "She looks like you, you know."

Interest flickered in Martin's eyes along with the hint of a smile. "Yes?" Obviously, that touched a nerve with the conceited bastard. But the moment passed quickly, and the near-smile glided into an oily sneer. "Then my imagination will have to serve me well. *Au revoir,* Mr. Hughes."

Garrett's imagination churned up an idea. If Martin could just see Tara's smile, hear her laugh. Could anyone who knew her not want her in his life?

Especially the only person in the world who could have created her?

If his plan didn't work, he had nothing to lose, whereas Tara and Jacques Martin had everything to gain if it did.

"I think it would be only natural to want to know what your father or daughter looked like, especially if you were aware of a strong family resemblance."

Jacques Martin pursed his lips.

"Like that." Garrett pointed to the man's mouth and smiled. "She looks just like you when you do that," he lied.

Martin's mouth flattened into a near-smile.

Garrett took that as progress and pressed ahead. "I understand why you don't want your wife to know about Tara," he lied again. "But that shouldn't stop you from meeting her."

"Non." Martin shook his head. "That will only open a door that should remain closed. I cannot chance that she might begin making the demands to see me."

Garrett pushed on, fully aware he was treading on dangerous ground. "What if it's done in such a way that she doesn't suspect who you are?"

He'd reached the point-of-no-return, and suddenly it felt as if the air in Garrett's lungs wasn't enough to sustain speech. He dropped his arms and shifted to give his chest room to expand, astounded to see Martin follow his lead. The man was invested in the conversation! A jolt shot through him. Was it possible this might actually work?

Martin's head tilted in question. "And how would you suggest that should be accomplished, Monsieur Hughes?"

Garrett held the breath steady as it left his lungs. "Perhaps we could arrange for a chance meeting. Somewhere you might easily go alone without raising your wife's suspicion."

Martin's eyes narrowed. "Go on. I am listening."

"Saturday morning, we could be at Place des Vosges at…let's say eleven o'clock?" Paris's oldest square was close to home and one of Garrett's favorite places. "You could be there and engage us in conversation. Perhaps share a bench with us."

"And you believe this Tara O'Malley will charm me, win my affection, and I will choose to inform her of my identity." There was no question in the tone.

If he looked very closely, Garrett could see a hardness that he didn't want to notice tightening the edges of Martin's mouth. He shifted his gaze to look directly in his host's eyes. "Yes, sir. I believe exactly that."

"And if I am not won over, what then?"

The twist in Garrett's stomach caught his heart as it sank, far too aware he was offering up Tara, the woman he loved, as a dispensable pawn in this risky game.

"I promise not to tell her who you are." Garrett jerked a business card from his pocket. He jotted Tara's number on the back and threw it on the desk in front of the man. "That's her number. I'll leave it up to you to contact her when you feel it's appropriate." That probably wouldn't be until Mrs. Jacques Martin number three was out of the picture, but Garrett felt reasonably sure it would happen someday. Maybe sooner than later.

A wall of silence fell between them and remained for what seemed like an eternity. Finally, Martin picked up the card. He turned it over to Garrett's information. "Soulard? Ah, the new beer I have been hearing about, yes?"

Garrett's ears perked up at the friendliness in the tone. Maybe they were getting somewhere. "Yes, that's right. We're a fledgling company, but we're doing very well."

The tips of Martin's fingers turned white as he gripped the corner of the card, and he shot Garrett a menacing look. "I have many friends in positions of power, Garrett Hughes. If this woman…this Tara…attempts to make any contact with me, it could be very, very bad for your 'fledgling company.'"

The ice in his voice sent a chill up Garrett's spine, but he kept his gaze locked with Jacques Martin's. Soulard. Everything he'd worked so hard for. And Henri…*damn! Damn! Damn!* He held out a hand that he willed not to tremble. "And I give you my word that will not happen."

Martin studied him for a moment longer then grasped his hand with a firm shake, turning them so that his was on top, in the position of control. "I trust you are as honest and intelligent as you seem. I will be at Place des Vosges Saturday morning."

Garrett turned and made his way out the door on legs that were stiff and wooden, breathing deeply to battle the nausea churning up his insides.

"Au revoir, madame." He nodded to Jacques Martin's third wife as he passed.

"Au revoir, monsieur," she answered, her cheeks blazing with color.

How much had she heard…or suspected?

No doubt, Jacques Martin was already rehearsing the lie he would use to calm her down. It would be interesting to see what happened when the Frenchman's icy manner clashed with his wife's heated one, but Garrett had no desire to stick around for that collision.

It was the Fourth of July.

Paris might have a fireworks display after all.

Garrett prayed that Henri and Soulard didn't get burned by the fallout of the explosion.

"You can't get 'em like this in Paducah, and certainly not in Taylor's Grove." Tara studied the meaty olive before popping it into her mouth. She rolled it around, like Garrett had taught her, appreciating the silky texture and allowing the subtle flavor of the oil to prepare her tongue for the burst of flavor. When she bit into it, the briny tang brought her taste buds to full attention. She held the plate out to Garrett, who declined the offer.

"You seem preoccupied." She pointed to the Scotch he'd chosen tonight over his usual wine. "Is everything okay?"

"Sorry. Hard day at work." He smiled and tilted Tara's face up with a finger under her chin. "Let me get my mind back where it belongs."

The kiss with a Scotch chaser brought a yummy warmth to her lips and a smile to accompany it. "That makes my two Jacques Martin strikeouts today bearable."

Garrett's smile wavered. "No luck, huh?" She shook her head as he pulled a pen and his copy of her list from his pocket. He drew a line through the top name. "This one isn't him, either."

"Thanks for checking, though." She got comfortable again with her head against his shoulder. It was too hot to sit so close on the terrace, but she couldn't resist the opportunity to relax in his arms and pretend that their time together wasn't waning.

Garrett didn't seem to mind. He'd chosen the bench over the separate chairs and pulled her close when they sat down.

He cleared his throat, and the way his body stiffened

against her side told her he was about to say something that made him uncomfortable.

"I know we've talked about it a little, but what will you do, really, if you locate your birth father and he won't meet you? I mean, he could refuse to even see you."

Bless his heart. Garrett was so concerned about how this ordeal would affect her. "I won't take no for an answer. I've come too far for that." She kept her head on his shoulder, but laid her hand against his chest. "You've still got a lot to learn about me, and my stubbornness is one of those faults you're going to run into."

His heartbeat quickened under her palm. "What if he threatens you? Or—" He stopped abruptly, and the concern in his voice pulled her around to face him. The worry she'd heard was etched in his face.

"If he throws me out?" She shrugged. "I'll still have accomplished what I came for. I'll have *seen* him."

Garrett took a deep swallow of his Scotch and a grimace followed. "But if *I* find him, he could threaten me. Or Dylan. Or Soulard."

Anger flashed through her at the thought. "He wouldn't dare. I'd get the law involved. I assume there are laws here to protect the innocent? And why would he threaten you or Dylan? Or Soulard…?"

Garrett didn't answer. Just stared mutely at her flat across the way. His silence jolted a question from her mind.

"What's with the worry all of a sudden?" She leaned in front of him to capture his attention. "Did something happen today?"

He glanced at her, then away, and shook his head. "No, of course not. I was just imagining scenarios."

She hadn't realized how seriously he was taking all this. Coming off the huge media blitz, his head was obviously wrapped around the future of the company. And he was always superprotective of Dylan.

Taking him up on his offer to help her search for her

father had been a mistake. He didn't need another responsibility or anything else to worry about.

"Tell you what." She interlaced her fingers with his. "Forget about looking for Jacques Martin. If it's meant for me to find him, I'll do it on my own. And if I don't find him, so be it." The worry lines on his forehead relaxed a bit, but they didn't disappear completely.

She pressed on. "Come straight home after work from now on. That will give you more time with Dylan." She shrugged her eyebrows playfully. "And if you play more catch with him, he might tire out faster and go to bed earlier, which will give you more time with me…" She moved to straddle his lap. "To explore my very…naughty…stubborn side."

His eyes met hers and the worry wrinkles deepened again. His glance shifted to her eyebrow ring and seemed to fixate there. "I wish we had more time." He touched the piercing with a fingertip. "I need to know…want to know… everything about you."

She captured his attention by placing his palm against her breast. "You want to know how I'm going to react when I'm placed in, shall we say…different positions?"

She rocked forward and pressed her mouth to his for the most erotic kiss she knew how to give. When she pulled away, she met his dark gaze and lowered her voice. "Take me inside and you can find out."

Without so much as a grunt, he stood up.

She wrapped her legs around his waist and let him carry her to his bedroom, and, once there, she took control of the situation, making good on her promise.

But, try as she might to get him to relax, intuition told her at least one of his brains was focused somewhere else.

FAITH WAS WORRIED TO the point of being almost frantic. Sawyer usually didn't stay out fishing this late.

It was nearly dark, and most of Taylor's Grove's population had vacated the town to watch the fireworks display at Kentucky Dam.

The day with the kids at the cabin had been pleasant although it wasn't the same with Tara and Sawyer absent. But Thea, Trenton and Emma, who claimed to be "the nearest thing to a daughter without all the pain involved," had kept her laughing for a good chunk of the time.

Any mention of Tara had usually involved something funny. But Sawyer's name had come up with a forced infrequency that dampened her spirit as much as the fake rain they'd lied to Tara about.

Just before nine o'clock, after a wait that had seemed a lifetime but was actually only a little over three hours, Faith heard the truck in the driveway and said a word of thanks that her husband hadn't fallen overboard and hit his head on the boat and drowned.

He probably wouldn't make the effort to see her, so she went outside.

"Hey." She spoke quietly as she approached and watched him flinch at the sound of her voice.

"Hey, Faith." He glanced up as he cranked the boat trailer loose from the hitch. "Trent called. He said y'all went to the cabin. Did you have a good day?"

The gentleness in his tone made her breath quiver in her chest. "It was nice." She hesitated. "Not like when we're all together, though."

He nodded and it felt like agreement whether he meant it as such or not. He picked up the tongue of the trailer and guided it back a few feet to its regular spot under the carport. The muscles in his arms and back bulged under the exertion, and the sight caused a flutter in her belly.

She closed her eyes, not wanting to need him, not needing to want him, so desperately. When she opened them, he was rubbing some grease off his palms onto his jeans, which was a little better, but still reminded her he was all man. She moved even closer to where he stood.

She glanced around nervously for a conversation starter. The boat was already covered, and she didn't see a cooler anywhere. "Did you catch any?"

"A few. Couple of pretty nice ones, but I let them go. Didn't really feel like messing with cleaning them." He pulled a rag from his back pocket, and lovingly rubbed away the dab of grease he'd gotten on the hull. Satisfied, he rammed the rag back where he got it. He leaned his back against the boat and hooked his thumbs in his front pocket. "Could we, uh…talk for a little while?"

"Sure!" She cleared her throat to subdue the eagerness in her tone. "Do…do you want to come in? I have some strawberry lemonade made. And rhubarb pie."

Rhubarb was his favorite, so passing it up would send her a distinct message. Her breath stopped as she waited for his answer.

Darkness had fallen while he put the boat to bed, but she saw his eyes flash in the moonlight. "Sounds good." He nodded, and her heart answered by picking up the quick rhythm.

She waited for him to fall into step beside her. "I've been going through your mom's stuff, making piles to keep, throw away and give away."

When he opened the door for her, his hand touched the small of her back. It was probably a reflexive move, but she pretended it was on purpose and relished the burst of warmth it sent through her.

While she cut the pie and poured the lemonade, they made small talk about the family treasures she'd discovered in the back of closets. They moved to the table on the back porch and the conversation moved with them to the kids. Even the talk about Tara stayed amiable.

"She thinks she's in love?" Sawyer chewed a bite of pie slowly. "That's a little impetuous, even for Tara. Don't you think?"

"I agree. But she's just like—" *you* was on her tongue,

but she bit it back "—an old mule about things. She'll have to figure it out on her own." The first sip of tart lemonade made Faith's mouth pucker, and the flutter started again when Sawyer grinned. "A little heavy on the lemon," she warned, and shifted her focus back to Tara. "She'll be home in a couple of weeks. Once she's away from him, he'll lose his appeal."

Sawyer laid his fork down. "Unless it's really love. Then being away from each other's going to make them miserable."

The question in his eyes was unmistakable. And, if he'd only asked, she'd have gladly told him how utterly miserable she was without him. But he didn't ask. And he didn't say he forgave her. And he didn't ask her to come back home. She waited, but the words didn't come.

Instead, he went back to his pie, and she pretended the drift in conversation hadn't happened. "Trent was surprised you didn't ask him to go fishing with you today." Actually, Trenton had been peeved when he found out he'd been left behind. Fishing with Dad had always been part of his Fourth of July.

"I had things I needed to think about. It was best for me to be alone." Sawyer wiped his mouth with his napkin and laid it beside his plate. "The pie was delicious. Thanks."

"You're welcome."

He began to rub his lip with the tip of his finger and her senses went on alert. "I need to tell you something, Faith. I want you to hear it from me first. Not out in town."

Her fork rattled against the plate, and she let it slide from her grip. "What is it?"

"Arlo came to see me yesterday."

The president of the Board of Fellowship's name made the air rush from her lungs. "Already?" Her voice was a hushed whisper with no force behind it. She and Sawyer had just separated Saturday, and this was only Tuesday. Surely no one would be pushing them yet.

"He said the board's meeting next week." Sawyer's eyes dropped to his hands folded in front of him on the table.

Faith's breathing came faster, and her head swam from the excess of oxygen.

"He's got some obvious concerns." Sawyer's eyes rose to lock with hers. The support was what she needed, and her breathing slowed as he continued. "And Sue's raising a big stink about our separation—just like we knew she would. Her argument's that we're being so secretive, it has to be something earth-shattering."

Faith's mind flipped back and forth as she considered Ollie's advice yesterday. "I told you I didn't care who knew, Sawyer, and I don't, but I've been thinking…" Scrunching her fingers to make quotation marks in the air she said "'The secret' is more Tara's than ours to share. I was going to leave it up to her."

He nodded. "That's what I want, too. I'm glad we're in agreement about it."

Faith voiced her thoughts. "Sue's going to keep worrying the snot out of everybody until she gets some answers."

"She may get them. She may not." Sawyer leaned back to rest his elbows on the arm of the chair and spread his hands. "We'll just wait and see."

Faith picked up his plate and stuck it under hers, which still contained half a piece of pie. "Tara won't be home until after the meeting. So, if the board meets next week, what does Arlo think will happen?"

"Oh, he was pretty adamant about that—" Sawyer swallowed hard. "Sue's already got the votes lined up. They're going to call for my resignation."

CHAPTER NINETEEN

"And I think he'll do it, Henri." Garrett pushed his *flammkuchen* aside. "Tara's father may be the most despicable son of a bitch I've ever met."

He'd barely touched his lunch, and, since he'd begun his tale to Henri about yesterday's ordeal with Jacques Martin, his friend hadn't touched his, either, seemingly determined to drink his meal instead. A special section of hell was probably designated for those people who wasted a meal from a Paris brasserie. To have wasted two servings seemed especially heinous.

But Garrett had been badly mistaken when he thought he'd be able to eat after filling Henri in on the details. The looks of horror that kept cracking the Frenchman's perfect facade were shredding Garrett's insides almost as much as the information he was hiding from Tara.

"Several times I started to level with her, but the damn tattoos and piercings kept reminding me of Angie and her wild ways and I'd remember that she has a bit of a wild side, too. I mean, we haven't known each other very long. What if…" The waiter brought Henri's third martini while Garrett declined a second glass of sauvignon blanc. "What if she decides she *has* to see him no matter the consequences?"

"And Tara *does* have the wild hair." Henri pointed a philosophical finger upward as he sipped his drink. "What if you and she break up and she desires to hurt you? The women like the revenge."

"I don't believe Tara would ever stoop that low."

"The blood of the son of a bitch runs in her veins, *oui?*" Henri growled into his glass. "And you did not believe Angie would ever leave Dylan. *C'est vrai?*"

Garrett flinched as the comment pierced the protective area of his psyche. Yes, he'd ignored signs that Angie was spiraling out of control. He'd battered himself for years over that one. But for Henri to bring it up right now was out-of-character.

"That's your last drink, Henri. You're getting drunk and mean, and I'm cutting you off."

Henri sneered. "You would cut me off from the last drink I may get in a very long while? They do not serve the cocktails in prison, *mon ami.*"

"You're not going to prison." Garrett massaged the back of his neck where the muscles were in knots. "No matter what happens, I'm not going to let anyone know—" he lowered his voice to a whisper "—where I got his address. Not Tara. Not anyone. I told you your secret is safe with me, and it is. I promise."

Henri sat the drink on the table, looking more downcast than Garrett could ever imagine. "I am sorry, my dear friend. I say the cruel things in anger. I only wanted to help Tara, and now the sweet soufflé goes *poof!* into my face." He drummed his fingertips on the table.

"If we'd been together longer, I'd feel more comfortable telling her the truth. But right now…" Garrett ran his hand through his hair. "I just can't. And I feel like such a lying sack of shit because I can't."

Henri took another drink, and his mouth pulled into a deeper frown. "Is the sack of shit lying as in telling an untruth? You cannot know what it is because the sack disguises what is inside? Or is the sack of shit lying on the ground doing nothing and is therefore worthless?"

"You can take whichever meaning you want, Henri." A remorseful sigh pushed from Garrett's lungs. "Either one fits me perfectly."

What he'd done hit him with the impact of a sledgehammer to his chest.

If things with Martin worked out, Tara surely would forgive the underhanded means he'd used to obtain the end. If they didn't work out—if Jacques Martin never made contact—Garrett would have to live with his lie, but Tara's exemption from the heartbreak of the rejection would serve as his consolation.

His gut churned the way it used to during a championship baseball game. In his mind's eye, he was once again standing in the batter's box. The pitcher had just given all he had to a well-executed curveball. Garrett had swung and connected, and the ball was hurtling into the stands.

Now he had to wait for his vision to clear to see if he'd hit it foul or if he'd scored the game-winning home run.

"TARA HAD TUNA ON HER pizza today, Dad." Dylan made a retching sound and squinched his face into a mask of horror. "Doesn't that sound icky?"

"It does sound icky, sport. But let's leave the sound effects off at the dinner table, okay?" Amusement twinkled in Garrett's eyes when he turned back to Tara. "Did you do that on purpose?"

"No." She reached over and gave a gentle tweak to Dylan's nose. "And I shouldn't have even told you, you little twerp."

Dylan giggled around his last forkful of mashed potatoes.

"I was craving pizza, and I couldn't translate the toppings, so I just pointed to one." She squinched her face to match Dylan's. "I chose poorly."

Garrett's laugh heated the already warm night air. She took a sip of the sweet iced tea she'd made to go along with the special Southern dinner she'd prepared of country-fried steak and gravy, mashed potatoes, green beans, fried okra and biscuits.

"You were hungry." She pointed to Garrett's plate, which looked as if it had been licked clean of his second round of helpings.

He nodded. "I didn't eat much lunch. Had too much on my mind." The tight lines around his eyes softened, and his lips relaxed enough for the scar to deepen. "But this meal—whew!" He leaned back and patted his stomach. "Gave me back my appetite."

"You want to talk about whatever's on your mind?" Tara prodded. He seemed better than last night, but something was still eating at him.

He winked and gave her a gentle smile. "Later."

The way he said the word tightened a coil deep inside her. Oh, for heaven sakes! The things this man could do to her with one word.

"Dylan!" A child's voice called from below, and Dylan ran across the terrace to the opening that accessed the courtyard beneath their terrace.

"Sit." She ordered Garrett back into his seat when he started to help her clear the table.

Dylan ran back to the table. "Jules has a new puppy! Can I go see it?"

"Sure." Garrett pointed to the opening. "Yell at me when you get down there and when you start to come back up."

Dylan nodded.

"Be back in a half hour."

"I will," the boy promised.

A little enticement would help him get back on time. "I fixed ambrosia for dessert," Tara informed him.

He cocked his head, giving her a quizzical look that made him a miniversion of Garrett. "Was it broken?"

"What?" It was her turn to be confused.

"You said you fixed it."

Sheesh! Nothing got by the little scamp. "I *prepared* ambrosia for dessert," she explained. "We'll have it when you get back."

"Okay." He took off at a full gallop and they heard the front door slam behind him.

Tara shook her head in feigned exasperation. "Guess I thought some Southern cooking would infuse some of the jargon into him."

Garrett stood and stretched. "I haven't had a meal like that since I've been here. You're a good cook."

She grinned. "When I get the hankering."

Garrett chuckled as they moved to the railing to watch for Dylan's appearance in the courtyard below. The little boy with the new puppy held it up proudly to show them, and they praised and cooed at it from one floor up.

In no time, a red-faced Dylan scampered into view, waving at them and then turning his complete attention to the neighborhood's newest member.

Garrett took her hand as they walked back to the table. "I'm up now, so you're going to let me help with these dishes." His stern voice didn't match the smile that teased at his lips.

She held up their locked hands. "Guess we have to let go, first."

He stacked the plates as she took care of the empty serving dishes. Not a scrap of leftovers for tomorrow's lunch. Her mom always said that was a good sign.

"So what did you do today, other than cook…and order an icky pizza?" He didn't ask about her Jacques Martin quest for the day, so she didn't mention it.

He was obviously aware she'd tell him when she found the right one, so for once, she left her elusive birth father out of the conversation. Besides, last night the subject had made him antsy. She didn't want a repeat performance of that.

"I went to Sacré Coeur." She loaded the dishes into the dishwasher as Garrett put things back into the fridge and cabinets.

"Oh? Did you take the funicular up to it?"

"No, I wanted to walk the hill," she answered. "The basilica was so beautiful, and the view from up there? Spectacular!" She chatted on about the Montmartre area's quaint streets.

"What else did you see?" He wet the dishcloth and wiped the crumbs and drips from the countertops.

"Well, I went to the cemetery and then I roamed around the Moulin Rouge area, but I didn't go in the theater." She paused, studying which button to push. She chose one and gave a satisfied smirk when the sound of water met her ears. "Man, those sex shops around there are sleazy. Not what I expected."

Garrett threw the dishcloth into the sink and pulled her into his arms. "Not a place I want you going without me, either."

His mouth came down on hers hard and insistent in a kiss that left her breathless and quivering. When he straightened and their lips parted, his arms remained locked around her as if he knew she would need the extra support.

And she did.

She leaned back and shook her finger. "You shouldn't kiss me like that so early in the evening. It sends my mind to places it shouldn't be. Gives me a terrible hankering for you."

He grinned, but then his eyes grew dark, his face serious. "I've got something I want to talk to you about." He nodded toward the door. "But we need to go back outside and listen for Dylan."

Her stomach squeezed at the intensity of his tone. "Is everything okay?"

"It will be if I can get you to consider something with an open mind." With a hand on her back, he led her outside to the terrace and the area with the railing.

"You sure are being cryptic." She peered into the courtyard below, but Dylan hadn't reappeared. He still had about ten minutes of his half hour remaining. She leaned an elbow on the wrought-iron barrier, giving Garrett her full attention.

"I don't mean to be." Garrett's voice was husky. "Fact is, I want to lay it all out for you." He faced her, leaning on his elbow. "I love you, Tara. We've said that's crazy to say this soon, but it's how I feel. But…" He paused and took her hand. "I'm not crazy enough to think we know each other as well as we need to in order to make any commitments."

For a minute there, she'd had the crazy idea he was going to propose, and it had her heart thudding so hard she could feel it from her temples to her toes. His last sentence calmed that quaking some, but she still couldn't trust her voice not to squeak.

Garrett didn't give her time to respond anyway. He plunged ahead with his proposal of a different kind. "I want you to consider staying longer. You've said yourself, you really don't have to be back until August. Stay a few more weeks."

"My ticket…"

"Can be changed. I'll pay the fee. Stay with me and Dylan, Tara." He let go of her hand and slid his fingers into the sides of her hair. "Let's use whatever time we have to explore this thing between us. It feels more right to me than any relationship ever has."

Tara stood speechless for a moment, her brain whirring too fast for her mouth to catch up.

Garrett seemed to understand. He leaned in to capture her mouth with another kiss that was soft and beguiling, packed with emotion.

More time with Garrett and Dylan was exactly what her heart had been yearning for, and it leaped in her chest as she considered his offer. "I would love that."

"Dad?" Dylan's voice broke the moment. He stood in the courtyard below, hands on hips. "I called you three times before you heard me," he chided, but his grin said he really didn't mind.

"Sorry, sport. Didn't hear you."

"Yeah, because you and Tara were kissing. I'm on my way up," he called as he disappeared from view.

Garrett's gaze returned to hers, his hands still in her hair. "That was a yes from you, I think?"

She nodded. "That was an enthusiastic yes from me."

"Good."

His mouth closed down on hers again, and it was his kiss that she felt this time from her temples to her toes.

(Overlapping text from previous page, partially visible at top)

CHAPTER TWENTY

"AND IT'LL GIVE ME MORE time to look for you-know-who and visit some places I haven't had time for yet."

The verdant, rolling hills of the French countryside came into view as Tara's train pulled out of the station, while images of the opulence of Versailles still spun in her head. Trying to accurately describe the place to Emma had proven futile, and even the photos she'd taken wouldn't do justice to the unfathomable beauty of the palace and its grounds.

"Garrett says we can take a weekend trip to the Loire Valley," she continued. "And we can do a weekend in Brussels, too, which is only four hours away. Isn't that crazy? He can be in Brussels, Belgium, in about the same time it takes us to get to St. Louis."

"What's crazy is my best friend's falling in love with a guy I've never met, who lives across the ocean, and she's pretending that she's extending her trip because she wants to see more of the country."

Tara grinned at the exasperation in Emma's tone. Ms. Counselor could take anything a troubled teen threw at her with calm patience, but Tara's quirky manner could send her into a dither faster than a bluegill on a cricket.

"I can't help it, Emma." Soul-lifting fields of sunflowers appeared in the distance. The train's speed increased, and Tara could feel the thrum of the movement low in her belly. "I've got a feeling I'm headed toward something… something big. Yes, I want more time with Garrett and

Dylan. I love being with them. But it's more than that. My father's here and he's alive, and I'm on the verge of locating him. I just know it.

The woman occupying the seat in front of her turned and gave a sympathetic glance, so Tara lowered her voice. "I only have nine addresses left. My odds have got to be getting better."

"Now I remember why we only went to Vegas once." The train was quiet enough for Tara to hear the sigh all the way from Kentucky to France. "I'm just jealous. Garrett's getting your whole summer. By the time you get back, we'll be heading back to work, and there won't be time for any of those things we'd planned to do."

"We'll still take that road trip to Memphis," Tara promised. "Graceland's on the to-do list this summer, no matter what else comes up."

"Thank you. Thank you very much."

Emma's barely recognizable imitation of Elvis sent Tara into a fit of the giggles. "That was god-awful."

"Yeah? Well, you ought to try it with drool running from a totally numb bottom lip."

Tara rolled her eyes. "One little filling, you baby. Try cutting off half your hand."

"I'll leave that to you."

The words were blotchy, and Tara realized they were about to lose reception. "Hey, you're cutting out, but before I lose you, do you think my mom and dad are doing okay?"

The line went silent, and Tara checked her phone. Call Ended was soon replaced by No Service.

She let out a frustrated sigh. Dad went fishing July Fourth. The family had a picnic at the cabin and had included Emma. Things were back to normal; she just needed to cool it with the worrying.

For the millionth time since she'd arrived in this country, she imagined how it would be when she met her father. He would smile, embrace her, introduce her proudly to his family. It seemed strange to think other siblings might be waiting in the wings to make their appearance on her life's stage.

She pressed her forehead to the train window, turning her attention to the landscape outside.

This trip was the most important journey of her life.

She didn't want to miss a single detail.

"WE MISSED YOU AT Ladies' Prayer Group, Faith. And the prayer meeting Wednesday night."

The voice behind her caused Faith's teeth to clench involuntarily. She'd known that Sue would make a beeline to her if she stepped even one foot outside. But she was tired of feeling like a prisoner in her mother-in-law's house. Besides, she could hardly do the gardening at night.

Faith tossed the handful of weeds into the bucket without turning around. "I didn't feel like going." She grabbed another clump of chickweed.

"All the more reason you should've been there. When we're at our lowest, we need to be lifted up. You need prayer right now more than anyone else I know."

Faith could swear she heard a smile in Sue's condescension. "Prayer I need." The chickweed broke loose. She tossed it away and turned to face her neighbor. Yes, indeed, the woman had a smug, mule-eating-briars grin on her face. "Gossip I can do without."

"Avoiding people isn't going to stop the gossip." Sue wrinkled her nose and sniffed as if the clean air harbored some kind of stench.

"Maybe not. But it gives me a rationale for avoiding people I don't like." Faith gave a fake grin of her own. "Like you."

"Don't blame me for your personal problems." There was the anger that always lay just below the surface of Sue's insecurity. It never took much scratching to bring it to the top. Fact was, Faith had always suspected Sue enjoyed being mad. She seemed to delight in telling people off, and this morning she was going to get a chance to start her day on the upswing.

"I'm not blaming you for *my* personal problems. I'm blaming you for leading the charge against my husband." The words left Faith's mouth in a much calmer state than they'd been formed.

"*Somebody* has to take the reins in a situation like this."

Faith snorted. "You mean, somebody has to stir the *pile*. So tell me, Sue, just what kind of situation are you making this out to be?"

Sue's fisted hands rested on her hips and her head wobbled as she spewed her venom. "One where the preacher and his wife are having serious enough marital problems that they separate, yet they won't tell even their closest friends what's going on. It looks bad. Real bad. And I'm not going to sit around and wait until the Taylor's Grove Church becomes the laughing stock of Marshall County."

Faith pulled off her gardening gloves. "Have you and Ed ever had problems, Sue?"

"Well, of course we've had problems. Every married couple has problems."

Faith leaned forward and used a stage whisper. "Did you want those problems talked about?"

"*I* didn't put them on public display by moving out of the house." The smug smile came back out to play at the edges of her mouth.

"And neither did Sawyer." Faith took the gloves in one hand and slapped them against the other to knock the dirt off, imagining the hand was Sue's smirk. "But he's who you're going after."

Sue's chin lifted. "He's the leader of the church."

"Or maybe he's the easier of the two targets." Faith opened the cage on her own anger. "You know if you come after me, I won't take any of your crap."

Sue gasped and Faith rolled her eyes at the drama.

"Oh, like you've never heard the word before. Your daddy started the church and you control the purse and therefore you *think* you control Sawyer." Maybe Sue had been right all these years. Telling somebody off *did* feel good! "What you may not realize is that Sawyer doesn't just put up with your *crap* because of your position. He genuinely likes you, Sue, which isn't true of most of the people in this community. He somehow manages to see through your hateful, mean ways to some goodness inside you—though goodness knows where. Did you know that? Sawyer's your staunchest supporter. 'Sue has a good heart,' he always says. 'She means well.' Well, look at where *that* faith in humanity has gotten him."

Sue's face was the color of the beet Faith had unearthed a few minutes earlier. "I'll make you sorry you ever crossed me, Faith Franklin. I'll get to the bottom of this secret you're harboring, and when I do, I'll have you run out of town on a rail. And your husband, too. He'll never lead another church in this county or anywhere near here, if I have my say."

"Oh, that's what you do best, Sue. You have your say… whether it's the truth or not." Faith took a menacing step in the woman's direction, brandishing the weeding fork she still held. "Now, get out of my yard before I throw you out. Lacy's plants don't need any more of your…fertilizer."

Sue nearly ran from the yard.

Faith watched with amusement, breathing hard and thinking the woman might actually vault over the gate in her haste to leave.

She gathered up the gardening tools, the task having suddenly lost its appeal. Guilt tightened her chest for participating in such an ugly scene in Lacy's lovely place of tranquility.

She needed to finish the calls she'd started two days ago, and then she'd go see Sawyer and tell him what had just happened. He'd been sure the Board of Fellowship would follow Sue's lead. Well, her tirade had pretty much put the last nail in that coffin.

The house was cool and stepping inside was like putting a soothing balm on her temper.

Faith sat down at the table with the list of numbers she'd jotted down in her quest for Jacques Martin and picked up the phone.

The placement office at Murray State didn't have any information on the former student, nor did the Office of Alumni Affairs. But the woman there had been most helpful. She'd suggested Faith use the yearbook from her college sorority to help contact her sorority sisters—one of them might have information on Jacques Martin.

It was a splendid plan, and had kept Faith busy the past two days catching up with old friends and rehashing old times.

She dialed Tina Lofton's number and listened to it ring. No answer. No answering machine. No voice mail. She'd try that one again later.

On to Mary Jane Mitchell. She had only the first three numbers punched in when the phone vibrated in her hand.

"Faith? It's Cheryl Wheeler. Cheryl Gates Wheeler. I got your message."

An image of Cheryl Gates as she looked thirty years ago settled in Faith's mind. "It's so good to hear from you, Cheryl. Thanks for calling me back."

They chatted for a while, catching up on the years that had been swept away like they'd been caught in a flash flood.

"So, Cheryl, do you remember Jacques Martin?" Faith tried to modulate her voice so it didn't sound too full of excitement…or trepidation.

"That hot French guy? Nobody could forget him." Cheryl laughed. "Didn't you two hook up on graduation night?"

Hearing the secret she'd harbored for so many years spoken aloud as if it were common knowledge caused Faith's throat to tighten. When Cheryl said it, it sounded so worldly and modern, So opposite of the real her, but perhaps the woman she might have been if she'd not spent the past twenty-nine years as the preacher's wife in Taylor's Grove.

"Yeah, just that once, though." She forced a smile, trying to borrow that worldly persona. She'd practiced what she would say and fell easily into the lie. "But my husband and I are thinking about a trip to France, and I thought I might try to look Jacques up. Would you happen to know if he's still in Paris?"

"He *is* still in Paris," Cheryl answered, and Faith tilted the phone away from her mouth and nose to keep her sporadic breathing from sounding creepy. "Or, at least, he was two years ago. Kay and George Yancy had dinner with him. You remember Kay and George? George and Jacques were fraternity brothers."

Faith swerved the phone down to her mouth. "Yeah, I remember Kay and George well." Her hand shook as she grabbed the pen and notepad.

"Well, they live in Frankfort now. George is a state congressman." That came as no surprise. "But we see them occasionally. I'm sure they could put you in touch with him."

Her? In touch with Jacques? Lord, no! "That would be great. Could you give me their number?" Faith's throat felt as tight as her grip on the pen.

"Sure, just let me get Kay's personal number, one second."

A few seconds later Cheryl returned to the phone with that fateful number and Faith jotted it down on her notepad.

"Just so you know, Faith, I tried calling Kay a few days ago and found out she and George are on a cruise. They won't be home until Sunday, so, if I were you, I'd wait until Monday or Tuesday to call."

"That's no problem. I'm not in any hurry." Faith's throat relaxed a little, knowing she had a few days' reprieve before she had to act on this. "But thanks for the number, Cheryl. I really appreciate it."

"Oh, you're welcome. We should get together sometime."

"Yes, definitely, when life isn't so hectic," Faith answered. *Which is never.*

"I hear you." Cheryl paused, and Faith didn't pick up the conversation. "Well, I'll let you go. I hope you enjoy your trip."

Trip? Oh, the made-up trip to France. "Yes, thank you. Hopefully we'll actually end up going." Adding the qualifier softened the lie in her mind. "Thanks again, Cheryl."

After the goodbyes, Faith stared at the number she'd scribbled. Her hand had been shaking so much, it would be difficult for anybody but her to make it out.

Kay. Tara. Jacques.

Now, with the possibility of Jacques being as close as three calls away, Faith's courage began to slip.

She hadn't thought about the possibility of Jacques Martin's return to *her* life. She'd imagined Tara meeting him. Coming back to Taylor's Grove, thrilled with the new discovery. She'd never considered that the man himself might show up, too.

The air conditioner kicked on, and the vent above her head directed a cold breeze down her back, causing a shiver to course through her.

What would it be like to see Jacques Martin again? Would she have heart palpitations? Yeah, but not because of any attraction to him.

Because of Sawyer.

With everything else he was going through, could she do this to him, knowing it could be the end of the marriage she wanted so desperately to save?

The choice had come down to choosing her daughter's happiness or her husband's and therefore her own.

A tear fell on the paper, smearing the ink and obliterating the last two numbers.

She might have considered that as a sign not to start the sequence of actions if the number wasn't already etched into her brain.

CHAPTER TWENTY-ONE

THE MATTER WAS OUT OF Garrett's hands now. He could only hope things went as he'd planned and that he hadn't made a mistake.

It all seemed a little surreal that Saturday morning had come at last. That they were strolling hand in hand toward a bench where, unbeknownst to Tara, they would await the meeting with her birth father. He, with his heart in his mouth, hardly able to concentrate enough to put together a coherent sentence. She, in her yellow dress, smiling and bright.

"You look like a freshly picked sunflower...or maybe a drop of the sun." He kissed her hand as they walked. "You've certainly brought light and warmth into my life... and Dylan's."

The smile she rewarded him with both soothed his heart and made it ache.

For the millionth time, he wondered if Tara would pick up a familial vibe or notice a resemblance between her father and herself.... Though he'd exaggerated the similarity in looks in order to appeal to Jacques Martin's ego, it definitely existed. Her mouth was an exact copy, but her eyes and nose belonged to her mom.

As they approached Place des Vosges, another worry niggled at his brain. Why in the hell, with Paris's abundance of parks, had he chosen *this* particular place for their meeting? It seemed a cruel twist of fate.

Paris's oldest square, beautiful in its symmetry, had

drawn its share of famous residents, and Parisians and visitors were still drawn to its beauty.

But it was also a well-known place for dueling, for God's sake, and *that* irony caused the sweet morning air to leave a bitter taste on Garrett's tongue as he spoke.

"King Henri the second was wounded here in a tournament." Garrett guided Tara to an empty bench. A quick glance around the immediate area turned up no Jacques Martin, which relieved and agitated Garrett at the same time. "He died of the wounds."

"Poor Henri."

"Yeah." He tried to ignore the irony in that statement, too, and changed the subject by pointing to *maison* number six. "Victor Hugo lived there. It's a museum now that houses some of his things. Did you know he went mad?"

He watched Tara's mouth curve down at the corners. "No, but I can believe it. I've never cared for *Les Mis*. I mean, it was uplifting, but the story was so sad."

"It must not have given him much joy, either. He took to carving furniture…with his teeth, earning him the nickname Beaver Hugo."

Laughter rippled out of her. "You're kidding, right?"

Garrett held up three fingers. "Boy Scout's honor. Well, not about the nickname, but the part about carving out furniture with his teeth. Or, at least, that's what I've read." He grinned. "Probably started out as a pencil chewer."

"So maybe the madness was caused from all the lead he ingested." She said it with a straight face that dissolved into a giggle. "Nope, I don't believe you."

"God, you're beautiful when you laugh." He nabbed her smile with a kiss that she returned with enough enthusiasm to make him wish they were home in bed.

She jumped, then her lips tore away from him, and she leaned over. "Oh, look!" she cooed.

A small blue ball lay at her feet with a tiny Yorkie rushing toward it in pursuit.

Garrett looked up to see Jacques Martin watching them intently, and his breath froze in his chest.

He counted the man's steps as he approached although instinct had already told him the distance between them.

Ten paces.

TARA PICKED UP THE BALL as the Yorkie skidded to a halt at her feet.

He didn't bark, just looked at her with bright, expectant eyes, twitching with excitement. The ball she held matched the dog's turquoise collar, which was set with jewels that sparkled in the sunlight like real diamonds.

Surely not. But the man who approached them—the dog's owner—had an affluent air about him that screamed "Money!" and changed her mind to *maybe so.*

"Bonjour, madame...monsieur." He rattled off something she didn't understand, and, as she had gotten used to doing, she turned to Garrett for a translation.

His eyes cut to the stranger and back. "He said he's sorry for the clumsy throw."

"Ah, English?" the man asked.

"American." Tara leaned over to allow the dog to sniff her hand. He rewarded her with a couple of licks. "Can I pick him up?"

"But, of course." The Frenchman nodded toward the dog's continued licks. "Attila likes you."

She chuckled at the name. "Attila the Hun?" The tiny dog felt almost weightless in her hand and barely made an indent on her dress when she placed him on her lap. He had way too much energy to just lie there, though, and scrambled up to lick her face. She laughed as he covered her nose with doggy kisses. "More like Attila the Honey, if you ask me."

A wide smile split the Frenchman's face and his dark eyes brightened. "You make a good joke."

Nice-looking for a middle-aged guy, the man was of

medium height and build, with dark hair combed back
from his face. Heavy brows framed dark brown eyes with
a keen and perceptive gaze that seemed to miss nothing.
His pink shirt was crisp and tucked neatly into trousers
that appeared to be of black silk. Expensive-looking black
leather shoes and belt. A leash that matched the dog's collar dangled from his hand. His whole demeanor exuded
elegance—something she'd grown used to in Paris.

Attila flipped around, looking at her over his shoulder,
and wagged his almost nonexistent tail.

"He wants you to throw the ball, but not too far."

Tara waited for a strolling couple to get past and then
tossed the ball a few yards away.

Attila shot from her lap, catching up with the ball before it stopped rolling. He stretched his little mouth wide to
pick it up and skipped his way back, jumping on the bench
beside her and placing it back in her lap.

"What a good boy you are!" Tara scratched behind his
ears, and he closed his eyes and tilted his head to give her
full access to his favorite spot. "He's so adorable. How
old is he?"

"Seven months." Pride showed in their visitor's eyes almost as if he were talking about his child.

Tara scooted closer to Garrett and pointed to the empty
space beside her. "Would you like to sit down?"

The man gave a slow nod. "Thank you. You are very
kind."

"Yes, she is." Garrett gave her leg a pat. Attila added
his approval by stretching over Tara and licking his hand.

When the gentleman sat down beside her, the pleasant
fragrance of his cologne filled her head. Unlike the light,
clean aroma that surrounded Garrett, this was a heavier
scent, exotic and mysterious. Perhaps a good match to the
man who wore it. But the two extremes dueled for domi-
nance in the air around her, with a distinct advantage determined by the way she tilted her head.

She picked Attila up and buried her nose in the soft fur, finding a third scent that was decidedly feminine. "You smell good." She rubbed her nose against him again, and he licked her cheek in response.

"My wife's *parfum*." The man rolled his eyes. "I tell her a dog with such a name should not smell like a woman, but she puts a little on her hands and strokes it into his fur."

Tara fought back her own eye roll. She couldn't imagine her mom putting perfume on a dog. And never in her wildest imagination could she imagine her dad walking a dog that wore a diamond-studded collar. The absurdity almost dislodged a snort she kept at bay only through sheer will.

She tossed the ball again, and the dog sprang from the bench.

The Frenchman's laugh was low. "He already has you trained. Now he will allow you to throw the ball for him all day."

"That's okay." Tara clapped when Attila grabbed the ball and held it up like he was showing off his prowess. "We don't have any place we need to be for a while."

"So you are American?" The man gave her a sidelong glance and passed a hand over his brow. The heavy Rolex on his wrist glinted in the sun—another thing she couldn't imagine ever seeing on her dad. If Sawyer were ever given such a thing, he would sell it and send the money to some mission.

"Yes, I'm from Kentucky," she answered.

"Ah!" Attila jumped onto the bench between them and the man took his turn at throwing. "I have visited Kentucky, I believe. But only once, and that was many years ago."

Garrett jerked beside her, coughing hard several times.

"You okay?" she asked and he nodded. She turned back to the stranger. "You should go back there sometime." Most of the French people she'd talked with on this trip weren't familiar with Kentucky. It was nice to converse with someone who had some familiarity with the place. "It's really beautiful on Kentucky Lake in the summer."

The Frenchman shrugged. "Perhaps I'll return someday."

Garrett coughed again, this time louder and harder. She hoped he wasn't coming down with something.

"Hey, babe." Apparently he'd gotten the coughing under control enough to speak. "I'm going to find a bottle of water. Be right back, okay?"

She nodded.

"You want anything?"

She shook her head. "No. I'm good."

"Your husband?" The man nodded toward Garrett as he left.

"Boyfriend." The words felt good on her lips. She couldn't keep from smiling, waving bye to him when he glanced back over his shoulder.

The man pointed to the half hand she'd waved with. "You have had an accident."

"A wreck on a motorcycle." She ran her fingertip up the scar on her arm. "But I've since sworn off those things." She held her hand out for a shake. "I'm Tara O'Malley, by the way."

"I am—" he paused to throw the ball for the dog whose energy didn't seem to be waning in the least "—François Martin."

All of the moisture in Tara's mouth abandoned her at the sound of the man's surname. "Martin?" The word came out as a croak.

"*Oui,* Martin. It is the most common surname in Paris." He gave an apologetic shrug. "Much like Smith or Jones in the U.S."

Tara nodded mutely. She already knew that, but to have an actual Martin sitting beside her seemed an amazing coincidence. She'd been feeling like she was getting close to finding her father. Maybe this man was here to help.

"I, uh." She sucked in a breath. "I've been looking for a friend of my family while I'm here, and *his* name is Martin. Jacques Martin. You wouldn't happen to know anyone by that name, would you?"

A hint of laughter lit the man's eyes before he gave her a small smile. "*Oui,* Tara O'Malley. I know two men who have the name of Jacques Martin." He held up two fingers and ticked the names off. "My father's name was Jacques Martin, though he died many years ago. And my son is also Jacques Martin. He is fifteen years old and could not be the friend of your family, I think."

"No." Tara's chest heaved with disappointment. She tossed the ball for the waiting Attila. "You don't know of any others. Cousins…?"

The man shook his head, his heavy brows drawing in and nearly touching. "No, but as I said before, there are many Martins, and Jacques is also very common."

Garrett headed back toward them from across the park, and a spark of joy lit Tara's insides at the sight of him. Thankfully, he'd ignored her when she declined the offer of a drink. He held a bottle in each hand.

"Are you originally from Paris?" She continued to make conversation.

"Yes. I was born here and have lived here most of my life although I also travel extensively." The touch of pride was evident again.

"It's such a beautiful place." Tara rolled her shoulders to loosen the muscles that had tightened when the man told her his name. "I'm glad I got to come see it for myself."

The Frenchman's eyes met hers directly. "Yes, she is a beauty." He swallowed hard before he glanced away, obviously moved by his love for the city. "I have much to be proud of."

The wistful timbre of his voice and the sudden serious tone the conversation had taken made Tara a little uncomfortable. A shiver scampered up her spine, though there was no logical reason for it. But Tara sensed sadness in this person. Perhaps he'd experienced a recent loss...or maybe he was the type of wealthy person who was never quite satisfied no matter how much he had.

"Here you go."

Garrett's familiar voice wrapped her in instant warmth. She took the Orangina he proffered, enjoying the solidness of him as he settled down beside her again. She downed the small bottle of liquid in two gulps, the cool drink soothing her parched throat.

Garrett laughed. "Thought you weren't thirsty."

"I'm glad you knew better than I did." Pointing to her companion, she added, "I should introduce you two. Garrett Hughes, meet François Martin."

She should have timed it better, should have allowed Garrett to swallow what was in his mouth. Instead, she watched him choke when the name Martin left her lips. He managed not to spew Orangina, but his face turned so red she was afraid he was going to burst a blood vessel. His body jerked with spasms and he finally gave in to a series of long, loud coughs.

"Sorry." At last, he got himself under control enough to extend his hand. "*François* Martin, is it?"

"Yes, that is correct." François's hand dropped to caress Attila's head, his several-carat diamond ring glinting sunlight into Tara's face.

She turned to face Garrett. "His father and his son are *both* Jacques Martin."

Sympathy softened Garrett's features as he brushed the back of his finger to her face. She gave him a soft smile and kissed the finger.

The weight of his arm settled on her shoulder and he pulled her to him in a quick hug. "I'm sorry, baby," he whispered into her hair and then kissed the same spot.

She winked to let him know everything was okay.

Attila's energy had finally run out, and he snuggled

into Tara's lap. A tiny snore escaped, which made them all laugh.

"Ah, the excitement of the day has tired out the great Attila the Honey." François stood and held out his arms. Tara handed the sleeping dog to him, and François gathered him to his chest. "I think it is time for us to say *au revoir.*"

A sudden restlessness spurred Tara to her feet. "It was nice to meet you, Monsieur Martin." She gave Attila a final scratch, her eyes tangling with François's dark gaze. "If you're ever back in Kentucky near Paducah, please look me up."

"Thank you, lovely Tara." François's hand rested briefly on top of hers. "I shall remember your generous invitation. *Au revoir,* my dear."

As he left them, Tara tracked his movement until he was completely lost from sight, then she plopped back down beside Garrett. "Can you believe that? A Martin. Right here beside me."

"Yeah, that was quite a coincidence," he said, but without any enthusiasm. "C'mon, Tara." He stood up and held his hand out. "Let's go see the crafty stuff Hugo cut his teeth on."

She let Garrett take the lead, her mind still occupied by the new acquaintance she'd made.

Allowing her hopes to get too high would be a mistake. But her growing love for the Hughes guys and the conviction that nothing happened by chance made her heart feel like it could soar with happiness.

Luckily, Garrett's grip on her hand kept her firmly grounded.

FAITH HAD CALLED TO TELL him she was on her way, so Sawyer was waiting for her at the back door when she arrived.

She hadn't been back to the house since she'd left a week ago yesterday. It felt odd to be welcomed into her own home. She glanced around, relieved to see he was keeping the place clean. But, of course, he would be. Sawyer's standard of clean living reached into even the tiniest crevices of his life.

A faint aroma of burned food hinted that his cooking skills hadn't improved, though.

"I was glad to see you at church tonight." He handed her a glass of iced tea, their fingers touching as she took it. If he felt the jolt from the touch like she had, he gave no indication.

"You preached a good sermon." She took a sip, finding the strong brew sweetened and *lemoned* exactly the way she liked it. "You always do."

She'd skipped the morning service for the second week in a row, but Ollie had come by on his way this evening and talked her into accompanying him. He convinced her that a show of confidence and solidarity with Sawyer might encourage the Board of Fellowship to stop and consider what they were doing.

She was glad she'd taken his advice. It also put that first-time awkwardness behind her, although the stares and whispers had sent her into the mother of all hot flashes.

But she'd survived.

And now she knew she could.

Sawyer nodded toward the den. "Let's go in there where we'll be comfortable."

Finding her favorite spot on the sofa, she slipped off her shoes and pulled her legs up under her, making herself at home. Sawyer sat in his recliner, but he didn't kick it back.

"You first," she said.

When he'd invited her to come by after church, she'd hoped he was going to ask her to move back home. If he did, it would make what she wanted to talk about much easier.

But the distance he kept didn't bode well that reconciliation would be their topic of conversation. She steeled herself against whatever the purpose of this visit turned out to be.

"Well, I'm sure you've already thought about it, but we haven't talked about it." Sawyer leaned forward and rested his elbows on his knees. "If I lose the church, we'll have to put the house up for sale. I've been studying our finances all week, and I just don't see any other way. Selling Mom's house and the cabin will help, but it won't pay off the mortgage." He leaned back and passed a hand across his eyes. "Of course…if another church will have me…it would mean a move anyway."

If another church will have me. If was the definitive word. Their future together was not so definitive though— *have me*, not *have us*.

Before all this, he'd always referred to them as a team.

Guilt pushed a heavy finger into her chest. The house they'd planned and built together. The place where they'd raised their family. Their sanctuary from the world.

All of it would be lost.

Because of her lie?

Yes. But what it actually came down to was her lack of faith in Sawyer's love.

If she'd trusted his love enough to tell him the truth all those years ago, they wouldn't be going through this now.

She would never make that mistake again.

"We'll do whatever we have to do." She deliberately chose the plural form and felt some of the guilt seep away with her words. "Sell the house. Sell both houses and the cabin. I'll get a job. I'll get two jobs. It's not like I have kids to stay home for anymore."

His tired eyes regarded her for a moment over the rim of his glass. He opened his mouth to say something, and then closed it, setting his drink down with a shrug. "Thanks for not going all emotional on me. I don't think I could've stood that."

"I'm giving up emotional…except with Sue." She saw

his chin buckle at that admission, but Faith wasn't here to mince words. They'd already been through yesterday's argument with Sue. No use pretending it hadn't happened. "I've decided that logical's a better fit at my age."

"It looks good on you." Her heart fluttered as she watched the corners of his mouth turn up, and the tiniest light of interest flare in his eyes. "But then, everything looks good on you."

His tender smile and flirtation made her heart race. But she couldn't let herself get carried away. The news she bore would douse that flicker in a hurry.

And there was no use letting the flirtation go any further. Building hope only to dash it again was cruel to them both. So, without preamble, she blurted, "I've found a promising connection to Jacques Martin, and I think I can get his address for Tara."

Sure enough, all the emotion drained from his face and the flame went out, leaving behind a white mask, devoid of expression.

"I got it Friday." She plunged ahead, just wanting to get this—all of it—over with. "But I didn't bring it up because I can't do anything about it until tomorrow, and I wasn't sure what to do about it anyway."

"What do you mean you're not sure what to do about it?" Sawyer's fingertip brushed his lip, back and forth.

"I have the number for someone who may be able to give me his number and address." She took a fortifying breath to help her get through this next part. "But I think I need to leave it up to you whether or not I make the call."

His head tilted in question. "Me? Why?"

"Because you appear to be the one with the most at stake."

His lips pressed together into a thin line. "Because, if she finds her birth father, she may push me out of her life."

"I don't think that's going to happen. But it's possible he could visit if they hit it off. She might bring him here to show off where she grew up. Next to Tara, you seem to be the one who could be the most affected, so the decision of whether I call or not has to be yours. I refuse to do anything else that might screw your life up worse than I have already."

"You haven't screwed my life up, Faith." The voice was flat again, almost robotic, so the words, placating as they were, didn't live up to their intention.

She snorted in return. "Well, I haven't made it a rose garden lately."

She wasn't interested in debating the issue. It was all water under the bridge, and she dismissed it with a wave of her hand. "I'm not here to discuss that. I just need to know whether to make the call in the morning or not?"

Sawyer leaned forward again, studying his tightly clasped hands. "The whole time she's been over there, I've been praying that she wouldn't find him. That's selfish, I know. It was me I was worried about." His eyes drifted up to meet hers. "What kind of father would I be if I put my happiness ahead of hers?" He paused and shook his head. "Not the kind I *want* to be." He sat up straight, opening his hands to rest them on the arms of the chair. "Make the call, Faith. She needs this, and in some weird way that I don't understand, maybe I need it, too."

His fingers brushed at the corner of his eye, and Faith's throat constricted. "You're sure?"

"I'm committed," he answered. "But the truth is that I understand a little better how Abraham must have felt when he was leading Isaac up the side of that mountain."

She nodded. "I'll call first thing in the morning."

CHAPTER TWENTY-TWO

GARRETT WATCHED THE FIRST light of dawn break through the bedroom window and catch in Tara's wild curls. Snuggled against his side, her naked breasts rising and falling to the rhythm of her soft breathing, she had the countenance of an angel—or so he'd been thinking. But the fiery glow suddenly surrounding her reminded him what a she-devil she could be in bed—a tempting red-haired seductress whose magic brought out a passion that he'd buried years ago and had all but forgotten.

She stirred in her sleep and he felt himself stir in response, despite his lack of shut-eye the past two nights.

Since Saturday, he'd been waiting for the call that hadn't come—the invitation he'd been sure Jacques Martin would extend to Tara to join his life after their encounter.

Seeing the fulfillment of her quest sitting next to her, while she remained so blissfully unaware brought out a protective instinct in Garrett that he'd thought was reserved for only Dylan. He wanted to grab Martin and shake him until he loosened the part of the man's brain that would allow him to think clearly instead of filtering everything through his wallet.

Just wake her and tell her the truth. Lay out the entire story about Martin's fears of losing his wife and his fortune, his threat to Soulard. Make her promise never to approach the man.

Tara stirred again, shifting her head slightly. The sunlight had eased over enough to catch in the ring that decorated her thin brow line. It flashed like the beacon from a lighthouse, warning of dangerous waters.

Warnings he'd ignored from Angie.

I hate you.

His insides coiled into a hard knot pulling from his stomach to his throat.

He closed his eyes, taking long, deep breaths, and ran a hand over his sweat-drenched face.

Tara was nothing like Angie, and he couldn't continue this asinine habit of allowing his guilt over his wife's death control the workings of his heart.

If any warning was truly flashing, it was the one in his brain to guard against broken promises.

He'd promised Henri to keep his secret safe. He'd, also, given Martin his word he wouldn't interfere.

A man was only as good as his word.

And he'd learned the hard way that he had no business trying to control other people's lives.

But he had to believe that Jacques Martin would make that call. It might take a few years, but it would happen. And, when it did, he would be there with Tara in his arms, holding her, protecting her, dancing with her in her time of joy.

He opened his eyes to find her watching him, sunlight on her face and lovelight in her eyes.

"Good morning." She slipped her arm around his waist and her leg moved subtly between his. Not quite as subtly, she pressed against him in unspoken invitation.

"Good morning." He kissed the brow ring and then let his lips wander to her nose, her mouth and on to her neck.

Her contented sigh feathered around his ear. "I love you, Garrett."

The words spread through him like wildfire across a

dry plain. He moved lower, covering her with kisses, igniting her heat with his mouth and hands, fanning the flame.

The blaze raged hotter, an inferno that burned away any lingering doubts of whether true love could grow in such a short span of time. Garrett allowed it to consume him, reaching for only the slightest protection as the combustion moved toward their collective core, shattering them both in a simultaneous cataclysm of passion.

He held her tightly until the delicious spasms subsided and her breathing returned to normal. He loosened his hold then, but only with his arms. His heart gripped tighter than ever.

"Wow," she whispered. "I never knew it could be like that. Like this. Just...wow."

The room was bright now with a light that Garrett wasn't sure originated from the sun. An ember from the wildfire continued to burn in his heart, waiting for the next piece of kindling—a touch or a whisper—to make it burst into flame.

Wildfire could be destructive, he knew, but it could also be beneficial in the larger scheme of things. Though its uncontrollable blaze moved through an area with thoughtless destruction, the final result was ultimately freshening.

Wildfire had wiped the area of his heart clean, destroying the leftover debris from times past. It had burned away the rubble of that which was dead.

It had cleared a space for new growth.

At 9:07 a.m. Monday, Faith made the call to Kay Yancy, whose only recollection of Faith was that she'd slept with Jacques Martin graduation night.

A reluctance in Kay's tone had Faith doubting whether securing Jacques's number was going to be possible—even with the plausible lie about the intended trip to Paris.

"Jacques's very different than he was at Murray." Kay's

voice held a hint of warning. "He's very private. And very wealthy. A bit of a snob, actually."

"Oh, what a shame. He was such a neat person back then." Faith's heart quivered at the thought of what she might be putting Tara through, but she pressed on with her made-up story. "I'll give him a call and feel him out before we make the trip. If he doesn't seem interested in getting together, I won't push it."

"Well." There was a long pause on the other end. "Here's his address and phone number." Kay quickly relayed the information. "But this is his place of business. We've never been invited to his home."

"Oh, this will be just fi-fine." Faith's throat went dry as the nonchalant attitude dissolved. The numbers and letters she'd written down were scrawled across the page as if the hand that wrote them belonged to someone recovering from a stroke.

She didn't press Kay to chat. They had little in common. So she thanked her acquaintance, said her goodbyes and hung up.

Then she punched in Tara's number before she lost her nerve.

"So, IF I GET HOME ON THE second, I can sleep all day on the third, make the meeting the morning of the fourth and spend the rest of that day getting things ready for the kids on the fifth. What do you think, Ethel?" Tara made some quick notes in the back of her journal. When she finished this call, she'd contact the airlines and change her returning flight, so she wanted to make sure she had her dates correct.

Ethel, the school's ancient secretary, gave one of her trademark cackles. "You can do that at your age, doll. I'd have to sleep for a week to recover from the jet lag."

"I'm actually gaining time coming back," Tara explained. The phone beeped and she glanced down before she spoke again. "Hey, Ethel, my mom's calling, so I'm going to let you go now. I'll see you August fourth."

"See you, doll. Have fun."

Tara was all smiles as she retrieved the other call. Three more weeks with Garrett and Dylan! "Hi, Mama."

"Hi, sweetpea."

Her mom's voice sounded off, and Tara gripped the phone a little tighter. "You okay? You sound upset."

"I have...I have Jacques Martin's business address and phone number...if you still want it."

A violent shudder echoed in Tara's speech. "You—you have it? H-how?"

She heard the deep intake of breath on the other end of the line. "One of my sorority sisters from Murray knew someone who's been in touch with him fairly recently."

"That's unbelievable." Tara was thankful for the chair beneath her as she felt her legs go weak. But she wished she hadn't just drunk that double espresso. Her heart was galloping at a scary pace. "Yeah. Yeah, I still want it."

"Kay says that he's really wealthy, and quite a snob." The warning in her mom's tone was clear. "Are you sure you want to go through with this?"

The pounding in Tara's temples said she wasn't sure of anything at that moment, but her mouth ran ahead of her brain. "I'm sure."

"Do you have something to write on?"

Tara glanced down, a little surprised to find a pen already in her hand and her journal opened in front of her. Oh yeah, she'd been talking to Ethel and jotting down dates.

Was that only a minute ago?

"Gah." She swallowed, trying to wet her parched throat. "Got it."

Her mom spoke slowly, spelling out the name of the street. "Do you know where that is?"

"No." Tara pulled out her map. "I can find it, though."

"First make sure it's not in a bad part of town, and don't

go by yourself. Take Garrett with you." It was unclear if she meant for safety or moral support. "Kay said he's very private."

Tara flinched. "So, you're saying he might not welcome a long-lost daughter from Podunk, Kentucky."

"I'm saying just be careful, precious. Guard your heart." Tears were evident in her mom's voice.

"I will, Mama." Her own eyes blurred, and she wasn't sure if the tears were joy, fear or something else entirely.

"And call me afterward. Okay?"

"Okay." Tara glanced at her watch. It was after four. She couldn't let this wait until tomorrow. "I need to go now."

I need to go now!

"Okay, baby. I love you, and I'm praying for you."

Tara found comfort in those words. "You always are. Thanks, Mama. I love you, too. Bye."

Tara ran a shaky hand over her face. She needed grounding. Without a second thought, she called Garrett. It went to voice mail, which meant he was in a meeting. She knew the protocol. If it was an emergency, call the business line and the secretary would get him out of the meeting.

She hung up.

This wasn't an emergency. If the secretary interrupted the meeting, he would panic and think something had happened to Dylan.

She opened up the map and found the street. It wasn't too far away from the café where she sat. Too far to walk maybe, but a cab would get her there in ten minutes. Fifteen tops.

Her breathing became erratic.

In fifteen minutes, she could be meeting her birth father!

He might not want to see her.

If she called, he might turn down a request to meet. But if she went to his place of business, she had a good chance of at least seeing him.

She looked at her blue sundress. It was classy and went

well with her coloring. Her hair was fairly tame today since the humidity was low.

She dug in her purse and found a tin of strong mints, popping a couple in her mouth.

Coffee breath taken care of.

She took a few bills out of her wallet to cover her check and laid them carefully on the table.

She was ready. She could do this.

Her knees felt weak, but she willed them to hold her up long enough to hail a taxi.

The driver nodded that he understood the address, and then she was whizzing through the Parisian traffic…on a magic carpet ride to meet her father.

She punched Garrett's number into the phone again, and once again listened as it went to voice mail.

"Garrett, it's Tara. Mama called and she's managed to get Jacques Martin's address and phone number from somebody she knew in college." She was giddy with excitement now, and the words rushed out. "I'm…I'm going to see him! Right now! I decided not to call first. It's his business address, so I figure I'll at least get a glimpse of him if…if nothing else." She knew she was rambling. "I'll tell you all about it when I get home. Wish me luck. I love you."

She put the phone away. Then, on second thought, she got it back out. She needed to think about what she was going to say, and she didn't want anything interrupting her thoughts the rest of the way there.

Not even Garrett.

She turned off her phone.

GARRETT CHECKED HIS phone as he headed back to his office.

Two calls from Tara. Odd. But the meeting hadn't been interrupted, so there was no emergency.

He dropped the legal pad on his desk.

The last call came in four minutes ago, and she'd left a voice mail that time.

"Garrett, it's Tara. Mama called and she's managed to get Jacques Martin's address and phone number from somebody she knew in college. I'm…I'm going to see him! Right now!"

Oh, God. No.

"…his business address, so I figure I'll at least get a glimpse of him if…if nothing else. I'll tell you all about it when I get home. Wish me luck. I love you."

Garrett's head spun, and he leaned on the desk with both hands.

Tara was on her way to Jacques Martin.

Bloody hell!

He had to talk her out of this.

Her phone went to voice mail.

Damn it.

Think!

He pressed a hand to his forehead, vaguely noticing that both were covered in sweat.

Call Martin and warn him she's on the way.

But he didn't have the number. He'd given Henri the original back and destroyed his copy, like he'd promised.

The sound of panting echoed in his ears, and he realized it was his own.

Where was Tara? Was she out in the city somewhere or had she gone from home?

Either way, she had a head start. He couldn't ask Henri for the number again. Too great a risk. And there was no time, besides.

Garrett rushed from his office, stopping just long enough to let the secretary know he was leaving. Then he was hailing a taxi and spewing Jacques Martin's address from memory.

His only hope—Soulard's only hope—was to make it there before Tara did.

He called her number repeatedly during the ride, giving up, finally, and leaving a voice mail.

"Tara, if you get this message before you get to Jacques Martin's address, please don't go in. I'll explain everything. Just wait for me outside. I love you."

me said you on lithographs information and to support
Allen maddison, please that good i'll remember you find
supervisor me suitable into you.

CHAPTER TWENTY-THREE

TARA STOOD IN FRONT OF the imposing building, trying to
bring her breathing down to something that resembled normal rate.

The taxi ride had taken longer than she'd anticipated
with a couple of fast sprints through harrowing tunnels
that had her clutching her seat and thinking of Princess Di.

Amazingly, several times the fact that she was headed to
meet Jacques Martin slipped from her mind as she feared
for her life. Then, the purpose of the taxi ride would pop
back into her mind and she would clench her teeth and
hope that meeting her father would still remain an option
in this lifetime.

She should probably spend some time in contempla-
tion of the fabulous architecture of the building, but later
seemed like a better time for that activity. Right then, she
needed to get on with the task at hand before she lost her
nerve…or her chance.

And she had no guarantee Jacques Martin would even
be in, or that he would welcome her unannounced visit.

She opened the massive door and stepped into a huge
corridor whose pink granite floors cast a rosy hue to the
ivory walls—an effect she found both charming and soothing. What appeared to be suites of offices lined the sides
of the wide hallway. A large lobby opened up the center of
the first floor, and beyond it was another corridor, identical to the one she was standing in.

She felt as if she'd just fallen down the hole with Alice

and needed one of those mushrooms that made her larger—
and more significant.

At least one breath came easier when she located the
directory on the wall, but when she came to the name, it
went erratic again. *Jacques Martin, le concessionnaire,
137.* She touched her finger to the glass, leaving a smudge
after she removed it.

She began walking, checking the numbers on the doors.
All lower one hundreds. When she reached the lobby, dismay brought her to a halt. Seven more identical corridors.
Three continued toward the back of the building. Two came
into the lobby on her left, and two on her right.

She stood there for a minute, not sure which way to go
next, wishing she'd waited till Garrett could have come
with her and divided up the territory. Then her eyes fell
on the ornate golden numbers above each corner of the
hallways.

On her left, 190 and 180. On the right, 120 and 130. She
walked with a purposeful gait down the right-hand 130 corridor until she stood before 137.

Jacques Martin, le concessionnaire.

She had no idea what that meant, and it made not one
iota of difference to her.

The coolness of the suite hit her, as did the coolness of
the drop-dead gorgeous receptionist whose crisp welcome
held the warmth of a freshly dug radish.

"Bonjour, madame."

"Bonjour, madame," Tara answered, hoping *madame*
was okay to use even though she was pretty sure the woman
was younger than she. "Um." Tension closed her throat and
her mouth went dry, causing her to pause. *"Je m'appelle*
Tara O'Malley. *Je...uh...*crap!" She forgot the words. Closing her eyes, she "read" them from her frontal lobe. *"Je
cherche Jacques Martin. Est-il ici?"* She opened her eyes
and smiled in relief.

The receptionist, who may have been younger but had a

much older air about her, didn't smile, but looked Tara up and down thoroughly, pausing at the missing fingers long enough to wrinkle her nose in distaste. Tara had seen it happen before, but coming from the embodiment of feminine perfection, the gesture made her flush. "And do you have an appointment, Ms. O'Malley?" The young woman's English pushed through a thick accent.

"No. I just decided to pop in." *Seriously? Pop in?* "Monsieur Martin is an old friend of my family's. I was in town, and I promised my mother I would stop in and say hello. They were friends in college." Tara fought the urge to cover her mouth with her hand to stop her talking.

"Jacques is very busy." The use of the man's first name, and the way she said it, made Tara think this was more than a boss-receptionist relationship. "I will see if he wants to take time for you." Her tone said he wouldn't.

The young woman rose from her seat like Venus in a red peplum halter over a black-and-white polka-dotted pencil skirt. Tara gawked at her red patent leather five-inch stilettos as she walked away from the desk.

Who dressed like that for work? Even in Paris.

The sound of a door opening stopped the young woman's forward movement, but Tara's eyes continued to where François Martin appeared in an office doorway.

"Yvette." He took a couple of steps in the woman's direction before his eyes landed on Tara.

"François?" Tara felt her face break into a smile at this happy coincidence.

For the second time since she'd entered the suite, her smile wasn't returned. François's face turned hard and cold, the look in his eyes even colder.

Tara gave a little wave and took a couple of steps in his direction. "It's me. Tara O'Malley. We met at the park Saturday. The Place des Vosges? We shared a bench and I played with Attila."

The receptionist swung around to glare at her. "You met

Jacques at Place des Vosges Saturday? And why do you call him François?" Her icy stare jerked toward François and she said something Tara wouldn't have understood even if her consciousness hadn't stalled on the first part of what the woman had said.

She'd called him Jacques.

"Your name is Jacques?" Tara's brain was slow to download the meaning behind this discrepancy, but her heart heard the message loud and clear and took off faster than the taxi she'd arrived in. She pointed a quivering finger. "You're Jacques Martin?"

"I want you to leave. Now." He bit the words out.

Tara's mind whirred, trying to make sense of what was happening while protecting her psyche from the encroaching attack. Comprehension breached the barrier quickly. "Meeting you was no coincidence, was it? You knew who I was Saturday…knew I was your daughter."

The young woman's face contorted into a mask of disgust. "Your daughter?" She pointed to Tara's hand and barked a mean laugh. "This…this freak?"

Tara recoiled from the blow as the ice queen melted into a puddle of condemnation, French words spitting out like poison from a cobra.

Temporarily forgotten by the woman and the man, whose placating words seemed to be falling on deaf ears, Tara took a moment to rise from the verbal punch that had knocked the wind out of her and take stock of what she knew.

François Martin, the man she'd had such a lovely conversation with in the park…the man with the precious, well-behaved dog…was her father, *Jacques Martin*. He'd lied about his name because he didn't want her to know who he was.

But how did he know who *she* was? How did he find out she even existed? How did it happen that *he* found *her* when the number of people who knew of their relationship could be counted on her fingers—even with some of them gone?

Someone had alerted him.

Someone arranged the meeting in the park without her knowledge.

Someone wanted to give *him* the opportunity, but not her.

Her stomach drew into a hard knot, making her queasy. *Please don't let me throw up now.*

Who would do such a thing? Who would make such a cruel, heartless arrangement when she'd come so far and gone to such lengths?

The door of the suite opened, and the place went quiet as her companions' squabble was sidetracked by someone's entrance.

Tara swung around to face the door.

"Garrett?"

She hadn't given him the address in her voice mail, had she?

"Get out of my office." The words spewed from Jacques Martin's lips. "Both of you. Get out, and never let me see your faces again."

Tara heard the command, yet her feet stood firmly planted to the spot. Any movement was going to take her over an emotional abyss, and so she stood motionless, listening to the growl and the shrieks from the couple behind her, unable to tear her eyes from Garrett's face.

He didn't have to say a word. The answers to her questions were all there in the grim set of his mouth.

A pain unlike anything she'd ever experienced sliced through her and lodged in her chest.

"No."

Garrett read the word on Tara's lips, and watched the question in her eyes dissolve into anguish. Her look speared him from across the room, but he ignored the warning and moved closer.

"Monsieur Hughes, I advise you to leave, and take your girlfriend with you." The threat was evident in Martin's tone. "I have lost my patience with you both."

"Give me a minute, will you?" Garrett shot a look the man's way, but continued moving toward Tara, needing to touch her, hold her. Her look chilled him and, with every step, the wall of ice between them grew thicker.

"Tara," he said gently. "I can explain. You just need to hear me out." He held out his hand, but she stepped around him, out of reach.

"You…both—" her eyes darted from him to her father "—should be ashamed."

The words brought an eerie moment of silence to the room, and then Martin sneered. "Her mother spread her legs easily," he said in French. "The daughter of the whore should be ashamed. And you have had your minute. Now go say goodbye to your Soulard beer."

A double helix of anger and frustration spiraled through Garrett, twisting everything in its path. "I didn't tell her. I kept my word." He bit out the words through clenched teeth. "Tara, tell him how you found him."

"Mama got your address from one of her sorority sisters at Murray." Tara addressed Martin with her chin lifted, but the defiant pose couldn't mask the hurt brimming in her eyes. "I should've listened to her. Coming here was a mistake." With a dismissive toss of her head, she stalked toward the door.

"Wait, Tara," Garrett called after her, but she ignored him. He would run to catch up in a minute, but first he would have his say.

Garrett locked gazes with Martin and dared him to look away. "You've just thrown away what would've been the best thing to ever happen to you, Monsieur Martin. Something that would've given depth to your shallow existence."

He pointed to the closing door. "And you may think you're all big and powerful because you can crush Soulard for no reason. But nothing you have makes you deserving of Tara. She was a gift of love, and unlike that one—" he nodded toward Yvette "—wanted nothing but love in return."

He left, keeping his dignity until the office door closed. Then he broke into a jog.

Tara wasn't in the corridor, as he'd expected, nor was she anywhere in sight. He ran through the lobby, looking this way and that. People stared at him as he jostled past groups and bumped into those standing in his way.

Where was she? His gut clenched into a knot. How could she have disappeared so quickly?

He exited the building at full speed and spotted her standing at the curb. "Tara!"

She ignored him and waved at an approaching taxi. It swept by her, giving him a chance to catch up.

He touched her shoulder and felt her flinch. When she spun around, he could see the wetness on her cheeks, and the accusation in her eyes made him flinch in return.

"How could you, Garrett?" She ran her hand through the top of her hair, sweeping off the band that was keeping the curls back. They sprang loose in a wild riot around her face that animated her speech as she punched a finger in his direction. "How could you do this to me?"

He caught her hand in midair. "I didn't mean for it to turn out like this." She winced, and he realized he'd squeezed her injured hand. He loosened his grip, and she jerked her hand from his. "When I found Martin, he didn't want to meet you. In fact, he threatened to ruin Soulard if I didn't keep you away."

"And you didn't tell me? Why?" She pinned him with narrowed eyes.

"I should have."

"But you didn't. Why?"

"I was concerned, if we ever broke up, you might retaliate by going to him anyway...." He shrugged, refusing to dig himself any deeper into the ridiculous hole he'd started.

Her look was incredulous. "You really think I could ever be *that* vindictive? That I would try to ruin your career over a failed relationship? What kind of person do you think I am?"

"I didn't think. I reacted like I would've with Angie."

"Because Angie and I are so much alike...with the tattoos and piercings and all." She shook her head in disgust and a deep breath shook her chest.

Garrett pressed on, wanting to get the whole story out so she'd have a clear picture. "Martin refused to see you, but I thought, if he could just meet you, he'd fall in love with you like I have." Her eyes filled with tears again, but she didn't say anything. "So I arranged for him to meet us in the park, and I gave him my word I would leave it up to him to contact you."

Her chin quivered and Garrett felt the tremor deep inside. "But he didn't contact me." She sniffed, fighting the tears. "And he wasn't going to, was he? Why? Would I be so terrible to claim as a daughter?"

"It's not you, baby." Garrett laid his hands on her shoulders and leaned down until his eyes and hers were even. "It's his wife. The receptionist." Tara frowned, but understanding dawned through the shimmer of her tears. "He's giving money to two other out-of-wedlock children. His wife, who is his third and younger than you, by the way, is jealous the kids are taking too much of his wealth. She threatened divorce if it happened again."

"So the freak had a price tag attached." Tara wiped a hand down her face.

"What does that mean? You lost me."

She cut her eyes away and waved her hand. "Never mind."

He slid his grip down her arms and attempted to pull her into a hug, but she shook her head and pulled away. "So you were going to let me go home...go on for the rest of my life...never knowing I'd met my birth father?"

"I thought he would come around eventually, and that, until then, what you didn't know wouldn't hurt you."

"Augh!" The sadness in her eyes morphed into anger. "How could you do that? You took the choice away from me, and gave it to him. And neither of those choices was yours to make."

Her logic made his own seem horribly flawed in hindsight. "I'm sorry. I screwed up."

Her eyes narrowed again. "How did you find him, anyway? This address wasn't on my list."

His promise to Henri flashed through Garrett's mind. Damn it! "I can't tell you. I promised I wouldn't because it could get someone in a lot of trouble."

Her eyebrows shot up, and it seemed as if her face became all eyes. "Ah! More knowledge about my father that I can't be trusted with." She threw her hands in the air, which brought a taxi to a screeching halt at the curb beside her.

When she jerked the door open, Garrett moved to join her, but she blocked the way, shaking her head. "No, Garrett. I need to be alone."

"We haven't finished talking." He held the door as she climbed in, his jaws aching with tension.

"We have for now." She pulled the door closed, and he heard the lock snap.

The sound caught in his ear, its finality jarring loose memories that ran a shudder up his spine.

He touched his phone, poised for the text message he feared might follow in the taxi's wake.

None came.

He raised his hand to hail a taxi, wondering whether Tara was going home or if she was headed somewhere else.

They would talk later when they both had clearer heads.

Right then, he needed to get back and talk to his bosses at Soulard and hope he hadn't signed a death sentence for the company.

TARA HELD HER COMPOSURE fairly well as the taxi careened through the streets of Paris. She didn't go back to her flat. Couldn't. Not yet.

The hurt she felt wouldn't let her listen to Garrett's explanation again right then. Wouldn't let her get into what was sure to bloom into an argument in front of Dylan.

Tears glided from her eyes, but she held in the sobs.

The taxi dropped her off at the Tuileries—the gardens adjacent to the Louvre. The place brimmed with people, but she felt protected in her anonymity. Everyone here had cried at one time or another, and she likely wasn't the only one crying there even at that moment.

She found a small space at the end of a crowded bench and allowed the tears to continue falling, confident they weren't too noticeable behind her large sunglasses.

They slowed, and while she wasn't feeling better, she at least got her breathing under some control. So when the phone rang and she saw it wasn't Garrett but her dad, she answered with a modicum of confidence that she could handle this conversation.

Boy, was she wrong.

"Hi, lovebug."

Just the sound of her dad's voice brought all of the wicked pain to the surface.

"Oh, Daddy…" She cried, channeling her inner four-year-old with giant sobs that garnered looks of curiosity and pity from the people near her. "Jacques Martin didn't want anything to do with me. Told me to get out. And his wife called me a fr-fr-freak."

"Hey…hey," the familiar, gentle voice soothed across the line. "Calm down. It's okay."

"No, it's not okay," she blubbered. "Nothing's okay. Garrett found him a week ago, but he doesn't trust me enough to tell me *how*. And then he set up a secret meeting between Jacques and me, but he didn't trust me enough to tell me the man I met was my father. He left it all to Jacques…who doesn't want me."

"I'm sorry, sweetheart. I'm not following all this, but it sounds like you've been treated badly. Just tell me how I can help."

"You can't. Nobody can. My birth father doesn't want anything to do with me, and the man I'm in love with doesn't trust me."

"But *we* love you. Your family…your friends…your students. The people here love you and trust you. You're in a strange place with strange people, but your life is back here. Nothing about the way *we* feel about you has changed."

That made her cry harder.

Tension infused her dad's voice when he spoke again. "Tell you what…I'm going to have your mom call you, okay? I think she might be better over the phone than I am."

"O-okay. Isn't she there?"

"No, she's at Mom's. I'll call her right now and have her call you, okay? It'll just take a couple of minutes."

"Okay. Th-thanks, Dad."

"Love you, baby."

"I know." She broke down sobbing again, words not coming in response to her dad's goodbye. She waved pitifully, knowing he couldn't see her, but wishing he was there.

When her phone rang again, she answered her mom's call with another loud sob.

FAITH'S HEART ACHED AS only a mother's could.

If she could've gotten her hands on Jacques Martin at that moment, she could've easily rendered him incapable of fathering any more children with just a few twists—and thoroughly enjoyed herself in the process.

She didn't pass judgment on Garrett for his part in this. It sounded as if he'd tried, though his attempts to help were obviously misguided.

She cried in sympathy for Tara's disappointment and hurt and for her own frustration that this was not in the realm of things she could kiss and make all better.

As Tara talked, her desolate tone chilled Faith's soul. It wasn't fair that Garrett was involved. Her daughter needed someone's arms around her.

She needed someone's arm around her, too. She longed for Sawyer's quiet calm.

"And he actually threatened Garrett's company?" Faith broke into Tara's lengthy blow-by-blow of what had happened, incredulous at the extent of Jacques Martin's vindictiveness. Obviously, life had changed the pleasant young man who always had a smile for everyone.

Tara, who seemed calmer now and could put several sentences together without her breath snubbing, filled in missing details of the backstory.

As Faith listened, a noise outside pulled her attention to the window.

Sawyer had pulled into the driveway.

Bless him! He knew she needed him, and he'd come to be with her.

The ache in her chest eased, knowing in a few minutes she wouldn't be alone. He would be in here with her. Would hold her. Comfort her. And together they would lift Tara up and hold her from across the distance.

This was it. This horrible incident was the catalyst meant to reunite them.

Healing would begin. Maybe already had begun.

Then she noticed what she hadn't before.

Sawyer hadn't pulled into the driveway. He'd backed in.

She watched in disbelief as he got out of the truck and gingerly hooked up the trailer to his bass boat.

He was going fishing!

At a time like this? When she needed him? Knowing that she *and* Tara both needed him?

He made quick work of the task as Tara continued to

talk. Faith only added supportive, guttural phrases, "uh-huh…right," at the appropriate lulls.

Sooner than she could've imagined, he pulled out of the drive, bass boat in tow.

Tara's story gave an excuse to cry openly, so she did.

But she cried not only for her daughter now, but also for herself.

Sawyer's action this time, even more than his inability to make love to her, screamed the message she hadn't wanted to acknowledge but which came through now with horrible clarity.

Their marriage was over.

CHAPTER TWENTY-FOUR

THE LAST TIME GARRETT had endured a day this bad was when Angie died.

For the past five hours since leaving Jacques Martin's office, he'd been sequestered with the *cadres supérieurs,* the upper management at Soulard, who'd brought in the *président-directeur général* after one hour. And a couple of hours later, the owners had been pulled in via teleconference from Brussels.

When all was said and done, they'd decided to do nothing at this point. The initial panic that stemmed around the possible identity of Martin's powerful friends gave way to logic that there was simply no way of knowing who these people were without confronting the man himself. That idea was vetoed because it would push the power in Martin's direction. Plus there was always the chance he would come to his senses and not do anything.

Garrett's gut told him otherwise.

But for now, a wait-and-see attitude had been adopted.

The construction worker in Garrett's brain had a jackhammer running full bore as he made his way home. His temples throbbed, his throat ached, he was starved, and talking with Tara was still on the agenda.

He did get to utter his one bit of good news to Henri's pale expression when his friend met him at his apartment door. "You can relax, Henri. I told them a private investigator found Martin for me, which isn't a lie. You did your investigation in private. That subject never came up again."

Henri's shoulders slumped with relief. "*Merci beaucoup,* Garrett. I also spoke with Tara when she got home. I told her the truth about generating the list."

"Thanks, man." Garrett shrugged out of his jacket and tossed it on the couch. "And thanks for watching Dylan— was he good for you?"

"Dylan is always good for me. He played with the new puppy downstairs, ate a good dinner and fell asleep quickly."

"And Tara? How is she?"

Henri tilted his head with a shrug. "Sad."

Garrett glanced across the terrace. "Better than angry, I suppose." The lights of her flat were still on.

"I am not so sure of that." Henri's look was guarded and fretful, and neither boded well for what lay in store. "So tell me…what is the plan at Soulard?"

Garrett pressed his fingers into his forehead and rubbed hard. "It's difficult to know what to do because we don't know what direction Martin's strike will come from, if it comes at all. So, for now, we're going to sit tight and not do anything."

Henri's pursed lips curved down at the corners. "I suppose that is all we can do." His eyelids drooped with exhaustion. The past few hours had been hell for him, as well.

"Go on home, Henri." Garrett clapped his friend's back, trying to lighten the mood. "I'll get Tara to talk with me here or on the terrace."

"You are certain she will?"

"No," he answered honestly. "But, if she'll talk to me at all, we need to be alone."

"*Je comprends.*" Henri laid his suit coat gingerly over his arm. "*Bon chance, mon ami. À demain.*"

"Yeah, I'll see you tomorrow."

Garrett saw him out and then wasted no time heading for Tara's.

She evidently had been watching for him because she

came out on the terrace and met him halfway. He hoped that was a good sign, but one glance at her red, swollen eyes told him it wasn't.

The pounding jackhammer shifted into high.

Her rigid stance, with her arms locked across her chest as if it were freezing out rather than ninety degrees, held no welcome, and the hug he'd wished for didn't come, so he shoved his hands into his pockets for lack of anything better to do and waited for her to begin the conversation. Giving her control of the situation was a must, even though it went against every fiber of his being.

The fact was he'd gone behind her back, good intentions notwithstanding. He had to face the consequences.

"Henri told me what he did." Her voice was quiet and low, her tone calm. "How he found my fa—Jacques Martin. I'm grateful for the lengths you both went to, and I'm sorry my actions put Soulard in jeopardy. If I'd had any inkling, I wouldn't have gone to see him."

Garrett pulled his hands from his pockets, opening his arms to her. But she ignored the gesture, so he rested them on his hips. "I should've told you everything. Should've leveled with you from the start."

Her eyes met his straight on. "Yeah. You should have." She glanced away, running a hand through the top of her hair, sliding the other into a side pocket on her dress.

The outfit was the same she'd had on in Martin's office. There it'd looked fresh and crisp. Now, it was wrinkled as if she'd been wallowing in it, which, he realized, was probably exactly what she'd been doing. The thought pinched his heart.

"It might *not* have changed the way things turned out, but I keep wondering if it *could* have." The wistfulness in her voice clawed at his insides. "If I'd approached him differently. In my own way. I'm good with people. With students and parents. Even the difficult ones."

Garrett recalled the conversation with their mutual

friend in the States and the guilt in his stomach took on more weight. "Josh told me that."

"But you didn't believe him because anybody with my… interesting characteristics…" a bitter note edged into her voice as she held up her half hand "…couldn't be someone others would trust."

Her words slammed into him, momentarily shattering his resolve to relinquish the control. He stepped toward her, and she stepped back before he caught himself. He didn't want her to leave. Things would be okay if he could just keep her talking. "When he told me that, I didn't know you well. Now I do, and the trust is there. Believe me."

"That's the problem, Garrett." Her voice grew quiet—ominously so—and the hairs on the back of his neck rose. "I don't know when I can believe you and when I'm being judged on the Angie scale." Tears cascaded down her cheeks, scalding Garrett's heart with their honesty. "I love you, but love can't sustain a relationship. There has to be trust, and we're just not there yet."

His heart caught on her last word and pounded it into his brain. "But we'll get there."

"We don't have time." She shook her head. "Even another three weeks isn't enough to build anything that can sustain the time and distance we're up against." She took a deep breath and he watched it shudder in her chest. The next one he took responded in kind.

"Don't, Tara." He held a palm up to make her stop talking. Giving her control was a mistake, and he had to slow this train down and veer it away from the cliff it was hurdling toward. Then she reached out and took his hand, and the gesture came so unexpectedly…so gently and so unlike anything Angie would've ever done, it threw his game off and shocked him into silence.

"I've decided not to change my ticket," she went on. "I'm going home on the fifteenth like I originally planned. It'll be better for everybody this way."

He found his voice again and opened his mouth to protest, but she countered with her coup de grâce.

"Especially Dylan."

His heart stalled in his chest, and his head felt like it would explode with the acknowledgment that she was right. This sure as hell felt like the worst that could happen, but devastating Dylan would trump everything.

"I love you, Tara," he said simply.

She nodded. "Yeah. I think you do."

Their eyes met for one horrible and tender moment that held all the passion of what they'd had together...and all the regrets of what might have been.

Then she turned and ran back to her door, flipping off the light on the terrace.

Leaving him in the dark.

TARA WAS STARTLED AWAKE and glanced at her clock.

Six fifty-two. Someone was knocking on her front door.

Garrett. He probably didn't come across the terrace because he didn't want Dylan to know he was talking to her. On his way to work? She realized she hadn't even asked what happened when he returned to the office last night. If he was going in this early, things must not have gone well.

She lay there, listening to him knock a second time, thinking how she didn't need to begin her day like this. It was going to be difficult enough without hearing his pleas for reconciliation right off the bat.

She blinked, trying to rid her eyes of the two hours of sleep she'd managed, but sandbags had replaced her eyelids. With all the crying she'd done, she probably should be thankful they'd even open.

Garrett knocked again, more persistent this time, and she resigned herself to the fact that he wasn't going away. She stumbled from the bed still in yesterday's clothes, grimacing at the achy feeling that suffused her entire body.

She'd caught a bad case of heartbreak flu.

"I'm comin'." Her voice crackled as if she were ninety.

She stopped at the door and took a deep breath to brace for the onslaught of emotion. Then she swung it open, and her chin hit her chest.

"Dad!"

"Hi, lovebug."

Sawyer O'Malley didn't look quite as bad as she did, but he was running a close second. Tired and rumpled and unshaven, he was the most wonderful thing her eyes could've beheld at that moment.

He dropped his small bag and held out his arms, and Tara fell into his warm embrace, sobbing her joy and anguish.

"What are...you doing...here?" She jerked her way through the obvious question.

He didn't let go. Just kept holding her while he spoke, rocking back and forth in a soothing motion. "You sounded so miserable yesterday when I talked to you. I couldn't stand the thought of you facing all of this alone."

"But, Dad...this is Paris. It's...not like driving...from Taylor's Grove...to Paducah. How'd you get here...so fast?" Her tears were leaving a wet spot on his shirt, but she didn't care. Her dad was there, holding her, and suddenly her topsy-turvy world had righted a bit.

"I bought a ticket, drove to St. Louis and got on a plane." He kissed the top of her head. "The seven-hour difference helped. It was still morning at home when I talked to you."

She loosened her grip so she could lean back and look him in the eye. "You shouldn't have come. But I'm so glad you're here."

"Me, too." He gathered her to his chest in a tight squeeze. "But if I don't get some coffee soon, I'm going to collapse."

She pulled away with a smile, the first one she'd felt in what seemed like forever. "I can help with that."

She showed him around her apartment and let him freshen up while she prepared breakfast. Her appetite still hadn't returned but she forced down a few bites of bacon, eggs and toast to help ease her splitting headache while she shared all the gruesome details of the visit with Jacques Martin.

Pain radiated from her dad's eyes as he listened, and every so often he'd shake his head in disgust or sympathy or whatever the appropriate emotion was at the time.

She didn't say too much about Garrett—only that she'd ended the relationship and how that seemed to be the smart thing to do. And, for the most part, her dad withheld advice.

"It just felt so right, Dad."

Her tears turned on again, and he took her hand, his touch as gentle as his voice. "Maybe it *is* right."

That certainly wasn't what she'd expected. "But not if the trust isn't there."

"No, trust is important." He swallowed hard. "It has to be earned, and that takes time."

"Time Garrett and I don't have." She shrugged. "I'm leaving Saturday." She paused, realizing she'd been talking only about herself since he'd arrived. "Are you staying till then?"

He smiled, but sadness darkened his eyes. "No. Actually, my return flight leaves at three, and I have to be back at the airport at one, so I'll need to leave here by noon."

"What? It's seven already! You're only here for five hours?"

"I have an important meeting at the church tomorrow. I have to be back for it."

"So you came all this way...?"

"To show my daughter—" He looked at her then with an intensity she'd rarely seen except when her dad was preaching. He tapped his chest at the place over his heart. "To show *my daughter*...who is more precious to me than life itself...how much she's loved and treasured. And that I'll *always* be there for her."

Tara's heart swelled so large it pushed the air from her

lungs and for a moment she couldn't speak. "I'm sorry for what I've put you through, Dad," she managed, at last. "I'm not sure I deserve you."

"None of us deserve the blessings we're given. That's what makes them special."

She glanced out the window and saw Garrett and Dylan stirring in their apartment. They'd blessed her life. She could only hope that in some small way she'd blessed them, too. And the best way to assure that she remained a blessing, at least to Dylan, was to leave while things were good between them.

She made her mind up quickly. "I'm going to call the airlines and see if I can move my flight up to today. I want to go home with you."

Her dad's eyes widened. "Are you sure you want to do that?"

Her heart, which had grown so large a minute ago, started to wither. She knew if she stayed, it would shrivel up to nothing in no time flat. "I came to Paris to find out who I am, and now I know. I'm Tara O'Malley from Taylor's Grove, Kentucky...and I'm proud of that," she said more to herself than to him. "I need to go home, need to get back to my life."

"But...?"

"No buts." Resolve brought her to her feet. She had a plan of action. It may not be the best one, but at least she wouldn't be wallowing in sorrow here for four more lonely days.

She could wallow at home just as easily...surrounded by people who loved her.

"I'm going to shower and pack."

"Can you be ready by eleven-thirty?" Her dad's eyes held a strange glint.

"Yeah. Why?"

"I have one thing I want to see during this whirlwind trip to Paris."

She gave a small laugh. He was so predictable. "Notre-Dame's not far. I'll hurry and maybe we'll even have time to walk there."

He shooed her in the direction of the bedroom. "Go on. I need to call your mom."

Tara grabbed her luggage from the hall closet and hurried to her room to begin stuffing it with clothes.

IT WAS JUST AFTER MIDNIGHT, but Faith wasn't asleep. She wasn't even in bed. She'd been staring at the same words on the same page for a long while, debating with herself whether to call the sheriff and report Sawyer as missing.

He'd texted her around five saying he'd talk to her tomorrow. She'd been so hurt and angry he'd gone fishing, she hadn't texted him back.

But an hour or so ago, she swallowed her pride and called him because he still hadn't returned from the lake and all sorts of scenarios had started messing with her mind. Most of them centered around him falling out of the boat and being knocked unconscious and drowning.

Of course, he'd specifically texted tomorrow, so he could be ignoring her calls or might even have his phone turned off. He did that sometimes when he needed to think.

She picked up her car keys. She would just drive over to the house. He might've taken the boat home since her car wasn't taking up the extra space in the garage. She could run over there and peek in the garage window....

Her phone rang, shattering her thoughts. The caller ID said it was Sawyer, but what if someone had found his phone in an empty boat?

Panic flooded adrenaline through her system. "Hello?" she practically screamed into the phone.

"Whoa!"

"Don't whoa me!" she snapped. All of the frustration that had been bottled up since morning came spewing out. "Where are you? It's after midnight and you haven't brought the boat back and you haven't been answering my calls and I've been imagining your dead, unconscious body floating around some dark cove on Kentucky Lake."

He laughed? How dare he?

"Dead *and* unconscious, huh?"

"You know what I mean. I've been scared out of my wits."

"I'm in Paris, Faith."

"Well, you could've at least told me you were going down there." She huffed. "Is there a tournament?"

He chuckled again. "Not Paris, Tennessee. Paris, France. I'm with Tara."

Faith's knees buckled, and she plopped down on the floor. "You're in France? With Tara?"

"I couldn't stand the thought of her being over here alone, dealing with all she's going through."

Faith winced at the raw emotion in his voice. "Oh, Sawyer. How's she doing?"

"Hurting. Depressed."

Shock began to dissolve her brain matter into a mishmash of relief and worry, releasing a flood of questions into her brain. "How'd you get there so fast? Why didn't you tell me you were going?"

"I left as soon as I could get the arrangements made, and I didn't tell you because I knew you would try to talk me out of it."

She nodded, even though he couldn't see her. She would most definitely have tried to talk him out of such an extravagant trip, especially with their income on the chopping block… Oh, Lord! "Did you forget the meeting with the Board of Fellowship tomorrow night?" With him not there to defend himself, Sue would ramrod her way through the process in record time.

"I didn't forget." The weariness in his tone caught in her chest and squeezed her heart. "I'm booked on a return flight this afternoon. Tara's decided to come home with me. She's going to try to change her ticket to that flight."

"Ah…" A worried gasp escaped from Faith's lungs. "How are we going to pay for all this, Sawyer? If you lose the church…?"

"Don't worry about the money. Everything's already taken care of." The gentle voice lowered. "Love always finds a way."

The reality of the situation finally rooted in Faith's mind, warming her through and through. Sawyer, bless his heart, had gone all the way to Paris, France, to take care of his daughter. *His* daughter, regardless of the circumstances surrounding her conception. He'd used their savings, no doubt. But that didn't matter because he was there for Tara, taking care of everything…like he'd always done. And Faith could feel his steadfast love holding *her* up, too.

"You're a wonderful man, Sawyer." Faith hoped her voice could convey a tiny part of the pride she felt. "Tara's so blessed to have you in her life."

"I'm the one who's blessed, Faith."

She couldn't stifle the sob that sprang from her lips.

"Hey, don't cry." His soothing voice caressed her from across the miles…across an ocean. "I'm going to let you go now. I'll call you when we get back into St. Louis. But adding in the four-hour drive, it might be late when I get home."

"I don't care how late it is. I'll be up."

"Yeah, I figured that." She heard the smile in his voice.

A final question popped into her mind. "But if you drove the truck to St. Louis, what did you do with the boat? It's not here."

There was a long pause, and then an even longer breath. "I sold it."

Faith felt another blow to her system that shook her to the core. "You sold your dad's bass boat? Why?"

"I used the money to come to Paris."

"But, Sawyer, you loved that boat." Faith couldn't stop

the tears now if she wanted to, and her voice started to blubber as her nose and throat clogged.

"No, the boat was nice to have, but I love my family. Trust me, it was a small price to pay for the love I get in return. I'll talk to you later."

He hung up quickly, and Faith understood he didn't want to hear her cry. But that didn't stop her. She cried for Tara, for what she was enduring. And for the bass boat, the family heirloom...gone now.

But, most of all, she cried for the conclusions she had jumped to that morning.

Sawyer loved their children. All three of them.

And he loved her.

He proved it day after day...had proven it as long as she'd known him.

He would get home, and they would work out their problems.

"'Love always finds a way.'"

She branded his promise on her heart.

GARRETT FELT THE TENSION as soon as he walked in the door at Soulard.

Far from the usual morning bustle of activity and conversations, people were scurrying around like scared mice, speaking in hushed whispers, eyes wide with alarm or narrowed and tight with agitation.

Through the conference-room window, he saw the same group he'd met with last night, but two others had been added to the group. Adrienne Goffinet, Soulard's brilliant young attorney, and a middle-aged man he didn't recognize, but who was speaking and had everyone's attention. Adrienne's face was ashen and drawn into a scowl.

It took only a quick glance for the solemn atmosphere in the conference room to creep into Garrett's gut and chill him to the bone...only another few seconds to know that Jacques Martin was behind it.

He'd barely had time to set his briefcase on his desk before Henri came in and closed the door. His friend held no coffee. This was even worse than he'd thought.

"What's happened, Henri?"

"C'est mauvais, Garrett. C'est très, très mauvais."

"Tell me what's happened, damn it!"

Henri unbuttoned the top button on his shirt and loosened his tie. "An official is here from *le CFE.*"

An official from the *Centre de Formalités des Entreprises* was here? Henri was right. This was very bad. "What does he want? Do you know?" Garrett empathized with Henri's loosening of his tie. His own felt like a noose around his throat now.

"I hear the rumor there is a threat to close the company temporarily. Important documents are missing from the Soulard file."

"Shit!" Garrett's ability to stand left him in a rush and he dropped into his chair. The terror he felt was reflected in Henri's eyes.

How long was temporarily?

Adrienne had often complained of the hellish number of documents the CFE required to start up the company. But it was beyond belief that the attorney, who was meticulous to the point that Garrett suspected she might have OCD, could've missed anything. It had taken her months to complete all the required paperwork. That was three years ago. How was it that missing documents were just being discovered today? "This is Jacques Martin's doing." The coincidence was too great for Garrett to attribute the crisis to anyone else.

Henri nodded gravely as he pulled up a chair and sat down. "I fear you are correct."

Neither of them said anything for a long minute. What was there to say? What was done couldn't be undone. He'd screwed up royally, and they both knew it.

Henri rested his arms on the desk and leaned forward, his voice low and sympathetic. "What about you and Tara?"

Garrett glanced away, unwilling to share the full depth of the grief churning low in his belly. "Well, let's just say if bad news was counted like hits in baseball, this morning I'd be batting a thousand."

CHAPTER TWENTY-FIVE

"ARE YOU READY?" Her dad gave the living room one final inspection.

Tara had contacted the landlord and made arrangements for the cleaning service to come by. They'd assured her they would take care of any food left in the cabinets and refrigerator. She'd stripped the bed and left all the linens on the washer, and checked under the bed and in the closets for anything left behind. And she'd taken care of the trash.

Everything was done.

Well…there was one thing left to do. The most heartbreaking thing. But it was inevitable.

"Just one more thing, Dad. Come here. I want you to meet somebody."

Dylan looked up from his book when they stepped onto the terrace. He was all smiles and boyhood charm, and, for a few agonizing seconds, Tara thought her heart would stop for good.

She called on all her teacher reserves that kept her from bawling whenever she read a sad story to her classes.

"Hey, Dylan." She motioned him over. "I want to introduce you to someone."

He placed his book on the bench and came running at her invitation, stopping by her dad with a big grin that said "See how fast I am?"

Tara stooped down and put her arm around his waist. "You remember I told you I was looking for my father?"

He nodded. No use complicating this more than necessary. "Well, I found him," she said simply.

Dylan's expression of wonder made him look so much like Garrett, she had to cut her eyes away to breathe. She pointed. "This is my dad from Kentucky, Sawyer O'Malley. Dad, this is Dylan Hughes."

Dylan's face turned somber for a moment, and he stuck out his hand. *"Bonjour, Monsieur O'Malley. Comment allez-vous?"* The formal facial expression gave way to a wide grin. "That means hi."

Tara could tell by her dad's smile that the child had already won him over. He laughed and grasped the little boy's hand. "Well, bone jur to you, too, bud."

"Hey, my dad calls me bud sometimes!"

A tremor shot through Tara at the mention of Garrett. She stood up and patted Dylan on the back. "My dad has come to…uh…" Lord, this was even harder than she had imagined. "To take me back home. So, I guess I have to say bye."

In a nanosecond, Dylan's happy expression went south. "But I don't want you to go."

Tara knelt down again and took his hand. "I know it's hard. It's hard for me, too. But remember when we talked that day at the Luxembourg Gardens, and I told you I'd have to leave sometime soon?" His bottom lip protruded as he nodded. "Well, everything I told you that day is still true. Your dad—" She paused and swallowed. "Your dad has my number, and I want you to call me anytime you want. As often as you want."

"But talking on the phone's not the same as being with you."

Tara shrugged. "I know. But it's the next best thing for people who live so far apart. And I have something for you that will make it seem like I'm still here, sort of." She reached into her tote and pulled out the purple Crown Royal bag containing the GPS locator and all the homemade tokens. "I want you to keep this so you and your dad can do lots of geocaching and find lots of treasures. And I want you to call me every time you find one."

"Wow!" The surprise brought a smile to Dylan's lips and Tara's heartache eased a smidgen when he took the bag. "Thanks!"

She pulled a card from her tote. "I wrote down the addresses of some geocaching clubs that meet here in Paris. I thought y'all might consider joining one."

"I wish you could be here to join it with us." Dylan's eyes grew cloudy. She had to get this over with quickly or it was going to be a major trauma for them both.

She raised her chin. "I wish I could, too." A sob was building in her chest. Its weight pulled at her heart. "But I really have to go now, so give me a hug, and let me get out of here."

He grabbed her around the neck with such force she struggled to stay upright. "I love you," he said.

She nodded. "I love you, too."

She let him break the hug first, and then she stood up. "Call me tomorrow, okay?"

"Okay."

When they turned away, her dad's arm came around her shoulder and she leaned into him, appreciating the support.

"Hey, Tara," Dylan called.

They stopped and turned back around as the little boy came running to her, holding out one of the tokens they'd made together. "You'll need this in case you find a treasure." His innocent grin told her he didn't realize the devastating consequences his parting gift would wreak on her emotions.

She took the token and squeezed it. "I think I've already found one." She gave him a quick peck on the top of his head and somehow managed to hold her outburst until she and her dad were safely back in her flat with the door closed.

Then the dam broke, rendering her amazed at the volume of tears her body could still produce. They had to be nearly all gone by now.

Her dad held her, silently rocking back and forth again, until this wave passed.

"What a great kid," he said.

She nodded and blew her nose on the tissue he handed her. "Dylan's the best."

"I was talking about you."

His joke brought a wan smile to her lips.

"Are you ready now?" He glanced at his watch as she flipped out the lights.

"Yeah." She opened the door to let him pass. "But we'll have to take a taxi to Notre-Dame. There's not enough time to walk."

He took the handle of her duffel and rolled it out the door. "I don't want to go to Notre-Dame. I want to meet Jacques Martin."

Tara's startled movement slammed the door behind them, and its echo surrounded them in the dark corridor. She slapped the light switch on to find her dad's calm expression looming in front of her.

"No, we can't." She wasn't about to face the jerk or his condescending wife again.

Her dad nodded calmly. "Yeah, we can." He punched the button to call the elevator.

"He was mad yesterday, Dad." She had to make him understand. "And he threatened Soulard. No telling what he might do if I or anybody connected to me shows up again."

The doors opened and they stepped inside. "I've made up my mind," he said matter-of-factly. "You can either give me the address, or I can call Faith and get it."

Tara sighed dramatically and didn't answer. She seethed in silence the rest of the way down, her brain whirring to come up with a way to talk her dad out of this absurdity. As they stepped off the elevator and made their way through the myriad passages, she tried to fight her growing anxiety by pointing out the items she used as markers to help her find her way through the building.

When they finally made their way to Madame LeClerc's post, the woman seemed truly sorry to see Tara go and hugged her, muttering things in French Tara didn't understand, but they sounded kind.

Something niggled at Tara, though, and when they stepped into the open air, she narrowed her eyes to look at her dad. "So…how'd you get past Ironpants LeClerc this morning? The woman is a guard dog."

Her dad shrugged. "It seems Madame LeClerc might be a pushover for the American Southern accent."

Tara shook her head. "It didn't work for me."

"Let me qualify that." His grin turned positively boyish. "Madame LeClerc might be a pushover for the American *male* Southern accent."

"Daddy!" Tara was aghast. "You flirted?"

"You do what you have to do." He sped up his steps. "And I have to speak to Jacques Martin."

BY THE TIME GARRETT MADE it into the conference room, the seats were all gone and there was standing room only. Not a breath of air stirred.

The only other time the entire staff had been crammed in like that was on opening day. Then, the atmosphere had sizzled with excitement. Today, it was sultry and stifling.

The owners, the president, the upper management—all the people he'd met with last night—regarded him solemnly when he entered. They were joined at the front table by the representative from the CFE and the company attorney, both of whom had no reason to look at him, and didn't.

He was almost grateful the less crowded area was in the back of the room, where he'd be shielded from the intensity of some of the accusing glares.

As he made his way to the back, his phone vibrated in his pocket.

Shit! In his haste, he'd forgotten to turn it off. He pulled it out to do so, but stopped short at the sight of Tara's name on the ID.

His heart catapulted into a gallop. Had she changed her mind about the break-up?

Damn! He couldn't take the call. Not now. As difficult as it was to do, he pushed *Ignore* and sent her to voice mail. Then he slipped the phone back into his pocket.

Only a minute later, he felt the vibration again. People were still filing in, filling up the empty spaces and using up what little remained of the air conditioning…and the oxygen.

He pulled his phone out and glanced at it.

A text from Tara. Nothing good *ever* came to him in a text. He broke out in a cold sweat, suddenly aware of rivulets of perspiration coursing down his back, his shirt clinging to his clammy skin as he leaned against the wall.

I called. No answer. I'm going back home today. Thanks for everything. Sorry things didn't work out and for any trouble I've caused. Please let Dylan call me anytime he wants, but please don't call yourself. It will only make the pain worse.

Garrett closed his eyes and wiped a hand down his face. A nudge startled him, and he opened his eyes to find Henri standing beside him, holding out a crisp white handkerchief.

"Is this in case I want to surrender?" he asked, and held the phone so Henri could read it.

His friend's deep sigh sucked the last good breath from the surrounding air.

Garrett turned the phone off and dropped it in his pocket as one of Soulard's owners started to speak.

CHAPTER TWENTY-SIX

TARA PAUSED OUTSIDE THE door of Jacques Martin's office. "Dad." She would make one last attempt to talk him out of this, but her pleas had fallen on deaf ears in the taxi. "This really isn't a good idea, and it could make things horrible for Soulard."

Her dad placed his hands on her shoulders and leaned down to look her directly in the eyes. "Tara, I believe in a master plan. If my meeting him is part of that plan, it will happen. If it's not, he won't be here." He smiled and gave her shoulders a light squeeze. "Besides, I've prayed about what to say, and I don't think what I want to tell him will be harmful to Soulard, Jacques's wife or anybody else."

Her dad had never given her any reason to doubt that he only wanted what was best for her. She needed to trust him now. "Okay." She nodded. "Let's do this."

Sawyer opened the door and stepped back to let Tara enter first. Thank heavens, the waiting room was empty again. Just what kind of business never had any customers?

Yvette Martin's eyes widened at the sight of Tara, and she snarled something in French as she came to her feet. Pointing to the door, she raised her voice. "Get out. Now!"

Sawyer ignored the directive and pushed past Tara, extending his hand to the young woman. "Well now, there's no reason to get all huffy. Hi there. I'm Sawyer O'Malley. Tara's dad."

"I don't care who you are." She spoke through gritted

teeth. "This is a private office, and I am instructing you to get out now."

Sawyer shifted his look between the two women and grinned. "Whooee! There's no use getting all worked up like this. I just want—"

"Jacques!" Yvette turned toward the closed door down the hall and shouted.

While she continued shouting in French, Sawyer gave her an innocent shrug. "See there. You already knew what I wanted without me even having to ask."

The office door flew open, and a red-faced Jacques Martin marched out, shoulders squared and obviously ready to tangle.

Sawyer rushed to meet him as Tara gawked, rooted to where she stood.

Her dad extended his hand once more, and again it was ignored. "Hello, Mr. Martin," he said calmly. "I know this is a surprise, but I couldn't pass up what might be my only opportunity to ever meet Tara's birth father."

"She is *not* my daughter. Now get out."

Her heartbeat, which was already fast, didn't accelerate. Her stomach did no additional churning. In fact, his words had no effect on Tara this time. Perhaps the tears had done their job and left her numb…or maybe having her dad there with her made all the difference.

Sawyer turned to Tara and held out his hand to her.

She moved to where he stood, taking the hand he proffered, relaxing in his firm but gentle grip.

He turned back to Martin. "You're right. She's not your daughter. She's *my* daughter, and I thank God every day for her."

Tara's face heated, but she noticed Martin's had lost some of its earlier color.

"And I want to thank *you*, Mr. Martin. Without you, I'd have no Tara." Her dad's voice lowered. "You see, my wife and I produced two other children whom I love very much, but nothing I could ever have done would've allowed me to produce Tara. Only you could do that."

Sawyer looked at Tara, and the smile he gave her held so much love she thought her heart would burst from it. She smiled back through eyes that brimmed with happy tears.

He tightened his grip on her hand before turning back to Martin while Tara stole a quick glance toward Yvette. The young wife was perched on her seat, arms crossed tightly, eyes boring into nothing but the top of the desk.

"And so I came here today," Sawyer continued, "simply to let you know how much you've blessed my life, and I've asked God to bless you in whatever way he sees fit. Rest assured, you'll be in my prayers often."

Martin said nothing, but just for a moment, Tara thought she could see a resemblance to the kind man she met at Place des Vosges.

Her dad faced her. "Ready?"

A chuckle floated out of her on a bubble of joy. "Yep."

She kept her arm linked through her dad's as they left the office, carrying in her heart a certainty that she was bound to this man with a bond even deeper than blood.

GARRETT HAD ALWAYS heard that 95 percent of the things you worry about never happen.

Just his luck that this incident lay in the remaining 5 percent.

The owners had announced, to the groans of shock and dismay from the audience, the immediate, temporary closing of Soulard until such time as this crisis could be resolved. Because most of the missing forms were those dealing with the labor force, it would be inadvisable to keep the brewery open until the documents were back in place.

Guilt that he had caused this whole, nightmarish fiasco was eating Garrett's insides like acid. Bile had actually risen into his throat when the official announcement was made.

He'd made up his mind to offer his resignation as soon as the meeting adjourned. It might not help anything, but if there was a chance it would call off the jackal that was Jacques Martin, it would be worth a try.

He and Dylan could make it for a while. He'd never touched the insurance money from Angie's death, which was tucked away in savings for Dylan's future, but he could borrow against it if a crisis arose.

Damn, he was going to be sick if he didn't get out of this room soon. He wiped his face with Henri's handkerchief. The walls were closing in on him, squeezing the breath out of his lungs.

The CFE representative was droning on and on with his apologies and reiterating the importance of having all required paperwork complete, and how he couldn't accept the copies on hand because all official documents must be originals.

It was a highly unusual breach of protocol for the receptionist to interrupt a meeting, especially one of such magnitude, and a nervous titter moved through the crowd when she pecked on the door and entered, waving a piece of paper.

She handed it to the man from CFE, who frowned and apologized, but then pulled out his cell phone and stepped from the room to make what was assumed to be an urgent call.

People remained oddly quiet, maybe wondering what else could possibly have happened that would rank high enough to interrupt this meeting. There were a few nervous whispers around him, which Garrett didn't try to discern. Instead, he studied the grim faces of those who sat in silence. He, at least, had some income to fall back on. Some of these people were the sole providers for their families. They wouldn't be able to wait around for months to be called back to Soulard.

The man from CFE returned to the front of the room. The room fell silent, and he cleared his throat.

"I have just received a call," he began in his smooth French, which Garrett had no trouble following, "and I must offer my personal apology to each of you for the turmoil you have been through this day." He paused and cleared his throat again, and Garrett wondered what else could be so difficult for him to say that he hadn't already said.

"Just say it," Garrett muttered under his breath, causing several people around him to look his way.

"It appears a grave error has been made. The documents for Soulard Brewery have been located and are all accounted for. The brewery is in no danger of being closed. You may all return to work immediately." He stopped and gave the owners a sheepish look. "Or as soon as you are instructed to do so."

The loud cheer that filled the room soon gave way to a myriad of mixed emotions. Some people cried tears of joy. Others laughed and hugged. Still others spoke in harsh, angry tones that they'd been made to suffer for several hours over what turned out to be nothing.

Garrett slid to the floor in a sweaty heap of happiness, anger and frustration.

Had Jacques Martin gone to this extreme just to flex his muscles and show his strength?

What a bastard!

Tara was fortunate Martin didn't have a part in her life. Perhaps someday she would realize that.

Garrett pulled his phone out and switched it on, hoping to find another call from her, but there wasn't one.

Perhaps, if *he* was fortunate, he might have a part in her life again.

They had been good together.

Perhaps someday she would realize that, too.

FAITH RUSHED TO MEET SAWYER when he pulled into the driveway, getting there even before he could switch the motor off. To her surprise, Tara was waking up in the passenger seat.

Faith opened the door for her sleepy daughter. "I didn't expect to see you, sweetheart. I thought Sawyer would drop you off in Paducah."

Tara shook her head as she lumbered from the truck and grabbed Faith into the tightest hug she'd felt from her eldest child in years.

"I didn't want to go to my place tonight. I wanted to come *home*." Her heavy emphasis on the word brought a warm glow to Faith's heart. "Oh, Mama, I'm so sorry for everything y'all have been through. Dad filled me in, and I feel just awful." She started to whimper, and Faith recognized that it was exhaustion coupled with jet lag speaking. Tara had been through a lot the past couple of days.

They all had.

She cooed soothingly while Sawyer came around the truck. She'd never seen him as disheveled as he was right then, but he'd never looked sexier. When their eyes locked, she recognized the flame burning in his gaze, and felt the spark from it deep within her.

He spread his arms and pulled them both to his chest, voicing a quiet prayer of thanks.

It was just after eight, and the sun hadn't set yet, so they were very much on display to the people that passed. A few passersby waved or tooted their horns in greeting.

"Let's go inside for a bit." Faith tilted her head toward the door.

"I'll wait for you out here." Tara staggered back to the truck and crawled into the backseat.

"I don't want to go inside." Sawyer pulled Faith against him and locked his arms around her. "I want the world to see me kiss my wife." His lips captured hers in a knee-weakening kiss, and his obvious erection pressed boldly against her. It went on far longer than she would've ever imagined, his tongue blissfully exploring the deepest reaches of her mouth, and Faith became vaguely aware of the loud blaring horns, catcalls and applause from the residents of Taylor's Grove.

"Sawyer, we're becoming a spectacle," she gently chided when they finally came up for air.

"I don't care." His eyes remained locked on hers with a burning intensity that said he wasn't aware anyone else was around. His arms loosened from around her back, moved up her arms and shoulders to cup her face. "Forgive me, Faith. I've been such a fool these past few weeks. Come home with me, now. Let me make love to you. Let me show you how blessed I am to have you as my wife and the mother of my children…my three precious, wonderful children."

"Jacques Martin…?" The name pushed from her lips on a rush of air.

"And *you* gave me a blessing beyond value. And I want to spend the rest of my life showing you how grateful I am." He lowered his lips to hers slowly this time, and hers trembled at the tenderness in his touch.

No longer caring who was watching, she slipped her arms around his neck and pressed her cheek to his when their lips slid apart. "Take me home," she whispered. "I'll get my stuff tomorrow."

He growled hungrily in response, and she laughed at the pleasant shiver the sound sent through her.

He led her to the truck and gallantly opened the passenger door for her. A soft snore came from the backseat as she buckled her seat belt.

Faith breathed a deep, lung-filling breath. What tomorrow would hold for them was a mystery, but the happiness she felt right then was enough to sustain her for a long while.

As Sawyer backed the truck out of the driveway, she glanced toward her neighbor's house to the north.

Sue Marsden had come outside, no doubt checking to see what all the commotion was about.

And if her crossed arms and angry glare were any indication, she wasn't at all happy with what she'd observed.

CHAPTER TWENTY-SEVEN

GARRETT WALKED INTO HIS office and slapped a hand to his backside. Yep, his ass was still there. After the chewing it had just received, he was surprised there was anything left.

The president and the upper management had pretty much ignored him yesterday after the horrendous threat had passed. Spirits had been much too high to do anything that would bring them down. But this morning, the president had wasted no time. He couldn't be sure the incident had been Jacques Martin's doing, but he needed someone to blame, and Garrett seemed like the logical choice.

He'd been lambasted for his actions and told he needed to keep his girlfriend "under control."

Garrett didn't bother to correct his boss about his now-defunct relationship. He was having a hard enough time accepting that himself.

God, he missed Tara.

He shut his door and went over to stand by the window, looking out on the city.

Control Tara, indeed. He snorted and gave his head a shake. There was no controlling Tara...nor did he have any desire to control Tara.

He *had* wanted to control Angie, and, damn it, she'd ended up controlling him.

And still was.

He balled his hand into a fist and hammered the butt end into the wall.

Tara was right. Angie haunted him. He lived his life

in fear of Angie, running from memories that dredged up guilt, so afraid of making the same mistakes again.

This time it had cost him plenty—almost everything, in fact.

Well, no more. He couldn't keep putting Dylan—or himself—through this.

The time to stop running was now. He had to face his fears and put Angie's ghost to rest at last.

He drew a deep breath and felt his head clear completely for the first time in four years.

And for the first time in four years, he knew exactly what his next move needed to be.

He strode from his office to Henri's with a purposeful stride, barging in on his surprised friend without bothering to knock.

"Henri," he said. "We need to talk."

THE CROWD WAS SO LARGE for the Board of Fellowship meeting, it had to be moved from the pastor's study to the Fellowship Hall of the church.

Remains from the Wednesday night potluck had to be cleaned up first, but, with so many hands there to help, that task didn't take long.

Faith knew she should be upset about the single item on the agenda, but she wasn't. Her breath came easily, her heart beat at a normal speed. Her family was all there together—Tara on one side of her, Thea on the other, Trenton between Thea and Sawyer. Even Emma was there on the far side of Tara. They were a loving, united front and nothing that happened tonight would change that.

Ollie had stopped by for a few minutes as they were leaving for the church. He asked if he could play them one song, then he'd pulled out his violin and played the old hymn "Wherever He Leads, I'll Go."

The song had been playing in Faith's head ever since.

Like Sawyer always said, there was a master plan, and

they were all part of it. If that plan included a move away from Taylor's Grove, so be it. As long as she could be with Sawyer, she'd go to the ends of the earth.

A hush fell over the group as Arlo James began the meeting with roll call. All five members were there, and, as Faith considered each one, she was pretty sure she knew how four of the votes would go.

Sue Marsden played Duane Abell like a puppet. He always voted with her on everything. On the other hand, Arlo and Sawyer were fishing buddies, and Johnny Bob Luther treated Sawyer like a son, so it was doubtful either of them would vote against him now.

That left Miss Beulah May Johnson, a matriarch of the church, who sometimes threw out pearls of wisdom the size of golf balls, and other times was sillier than a pet coon.

Her flights of fancy hadn't come on with old age. She'd always been that way, and everybody accepted what she said with a grain of salt.

But how Miss Beulah May would vote was anybody's guess.

Sawyer was listed on the agenda under New Business, and because there were no Committee Reports and no Old Business, his position came up quickly.

It was Sue, of course, who made the motion to "relieve Pastor Sawyer from his duties due to gross lack of leadership and lack of transparency in his personal life as behooved a spiritual shepherd."

Faith felt her hackles rise at the ridiculous drivel, but as expected, Duane seconded the motion.

Then came the call for discussion.

Tank Wallis was the first to speak. "Sue's motion seems to be based on old facts," he said. "Not current ones. Everybody in town knows Sawyer and Faith are back together. And their actions in Lacy's front yard last night were pretty transparent to anyone looking on. I think the motion should be withdrawn."

Sue butted in without being called on. "Their actions in Lacy's front yard last night make my point. A preacher and his wife shouldn't behave in such a vulgar manner."

"I'm kinda sorry I slept through it," Tara whispered, and Faith gave her a wink.

"And," Sue continued, "I believe they only made a show of reconciliation because they knew what was coming. If we let him off tonight, she might still move her things out tomorrow. They're just trying to buy some time and weasel the church out of his salary for another month."

"Oh, that's ridiculous, Sue." Faith recognized Ivadawn's loud voice from the back.

"It's not ridiculous. We still have no idea what any of this separation was about, and why everything suddenly became so hunky-dory when Tara got home. If we don't know the reason, how can we be sure it won't come around again?"

Tara had flinched at the mention of her name, and Faith felt her own spine stiffen. Her child had been through way too much lately, and it had shown in her mood today.

Faith had never seen Tara so down—not even when Louis had come home from Honduras with a wife on his arm. It hadn't bothered her to speak of Jacques Martin, but any mention of Garrett Hughes made her mood plummet lower than a snake's belly.

Faith reached for Tara's hand too late. Her daughter was already on her feet.

"I can't believe this has even gotten this far." Tara shook her head in disgust as she addressed the crowd. "What business is my parents' separation to anybody here except them? And y'all know my dad is the finest example of a loving spirit Taylor's Grove has ever known. I was in Paris, alone and sick at heart, and as soon as he heard that, he sold his bass boat—you know...the one that belonged to Grandpa Ian?" There were a few gasps from people who knew what a sacrifice that was, and Faith's throat tightened.

"Yeah, that one. He sold it in order to have the money to come see about me. If that's not love, I don't know what is." She looked directly at Sue. "And neither do you."

A bubble of pride swelled in Faith's chest. Her daughter had become quite a woman.

"Well, of course, you're going to be on his side," Sue snapped. "You're his daughter."

"Yes, I am." Tara turned a beaming smile toward Sawyer. "And proud of it."

"I understand Sue's point," Randall Lively called out. "The preacher needs to be somebody you can go to with your troubles. If he's too worried 'bout his own, he ain't likely to be too interested in mine."

A few nods and grunts of agreement followed.

"Everybody's got troubles, Ran," Tank growled.

"And maybe that's what we need to think about." Ollie stood up from his seat in the front row. "We all have our troubles—that's no secret and it shouldn't be a big deal. So why keep secrets?"

Where was he going with this? For the first time that evening, Faith squirmed uncomfortably in her seat.

"Let's just let it all out." Ollie swept his arm dramatically. "You see, I have the mother of all secrets."

Faith felt herself blanch. *No, Ollie. Please, don't.*

"Years ago," Ollie said, "when I was a much younger man and had just been told I was probably gonna lose my sight, I was depressed. Mightily so." Faith clasped her hands together to stop the trembling. "I couldn't sleep at night, so I took to walking the streets of town. I was trying to memorize everything so I'd have the images in my brain when I couldn't see them with my eyes anymore."

He paused and looked around slowly. "Y'all have no idea the things that happen in this town after the sun goes down…but I've seen them all. I have the mother of all secrets because, you see, I *know* the secrets."

Ollie's gaze shifted from one side of the room to the

other, but he couldn't see who was sitting where, so his eyes held no accusation. "I've seen the cars driving into garages at night, occupying the space where the out-of-town spouse's car usually sits. I've seen the clandestine meetings in the dark parking lot behind the school." He smiled. "Yes, kids, I've known for years about the smoking and drinking that goes on down by the marina when it's closed for the night. And the skinny-dipping, too."

An embarrassed laugh passed through the crowd.

Ollie shook his head sadly. "I've heard the arguments and seen the abuse through windows that weren't quite closed and shuttered all the way." He sighed. "And I'm here to tell you tonight, that if you demand complete transparency from the preacher, I'm gonna unload everything I know about everybody. If the preacher can't have secrets, ain't nobody gonna have secrets."

There was a long, anxious moment of silence before Nell Bradley stood up. "Y'all are just turning this meeting into a big gossip session, and I for one won't stand here and listen to it."

"Yeah!" A number of people shouted their agreement while Nell excused her way across the row of people sitting by her.

"We don't need this!" one particularly hostile voice shouted from the back. Faith thought it was Bobo Hudson, but she couldn't be sure.

"You're right," Ollie agreed. "We don't need this. Maybe we don't need transparency. Maybe all we need is love. We all have secrets, and we love each other in spite of them. If we knew everything about each other, I don't think we'd love each other nearly as much."

That brought a much-needed laugh of relief.

Miss Beulah May stood up. "I think we just all need to relax. And I believe I'll go home now and pour myself a good stiff shot of bourbon."

"Miss Beulah May!" Sue's chin dropped to her chest. "You can't say things like that in church!"

Miss Beulah May gave a smile and a pageant-queen wave to the crowd. "I think I just did." She looked very pleased with herself as she moseyed her way to the door.

"You just lost your swing vote, Sue." Tank gave a delighted laugh.

Johnny Bob Luther stood up in the middle of the aisle. "I reckon the preacher ain't gotta be perfect. He just needs to be better'n me." He slapped Sawyer on the back as he passed him. "And I reckon he is."

The meeting dissolved with that. People started talking, moving about and leaving.

"Sit down!" Sue snarled, but everybody ignored her. "This meeting's not over yet."

"Yes, it is," Arlo shouted over the noise. "The motion's withdrawn. This meeting's adjourned."

Sue slammed her palm to the table. "You can't do that!"

Arlo smiled at her and did a good imitation of Miss Beulah May's wave. "I think I just did."

The outpouring of love Faith felt from the congregation filled her heart to the brim. This was why they'd stayed in Taylor's Grove all these years. It was a good place. A loving place. It wasn't perfect, but, like a successful marriage, you took the good with the bad, for better or worse.

Sawyer's arms slid around her waist in a hug from behind. "I love you." He kissed her ear. "I've been too lax about showing it in public, but that's all changed."

Palming his cheek, she pressed his face to hers. "I'm never going to get tired of it, either." As he moved away, she held her arms out to Ollie, who had moved within reach of her, and hugged him across the folding chair. "You said what nobody else could, Ollie. I'll never be able to thank you enough."

"I only spoke the truth. We're not made to be perfect.

The blessing lies within the fact that we're loved in spite of our imperfections."

"Amen," she agreed.

"You have a good man, Faith."

She glanced at her husband, who, at the moment, was hugging all three of his children at once. "The best," she said.

"Don't ever forget to tell him that."

"I won't," she promised.

And she never did.

CHAPTER TWENTY-EIGHT

TARA OPENED HER EYES to the bright morning sun. *Eighty-nine days.*

"Stop it!" She wrapped the pillow around her head as if that could stifle her thoughts.

Since the day she'd returned home from Paris, the first thought to pop into her mind every morning was how long it had been since she'd seen Garrett and Dylan.

It was crazy, but despite her best efforts, she just couldn't get beyond the man and his little boy. It was like her brain wanted to move on, but her heart remained rooted in the concrete of that terrace in Paris.

The first couple of weeks after she'd left, Dylan had called every day. But toward the middle of August, his calls became fewer and fewer, eventually dwindling to none. She supposed it was a good sign that she'd been forgotten.

The pillow made her feel like she was smothering herself. She uncovered her head.

One day she'd want to date again, and she would allow herself to love someone else.

Today just wasn't that day.

But she did at least have a plan that would keep her busy for the next three days—the annual O'Malley Columbus Day weekend at the cabin.

She'd stayed up late last night getting all her students' essays graded, so the entire weekend would be work-free.

She hurried through breakfast and a shower, anxious

to get to the lake, where there would be so much laughter and talk that her mind would have little chance to wander.

She grabbed her phone on the way out the door, listening to the voice mail from Emma as she walked to the car.

"Hey, I got booked into a much-needed massage today, but it's not until eleven. Go on without me. I'll drive up later."

"Darn," Tara muttered. She'd looked forward to having Emma with her on the drive. She reached over and tuned her radio to a heavy metal station, setting the volume to a few decibels below painful.

The changing foliage with its stunning array of crisp golds and fiery reds filled the roadside, and she tried to lose herself in the passing images. But her thoughts kept diverting back to Paris and how the city would look in autumn... how much Dylan would have grown...how Garrett's eyes could set her on fire with a simple glance.

The cabin came into sight, drawing an audible groan from her. She was the first to arrive. Where was everybody?

She pulled out her phone and punched her mom's number. Her mom picked up after just one ring.

"Morning, Tara," she said brightly.

"Hey, Mom, where are you? I'm the first one here." She unlocked the door and tossed her bag on the floor of the front bedroom.

"We're on our way. I took food up yesterday, so everything's there. Start a pot of coffee, would you?"

"Okay. See you in a bit."

She made coffee the O'Malley way—extra strong. The aroma took her back to mornings in Paris when Garrett would bring her coffee in bed. She sighed and stepped away from the coffeemaker...and the memory.

A car door slammed, which probably meant either Trent or Thea had arrived. She headed to the front door to greet her sibling, and was barely halfway across the living room when the screen door opened and Garrett stepped in.

Tara's brain stalled as her feet came to an abrupt halt. An unseen force knocked the breath from her lungs, and she stood there gaping and mute.

His hands went to his hips and he filled the doorway, barring escape in that direction if she'd been so inclined, which she wasn't. "Hi," he said, and she could read the wariness in his eyes. The scar on his upper lip disappeared as his lips pressed together tightly.

The momentary numbness passed and feeling rushed back through her extremities. Her first inclination was to run to him, but she held herself motionless.

"Hi," she answered. "What are you doing here?"

"I came to talk to you. Can we do that?"

"I guess so." She tried to right her world, which had been jerked completely off its axis. "How did you know where I was?"

His face relaxed enough to allow a small smile. "This weekend has been planned for...well, for a long time. Your dad and I started talking on the phone the week after you left Paris, and your parents invited me here for this weekend."

"You came all the way from Paris for the weekend?" And her mom and dad had encouraged that?

"No." He shook his head and the smile disappeared. "Look. Can we sit down? I'll explain everything."

His presence filled the room...the whole cabin, and Tara needed fresh air to clear her wobbly thoughts. "Let's walk down to the lake." She tilted her head in the direction of the back door. When she moved, he followed, but she noticed he was careful not to touch her. Was that for her benefit or his?

"You want coffee?" she asked as they passed through the kitchen.

"Not yet. My heart's racing enough without it."

She smiled at his honesty, knowing exactly how he felt, although she didn't say so.

They stepped into the brisk autumn air coming off the lake. Tara breathed it deep into her lungs, hoping it would clear the conflicting emotions this man's presence caused.

"Where's Dylan?" She cast him a sidelong glance, still not trusting a direct eye-to-eye gaze.

"He's with your mom and dad. We stayed with them last night."

Her parents had invited Garrett and Dylan to stay with them in Taylor's Grove…and hadn't called her? Hadn't warned her they were coming? They knew how heartbroken she was over Garrett. Did they think closure would get her over her depression?

That brought her around to face him straight on. "Garrett…please tell me what's going on."

His chest heaved as he took a breath, then let it out, and his gaze bored into hers, pinning her to the spot. "Tara," he said. "I love you."

IT PROBABLY WASN'T THE best place to start, but it was the truth, and Garrett wanted her to know where he was coming from. No secrets. No ghosts.

She tilted her head in question and slid her hands into her back pockets—a stance that kept her elbows back and placed her heart right out there. An encouraging sign. "Did Mama and Dad know you were going to say that?"

He nodded. "They told me that to win your trust, I was just going to have to lay it all out there."

"Go on." She started to gnaw on her bottom lip.

"After you left, I did some soul-searching, and I realized you were right. You *couldn't* trust me. Hell, I couldn't trust myself. I was afraid. Running away from my past. Running away from Angie. I'd pulled Dylan away from the family he needed…the family who needed him and me… at the time when we all needed each other the most. And

I'd done it because I didn't want to deal with the memories and the guilt." He paused.

Her nod was encouraging, but a shrug followed in its wake. "Great. But I'm still not getting it."

"Dylan and I moved back to St. Louis last month."

An audible gasp rushed from her lungs as her eyes widened.

"I quit Soulard, sublet the flat and we moved back home. A friend from college had been in contact with me for several years about starting a new marketing firm in St. Louis. I'd always turned him down before, but this time, we decided to go for it."

For the first time, he edged closer to her. She didn't move, but her eyes clouded. "What about Henri?"

His heart twinged at the mention of his best friend, who he missed like hell. "He wasn't happy about it, but we both knew it was for the best. We'll visit." He held out his hand, and when she placed hers in it, his heart twinged in a different way that he didn't dare stop to analyze. It felt promising. And, if it wasn't, he didn't want to know yet. "I was hoping you and I could do that, too. Take turns visiting on weekends and during school breaks. Dylan and I can come down here. You can come up there. I just want you back in our lives, Tara. We can take it as slow as you want. Or as fast. Just give us a chance."

The words had barely left his mouth before she was in his arms. Her hands clasped around his neck and she kissed him with a fervor he hadn't allowed himself to think about for months.

"I'm so glad you're here! I love you, Garrett." The words poured out, straight from her heart to his. "And I love Dylan. But things happened so fast, and I was so upset and confused. Trust takes time…I learned that from a very wise man. I knew in my heart that I'd screwed up by not giving us the time we needed to work through the trust issue. And I've been *miserable* for the past eighty-nine days because of it."

He laughed at her exactness while she laughed and cried at the same time.

He kissed her again then pulled her to his chest, against his heart. "God, I missed you. Your parents kept telling me you were miserable, but I didn't think there was any way you could be as miserable as I felt."

"At least you had Dylan." She sniffed. "All I had were memories." She gave him a squeeze. "But not anymore. I can't believe you're here."

He kissed the top of her hair where the morning sun was burnishing the copper tresses. "Believe it."

She leaned back in his arms and he brushed back the damp hair that had stuck to the tears on her cheeks, brushed the eyebrow ring with his thumb and kissed it.

"How'd you get my dad's number?" she asked.

That brought a chuckle. "As opposed to your other elusive father, Sawyer O'Malley was listed in the online phone book."

She narrowed her eyes and gave him a pretend pout. "I don't know who you're referring to. I only have one dad."

The sound of car doors slamming came from the front of the cabin. She grabbed his hand and took off running in that direction.

They rounded the corner as Dylan was skipping up the sidewalk, chattering excitedly to Faith and Sawyer.

"Dylan!" Tara called.

The unbridled joy on his son's face when he turned and saw Tara would stay with Garrett for the rest of his life.

"Tara!" Dylan ran to them, and they swooped him off the ground in an ecstatic, three-way hug.

Garrett's arms were full, but his heart was fuller. If he let go of Dylan and Tara right then, he would float away on happiness.

Over Tara's head, he watched Sawyer stop and eye them for a moment, then he nodded, and Garrett nodded back. The exchange was brief, but its meaning unmistakable. Sawyer O'Malley had just given his daughter away.

EPILOGUE

June of the following year

"FAITH, YOU LOOK STUNNING."

"Thanks, sweetheart." She smiled at him, and Garrett watched the soft blush rise from the round neck of her pink dress.

"And the pink is perfect." He pointed to the hot pink streak of hair that swept through her bangs.

She fingered it self-consciously and shrugged. "Hey, this is Paris, right?"

"I think it's lovely."

Garrett turned at the sound of his mom's voice as she slid her arm around his waist.

"And you are a vision of beauty in that blue," he told her.

She slapped her chest in mock horror. "Oh God, it's getting deep, and I'm in open-toed shoes." She grinned up at him. "But Henri's shoveling it out more than you are."

Over her head, Garrett could see his friend talking with Thea and Emma, most certainly in his element. Garrett had warned Tara that taking Henri up on his offer to have her sister and her best friend stay with him might be a mistake, but she'd insisted everything would be fine with Trent there.

Garrett sighed. They were all adults, and today, he wasn't going to worry about anything.

His phone vibrated and he pulled it out of his pocket and read the text.

I'm ready (again). I love you.

He smiled at their private joke. Switching off the phone, he clapped his hands loudly.

"All right, people. It's showtime."

The few guests took their seats as the wedding party found their places.

Garrett nodded to the harpist, and she began.

THE STRAINS OF "ODE TO JOY" floated through the open door.

Tara took a deep breath and gave her dad a smile.

"Ready to make this official in God's eyes?" he asked. He was the only one in on the secret that, because of French law, a civil ceremony had already taken place.

"I've never been more ready, Dad."

She took the arm he proffered, and they stepped through the door onto the terrace.

Her eyes locked with Garrett's, and her heart swelled at the look on his ruggedly handsome face. "I love you," he mouthed, and she felt her answering smile spread across her face.

She shifted her eyes to Dylan, who was standing in front of his dad, and kissed the air in his direction. He giggled and blew her a kiss in return. It caught in her throat, lodging on a bubble of joy her heart had released.

When she reached the wedding party, Emma took her flowers as her dad kissed her on the cheek and then moved to stand beside the French minister.

Garrett reached for one hand and Dylan for the other, and, as the three of them exchanged their vows, she recalled the first time she'd stood on this terrace during the raging storm.

She'd sought shelter, and she'd found it in the hearts of these two guys.

She understood how her dad felt now. Dylan wasn't hers by blood, but that didn't make any difference to her heart.

Garrett was hers, and Dylan was hers.
They were a family.
And they would stay a family forever.

*****

JUST ONE MORE NIGHT

BY
FIONA BRAND

Fiona Brand lives in the sunny Bay of Islands, New Zealand. Now that both her sons are grown, she continues to love writing books and gardening. After a life-changing time in which she met Christ, she has undertaken study for a bachelor of theology and has become a member of The Order of St Luke, Christ's healing ministry.

To the Lord, whose "word is a lamp unto my feet, and a light unto my path."
—*Psalms* 119

For God so loved the world that he gave his one and only Son, that whoever believes in him shall not perish but have eternal life.
—*John* 3:16

Many thanks to Stacy Boyd, Allison Carroll and all of the editorial staff who work so hard to help shape and polish each book, and always do a fabulous job.

One

Elena Lyon would never get a man in her life until she surgically removed every last reminder of Nick Messena from hers!

Number one on her purge list was getting rid of the beach villa located in Dolphin Bay, New Zealand, in which she had spent one disastrous, passionate night with Messena.

As she strolled down one of Auckland's busiest streets, eyes peeled for the real estate agency she had chosen to handle the sale, a large sign emblazoned with the name Messena Construction shimmered into view, seeming to float in the brassy summer heat.

Automatic tension hummed, even though the likelihood that Nick, who spent most of his time overseas, was at the busy construction site was small.

Although, the sudden conviction that he was there, and watching her, was strong enough to stop her in her tracks.

Taking a deep breath, she dismissed the overreaction which was completely at odds with her usual calm precision and girded herself to walk past the brash, noisy work site. Gaze averted from a trio of bare-chested construction workers, Elena decided she couldn't wait to sell the beach villa. Every time she visited, it seemed to hold whispering echoes of the intense emotions that, six years ago, had been her downfall.

Emotions that hadn't appeared to affect the dark and dangerously unreliable CEO of Messena Construction in the slightest.

The rich, heady notes of a tango emanating from her handbag distracted Elena from an embarrassingly loud series of whistles and catcalls.

A breeze whipped glossy, dark tendrils loose from her neat French pleat as she retrieved the phone. Pushing her glasses a little higher on the delicate bridge of her nose, she peered at the number glowing on her screen.

Nick Messena.

Her heart slammed once, hard. The sticky heat and background hum of Friday afternoon traffic dissolved and she was abruptly transported back six years....

To the dim heat of what had then been her aunt Katherine's beach villa, tropical rain pounding on the roof. Nick Messena's muscular, tanned body sprawled heavily across hers—

Cheeks suddenly overwarm, she checked the phone, which had stopped ringing. A message flashed on the screen. She had voice mail.

Her jaw locked. It had to be a coincidence that Nick had rung this afternoon when she was planning one of her infrequent trips back to Dolphin Bay.

Her fingers tightened on the utilitarian black cell, the perfect no-nonsense match for her handbag. Out of the blue, Nick had started ringing her a week ago at her apartment in Sydney. Unfortunately, she had been off guard enough to actually pick up the first call, then mesmerized enough by the sexy timbre of his voice that she'd been incapable of slamming the phone down.

To make matters worse, somehow, she had ended up agreeing to meet him for dinner, as if the searing hours she'd spent locked in his arms all those years ago had never happened.

Of course, she hadn't gone, and she hadn't canceled, either. She had stood him up.

Behaving in such a way, without manners or consideration, had gone against the grain. But the jab of guilt had been swamped by a warming satisfaction that finally, six years on, Messena had gotten a tiny taste of the disappointment she had felt.

The screen continued to flash its message.

Don't listen. Just delete the message.

The internal directives came a split second too late. Her thumb had already stabbed the button that activated her voice mail.

Nick's deep, curt voice filled her ear, shooting a hot tingle down her spine and making her stomach clench.

This message was simple, his number and the same arrogant demand he'd left on her answerphone a number of times since their initial conversation: *Call me.*

For a split second the busy street and the brassy glare of the sun glittering off cars dissolved in a red mist.

After six years? During which time he had utterly ignored her existence and the fact that he had ditched her after just one night.

Like that was going to happen.

Annoyed with herself for being weak enough to listen to the message, she dropped the phone back into her purse and stepped off the curb. No matter how much she had once wanted Nick to call, she had never fallen into the trap of chasing after a man she knew was not interested in her personally.

To her certain knowledge Nick Messena had only ever wanted two things from her. Lately, it was the recovery of a missing ring that Nick had mistakenly decided his father had gifted to her aunt. A scenario that resurrected the scandalous lie that her aunt Katherine—the Messena family's housekeeper—had been engaged in a steamy affair with Stefano Messena, Nick's father.

Six years ago, Nick's needs had been a whole lot simpler: he had wanted sex.

The blast of a car horn jerked her attention back to the busy street. Adrenaline rocketing through her veins, Elena hurried out of the path of a bus and stepped into the air-conditioned coolness of an exclusive mall.

She couldn't believe how stupid she had been to walk across a busy street without taking careful note of the traffic. Almost as stupid as she'd been six years ago on her birthday when she'd been lonely enough to break every personal rule she'd had and agree to a blind date.

The date, organized by so-called friends, had turned out to be with Messena, the man she'd had a hopeless crush on for most of her teenage years.

At age twenty-two, with a double degree in business and psychology, she should have been wary of such an improbable situation. Messena had been hot and in demand. With her long dark hair and creamy skin, and her legs—her best feature—she had been passable. But with her propensity to be just a little plump, she hadn't been in Messena's league.

Despite knowing that, her normal common sense had let her down. She had made the fatal mistake of believing in the heated gleam in Nick's gaze and the off-the-register passion. She had thought that Messena, once branded a master of seduction by one notorious tabloid, was sincere.

Heart still pumping too fast, she strolled through the rich, soothing interior of the mall, which, as luck would have it, was the one that contained the premises for Coastal Realty.

The receptionist—a lean, elegant redhead—showed her into Evan Cutler's office.

Cutler, who specialized in waterfront developments and central city apartments, shot to his feet as she stepped through the door. Shadow and light flickered over an expanse of dove-gray carpet, alerting Elena to the fact that Cutler wasn't the sole occupant of the room.

A second man, large enough to block the sunlight that would otherwise have flooded through a window, turned, his black jacket stretched taut across broad shoulders, his tousled dark hair shot through with lighter streaks that gleamed like hot gold.

A second shot of adrenaline zinged through her veins. *"You."*

Nick Messena. Six feet two inches of sleekly muscled male, with a firm jaw and the kind of clean, chiseled cheekbones that still made her mouth water.

He wasn't male-model perfect. Despite the fact that he was a wealthy businessman, somewhere along the way he had gotten a broken nose and a couple of nicks on one cheekbone. The battered, faintly dangerous look, combined with a dark five-o'clock shadow—and that wicked body—and there was no doubting he was potent. A dry, low-key charm and a reputation with women that scorched, and Nick was officially hot.

Her stomach sank when she noticed the phone in his hand.

Eyes a light, piercing shade of green, clashed with hers. "And you didn't pick up my call, because…?"

The low, faintly gravelly rasp of his voice, as if he had just rolled out of a tangled, rumpled bed, made her stomach tighten. "I was busy."

"I noticed. You should check the street before you cross."

Fiery irritation canceled out her embarrassment and other more disturbing sensations that had coiled in the pit of her stomach. Positioned at the window, Nick would have had a clear view of her walking down the street as he had phoned. "Since when have you been so concerned about my welfare?"

He slipped the phone into his jacket pocket. "Why wouldn't I be? I've known you and your family most of my life."

The easy comment, as if their families were on friendly terms and there hadn't been a scandal, as if he hadn't slept with her, made her bristle. "I guess if anything happened to me, you might not get what you want."

The second the words were out Elena felt ashamed. As ruffled and annoyed as she was by Nick, she didn't for a moment think he was that cold and calculating. If the assertion that her aunt and Stefano Messena had been having an affair when they were killed in a car accident, *the same night she and Nick had made love,* had hurt the Lyon family, it went without saying it had hurt the Messenas.

Her jaw tightened at Nick's lightning perusal of her olive-green dress and black cotton jacket, and the way his attention lingered on her one and only vice, her shoes. The clothes were designer labels and expensive, but she was suddenly intensely aware that the dark colors in the middle of summer looked dull and boring. Unlike the shoes, which were strappy and outrageously feminine, the crisp tailoring and straight lines were more about hiding curves than displaying them.

Nick's gaze rested briefly on her mouth. "And what is it, exactly, that you think I want?"

A question that shouldn't be loaded, but suddenly was, made her breath hitch in her throat. Although the thought that Nick could possibly have any personal interest in her now was ridiculous.

And she was absolutely not interested in him. Despite the hot looks, *GQ* style and killer charm, he had a blunt, masculine toughness that had always set her subtly on edge.

Although she could never allow herself to forget that, through some weird alchemy, that same quality had once cut through her defenses like a hot knife through butter. "I already told you I have no idea where your lost jewelry is."

"But you are on your way back to Dolphin Bay."

"I have better reasons for going there than looking for your mythical lost ring." She lifted her chin, abruptly certain that Nick's search for the ring, something that the female members of his family could have done, was a ploy and that he had another, shadowy, agenda. Although what that agenda could be, she had no clue. "More to the point, how did you find out I would be here?"

"You haven't been returning my calls, so I rang Zane."

Her annoyance level increased another notch that Nick had intruded even further into her life by calling his cousin, and her boss, Zane Atraeus. "Zane is in Florida."

Nick's expression didn't alter. "Like I said, you haven't returned my calls, and you didn't turn up for our…appointment in Sydney. You left me no choice."

Elena's cheeks warmed at his blunt reference to the

fact that she had failed to meet him for what had sounded more like a date than a business meeting at one of Sydney's most expensive restaurants.

She had never in her life missed an appointment, or even been late for one, but the idea that Nick's father had paid her aunt off with jewelry, *the standard currency for a mistress,* had been deeply insulting. "I told you over the phone, I don't believe your father gave Aunt Katherine anything. Why would he?"

His expression was oddly neutral. "They were having an affair."

She made an effort to control the automatic fury that gripped her at Nick's stubborn belief that her aunt had conducted a sneaky, underhanded affair with her employer.

Quite apart from the fact that her aunt had considered Nick's mother, Luisa Messena, to be her friend, she had been a woman of strong morals. And there was one powerful, abiding reason her aunt would never have gotten involved with Stefano, or any man.

Thirty years ago Katherine Lyon had fallen in love, completely, irrevocably, and he had *died.*

In the Lyon family the legend of Katherine's unrequited love was well respected. Lyons were not known for being either passionate or tempestuous. They were more the steady-as-you-go type of people who tended to choose solid careers and marry sensibly. In days gone by they had been admirable servants and thrifty farmers. Unrequited love, or love lost in any form was a novelty.

Elena didn't know who Aunt Katherine's lover had been because her aunt had point-blank refused to talk about him. All she knew was that her aunt, an exceptionally beautiful woman, had remained determinedly single and had stated she would never love again.

Elena's fingers tightened on the strap of her handbag. "No. They were not having an affair. Lyon women are not, and never have been, the playthings of wealthy men."

Cutler cleared his throat. "I see you two have met."

Elena turned her gaze on the real estate agent, who was a small, balding man with a precise manner. There were no confusing shades with Cutler, which was why she had chosen him. He was factual and efficient, attributes she could relate to in her own career as a personal assistant.

Although, it seemed the instant she had any contact with Nick Messena, her usual calm, methodical process evaporated and she found herself plunged into the kind of passionate emotional excess that was distinctly un-Lyon-like. "We're acquainted."

Nick's brows jerked together. "I seem to remember it was a little more than that."

Elena gave up the attempt to avoid the confrontation Nick was angling for and glared back. "If you were a gentleman, you wouldn't mention the past."

"As I recall from a previous conversation, I'm no gentleman."

Elena blushed at his reference to the accusation she had flung at him during a chance meeting in Dolphin Bay, a couple of months after their one night together. That he was arrogant and ruthless and emotionally incapable of sustaining a relationship. "I don't see why I should help drag the Lyon name through the mud one more time just because you want to get your hands on some clunky old piece of jewelry you've managed to lose."

His brows jerked together. "I didn't lose anything, and you already know that the missing piece of jewelry is a diamond ring."

And knowing the Messena family and their extreme wealth, the diamond would be large, breathtakingly expensive and probably old. "Aunt Katherine would have zero interest in a diamond ring. In case you didn't notice, she was something of a feminist and she almost never wore jewelry. Besides, if she was having a *secret* affair with your father, what possible interest would she have in wearing an expensive ring that proclaimed that fact?"

Nick's gaze cooled perceptibly. "Granted. Nevertheless, the ring is gone."

Cutler cleared his throat and gestured that she take a seat. "Mr. Messena has expressed interest in the villa you've inherited in Dolphin Bay. He proposed a swap with one of his new waterfront apartments here in Auckland, which is why I invited him to this meeting."

Elena suppressed her knee-jerk desire to say that, as keen as she was to sell, there was no way she would part with the villa to a Messena. "That's very interesting," she said smoothly. "But at the moment I'm keeping my options open."

Still terminally on edge at Nick's brooding presence, Elena debated stalking out of the office in protest at the way her meeting with Cutler had been hijacked.

In the end, feeling a little sorry for Cutler, she sat in one of the comfortable leather seats he had indicated. She soothed herself with the thought that if Nick Messena, the quintessential entrepreneur and businessman, wanted to make her an offer, then she should hear it, even if only for the pleasure of saying no.

Instead of sitting in the other available chair, Nick propped himself on the edge of Cutler's desk. The casual lounging position had the effect of making him look even larger and more muscular as he loomed over her.

"It's a good deal. The apartments are in the Viaduct and they're selling fast."

The Viaduct was the waterfront area just off the central heart of the city, which overlooked the marina. It was both picturesque and filled with wonderful restaurants and cafés. As an area, it was at the top of her wish list because it would be so easy to rent out the apartment. A trade would eliminate the need to take out a mortgage to afford a waterfront apartment, something the money from selling the villa wouldn't cover completely.

Nick's gaze skimmed her hair, making her aware that, during her dash across the road, silky wisps had escaped to trail and cling to her cheeks and neck. "I'll consider a straight swap."

Elena stiffened and wondered if Nick was reading her mind. A swap would mean she wouldn't have to go into debt, which was tempting. "The villa has four bedrooms. I'd want at least two in an apartment."

He shrugged. "I'll throw in a third bedroom, a dedicated parking space, and access to the pool and fitness center."

Three bedrooms. Elena blinked as a rosy future without the encumbrance of a mortgage opened up. She caught the calculating gleam in Nick's eye and realized the deal was too good. There could be only one reason for that. It had strings.

He was deliberately dangling the property because he wanted her to help him find the missing ring, which he no doubt thought, since she didn't personally have it, must still be in the old villa somewhere.

Over her dead body.

Elena swallowed the desire to grasp at what was an exceptionally good real estate deal.

She couldn't do it if it involved selling out in any way

to a Messena. Maybe it was a subtle point, but after the damage done to her aunt's reputation, even if it was years in the past, *and after her own seduction,* she was determined to make a stand.

Lyon property was not for sale to a Messena, just like Lyon women were not for sale. She met Nick's gaze squarely. "No."

Cutler's disbelief was not mirrored on Nick's face. His gaze was riveted on her, as if in that moment he found her completely, utterly fascinating.

Another small heated tingle shot down her spine and lodged in her stomach.

As if, in some perverse way, he had liked it that she had said no.

Two

Elena dragged her gaze from the magnetic power of Nick's and fought the crazy urge to stay and continue sparring with him.

Pushing to her feet, she bid Cutler good day, picked up her handbag and stepped out the door. Nick was close enough behind her that the sudden overpowering sense that she was being pursued sent another hot, forbidden thrill zinging through her.

The door snapped closed. Nick's firm tread confirmed that he was in pursuit and the faint, heady whiff of his cologne made her stomach clench. Clamping down on the wimpy feeling that she was prey and Nick was a large, disgruntled predator, Elena lengthened her stride and walked briskly past the receptionist out into the mall.

She had just stepped out of air-conditioned coolness into the humid heat of the street when a large tanned hand curled briefly around her upper arm. "What I don't get is why you're still so angry."

Elena spun and faced Nick, although that was a mistake because she was suddenly close enough that she could see a pulse jumping along the line of his jaw.

She tilted her chin to meet his gaze, unbearably aware that while she was quite tall at five foot eight, Nick was several inches taller and broad enough that he actually made her feel feminine and fragile. "You shouldn't have crashed my meeting with Cutler or tried to pressure me when you knew ahead of time how I felt."

There was an odd, vibrating pause. "I'm sorry if I hurt you six years ago, but after what happened that night it couldn't be any other way."

His words, the fact that he obviously thought she had fallen for him six years ago, dropped into a pool of silence that seemed to expand and spread around them, blotting out the street noise. She dragged her gaze from the taut planes of his cheekbones, the inky crescents of his lashes. "Are you referring to the accident, or the fact that you were already involved with someone else called *Tiffany?*" A girlfriend he'd apparently had stashed away in Dubai.

Nick frowned. "The relationship with Tiffany was already ending."

Elena found herself staring at the V of bronzed flesh bared by the pale peach T-shirt Nick was wearing beneath his black jacket. Peach. It was a feminine color, but on Nick the color looked sexy and hot, emphasizing the tough, stubbled line of his jaw and the cool gleam of his eyes. "I read about Tiffany in an article that was published a whole month later."

She would never forget because the statement that Nick Messena and his gorgeous model girlfriend were in love had finally convinced her that a relationship with him had never been viable.

"You shouldn't believe anything printed in a tabloid. We broke up as soon as I got back to Dubai."

Elena ruthlessly suppressed the sudden, wild, improbable notion that Nick had ended his relationship with Tiffany because of her.

That was the kind of flawed thinking that had seen her climbing into bed with him in the first place. "That still didn't make it all right to sleep with me when you had no intention of ever following up."

A hint of color rimmed Nick's cheekbones. "No, it didn't. If you'll recall, I did apologize."

Her jaw tightened. As if it had all been a gigantic mistake. "So why, exactly, did you finish with Tiffany?"

She shouldn't have the slightest interest. Nick Messena meant nothing to her—absolutely nothing—but suddenly she desperately needed to know.

He dragged long, tanned fingers through his hair, his expression just a little bad-tempered and terminally, broodingly sexy. "How would I know why?" he growled. "Men don't know that stuff. It ended, like it always does."

She blinked at his statement that his relationships always ended. For reasons she didn't want to go into, there was something profoundly depressing in that thought.

She stared at his wide mouth and the fuller bottom lip, which was decorated with a small, jagged scar. She couldn't remember the scar being there six years ago. It suggested he had since been involved in a fight.

Probably a brawl on one of his construction sites.

Against all good sense, the heady tension she had so far failed to defuse tightened another notch. Feeling, as she was, unsettled by memories of the past, distinctly vulnerable and on edge from the blast of Nick's potent sexuality, it was not a good idea to imagine Nick Messena in warrior mode.

She dragged her gaze from his mouth and the vivid memory of what it had felt like to be kissed by Nick. "Maybe you go about things in the wrong way?"

He stared at her, transfixed. "How, exactly, should I 'go about' things?"

She took a deep breath and tried to ignore the piercing power of his gaze. "Conversation is not a bad starter." That had been something that had been distinctly lacking in their night together.

"I talk."

The gravelly irritation in his voice, the way his gaze lingered on her mouth, made her suddenly intensely aware that he, too, was remembering *that* night.

She could feel her cheeks warming all over again that she had actually offered Nick advice about improving his relationships. Advice had so far failed to be her forte, despite the psychology classes she had passed.

The heat that rose off the sidewalk and floated in the air seemed to increase in intensity, opening up every pore. Perspiration trickled down the groove of her spine and between her breasts. She longed to shrug out of the overlarge jacket, but she would rather die of heatstroke than take off one item of clothing in Nick's presence. "Women need more than sex. They need to be appreciated and...liked."

They needed to be loved.

He glanced down the street as if he was looking for someone. "I like women."

A muscular black four-wheel-drive vehicle braked to a halt in a restricted parking zone a few steps away; a horn blared. Nick lifted a hand at the driver. "That's my Jeep. If you want, I can give you a ride."

The words, the unconscious innuendo, sent another small, sensual dart through her. Climb into a vehicle with tinted windows with Nick Messena? *Never again.* "I don't need a ride."

His mouth quirked. "Just like you don't need my apartment or, I'm guessing, anything else I've got to offer."

Reaching out a finger, he gently relocated her glasses, which had once again slipped, back onto the bridge of her nose. "Why do you wear these things?"

She blinked at the small, intimate gesture. "You know I'm shortsighted."

"You should get contacts."

"Why?" But the moment she asked the question she realized what had prompted the suggestion. Fiery outrage poured through her. "So I can get a man?"

He frowned. "That wasn't what I meant, but last I heard there's nothing wrong with that...yet."

Her chin jerked up another notch. "I'm curious, what else should I change? My clothes? My shoes? How about my hair?"

"Don't change the shoes," he said on a soft growl. "Your hair is fine. It's gorgeous." He touched a loose strand with one finger. "I just don't like whatever it is you do with it."

Elena tried not to respond to the ripple of sensation that flowed out from that small touch, or to love it that he thought her hair was gorgeous. It would take more than a bit of judicious flattery to change the fact that she was hurt—and now more than a little bit mad. "It's called a French pleat." She drew a swift breath. "What else is wrong?"

He muttered something short and indistinct that she didn't quite catch. "There's no point asking me this stuff. I'm not exactly an expert."

"Meaning that I need expert help."

He pinched the bridge of his nose. "How did we get onto this? It's starting to remind me of a conversation with my sisters. And before you say it, no, I can categorically say I have never thought of you as a sister."

His gaze, as it once again dropped to her mouth, carried the same fascinated gleam she had noticed in Cutler's office. Her breath stopped in her throat at the heart-pounding thought that he was actually considering kissing her. *Despite all of her deficiencies.*

A horn blast from a delivery vehicle that wanted the restricted parking place jerked her attention away from the tough line of Nick's jaw.

A split second later the passenger door of the Jeep popped open. Nick ignored the waiting vehicle. "Damn, I did hurt you," he said softly.

Elena tried to suppress a small stab of panic that, after six years of stoically burying the past, she had clearly lost control to the point that she had revealed her vulnerability to Nick.

Pinning a bright smile on her face, she attempted to smooth out the moment by checking her watch, as if she was in a hurry. "It was a blind date. Everyone knows they never turn out."

"It wasn't a blind date for me."

The flat tone of Nick's voice jerked her gaze back to his.

Nick's expression was oddly taut. "Six years ago I happened to overhear that a friend of yours had organized a blind date for you with Geoffrey Smale. I told Smale to get lost and took his place. I knew you were the girl I was taking out, and I slept with you for one reason— because I liked you."

* * *

Broodingly, Nick climbed into the passenger-side seat of the Jeep. He shot an apologetic glance at his younger brother, Kyle, as he fastened his seat belt.

Kyle, who had a military background and a wholly unexpected genius for financial investment, accelerated away from the curb. "She looked familiar. New girl?"

"No." *Yes.*

Nick frowned at the surge of desire that that thought initiated. The kind of edgy tension he hadn't felt in a very long time—six long years to be exact. "That's Elena Lyon, from Dolphin Bay. She works for the Atraeus Group."

Kyle's expression cleared as he stopped for a set of lights. "Elena. That explains it. Zane's PA. And Katherine's niece." He sent Nick an assessing look. "Didn't think she would be your type."

Nick found himself frowning at the blunt message. Kyle knew he was the one who had found their father's car, which had slid off the road in bad weather, then rolled.

His stomach tightened on a raft of memories. Memories that had faded with time, but that were still edged with grief and guilt.

If he hadn't been in bed with Elena, captivated by the same irresistible obsession that had been at the heart of his father's supposed betrayal, *with another Lyon woman,* he might have reached the crash site in time to make a difference.

The coroner's report had claimed that both his father and Katherine had survived the impact for a time. If he had left Elena at her door that night and driven home, there was a slim possibility he might have saved them.

Nick stared broodingly at the line of traffic backed up

for a set of lights. Kyle was right. He shouldn't be thinking about Elena.

The trouble was, lately, after the discovery of a diary and the stunning possibility that his father had not been having an affair with Katherine, he hadn't been able to stop thinking about Elena. "So…what is my type?"

Kyle looked wary. "Uh—they're usually blonde."

With long legs and confidence to burn. The exact opposite of Elena, with her dark eyes, her vulnerability and enticing, sultry curves.

Feeling in need of air, Nick activated the electric window. "I don't always date blondes."

"Hey, I won't judge you."

Although, for a while, it had been blondes or nothing, because dating dark-haired girls had cut too close to the bone. For a couple of years the memory of his night with Elena had been too viscerally tied into his grief and the gnawing guilt that he had failed to save his father.

Kyle sent him the kind of neutral, male look that said he'd noted Nick's interest in Elena, but wasn't going to probe any further. It was the kind of unspoken acceptance that short-circuited the need for a conversation, and which suited Nick.

His feelings for Elena were clear-cut enough. He wanted her back in his bed, but he wasn't prepared to think beyond that point.

Kyle turned into the underground parking building of the Messena building. "Any success locating the ring?"

Nick unfastened his seat belt as Kyle pulled into a space. "I've been asked that question a lot lately."

By his mother, his older brother, Gabriel and a selection of great-aunts and -uncles who were concerned about the loss of an important heirloom piece. Last but not least, the insurance assessor who, while engaged in a revaluing exercise, had discovered the ring was missing.

Climbing out of the Jeep, Nick slammed the door. "I'm beginning to feel like Frodo Baggins."

Kyle extracted his briefcase, locked the vehicle and tossed him the keys. "If that's the little guy off *Lord of the Rings,* he had prettier eyes."

"He also had friends who helped him."

Kyle grinned good-naturedly. "Cool. Just don't expect me to be one of them. My detective skills are zero. "

Nick tapped in the security PIN to access the elevator. "Anyone ever tell you you're irritating?"

"My last blonde girlfriend."

Nick hit the floor number that would take them to Gabriel's suite of offices and a discussion about diversifying his business interests. "I don't recall your last girlfriend."

Of all the Messena clan, Kyle was the quietest and the hardest to read. Maybe because of his time in Special Forces, or the fact that he had lost his wife and child to the horror of a terror attack, he had grown to be perceptibly different to them all.

"That was because I was on an overseas posting."

"She was foreign?"

"No. A military brat."

"What happened?"

He shrugged, his expression cagey. "We both moved on."

Nick studied Kyle's clean profile. With his obdurate jaw and the short, crisp cut of his hair, even in a sleek business suit he still managed to look dangerous. "So it wasn't serious."

"No."

Kyle's clear-cut indifference about his last casual relationship struck an odd chord with Nick. Kyle had cared about his wife and child, to the point that he hadn't cared about anyone since.

Nick hadn't lost a wife and child, not even close, but it was also true that for years, ever since their father had died, *and the night with Elena,* he had not been able to form a relationship.

The elevator doors slid open. Moving on automatic pilot, Nick strolled with Kyle through the familiar, hushed and expensive interior of the bank.

Normally, his social life was neatly compartmentalized and didn't impinge on the long hours he worked. But lately his social life had ground to a halt.

Dispassionately he examined the intensity of his focus on Elena, which, according to his PA, had made him irritable and terminally bad-tempered. He had considered dating, but every time he picked up the phone he found himself replacing it without making the call.

The blunt fact was that finding out that the past was not set in stone had been like opening up a Pandora's box. In that moment a raft of thoughts and emotions had hit him like a kick in the chest. Among them the stubborn, visceral need to reclaim Elena.

He couldn't fathom the need, and despite every effort, he hadn't been able to reason it away. It was just there.

The thought of making love with Elena made every muscle in his body tighten. The response, in itself, was singular. Usually when he finished a relationship it was over, his approach to dating and sex as cut-and-dried as his approach to contracting and completing a business deal.

But for some reason those few hours with Elena had stuck in his mind. Maybe the explanation was simply that what they'd shared had been over almost before it had begun. There hadn't been a cooling-off period when the usual frustrations over his commitment to his business kicked in.

But as much as he wanted Elena, bed would have to wait. His first priority had to be to obtain answers and closure. Although every time he got close to Elena the concept of closure crashed and burned.

Despite the buttoned-down clothing and schoolmarm hair, there had always been something irresistibly, tantalizingly sensual about Elena. She had probably noticed he'd been having trouble keeping his hands off her.

It was no wonder she had practically run from him in Cutler's office.

Nick had *liked* her.

A surge of delighted warmth shimmered through Elena as she strolled through a small park.

Six years ago Nick had cared enough to step in and protect her from a date that would have been uncomfortable, at best. More probably it would have ended in an embarrassing struggle, because Geoffrey Smale had a reputation for not taking no for an answer.

Feeling distinctly unsettled and on edge at this new view of the past, Elena made a beeline for the nearest park bench and sat down.

For six years she had been mad at Nick. Now she didn't know quite what to feel, except that, lurking beneath all of the confusion, being discarded by him all those years ago still hurt.

The problem was that as a teenager she'd had a thing for him. Summers spent in Dolphin Bay, visiting her aunt and watching a bronzed, muscular Nick surfing, had definitely contributed to the fascination.

Walking away from the night they'd spent together would have been easier if he had been a complete stranger, but he hadn't been. Because of her summers with her aunt at the original Lyon homestead on the beach, and because of Katherine's work for his family as a housekeeper, Elena had felt connected to Nick.

Too restless to sit, she checked her watch and strolled back in the direction of the Atraeus Hotel, where she was staying.

As she approached a set of exclusive boutiques a glass door swung open, and a sleek woman wearing a kingfisher-blue dress that showed off her perfect golden tan stepped out onto the street.

The door closed on a waft of some gorgeous perfume, and in the process Elena's reflection—that of a slightly overweight woman dressed in a plain dress and jacket, and wearing glasses—flashed back at her.

Even her handbag looked heavy and just a little boring. The only things that looked right were her shoes, which were pretty but didn't really go with the rest of her outfit.

Not just a victim, a *fashion* victim.

Nick's words came back to haunt her.

He didn't like her glasses or the way she did her hair. He hadn't mentioned her clothes, but she was seeing them through his eyes, and she was ready to admit that they were just as clunky, just as boring as the glasses and her hair.

As much as she resented his opinion, he was right. Something had to change. *She* had to change.

She could no longer immerse herself in work and avoid the fact that another birthday had just flown by. She was twenty-eight. Two more years and she would be thirty.

If she wasn't careful she would be thirty and alone.

Or she could change her life so that she would be thirty and immersed in a passionate love relationship.

Feeling electrified, as if she was standing on the edge

of a precipice, about to take a perilous leap into the unknown, she studied the elegant writing on the glass frontage of the store. A tingling sense of fate taking a hand gripped her.

It wasn't a store, exactly. It was a very exclusive and expensive health and beauty spa. The kind of place she was routinely around because her employer, the Atraeus Group, numbered a few very high-quality spa facilities among its resort properties. Of course, she had never personally utilized any of those spa facilities.

But that was the old Elena.

Her jaw firmed. She had made a decision to change. By the time she was finished, she would be, if not as pretty, at least as sleek and stylish and confident as the woman in the blue dress.

The idea gained momentum. She would no longer allow herself to feel inadequate and excluded, which would mean inner as well as outward change.

She could walk in those doors now if she wanted. She had the money. After years of saving her very good salary, she had more than enough to pay for a makeover.

Feeling a little dizzy at the notion that she didn't have to stay as she was, that she had the power to change herself, she stepped up to the exquisite white-and-gold portal. Taking a deep breath, she pushed the door wide and stepped inside.

After an initial hour-long consultation with a stylist called Giorgio, during which he had casually ticked almost every box on the interview form he had used, Elena signed on for every treatment recommended.

First up was weight loss and detox, which included a week in a secluded health spa. That was followed by a comprehensive fitness program and an introduction to her new personal trainer. A series of beauty and pamper treatments, and a comprehensive hair, makeup and wardrobe makeover completed her program.

The initial week at their spa facility would cost a staggering amount, but she was desperate.

According to Giorgio she wasn't desperate; she was worth it.

Elena wasn't about to split hairs. As long as the spa could carry out its promise and transform her, she was happy to pay.

Her heart sped up at the changes she was about to make. Hope flooded her.

The next time she saw Nick Messena, things would be different. *She* would be different.

Three

One month later, Nick Messena watched, green gaze cool, as Elena Lyon walked with measured elegance down the aisle toward him, every step precisely, perfectly timed with the beat of the Wedding March.

Mellow afternoon sunlight poured through stained glass windows, illuminating the startling changes she had made, from her long, stylishly cut, midnight-dark hair to the tips of her outrageously sexy pink high heels. Her bridesmaid's dress, a sophisticated confection of pink lace and silk that he privately thought was just a little too revealing, clung to lush, gentle curves and a mouthwateringly tiny waist.

As the bride reached the altar, Elena's gaze rested briefly on Kyle who was Gabriel's groomsman, then locked with his. With grim satisfaction, he noted that she hadn't realized he had changed roles with Kyle and taken over as Gabriel's best man. If she had, he was cer-

tain she would have very quickly and efficiently organized someone else to take her place as maid of honor.

Dragging her gaze free, Elena briskly took charge of
the flower girl, Gabriel and Gemma's daughter Sanchia,
who had just finished tossing rose petals. Nick's brows
jerked together as he took stock of some of the changes
he had barely had time to register at the prewedding dinner the previous evening. For the first time he noticed a
tiny, discreet sparkle to one side of Elena's delicate nose.
A piercing.

Every muscle in his body tightened at the small, exotic touch. His elusive ex-lover had lost weight, cut her
hair and ditched the dull, shapeless clothing she had worn
like a uniform. In the space of a few weeks, Elena had
morphed from softly curved, bespectacled and repres-
sively buttoned-down, into an exotically hot and sensuous swan.

Jaw clamped, Nick transferred his attention to the
bride, Gemma O'Neill, as she stood beside his brother.

As the ceremony proceeded, Elena kept her attention
fixed on the priest. Fascinated by her intention to utterly
ignore him, Nick took the opportunity to study the newly
sculpted contours of Elena's cheekbones, her shell-like
lobes decorated with pink pearls and tiny pink jewels.

The sexily ruffled haircut seemed to sum up the
changes Elena had made: less, but a whole lot more.

As Nick handed the ring to Gabriel, Elena's dark gaze
clashed with his for a pulse-pounding moment. The
starry, romantic softness he glimpsed died an instant
death, replaced by the familiar professional blandness
that made his jaw tighten.

The cool neutrality was distinctly at odds with the way
Elena had used to look at him. It was light-years away

from the ingenuous passion that had burned him from the inside out when they had made love.

A delicate, sophisticated perfume wafted around him. The tantalizing scent, like Elena's designer wardrobe, her new, sleek body shape and the ultramodern haircut—all clearly the product of a ruthless makeover artist—set him even more sensually on edge.

Gabriel turned to take the hand of the woman he had pledged to marry.

A flash of Elena's pink dress, as she bent down to whisper something to Sanchia, drew Nick's gaze, along with another tempting flash of cleavage.

With a brisk elegance that underlined the fact that the old Elena was long gone, she repositioned Sanchia next to Gemma. Nick clamped down on his impatience as the ceremony proceeded at a snail's pace.

Elena had been avoiding him for the past twenty-four hours, ever since she had arrived in Dolphin Bay. The one time he had managed to get her alone—last night to discuss meeting at the beach villa—she had successfully stonewalled him. Now his temper was on a slow burn. Whether she liked it or not, they would conclude their business this weekend.

Distantly, he registered that Gabriel was kissing his new bride. With grim patience, Nick waited out the signing of the register in the small, adjacent vestry.

As Gabriel swung his small daughter up into his arms, Elena's gaze, unexpectedly misty and soft, connected with his again, long enough for him to register two salient facts. The contact lenses with which she had replaced her trademark glasses were not the regular, transparent type. They were a dark chocolate brown that completely obliterated the usual, cheerful golden brown of her irises.

More importantly, despite her cool control and her

efforts to pretend that he didn't exist, he was aware in that moment that for Elena, he very palpably *did* exist.

Every muscle in his body tightened at the knowledge that despite her refusals to meet with him, despite the fact that every time they did meet they ended up arguing, Elena still wanted him.

With an effort of will, Nick kept his expression neutral as he signed as a witness to the ceremony. In a few minutes he would walk down the aisle with Elena on his arm. It was the window of opportunity he had planned for when he had arranged to change places with Kyle.

Negotiation was not his best talent; that was Gabriel's forte. Nick was more suited to the blunt, laconic cadences of construction sites. A world of black and white, where "yes" meant *yes* and "no" meant *no* and not some murky, frustrating shade in between.

As the music swelled and Elena looped her arm through his, the issue of retrieving an heirloom ring and unraveling the mystery of his father's link with Elena's aunt faded.

With Elena's delicately enticing perfume filling his nostrils again, Nick acknowledged that the only "yes" he really wanted from Elena was the one she had given him six years ago.

Elena steeled herself against the tiny electrical charge that coursed through her as she settled her palm lightly on Nick's arm.

Nick sent her another assessing glance. Despite her intention to be cool and distant and, as she'd done the previous evening, pretend that she didn't look a whole lot different than she had a month ago, Elena's pulse rate accelerated. Even though she knew she looked her very best, thanks to the efforts of the beauty spa, she was still adjusting to the changes. Having Nick Messena put her new look under a microscope, *and wondering if he liked what he saw,* was unexpectedly nerve-racking.

Nick bent his head close enough that she caught an intriguing whiff of his cologne. "Is that a tattoo on your shoulder?"

Elena stiffened at the blunt question and the hint of disapproval that went with it. "It's a transfer. I'm *thinking* about a tattoo."

There was a small tense silence. "You don't need it."

The flat statement made her bristle. "*I* think I need it and Giorgio thought it looked very good."

"Damn," he said softly. "Who is Giorgio?"

A small thrill went through her at the sudden, blinding thought that Nick was jealous, although she refused to allow herself to buy into that fantasy.

From what she knew personally and had read in magazines and tabloids, Nick Messena didn't have a jealous bone in his body. Most of his liaisons were so brief there was no time for an emotion as deep and powerful as jealousy to form. "Giorgio is…a friend."

She caught the barest hint of annoyance in his expression, and a small but satisfying surge of feminine power coursed through her at the decision not to disclose her true relationship with Giorgio. It was absolutely none of Nick's business that Giorgio was her personal beauty consultant.

In that moment she remembered Robert Corrado, another very new friend who had the potential to be much more. After just a couple of dates, it was too early to tell if Robert was poised to be the love of her life, but right now he was a touchstone she desperately needed.

Taking a deep breath, she tried to recall exactly what

Robert looked like as they followed Gabriel, Gemma and Sanchia down the aisle.

She felt Nick's gaze once again on her profile. "You've lost weight."

Her jaw clenched at the excruciating conversation opener. It was not the response she had envisaged, but all the same, a small renegade part of her was happy that he had noticed.

Her new hourglass shape constantly surprised her. The diet, combined with a rigorous exercise regime had produced a totally unexpected body. She still had curves, albeit more streamlined than they used to be, and they were now combined with a tiny waist.

She was still amazed that the loss of such a small amount of weight had made such a difference. If she had realized how little had stood between her and a totally new body, she would have opted for diet and exercise years ago. "Can't you come up with a better conversational opener than that?"

"Maybe I'm out of touch. What am I supposed to say?"

"According to a gossip columnist you're not in the least out of touch. If you want to make conversation, you could try concentrating on positives."

"I thought that was a positive." Nick frowned. "Which columnist?"

Elena drew a swift breath. After her unscheduled meeting with Nick in Auckland she had, by pure chance, read that he had dated a gorgeous model that same night. She said the name.

His expression cleared. "The story about Melanie."

"Melanie. Rhymes with Tiffany."

Nick's gaze sliced back to hers. "She's a friend of my sister, and it was a family dinner. There was no date. Have you managed to sell the villa yet?"

"Not yet, but I've received an offer, which I'm considering."

The muscles beneath her fingers tensed. She caught his flash of annoyance. "Whatever you've been offered, I'll top it by ten percent."

Elena stared ahead, keeping her gaze glued to the tulle of Gemma's veil. "I don't understand why you want the villa."

"It's beachfront. It's an investment I won't lose on, plus it seems to be the only way I can get you to agree to help me search for the ring."

"I've looked. It's not there."

"Did you check the attic?"

"I'm working my way through it. I haven't found anything yet, and I've searched through almost everything."

Her aunt had been a collector of all sorts of memorabilia. Elena had sorted through all the recent boxes, everything else she had opened lately was going back progressively in time.

There was a small, grim silence. "If you won't consider my purchase offer, will you let me have a look through before you sell?"

Her jaw set. "I can't see Aunt Katherine putting a valuable piece of jewelry in an attic."

"My father noted in a diary that he had given the ring to Katherine. You haven't found it anywhere else, which means it's entirely probable that it's in the house, somewhere."

Elena loosened her grip on the small bouquet she was holding. Nick's frustration that he wasn't getting what he wanted was palpable. Against all the odds, she had to fight a knee-jerk impulse to cave and offer to help him.

Determinedly, she crushed the old overgenerous Elena: *the doormat.*

According to Giorgio her fatal weakness was that she liked to please men. The reason she had rushed around and done so much for her Atraeus bosses was that it satisfied her need to be needed. She was substituting pleasing powerful men for a genuine love relationship in which she was entitled to receive care and nurturing.

The discovery had been life altering. On the strength of it, she intended to quit her job as a PA, because she figured that the temptation to revert to her old habit of rushing to please would be so ingrained it would be hard to resist. Instead, she planned to branch out in a new, more creative direction. Now that she'd come this far, she couldn't go back to being the old, downtrodden Elena.

Aware that Nick was waiting for an answer she crushed the impulse to say an outright yes. "I don't think you'll find anything, but since you're so insistent, I'm willing for you to come and have a look through the house for yourself."

"When? I'm flying out early tomorrow morning and I won't be back for a month."

In which time, if she accepted the offer she was considering, the villa could be sold. She frowned at the way Nick had neatly cornered her. "I suppose I could spare a couple of hours tonight. If I help you sort through the final trunks, one hour should do it."

"Done." Nick lifted a hand in brief acknowledgment of an elderly man Elena recognized as Mario Atraeus. Seated next to him was a gorgeous brunette, Eva Atraeus, Mario's adopted daughter.

Elena's hand tightened on Nick's arm in a weird, instant reflex. Nick's gaze clashed with hers. "What's wrong?"

"Nothing." She had just remembered a photograph she stumbled across a couple of months ago in a glossy women's magazine of Nick partnering Eva at a charity function. They had looked perfect together. Nick with his strong masculine good looks, Eva, with her olive skin and tawny hair, looking like an exotic flower by his side.

The music swelled to a crescendo as Gabriel and Gemma, with Sanchia in tow, stopped to greet an elderly matriarch of the Messena clan instead of leaving the church.

Pressed forward by people behind, Elena found herself impelled onto the front steps of the church, into a shower of confetti and rice.

A dark-haired young man wearing a checked shirt loomed out of the waiting crowd. He lifted a large camera and began snapping them as if they were the married couple. Embarrassment clutched at Elena. It wasn't the official photographer, which meant he was probably a journalist. "He's making a mistake."

Another wave of confetti had Nick tucking her in closer against his side. "A reporter making a mistake? It won't be the first time."

"Aren't you worried?"

"Not particularly."

A cluster of guests exiting the church jostled Elena, so that she found herself plastered against Nick's chest.

"I said I wasn't going to do this," he muttered.

A split second later his head dipped and his mouth came down on hers.

Four

Instead of pulling away as she should have, Elena froze, an odd feminine delight flowing through her at the softness of his mouth, the faint abrasion of his jaw. Nick's hands settled at her waist, steadying her against him as he angled his jaw and deepened the kiss.

She registered that Nick was aroused. For a dizzying moment time seemed to slow, stop, then an eruption of applause, a raft of excited comments and the motorized click of the reporter's camera brought her back to her senses.

Nick lifted his head. "We need to move."

His arm closed around her waist, urging her off the steps. At that moment Gemma and Gabriel appeared in the doors of the church, and the attention of the reporter and the guests shifted.

Someone clapped Nick on the shoulder. "For a minute there I thought I was attending the wrong wedding, but as soon as I recognized you I knew you couldn't be the groom."

Relieved by the distraction, Elena freed herself from Nick's hold and the haze of unscripted passion.

Nick half turned to shake hands with a large, tanned man wearing a sleek suit teamed with an Akubra hat, the Australian equivalent of a cowboy. "You know me, Nate. Married to the job."

Elena noticed that the young guy in the checked shirt who had been snapping photos had sidled close and seemed to be listening. Before she could decide whether he was lingering with deliberate intent or if it was sheer coincidence, Nick introduced her to Nate Cavendish.

As soon as Elena heard the name she recognized Cavendish as an Australian cattleman with a legendary reputation as one of the richest and most elusive bachelors in Australia.

Feeling flustered and unsettled, her mind still locked on Nick's statement that he was married to the job, she shook Nate's hand.

Nate gave her a curious look as if he found her familiar but couldn't quite place her. Not surprising, since she had bumped into him at Atraeus parties a couple of times in the past when she had been the "old" Elena. "You must be Nick's new girl."

"No," she said blandly. "I'm not that interested. Too busy shopping around."

Nick's gaze touched on hers, promising retribution. "It's what you might call an interesting arrangement."

Nate shook his head. "Sounds like she's got you on your knees."

Nick shrugged, his expression cooling as he noticed the journalist. "Another one bites the dust."

"That's for sure." Nate tipped his hat at Elena and

walked toward the guests clustered around Gabriel and Gemma.

Nick's gaze was glacially cold as he watched the reporter jog toward a car and drive away at speed.

Elena's stomach sank. After working years for the Atraeus family, she had an instinct about the press. The only reason the reporter was leaving was because he had a story.

Nick's palm landed in the small of her back. He moved her out of the way of the crowd as Gemma and Gabriel strolled toward their waiting limousine. But the effect that one small touch had on Elena was far from casual, zapping her straight back to the unsettling heat of the kiss.

Nick's brows jerked together as she instantly moved away from his touch. A split second later a vibrating sound distracted him.

Sliding his phone out of his pocket, he stepped a couple of paces away to answer the call.

While he conducted a discussion about closing some deal on a resort purchase, Elena struggled to compose herself as she watched the bridal car leave.

A second limousine slid into place. The one that would transport her, Nick and Kyle to the Dolphin Bay Resort for the wedding photographs.

Her stomach churned at the thought. There was no quick exit today. She would have to share the intimate space of the limousine with Nick then, sit with him at the reception.

Too late to wish she hadn't allowed that kiss or the conversation that had followed. Before today she would have said she didn't have a flirtatious bone in her body. But sometime between the altar and the church gate she had learned to flirt.

Because she was still fatally attracted to Nick.

Elena drew a breath and let it out slowly.

She should never have allowed Nick to kiss her.

Her only excuse was that she had been so distracted by Gemma finally getting her happy-ever-after ending that she had dropped her guard.

But Nick had just reminded her of exactly why she couldn't afford him in her life.

Nick Messena, like Nate Cavendish, was not husband material for one simple reason: no woman could ever compete with the excitement and challenge of his business.

Nick terminated his conversation and turned back to her, his gaze settling on her, narrowed and intent. "Looks like our ride is here."

Elena's heart thumped once, hard, as Nick's words spun her back to their conversation on the sidewalk in Auckland. The breath locked in her throat as she finally allowed the knowledge that Nick was genuinely attracted to her to sink in. More, that he had been attracted to her six years ago, *before* she had changed her appearance.

The knowledge that he had wanted her even when she had been a little overweight and frumpy was difficult to process. She was absolutely not like the normal run of his girlfriends. It meant that *he liked her for herself.*

The sudden blinding thought that, if she wanted, she could end the empty years of fruitless and boring dating and make love with Nick sent heat flooding through her.

Nick was making no bones about the fact that he wanted her—

"Are you good to go?"

Elena drew a deep breath and tried to slide back into her professional PA mode. But with Nick looming over her, a smudge of lipstick at the corner of his mouth, it was difficult to focus. "I am, but you're not."

Extracting a handkerchief from a small, secret pocket at the waist of her dress, she handed it to him. "You have lipstick on your mouth."

Taking the handkerchief, he wiped his mouth. "An occupational hazard at weddings."

When he attempted to give the handkerchief back, she forced a smile. "Keep it. I don't want it back."

The last thing she needed was a keepsake to remind her that she had been on the verge of making a second mistake.

Slipping the handkerchief into his trousers' pocket, he jerked his head in the direction of the limousine. "If you're ready, looks like the official photo shoot is about to begin." He sent her a quick, rueful grin. "Don't know about you, but it's not exactly my favorite pastime."

Elena dragged her gaze from Nick's and the killer charm that she absolutely did not want to be ensnared by. "I have no problem with having my photo taken."

Not since she had taken one of the intensive courses offered at the health spa. She had been styled and made up by professionals and taught how to angle her face and smile. After two intimidating hours beneath glaring lights, a camera pointed at her face, she had finally conquered her fear of the lens.

A good thirty minutes later, after posing for endless photographs while the guests sipped champagne and circulated in the grounds of the Dolphin Bay Resort, Elena found herself seated next to Nick at the reception.

Held in a large room, which had been festooned with white roses, glossy dark green foliage and trailing, fragrant jasmine, the wedding was the culmination of a romantic dream.

A further hour of speeches, champagne and exquisite food later, the orchestra struck a chord. Growing more tense by the second, Elena watched as Gabriel and Gemma took the floor. According to tradition she and Nick were up next.

Nick held out one large, tanned and scarred hand. "I think that's our cue."

Elena took his hand, tensing at the tingling heat of his touch, the faint abrasion of calluses gained on construction sites and while indulging his other passion: sailing.

One hand settled at her waist, drawing her in close at the first sweeping step of a waltz. Elena's breath hitched in her throat as her breasts brushed his chest. Stiffening slightly, she pulled back, although it was hard to enjoy dancing, which she loved, when maintaining a rigid distance.

Nick sent her a neutral glance. "You should relax."

Another couple who had just joined the general surge onto the floor danced too close and jostled her.

Nick frowned. "And that's why." With easy strength he pulled her closer.

Feeling a little breathless, Elena stared at the tough line of Nick's jaw and decided to stay there.

"That's better."

As Nick twirled her past Gabriel and Gemma, Elena tried to relax. Another hour and she could leave. Tension hit her again at that thought because she would be leaving with Nick, a scenario that ran a little too close to what had taken place six years ago. The music switched to a slower, steamier waltz.

Instead of releasing her, Nick continued to dance, keeping her close. "How long have you known Gemma?"

Heart pounding with the curious, humming excitement of being so close to Nick, Elena forced herself to concentrate on answering his question. "Since I started coming to Dolphin Bay for my vacations when I was seventeen."

"I remember seeing you on the beach."

Elena could feel her cheeks warming at the memory of just how much time she used to spend watching Nick on his surfboard or messing around on boats. "I used to read on the beach a lot."

"But not anymore?"

She steeled herself against the curiosity of his gaze, his sudden unnerving focus. "These days, I have other things to occupy my time."

He lifted a brow. "Let me guess—a gym membership."

"Fitness is important."

"So, what's behind the sudden transformation?"

Elena stiffened against the urge to blurt out that he had been the trigger. "I simply wanted to make the best of myself."

They danced beneath a huge, central chandelier, the light flowing across the strong planes and angles of Nick's face, highlighting the various nicks and scars.

He tucked her in a little closer for a turn. "I liked the color your eyes used to be. They were a pretty sherry brown, you shouldn't have changed that."

Elena blinked at the complete unexpectedness of his comment. "I didn't think you'd noticed."

No one else had, including herself. A little breathlessly she made a mental note to go back to clear contacts.

"And what about these?" he growled. His thumb brushed over one lobe then swept upward, tracing the curve of her ear, initiating a white-hot shimmer of heat.

He hooked coiling strands of hair behind one ear to further investigate, his breath washing over the curve of her neck, disarming her even further. "How many piercings?"

Despite her intense concentration on staying in step, Elena wobbled. When she corrected, she was close enough to Nick that she was now pressed lightly against his chest and his thighs brushed hers with every step. "One didn't seem to be enough, so I got three. On my lobes, that is."

His gaze sharpened. "There are piercings...else-where?"

Her heart thumped at the sudden intensity of his expression, the melting heat in his eyes. She swallowed, her mouth suddenly dry. "Just one. A navel piercing."

He was silent for a long, drawn-out moment, in which time the air seemed to thicken as the music took on a slower, slumberous rhythm. A tango.

Nick's hand tightened on her waist, drawing her infinitesimally closer. "Anything else I should know?"

She drew a quick, shallow breath as the heat from his big body closed around her. The passionate music, which she loved, throbbed, heightening her senses. Her nostrils seemed filled with his scent. The heat from his hand at her waist, his palm locked against hers, burned as if they were locked into some kind of electrical current.

She squashed the insane urge to sway a little closer. Wrong man, wrong place and a totally wrong time to road test this new direction in her life.

The whole point was to change her life, not repeat her old mistake.

Although, the heady thought that she could repeat it, if she wanted, made her mouth go dry. She hadn't missed the heat in Nick's gaze, or when he'd pulled her close, that he was semiaroused. "Only if you were my lover, which you're not."

"You've got a guy."

She frowned at the flat statement, the slight tightening of his hold. As if in some small way Nick considered that she belonged to him, which was ridiculous. "I date." Her chin came up. "I'm seeing someone at the moment."

His gaze narrowed with a mixture of disbelief and displeasure. "Who?"

A small startled thrill shot through her at the sudden notion that Nick didn't like it one little bit that there was a man in her life, even if the dating was still on a superficial level.

A little drunk on the rush of power that, in a room teeming with beautiful women, *she* was the center of his attention, she touched her tongue to her top lip. It was a gesture she became aware was an unconscious tease as his focus switched to her mouth.

Abruptly embarrassed, she closed her mouth and stared over Nick's shoulder at another pair of dancers whirling past. "You won't know him."

"Let me guess," he muttered. "Giorgio."

Elena blushed at the mistaken conclusion. A conclusion Nick had arrived at because she had deliberately failed to clarify who, exactly, Giorgio was. "Uh—actually, his name is Robert. Robert Corrado."

There was a stark silence. "You have *two* guys?"

She wasn't sure if the two tentative pecks on the mouth she had allowed, and which had been devoid of anything like the electrifying pleasure she had experienced when Nick kissed her, qualified Robert to be her *guy*. "Just the one."

Nick's gaze bored into hers, narrowed and glittering. "So Giorgio's past history?"

Elena tried to dampen down the addictive little charge of excitement that went through her at Nick's obvious displeasure. "Giorgio's my beauty consultant."

Nick muttered something short and succinct under his

breath. Another slow, gliding turn and they were outside on a shadowy patio with the light of the setting sun glowing through palm fronds and gleaming off a limpid pool.

Nick relinquished his hold, his jaw set, his gaze brooding and distinctly irritable. "Is Corrado the one you got the piercings for?"

The question, as if he had every right to expect an answer, made her world tilt again.

She had speculated before, but now she *knew*.

Nick was jealous.

Five

Elena dragged her gaze from Nick's and looked out past the pool and the palms to the ocean. Anything to stop the crazy pull of attraction and the dangerous knowledge that Nick really did want her.

The fact that he had been attracted to her before she had lost weight—that he actually liked her simply for who she was—was bad enough. But his brooding temper, as if the one night they had shared had somehow given him rights, was an undertow she wasn't sure she could resist. "Not that it's any of your business, but Robert doesn't care for piercings."

He definitely didn't know about the one she had gotten in her navel, or the pretty jeweled studs she had bought to go with her new selection of bikinis.

"So you didn't get the piercings for him."

The under note of satisfaction in Nick's voice, as if she had gotten the piercings for him, ruffled her even further. "I didn't get the piercings for *anyone*."

But even as she said the words, her heart plummeted. She had tried to convince herself that the piercings were just a part of the process of change, a signpost that declared that she wasn't thirty—yet. But the stark reality was that she had gotten them because they were pretty and sexy and practically screamed that she was available. She had gotten them for Nick.

"You haven't slept with Corrado."

Annoyed at the way Nick had dismissed Robert, Elena stepped farther out onto the patio, neatly evading his gaze. "That's none of your business. Robert's a nice man." He was safe and controllable, as different from Nick as a tame tabby from a prowling tiger. "He's definitely not fixated on piercings."

"Ouch. That puts me in my place." Nick dragged at his tie. Strolling to the wrought iron railing that enclosed part of the patio, he pulled the tie off altogether, folded it and shoved it into his pocket.

Drawn to join him, even though she knew it was a mistake, Elena averted her gaze from the slice of brown flesh revealed by the buttons he had unfastened.

The balmy evening seemed to get hotter as she became aware that Nick was studying the studs in her ear and the tiny glimpse of the butterfly transfer. "I'm guessing from the pink earring that there's a pink jewel in your navel?"

The accuracy of his guess made her stiffen. The old adage "give him an inch and he'll take a mile" came back to haunt her. "You shouldn't flirt with me."

"Why not? It makes a change from arguing, and after tonight we may never see each other again."

Elena froze. The attraction that shimmered through her, keeping her breathless and on edge, winked out. She stared at the strong line of his jaw, the sexy hollows of his cheekbones, aware that, somehow, she had been silly enough, vulnerable enough, to allow Nick to slide through her defenses. To start buying into the notion that just because he found her attractive it meant *he* had changed.

The day Nick Messena changed his stripes she would grow wings and fly.

Lifting her chin, she met his gaze squarely. "*If* you find the ring." The instant the words were out, she wished she could recall them. They had sounded needy, as if she was looking for a way to hang on to him.

Nick glanced out over the pool, the sun turning the tawny streaks in his dark hair molten. "You make it sound like a quest. I'm not that romantic."

No, his focus was always relentlessly practical, which was what made him so successful in business.

Swallowing a sudden ache in her throat, Elena did what she should have done in the first place: she turned on her heel and walked back to the reception. As she strolled, Nick's presence behind her made her tense. By the time she reached her table he was close enough that he held her chair as she sat down.

He dropped into the seat beside her and poured ice water into her glass before filling his own.

Elena picked up the glass. The nice manners, which would have been soothing in another man, unsettled her even further. "If Aunt Katherine did receive the ring, then I guess all the gossip was true."

Nick sat back in his seat. "I don't want it to be true, either," he said quietly.

For a split second she was caught and held by the somberness of his expression.

A set of memories from her summers on the beach at Dolphin Bay flickered, of Nick yachting with his father.

It had usually been just the two of them, sailing, making repairs and cleaning the boat after a day out.

One thing had always been very obvious: that Nick had loved his father. Suddenly, his real agenda was very clear to Elena. He wasn't just searching for a valuable heirloom. He was doing something much more important: he was trying to make sense of the past. "You don't want to find the ring, do you?"

"Not if it meant an affair."

"You think they weren't having an affair?"

"I'm hoping there's another reason they spent time together."

Her stomach tightened at the knowledge that Nick was trying to clear his father, a process that would also clear her aunt. That despite his reputation there were depths to Nick that were honorable and true and *likable*.

That she and Nick shared something in common.

Elena watched as Nick drank, the muscles of his throat working smoothly. At that moment Gemma signaled to her.

Relieved at the interruption, Elena rose from her seat. She felt unsettled, electrified. Every time she thought she had Nick figured out, something changed, the ground shifting under her feet.

After a quick hug, Gemma stepped back. Almost instantly, she tossed the bouquet. Surprised, Elena caught the fragrant, trailing bunch of white roses, orchids and orange blossom.

Feeling embattled, she dipped her head and inhaled the delicious fragrance. Her throat closed up. After years of brisk practicality as a PA, she was on the verge of losing control and crying on the spot because she realized just how much she wanted what Gemma had: a happy ending with a man who truly, honorably loved her. "You should have given it to someone else."

Gemma frowned. "No way. You're my best friend and, just look at you, you're gorgeous. Men will be falling all over you." She gave her another hug. "I won't be happy until you're married. Who's that guy you're seeing in Sydney?"

Elena carefully avoided Gemma's gaze on the pretext that she was examining the faintly crushed flowers. "Robert."

Gemma grinned and hooked her arm through Gabriel's, snuggling into his side. "Then marry him. But only if you're in love."

Elena forced a smile. "Great idea. First he has to propose."

Elena walked back to her seat, clutching the bouquet. She was acutely aware that Nick, who was standing talking with a group of friends, had watched the exchange.

Gray-haired Marge Hamilton, an old character in Dolphin Bay, with a legendary reputation for gossip in a town that abounded with it, made a beeline for her. "Caught the bouquet I see. Clever girl."

"Actually, it was given to me—"

Marge's gaze narrowed, but there was a pleased glint in the speculation. "You'll be next down the aisle and, I must say, it's about time."

Elena's discomfort escalated. Nick was close enough that he could hear every word. But as embarrassing as the conversation was, she would never forget that, despite Marge's love of gossip, she had been fiercely supportive of her aunt when the scandal had erupted.

Elena dredged up a smile. "As a matter of fact, I'm working on it."

Marge's gaze swiveled to her left hand. A small frown

formed when she noted the third finger was bare. "Sounds like you have someone in mind. What's his name, dear?"

Elena's fingers tightened on the bouquet as she tried to make herself say Robert's name, but somehow she just couldn't seem to get it out. Something snapped at the base of the bouquet. There was a small clunk as a small plastic horseshoe, included for luck, dropped to the floor. "He's...from Sydney."

"Not that hot young Atraeus boy?" Marge sent a disapproving glance at Zane, who had flown in from Florida and happened to be leaning on the bar, a beer in his hand.

"*Zane?* He's my boss. No, his name is—"

Marge frowned. "At one point we thought you actually might snaffle one of those Atraeus boys. Although, any one of them is a wild handful."

Elena could feel herself stiffening at the idea that she was hunting for a husband in her workplace and, worse, the suggestion that the whole of Dolphin Bay was speculating on whether or not she could actually succeed. "I *work* for the Atraeus Group. It would be highly unprofessional to mix business—"

Nick's arm curved around her waist as casually as if they were a couple. His breath feathered her cheek, sending heat flooding through her.

"Were you about to say 'with pleasure'?"

Marge blinked as if she couldn't quite believe what she was witnessing. "I can see why you didn't want to say his name, dear. A little premature to announce it at a family wedding."

With surprising nimbleness she extracted a gleaming smartphone from her evening bag and snapped a picture. Beaming, she hurried off.

Elena disengaged herself from Nick's hold. "I was

about to say that it would be unprofessional to mix business with a *personal relationship.*"

"Last I heard, personal relationships should be about pleasure."

"Commitment would be the quality I'd be looking for."

She noted Marge sharing the photo with one of her cronies. "The story will be all over town before the sun sets."

"That fast?"

"You better believe it. And, unfortunately, she has the picture to prove it."

"I must admit I didn't expect her to have a phone with a camera." Nick looked abashed.

Infuriatingly, it only made him look sexier. Elena had to steel herself against the almost irresistible impulse to smile back and forgive him, and forget that he hadn't responded to her probe about commitment. "Never underestimate a woman with a lilac rinse and a double string of pearls."

"Damn. Sorry, babe, it'll be a five-minute wonder—"

"Approximately the length of time your relationships last?" But, despite her knee-jerk attempt to freeze him out, Elena melted inside at the casual way Nick had called her "babe," as if they were intimately attached. As if she really were his girl.

Taking a deep breath, she forced herself to recall every magazine article or gossip columnist's piece she had ever read about Nick. And every one of the gorgeous girls with whom he'd been photographed.

Nick's expression sobered. "Okay, I guess I deserved that."

Elena set the gorgeous bouquet down on the table. "So, why did you do it?"

Nick's gaze was laced with impatience. "You should

ignore the gossips. They've had me married off a dozen times. I'm still single."

Elena pulled out her chair and sat down. She couldn't quite dredge up a light smile or a quip for the simple reason that a small, tender part of her didn't want there to be *any* gossip about her and Nick. The night she had spent with Nick, as disastrous as it was, had been an intensely private experience.

She didn't know if she would ever feel anything like it again. In six years she hadn't had so much as a glimmer of the searing, shimmering heat that had gripped her while she'd been in Nick's arms.

If people gossiped about them now, assuming they were sleeping together, that night would be sullied.

Nick frowned. "Is this about Robert?"

Elena almost made the mistake of saying *who?* "Robert isn't possessive." He hadn't had time to be, yet.

"A New Age guy."

She tried to focus on couples slow dancing to another dreamy waltz as Nick took the chair beside her. "What's so wrong with that?"

"Nothing, I guess, just so long as that's what you really want."

Elena's chest squeezed tight at the wording, which seemed to suggest that she had some kind of choice, between Robert and Nick.

Somehow, within the space of a few short hours the situation between them had gotten out of hand. She didn't think she could afford to be around Nick much longer. They needed to resolve the issue of the ring, and whatever else it was he was looking for, tonight.

She pushed to her feet again, so fast that her chair threatened to tip over.

Nick said something curt beneath his breath as he rose

to his feet and caught the chair in one smooth movement. In the process, her shoulder bumped his chest and the top of her head brushed his jaw.

He reached out to steady her, his fingers leaving an imprint of heat on her upper arm. Elena stiffened at her response to his touch, light as it was. She instantly moved away, disengaging.

Blinking a little at the strobing lights on the dance floor, and because her new contacts were starting to make her eyes feel dry and itchy, she collected the pink, beaded purse that went with her dress. "If you want to look for the ring, I'm ready now. The sooner we get this over and done with the better."

She was still clearly vulnerable when it came to Nick, but that just meant she had to work harder at being immune.

As she strolled with Nick out of the lavish resort, she tried to fill her mind with all of the positive, romantic things she could plan to do with Robert.

Intimate, candlelit dinners, walks on the beach, romantic nights spent together in the large bed she had recently installed in her Sydney apartment.

Unfortunately, every time she tried to picture Robert in her bed, tangled in her very expensive silk sheets, his features changed, becoming a little more hawkish and battered, his jaw solid, his gaze piercing.

Annoyed with the heated tension that reverberated through her at the thought of Nick naked and sprawled in her bed, she banished the disruptive image.

Six

Tension coursed through Nick as he walked through the resort foyer and down the front steps. Outside the sun had set, leaving a golden glow in the west. The air was still and balmy, the cool of evening infusing the air with a soft dampness.

"My car's this way." He indicated the resort's staff parking lot.

Elena paused beside his Jeep, which was parked in the manager's space. "No towing service in Dolphin Bay?"

"Not for a Messena."

She waited while he unlocked the Jeep. "I keep forgetting you're related to the Atraeus family. Nothing like a bit of nepotism."

He controlled the automatic desire to flirt back and held the door while Elena climbed in. As she did so, the flimsy skirt of her dress shimmied back, revealing elegant, shapely legs and the ultra-sexy high heels.

He found himself relaxing for the first time since Elena's pronouncement that she had a boyfriend. Although the hot pulse of jealousy that Elena had not only been ignoring his calls, but that sometime in the past few weeks she had started dating someone else, was still on a slow burn.

Robert Corrado. Grimly, he noted the name.

It was familiar, which meant he probably moved in business circles. Given that Elena was Zane's PA, she had probably met him in conjunction with her work for the Atraeus Group.

The thought that Corrado could be a businessman, and very likely wealthy, didn't please Nick. He would call his personnel manager and get him to run a check on Corrado first thing in the morning.

Jaw taut, he swung into the cab. The door closed with a thunk, and Elena's delicate, tantalizing perfume scented the air, making the enclosed space seem even smaller and more intimate.

The drive to the villa, with its steep bush-clad gullies and winding road, took a good fifteen minutes despite the fact that the property was literally next door to the resort, tucked into a small private curve of Dolphin Bay.

Security lights flicked on as he turned into the cypress-lined gravel drive. He checked out the for-sale sign and noted that it didn't have a Sold sticker across it yet.

Satisfaction eased some of his tension. He didn't need another property, and with its links to his father's past he shouldn't want this one. His offer to Elena had been a tactic, pure and simple, a sweetener to give him the opening he needed to research the past.

Although, once he had decided to make the purchase, the desire to own the property had taken on a life of its own.

On thinking it through, he had decided that his motives were impractical and self-centered. In buying the villa he hoped to somehow soothe over the past and cement a link with Elena.

Whichever way he looked at it, the whole concept was flawed. It presupposed that he wanted a relationship.

The second he brought the Jeep to a halt, Elena sent him a bright professional smile and unfastened her seat belt. "Let's get this over and done with."

With crisp movements, she opened her door and stepped out onto the drive.

Jaw tightening at the unsubtle hint that, far from being irresistibly attracted, Elena couldn't wait to get rid of him, Nick locked the Jeep.

He padded behind Elena, studying the smooth walls glowing a soft, inviting honey, the palms and lush plantings.

Elena was being difficult about the property, but he was certain he could bring her around. With the deal he was negotiating to buy a majority share in the Dolphin Bay Resort, in partnership with the Atraeus Group, it made sense to add the property to the resort's portfolio.

As Elena unlocked the front door, the sense of stepping back in time was so powerful that he almost reached out to pull her close. It was a blunt reminder that almost everything about a liaison with Elena had been wrong from the beginning, and six years on, nothing had changed.

The tabloids exaggerated his love life. Mostly he just dated because he liked female company and he liked to relax. If he wanted to take things further, it was a considered move with nothing left to chance, including the possibility that he might be drawn into any kind of commitment.

With Elena the situation had always been frustratingly

different; *she* was different. For a start, she had never set out to attract him.

Six years ago he had muscled in on her blind date because he had overheard a conversation in a café and gotten annoyed that her friend had set her up with a guy who could quite possibly be dangerous.

But, if he was honest, that had only been an excuse. Elena had been on the periphery of his life for years. She was obviously naive and tantalizingly sweet, and the idea that some other guy could date Elena and maybe make love to her had quite simply ticked him off.

She had been a virgin.

The moment he had logged that fact was still burned indelibly into his mind.

The maelstrom of emotions that had hit him had been fierce, but tempered by caution. At that point he'd had no room in his life for a relationship. His business had come first—he had been traveling constantly and working crazy hours. Elena had needed love, commitment, *marriage,* and he hadn't been in a position to offer her any of those things.

The accident and his father's death had slammed the lid on any further contact, but years later the pull of the attraction was just as powerful, just as frustrating.

Despite applying his usual logic—that no matter how hot the sex, a committed relationship didn't fit with his life—he still wanted Elena.

The fact that Elena wanted him despite all of the barriers she kept throwing up made every muscle in his body tighten. They were going to make love. He knew it, and he was certain, at some underlying level, so did she.

And now he was beginning to wonder if one night was going to be enough.

* * *

Elena stepped inside the villa and flicked on the hall light. Nick, tall and broad-shouldered behind her, instantly made the airy hall seem claustrophobic and cramped, triggering a vivid set of memories.

Nick closing the door six years ago and pulling her into his arms. The long passionate kiss, as if he couldn't get enough of her....

Elena's stomach tightened at the vivid replay. With one brisk step she reached the next series of light switches and flicked every one of them.

They didn't require that much light, since the boxes they needed to search were in the attic. She didn't care. With tension zinging through her, and Nick making no bones about the fact that he wouldn't be averse to repeating their one night together, she wasn't taking any risks.

The blazing lights illuminated the small sunroom to the left, the larger sitting room to the right and the stairs directly ahead.

Sending Nick a smile she was aware was overbright and strained, she started up the stairs. "Help yourself to a drink in the kitchen. I'll change and be right back."

There were four bedrooms upstairs. The doors to each were open, allowing air to circulate. Elena stepped inside the master bedroom she had claimed as her own. A room her aunt had refused to use and which was, incidentally, the same room she and Nick had shared six years ago.

With white walls and dramatic, midnight-dark floorboards, the bedroom was decorated in the typical Medinian style, with a four-poster dominating. Once a starkly romantic but empty testament to her aunt's lost love, Elena had worked hard to inject a little warmth.

Now, with its lush, piled cushions and rich pomegranate-red coverlet picked out in gold, the bed glowed like a warm, exotic nest. A lavish slice of paradise in an otherwise very simply furnished house.

Closing the door behind her, she began working on the line of silk-covered buttons that fastened the pink dress, her fingers fumbling in their haste.

As she hung the lavish cascade of silk and lace in her closet, her reflection, captured by an antique oval mirror on a stand, distracted her. In pink lingerie and high heels, her hair falling in soft waves around her face, jewels gleaming at her lobes and her navel, she looked like nothing so much as a high-priced courtesan.

Not a good thought to have when she was committed to spending the next two hours with Nick.

Dragging her gaze from an image she was still struggling to adjust to, she pulled on a summer dress in a rich shade of red.

Unfortunately the thin straps revealed the butterfly transfer on her shoulder. Maybe it was ridiculous, but she didn't want Nick to see the full extent of the fake tattoo. With all of the changes she had made, the addition of a tattoo now seemed like overkill and just a little desperate.

Unfastening the gorgeous pink heels, she slipped on a pair of comfortable red sandals that made the best of her spray-on tan, shrugged into a thin, black cardigan and walked downstairs.

When she entered the sitting room, she saw Nick's jacket tossed over the back of a chair. The French doors that led out to the garden were open, warm light spilling out onto a small patio.

As she flicked on another lamp, Nick stepped in out of the darkness, the scents of salt and sea flowing in with him. He half turned, locking the door behind him, and the simple, intimate motion of closing out the night made her heart squeeze tight.

With his jaw dark and stubbled, his shirt open at the throat, he looked rumpled and sexy and heartbreakingly like the young man she had used to daydream about on the beach.

Although the instant his cool, green gaze connected with hers that impression evaporated. "Are you ready?"

"Absolutely. This way." She started back up the stairs, her heart thumping faster as she registered Nick's tread behind her.

As she passed her bedroom, she noted that in her rush to get downstairs she had forgotten to close the door. The full weight of her decision to invite the *only* man she had a passionate past with to the scene of her seduction, hit home.

If she had been thinking straight she would have asked someone to come with them. A third person would have canceled out the tension and the angst.

Relieved when Nick didn't appear to notice her room or the exotic makeover she'd given the bed, she ascended another small flight of stairs. Pushing the door open into a small, airless attic, she switched on the light. Nick ducked underneath the low lintel and stepped inside.

He stared at the conglomeration of old furniture, trunks and boxes. "Did Katherine ever throw anything away?"

"Not that I've noticed. I suppose that if the ring is anywhere on the property, it'll be here."

As always when she thought of her aunt, Elena felt a sentimental softness and warmth. She knew Katherine had adored all of her nieces and nephews, but she and Elena had shared a special bond. She had often thought that had been because Katherine hadn't had children of her own.

Feeling stifled by the stale air and oppressive heat,

Elena walked to one end of the room to open a window. The sound of a corresponding click and a cooling flow of air told her that Nick had opened the window at the other end.

"Where do we start?" Nick picked up an ancient book, a dusty tome on Medinian history.

"Everything on that side of the room has been searched and sorted." She indicated a stack of trunks. "This is where we need to start."

"Cool. Sea trunks." Nick bent down to study one of the old leather trunks with their distinctive Medinian labeling. "When did these come out?"

"Probably in 1944. That's when the Lyon family immigrated to New Zealand."

"During the war, about the same time my family landed. I wonder if they traveled on the same ship."

"It's possible," Elena muttered. "Although, since your family owned the ships it was unlikely they would have socialized."

Nick flipped a trunk open. Another wave of dust rose in the air. "Let me get this right. My grandparents would have traveled first-class so they wouldn't have spoken to your relatives?"

Still feeling overheated, Elena ignored her longing to discard her cardigan. "The Lyons were market gardeners and domestic servants. They would have been on the lower decks."

With a muffled imprecation, Nick shrugged out of his tightly fitted waistcoat. Tossing it over the back of a chair, he unfastened another button on his shirt, revealing more brown, tanned skin.

Dragging her gaze from the way the shirt clung across his chest, Elena concentrated on her trunk, which was filled with yellowed, fragile magazines and newspapers.

Nick, by some painful coincidence, had opened a trunk filled with ancient women's foundation garments. He held up a pair of king-size knickers in heavy, serviceable cotton. "And the fact that some of them settled here in Dolphin Bay was just a coincidence, right?"

The tension sawing at her nerves morphed into annoyance. She had never paid any particular attention to her family's history of settlement, especially since her parents lived in Auckland. But now that Nick was pointing it out, the link seemed obvious. "Okay, so maybe they did meet."

Nick extracted a corset that appeared to rely on a network of small steel girders to control the hefty curves of one of her ancestors. "It was a little more than that. Pretty sure Katherine's grandparents worked for mine."

Elena vowed to burn the trunk, contents and all, at the earliest possible moment. "I suppose they could have been offered jobs."

He closed the lid on the evidence that past Lyon women had been sturdy, buxom specimens and pulled the lid off a tea chest. "So, maybe the Messena family aren't all monsters."

Feeling increasingly overheated and smothered by the cardigan, Elena discreetly undid the buttons and let it flap open. The neckline of her dress was scooped, revealing a hint of cleavage, but she would have to live with that. "I didn't say you were. Aunt Katherine liked working for your family."

The echoing silence that greeted her quiet comment, was a reminder of the cold rift that still existed between their families—the abyss that separated their lifestyles—and made her mood plummet.

Although she was fiercely glad she had ruined the camaraderie that had been building. Stuck in the confined space with Nick, the past linking them at every turn, she had needed the reminder.

Elena opened the trunk nearest her. A cloud of dust made her nose itch and her eyes feel even more irritated. She blinked to ease the burning sensation.

Too late to wish she'd taken the time to remove her colored contacts before she'd rejoined Nick.

Nick dumped an ancient bedpan, which looked like it had come out of the ark, on the floor. When she glanced at him, he caught her eye and lifted a brow, and the cool tension evaporated.

Suddenly irrationally happy, Elena tried to concentrate on her trunk, which appeared to be filled with items that might be found in a torturer's toolbox. She held up a pair of shackles that looked like restraints of some kind.

"Know what you're thinking." Nick grinned as he straightened, ducking his head to avoid the sloping ceiling. "They're not bondage." He closed the box of books he'd finished sorting through. "They're a piece of Medinian kitchen equipment, designed to hang hams in the pantry. We've got a set at home."

Elena replaced the shackles and tried not to melt at Nick's easy grin. She couldn't afford to slip back into the old addictive attraction. With just minutes to go before he was out of her life, now was not the time to soften.

She glanced at her watch, although her eyes were now watering enough that she had difficulty reading the dial.

"Are those contacts bothering you?"

"They're driving me nuts. I'll take them out when I go downstairs."

Once Nick was gone.

Nick closed the lid on the box with a snap that echoed through the night.

There was a moment of heavy silence in which the

tension that coiled between them pulled almost suffocatingly tight.

"Damn," he said softly. "Why are you so intent on resisting me?"

Seven

The words seemed to reverberate through the room.

Elena glared at Nick. "What I don't get is *why* you want me?"

"I've wanted you for six years."

"I've barely seen you in six years."

Nick frowned as a gust of wind hit the side of the house. "I've been busy."

Building up a fortune and dating a long line of beautiful girls who never seemed to hold his interest for long... and avoiding her like the plague because she would have reminded him of *that* night.

And in that moment Elena acknowledged a truth she had been avoiding for weeks.

Now, just when she was on the point of getting free and clear, and at absolutely the wrong time—while they were alone together—it dawned on her that Nick was just as fatally attracted as she.

Outside it had started to rain, large droplets exploding on the roof.

Elena rubbed at her eyes, which was exactly the wrong thing to do, as one of the contacts dropped out. Muttering beneath her breath, she began to search, although with the dim lighting and with both eyes stinging, she didn't expect to find it.

Sound exploded as the rain turned tropically heavy. Moist air swirled through the open window.

She was suddenly aware that Nick was close beside her.

"Sit down, before the other one drops out."

"No. I need to find the lens, although it's probably lost forever." Added to that, her eyes were still watering, which meant her mascara was running.

Swiping at the damp skin beneath her eyes, Elena continued to search the dusty floorboards.

Something glittered, but when she reached for it, it turned out to be a loose bead. At that moment the wind gusted, flinging the window wide. Jumping to her feet, she grabbed at the latch and jammed it closed.

A corresponding bang informed her that Nick had closed the other window. As she double-checked the latch, Nick loomed behind her, reflected in the glass.

"Don't you ever listen?" The low, impatient timbre of his voice cut through the heavy drumming on the roof. His hands closed around her arms, burning through the thin, damp cotton of her cardigan. "You need to sit down."

Obediently, Elena sat on an ancient chair. Nick crouched in front of her, but even so he loomed large, his shoulders broad, his bronzed skin gleaming through the transparent dampness of his shirt. The piercing lightness of his eyes pinned her. "Hold still while I get the other lens out for you."

Elena inhaled, her nostrils filling with his heat and scent. Her stomach clenched on the now-familiar jolt of sensual tension. "I don't need help. All I need is a few minutes in the bathroom—"

Cupping her jaw with one large hand, he peered into her eyes. "And some drops."

Nick was close enough that she could study the translucence of his irises, the intriguing scar on his nose to her heart's content. "How would you know?" But she was suddenly close enough to see.

"I've worn contacts for years. Hold still."

As Nick bent close, his breath mingled with hers. She swallowed and tried not to remember the softness and heat of the kiss they'd shared on the steps of the church.

With a deft movement he secured the second contact on the tip of his forefinger.

Reaching into his pocket, he pulled out a small container of eyedrops and a tiny lens case. Setting the drops on the top of a nearby trunk he placed the lens gently in the case and snapped it closed.

Before he could bulldoze her into letting him put the drops in, Elena picked up the small plastic bottle and inserted a droplet of the cooling solution in each eye. The relief was instant. Blinking, she waited for her vision to clear.

Nick pressed the folded handkerchief she had given him earlier in the day into her hand. "It's almost clean."

"Thank you." Elena dabbed in the corners and beneath both eyes, then, feeling self-conscious, peeled out of the damp cardigan. "What else have you got in those pockets?"

"Don't ask."

Acutely aware that if Nick had another item in his pockets, it was probably a condom, Elena peered into a dusty mirror propped against the wall.

For a disorienting moment she was surprised by the way she looked, the tousled hair and exotic curve of her cheekbones, the pale lushness of her mouth.

She had definitely made outward changes, but inside she wasn't nearly as confident as that image would suggest.

Although according to Giorgio, that would change once she resurrected her sex life.

The thought that she could resume her sex life, here, now, if she wanted, made her heart pound and put her even more on edge.

An hour later, they emptied the final trunk. "That's it." Relief filled Elena as she closed the lid. "If the ring isn't here, then Katherine didn't receive it. I've already been through everything else."

"You searched all of the desks and bureaus downstairs?"

Elena wiped her hands off on a cloth. "Every cupboard and drawer."

Absently, she picked up a photo album, which she'd decided to take downstairs.

Picking up the cloth, she wiped the cover of the album. Glancing at the first page of photos, her interest was piqued. Unusually, many of the photos were of the Messena family.

She was aware of Nick's gaze fixing on the album. Somewhere in the recesses of her mind disparate pieces of information fused into a conclusion she should have arrived at a long time ago. Nick had taken a special interest in any photo album he had come across.

As she tucked the album under her arm and bent to retrieve her damp cardigan, a small bundle of letters dropped out from between the pages. Bending, she picked them up. The envelopes were plain, although of very good parchment, a rich cream that seemed to glow in the stark light. They were tied together with a white satin ribbon that shimmered with a pearlized sheen.

Her throat closed up. Love letters.

The top envelope was addressed to her aunt. Heart beating just a little faster, because she knew without doubt that she had found a remnant of the relationship her aunt had kept secret until she died, Elena turned the small bundle over.

The name Carlos Messena leaped out at her, and the final piece in the puzzle of just why her aunt and Stefano Messena had been personally linked fell into place. "Mystery solved," she said softly.

Nick tossed the cloth he'd used to wipe his hands with over the back of a broken chair. Stepping over a pile of old newspapers that were destined for the fire, he took the letters.

"Uncle Carlos," he said quietly, satisfaction edging his voice. "My father was the first son, he was the second. Carlos died on active duty overseas around thirty years ago. So that's why Dad gave Katherine the ring. It was traditionally given to the brides of the second son in the family. If Katherine and Carlos had married, it would have been hers."

With careful movements, he untied the faded ribbon and fanned the letters out on the top of a trunk, checking the dates on each letter.

Holding her breath, because to read the personal exchanges, even now, seemed an invasion of privacy, Elena picked up the first letter. It was written in a strong, slanting hand, and she was instantly drawn into the clear narrative of a love affair that had ended almost before it had begun, after just one night together.

Empathy held her in thrall as she was drawn into the brief affair that had ended abruptly when Carlos, a naval officer, had shipped out.

Elena refolded the letter and replaced it back in its envelope. Nick passed her the contents of the envelope he had just opened. On plainer, cheaper paper, it was written in a different hand. There was no love letter, but in some ways the content was even more personal: a short note, a black-and-white snapshot of a toddler, a birth certificate and adoption papers for a baby named Michael Carlos.

The mystery of Stefano's relationship with Katherine was finally solved: he had been helping her find the child she had adopted out. A Messena child.

Nick studied the address on the final envelope. "Emilia Ambrosi." He shook his head. "She's a distant cousin of the Pearl House Ambrosis. I could be wrong, but as far as I know she still lives on Medinos." He let out a breath. "Medinos was the one place we didn't look."

Elena dragged her attention from the sparse details of the Messena child. "You knew Aunt Katherine had had a baby?"

"It seemed possible, but we had no proof."

Feeling stunned at the secret her aunt had kept, she handed Nick the note, the snapshot and the birth certificate.

Gathering up the letters, she tied them together with the ribbon and braced herself for the fact that Nick would be gone in a matter of minutes.

She should be happy they had solved the mystery and found closure. Her aunt had tragically lost Carlos, but she had at least experienced the heights—she had been *loved.* They hadn't found the ring but, at a guess, Katherine had sent it to her son, who was probably a resident on Medinos.

Elena made her way downstairs to the second level. Placing the album and the sadly rumpled cardigan on a side dresser in the hall, she washed her hands and face, then waited out in the hall while Nick did the same.

Curious to see if Aunt Katherine had included any further shots of her small son in the album, she flipped to the first page. Unexpectedly, it was dotted with snapshots of the Messena children when they had been babies.

Nick's gaze touched on hers as he exited the bathroom, and the awareness that had vibrated between them in the attic sprang to life again.

She closed the album with a faint snap. "You must have suspected all along that a Medinian engagement ring, a family heirloom, was a strange gift for a mistress."

With his waistcoat hanging open, his shirt unfastened partway down his chest, the sleeves rolled up over muscular forearms, Nick looked tough and masculine and faintly dissolute in the narrow confines of the hall. "It wouldn't be my choice."

The thought that Nick obviously gave gifts to women he loved and appreciated ignited a familiar coal of old hurt and anger. After their night together she hadn't rated so much as a phone call.

"What would you choose? Roses? Dinner? A tropical holiday?"

She seemed to remember reading an exposé from a former PA of Nick's and her claims that she had organized a number of tropical holidays for some of his shorter, more fiery flings.

His expression turned wary. "I don't normally send gifts. Not when—"

"Great strategy." She smiled brightly. "Why encourage the current woman when there's always another one queuing up?"

There was a moment of heavy silence during which the humid, overwarm night seemed to close in, isolating them in the dimly lit hall.

Nick frowned. "Last I heard there is no queue."

Probably because he was never in one place long enough for the queue to form. Nick was more a girl-in-every-port kind of guy.

Elena found herself blurting out a piece of advice he probably didn't want to hear. "Maybe if you slowed down and stayed in one place for long enough there would be."

And suddenly Nick was so close she could feel the heat radiating off him, smell the clean scents of soap and aftershave, and an electrifying whiff of fresh sweat generated by the stuffy, overheated attic.

She stared at a pulse beating along the strong column of his throat. Sweat shouldn't be sexy, she thought a little desperately, but it suddenly, very palpably, was.

Nick's hand landed on the wall beside her head, subtly fencing her in. "With my schedule, commitment has never been viable."

"Then maybe you should take control of your schedule. Not," she amended hastily, "that I have any interest in a committed relationship with you. I have—Robert."

She didn't, not really, and the small lie made her go hot all over. But suddenly it seemed very important that she should have someone, that she shouldn't look like a total loser in the relationship stakes.

Nick's brows jerked together. "I'm glad we're clear on that point."

"Totally. Crystal clear." But her heart pounded at the edge in Nick's voice, as if he hadn't been entirely happy at her mention of Robert. Or that she had nixed the whole idea of a relationship with him.

Nick cupped her jaw, the heat of his fingers warm and slightly rough against her skin. "So this is just friendship?"

He dipped his head, slowly enough that she could avoid the kiss if she wanted.

A shaft of heat burned through her as he touched his mouth to hers. She could move away. One step and she could end the dizzying delight that was sweeping through her that maybe, just maybe, they had turned some kind of corner when they had uncovered the reason behind his father's relationship with her aunt.

That now that the past was resolved, a relationship between them wasn't so impossible.

Heart pounding as the kiss deepened, she lifted up on her toes, one hand curving over Nick's broad shoulder as she hung on. The tingling heat that flooded her, the notion that they could have a future, were all achingly addictive. She couldn't remember feeling so alive.

Except, maybe, six years ago.

That thought should have stopped her in her tracks. But the gap of time, the emotional desert she'd trudged through, *after Nick,* had taught her a salutary lesson.

She needed to be loved, and she absolutely did not want to remain alone. So far the search for a husband had proved anticlimactic. Good character and an appealing outward appearance just didn't seem to generate the "in love" part of the equation. Bluntly put, so far there had been no chemistry.

On the other hand, while Nick failed every sensible requirement, with him there was nothing *but* chemistry.

If she could have the chemistry and the committed relationship with Nick, she would be…happy.

His mouth lifted. He released her jaw as if he was reluctant to do so, as if he hadn't wanted the kiss to end,
either.

Drawing a shaky breath, Elena relinquished her grip
on Nick's shoulder.

A relationship with Nick? Maybe even with a view
to marriage?

It was a major shift in her thinking. She didn't know
if Nick could be anything to her beyond a fatal attraction. All she knew was that with his gaze fixed on hers
and the unsettling awareness sizzling between them, the
possibility seemed to float in the air.

That, and the knowledge that she was about to lose
him in approximately two minutes.

She drew a swift breath. If she wanted Nick, she would
have to take a risk. She would have to fight for him.

The fingers of her free hand curled into one of the lapels of his waistcoat where it hung open, her thumb automatically sweeping over the small button.

Surprise at the small possessive gesture flared in his
gaze and was quickly replaced by a heat that took her
breath. "I have to leave early in the morning."

She did her best to conceal her shock at how quickly he
had cut to the chase and assumed that they would spend
the night together, and the instant stab of hurt evoked by
his blunt pronouncement that he had to leave. She had
already known he was flying out on business. "Yes."

"You don't mind?"

She did, like crazy, but she wasn't about to let him
know that. She had decided to take the risk of trying for a
relationship with Nick. That meant she had to toughen up
because a measure of hurt would naturally be involved.

She forced a smile. "I'm only here for a few days myself, then I need to be back in Sydney."

He wound a finger in her hair, the touch featherlight, and she tried not to love it too much. "For the record, my dating is usually on a casual basis. Most of it happens around yachting events when I'm racing."

That wasn't news to Elena. Her current Atraeus boss was a sailor, which meant there were quite often yachting magazines lying around in the office. Nick's name occasionally leaped out from the pages. "Which is quite often."

His breath wafted against her cheek, damp and warm and faintly scented with the champagne they'd drunk at the wedding. "Granted."

She inhaled and tried to drag her gaze from the slice of brown flesh and sprinkling of dark hair visible in the opening of his shirt. "But there have been a lot of women."

The album, which had been tucked under her arm, slipped and fell to the floor, as if to punctuate her statement.

His hands closed on the bare skin of her arms, his palms warm and faintly abrasive, sending darting rivulets of fire shimmering through her. "According to the tabloids. But we both know how reliable they are as a source of information."

Nick bent his head, bringing his mouth closer to hers. "If you don't want me to stay the night, just say so, and I'll leave you alone."

As he drew her close, she gripped the lapels of his shirt, preserving a small distance. Despite committing to a night with him, caution was kicking in. She needed more. "*Why* me?"

"For the same reason it's always been. I'm attracted to you. I like you."

A month ago, on a street in Auckland, he had said he

liked her. It wasn't enough, but coupled with the chemistry that vibrated between them and the fact that the rift between their families would now be healed, a relationship suddenly seemed viable.

Cupping Nick's stubbled jaw, she lifted up on her toes and kissed him. A split second later she found herself in his arms. With a heady sense of inevitability, she looped her arms around his neck, heat clenching low in her belly as she fitted herself even more closely against the hard angles and planes of his body.

After all the years of being calmly, methodically organized, of never losing her cool, there was something exhilarating about abandoning herself to a passionate interlude with Nick.

"That's better." He smiled, a glimpse of the uncomplicated charm that had always entrapped her, the kind of charm that made little kids flock around him and old ladies sit and chat. Except this time it was all for her and enticingly softer.

As Nick's mouth settled on hers, the reason he was so successful with women hit her. Despite the hard muscle and the wickedly hot exterior, he possessed a bedrock niceness that made women melt.

It was there in the way he noticed small things, like the color of her eyes and the fact that she was wearing contacts, the way he had rescued her from the blind date six years ago when he didn't have to get involved.

Her feet lost contact with the floor; the light of the hall faded to dim shadows as they stepped into a bedroom.

With a sense of inevitability, Elena noted the wide soft bed, with its lush piled cushions and rich red coverlet.

A lavish, traditional Medinian marriage bed, arrayed for a wedding. The room she had whimsically decorated.

The same room in which Nick had made love to her the last time.

Eight

Fitful moonlight shafted through a thick bridal veil of gauze festooning a tall sash window as Elena was set down on marble-smooth floorboards.

Nick shrugged out of his shirt, revealing sleekly powerful shoulders, a broad chest and washboard abs.

His mouth captured hers as he locked her against the furnace heat of his body. The hot shock of skin on skin momentarily made her head swim, but for all that, the kiss and the muscled hardness of his chest felt, oddly, like coming home.

Lifting up on her toes, she wound her arms around his neck and kissed him back. She felt the zipper of her dress glide down, the sudden looseness. Seconds later, she shrugged out of the straps and let the flimsy cotton float to the floor. Another long, drugging kiss and her bra was gone.

Bending, Nick took one breast into his mouth and for

long aching minutes the night seemed to slow, stop, as heat and sensation coiled tight.

She heard his rapid intake of breath. A split second later she found herself deposited on the silken-soft bed.

Feeling a little self-conscious and exposed, Elena slipped beneath the red coverlet, unexpected emotion catching in her throat as she watched Nick peel out of his trousers. She was used to seeing him in a modern setting as masculine, muscled and hot, but cloaked in moonlight and shadows, his bronzed skin gleaming in the glow of light from the hall, he was unexpectedly, fiercely beautiful, reminding her of paintings of Medinian warriors of old.

Dimly, she registered a rustling sound, like paper or foil. The bed depressed as Nick pulled the coverlet aside and came down beside her. The heat of his body sent a raw quiver through her as he pulled her close.

His gaze locked with hers, the softness she had noted in the hall giving her the reassurance she suddenly desperately needed.

He propped himself on one elbow, a frown creasing his brow. "Are you all right?"

She cupped his jaw and tried for a confident smile. "I'm fine."

One long finger stroked down her cheek. "Then why do I get the feeling that you're not quite comfortable with this?"

"Probably because I haven't done *this* in a while."

Something flared in his gaze. "How long?"

"Uh—around six years, I guess."

He said something soft beneath his breath. "Six years ago you slept with me."

The breath caught in her throat. "I guess, given what happened that night, you're not likely to forget."

"If the accident hadn't happened, I would still have remembered," he said quietly, "since you were a virgin."

For a split second she felt his indecision, the streak of masculine honor that had once been ingrained in Medinian culture. Abruptly afraid that he might abandon the whole idea of making love, that she might lose this chance to get him back in her life, she took a deep breath and boldly trailed a hand down his chest. "I'm not a virgin now."

He inhaled sharply and trapped her hand beneath his, then used it to pull her close so that she found herself half sprawled across his chest. "Good."

He rolled, taking her with him so that he was on top, his heavy weight pressing her down into the feather-soft mattress. Dipping his head, he kissed her mouth, her throat, and finally took one breast in his mouth.

Elena tensed, palms sliding across his shoulders, the sleek muscles of his back, as rivulets of fire seemed to spread out from that one point, culminating in a restless, aching throb.

He shifted his attention to her other breast, and in that moment heat and pleasure coiled and condensed, exploding into aching, shimmering pleasure as the night spun away.

Nick muttered something short and flat. Moments later his weight pressed her more deeply into the bed. She felt him between her legs, and relief flowed through her as slowly, achingly, he entered her.

The faint drag of what could only be a condom made her eyes fly open. The sound she had registered earlier suddenly made sense. Nick had sheathed himself, which meant he'd had the condom in his pocket.

The realization was like a cold dash of water. She shouldn't think about the condom. She shouldn't allow it to matter, but it did, because it meant he had been prepared to have sex with *someone,* not necessarily her.

Nick was oddly still, his expression taut as if he had gauged every one of the emotions that had just flitted across her face. "Something's wrong. Do you want me to stop?" A muscle pulsed along the side of his jaw. *"Yes, or no?"*

The words were quietly delivered, without any trace of frustration or need—just a simple question. Although she could see the effort it was costing him in the corded muscles of neck and shoulders.

The blunt, male way he had presented her with the choice brought her back to her original reason for making love: because she wanted another chance with him.

At the thought of losing him, contrarily, she wanted him with a fierce, no-holds-barred need that rocked her.

For every reason that shouldn't matter—because he was too elusive, too spoiled by the women he had dated and way too dangerous for her heart—he was the last man she could afford in her life.

And yet he was the only man to whom she had ever been truly, passionately attracted.

There was no logic to what she felt, no reason why he should smell and taste and *feel* right when no one else had ever come close.

Unless somehow, despite the frustration and anger and sheer loneliness of the past few years, she had somehow fallen for him, and he was *The One.*

She clamped down on the moment of shocked awareness. This was where she had gone wrong the first time with Nick—she had wanted too much, expected too much.

Every feminine instinct she had informed her that applying any form of pressure at this point would scare

Nick off, and she couldn't afford that. Framing his face with her hands, she drew his mouth to hers, distracting him from discovering that she might have done the one thing that seemed to scare men the most and fallen for him. "The answer is no, I don't want you to stop."

She promised herself she wouldn't cry as relief registered in his gaze and gently, slowly, he began to move.

There was a moment of utter stillness when he was fully sheathed and they were finally, truly one, and then he undid her completely by softly kissing her mouth.

His thumb brushed away a trickle of moisture that had somehow escaped one eye, then he pulled her closer still, holding her with exquisite care and tenderness as if he truly did love her. A heated, stirring pleasure that was still shatteringly familiar despite the passage of years, gripped her as they began to move.

Locked together in the deep well of the night, the angst and hurt of the past dissolved. Nothing mattered but the way Nick held her, the way he made her feel, as the coiling, burning intensity finally peaked and the night spun away.

In the early hours of the morning, Elena woke, curled in against the furnace heat of Nick's body. His arm was curved around her waist, keeping her close, as if even in sleep he couldn't bear to be parted from her.

A surge of pure joy went through her. She had taken the risk, and it was working. Nick had been tender and sweet, and the passion had, if anything, been even hotter, even more intense.

She was convinced that this time they really had a chance.

The false start six years ago had muddied the waters,

but the hurts of the past shrank to insignificance compared with the happiness and pleasure ahead.

She smiled as she sank back into sleep. All was forgiven. She couldn't let the past matter when they were on the verge of discovering the once-in-a-lifetime love she was certain was their destiny.

A chiming sound pulled Elena out of a deep, dreamless sleep. She rolled, automatically reaching for Nick. The pillow where his head had lain was still indented and warm, but that side of the large, voluminous bed was empty.

Moonlight flowed through the window, illuminating the fact that Nick was pulling on clothes with the kind of quick efficiency that denoted he was in a hurry. Silvery light gleamed over one cheekbone and the strong line of his jaw as he glanced at his watch.

The bronzed gleam of broad shoulders and the strong line of his back disappeared as he shrugged into his shirt.

His gaze touched on hers as he buttoned the shirt with quick efficiency. "I have to leave now, otherwise I'll miss my flight out."

Elena jackknifed, dragging the sheet with her and wrapping it around her breasts. The memory of Nick explaining his schedule the previous evening flooded back. "The flight to Sydney."

The side of the bed depressed as he pulled on socks and shoes. "I have a series of business meetings I can't cancel. They're important."

"Of course." More important than exploring the passion they had found together, or the spellbinding sense that they were on the verge of discovering something special.

She drew an impeded breath and killed the idea of suggesting that, since she lived in Sydney and was due back soon, maybe she could go with him. It was too soon to put that kind of pressure on their relationship.

She needed to remember one of the rules Giorgio had given her about dating: that men liked to feel as if they were the hunter, even if that wasn't strictly the case.

She forced one of her professional smiles. "Of course. I understand completely."

His gaze was oddly neutral as he collected his phone from the bedside table and shoved it into his pocket. A trickle of unease made her stomach tighten.

As if he had already distanced himself from what they had done.

Bending, he picked something up from the floor. When he straightened, she recognized the packet of love letters. "I'll return these."

"No problem. I'm sure your mother will be relieved to know that Stefano was helping Katherine find her adopted child."

Another lightning glance at his watch, then Nick leaned across the bed and kissed her, the caress perfunctory. "Thanks. It was…special."

Elena froze. The awkwardness of the moment expanded when she failed to respond, but she had quite suddenly reached the end of her resources.

She recognized this part. Nick had gotten what he wanted: closure for the scandal that had hurt his family and another night of convenient passion. Now he was trying to step away from any suggestion of a relationship by leaving as quickly as possible.

Her fingers tightened on the beautiful sheets as Nick strode from the room. She heard his step on the stairs, then the sound of the front door quietly closing. A few seconds later, the rumble of the Jeep's engine broke the stillness of early morning.

She blinked back the burning heat behind her eyes and resolved not to cry. She could see why Nick's relationships ended so easily. He had concluded a night of passion in the same way he conducted his business affairs: briefly and with his gaze fixed on the next goal.

The full folly of returning to the scene of her last mistake and sleeping with Nick again settled in. Dragging the silk sheet with her, she wrapped it around herself and walked to the freestanding oval mirror. The moonlight was incredibly flattering. She was actually, finally, attractive in the way she had longed to be.

Although that hadn't seemed to matter to Nick. It hadn't tipped the balance and made him fall for her.

Which, she realized, was exactly what she had secretly hoped when she had started on the whole process of improving her appearance.

Admitting that pleasing Nick had been her motivation to change was painful, but if she wanted to move on she had to be honest.

She had been stuck in relationship limbo for years. Just when she was on the verge of forming a positive, rewarding romantic friendship with a nice man, she had thrown herself at Nick again.

Hitching the sheet up, she walked to the window and dragged the thick drape of white gauze back. A pale glow in the east indicated that the sun would soon be up. She needed to shower, get dressed and make a plan.

She had made the mistake of allowing Nick to get to her, again.

But the fledgling love affair that had dogged her for six years was finally finished. There would be no replays.

She was finally over Nick Messena.

Nick grimly suppressed a yawn as he sipped an espresso during his flight to Sydney.

Kyle, who was with him to represent the bank's interests in the partnership deal he was negotiating with the Atraeus Group, turned a page of his newspaper. "Did you find the ring?"

Nick took another sip of coffee and waited for the caffeine to kick in. "Not yet."

Briefly he filled Kyle in on the love letters and the adoption papers they had found, and that he had stopped by and spoken to their mother before he had left Dolphin Bay.

That had been a priority. The stark relief on Luisa Messena's face had told him just how much she had been holding out for the information.

There was a small vibrating silence, which finally broke through the grim flatness that had gripped Nick ever since he had driven away from Dolphin Bay.

Kyle put his newspaper down. "You and Elena looked like you were getting on. Last I heard, she wasn't returning your calls—"

"We found some common ground."

"Something's happened." Kyle's gaze had taken on the spooky, penetrating look that was a legacy of his time in the SAS, New Zealand's Special Forces. Something about Kyle's calm neutrality inspired respect and actual fear in the high-powered financial magicians he dealt with on a daily basis. When he turned up with the scary eyes the deal usually got done in minutes.

Kyle shook his head. "You slept with her again."

Nick's fingers tightened on his coffee cup. "I shouldn't have confided in you six years ago."

Kyle shrugged. "Dad had just died. You were understandably emotional."

Nick finished his coffee and set his cup down on the seat tray with a click. "According to the family, I have the emotions of a block of stone."

"Whatever. You've slept with Elena Lyon twice. That's...complicated."

Wrong word, Nick thought. There had been nothing complicated about what they had done or how he had felt.

He had been caught up in the same visceral hit of attraction that had captured him the night his father had died. An attraction that had become inextricably bound up with loss and grief, and what he had believed was his father's betrayal.

With the knowledge that his father and Katherine had not been involved, he should have been able to view Elena in the same way he viewed other past lovers. As an attractive, smart woman who was in his life for a period of time.

But the realization that Elena hadn't ever slept with anyone but him had sounded the kind of warning bells he couldn't ignore.

His reaction had been knee-jerk. As addictive as those hours with Elena had been, after years of carefully avoiding emotional entanglements and commitment, he'd found he couldn't do a sudden, convenient U-turn.

As much as he had wanted to spend more time with her or, even more crazily, take her with him, the whole idea of being that close to someone again had made him break out in a cold sweat.

Kyle signaled to a flight attendant that he wanted a

refill for his coffee. "If you don't want to talk about it, that's cool, but you might need to take a look at this."

Nick took the tabloid newspaper Kyle had been reading and stared at the piece written about Gabriel and Gemma's wedding. The details of the ceremony were correct, but it wasn't his brother and his new bride in the grainy black-and-white wedding photos.

Someone had made a mistake and inserted a photo of himself and Elena kissing on the steps of the church. It was flanked by a shot of him helping Elena into the limousine when they were on their way to have the official photos taken. A third snap as they had left the reception together rounded out the article. Apparently they were now on their way to a secret honeymoon destination.

A trolley halted beside his seat. A pretty flight attendant offered to take his cup. Absently, Nick handed it to her, barely noticing her smile or the fact that she was blonde, leggy and gorgeous.

According to the tabloids, *according to Elena,* the flight attendant was his type.

Although not anymore.

Now, it seemed, he had a thing for brunettes. Fiery brunettes with hourglass figures and issues.

Just as the flight attendant was about to move on, she glanced at the newspaper and sent him a brilliant smile. "I thought I recognized you. Congratulations on your marriage."

"Uh—I'm not actually married."

She looked confused. "That's not you?"

"It's him," Kyle supplied unhelpfully. "They've split up already."

There was a moment of shocked silence. The flight attendant dredged up a brilliant, professional smile that was cold enough to freeze water. "Would you like me to get you anything more, sir?"

The words, *like marriage guidance or an actual heart,* hung in the air.

"He's happy," Kyle supplied, along with the killer smile that usually made women go weak at the knees. "We have everything we need."

The attendant gave Kyle a stunned look, then walked quickly off, her trolley rattling.

Nick folded the newspaper and gave it back to Kyle. "Thanks for making her think that I ditched my wife of just a few hours because I decided to turn gay."

Kyle disappeared behind his paper again. "Look on the bright side. At least now she thinks *I'm* the villain."

Broodingly, Nick returned to thinking about the second night he had spent with Elena. Another passion-filled encounter that was proving to be just as frustratingly memorable and addictive as the first.

He hadn't been able to resist her and the result was that Elena had gotten hurt.

Nick retrieved an envelope from his briefcase and stared at the faded copy of the birth certificate and the photograph of the toddler he had brought with him.

He had found the reason his father had been in the car with Katherine the night they had both died. Not because Stefano Messena had been having an affair, but for a reason that fitted with his character. His father had been helping Katherine locate her baby.

The reason he had passed the ring to Katherine was because it, and a sizable chunk of the Messena fortune, belonged to his long-lost cousin. His birth year was the same as Nick's, which would mean Michael Ambrosi would be his age: twenty-nine.

An image of his father the last time he had seen him

alive flashed through Nick's mind. His chest went tight at the vivid picture of Stefano Messena tying down a sail on his yacht, his expression relaxed as he enjoyed the methodical process. It was the picture of a man who liked to do everything right.

For the first time he examined the fact that he hadn't been able to let anyone close since his father had died.

Intellectually, he knew what his real problem was, or *had been.* He had known it the moment he saw the love letters and birth certificate hidden in Katherine Lyon's photo album.

Because he and his father had been so close, no matter how hard he'd tried he hadn't been able to disconnect and move on. He'd stayed locked in a stubborn mind-set of grief and denial. The last thing he had wanted was to immerse himself in another relationship.

His mother and his sisters had probed and poked at his inability to "open up." The words *dysfunction* and *avoidance* had figured largely in those conversations.

Nick had stepped around the whole issue. Maybe it was a male thing, but he figured that when he felt like becoming involved in a relationship, he would.

But something had changed in him in the instant he had discovered the possibility that Stefano Messena hadn't cheated on or betrayed anyone.

Emotion had grabbed at his stomach, his chest, powerful enough that for long seconds he hadn't been able to breathe.

His fingers tightened on the birth certificate.

Grimly he allowed himself to remember that night. The time spent waiting for the ambulance, even though he'd known it had been too late. The hurt and anger that had gripped him at the way his father had died.

He knew now that his father had just been unlucky.

The heavy rain had made the road slippery. He'd probably been driving so late because he wanted to get home.

Home to the wife and family he loved.

He slipped the birth certificate and the photograph back into the briefcase. The moment felt oddly symbolic.

Nick didn't personally care about the ring, which, in any case, rightfully belonged to Michael Ambrosi. He had what he wanted: he had his father back.

When they landed in Sydney the press was waiting in the arrivals lounge.

Nick groaned and put on his game face.

Kyle grinned. "Want me to take point?"

"Just promise not to speak."

"Name, rank and serial number only. Scout's honor."

"That would have meant more about an hour ago on the flight."

The questions, all centered on Elena, were predictable. Nick's reactions were not.

Instead of staying doggedly neutral, cold anger gripped him every time a journalist directed another intrusive or smutty question at him.

By the time he reached the taxi rank he was close to decking a couple of the tabloid hacks.

When they reached the Atraeus offices thirty minutes later, his normally nonexistent temper had cooled. But his lack of control pointed up a change in himself he hadn't expected.

Usually when he walked away from a liaison he felt detached, his focus firmly on his next work project.

Right at that moment, he was having trouble concentrating on anything but Elena.

What she was doing and how she was feeling *about him* was coming close to obsessing him.

The thought that she might actually get a tattoo or, worse, go back to the mysterious Robert, suddenly seemed a far more riveting issue than the resort package that would take his business portfolio to a new level.

As they stepped into an elevator, Nick took out his cell and put through a call to his PA, instigating a security check on Corrado. And, more importantly, requesting a full rundown on all of Corrado's business interests and a photo.

He hung up as the elevator doors opened up on the floor occupied by the Atraeus offices.

Constantine Atraeus, who was dealing with the negotiation himself, walked out and shook hands.

Constantine was both family and a friend. In his early thirties, he was incredibly wealthy, with a reputation for getting what he wanted. Although the powerful business persona was offset by a gorgeous, fascinatingly opinionated wife, Sienna, and now a cute young daughter.

Minutes later, with the deal on the table, Nick should have been over the moon. Instead, he found it difficult to focus. Kyle kept sending him questioning glances because it was taking him so long to read the paperwork.

A slim brunette with silky dark hair strolled into the room. Constantine's new legal brief. Apparently the last one had bitten the dust because he had tried to put a prenup on Sienna Atraeus. Sienna had seen him to the door, personally.

Nick forced himself to finish the clause he was reading, even though he knew he was going to have to go over it again because he hadn't understood a word.

The problem, he realized, was the legal brief. For a searing moment he had thought she was Elena, even though a second glance confirmed that she didn't look like Elena at all.

His gaze narrowed as he tracked her departure. His pulse was racing, his heart pounding as his inability to concentrate became clear.

He wanted Elena.

He wanted her back, in his arms and in his bed, which was a problem given that he had walked out on her that morning for the second time. If she ever spoke to him again, that in itself would be a miracle.

It had been difficult enough getting her to trust him the last time. The process had been slow and laborious. From the first phone call, it had taken weeks.

She had stood him up, refused his calls and done everything in her power to avoid him. He had managed to get close to her only through the good luck that his brother had gotten married to Elena's best friend.

If he wanted Elena back, he was going to have to engineer a situation that would give him the time he needed to convince her to give him another chance.

Two of his Atraeus cousins had employed kidnapping as a method of securing that quality time, although Nick didn't seriously think a kidnap situation would repair the rift with Elena. Both Constantine and Lucas had had long-standing relationships with their chosen brides, with the added bonus that love had been a powerful factor in each relationship.

It was a factor Nick could not rely on. He was certain that after a second one-night stand, Elena would no longer view him as a relationship prospect.

For a split second disorientation gripped him. He could kick himself for the mistake he'd made. He'd had Elena back in his arms, and then let her go.

He had further complicated the situation by leaving the field clear for Corrado.

If he wanted Elena back he was going to have to move

fast. Normal dating strategies wouldn't work; he was going to have to use the kind of logic he employed with business strategies.

With this new deal they would have a vital link in common: the Atraeus Group. He wouldn't exactly be her boss, but it would bring her into his orbit.

He'd had two chances with Elena and had blown them both.

He didn't know if he could create a third, but he had an edge he could exploit.

Try as she might, Elena couldn't hide the fact that she couldn't resist him.

Nine

Master of Seduction Meets His Match.

Elena stared in horror at the tabloid coverage of the wedding. She hadn't read many of the words; it was the image of the bride and groom that riveted her attention.

Someone had made a terrible mistake. A photo of her and Nick on the steps had been used instead of one of Gemma and Gabriel. The black-and-white print made her bridesmaid's dress look pale enough to be a bridal gown, and Nick looked the part with his morning suit. The shower of confetti and rice added the final touch.

There was nothing either scandalous or libelous about the brief article. If the photograph had been the correct one, it would have been perfectly nice, if boring, coverage of a high-end society wedding.

Acute embarrassment gripped her as she imagined the moment Nick saw the article and the photo, which portrayed the exact opposite of what he had wanted.

As wonderful as the night had been, something had gone wrong. They had been finished the moment Nick had walked out of the bedroom without a backward look.

She hadn't tried to cling to him, but that didn't alter the fact that watching Nick walk away a second time had hurt.

Or that in a single night she had been willing to sacrifice almost every part of her life to be with him, if only he had truly wanted her.

Elena snapped the paper closed. She could not be a victim again. She had changed her external appearance and now she needed to work hard at changing her actual life.

First up, she would take the new corporate position Constantine Atraeus had suggested she consider. With her executive PA skills, the psychology papers she had done at university and her recent experience of health and beauty spas, she was uniquely suited to reinvigorate the Atraeus spas.

She would be an executive, which suited her.

She was tired of catering to the whims of the mega-wealthy Atraeus bosses, who had appreciated her skills but who never really noticed her as a person.

A hum of excited possibility gave the future a rosy glow. She would probably need her own personal assistant, although that was a leap.

Two brief calls later, and her life was officially transformed.

Zane wasn't happy, since he had just gotten used to her taking care of every possible detail of his working day and travel arrangements. However, he was pragmatic. Since Elena had lost weight, his fiancée, Lilah, hadn't been entirely happy with her as a PA, much as she liked Elena. It was nothing personal, it was just that Lilah had a protective streak when it came to Zane.

"She might relax more after the wedding," Zane explained.

Elena hung up, a little dazed. She would never have believed it, but apparently she was now too pretty to be a PA.

She walked across to her hotel mirror and stared at her reflection. She looked pale and washed-out, but if Zane Atraeus said she was too pretty, then she was too pretty.

Nick had said she was beautiful.

She could feel herself melting inside at the memory of the way he had said those words, the deep timbre of his voice.

Jaw firming, she banished a memory that could only be termed needy and self-destructive.

Instead of going weak at the knees at any little hint of male appreciation from Nick, she needed to form an action plan. She needed rules.

Rule number one had to be: Do *not* get sucked back into Nick Messena's bed.

Rule number two was a repeat of the first.

She would make the rest up as she went along.

Critically, she studied the suit she was wearing. It was pink. She was over pink. The suit was also too feminine, too *pretty*.

She needed to edit her wardrobe and get rid of the ruffles and lace, anything that might possibly hint that she had once been a pushover.

From now on, red was going to be her favorite color.

She would also make a note to encourage Robert a little more. If she was in a proper relationship, it stood to reason that she would not be so vulnerable to a wolf like Nick Messena.

One month later, Elena opened her eyes as pads soaked in some delicately perfumed, astringent solution were removed from her now-refreshed eyes.

Yasmin, the head beauty therapist at the Atraeus Spa she had spent the past three weeks overhauling, smiled at her. "You can sit up now, and I'll start your nails. Can't have you looking anything less than perfectly groomed for your date. What was his name again?"

"Robert."

There was a small, polite silence. "Sounds like a ball of fire."

"He's steady and reliable. He's an accountant."

Yasmin wrinkled her pretty nose. "I've never dated one of those."

Elena reflected on the string of very pleasant dates she'd had with Robert. "He has a nice sense of humor."

Yasmin gave her a soothing smile as she selected a bottle of orchid-red nail polish and held it up. "That's important."

Elena nodded her approval of a color that normally she wouldn't have gone near. But with her transformation, suddenly reds and scarlets seemed to be her colors. Idly, she wondered what Nick would think of the nail polish.

She frowned and banished the thought.

Yasmin picked up one of Elena's hands and set to work on her cuticles. "So, tell me, what does Robert look like?"

Elena shifted her mind away from its stubborn propensity to dwell on Nick, and forced herself to concentrate on Robert. "He has green eyes and dark blond hair—"

Yasmin set one hand down and picked the other up. "Sounds a little like Nick Messena."

Except that Robert didn't have quite that piercing shade of green to his eyes, or the hot gold streaks in his hair. "Superficially."

"Well, if he looks anything like Nick Messena, he's got to be sexy."

"I wouldn't say Robert was sexy...exactly."

"What then?"

Elena watched as Yasmin perfectly and precisely painted a nail. "He's...nice. Clean-cut and extremely well-groomed. Medium build. He's definitely not pushy or ruthless."

Every attribute was the exact opposite of Nick's casual, hunky, killer charm. She had checked weeks ago before she had made the decision for a first date with Robert. After all, what was the point of repeating her mistake? She wanted a man who would be good for her. A man who would commit.

Yasmin painted another nail. "He sounds close to perfect."

"If there was a textbook definition for the perfect date, Robert would be it."

"Talking about perfect men, I saw a photo of Nick Messena in a magazine the other day." She shook her head. "I can't believe how *hot* he is. That broken nose... It shouldn't look good, but it is to *die* for."

Elena's jaw tightened against a fierce surge of jealousy. Swallowing, she tried to put a lid on the kind of primitive, unreasoning emotion that made her want to find the magazine Yasmin had been mooning over and confiscate it.

Jealousy meant she hadn't quite gotten Messena out of her system. It meant she still cared. "Why is it that a broken nose makes a guy more attractive?"

"Because he fights. Perfect men look like they're fresh out of the wrapper. Untried under pressure." She grinned. "I must admit, I like a guy who doesn't mind getting sweaty."

Elena blinked at the sudden image of Nick years ago when she'd walked past a construction site and glimpsed him with his shirt off, covered in dust and grease smears, a hard hat on his head. "I think we should talk about something else."

"Sure." Yasmin sent her a patient you're-the-client look.

The following day, after another pleasant date with Robert during which she had partnered him to one of his company dinners, Elena was packed and ready to fly back to New Zealand. She would spend a couple of days in Auckland, then travel on to Dolphin Bay where she was poised to add a new level of service to the resort business: a pamper weekend that included a relationship seminar she had designed herself.

Her stomach tightened a little as the taxi driver put her luggage into the trunk. Just because she was on her way back to Dolphin Bay didn't mean she would run into Nick. Chances were, he wouldn't even be in the country.

And even if he was, she had successfully avoided him for years. She could avoid him again.

He would get Elena back; it was just a matter of time.

Despite the fact that she had hung up on him again.

Broodingly, Nick placed his phone on the gleaming mahogany surface of his desk.

Not a good sign.

A familiar surge of frustration tightened every muscle in his body as he rose from his office chair, ignoring the cup of coffee steaming gently on his desk. Prowling to the French doors, he looked out over Dolphin Bay.

A heat haze hung on the horizon, melding sea and sky. Closer in, a small number of expensive yachts and launches floated on moorings, including his own yacht, *Saraband*.

Stepping out on the patio, he looked down over his new domain. He now owned a 51-percent share of the resort chain. It was a new turn in his business plan, but one that made sense with his close ties to the Atraeus family and their meshing interests.

Gripping the gleaming chrome rail, he surveyed the terraced levels of the resort complex. His eye was naturally drawn to gleaming turquoise pools below dotted with swimmers and fringed with cooling palms. Though it was the peaked roof of the villa in the adjacent curve of the bay that held his attention.

A hot flash of the night he'd spent with Elena blotted out the lavish tropical scene. The heat of the memory was followed by a replay of the hollow sensation that had gripped him when he had walked out of the villa just before sunrise.

His mother and his two sisters had read him the riot act about his dating regime a number of times.

He now no longer had the excuse of his father's so-called betrayal. As one of his sisters had pointed out, he was out of excuses. It was time he confronted his own reluctance to surrender to a relationship.

A tap on his office door jerked him out of his reverie. The door popped opened. Jenna, his new ultra-efficient PA, waved the file he had requested and placed it on his desk.

As he stepped back into the office, she sent him one of the bright, professional smiles that had begun to put his teeth on edge.

She paused at the door, her expression open and confident. "A group of us are going into town for lunch. You're welcome to join us if you'd like."

Nick dragged his gaze from the lure of the file, which he'd been waiting on. Absently he turned down the offer. Jenna was five-ten, slim and curvy in all the right places. He would have to be stone-cold dead not to notice that she was gorgeous in a quirky, cute way that would obsess a lot of men.

Although not him.

He should find her attractive. A couple of months ago, he would have. The red-haired receptionist in the lobby was also pretty, and a couple of the waitresses in the resort restaurant were stunning. The place was overrun with beautiful, available women, if only he was interested.

Opening the file, he began to skim read. Zane had given him a heads-up that a pamper weekend the Dolphin Bay Resort was scheduled to run in the next few days was Elena's pet project.

He was aware that she had quit her job as a PA and was now heading up a new department, developing the lucrative spa side of the resort business. The pamper weekend and seminar, designed for burned-out career women, was a pilot program she had designed and was entitled What Women Really Want: How to Get the Best Out of Your Life and Relationships.

His door opened again, but this time it was his twin sisters, Sophie and Francesca, who were home for a week's holiday.

They were identical twins, both gorgeous and outgoing with dark hair and dark eyes. Sophie tended to be calm and deceptively slow-moving with a legendary obsession with shoes, while Francesca was more flamboyant with a definite edge to her character.

Sophie, sleek in white jeans and a white tank, smiled. "We've come to take you out to lunch."

Francesca, looking exotic in a dress that was a rich shade of turquoise, made a beeline for his desk and perched on the edge, swinging one elegantly clad foot. "Mom's worried about you." She leaned over and filched his coffee. "Apparently you've gone cold turkey on dating for three months, and you're not sailing, either. She thinks you're sickening for something."

With the ease of long practice, he retrieved his coffee. "You'll have to try another tack. First of all, Mom isn't likely to worry when I'm doing exactly what she wants by not dating. And I've gone without dating for longer periods than three months before."

Sophie circled his desk and dropped into his chair. "When you were building your business and didn't have time for the fairer sex."

"News flash," Nick growled. "I'm still building the business."

Sophie picked up the file he'd dropped on the desk when he'd rescued his coffee and idly perused it. "But you have slowed down. Haven't you got some hotshot executive shark cutting deals and intimidating all of your subcontractors?"

Nick controlled the urge to remove the file from Sophie's grasp. "I've got a team of sharks. Ben Sabin is one of them."

Sophie looked arrested. "But you knew who I was talking about."

Nick frowned at Sophie's response to Ben Sabin, who had a reputation for being as tough on relationships as he was troubleshooting his jobs. He made a mental note to have a word with Sabin and make sure that he understood that Nick's sisters, both of them, were off-limits.

Francesca pushed off the edge of the desk, the movement impatient but graceful. "So what's up? Mom thinks you've fallen for someone and it isn't working out."

Nick dragged at his tie, suddenly feeling harassed and on edge. He should be used to the inquisition. His family was large and gregarious. They poked and pried into each other's lives, not because they were curious but because they genuinely cared.

As prying as his mother and his sisters could be, in an odd way he usually loved that they hassled him. He knew that if he ever got seriously messed with by a woman, they would be as territorial as a pack of wolves protecting their young.

Sophie frowned at the file. "Elena Lyon? Didn't you used to date her?"

Francesca's gaze sharpened. She strolled around the desk and peered at the file. "It was a blind date, only Nick wasn't blind. He set it up."

Nick frowned. "How do you *know* this stuff?"

Francesca looked surprised. "I used to study with Tara Smith who waited tables at the Dolphin Bay Coffee Shop. She overheard you telling Smale to find someone else to date and that if you ever heard he was trying to date Elena Lyon again, the next conversation would be outside, on the sidewalk." Francesca smiled. "Pretty sure that's verbatim. Tara's now a qualified accountant—she doesn't make mistakes."

Nick felt like pounding his head on the solid mahogany door of his office, but that would be a sign of weakness—something he couldn't afford around his sisters.

A small frown pleated Sophie's brow. "Elena was Gemma's bridesmaid, the girl in the picture when the tabloids mistakenly put the wrong photo in the paper."

Francesca went oddly still. "That would be the series of photos that fooled everyone into thinking Nick had gotten married."

There was a heavy silence as if a conclusion that only women could achieve had just been reached.

Sophie's expression morphed back to calm and serene. Nick groaned inside. He didn't know how they had connected the dots, but both of his twin sisters now knew exactly how interested he was in Elena Lyon.

Nick controlled another powerful urge to retrieve the file. If he did that, the inquisition would worsen.

Sophie turned another page, brow pleated, reminding him of nothing so much as a very glamorous, earnest female version of Sherlock Holmes. "Elena was the maid of honor at Gabriel's wedding." There was a significant pause. "Now she's coming back to Dolphin Bay for a weekend."

Francesca's gaze snapped to his. "Did she plan this?"

Nick's brows jerked together at the implication that Elena was scheming to trap him, when as of ten minutes ago she was still refusing to take his calls. "There is nothing planned about it. She doesn't know I'm here."

That was a mistake.

Nick pinched the bridge of his nose and tried to think, but something about the twin's double act interfered with normal brain function.

Francesca's look of horror sealed his fate. Five minutes ago he had been an object of careful examination and pity, but now he was a predator. It was strange how the conversations usually went that way.

Francesca fixed him with a fiery gaze. "If you're letting her come here and she doesn't know you own the hotel, well, that's…predatory."

Sophie ignored Francesca's outrage as she placed the file back on the desk and eyed him with the trademark calm authority that thirty years from now would probably be scaring grandkids. "Do you want her?"

In the quiet of the room the bald question was oddly shocking.

Nick's jaw clenched. As family inquisitions went, this one was over. "There is no relationship. Elena works for the Atraeus Group. She's coming to Dolphin Bay to work."

As far as he was concerned, technically, the relationship he was angling for would begin *after* Elena arrived.

An hour later, after a fraught lunch spent sidestepping further questions and a raft of romantic advice, Nick made it back to his desk.

Opening the file he'd been attempting to read earlier, he studied the letter that had come with the pamper weekend program. He would recognize Elena's elegant slanting signature anywhere.

Unfastening the pale pink sheet from the file fastener, he lifted it to his nostrils. The faint exotic scent of lilies assailed him, laced with a musky under note that set him sensually on edge.

Loosening his tie, he sat back in his seat and studied Elena's pamper weekend package. Though designed for women, men were welcome to attend.

He flicked through the pages until he arrived at a quiz. Gaze sharpening, he studied a sheet of multiple-choice questions entitled The Love Test.

The stated object of the quiz, one of the few elements of the package aimed at men, was to find out if the man in a woman's life knew how to really and truly love and appreciate her.

He flicked through the pages, twenty questions in all that ignored the more commonly perceived signs of a good relationship, such as flowers, gifts and dating. Instead the quiz wound through a psychological minefield, dealing with issues such as emotional honesty, the ability to understand a woman's needs, and with commitment.

As far as Nick could make out, the quiz didn't focus on what a man could aspire to romantically so much as highlight the age-old masculine traits that would make him stumble.

The question on when a relationship should be consummated was a case in point. For most men the answer to that question was simple. Sex was a priority, because in a man's mind until he had made a woman his completely, there was an element of uncertainty that didn't sit well with the male psyche.

Setting the test sheets down, he turned to the answers, frowning as he read through. The questions he had taken a guess at were all wrong.

As far as he could make out, no ordinary man could hope to score well. It would take an intellectual studying psychology or some kind of New Age paragon.

Like Robert Corrado.

His jaw tightened. From the few comments Elena had made, if Robert took the test, he would pass with flying colors. From the research Nick had done on Corrado, he was inclined to agree.

His fingers tightened on the page, crumpling it. As highly as he was certain Robert would score, he didn't think he was the kind of man to make a woman like Elena happy. She would be bored with him in a matter of months. Elena needed a man who wouldn't be intimidated by her formidable strength of character, her passionate intensity.

Nick was that man.

The moment was defining.

He straightened out the page of answers and reattached it to the file. Over the years, commitment had not been a part of any of his relationships.

But now, with the expansion of his business, and several highly paid executives taking the lion's share of the work, he didn't have quite so much to do.

He had time on his hands. And, as luck or fate would have it, once again Elena Lyon was in his equation.

And he was on the brink of losing her to another man.

In that moment, an internal tension he hadn't known existed relaxed, and the focused, masculine drive to attain and hold on to the woman he wanted, that had been missing for so many years, settled smoothly into place.

Six years had passed. Years in which Elena had been single and free, prey to any male who cared to claim her.

But not anymore.

Elena was his. He had hurt her—twice—but there was no way he was going to tamely stand aside and give Corrado a chance at her.

His resolve firmly in place, he checked the answer sheets to find the highest-scoring answers for each question. His frown increased as he read. Out of a possible score of sixty, with a couple of lucky guesses thrown in, he might have made five points. If that wasn't bad enough, the grading system, at odds with the smooth New Age language, was punitive. Thirty points, a pass in any man's language, was considered to be "indifferent." Ten points was "extremely poor." At five points he balanced on the cusp of "disastrous" and "a relationship mistake of catastrophic proportions."

Irritation coursed through him. There was no possibility that any red-blooded male could score well. But information was power and if he wasn't mistaken, he had just been given the key to getting Elena back.

The pamper weekend and the seminar provided the window of opportunity he needed.

Setting the sheet of answers back on top of the file, he walked through to the next office. He offered Alex Ridley, the hotel manager, a well-earned few days off, during which time he would manage the resort. An hour later, he had cleared his schedule for those three days.

Elena wouldn't be happy when she arrived and found him in residence, but he would cope with that hurdle when they got to it.

After the way he had messed up, he was well aware that negotiation wouldn't work. With the skills Elena had honed during her years as a personal assistant to his Atraeus cousins, she would ruthlessly cut him off. Desperate measures were required.

Picking up the quiz, he broodingly read through the questions again.

He didn't know if he would ever be in a position to do the quiz, but at this juncture he needed to be prepared for any eventuality. Picking up a pen, he systematically ticked the correct answer for each question. The 100-percent score entitled him to encircle the grade that assured him he was A Perfect Relationship Partner.

It was cheating.

But as far as he was concerned, when it came to getting Elena back, all was fair in love and war.

Ten

Elena crossed Dolphin Bay's county line just minutes short of midnight. The Dolphin Bay sign was briefly illuminated in the wash of headlights as she changed down for a curve and braked. The familiar arching entrance to the Messena Estate loomed, and her heart beat a brief, unwelcome tattoo in her chest.

She had to stop thinking about Nick. By now he would be thousands of miles away, probably on some sand-blasted site in Dubai and doing what was closest to his heart: making millions.

A tight corner loomed. She slowed even further as she drove through a bush reserve, the road slick with recent rain and the moonlight blocked by large, dripping ponga ferns arching over the road.

The massive plastered gateposts of the resort glowed softly ahead. Relieved, she turned onto the smoothly sealed resort road and accelerated, climbing steadily.

The lush rainforest gave way to reveal a breathtaking expanse of moonlit sea. Nestled amidst bush-clad hills and framed by the shimmering backdrop of the Pacific Ocean, the resort glittered, patently luxurious and very, very private.

Minutes later, she drew up outside a security gate.

The resort boasted a conference center, a world-class private golf course, a marina and a helipad. They catered to the luxury end of the market and were open for business 24/7, but for security reasons—mostly centered around the extremely wealthy clientele who stayed there and their privacy needs—the gates were locked from midnight until six in the morning.

Guest were issued key cards in advance, but weirdly, her key card envelope, which had been couriered to her, had been empty. Since she didn't yet have a card, on arrival she had to ring the reception desk so they could dispatch someone to unlock the gate and let her in. It all seemed unacceptably low-tech to Elena. She had already sent a very short email to the manager informing him that he needed to lift his game in this respect.

Once she checked in, apparently she would be issued a key card and could come and go as she pleased.

Jaw locked, she pushed the door open, climbed out into the balmy night and took a moment to stretch the kinks out. Just a few yards away, water lapped on honey-colored sand, the soothing rhythm underpinned by an onshore breeze flowing through the pohutukawa trees that overhung parts of the beach. During daylight hours, the stunning red blooms would provide a brilliant contrast to the intense blue of sea and sky.

She examined the fortresslike wrought iron gates, searching for the intercom. A small red light winked off to one side. Seconds later a receptionist with a smooth, warm voice answered her and assured her that someone would unlock the gate for her shortly.

Tiredness washed through Elena as she strolled across the short patch of perfectly mown grass that separated the driveway from the beach. Peeling out of her strappy red high heels, she stepped down onto the sand.

It was close on high tide. Letting her shoes dangle from her fingers, she walked a few steps until she was ankle deep in the creamy wash of the waves, drawn by the sheer romantic beauty of the moon suspended over the water.

The throaty rumble of an engine broke the soothing moment. Reluctantly, she retraced her steps. Powerful headlights speared the murky darkness, pinning her. The SUV, which was black and glossy with expensive, chunky lines, came to a smooth halt behind the wrought iron gates, the engine idling.

The driver didn't immediately climb out. Frustrated, she attempted to identify who it was behind the wheel, but the glaring halogen headlights had killed her night vision. A peculiar sense of premonition tightened low in her belly.

The door swung open. A broad-shouldered figure swung smoothly out from behind the wheel and the premonition coalesced into knowledge.

Despite the fact that she was braced for the reaction, her stomach plunged. Dressed in faded jeans and designer trainers, a soft muscle T-shirt molding the contours of his chest and leaving tanned biceps bare, Nick looked as tall, dark and dangerous as the last time she had seen him, *naked and in her bed*.

She went hot, then cold, then hot again. A weird pastiche of emotions seized her: embarrassment, dismay, a familiar sharp awareness, a jolt of old fury.

He gave her a lightning-fast once-over, making her aware of the messy strands of hair blowing around her cheeks and her sand-covered feet. Despite the fact that she was dressed for work in a tailored gray suit, she suddenly felt underdressed.

"Nick." She reached for the smooth professionalism that went with the suit, the elegant shoes and her new executive status. "This is a surprise."

And his presence threw some light on the resort's failure to supply her with a key card. Obviously, for some reason of his own, Nick had wanted another conversation.

His gaze, between the bars, was considering. "Not my fault. You didn't return my calls."

Two phone calls, four weeks and two days out? After she had been dumped—*for the second time*—by a man who had a reputation for running through women?

She held on to her temper with difficulty. "Sorry. I've been a little busy lately."

"You've cut your hair."

"It was time for a change."

A whole lot of changes. The feathery, pixie cut went well with her new executive job. Plus, the new, sharper style made her feel that she was moving on emotionally.

His gaze was distant as he depressed a remote for the gate and she wondered if she'd imagined the initial flash of masculine interest.

With careful precision, she deposited the red shoes on the passenger seat of her car. "What are you doing here?"

The weird sense of premonition that had gripped her was back. In none of her contacts with the Dolphin Bay Resort had Nick's name been mentioned. He wasn't listed on the website or in any of the correspondence she'd received from the resort when she had set up the seminar. "Tell me you're a guest."

Although, he couldn't be a guest. His family's enormous luxury house was just up the road and guests didn't open gates.

His gaze connected with hers, sending chills zinging down her spine again, and the brief fantasy that this was just as much of a surprise to Nick as it was to her evaporated. He had been expecting her.

"I'm not a guest. Haven't you heard? As of two days ago, I'm a part owner of the Dolphin Bay Resort."

Elena parked her car outside the reception area. She was now officially in shock.

Although maybe she should have seen this coming. She knew Nick had been working on some deal at Gabriel and Gemma's wedding. She just hadn't put it together with the news that the Atraeus family were shifting shares around within the family.

She had assumed that an Atraeus would take over the New Zealand side of the resort business. She had forgotten that Nick Messena was an Atraeus on his mother's side.

Nick insisted on helping her with her bags, then waited while she checked in at the reception desk. The owner of the smooth voice was a tall redhead with a spectacular figure and a pleasant manner. Once Elena had signed the register and obtained a site map of the resort, she looped the strap of her handbag over her shoulder, picked up her briefcase and reached for her overnight suitcase. Nick beat her to it.

"I'll show you to your cottage."

"I have a map. I can find my own way."

"It's no problem. All part of the service."

Briefly, she considered trying to wrestle the case back then, gave up on the notion and reluctantly followed Nick as he stepped back out into the night. The resort wasn't a high-rise complex—it comprised a number of layers of apartments and cottages, each set in their own lushly landscaped areas to preserve privacy. Her cottage was located in sector C. According to the map, it couldn't be more than one hundred yards away.

As she strolled, she kept an eye on the curving path, which had narrowed, meaning that she had to move closer to Nick.

In her eagerness to keep distance between them, one of her heels slipped off the edge and sank into a thick layer of shells. His hand landed in the small of her back, steadying her. She stiffened, moving away from the heat of his palm, careful not to stumble again.

He indicated a branching pathway and an attractive hardwood building nestled among palms. A tinkling fountain was positioned to one side.

Seconds later, relieved, she slid her key card into the lock and opened her door. Soft light automatically filled the small, inviting hallway. She set her handbag and her briefcase down on the exquisite hardwood floors and turned to collect her case.

Moonlight glinted on the tough line of Nick's jaw. "Now that you're here,' he said with a smooth confidence that set her teeth on edge, "we can finally talk."

"It's late. And this conversation was over a long time ago." If memory served her correctly, it had involved three words and the last one had been "special."

His jaw tightened, the first kink in his composure

she'd seen so far, and suddenly the ball was back in her part of the court.

He set the case down. "I know I behaved badly last month, but I was hoping we could—"

"What, Nick?" She checked her watch, anything to take her mind off the riveting notion that Nick was working up to doing the one thing she had wanted when she had woken up after their night together. He was on the verge of suggesting they spend some time together.

The luminous dial indicated it was almost one in the morning.

He stepped a little closer. The wash of golden light from the porch of her cottage gleamed off his mouth-watering cheekbones. "Since you're here for the weekend I was hoping we could spend some time together." Startled that he had actually said the words, she dragged her gaze from the odd diffidence of his. It occurred to her that he seemed sorry that he had hurt her. As if he really did want—

She forced herself to edit that line of thought. This was Nick. She would not be fooled again.

Taking a deep breath, she dismissed the old, automatic desire to soften, to do exactly what *he* wanted. "I can't think why."

"Because I want another chance with you."

The words were flatly stated, and they sent an electrifying thrill through her. For a split second she was riveted to the spot, quite frankly stunned, then she pulled herself up short. "When did you decide this?"

"A month ago."

She blinked. "I don't believe you."

He shrugged. "It's the truth."

His gaze dropped to her mouth.

Did he actually want to kiss her?

She should be furious, but for the first time in years, armed by hurt, she felt in control of her emotions and entirely capable of resisting him.

Heart pounding, high on an addictive, giddy sense of victory, she held her ground. "I don't understand why."

"This is why." He stepped closer, filling the doorway, his gaze fastened on hers and, like a switch flicking on, her whole body was suddenly alive and humming.

Nick's breath wafted against her cheek, warm and laced with the faintest hint of coffee. After a month of misery and platonic dating, the thought of kissing Nick Messena should leave her utterly cold. Unfortunately, it didn't.

"Thanks for carrying my bag." With a deliberate motion, Elena took a half step back into the hall, closed the door and leaned back on it. Her heart was pounding out of control. She felt weird and slightly feverish, and there it was. Her problem.

Nick Messena, unfortunately, still qualified as a fatal attraction. Close to irresistible and very, very bad for her.

Just like the last time, he was making no bones about the fact that he wanted her, and that in itself was very seductive.

But touching Nick Messena, kissing him—doing anything at all with him—was crazy. He was the boyfriend no self-respecting woman should allow herself to have... except in her fantasies.

She touched her lips, which felt sensitive and tender, even though she hadn't been kissed.

So, okay...Nick Messena still affected her, but she was almost certain that for him there was little or no emotion involved.

He was all about the chase. Commitment was not his middle name.

But after what had happened the last time they had met, it was definitely hers.

Nick's pulse settled into a steady beat as he walked to his own cottage, which was situated next door to Elena's.

The encounter hadn't gone well, but he had been braced for that.

He'd made love to her and left her—twice. He was going to have a tough time reclaiming her trust.

His pulse picked up a notch as he glimpsed Elena, just visible through the wide glass doors in her sitting room, easing slim, delicately arched feet out of her shoes.

With the addition of the red shoes, the gray suit, which could have been dull and businesslike, was cutting-edge and outrageously sexy.

He watched as she walked into the kitchenette, her stride measured, her spine straight, before she finally disappeared from view. It was an award-winning act, but no amount of control could completely repress the sleek, feminine sway to her hips or the fire he knew was stored behind those guarded eyes.

The red shoes said it all. The passion was still there.

He had made a mistake in leaving her. He should have kept her with him, but it was too late to turn the clock back now.

On the plus side, he finally had her back in his territory. He had three days, and the clock was ticking.

Unlocking his door, he stepped inside and walked through to his shower. Now all he had to do was convince her that the chemistry that exploded between them was worth another try. She hadn't let him kiss her, but it had been close.

Satisfaction eased some of his tension as he peeled out of his clothing and stepped beneath twin jets of cool water.

The night hadn't been a complete washout.

Despite the fact that she had closed the door in his face, he was certain that Elena Lyon still wanted him.

Eleven

The next morning, Elena dressed with care for the official part of the program: the What Women Really Want seminar.

Keeping her mind firmly off the fact that, despite everything, she was still attracted to Nick, she studied the filmy pink-and-orange halter top and white resort-style pants. The hot, tropical colors of the top revealed her smooth golden tan and a hint of cleavage. The pants clung to her hips and floated around her ankles, making the most of her new figure.

The outfit was perfect for a luxury resort, but even so she was tempted to retreat behind the business persona that had been her protective armor for years. Picking up pretty pink-and-gold earrings, she determinedly fitted them to her lobes.

The sound of a door closing in the cottage next door distracted her. A glimpse of Nick, dressed in narrow dark pants and a dark polo, strolling in the direction of the resort, made her heart slam against the wall of her chest.

The path he was using was the same one that led to her cottage and one other. Since she had heard a door close and then had seen Nick strolling *away* from the cottages, there was no way he could be just casually strolling before breakfast. He was living in the cottage next door.

Last night, after Nick had left, she hadn't given any thought to where he was staying. She had been too relieved that she had managed to say "no," and too busy going over every nuance of the exchange.

But the fact that Nick had stooped to the tactic with the key card and put her in a cottage next door to his underlined that he was serious about wanting her back.

She took a deep breath and let it out slowly. Just because Nick was next door didn't change anything. When he realized that she meant what she had said, he would soon switch his attention to one of the many gorgeous women she was sure would be at the resort.

After spraying herself with an ultrafeminine floral perfume, she picked up her folder of workshop notes and the quiz and strolled out of the cottage.

The restaurant was buzzing with guests enjoying breakfast and sitting on the terrace looking out over the stunning views. Relieved to see that Nick was not among the diners, Elena chose a secluded table, and ordered items that were listed on her diet maintenance plan.

Half an hour later, fortified by fresh fruit, yogurt and green tea, Elena strolled into the conference center and froze.

In a sea of femininity, Nick, dressed in black, his shoulders broad, biceps tanned, was a shady counterpart to the preponderance of white cotton, expensive jewelry and flashes of bright resort wear.

His head turned and her heart jolted as his gaze locked with hers.

Jaw firming against the instant heightened awareness and a too-vivid flashback of the previous night, Elena quickly walked to the podium and made an effort to ignore him.

Setting her folder and her laptop down on the table next to the lectern, she booted up the laptop and connected with the large state-of-the-art computerized screen. Briskly, she opened the file and checked that there were no glitches with the software. With the first slide displayed, she was good to go.

A wave of excited feminine laughter attracted her attention. A group of half a dozen of the youngest, prettiest women was clustered around Nick. *Like bees to a honeypot.*

The knowledge that, just as she'd thought, Nick was in the process of hooking up with one of the very pretty women in her seminar made her freeze in place.

She sloshed water from a jug into the tumbler beside it, barely noticing when some spilled onto the table. Setting the jug down with a sharp crack, she looked for a napkin to wipe up the spill. It shouldn't matter that Nick was making conquests, setting up his next romantic episode.

She couldn't find a napkin. Irritation morphing into annoyance, she found a notepad, which she dropped on top of the small puddle.

A sexy rumble of masculine laughter punctuated by a husky feminine voice calling to Nick jerked her head up. She was in time to see a tawny-haired woman with the kind of sultry beauty and lean, curvaceous figure that graced lingerie billboards, fling herself at Nick.

Nick's arms closed around the goddesslike creature, pulling her into a loose clinch.

In that moment, Elena registered two salient facts. Firstly, that the woman Nick was now hugging casually against his side was Nick's cousin, although only by adoption, Eva Atraeus. Secondly, that Eva *was* the kind of woman who graced underwear billboards.

Once a very successful model and now the owner of her own wedding-planning business, Eva was the feminine equivalent of a black sheep in the Atraeus family. Single and determinedly strong-willed, she had sidestepped her adoptive father's efforts to maneuver her into an advantageous marriage. Instead, she had become notorious for serially dating a number of tabloid bad boys.

Elena's stomach tightened as she watched the casual but intimate exchange. It was clear that Nick and Eva knew each other very well.

Who Nick hugged shouldn't matter. Nick Messena didn't belong to her, and he was not husband material.

He'd had his chance, *twice*.

Scrunching up the sopping wet little pad, she tossed it into a nearby trash can. Grimly, she concentrated on stacking her notes neatly on the podium and remembering her last date with Robert. Frustratingly, she couldn't recall the name of the restaurant or what she had eaten. Her one abiding memory was that she had learned just a little too much about Australian tax law.

She checked her watch. She had given herself plenty of time to set up, and consequently had a good fifteen minutes left until the official start time to mingle with her clients.

Extracting her name tag from her handbag, she fastened it on to the left shoulder of her top then walked down onto the floor of the conference room to circulate.

Nick cut her off just as she reached a table set up with coffee, green tea, a selection of wheatgrass and vegetable juices, and platters of fresh fruit. "Looks like a good turnout. Congratulations."

Elena pointedly checked her wristwatch. "We start in just a few minutes."

"I'm aware of the start time. I'm sitting in on the seminar."

Elena reached for a teacup, her careful calm already threatening to evaporate. "You can't stay."

Nick's expression was oddly neutral. "It's my resort. I'm entitled to make sure that what you're doing works for the level of service and luxury we provide."

Elena tensed at the thought of Nick sitting in on her seminar. Jaw tight, she poured herself a cup of green tea. "Constantine approved the program—"

"In the same week he handed over control to me."

With calm precision, Elena set the cup on its saucer, added a slice of lemon and tried to control an irrational spurt of panic. If Nick wanted to crash the seminar she couldn't stop him.

Last night, before she had gone to bed, she had used her priority clearance to check the Atraeus computer files for the details of the resort deal. Nick owned 51 percent. It was a reality she couldn't fight. Not only was he the majority shareholder, it would appear he was also now the current manager.

Technically, he was also her employer for the entire New Zealand group of resorts.

She held the steaming green tea in front of her like a shield. The thin, astringent scent, which she was still trying to accustom herself to, wafted to her nostrils, making her long for the richness of coffee, although she quickly quashed the thought. She was intent on cutting anything bad out of her life. Like Nick Messena, coffee was banned. "The seminar is of no possible interest to you. It's designed for women—"

"There are other men here."

Two men, both booked in by their wives. She had already checked both of them out and couldn't help noticing that they were oddly similar in appearance. Both were medium height and trim as if they ate sensibly and exercised regularly. They were also well dressed and extremely well-groomed. *Like Robert.*

With an effort of will, Elena called up Robert's image again. Right now, with Nick looming over her looking muscular and tanned, as relaxed as a big hunting cat, Robert was a touchstone she desperately needed.

Although, distressingly, she was having trouble remembering exactly what he looked like. Whenever she tried to concentrate on Robert's face, Nick Messena's strong, slightly battered features swam into view.

She kept her expression pleasant as she sipped the bitter tea and tried not to watch longingly as Nick helped himself to black coffee, adding cream and two sugars.

A clear indication that he was settling in for the duration.

She took a sip of tea and couldn't quite control her grimace. "I decided to throw the seminar open to men who were interested in improving their relationships."

"And I'm not?"

She met his gaze squarely. "You said it, not me."

"The question was rhetorical. As it happens, now that the nature of my business is changing, I'm going to have a lot more time on my hands to dedicate to…relationships."

Elena almost choked on another mouthful of tea. She glanced at Eva who had just helped herself to coffee. Unbidden, her mind made an instant wild leap. As an Atraeus employee she had heard the rumor that Eva's father, Mario, who was terminally ill, had been trying to force a match between Eva and Gabriel Messena.

The rumor had been confirmed by Gabriel's new wife, Gemma. Since Gabriel had just married, that meant Mario would be looking for another bridegroom for his headstrong daughter. Of course Nick, as the second Messena son, would be Mario's natural choice.

"No way," Nick said flatly.

Startled, Elena carefully set her tea down before she had another spill. "No way, what?"

"Eva and I are just good friends."

Elena could feel her careful control shattering, the veneer of politeness zapped by a hot burn of emotion she had no hope of controlling. "Then why is she here?"

Somewhere in the recesses of her brain she registered that she must have taken a half step toward Nick, because suddenly she was close enough that she could feel the heat from his body, smell the clean scents of soap and masculine cologne.

Nick's gaze narrowed. "You're jealous."

Elena stared at the taut line of Nick's jaw and a small scar that was almost as fascinating as the nick across the bridge of his nose. "That would be when hell freezes over."

"You don't have to worry. I'm not interested in Eva. After last night you have to know that I want you back."

A tingling thrill shot through her, cutting through the annoyance that he knew she was jealous.

He still wanted her.

A surge of delight mixed with an odd little rush of feminine power put a flush on her cheeks and jerked her chin up a little higher.

But a familiar dash of panic doused the surge of excitement. The last thing she needed to know now was that, after everything that had gone wrong, there was a chance for them after all.

He had left her twice. She should be over him, but clearly she wasn't because the dangerous, electrifying attraction was still there.

Six years. The time that had passed since they had first slept together was a dose of reality she badly needed.

Those years had been lonely and more than a little depressing because she had been unable to settle into another relationship. Like any other woman her age, she had wanted to be loved and connected to somebody special. She had wanted all the trappings of marriage, the warmth and commitment, the family home, the babies.

She hadn't come close, because in her heart of hearts she hadn't been able to move on. She had still been in love with Nick.

She went still inside, the hubbub of conversation receding as she examined the extremity of her emotions, the single-minded way she had clung to the one man who had never really wanted her.

Could she possibly still be in love with Nick?

The thought settled in with a searing, depressing finality. If so, she had loved him through her teens and for all of her adult life, eleven years and counting, with almost no encouragement at all. The chances that she could walk away from him now and get over him didn't look good.

She knew her nature. As controlled and methodical as she was in her daily life, she was also aware of a lurking streak of passionate extremity that seemed to be a part of her emotional make up. Like her aunt Katherine, she obviously had a deep need for a lasting, true love. The kind of love that was neither light nor casual, and which possessed the terrible propensity for things to go wrong.

Nick set his coffee down, untouched. "Eva's a wedding planner. This resort is one of her most requested wedding venues."

Unbidden relief made her knees feel suddenly as weak as water. "If all you want is to gauge the effectiveness of the seminar, you don't need to attend. The head therapist of the spa facility is sitting in."

Nick crossed his arms over his chest. "I'm not leaving, babe."

A secret little thrill shot down her spine at Nick's casual use of "babe," a term that carried the heady subtext that they were a couple and he was stubbornly bent on proving that fact.

A little desperately she skimmed the room and tried to restore her perspective. "I am not your *babe*."

Ignoring the steady way he watched her, she checked her watch, set her tea back down on the table and walked back to the podium.

Once the first session started it was easier to focus. Nick, true to his word, hadn't left but was occupying a seat near the back of the room. She would have to tolerate his presence until he got tired of material he could have absolutely no interest in and left. The other two men, Harold and Irvine, obviously keen to learn, were seated in the front row.

After introducing the other speakers who were there for the day, Elena surrendered the podium to a beauty therapist who wanted to talk about the latest skin-care technology. While that was going on Elena handed out her quiz.

When she reached Nick's row, which was occupied by Eva and a couple of the more elderly women, she bypassed him without handing out a quiz sheet.

A lean hand briefly curled around her wrist, stopping

her in her tracks. "Whatever that is you're handing out, I'd like to see it."

Reluctantly she handed him the quiz. "It's not something you'd be interested in."

He studied the sheet. "As it happens, I'm pretty sure I do know what women really want."

Her temper snapped at a sudden visual of Nick with dozens of women marching through his bedroom. "Sex doesn't count."

He went still. "Maybe I'm not all about sex. You think I'll score low?"

"I think your score will be catastrophic. Most men can't get above thirty percent."

"What would you say if I believe I can score at least eighty?"

"I'd say that was impossible."

"Then you wouldn't mind a wager on that?"

She drew a swift breath. "Name it."

"You in my bed, for one more night."

She blinked at the sudden flash of heat evoked by that image.

Although, he would never get past 10 percent. She had tried the test on her male hairdresser who was used to dealing with women all day. He had aced it at 55 percent. Nick definitely didn't have a chance. "What do I get when you lose?"

"A free rein to make whatever changes you want to our spa services. And I'll leave you alone."

She met his gaze. "Done."

There was a small smattering of applause.

Embarrassed, Elena swung around to find that the entire seminar group had stopped to listen, including the beauty therapist.

The elderly lady sitting next to Nick said, "When can he do the test?"

"Now would be a good time," Elena muttered grimly.

Twenty minutes later, Elena studied Nick's test with disbelief. She had checked through on her answer sheet, a sheet that only she had access to, twice. He had scored 85 percent, and she was almost certain that he had fluffed one of the easy questions to show off.

She thought she knew Nick through and through, although she was aware that there were private glimpses of his life, like his relationship with his father, which informed her that Nick had a very private side.

Still, could she have been so wrong, and the baddest of the bad boys wasn't so bad after all?

She walked over to where Nick was standing drinking wheatgrass juice and eating sushi with an expression on his face that suggested he wasn't entirely sure that either item qualified as food. "How did you do it?"

"What was my score?"

When she told him, Nick set his wheatgrass juice down, his gaze oddly wary. "When do I get my prize?"

Elena's stomach did a somersault as the completely unacceptable sensual excitement that had proved to be her downfall, twice, leaped to life.

Her reaction made no sense, because she had no interest in a slice of the relationship cake—she wanted the whole thing. She wanted to be desperately in love with a gorgeous guy who was just as in love with her.

She wanted to wallow in the attention and the nurturing warmth of being with someone who not only wanted her but who couldn't live without her.

Nick was not that man.

At six, as part of the pamper weekend package, they were all due to go on a sunset cruise. The cruise would

take up a substantial part of the evening. By the time
they got back there wouldn't be much of the evening
left. "Tonight."

Twelve

Nick knocked on her door at six. Feeling more than a little nervous, she checked her appearance. For the first time in her life she was wearing a bikini, a daring jungle print, concealed by a filmy green cotton tunic that fell to midthigh and was belted at her hips. The look was casual, chic and sexy.

Applying a last waft of perfume, she picked up her beach bag, slipped on matching emerald-green sandals and strolled to the door. When she opened it, Nick, still dressed in the dark trousers and polo, was lounging in the small portico talking on his cell.

His gaze skimmed the emerald-green cover-up and the length of tanned leg it revealed as he hung up. "There's been a change of plan. The motor on the resort's yacht is leaking oil, so we'll be taking mine."

Saraband.

Elena's pulse kicked up another notch at the mention

of Nick's yacht. She had seen it moored out in the bay. It was large, with elegant, racy lines.

He checked his wristwatch. "The catering staff is stocking *Saraband,* but before we cast off I need to collect a spare radio." He nodded in the direction of his Jeep, which she could glimpse, parked just beyond the trees that screened her cottage.

Long minutes later, emotion grabbed at her as Nick drove onto the manicured grounds of the Messena family home. She used to visit on occasion when her aunt was working here, but she had never actually been invited.

The house itself was a large, Victorian old lady with a colonnaded entrance and wraparound verandas top and bottom, giving it a grand, colonial air.

Ultrasensitive to Nick's presence and the knowledge that she had agreed to sleep with him again, *tonight,* Elena climbed out of the Jeep before Nick could get around to help her.

Nick strolled up the steps with her and held the front door.

Removing her sunglasses, Elena stepped into the shady hall.

Nick gestured at a large, airy sitting room with comfortable cream couches floating on a gleaming hardwood floor. French doors led onto a patio, a sweep of green lawn added to the feeling of tranquillity. "Make yourself at home—I won't be long. Eva's staying here for the duration of the retreat but, other than her, the house is empty."

Elena stiffened at the mention of Eva's name.

Firming her chin, she banished the too-familiar insecurities. She had committed to spend the night with Nick. She would not lose her nerve or allow herself to imagine that she wasn't attractive enough for him. It wasn't as if they had never spent a night together. They had. Twice.

Taking a steadying breath, she checked out the sun-washed patio with its pretty planters overflowing with gardenias and star jasmine, then stepped back inside, blinking as her vision adjusted to the shady dimness.

She had already reasoned out her approach. The whole idea of challenging Nick to the quiz had been a mistake. She would never in her wildest dreams have imagined that he could score so highly.

Now that he had, it was up to her to create a positive for herself out of the experience. It was an ideal opportunity to demystify the exciting passion that she now realized had blocked her from experiencing the true love she needed.

Both other times their lovemaking had been spontaneous and a little wild. This time she was determined that out-of-control passion would not be a factor. If Nick wanted to get her into bed, he would have to woo her, something she was convinced—despite his meteoric test score—that he would fail at, miserably.

Once he was exposed as superficial, unfeeling, basically dysfunctional and terrible husband material, she should be able to forget him and move on.

In theory....

She strolled to a sideboard covered with family photographs. Idly she studied an old-fashioned, touched-up wedding photo of Stefano and Luisa, and a variety of baby and family photos. She halted beside a large framed color photo of a plump, bespectacled boy in a wheelchair. It was clearly one of the Messena children, or perhaps a cousin, although she couldn't ever remember anyone mentioning that there was a disabled member of the family.

She studied the young teenager's nose, which had been broken at some point, perhaps in the accident that had injured him, and froze, drawn by an inescapable sense of familiarity. A split second later she was aware that Nick was in the room. When she turned, she logged that he had changed into faded, glove-soft denims and a white, V-necked T-shirt that hugged his shoulders and chest. A duffel bag was slung over one shoulder and he was carrying the spare radio he needed.

She looked at the framed photo of the boy in the wheelchair then transferred her gaze to Nick's nose.

The wariness of his expression killed any uncertainty she might have had stone dead. "That's you."

"At age sixteen."

She could feel the firm emotional ground she had been occupying shift, throwing her subtly off balance. She could remember her aunt mentioning that Nick had had an accident, she had just never imagined it had been that bad.

Just when she thought she had Nick in focus, something changed and she had to reevaluate. The last thing she wanted to learn now was that Nick had a past hurt, that he had been vulnerable, that maybe there were depths she had missed. "What happened?"

"A rugby accident." He shrugged. "It's old history now. I was playing in a trial game for a place at Auckland Boy's Grammar and their rugby academy. I got hit with a bad tackle and broke my back."

Nodding his head at the door, he indicated that they needed to leave, but Elena wasn't finished.

"How long were you overweight?"

He held the door for her, his expression now distinctly impatient. "About a year. Until I started to walk again."

"Long enough not to like how it felt."

"I guess you could say that."

Her mind racing, Elena followed him outside and

neatly avoided his offer of assistance as she climbed into the Jeep's front passenger seat.

Her fingers fumbling as she fastened the seat belt, she tried to move briskly past this setback. She thought she'd had Nick all figured out, that he was callous and shallow, but it was worse than that.

He had a nice streak, a compassionate, protective instinct that she could relate to with every cell of her body. When she was a kid, she had automatically protected every other overweight kid. She hadn't been able to help it; she had felt their vulnerability when they got picked on.

Nick shared that trait in common with her because he had been in that same depressing place, *and* with the glasses. "Is that why you stepped in as my blind date, then slept with me?"

Nick frowned. "The reason I stepped in on your blind date is that I couldn't stand the thought of Smale getting his hands on you. And it wasn't just because I wanted to protect you," he said grimly. "Babe, believe it. I wanted you for myself."

Nick maneuvered the *Saraband* into a sheltered crescent bay on Honeymoon Island, a small jewel of an island about three miles offshore from the resort.

He started lowering the anchor. While he waited for the chain to stop feeding out, he looked over the bow.

Elena had spent the first part of the trip circulating with the clients, but for the past fifteen minutes she had been a solitary figure sitting on the bow, staring out to sea.

Nick jammed his finger on the button, stopping the anchor chain from feeding out. Impatience ate at his normally rock-solid composure while he waited for the yacht to swing around in the breeze. He took a further minute to check line-of-sight bearings to ensure that the anchor had locked securely on to the seabed and that they weren't drifting. By the time he walked out onto the deck, the first boat, with Elena aboard, was already heading for the bay.

His gaze was remote as he slipped a pair of dark glasses onto the bridge of his nose. No doubt about it, she was avoiding him.

Not that he would let her do that for long.

She needed some space. He might not be the sensitive, New Age guy she thought she wanted. Over the next few hours he intended to prove to her that he was the man she needed.

Two hours later, annoyed with the champagne and the canapés, and the fact that Elena seemed intent on having long, heartfelt conversations with the two men attending the seminar, Harold and Irvine, Nick decided to take action.

He didn't dislike Harold, though something about Irvine set him on edge. Though both were married, he wasn't about to underestimate either of them. Harold, at least, was a carbon copy of the guy Elena was lining up to be her future husband.

By the time he had extracted himself from a conversation with a pretty blonde, the kind of friendly, confident woman he was normally attracted to, Elena had disappeared.

Annoyed, he skimmed the beach and the array of bathers lying beneath colorful resort beach umbrellas. There was no flash of the green tunic Elena had been wearing. After having a quick word with Harold, who was now immersed in a book, he followed a lone set of footprints.

Rounding a corner, he found a small private beach

overhung with pohutukawa trees in blossom, their deep red flowers a rich accent to gray-green leaves and honey-colored sand. Beneath the tree, in a pool of dappled shade, lay Elena's beach bag and the green tunic.

He looked out to sea and saw her swimming with slow, leisurely grace. His jaw tightened when he saw a second swimmer closing in on Elena. Irvine.

Out of habit, suspicious of the motives of men who wanted to come on a course designed for women, he had done some checking and received the information just minutes before. Harold had proved to be exactly as he appeared, a businessman intent on trying to please a dominant wife. Irvine, however, had a background that was distinctly unpleasant.

Nick shrugged out of his T-shirt and peeled off his jeans, revealing the swimming trunks he was wearing beneath. Jogging to the water, he waded to the break line. A few quick strokes through choppy waves and he was gliding through deep water.

A piercing shriek shoved raw adrenaline through his veins. Irvine was treading water beside Elena, holding his nose. Relief eased some of his tension as he logged the fact that it was Irvine, not Elena, who had shrieked. The source of the outraged cry was clear in the bloody nose Irvine was nursing.

An odd mixture of pride and satisfaction coursed through Nick as he saw Elena slicing through the waves toward him, her strokes workmanlike and efficient. Irvine had clearly thought he had caught Elena vulnerable and alone—no doubt his favorite modus operandi—and she had quickly dispelled that idea with a solid punch to the nose.

Irvine finally noticed Nick, and went white as a sheet.

Nick didn't need to utter a threat—the long steady look was message enough. He would deal with Irvine later.

Elena splashed to a halt beside him. "Did you see what Irvine did?"

Nick watched Irvine's progress as he gave them a wide berth and dog-paddled haltingly in the direction of the crowded beach. "I was too busy trying to get to you in time."

She treaded water. "You knew about Irvine?"

Nick dragged his gaze from the tantalizing view through the water of a sexy jungle-print bikini and the curves it revealed. "I ran a security check on him this morning. I received the results a few minutes ago."

Nick's hands closed around Elena's arms as the swell pushed her in close against him. "He has a police record and no wife. Did he touch you?"

The question was rough and flat, but the thought that Irvine had laid hands on Elena sent a cold fire shooting through his veins.

"He didn't touch me—he didn't get the chance. It was more what he said."

"Let me guess, he wanted 'sexual therapy' to help him with his problems?"

Another wave drove Elena closer still, so that their legs tangled and their bodies bumped. Automatically, she grasped his shoulders. "That's what's stated on his police record?"

"He targets therapists. Lately he's been doing the rounds of the health spas. Although this will be his last attempt."

"You're going to get him." Her gaze was intense and laced with the kind of admiration that made his heart swell in his chest. Finally, he was doing something right. He stared, mesmerized at her golden, flowerlike irises

and wondered how she could ever have reached the conclusion that she had to change those. "I'll sic my lawyers
onto him as soon as we get in."

Leaning forward, she touched her mouth to his.
"Thank you."

The kiss deepened. He fitted her close against him,
acutely aware of the smoothness of her skin against his,
the tiny span of her waist and the delicacy of her curves.

The moment when he had realized that Irvine had
swum after her replayed itself.

Unconsciously, his hold on Elena tightened. He had let
her out of his sight, too busy brooding over the easy way
she had shut him out, and Irvine had taken his chance.
That wouldn't happen again. From now on, he would
make certain that Elena was protected at all times.

Messena women routinely required protection because
the amount of wealth his family possessed made them a
target. Elena hadn't agreed to a relationship with him—
yet—but even so, she would accept his protection. There
was a small clause in all Atraeus and Messena employ-
ment contracts he could exploit if he needed to.

She wouldn't like it, but as far as he was concerned,
until Irvine was put behind bars, Elena wouldn't move
more than a few paces without either him or a bodyguard
protecting her.

When she pulled back and released her hold, Nick had
to forcibly restrain himself from reaching for her again.
Instead, when she indicated that she wanted to head for
shore, he contented himself with swimming with slow,
leisurely strokes so she could easily keep pace.

As he waded from the water, satisfaction eased some
of his tension when he saw Irvine still struggling in the
surf, holding his nose.

When Elena stepped out of the water and Nick got his

first real look at the bikini, he felt as though he'd been punched in the stomach. With her hair a satiny cap, her skin sleek with water, she was both exotic and stunning. The bikini revealed long, elegant legs and the kind of slim, curvaceous figure that made his mouth water, the bright jungle print giving Elena's skin a tawny glow.

He had always registered that she was pretty and attractive, but now she took his breath.

As Elena reached for the towel she had tossed down on the sand, a scuffling sound attracted Nick's attention. Harold, the carbon copy of the sainted Robert, was walking over the rocks, his gaze firmly fixed on Elena.

"That's it," he muttered. "No more men on your weekend seminars."

Elena wrapped the towel around herself and knotted it, successfully concealing almost every part of the bikini but the halter tie around her neck. Her first outing in the skimpy swimming costume had been a disaster. After the unhealthy way Irvine had looked at her, his eyes practically glowing, she was over revealing her new body. "Harold's harmless."

The complete opposite of Nick, who, with his gaze narrowed and glittering as he regarded Harold's halting progress, looked both tough and formidable. "Like Irvine?"

A shudder went through her. "Point made."

She noted that Harold's gaze was riveted on her chest. Her stomach plunged. She suddenly wished she hadn't spent so much time talking to Harold, who seemed to have misconstrued her intentions. "Do you think—?"

Nick said something short and sharp beneath his breath. "You should know by now that if you spend time with a guy, chances are he's going to think you're interested in him."

Elena recoiled from the concept of Harold falling in clinging lust with her. Reinventing herself and wearing the alluring clothes she had always longed to wear had an unexpected dark side. "That hasn't been my experience."

Nick's gaze sliced back to hers. "You've dated. I checked."

"You *pried* into my personal life?"

"You work for the Atraeus Group. We now share a database in common."

"You accessed my personal file." A file that did contain a list of the men she had dated. Working as a PA to both Lucas then Zane Atraeus, she was privy to confidential information and anyone she dated was also scrutinized.

Elena's intense irritation that Nick was poking his nose into her private affairs was almost instantly replaced by a spiraling sense of delight that he was worried enough to do so.

Her attention was momentarily diverted as Harold unfastened his shirt and tossed it on the sand, revealing an unexpectedly tanned, toned torso. "I don't think I'll include men in the pamper program again."

Nick's head swung in Harold's direction, and he muttered a soft oath. "Include men, babe, and you can bank on it that I'll be there."

The blunt possessiveness of his attitude, combined with the way he had come after her to protect her from Irvine, filled Elena with the kind of wild, improbable hope she knew she should squash. Hope messed with her focus. She needed to approach this night together exactly as Nick would—as a pleasurable interlude from which she could walk away unscathed.

Nick's gaze dropped to her mouth. "If you want to get rid of Harold, you should kiss me again."

A shaft of heat at the prospect of another passionate, off-the-register kiss seared through her. "It's not exactly professional."

"The hell with professional."

As Nick's hands settled at her waist, the clinical list of things she would absolutely not allow was swamped by another wave of pure desire. Before she could stop herself, mouth dry, heart pounding a wild tattoo, she stepped close and slid her palms over the muscled swell of his shoulders.

Without the cool water that had swirled around them out at sea, Nick's skin was hot to the touch. Taking a deep breath, she went up on her toes and fitted herself more closely against him.

The instant her mouth touched his, she forgot about Irvine and Harold, and she forgot about the strategy she'd decided upon. Streamers of heat seemed to shimmer out from each point of contact as Nick gathered her closer still, his arms a solid bar in the small of her back.

A small thrill went through her as her feet left the ground and she found it necessary to wind her arms around Nick's neck and hang on. The situation was absolutely contrary to her plan to control her emotions and keep her heart intact, to inform Nick that she was not the easy, forgettable conquest she'd been in the past.

Dimly, she registered that the towel had peeled away and that she was sealed against Nick from thigh to mouth. Long, dizzying minutes later, a rhythmic, vibrating sound broke the dazed grip of passion.

Elena identified the sound as the ringtone of a cell, emanating from Nick's jeans, which were tossed on the sand beside her beach bag.

With a searing glance, Nick released his hold on her.

Stumbling a little in the sand and again conscious of the brevity of the bikini, Elena noticed that Harold had disappeared. She snatched up her tunic.

By the time she'd pulled the filmy tunic over her head and smoothed it down over her hips, Nick had walked several paces away. His back was turned for privacy and he seemed totally immersed in his call.

She caught the phrases "construction crew" and "form work," which meant the call was work related.

Despite the heat that radiated from the sand and seemed to float on the air, Elena felt abruptly chilled at the swiftness with which Nick had switched from passion to work.

Retrieving her towel, she tried not to focus on the pang of hurt, or a bone-deep, all-too-familiar sense of inevitability.

Of course work would come first with Nick. Hadn't it always? It wasn't as if she had ever proved to be a fascinating, irresistible lover to him.

What they had shared was passionate, and to her, beautiful and unique, but it was as if she had never truly connected with Nick. She was certain Nick had the capacity to return love, she just didn't believe it would be with her on the receiving end.

She rummaged in her green tote, found her sunglasses and jammed them onto the bridge of her nose. In the process, her fingers brushed against a book of lovemaking techniques she had bought online. Her cheeks warmed at the research she'd embarked upon because she felt so hopelessly out of her depth in that area. It was part of her general makeover; although the whole idea of planning lovemaking became irrelevant around Nick. It just happened.

She was still reeling from the last kiss and the notion that he wanted her as much as she wanted him.

As if he couldn't get enough of her.

Nick pulled on his jeans and T-shirt and slipped the phone into his pocket. "Time to go."

The searing reality of what would happen when they got back to the resort stopped the breath in her throat. "We've only been here an hour."

"An hour too long, as far as I'm concerned." Snagging her towel and beach bag, Nick held out his hand to her.

Elena's breath caught in her throat at the sudden softness in his gaze, an out-of-the-blue sense of connection that caught her off guard. It was the kind of warming intimacy she had dreamed about and wanted. As if they were friends as well as lovers. Something caught in her throat, her heart, abruptly turning her plans upside down. A conviction that there really was something special between them, something that refused to fade away and die, despite the attempts both of them had made to starve it out of existence.

Nick might not recognize what it was, yet, but she did. It was love.

And not just any love. If she wasn't mistaken, this was the bona fide, once-in-a-lifetime love she had dreamed about. The dangerous kind of love that broke hearts and changed lives, and which she had longed for ever since that one night with Nick six years ago.

From one heartbeat to the next the conflict of making love with Nick when she was supposed to be keeping him at arm's length zapped out of existence to be replaced with a new, clear-cut priority.

Making love with Nick was no longer an untenable risk or an exercise in control; it was imperative.

As crazy as it seemed with everything that had gone

wrong, they were at a crucial tipping point in their relationship. Now was not the time to shrink back and make conservative choices; passion was called for.

By some fateful chance, Nick had taken her quiz and given her an insight into aspects of his personality she would not have believed were there. The kind of warmth and consideration that would make him perfect husband material.

On the heels of that, she had unraveled a piece of his past in the disabled, overweight boy with glasses he had once been.

She had agreed to spend the night in his bed.

Her heart pounded at the thought of the passionate hours that lay ahead, their third night together.

Nick had gone out on a limb to get her back, even if he couldn't quite express his intentions, yet. She was now convinced that the risk she had taken twice before, and which each time had failed, was now viable.

It was up to her to help Nick feel emotionally secure enough to make the final step into an actual relationship. To do what, in her heart of hearts, she had wanted him to for years: to finally fall in love with her.

Thirteen

Nick marshaled the guests back onto the yacht with the promise of free champagne, cocktails and dessert when they reached the resort. The regular manager would probably have a heart attack when he saw the damage to his bottom line on this particular venture, but the way Nick saw it, his night with Elena took precedence.

He had engineered a window of opportunity. He wasn't going to let that time be eroded because clients wanted more time on the beach.

When Irvine stepped aboard, Nick intercepted him and suggested they both go below.

Irvine's expression turned belligerent. "You can't give me orders. I'm a paying guest."

Nick stepped a little closer to Irvine, deliberately crowding him and at the same time blocking him, and their very private conversation, from the rest of the guests. "You also tried to molest Ms. Lyon."

His gaze turned steely. "You can't prove that."

"Maybe not, but we can have some fun trying."

Irvine tried to peer over his shoulder. "Now I'm scared. Elena wouldn't lay charges."

Aware that Elena was conducting a conversation with some of the guests on the bow, Nick moved to block Irvine's view. "Let me see. This would be the same Elena Lyon who has a double degree that she shelved in favor of being Lucas Atraeus's personal assistant for five years."

Irvine's Adam's apple bobbed. "*The* Lucas Atraeus—?"

"Who engineered a number of mining company and resort takeovers and tipped over a major construction company that tried to use substandard steel on one of his developments." Nick crossed his arms over his chest. "Elena might look little and cute, but she orchestrated Lucas's schedule, monitored his calls, including the death threats, and deployed security when required."

Irvine paled. "I don't get it. If she's that high-powered, what's she doing in Dolphin Bay?"

"Spending time with me." Nick jerked his chin in the direction of the two inflatable boats that, on his instructions, hadn't yet been tied at the stern and were still bobbing against the side of the yacht. "I'll make things even simpler for you. If you don't go below, you can stay on the island until I come back to get you. After that, it's a one way trip to the Dolphin Bay Police Station."

After a taut moment, Irvine visibly deflated. With a shrug, he started down the stairs.

Nick followed him and indicated a seat in the dining area, positioned so Nick could keep an eye on him while he was at the wheel.

Expression set, Irvine sat. "Who could know that there would be a police station in a hick town like this?"

"Just one guy—that's all Dolphin Bay needs. And as

luck would have it, he happens to be a relative." A distant uncle, on his mother's side.

Irvine seemed to shrink into himself even further at that last piece of information. Satisfied that he was contained for the moment, Nick went topside and skimmed the deck, looking for Harold. Relief filled him as he noted that Harold had evidently given up on Elena and now seemed to be directing all of his charm toward Eva.

Eva caught his gaze for a split second and winked.

Grim humor lightened Nick's mood as he logged exactly what she was doing—running interference. Somehow, with the scary talent Eva had for figuring out exactly what was going on in men's heads, she had summed up the situation and taken charge of Harold before Nick chucked him over the side.

Minutes later, after starting the yacht's motor, then weighing anchor, Nick took the wheel. A faint, enticingly feminine floral scent informed him that Elena was close. Turning his head, he met her frowning gaze.

"What did you do with Irvine?"

"Don't worry, I didn't hit him. He's in containment." He indicated the glass panel that gave a view into the dining room below.

Satisfaction eased the tension on Elena's face. "Good, I don't want him causing trouble for any of my clients. Bad for business."

"That's my girl."

Her gaze locked with his, the absence of levity informing him that she hadn't liked the situation with Harold or Irvine one little bit. Her reaction was a stark reminder that no matter how strong or efficient Elena seemed, when it came to men she was in definite need of protection.

He had to resist the urge to pull her close and tuck

her against his side. There was no need for the primitive methods he had employed on the beach. Irvine was controlled and he had made arrangements to have him removed from the resort as soon as they reached Dolphin Bay.

As much as he would like to lay a formal complaint againt Irvine, he was aware there wasn't anything concrete that Irvine could be charged with since all he had done was make an advance, which Elena had rebuffed. Besides, police procedure took time. Elena was exclusively his for just a few hours. He wasn't going to waste that time trying to get Irvine locked up.

His jaw tightened at the thought that one more night might be all they'd have. The desire for more than a sexual liaison settled in more powerfully. The thought process was new, but he was adjusting.

Elena crossed her arms over her chest as the yacht picked up speed, hugging the thin fabric of her tunic against her skin. She sent a worried glance in Eva's direction. "Will Eva be okay?"

Satisfaction at Elena's total rejection of Harold, with his smooth good looks, eased some of Nick's tension. He spared another glance for Eva and Harold, and noted the change in Harold's body language. The expansive confidence was gone and his shoulders had slumped. He no longer seemed to be enjoying the conversation. "Don't worry about Eva. She can spot 'married' from a mile off."

"A consequence of being in the wedding business, I suppose."

Nick lifted a hand at the deckhand who had secured the inflatables. "Eva came from a broken home before Mario adopted her. She's never placed much trust in relationships."

Elena slipped sunglasses onto the bridge of her nose

and gripped a railing as the yacht picked up speed. "Sounds like a family trait."

Aware that Elena was maneuvering the conversation into personal territory he usually avoided, Nick made an attempt to relax. "Maybe."

A heavy silence formed, the kind of waiting silence he had gotten all too used to with his own family.

Elena sent him a frustrated look. "Trying to get information out of you is like talking to a sphinx."

"Seems to me I've heard that phrase somewhere before."

"Let me guess… Your sisters." She tucked errant strands of hair behind one ear, revealing the three tiny blue-green jewels that sparkled like droplets of light in her lobe.

"And the head inquisitor—my mom." He steered around a curving lacework of rocks and reefs that partially enclosed the bay. "What, exactly, do you want to know?"

She met his gaze squarely. "What you like to eat for breakfast, because we've never actually had breakfast together. Why you went into construction when the family business is banking, and…" She hesitated, her chin coming up. "What's your idea of a romantic date?"

"I like coffee and toast for breakfast, I went into construction because while I was disabled Dad taught me how to design and build a boat, and my favorite date is… anything to do with a yacht. Don't you want to ask me about my relationship dysfunction?"

"I intended to skirt around that question, but now that you've brought it up, why haven't you ever been in a long-term relationship?"

In the instant she asked the question, the answer was crystal clear to Nick. Because he had never quite been able to forget what it had felt like making love with Elena. Or that she had waited until she was twenty-two to make love, and then she had chosen *him*.

His jaw clamped against the uncharacteristic urge to spill that very private, intimate revelation. "I've got a busy schedule."

"Not too busy to date, at last count, twenty-three girls in the last two years. That's not quite one a month."

Fierce satisfaction filled him at the clear evidence that Elena was jealous. There could be no other reason for the meticulous investigation of his dating past. "That many?"

Her gaze was fiery and accusing. "I thought it would be more."

He increased speed as the water changed color from murky green to indigo, signaling deep water and a cold ocean current. Against all the odds, he was suddenly enjoying the exchange. "You should stop reading the gossip columnists. Some of those so-called dates were business acquaintances or friends."

"Huh."

He suppressed a grin and the urge to pull Elena close, despite her prickly mood. Instead, he made an adjustment to the wheel. With no more rocks or reefs to navigate, and the bow pointed in the direction of the resort's small marina, he could relax more. He found there was something oddly sweet about just being with Elena.

Glancing down into the dining room below, he noted that Irvine was still sitting exactly where Nick had placed him, although his face was now an interesting shade of green.

The conversation he'd had with Irvine replayed. It occurred to Nick that the reason he hadn't been able to walk away from Elena this time was exactly the same reason Irvine needed to back up a step.

Elena had changed over the years, even since their meeting in Cutler's office in Auckland, morphing from the quiet, introverted girl who used to watch him from the beach into a fiery, exciting butterfly with a will of steel.

His stomach tightened. She was gorgeous and fascinating. He could understand why Harold and Irvine had been dazzled, why she could keep a successful businessman like Robert Corrado on ice while she pursued her new career.

If there had ever truly been anything soft or yielding about Elena, like her old image, it was long gone.

Elena turned her head away from him, into the wind, the movement presenting him with the pure line of her profile and emphasizing her independence. After years of single life, it occurred to Nick that she was happy with her own company. Abruptly annoyed by that streak of independence, a strength that informed Nick that, as attracted as Elena was to him she didn't need him in her life, he finally gave in to the urge to pull her close.

She softened almost instantly, fitting easily into his side. Despite that, he was uneasily aware that something important was missing between them. That something was trust.

He needed to come clean about the quiz and release her from the night she had forfeited.

But that was a risk he wasn't prepared to take. If he released Elena before he'd had a chance to bind her to him in the hours ahead, he wasn't certain he would be able to convince her that she should refocus her attention.

Away from Robert Corrado and onto *him*.

Elena, still uneasily aware of both Harold and Irvine, was more than happy to leave the yacht with her clients when they docked at the small jetty.

With satisfaction, she noted both Irvine and Harold being ushered by Nick into a resort vehicle that appeared to also contain their luggage. The driver of the vehicle was one of the gardeners she'd noticed, a burly man who looked as though he had once been a boxer.

Nick strolled alongside her as she entered the resort restaurant. Waiters were already circulating with trays of champagne and canapés. Lifting two flutes from a tray, he pressed one into her hand then began ushering her toward the door.

"We're leaving now?" she asked.

"It is almost eight."

A small thrill of excitement shot through Elena. She had thought they might have dinner and maybe dance on the terrace, but Nick's hurry to get her to himself was somehow more alluring than a slow, measured seduction.

And technically their bargain terminated at midnight. Her stomach clenched at the thought of four hours alone with Nick. "Uh—what about dinner?"

He stopped, his hand on the doorknob. "We can get room service. Although, if you'd prefer to stay here for dinner, we can do that."

His expression was oddly neutral, his voice clipped. If she didn't know Nick better, she would think that eating here and losing time alone together didn't really matter, but she knew the opposite to be true, and in a flash she got him.

Nick was utterly male. Naturally, he didn't like emotion, and in the world he moved, showing any form of emotion would be deemed a weakness. She knew that much from working with both Lucas and Zane Atraeus. The only time they truly relaxed was when they were with their families.

Carla and Lilah had made comments that when their

men felt the most, they closed up even more. Getting actual words out of them was like squeezing blood out of the proverbial stone.

Carla and Lilah had been describing Lucas and Zane, but the description also fit Nick.

Her heart pounded at a breakthrough that put a different slant on some of the starkest moments in her relationship with Nick and made sense of his extreme reaction to his father's death. Nick walked away, not because he didn't care, but because he cared too much. "I don't need to eat."

"I was hoping you would say that."

She took a hurried gulp of the fizzy champagne so it wouldn't spill as they walked. The walkway was smooth enough, but with the shadowy shapes of palms and thick tropical plantings plunging parts of it into deep shadow it would be easy to stumble. She took another sip and noticed the moon was up. "I'm for room service."

His quick grin made her stomach flip. She hadn't thought the night would be fun. She'd thought it would be too fraught with the tensions that seemed to be a natural part of their relationship.

The fact that she was applying the term "relationship" to herself and Nick sent a small, effervescent thrill shimmering all the way to her toes. Finally, after years of being stalled, and just when she had thought all was lost, they were finally in an actual relationship. She felt like hugging him, she felt like dancing—

"Okay, what's going on?"

Nick was eyeing her with caution, which made her feel even more giddily happy, because it was clear he had noted what she was feeling. He was *reading* her mood.

There was only one reason for that to happen. He was concerned about her happiness; he was beginning to *care*.

It wasn't love, yet, but they were definitely getting closer. "I'm…" She suppressed the dangerous, undisciplined urge to blurt out that she was head over heels in love with him and had been for years. "I'm happy."

His gaze slid to the half-empty flute.

Elena took a deep breath and tried to drag her gaze from the fascinating pulse beating on the side of his jaw. "It's not the champagne." She examined the pale liquid with its pretty bubbles and without regret tossed what was left into the depths of a leafy green shrub. "I don't need champagne to spend the night with you."

To make gorgeous, tender, maybe even adventurous love with the man she loved.

For a split second the night seemed to go still, the tension thick enough to cut. "You don't have to sleep with me if you don't want. The quiz was a spur-of-the-moment thing. I shouldn't have—"

"We have a bargain. You *can't* back out."

Startlement registered in his expression. Relief flooded Elena. She had been desperately afraid he was going to release her from their deal. By her estimation the next few hours together were crucial. If they didn't make love and dissolve the last frustrating, invisible barriers between them, they might never have another chance.

In response, Nick reeled her in close with his free hand, fitting her tightly enough against him that she could feel his masculine arousal. "Does this feel like I'm backing out?"

The breath hitched in her throat at the graphic knowledge that Nick very definitely wanted her. "No."

"Good, because I'm not."

He took the flute from her and set it down with his own on the arm of a nearby wooden bench. Taking her hand, he drew her down the short path to his cottage.

The warm light from his porch washed over taut cheekbones and the solid line of his jaw as, without releasing her hand, he unlocked the door and pushed it wide.

Instead of standing to one side to allow her to precede him, Nick stepped toward her. At first, Elena thought he wanted to kiss her, then the world spun dizzily as he swung her into his arms.

Startled, Elena clutched at Nick's shoulders as he stepped into the lit hall and kicked the door closed behind him. Seconds later he set her on her feet in the middle of a large room lit by the flicker of candles and smelling of flowers. Heart still pounding, and pleasure humming through her at a gesture that was traditionally shared by a bride and groom, Elena inhaled the perfume of lavish bunches of white roses.

Nick took his cell out of his pocket and placed it on a workstation in a small alcove that also contained a laptop and a file. The small action made her intensely aware that, for the first time ever, she was in Nick's personal quarters—not his home, because the resort cottage was only a temporary accommodation, but in his private space.

Elena strolled to one of the vases of flowers.

"Do you like them?"

Throat tight with emotion, Elena touched a delicate petal with one fingertip. She was trying to be sensible and pragmatic, trying not to get her hopes too high, but she couldn't *not* feel wonder and pleasure at the trouble Nick had gone to.

Even though the room, with its candles and flowers, had most probably been staged by one of the resort professionals, it was still quite possibly the most romantic gesture any man had ever made. More wonderful than the traditional red roses Robert had sent to her. Even though she had been thrilled to receive the bouquet, thrilled at the fact that for the first time in her life she was being wooed, Robert's dozen red roses hadn't made her heart squeeze tight.

Blinking back the moisture that seemed to be filling her eyes, she straightened. "I love white roses. How did you know?"

"I got my PA to research what flowers you liked." Nick picked up a remote from a low teak coffee table and pressed a button. A tango filled the air, sending an instant thrill down her spine and spinning her back to the steamy tango they had danced at Gemma's wedding.

Determinedly, she dismissed the small core of disappointment that had formed at the systematic, logical way Nick had selected the flowers for their night together. Using a PA was a very corporate solution. She should know; she had done similar personal tasks herself for her Atraeus bosses.

Nick may not have personally known what flowers she liked, he may not have staged the room, but he had arranged it for her pleasure.

She forced herself to move on from the flowers and examined the rest of the interior. Furnished with dark leather couches, low tables and exotic teak armoires, the stark masculinity was relieved by a pile of yachting books on a side table and an envelope of what looked like family snapshots.

The family photos, some of which had slid out of the envelope, riveted her attention because they proved that Nick loved his family, that at a bedrock level, relationships were vitally important to him.

She sensed Nick's approach a moment before he turned her around and drew her into his arms. The tango wound its sinuous way through the candlelit room as she allowed him to pull her closer still and the night seemed to take on an aching throb. Filled with an utter sense of rightness, Elena wound her arms around Nick's neck and went up on her toes to touch her mouth to his.

Long, drugging seconds later, Nick lifted his head. "That's the first time you've actually kissed me properly."

"I've changed." Elena concentrated on keeping her expression serene. As tempted as she was to let Nick take control, to simply abandon herself to sensation, she couldn't afford to get lost in a whirlwind of passion as she had done on the last two occasions. To maximize her chances of success with him, she needed to keep her head and control her responses.

Threading her fingers through Nick's hair, she pulled his mouth back to hers.

Conditions were not ideal for the love scene she had thought would take place. For one thing, she hadn't had time to slip into the sexy lingerie, or the jersey silk dress she had intended to wear. She hadn't had the chance to shower or use the expensive body lotion she had bought, which would have been a more pleasant alternative to the residue of sea salt on her skin.

She couldn't allow any of that to matter. Luckily, she had remembered to pack the book of lovemaking techniques in her beach bag, intending to read it on the beach, so at least she could attempt to be a little more sophisticated than she'd been on previous occasions.

As if in response to the sensuality sizzling in the air, the tango music grew smokier.

Feeling a little nervy, Elena dragged at the buttons of Nick's shirt. As she unfastened the last button, she watched, mouth dry as Nick shrugged out of it, letting the limp cotton drop to the floor.

With his shirt off, his shoulders muscular and gleaming in the glow of candlelight, his chest broad and abs washboard tight, Nick was beautiful in a completely masculine way. The dark hair sprinkled across his chest and arrowed to the waistband of his pants, adding an earthy edge that made her pulse race. He pulled her close for another kiss, this one deeper, longer than the last.

Once again, determined to take the initiative, Elena found the waistband of Nick's pants and tugged, pulling Nick with her as she walked backward in the direction of the bedrooms.

If this cottage was the same as hers, and so far it looked identical, the master bedroom would be a short walk down the hall and to the left, with a set of doors opening out onto the terrace.

She managed to maneuver a step to the right so she could grab the strap of her beach bag on the way.

Nick lifted his head, his brows jerking together when he noticed the bag, but by then they were in the hall and the ultimate destination of the bedroom was clear.

The plan stalled for a few seconds when Nick planted one hand on the doorjamb, preventing further progress. He cupped her jaw, sliding the pad of his thumb over her bottom lip in a caress that made her head spin. "Maybe we should slow this down—"

"You mean wait?" A little breathlessly, Elena tugged at the annoyingly difficult fastening of his jeans. By now, Nick should have been naked.

Fourteen

Nick's palm curled around to cup her nape. "Are you sure this is what you want? I had planned something a little more—"

She found the zipper and dragged it down.

Nick made an odd groaning sound. "Uh, never mind…" With a deft movement, he undid what looked like a double fastening and peeled out of the jeans.

Elena's mouth went dry. With Nick wearing nothing more than the swimming trunks he'd had on beneath his jeans while she was still fully dressed, the sexual initiative should have been hers, a clear message to him that she was no longer a novice at this. But with the golden wash of light from the sitting room flaring over taut, bronzed muscles and adding a heated gleam to his gaze, there was no hint that Nick had registered the dominating tactic. He looked utterly, spectacularly at home in his own skin.

Seconds later, in a further reversal, Elena found herself propelled gently backward into the bedroom. She remembered to hang on to the strap of the bag, which had slipped off her shoulder and hooked around her wrist. Having to concentrate on keeping the bag and the book with her was an unexpected boon, because the sensual control she'd worked so hard to establish was rapidly dissolving into an array of delicious sensations that made it very hard to think.

Nick's fingers brushed her nape. Heat surged through her as she felt the neckline of her tunic loosen. Cool air flowed against her skin as the tunic slipped to her waist, trapping her arms.

Nick took advantage of her trapped arms to bend and brush his lips over one shoulder. The featherlight kiss sent another throb of sensual heat through her, before she dropped her bag and finally managed to wriggle her arms free.

A split second later the entire tunic floated to the floor, informing her that while she had been concentrating on the logistics of moving Nick into the bedroom, his fingers had been busy undoing the entire line of buttons that ran down her back.

A wave of melting heat zinged through her as Nick's hands cupped her breasts through the thin Lycra of her bikini. Dipping his head, he took one breast into his mouth, and for long, shimmering moments she lost focus as the aching throb low in her belly gathered and tightened.

Dimly, she noted that this part of the seduction was not going to plan. She had hoped to keep all of her clothes on until the last moment. Somehow things had deteriorated to the point that she was in danger of being naked first and once more irresistibly propelled into a whirlpool of passion.

Nick transferred his attention to her mouth. Without thinking, her arms coiled around his neck as she arched into the kiss and fitted herself more closely against him. With a slick movement, he picked her up and deposited her on the bed, following her down and sprawling beside her.

She felt a tug at her hips, the coolness of air as her bikini bottoms were stripped down her legs. Her brain snapped back into gear when she realized that for a few seconds she had allowed herself to drift in a pleasurable daze and now was completely naked.

Bracing her palms on Nick's chest, she pushed.

He frowned. "You want to be on top?"

She drew a deep breath. "Yes." The position was the most basic in the book, but it had the advantage of being easy to remember.

Obligingly, he subsided onto his back. Taking a deep breath, Elena began the business of peeling the swim trunks down. With Nick now impressively naked and the trunks in her hand she realized she had forgotten one crucial step: the condom.

Mouth dry, she clambered off the bed and rummaged in her beach bag until she found the box of condoms she had bought earlier in the day. Feeling a little panicked because she sensed the ambiance was deteriorating, she selected one at random. In the process a number of the packets flew onto the floor.

Nick slid off the bed. His light green gaze pinned her. "When did you buy these?"

The sudden grim tension made her freeze in place. "Yesterday."

"Then they're not for Corrado."

"No." She blinked at the idea that she would want to sleep with Robert. Although that concept was overridden by a far more riveting one. Nick was jealous of Robert. "I haven't slept with Robert."

Nick released her wrist, relief registering in his gaze. "Good."

The conversation was blunt and inconclusive, but the fragile hope that had been slowly, but gradually, growing over the past two days unfurled a little more.

With an easy, fluid motion, Nick picked up the box and began shoveling condoms back into it. "These look… interesting."

"I just grabbed the first box I found." And unfortunately, it seemed to be filled with an assortment of acidic colors and strange ribbed shapes.

As she attempted to tear open one of the packets, Nick picked her up with easy strength and deposited her back on the bed with him, pulling her close. The rough heat of his palms at her hips, gliding to the small of her back, urged her closer still.

The foil packet tore across. A black, ribbed shape emerged. Nick made a choked sound—a split second later he kissed her.

Swamped by a sudden sensual overload, she kissed him back. Long seconds later, she surfaced. The condom was still clutched in one hand; she had almost forgotten it. Not good.

Pulling free, she eased down Nick's body.

Obligingly, he allowed her to fit the condom. She had almost mastered the art of rolling it on when, jaw taut, Nick stayed her hand.

In a strained voice he muttered, "Maybe you should let me do that."

With an expert motion he completed the sheathing. Face oddly taut, he pulled her beneath him. Before she could protest, he kissed her, his gaze soft, his mouth quirked. "Sorry, babe. You can be on top next."

Babe. A quiver of pleasure went through her at the easy endearment. Entranced by Nick's heat and weight, his clean masculine scent laced with sea salt, it suddenly ceased to matter that her plan had been overridden, or that she'd had a plan at all.

She was with the man she loved with all her heart. As he came down between her legs in the intense, heated joining that seared her to her very core, she had a split second to log that, as inspiring as the book with its chapters of advice was, in that moment it ceased to have any relevance.

Lost in coiling shimmers of sensation with Nick, she had everything she needed and more.

A rapping at the door pulled Elena out of a deep, dreamless sleep. Nick was sprawled next to her, the sheet low around his hips, sunlight flowing across the strong, muscular lines of his back.

Suppressing the urge to ignore whoever was at the door and snuggle back against him, she glanced at the bedside clock, which confirmed that it was late, past nine.

Another rap had her sliding out of bed. Grabbing a white terry-cloth robe she found draped over a chair, she finger-combed her hair as she padded to the front door.

Her first thought—that it was someone from the hotel wanting to speak to Nick—died when, through a window she glimpsed two feminine figures. Both were casually, if elegantly dressed, which suggested they were guests.

It occurred to her that they could be clients from her seminar who'd decided that What Women Really Want meant some kind of license to pursue Nick.

If that was the case, she thought, becoming more

annoyed by the second, they were about to be disappointed. The days of Nick being pursued by gorgeous young things who thought he was free were over. Nick was no longer free: he was *hers*.

A rosy glow spread through her at the thought. Suddenly, wearing a bathrobe to the door had its upside. She was in Nick's cabin. It was obvious she had been in his bed.

She wrenched the door open and froze.

"Elena?" Francesca Messena, dressed in snug jeans, red heels and a filmy red shirt peered at her. "We knocked on your door—"

"When you didn't answer, we figured you must be here." Sophie Messena, cool and serene in an oversize white linen shirt and white leggings, frowned. "Are you all right? Honey, can you speak?"

Elena clutched at the lapels of her bathrobe, which had begun to gape, but it was too late, Sophie and Francesca had already zeroed in on the red mark at the base of her neck. "I'm fine. Never better."

Sophie glanced at her twin. "She doesn't look fine." Her voice turned imperious. "Where's Nick?"

Francesca gave Elena a sympathetic look. "We heard about the bet."

"What bet?" Elena attempted to block the doorway, but she was too slow. The Messena twins, both taller than her by several inches, and as lithe and graceful as cats, had already flowed past her into the hall.

"It wasn't a bet," a gravelly voice interjected. "It was a wager."

A split second later, Nick, strolled out of the bedroom dressed in jeans, hair ruffled, his torso bare. If there had ever been any doubt for the twins about what they had spent the night doing, it was gone.

Nick's gaze pinned her. Linking his fingers with hers, he drew her close, then casually draped an arm around her waist, holding her against his side. "Let me guess who told you. Eva."

Francesca picked up Nick's shirt, which was still lying on the floor from the previous evening, and pointedly tossed it over the back of a chair. "We're not at liberty to reveal our source."

"You should say sources," Sophie corrected her twin. "Then he gets left guessing."

Francesca lifted a brow. "Hmm. Obviously, you're much better at this than me."

Sophie folded her arms across her chest as if she was settling in for the duration. "I'm in retail. It leads to wisdom."

Nick's arm tightened around her. "Now that you've had your say and seen that Elena survived the night, you can leave. I love you, but you've got approximately..." He consulted his wristwatch. "Five minutes before we start making love again."

"Before what?" Francesca's brows jerked together. "You wouldn't dare."

Sophie ignored Nick and looked directly at Elena. "I heard the wager was for one night. You should leave if you want."

Elena was abruptly tired of the intervention, as well-meaning as it was. "It's not about one night," she said firmly. "We're in love. This is about the rest of our lives."

There was a ringing silence.

Francesca sent Nick a level look. "Then I guess congratulations are in order."

After breakfast, Nick suggested they leave for Auckland and his apartment, where they could be guaranteed privacy for a few days. The seminar was technically finished. There was no need for Elena to go to the main part of the resort, and since she wasn't a guest, she didn't have to check out. Her car was a rental, so it was easy enough to arrange to have it collected from the resort, which meant she could travel with him.

Elena was happy to pack and leave. Ever since the twins had burst in she had felt unsettled and on edge. Nick had been nice. More, he had been charming, but the good manners and consideration were oddly distancing.

She found herself desperately wanting him to revert to type, to be blunt and irritable or even outright annoying. She would rather fight with him than endure this sense of being held at arm's length.

On the bright side, they were going to spend the next few days together, before she had to fly back to Sydney, and Nick had mentioned a sailing holiday. It wasn't everything she wanted, but it was a positive start.

The drive to Auckland took three hours. Exhausted from an almost sleepless night, Elena dozed most of the way and woke as Nick pulled into an underground parking lot.

Minutes later, they walked into his penthouse, which had a breathtaking view of the Waitemata Harbour.

The penthouse itself was huge, large enough to fit three normal-size houses into, with expanses of blond wood flooring and an entire wall of glass.

Nick showed her to a room. Her heart beat a little faster until he dropped his bag beside hers. With relief she realized they were sharing his room.

Feeling happier and almost relaxed, Elena strolled through the apartment and checked out the kitchen before stepping out onto a patio complete with swimming pool and planters overflowing with tropical shrubs.

While she was admiring a particularly beautiful bromeliad with tiger stripes and a brilliant pink throat, Nick's arms came around her from behind.

"I have to apologize for my family. Sophie and Francesca should have stayed out of it."

She turned in his grasp and braced her hands on his arms, preserving a slight distance. "You mean stayed out of our relationship?"

"Uh-huh."

Elena frowned, but Nick had already drawn her close and the feel of his lips on the side of her neck was making it difficult to think. Just before he kissed her, it occurred to her that Nick had carefully avoided saying the word *relationship*.

Elena woke to the dim grayness of early evening in a tangle of sheets. Nick's arm was draped heavily across her waist, as if even in sleep he wanted to keep her close.

Easing herself from the bed so as not to wake him, she picked up his shirt, which was puddled on the floor, shrugged into it and padded to the bathroom.

The reflection that bounced back at her stopped her in her tracks. Dressed in the oversize shirt, with her hair ruffled, eyes still slumberous from sleep and faint red marks from Nick's stubble on her jaw and neck, she looked like a woman who had been well loved.

Her cheeks warmed at the memory of the few hours they'd spent in bed. The lovemaking had been sweet and gorgeous and very tender. While she hadn't gotten a chance to consult the book, mainly because Nick had snatched it out of her grip and tossed it over the balcony, she had gotten to be on top, *twice*.

Elena used the facilities, and washed her hands and face. Feeling absurdly happy, she studied Nick's razor and the various toiletries lined up on the vanity, and gave in to the urge to take the top off his bottle of aftershave. The familiar resinous scent made her stomach clench and her toes curl.

Strolling out to the kitchen, she poured herself a glass of water then walked through the sitting room, fingers trailing over sleek, minimalist furniture. The thought that this could be her home for the foreseeable future filled her with a rosy glow.

Although nothing was settled, she reminded herself. Nick was clearly still adjusting; they would be taking this one step at a time.

A familiar humming sound caught her attention. Nick's phone was vibrating on the masculine work desk in the alcove. Moving quickly, she snatched up the phone and thumbed the Off button. The absolute last thing she wanted now was for Nick to wake up and shift straight into work mode, ending their interlude.

Holding her breath for long seconds, Elena listened hard, but the only sound she could hear was Nick's slow, regular breathing, indicating that he was still deeply asleep.

She placed the phone carefully down beside a file, and froze when she saw her name on a sheet of paper that had slipped partway out of the folder.

Flipping the cover sheet open, she found a note from Constantine Atraeus, her boss, indicating that he was sending Nick materials he had requested.

The materials turned out to be her proposal for the seminar, the quiz she had devised *and a copy of the answer sheet*.

Knees weak, Elena sat down in the swivel chair pulled up at the desk and spread the sheets out.

The tension that had started at Francesca and Sophie's

intrusive questioning, followed by Nick's evasive behavior, coalesced into knowledge.

At some point, way before she had ever gotten to Dolphin Bay to run the seminar, Nick had filled out the quiz, marking every question with the correct answer.

The mystery behind Nick's high score was solved.

He had cheated.

Fingers shaking with a fine tremor, she double-checked the folder in case she had missed something.

Such as a real, fumbled effort at the quiz. Anything that might indicate that Nick Messena had an actual beating heart and not an agenda that was as cold in the bedroom as it was in the boardroom.

There was one final piece of correspondence. It was a memo to the manager of the Dolphin Bay Resort, granting him a week's leave covering the period of the seminar.

Clearing the way for seduction, because Nick had known how weak her defenses had been, that given long enough, she wouldn't be able to resist him.

Setting the letter down, Elena walked back to the kitchen, replaced her glass on the counter and looked blindly out onto the patio with its lengthening shadows.

Her head was pounding and her chest was tight. Why had Nick done such a thing? And why with *her,* out of all the women he could choose?

In her heart of hearts she wanted it to be because, secretly, he had always been falling for her, that he was just as much a victim of the intense, magical chemistry that had held her in thrall as she had been.

But the weight of evidence didn't add up to that conclusion. Three short flings with a man who was known for his tendency to go through women. A seminar Nick had maneuvered his way into, with her accommodation placed conveniently next door to his. The champagne and the carefully staged room, the scene set for seduction.

The fact that he had cheated on the quiz, as hurtful as that had been, was only the clincher.

A bubble of misery built in her chest. She had wondered what the invisible, unbreachable barrier was with Nick. Now she knew. It was his own well-established protection against intimacy.

The twins busting in now made perfect sense. They were his sisters; they knew exactly how he operated. They had been trying to protect her, trying to tell her that despite Nick's pursuit of her, he didn't intend to allow a relationship to grow. All he had wanted was the thrill of the chase, with the prize of a few passionate hours in bed.

She had stupidly ignored the twins and her own instincts, choosing to cling to a fantasy that she wanted, but which had no substance. In so doing, she had allowed Nick to succeed at the one thing she had vowed she wouldn't allow.

He had made her fall in love with him all over again.

Fifteen

Nick came out of sleep fast, drawn by the utter silence that seemed to hang over the apartment like a shroud and the taut sense that he had slept too long.

Instantly alert, he rolled out of the empty bed. The first thing he noticed as he pulled on his trousers was that Elena's suitcase, which he had set down beside the dresser, was gone.

Stomach tight, he finished dressing, grabbed a fresh jacket from the wardrobe and found the Jeep keys. As he strode through the apartment he automatically took stock. Every trace that Elena had ever been there was gone.

The knowledge that something had gone badly wrong was confirmed by a copy of the quiz, and the incriminating answer sheet, placed side by side on a coffee table.

Too late to wish he'd told Elena what he'd done, or that he'd shoved the file in a drawer out of sight until he'd had the chance to come clean. But yesterday, after the showdown with the twins and Elena's quiet statement that she was in love with him, he had been stunningly aware that it was decision time.

Either he committed to Elena or he lost her. But knowing that he should commit—more, that Elena needed him to commit—didn't make it any easier to step over an invisible line he had carefully avoided for years.

Grabbing his phone, he stepped out of the apartment and took the elevator to the lobby. He speed-dialed Elena's number. He didn't expect her to pick up, and he was right.

When the elevator doors opened, he strode out of the building and was just in time to see a taxi pull away from the curb and disappear into traffic. He controlled the impulse to follow her in the Jeep.

He already knew her destination. Elena was smart and highly organized, and as a former Atraeus PA she had a lot of contacts in the travel industry. She would have booked a flight out of Auckland. He could try and stop her, but he wouldn't succeed. She would be back in Sydney within hours.

Stomach coiling in panic he took the elevator back to his apartment and threw on clean clothes. Minutes later, he was in traffic. It was rush hour and took an agonizing hour to do the normal thirty-minute drive to the airport.

During that time he made a number of calls, but every time he came close to making a breakthrough and discovering what flight Elena had booked, he was stymied. Elena, it seemed, had invoked the Atraeus name and chartered a flight. Now, apparently, there was a code of silence.

He found himself considering the caliber of the woman who had started out as a PA, then turned herself into one of the Atraeus Group's leading executives. It was just one more facet of Elena's quiet determination to succeed.

Now she was leaving with the kind of quiet, unshakable efficiency that told him she wouldn't be back, and he couldn't blame her

He had made a mistake. It was the same mistake he had made twice before with Elena. He had been irresistibly attracted but had failed to be honest with her about where he was in the relationship stakes.

He had changed. The problem was that the process of change had been agonizingly slow and the urge to protect himself had become so ingrained that he'd closed down even when he'd wanted to open up.

The quiz had been a case in point. Instead of being up front with Elena, *exposing himself to vulnerability,* he had used his knowledge of the quiz to leverage the intimacy he wanted without exposing any emotions.

Now that very protective behavior had backfired, ensuring that he would lose the one woman he desperately needed in his life.

He picked up his phone and stabbed the redial. When Elena once again refused to pick up, he tossed the phone on the passenger-side seat and drove.

Nick stepped off the evening flight from Auckland to Sydney, carrying his briefcase.

He hadn't brought luggage with him because he didn't need to. He was in Sydney often enough that he owned a waterfront apartment just minutes from the city center.

Twenty minutes later, he paid the taxi fare and walked into his apartment. A quick call to the private detective he had hired earlier on in the day and he had the information he needed.

The tactic was ruthless but, as it turned out, necessary.

Elena had arrived on her flight and gone straight to her apartment. She had stayed in her apartment all afternoon, the curtains drawn. Twenty minutes ago, she had taken a taxi to an expensive restaurant where she was having dinner with Corrado.

Nick's stomach hollowed out at the report. Corrado's name was like a death knell.

He grabbed his car keys and strode to the front door. The mirrored glass on one wall threw his reflection back at him. His hair was ruffled, as if he'd run his fingers through it repeatedly, which he had. His jaw was covered with a dark five-o'clock shadow because he hadn't stopped to shave, and somehow he had made the mistake of pulling on a mauve T-shirt with his suit jacket. The T-shirt was great for the beach; it looked a little alternative for downtown Sydney after five.

Fifteen minutes later, he cruised past the restaurant, the black Ferrari almost veering into oncoming traffic as he saw Elena and Corrado occupying a table by the window overlooking the street.

Jaw clenching at the blaring horns, he searched for a parking space and couldn't find one. Eventually he found a spot in an adjoining street and walked back in the direction of the restaurant.

He was just in time to see a troop of violinists stationing themselves around Elena and Corrado and a waiter arriving with a silver bucket of champagne.

His heart slammed in his chest. Corrado was proposing.

Something inside him snapped. He was pretty sure it was his heart. In that moment he knew with utter clarity that he loved Elena. He had loved her for years. There was no other explanation for his inability to forget her and move on.

Too late to wish that he could have found the courage to tell Elena that.

His family had termed his behavior a dysfunction caused by the supposed betrayal of his father, but they were wrong.

The situation with his father had definitely skewed things for Nick. He had walked away from a lot of emotions he wanted no part of, but that still hadn't stopped him falling for Elena.

He had been hurt, but his dysfunction hadn't been his inability to fall in love, just his objection to *being* in love.

Dazed at the discovery that he had found the woman he wanted to spend the rest of his life with *six years ago* and had somehow missed that fact, Nick walked up to the table and curtly asked the violinists to leave.

The music sawed to a stop as Elena shot to her feet, knocking over the flute that had just been filled with champagne. "What are you doing here?"

"Following you. I hired a private detective."

Elena blinked, her eyes oddly bright, her cheeks pale. "Why would you do that?"

"Because there's something I need to tell you—"

"Messena. I thought I recognized you." Corrado pushed to his feet, an annoyed expression on his face.

Doggedly, Nick ignored him, keeping his gaze on Elena. "We didn't get to talk, either last night or this morning, and we needed to."

He didn't need to shoot a look at Corrado to know that he had heard and understood that they had clearly spent the night together. It wasn't fair or ethical, but he was fighting for his life here.

Reaching into his jacket pocket, Nick pulled out the original copy of the quiz he had attempted without the answers and a letter he had written on the flight from Sydney, and handed both to Elena.

The quiz contained the raw, unadulterated truth about how bad he was at conducting a relationship. The letter contained the words he had never given her.

He didn't know if they would be enough.

Elena took the crumpled copy of the quiz and the letter.

Breath hitched in her throat, she set the letter on the table and examined the quiz first.

She knew the answers by heart. A quick scan of the boxes Nick had marked gave him a score that was terminally low. It was the test she had expected from him, reflecting his blunt practicality and pressurized work schedule, the ruthless streak that had seen him forge a billion-dollar construction business in the space of a few years.

It was also, she realized, a chronicled list of the non–politically correct traits that attracted her profoundly. Alpha male traits that could be both exciting and annoying, and which Corrado, despite looking the part, didn't have. "You cheated."

The hurt of finding the sheet seared through her again. "I thought you used it to get me into bed."

A woman from a neighboring table made an outraged sound. Elena ignored it, meeting Nick's gaze squarely.

"I did cheat," he said flatly. "I knew I wouldn't stand a chance with you, otherwise. Things were not exactly going smoothly and the opportunity was there to get you into bed so we could have the time together we needed. I took it."

Elena held her breath. "Why did you want time together, exactly?"

There was a small vibrating silence. "The same reason I arranged to be in Dolphin Bay during your seminar. I wanted what we should have had all along—a relationship."

Fingers shaking just a little, she set the quiz down and picked up the letter. Written on thick blue parchment, it looked old-fashioned but was definitely new and addressed to her.

Holding her breath, she carefully opened it and took the single sheet out. The writing was black and bold, the wording straightforward and very beautiful.

The flickering candles on the table shimmered, courtesy of the dampness in her eyes. Her throat closed up. It was a love letter.

Her fingers tightened on the page. Absurdly, she was shaking inside. She noticed that at some point Robert had left. It seemed oddly symptomatic of their short relationship that she hadn't noticed. "What took you so long?"

"Fear and stupidity," Nick said bluntly. "I've loved you for years."

He took her hand and went down on one knee. There was a burst of applause; the violins started again.

Nick reached into his pocket again and drew out a small box from a well-known and extremely expensive jeweler. Elena's heart pounded in her chest, and for a moment she couldn't breathe. After the black despair of the flight to Sydney, the situation was…unreal.

Nick extracted a ring, a gorgeous pale pink diamond solitaire that glittered and dazzled beneath the lights. "Elena Lyon, will you be my love and my wife?"

The words on the single page of romantic prose Nick had written, and which were now engraved on her heart, gave her the confidence she needed to hold out her left hand. "I will," she said shakily. "Just so long as you promise to never let me go."

"With all my heart." Nick slid the ring onto the third finger of her left hand; the fit was perfect. "From this day forward and forever."

He rose to his feet and pulled her into his arms, whispering, "Babe, I'm sorry I had to put you through this. If I could take it all back and start again, I would."

"It doesn't matter." And suddenly it didn't. She had been hurt—they had both been hurt—but the softness she loved was in his eyes, and suddenly loving Nick was no risk at all.

Epilogue

The wedding was a family affair, that is, both the Messena and the Lyon families, with a whole slew of Atraeus and Ambrosi relatives on the side.

The bride was stylish in white, with racy dashes of pink in her bouquet and ultramodern pink diamonds at her lobes.

Elena did her best not to cry and spoil her makeup as Nick slid the simple gold band, symbolizing love, faithfulness and eternity, onto her finger. When the priest declared they were man and wife, the words seemed to echo in the small, beautiful church, carrying a resonance she knew would continue on through their married life.

Elena's bridesmaid, Eva, on the arm of Kyle Messena, the best man, strolled behind them down the aisle. They halted at the door of the church and the press jostled to take photos.

Elena leaned into Nick, suddenly blissfully, absurdly

happy. "Let's hope they get the wedding story right this time."

Nick pulled her even closer, his hold protective as they made their way toward the waiting limousine. "No chance of a mistake this time. Pretty sure Eva's on record as saying she'll never marry, and Kyle's escorting her on sufferance. They're oil and water."

As brilliant and sunny as the day was, the wedding photos proved to be a trial. The Messena family did what all large families did; they argued. Sophie and Francesca were the worst. They loved Nick unreservedly, but they couldn't resist poking and prodding at him.

Their main issue was that they wanted to know what the aliens had done with their real brother, the bad-tempered, brooding, pain-in-the-ass one, and when would they be getting him back?

Nick had taken it all in good part, telling them that if they had an ax to grind over the fact that he had fallen in love, they would have to take it up with his wife.

Sophie and Francesca had grinned with delight, given Elena a thumbs-up and opened another bottle of champagne.

Halfway through the wedding dinner, which was held at sunset under the trees at the Dolphin Bay Resort, a guest they had all been waiting for arrived.

Tall, dark and with the clean, strong features that would always brand him a Messena, Katherine Lyon's long-lost son hadn't wanted to miss the wedding. Unfortunately, his flight from Medinos had been delayed, which meant he'd missed the actual ceremony.

Nick, who had gone to Medinos to meet with Michael Ambrosi just weeks before, made introductions.

Elena dispensed with the handshake and gave him a hug that was long overdue. After all, they were cousins.

After being thoroughly welcomed into the family fold, Michael took Elena and Nick aside and produced a small box.

Elena surveyed the antique diamond ring, nestled on top of the stack of love letters they had found in Katherine's attic, and finally understood why there had been so much fuss about it.

The pear-shaped diamond was set in soft, rich gold and radiated a pure, white light. The setting suggested that the ring was very, very old, the purity of the stone that it was extremely expensive.

Gorgeous as it was, Elena very quickly decided she much preferred the softness of the pink solitaire Nick had given her. "Aunt Katherine would have been proud to wear it."

Michael replaced the ring in its box. As Carlos's son, the ring was his to give to his future wife if he chose. It was just one of the many strands that now tied him irrevocably into a family that had been anxious to include him and make up for lost time.

As the sun sank into the sea, Nick pulled Elena onto the dance floor constructed beneath the trees. Illuminated by lights strung through the branches and just feet away from the waves lapping at the shore, it was the perfect way to end a perfect day.

A little farther out in the bay, Nick's yacht—the venue for their honeymoon—sat at anchor, lights beckoning.

Elena wound her arms around Nick's neck and went into his arms. "I have a confession. I used to watch you from the beach when I was a teenager."

Nick grinned. "I used to watch you from the yacht."

Elena smiled and leaned into Nick, melting against him as they danced.

No more unhappiness, no more uncertainty, she thought dreamily. *Just love.*

* * * * *

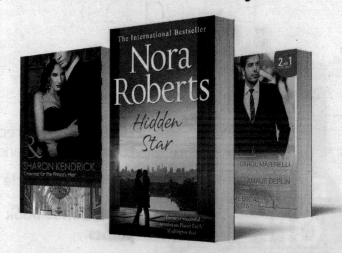